A Lantern in the Dark

An o'brien tale

Stacey Reynolds

© A Lantern in the Dark
Copyright: Stacey Reynolds
Published November 1, 2016
Createspace Independent Publishing
*This book is the intellectual property of the author. This book is licensed for your enjoyment. This book or any portion of it should not be copied, reproduced, or transmitted without the written permission of the author. You must not circulate this book in any format. The cover art was purchased legally through iStock. The characters of this book are fictional people. Any resemblance to real people is coincidental. Any mention of locations, landmarks, or business is strictly to create ambiance and a strong setting.

ISBN: 1540798518
ISBN 13: 9781540798510

This book is dedicated to my mother and father. My mother has always been my biggest fan and strongest ally. You listened when I cried, you picked me up when I fell, you taught me to cook and to pray and to love. You taught me to be kind and you also taught me not to take crap from anyone.

To my father. You were always the strong and silent papa bear. You were never one to show your feelings, but you showed your love through work and support and giving of yourself for your family. You taught us how to fight on the heavy bag when we were getting picked on. You taught us how to use a hammer and mow the lawn and everything else that was practical and needed teaching. You educated us. When I was ready to give up, you gave me a nudge. And as much as you disapproved of my adventurous side, you admired it in equal measure.

Thanks Mom and Dad. I love you.

PROLOGUE

Belfast, Northern Ireland, United Kingdom

Aidan was breathing heavily, sweat covering his brow and upper lip. He always knew on some level he was dreaming, but it didn't diminish the toll it took on him in the throes of it. It also didn't help with the disorientation, or confusion he felt, when he woke. He woke often with the sense of not knowing where he was. Occupational hazard. A captain in the British Army, he was with the Royal Irish Regiment, 2nd Battalion. He'd been to Afghanistan three times, and Iraq once, in the span of nine years. So he'd grown accustomed to the annoying habit of waking up in a confused state, not knowing where the hell he was, which time zone, which country, or which bed.

Looking around, he started to recognize the room. He was in his bedroom in his sparsely furnished flat. It was neat and clean, albeit a bit dated. Actually, it was his mother's flat in West Belfast. They'd kept it in the family, even after she'd married his da and moved to the Republic. As his chest slowed its heaving, he calmed with the realization that he was home. He'd only been having one of many recurring, shitty dreams that had been permanently etched into his psyche. He also remembered what day it was and that he was not going to be here for long.

Shaking off the little trip to third world shitsville, he got out of bed and walked into the sitting room. His phone was glowing with a silent alert. The text was from his brother Liam, in Dublin, telling him he would be there in three hours. It had come in ten minutes ago. He flipped up his laptop and checked his email. John Denario had contacted him again.

Captain Denario, USMC and battle buddy. He laughed when he saw there was an emoticon of a leprechaun hitchhiking on an airstrip holding a sign that read "America or bust. Will work for beer." How in the hell did Denario find these things? He went into the kitchen to start the kettle. He had no real food in the house due to the upcoming absence. He had cleaned and sanitized the fridge, leaving nothing but a bowl of baking soda on the top and bottom.

All he had to eat was a bag of pastry he'd picked up yesterday from Gran's house. He was the closest grandchild geographically, so Gran spoiled him accordingly. She also never tired of trying to marry him off to every friend's granddaughter, nurse, dental hygienist, waitress, and store clerk she met of marrying age. His grandda would just pat him on the shoulder and tell him that she meant well.

He wasn't interested in getting married, however. He'd known his share of women, cherished them all for the short time he'd been with them, but he knew he'd never marry. He didn't have a lifestyle that was cohesive to family life or to everlasting love. Women didn't like being left behind to worry and feel lonely. Children liked having their da around. No, he wouldn't be getting the happily ever after, and that was ok. He'd made his choices.

As he made his tea and placed a pastry on a plate, his mind flashed to another kitchen. It was the kitchen he would soon be staying in for three months. He closed his eyes as he remembered Branna and her friend bringing tea and coffee out to the sitting area, remembered Alanna's father giving Branna a letter, and her friend crying silently and leaving the kitchen. He remembered every bloody minute he'd been in her presence.

Long, silky blonde hair, not out of a bottle. She was what appeared to be the rare natural blonde, given by blood instead of by L'Oreal. Green eyes. Christ, those green eyes. They'd sparked with intelligence, bridled emotion. He remembered the way they'd burned when she'd slammed the door in his face, thinking he was Michael. And then he'd heard her sing, watched her head sway as she drew the bow across her fiddle. The only respite he'd had from the nightmares, recently, were the occasional, blissful dreams about her. Silky hair falling over his skin, beautiful mouth descending on him from above. Soft gasps and straining hips.

"Stop it," he said out loud. *Never going to happen, so quit thinking about her.* It occurred to him, in a moment of clarity, that moving next door to the lass for three months was probably not the best way to go about it.

Across the Atlantic
Topsail Island, NC

Alanna shot up from the couch, gasping and holding her chest. Her hair was stuck to her face from perspiration. She looked around the room in a panic until she remembered she had set her phone for a thirty minute nap. She laid back and let the sensations roll through her. Her heart was pounding and she had a distinct ache a little further south, having been awakened from yet one more steamy dream about the man she was not going to think about. She'd been having the dreams for months, mostly at night in the rare times that she slept deeply enough to dream.

It figures that the one time in her life that she felt true chemistry, mindless attraction, that the fiendish man lived across the ocean. The self imposed bachelor was about as unavailable as you could get. *I hope I never see you again, Aidan O'Brien.*

Some wishes were futile. This particular wish, however, was completely within the realm of possibility, considering he lived in Belfast. She forced herself off the couch, knowing that entertaining that particular ache while picturing that particular man was not healthy and not what she needed. She didn't need a man in her life, but she was also not going to obsess over a man she would probably never see again. Aidan O'Brien probably hadn't given her a second thought since he'd pulled out of her driveway last autumn. She pulled the pitcher of sweet tea out of the fridge, pouring it into a tall glass over ice. She had allowed herself the small nap, but her thesis wasn't going to write itself.

She was one month shy of a summer graduation from graduate school. Her internship and thesis findings were all that stood between school and the real world. Her unorthodox approach to PTSD treatment within the dynamics of the family unit had caused some head scratching with the stuffy, liberal professors at her university.

Classic approaches to Clinical Psychology were all well and good, but the traditional head shrinker bit only got you so far with the ass kicking sector. She knew a bit about what made her particular case studies tick, and talking about mommy with the aromatherapy candle burning wasn't going to cut it. By the end of this chapter in her life, she knew where she wanted to be. She wanted to be in a position to supersede the slow, archaic, broken system of the U.S. Veterans Administration.

She wanted to harness the non-profit sector for treatment alternatives, and to gain access to the best, the brightest, and the broken. She wanted to get them out of the VA waiting room and back in the driver's seat of their own lives. Motrin and Zoloft only got them so far. A therapy session once every two or three months, due to long wait lists, was no more than a check in the box for the politicians, and these vets weren't getting the treatment they needed.

Families were breaking, suicides were rising, and no one knew how to fix the red tape nightmare that these men and women were facing. At least not fast enough to help a whole new generation of combat vets that were lining up behind the old timers from WWII, Korea, and Vietnam.

That's where she was going to come in. But first she had to get this infernal paper done. She flipped her laptop open, pushing thoughts of another military man with blue eyes, wide shoulders, and a deep Irish burr firmly out of her mind.

1

Aidan had to laugh as his brother pulled up to his flat in Dublin. Liam's roommate was gone for the summer, but the place was packed to the point of bursting with O'Briens. He could have flown out of Belfast, but his family had insisted on seeing him off, and this was the easiest solution for everyone. His flight was around tea time, so this early morning gathering had everyone yawning and sucking caffeine by the cupful. Even his Gran Aoife and Grandda David were in attendance, which put four generations squashed under one tiny roof. It was chaos, but upon entering the place, he felt only joy. He felt loved.

"Are you all ready, brother? Three months is a long time for two suitcases and a carry-on." Michael was finishing up his man hug with a thump on the back.

Aidan answered, "Yes, I was able to send a footlocker ahead to John and Maria's home, so I should be all set. Shipping was a bit dear, but so is extra luggage so I decided to travel light." Branna came up to him, and he gave her a big bear hug. "Where are the babies this morning?" he asked.

"Oh, they are well occupied. Cora is in the bedroom singing and reading to them. She's very serious about her duties as the oldest child. Now remember, the spare key is hidden under the house between the far right piling and the joist. You will see an old tobacco tin wedged in there. That's where the key is. There's no alarm and that key will open all the exterior doors."

Aidan nodded. "Aye, I've got it. Don't worry, lass. I'll take care of the place. You'll need to e-mail the list of repairs that need done, and I will look the place over and see what else needs work. If you are going to take a hit on rent this summer, you'll at least get some free labor."

Branna just shook her head. "Just get what you can done, Aidan. And save receipts for the supplies you need. I don't want you going out of pocket."

He looked at his brother, hoping to get some reinforcements. Michael put his hands up, "Don't look at me. This is her business. She's the boss." He looked back at Branna and she had that chin up, her spine stiffened, and he knew better than to try and best her in an argument.

"I'm so jealous that you will be able to see Anna. You know, she graduates next month. Seven years of school, three degrees and working two jobs, and she is done next month. Poor thing has earned a break. I wish I could be there. Give her a congratulatory hug for me, will you?"

Aidan replied, "Yes, you mentioned her graduation last month. I'll send your regards. She knows to expect me late? I don't want to startle her by coming in the wee hours."

Branna just nodded, "Not to worry, Aidan. Just enjoy the beach and be careful. The training you are getting is top notch, but those boys don't play around. It is also hot as Hades in the summer, and humid. Lots of sunscreen and bug spray. Ticks, mosquitos, fire ants, black widows." Branna shuddered. "I love the South, but the bugs I could do without."

Brigid interrupted, pulling Aidan away. Michael leaned into Branna and spoke softly. "Don't think I missed the fact that you didn't actually answer that question." Branna just looked at him and wiggled her eyebrows which made Michael laugh out loud. "Sneaky, little hellcat."

Brigid hugged her brother and kissed his cheek. "I love you, dearthháir. Make sure to call me at least once a week. You know I can't do without news, and Cora will be put out if you don't give her a song now and then."

Aidan smoothed his hand down the back of her head. "I love you, too. You take care of little Colin until I can come back and teach him to throw a pig skin."

At this, Finn chimed in. "He'll be a footballer to be sure. You keep that barbarian rugby horde away from my boy!"

Aidan laughed and embraced his brother-in-law. "Take care of her," he whispered in his ear. Finn just looked thoughtfully at him, answering in his mild way. "Always, brother."

Aidan made his way through the brothers, sisters, and grandparents, and kissed the babies before finally settling in front of his mother and da. "Take care of yourself, my beautiful boy," Sorcha said, as she smoothed her hand over his cheek. Her endearment always brought a bit of a blush to his cheeks and warmth in his heart. He could remember her calling him that since he was a small boy.

"I will, Ma. Don't worry about me. Just check on Gran and Grandda and maybe on the flat if you can. I'll be home before you know it."

She teared up a little and her voice was shaky. "Yes, but then you'll transfer."

Sean put his hand around her shoulders. "Don't worry, love. He'll be a train and ferry ride away. Shropshire is not so very far."

She nodded and hugged Aidan fiercely. "I just don't want you to be alone, mo chroí," she whispered. Then she backed away, sweeping the tears from under her eyes.

Sean gave Aidan a pitying look and put one arm around him, leading him into the kitchen. "Do you need anything, son? Any traveling money?"

Aidan laughed. "Da, this isn't summer camp. I'm thirty-one years old."

Sean gave a self-deprecating shrug. "Old habits die hard."

Aidan put his hand on his father's shoulder. "I'll send you my number when I pick up a pre-paid phone in the states. You call me and keep me posted on everyone. I know Ma has a check up coming, and I want you to call me and tell me if she's still clear."

Sorcha had been cancer free for over ten years, but the entire family held their breath when she had a routine screening. "She's fine son. We are all fine. You go do this thing. We are so proud of how your career is going, so very proud. This is a good thing, and maybe it will be a nice change of pace. Spending the summer on the beach in America sounds like a pretty good venue for a training exercise."

Aidan nodded. "Oh, aye. I only saw it in the winter, but good God, Da. You and Ma should arrange to join me for a holiday. It's on a gorgeous stretch of beach. I'll not be suffering, and I already know a couple of people."

"Yes, so I've heard. Anna, is it?"

Aidan gave a startled look, like he'd been caught at something. "I meant John and Maria. He's the Marine I met in Afghanistan. As for Alanna, well I only met her briefly, but she's still next door. She seems like a good enough girl."

Aidan tried to sound casual, but Sean was no dummy. "Alanna? Is that her full name, then? Alanna Falk?" Aidan just nodded, not making eye contact.

"Interesting name, a pity I won't get to meet her." Aidan just shrugged and changed the subject. The last thing he needed was his parents sniffing out a potential mate for him. The ache in his mother's voice, Jesus wept. *I just don't want you to be alone, mo chroí.* He definitely didn't need them getting any ideas or false hope, or that sister-in-law of his. Because he had no interest in starting something with some American woman that he couldn't finish.

2

Aidan came off the airplane in Jacksonville, North Carolina with a stiff neck and a dry mouth. After hitting the water fountain with a vengeance, he walked toward arrivals. He hated flying. Not the actual act, but the feeling of being crammed into a tin can for umpteen hours. He'd slept a bit, since he could manage to fall asleep quickly and efficiently, like anyone who'd spent time in the military. It wasn't a deep or restful sleep, however. Not that he achieved that even in a bed. But sitting upright with a Chatty Cathy to his left and a child kicking his seat to his rear, the longest leg of the flight had been a little bit of hell.

That was without the consideration of three layovers in London, New York, and Charlotte. His ticket was funded, so the British government had found the rock bottom cheapest flight, which ended up taking a total of thirty plus hours. He left Dublin in the afternoon, and now he was standing in Albert J. Ellis Airport in sunny, North Carolina at o'dark thirty, over a day later.

He was grateful that his phone had kept up with the changes, because his body was rolling a *what the feck time is it* in a major way. He texted Denario from Charlotte and told him what time he was landing, since his flight was a bit delayed.

"Do I need to call the coroner?" Aidan smiled weakly at the sight of his old friend. He had a distinct, New Jersey accent, and he was a sight for sore eyes. The two men did a thumping man hug and began the snatch and grab off the luggage conveyer. The airport was tiny, so they only had to walk out the door to find the car, thirty feet away.

"So, how was the trip? By the looks of the itinerary, I'd have preferred a rectal exam."

Aidan laughed, shaking his head. "That's about the long and short of it. A short probe in the arse would have been merciful in comparison. How's Maria? I'm sorry you had to come out so late. She's not too put out, is she?"

John just waved a hand. "She's a Marine wife. Nothing phases her at this point. She was waddling around the house with a pint of Haagen Daz when I left. Can't get enough of the stuff."

Aidan smiled. "So she and the baby are getting along okay, then?"

John nodded. "This is the third. She's a pro at this point."

"Christ, you breed like an Irishman."

Denario just puffed his chest up with pride. "I'm a good Catholic boy and Italian stallion, my friend. You are going to have to work overtime if you want to catch me."

Aidan responded vehemently, "Oh, no. I'll leave that up to you and my siblings. Remember, I am a confirmed bachelor."

Denario looked at him a little more seriously as they loaded the bags into the hatch of his SUV. "A good woman makes life worth living, old friend. You mark my word. You will be changing your tune someday, and I will be having the last laugh."

Alanna woke in her bed, breath stuttering. She was sweating, even with the ocean breeze coming through the window. She'd been dreaming again, in vivid detail. She wouldn't mind the dreams so much if her subconscious mind had the decency to give her a happy ending before she woke up. And she didn't mean the fairytale type.

Considering her field of study was psychology and social work, Alanna didn't have to be Sigmund Freud to understand her infatuation with her dream lover. Considering her rather rocky start to intimacy, and her lack of practice in the sex department, she knew deep down that it wasn't so much about the man.

Aidan O'Brien was safe in that he was unattainable and conveniently beautiful, which made him good fantasizing material. Although she knew she had an unusual lack of sex drive and a non-existent dating life, she was for all intents and purposes a healthy twenty-five year old woman. The pent up sexual frustration had finally found an outlet.

Even after her lame attempts at dating had ended in the inevitable smooch and grab sessions, she never felt that burning passion that took the relationship to the next level. Twice, only twice had she taken that leap, and neither had gone well.

She sighed, stirring the remnants of her herbal tea. Her only consolation was that she didn't actually have to see the object of her infatuation, and relive the excruciating details of those dreams, while keeping a straight face.

She was graduating soon, and would enter the professional arena. At that point, she knew she needed to get back on the dating horse. She needed to find a nice, respectable southern boy who shared her values and didn't mind that his woman was a little on the sexually repressed side. She headed back to bed, hoping to get a few more hours of sleep before morning.

Aidan used his mini-LED light to look under the pilings. He found the tobacco tin right where Branna had told him it would be. He'd rushed Denario along, not wanting the headlights or car noise to disturb Alanna or the neighbors. The houses were close together and it was the middle of the night. No need to make a racket, considering the time. As he brought the can down, there was a distinct lack of clink. *Shit, no key.* He searched the ground around the piling and webbed out, searching high and low for a loose key.

He wasn't going to wake Alanna. She was working and going to school, and he was a big boy. He also wasn't going to bother Denario. The man had two kids and another on the way. He didn't need to come back out here in the middle of the night.

Aidan tried the door, hoping she'd left it unlocked for him. No such luck. He hid his gear under the house. It was out of sight and in a dry area, so it was fine until morning. When he did that, he realized there was a second set of stairs leading up to the wrap around deck. Bingo.

He grabbed his poncho.The night was warm and he didn't need much coverage. He also grabbed some sweats and a clean t-shirt and sweatshirt. He palmed his dopp kit and went up the stairs. The sliding door was also secured, as he expected it would be. He left the poncho liner on a chaise lounge on the deck, went down the side stairs and used the shower area to change into some comfortable clothes. He washed his face and brushed his teeth by trickling a little water from the faucet, and he felt like a new man. He also refilled the water bottle he had hanging off his ruck.

He walked back up the stairs and breathed in deeply of the sea air. After that cramped airplane, the lounger spread out under the stars looked like a bed for the gods. The ocean was a constant, comforting surge of crash and roll. As he laid down on the comfortable, cushioned lawn furniture, he found that it was slightly damp from humid air and ocean mist, so he flipped it over. He was instantly relaxed and at peace as he reclined his body, made a pillow from his sweatshirt, and let the stress of travel melt away. He was asleep within seconds.

Alanna had been stirring in and out of consciousness ever since she'd heard a car engine near the house. It was hard to tell where the cars were coming from, since it was the start of tourist season and she was surrounded by vacation homes. Her bedroom was overlooking the sea, so she never had to deal with headlights shining in the window, but the occasional car engine disturbed her sleep.

She'd almost drifted back off when she heard the distinct shift of what sounded like deck furniture. It wasn't loud or continuous, but her window was open. Granted, she could be a little paranoid at times. She lived alone, and from time to time she got unwanted attention. Sometimes she even felt like someone was watching her, but she knew that was her own paranoia. That particular creeper was out to sea in some foreign land and not an immediate problem.

Just when she'd convinced herself that she hadn't heard anything, she detected the rustle of some sort of canvas or fabric, a shifting of someone on the adjoining deck. Fear spiked through her. The rental schedule was cleared since Branna would be renovating. No one should be over there.

Aidan started emerging from sleep as he heard a door slide open. It took him a minute to figure out where he was, having crashed from the fatigue of travel. As his awareness started to surface, someone spoke.

"Okay, buddy. You take yourself off my deck and we will forget this happened. If you try anything funny, I will bash your skull in. Got it?" Aidan shot up and jumped to his feet in confusion, just as he saw the bat swing toward him. He instinctually ducked and dove at the assailant. He was groggy, but his instincts took over.

He came to awareness just as he felt a little, feminine body and heard a high pitched screech. "Ah fuck!" was all he could manage as he spun mid-fall to take the deck at his back, saving his new neighbor from two hundred plus pounds of Irishman landing on top of her. She went wild, limbs tangled, hair everywhere, hissing and punching from what she obviously thought was a threat.

"Alanna, lass! It's me, Aidan. It's okay!" The bat had thankfully been lost in the shuffle, but he didn't think he was getting through to her. Before she started screaming, he hugged her around her arms and lowered his voice, hoping that she would instinctually still to listen. "Be easy, Alanna. It's Aidan O'Brien. Calm down, lass. Shh."

His calm tone did in fact break through the chaos better than him trying to yell over her. She stiffened and scrambled off him. "Aidan? As in Branna's brother-in-law?" She was scooting backward as she spoke, and she scrambled for her bat.

It twisted his heart that he'd scared her so badly. "Yes, lass. Forgive me. I didn't mean to frighten you. Let's turn the light on, and you can see that it's me."

She stood up cautiously and flipped on the light. The first sight of her almost blinded him. She was just as beautiful as he remembered, maybe even more beautiful. The look on her face was wary and he cursed under his breath. "Christ, darlin'. I'm so sorry I gave you such a fright. You woke me and I didn't know where I was for a minute. I just saw that club coming at me and reacted. Did I hurt you?" He went to walk toward her and she stiffened. He stopped and ran his hand through his hair. "I won't come any closer; I just wanted to make sure you were okay."

Her body unclenched a bit and she took a deep breath. "I'm okay, I think you got the worst of it. If you don't mind me asking, what in heck are you doing here? You scared the crap out of me!" Her voice was raising and the look had switched from fear to fury.

Well, at least she isn't afraid of me anymore, he thought. He couldn't help the smile that he was failing to suppress. She was beautiful to be sure, but she was breathtaking when she was pissed. "What is so funny? I could have bashed your brains in, O'Brien!" She gripped the bat as if the idea still had some merit.

"Didn't Branna tell you I was coming in tonight?" he asked.

Confusion flickered in her eyes, but she cautiously leaned the bat against the house. "She didn't tell me you were coming at all.

I thought it was odd that the rental calendar was empty, but I just thought she was going to do some remodeling. She never said a word about you coming."

Aidan rubbed his shoulder where he'd landed on the deck. "Jesus, no wonder you came at me with a bat. Christ, girl. You should have called the police if you thought you had an intruder, not come out swinging. Have you taken leave of your senses? What if I had been a burglar or worse!" He didn't hide the irritation in his voice.

Alanna's brain was firing off too many emotions at once, especially after that spike of adrenaline, and the tussle with who she'd thought was a homeless guy or wayward drunk. Aidan freaking O'Brien was standing on her deck, looking every bit the hot soldier she remembered. What in the hell was going on? Had she summoned him from those steamy dreams? Was she dreaming now, and it was just getting more vivid? She looked him up and down before she could stop herself and was instantly disgusted with the way her thoughts were rolling.

Then she realized what he was saying, and the attitude she was getting, and she flipped right back around to her fighting mode. She pointed at him, walking up to his big body like a boss. "First of all, I can take care of myself. Don't get high and mighty with me, O'Brien or I will rethink the bat across your shins. Now, explain to me why you are sleeping on the porch in the middle of the night instead of inside like a normal person?"

That sharp tongue of hers should not have been a turn on. Not at all. But as she closed in on him with that finger pointed at him, eyes flaring, handing him his own ass, all he could think about was pulling her down on that lounger and kissing every inch of her. She seemed softer than she had a few months ago, like she'd eased up on the gym schedule and filled out a little. She was still lithe and fit, but she had a hint more curve, and the thought was dizzying. He was in such deep shit.

He kept his gaze off her body and took a deep breath. "She told me you were expecting me. She also told me there was a key in the tobacco tin under the house. When I didn't find a key, I decided to sleep under the stars and sort it all out in the morning. I tried to be quiet."

Alanna had the good conscience to look sheepish. "Oh, well that would be my fault. I took the spare key out of the tin. I was just worried, living here alone." What she didn't say is that she was fairly positive the tin had been moved a little. The key had never gone missing, but she'd found it behind the wrong piling, and there hadn't been a renter there that week. She continued, "I didn't want someone coming across it, so I have been keeping it in my house. Why didn't you just knock and ask me for it?"

Aidan sighed and took in her face with his eyes. "Branna said you worked two jobs and went to school. I didn't want to wake you if I didn't have to. I'm sorry I scared you. I didn't mean to put my hands on you. I just…reacted. I was half asleep. It was a long trip and honestly, I can think of worse places to sleep."

He gave her a sweet smile and those rolled r's and long vowels were doing funny things to her. "Jesus, O'Brien. Do you have to be so reasonable?" She gave a capitulating sigh, "Come inside. I'll find your key and get you settled." A smile danced across her face as he walked through her open door.

Aidan walked into Alanna's house and immediately approved. It was fresher than the other side. It had the feel of a home instead of a tired vacation rental. The other side was nice when he'd stayed there, but this was different. The layout was the same except everything was reversed. The woodwork was all white, as were the cabinets. The floor in the living room was knotty pine instead of carpeting. Her furniture was soft and white and looked like the type of place you'd curl up with a good book and a cup of tea. The accents were cobalt, and the blue and white combo was both clean and inviting. "Did you decorate? Your place is very nice."

She stopped and immediately looked at his feet. He'd taken his shoes off at the door and left them on the mat. Courteous and reasonable. Damn. "Yes, I moved my stuff in when Branna was making plans to leave. I painted, took out the touristy stuff, tried to make it comfortable. I splurged on this one little area of flooring. My dad put it in." She was reaching in a drawer and pulled out a set of keys. She took one off the ring as she spoke. "So, what brings you here? Are you staying the week?"

Aidan cleared his throat. He felt awkward for some reason. He was going to kill that little hellcat when he got back home. "Actually, I am here for three months. I did an exchange, and I am training with the Marines for a twelve week program. I can't believe Branna forgot to tell you." Her brows shot up in surprise.

"For God's sake, this is a fine mess." He mumbled under his breath. "Listen, lass. If this makes you uncomfortable I will try to find a place on the base. I can do the repairs during my time off and leave the place empty."

Jesus, Anna thought to herself. *He is completely serious. He would leave with his bags and no place to go if I asked him to.*

Anna stopped him before he could go any further. "Aidan, stop. Don't say another word. You aren't staying somewhere else. You just surprised me." She walked over and touched him for the first time since they'd wrestled on the deck. He shut his eyes, briefly, the zing of the contact cutting through him. Her small hand was warm on his forearm. When he opened them, she was looking at him with those bewitching green eyes. "You are welcome here. We are practically family when you think about it. Honestly, the idea of having a real neighbor for a while sounds down right appealing."

Her smile was genuine and he fixated on her beautiful mouth for longer than he should. Then he looked back up to those eyes. "Thank you, Alanna. I promise not to be too much trouble."

She looked at his face as if reacquainting herself. "Why do you call me Alanna? Hardly anyone calls me by my full name."

He shrugged. "It's a beautiful name. It suits you. Alanna Falk, a mix of Gaelic and Scandinavian. Do you know what it means?" She just stared at him, not answering. *I know what it means, but I want to hear you say it with that sexy-ass accent.* His eyes swept her face, her hair, and back to her eyes. "Beautiful Falcon" he said with a smile.

She cocked a brow. "Falcons bite."

He leaned in just a smidgen, "Aye, they do at that. But they can also be tamed to a strong hand."

She turned and walked toward the door, and he laughed when she said, "No one's managed yet."

Aidan walked into the house that was to be his home for the next three months and sighed. He'd brought all of his gear from under the house and set it in the master bedroom. Two bedrooms, two baths, and a view to die for. It wasn't as nice looking as Alanna's side, but it was nicer than his flat, to be sure. He could already see where the remodeling was needed, but it was a fine home. He turned to her and she handed him the keys. "I would have put some food in the fridge if I'd have known. Come over at seven and I'll whip up some vittles for you, before I leave for work." She was completely transformed. Her sweet southern drawl was like a balm that washed over him.

"You don't have to do that. I've kept you up late. Why don't you let me take you to breakfast?"

She waved a hand in dismissal. "I have failed miserably in my southern duties as hostess. I've assaulted you, insulted you, and the only way I'm going to keep my southern belle status is if I whip you up a nice, hearty breakfast. Seven a.m., you copy?"

He laughed, "Seven it is."

3

Seven a.m. came quickly considering Aidan had fallen asleep at three thirty, but he was bright eyed and bushy tailed at the prospect of having breakfast with Alanna. After a quick shower, he threw on a pair of shorts and a wrinkled St. Mary's t-shirt. He hadn't bothered to unpack last night. It was Friday morning, and he had a couple of days to get settled. He walked over to Alanna's house, via the adjoining deck, and her glass door was open, leaving only the screen. His heart squeezed as he paused on a knock.

She was passed out cold at her kitchen table, books and papers everywhere, her laptop left idle. He could hear the faint sound of her alarm clock buzzing from the bedroom, but she didn't stir. He half wanted to walk away and let the poor girl sleep, but she'd said she had to work. He slid in and went to the kitchen. Her coffee pot was ready to go. He just needed to hit the start button. He did, and then looked in her fridge. Lots of produce. He took out a tub of plain greek yogurt and some berries. He grabbed a peach from the fruit bowl. He rinsed it all, chopped it over the yogurt and took two cups off the hooks. She had honey and sugar by the coffee and tea area of the counter, so he drizzled a little honey over the yogurt as well. He brought it over to the table and knelt near her. He placed a gentle hand on her shoulder. God, she really was sound asleep, her breath soft and deep. "Wake up, Alanna." He spoke softly, and then he jostled her shoulder a little when she didn't stir. She gave a little, tired moan and opened her eyes.

Alanna didn't remember going to sleep. She also didn't remember getting up and starting the coffee. She smelled it though, so she must have. Then she felt a gentle nudge on her shoulder and her dream lover was whispering to her. *Huh, this is new. He's usually naked in my dreams, not bringing me coffee.* Then she opened her eyes and shot up in surprise.

"Oh! My God! What time is it?" She bumped the table with her knee, looking around disoriented. She saw some coffee slosh and panic hit her. "My papers! My laptop!" The hand was back on her shoulder. "It's all right. Calm down, woman. I moved it all to the desk."

She finally made eye contact and started to fully wake. Aidan O'Brien was kneeling next to her, smiling as he dabbed the coffee she'd spilled with a napkin. "Oh, God. They are going to kick me out of the southern belle club! Your breakfast! And I'm going to get fired!"

She heard him chuckle discreetly. "Don't get your knickers in a bunch. It's only ten after seven. Didn't you go to bed when I left?"

Relief flooded her face. She stood up and stretched, rolling her neck. "I tried, but I couldn't go back to sleep. I decided to work on my thesis." She looked at what he'd prepared and then back at him.

His face changed. "The door was open. I hope you don't mind. I heard your alarm going off and I knew you'd want me to wake you." Then he shrugged. "I figured you'd need a quick bite and some caffeine before you left. I'm sorry if I overstepped."

She put her finger to the rim of the coffee cup, one of two. He'd made her breakfast. "I am the worst neighbor in creation. I stood you up for breakfast."

He pulled her chair out. "Sit. Eat. I've been taking care of myself for a long time. It was a nice thought, but you need to worry about yourself. How much time do you have? Christ, you probably need to get ready. I'll go."

She pulled out the chair next to her. "Sit. Eat."

He looked at her, trying to decide whether to duck out. "God, am I that scary? Sit, O'Brien." Alanna gave it as an order, not a request. A strange look flickered over his face.

Yes, you are. You scare the hell out of me. Aidan didn't share that particular thought. He sat in the empty chair. "Well, you did come after me with a bat." Alanna giggled, and it was sweet and musical. He looked at her, loving the mischief in her eyes. "You think that's funny?"

She was covering her mouth over a bite of yogurt. "No, no. It was that ninja move you did when you flipped on your back. You have some skills for a big guy." She was positively impish.

"I was trying not to land on you, and you mock me. I've got nine stone on you, little girl. Next time, I'll just squash you like a wee bug." She got up and went to the fridge and he could have sworn she mumbled something along the lines of *promises, promises.*

"So, tell me about your training. What are you going to be doing with the Marines? It's amazing you hooked that up, Aidan. I can't imagine that it's an opportunity everyone gets."

Aidan shrugged. "I'll be with the transition teams. Infantry Marines. Small unit stuff."

Alanna was nodding, "My dad did some time on a MITT team. You are going to be doing some pretty cool stuff. Well, if you like blowing stuff up, driving big armored vehicles, shooting, fighting, you know....a regular day at the office."

Aidan was swallowing a sip of coffee. "Exactly. I can't wait."

She shook her head. "Boys and toys, and you get a beach house in the deal. You can bikini watch in your spare time." She could have sworn Aidan gave her an up and down appraisal, but it was quick.

Aidan was watching Alanna bend into the fridge to grab the cream and was barely keeping his composure. Her blonde hair was bound up on top of her head with little spikes sticking out. She had no make up on and was in cotton shorts and a pullover. Her smooth, beautiful legs led down to adorable little feet. Her get-up was unremarkable, but she was a vision as far as he was concerned.

"So, where is work for you? Branna said you had two jobs," Aidan asked.

She sat back down next to him and added cream to her coffee. "Cream?"

He nodded, "Please." She added some and they both stirred.

"Well, I have a part time job teaching fitness classes on base. Zumba and yoga, and an occasional spinning class. That doesn't pay a lot, but I enjoy it. I am actually doing a paid internship at the Heroic Spirit Concussion Recovery Clinic on base. It is a clinical psychology intern position. I won't be able to go for a doctorate, no money left, and honestly I just want to be done with school. I can work in certain positions with a masters. I just need to turn in my thesis paper, which should be done soon. I have a few more case studies to sum up and then I am done. Summer graduation."

She looked up from her breakfast and shrunk a little. "Am I geeking out on you? I'm babbling, sorry." She had his full attention though.

"I wouldn't have asked if I didn't want to hear about it. So, are we talking traumatic brain injuries? I've heard about the TBI clinics, here in the states."

Alanna nodded, "Sort of. That is what the main purpose of the clinic is. I am working in the PTSD treatment program." Aidan stiffened almost imperceptibly, but Alanna saw it. "My thesis and research is a longer story, but I'll tell you all about it when I have time to make you a proper meal. Now, we need to talk logistics. How are you going to get around? Are you renting a car? You can't be stuck here with no food and no wheels."

Aidan cleared his dishes and took her empty bowl as well. She waged a little custody battle as he took them. "You are not cleaning up on top of everything else," she ordered.

Aidan ignored her and started rinsing them, putting them in the dishwasher. "Denario has a Harley, so he is loaning me his old pick-up. If it rains, I'll pick him up on base. It's easier. He has a base sticker. I'll check in today and get credentials for getting on and off base, using the exchange and commissary. I won't have to officially go into work until Monday." Aidan picked up his coffee and refilled it. "Do you mind if I take this over with me? I'll bring it back."

Alanna was watching Aidan mill around in her kitchen and she was trying really hard not to think about the exquisite dream she'd had only hours ago. Now he was standing in her kitchen, in the flesh. He was too big for the space. Tall, masculine, and tough guy handsome. And that accent, good Lord. She was in utter deep shit.

"Alanna?"

She sharpened up. "I'm sorry, what was that?"

He smiled, "You were deep in thought."

You have no idea. Deep, deep shit. "Sorry, yes you can take the coffee. Why don't you take some filters and coffee over with you and some food?"

Aidan shook his head, "Don't worry about me. I'll do. John will take me to the grocer today. Now, I'm going to make my exit so you can get on with your day." He started to walk through the sliding door.

"Aidan," Alanna said. He turned. "Thank you for waking me up. I just…I get so tired, and sometimes I crash. I would have been late. Thank you."

He nodded. "This is the hard part, lass. It's the last mile. You're almost done." And somehow that simple statement comforted her more than anything her friends, professors, or family had ever said.

Alanna drove through the back gate of Camp Lejeune mentally kicking her own behind. She'd fallen asleep like a child that couldn't be trusted to put herself to bed. Not only had she failed to wake up, but she hadn't done one thing right since Aidan O'Brien had come to town. He was so steady, so quiet and kind. She met that gentlemanly grace with fumbling inadequacy and impure thoughts.

First on her list, as soon as she got out of this cell phone dead zone, was a little international face time with her best friend. How in the heck had she failed to mention that Aidan was coming here for three months? For God's sake, she could have shot him. She didn't take her gun out, assuming it had been a drunk vacationer that stumbled onto the wrong deck, but the bat. She groaned out loud. *You are dead meat O'Mara, or O'Brien, or whatever you are going by nowadays. Dead meat.* She wasn't going to be fooled for a second with the "I forgot" baby brain excuse. That little stinker was up to something, and poor Aidan had paid the price.

"Oh my God, Anna! How are you? I was just thinking about you!" Alanna's irritation dissolved, when she heard her sweet friend's voice.

"Oh, I'm fine. I just had breakfast with a wayfaring Irishman." Branna squealed so loud, it made Alanna grateful that the phone was on speaker and not against her ear. "Girl, you are pure trouble. Do you realize I came after him with a bat in the middle of the night?"

Cue the crickets. "I'm sorry, did you say bat?"

Alanna crooned sweetly, "Why yes, I did. I have custody of the spare key. He didn't want to wake me to get in the house. So in the middle of the night, he crept up on the deck and tried to sleep outside. I, having no idea he was coming, thought it was an axe murderer coming to kill me. So, I went after him with a bat." She paused for dramatic affect. "Excuse me, Branna. I know that isn't giggling that I hear. I broke the poor man's arm. I just left the hospital, where he was eating nasty cafeteria eggs, over-easy." God, she deserved an Emmy.

"Holy shit! You hit him? Oh my God, Anna! Why did you hit him? Is he okay? Jesus, this is my fault! Where was the key? Why did you move the key? Holy shit, his training! You broke his arm!"

Branna was screaming and Alanna considered letting her suffer a little longer, but was hit with a stab of conscience. Branna was starting to tear up a little.

"Just kidding. Gotcha." Alanna said calmly. Branna was silent, letting that sink in.

"You are seriously twisted. You know that? I can't believe I am friends with you."

Now it was Alanna's turn to giggle. "Don't even pretend you didn't deserve that."

Big sigh. "Okay, maybe I did. You can't tell Aidan I did it on purpose. He thinks I have baby brain. Twin baby brain. People feel so sorry for me that I can get away with murder. You can't blow my cover!"

"Why didn't you tell me he was coming? Have you lost your mind, girl?"

Branna was calm again and her answer was simple. "Because when you see the train coming, you have time to jump out of the way. You both needed a good collision." Scheming little hellcat, just like Michael said.

Alanna sighed. "Branna."

Her friend cut her off. "He needs something, Anna. I don't know what, but something. He'd deny it to the grave, but he is lonely. I also think that he is suffering from combat stress. I don't know if it was a specific incident or if it is the toll of four deployments. He is so strong, and he's as stubborn as the rest of the family. They don't have the same resources in the UK as they do in the US, and the Royal Irish Regiment is small and mostly reserves. They don't debrief them like the bigger units." Branna's voice was serious and a little pleading. "I just thought maybe you could be a quiet observer, tell me how he is doing?"

That got Alanna's attention. "He's not going to appreciate a grad school rookie trying to pry into his skull, Branna."

Branna answered, "That's not what I'm asking. Just be his friend, Anna. Please just be his friend and take care of him. He's one of the most amazing men I've ever known. I promise you, this won't be a chore."

Alanna mumbled something that made her best friend smile, "That's what I'm afraid of."

Denario was standing on Aidan's deck looking out at the ocean. "Nice digs. Must be nice to have a beach house in the family."

Aidan had his ruck thrown over his shoulder, all of his paperwork in order. "What's it like on base, is the housing good?"

Denario shrugged. "It is actually. The officer housing is older, built in the forties and fifties. Hardwood, fireplaces, lots of trees and playgrounds. I don't have a view, but the house is nice and you can't beat the neighbors." He winked.

"Aye, I'd imagine not," Aidan said with a grin.

Denario glanced at the adjoining deck. "Although, I don't imagine you'll be complaining about your neighbor, even if she does try to knock you into left field."

Aidan just grunted. "So, where to first?"

Denario took the hint and got back to business. "Let's get you checked in at First Battalion and get your letter from the C.O. It'll give you base privileges. Then we'll take a tour, stop and see Maria for lunch, grab the foot locker you mailed ahead, and finish up with a trip to the commissary. You need some chow and household stuff, I assume? Do you have a washer and dryer? You can do laundry at our house if you need to. The base laundry is ok, but it can get crowded."

Aidan shook his head. "There's a shared one downstairs. There's a common room with workout gear and a laundry set."

Denario lifted his brows, "Nice. You have quite a set up here. And we won't have any problem finding some muscle when you need to get that *Honey Do* list cracking. These boys work for burgers and beer."

Aidan laughed. "Great to know. Let me lock up and we can head out."

By lunchtime Aidan was completely blown away. He'd not toured the base when he'd come with Michael. The Captain and his family were living on the military base in family housing. When he'd come in the fall, they'd been wait-listed and living out in the neighboring town. Aidan couldn't believe the size of the military installation. He had never been on such a huge, well appointed military base. Movie theater, nice housing, swimming pools, an Officer's Club, several gyms. "You realize the rest of the world's military don't live like this?"

Denario just smiled at him. "This is nothing, you should see the Air Force. While we are sleeping on the ground with dirt in our ass cracks, those boys are eating surf and turf and typing away in central air." They walked up the drive and were greeted at the door by a very pregnant Maria. There was one child on her hip and the other around her leg.

"Hello Aidan, it's so wonderful to have you back." Maria hugged Aidan with one arm. She put the toddler down and walked into the house with the men trailing behind her. "John didn't tell me what you like to eat, so I hope you like pasta."

Aidan was bending down, greeting the little people who were very interested in their visitor. "Whatever you have will be perfect. I'm starved. Not a speck of food in the house yet."

Maria beamed. "You've come to the right place. We're both Italian-Americans. Over feeding guests is in the DNA."

As they sat and talked over a delicious lunch, Aidan looked around at the home they were living in. There were odds and ends that decorated the place and he could tell that they'd lived and traveled many places. Things from Europe and Asia, books on every subject, and travel guides to vineyards in California and hiking in the Rockies. It was just the sort of place he liked. No decorator could capture the true heart of a family like this.

"I feel like a Christmas goose, but I can't make myself stop. These local prawns are gorgeous, all together." Aidan said, stuffing another forkful of linguini in his mouth. Maria had her chin propped on her hand and was smiling.

John said with a grim tone, "Don't go getting all moony over that accent, woman."

Maria blushed, "Sorry, John. That I can't agree to. Why aren't you married, Aidan? I would have thought some beautiful woman would have snatched you up by now."

John sighed, "Don't start, Maria."

Aidan was blushing now. She shrugged innocently. "I'm just asking. It seems a tragic waste of a good man."

Aidan laughed and attempted a tactful, succinct explanation. "I just never thought I should pull a wife and kids into life in the army."

Maria rolled her eyes and stood up, waving a dismissive hand. "Oh no, don't tell me you're one of those." Aidan looked at John, baffled. She explained, "*If the military wanted me to have a wife and kids, they would have issued them to me.*" She said it in a husky, masculine voice with her hands on her hips. John was stifling a grin under his glass of tea. Aidan went to speak and she cut him off. "Listen, big man. This life is not for everyone, granted. But God didn't put you on this earth to be alone. He wants you to be loved, multiply, have a woman. Look at us."

She went over and put her arm around her husband and he instinctively covered her round belly with his hand. "We're in this together. I make him a better Marine. He makes me a stronger woman. This is as good as it gets." She kissed his friend on the mouth and walked over to the small children. "And these guys? They'll live all over the world; they're growing up strong and proud and patriotic." She gave him a direct look. "Don't be a chicken, Aidan. The water is fine."

At that, she turned and started clearing the table, as if the matter had been settled. Aidan looked at John, and John just grinned. "And that, my friend, is that." Both men started laughing and tucked into their dessert.

Alanna made it to work just in time to grab a cup of coffee and head to her cubicle. "Good morning, Anna. How is my favorite intern?"

Alanna looked up from her desk and smiled. "Good morning, Dr. Jennings. I'm a little tired, but ready to work." The doctor came into her work area and pulled up an extra seat. Alanna admired the woman in so many ways. She was attractive, but she didn't use her looks to her advantage. She was sharp, professional, and very hands-on with her staff and her patients.

"I'd love to sit in on your group sessions next week. What's on the schedule? Your approach has been so unique; I have been talking to a few of my colleagues in Virginia about your thesis and your sessions. "

Alanna preened under the praise. She cleared her throat and looked at her planner. "Ok, today and Monday I have individual sessions and I am helping another doctor with paperwork. Next Wednesday and Friday are my family days if that is what you were interested in observing. Wednesday evening is Dance with Daddy. I don't have any female patients right now, so I thought the name was okay. We are going to do some adaptive dancing with the patients and help them learn to be physical in their play with the kids. I have one man that is wheelchair bound, one prosthetic proficient patient, and three that are completely ambulatory. They obviously all have TBIs and are being treated for combat stress. One in particular doesn't like loud noises, and his two kids being rowdy has been a trigger for him. We are doing a little fun, aversion therapy. His wife said he hasn't picked the toddler up since he's been home. He also self medicates with alcohol. He's been told he has to be sober for this event, and his wife has assured me he will be."

The doctor was listening intently. "You are so amazing. You know your case histories really well. I wish some of my staff employees had your attention to detail. Now, what is this on Friday? It says *Night Soothing*. Is this for kids?"

Alanna shook her head, "No, it's couples therapy. I booked the Child Development Center and reserved the spaces we need for the couples that have kids. Childcare won't be an issue for anyone who comes. It's something we've been working on with the intimate partners. Nightmares are a big issue, as you know. We've worked on soothing techniques for the headaches, but I wanted to address the night terrors. Some of the wives say they are afraid to flip the light on or shake them awake. Sometimes it agitates the situation. So I have been reading a bit on touch therapy, and I wanted to try something in the yoga room. Are you up for it?"

"Anna, you are so creative with your approaches. I can't wait. My suggestion is for you to have a male helper in there, to actually show the techniques. Do you want me to try and scrounge up a male therapist?"

Alanna thought about it. "Yes, I was thinking about that, too. I asked Rick, and a couple of others, with no luck. I'll think of something. If not, I will use one of the female therapists."

The doctor nodded. "Anna, I wish we had a job opening for you. I know that the internship ends with your graduation. I want you to know that you are at the top of my list if we have a spot open up on the staff."

Alanna just smiled, "I understand. If you happen to hear of anything opening up from your friend in Virginia, please let me know. I am looking into some other non-profits. I could try the VA, but..." She trailed off, not wanting to seem too big for her britches.

"I understand. The VA has a lot of problems. Having huge caseloads where your patients get lost in the system is no-one's dream job. Something will come up. You are too good at what you do to be overlooked for long. Someone's going to snatch you up, and I will be rueing the day I didn't squeeze you onto my staff."

Aidan pulled the old truck into the carport of the beach house and wasn't surprised to find Alanna's car was gone. He stifled disappointment, trying to convince himself that he hadn't been secretly hoping to find her bikini clad, and lounging on the seaside. He unloaded the groceries armload by armload until the cab of the truck was empty. Then he brought in his ruck and footlocker.

He went into the house through the street side entrance and started arranging his groceries. He went to the outlet in the kitchen and plugged in the disposable cell phone he'd picked up at the base shopping center. He had phone cards to load minutes, and that was the easiest solution he could think of for not using his European phone.That bill would be astronomical within a few days.

After putting it all away, he went into his bedroom and began arranging all of his luggage into the closet and bureau. He took out an envelope that contained photos and began sticking them in the mirror frame. His brothers, Finn and Brigid with the babies, the twins, his parents and grandparents, and Tadgh. Brigid had printed them all off for him to take with him. He'd promised Cora that he would also place her painting in a place of honor in his new home. He smiled as he touched it. It was an ocean picture with a purple fish and an orange one. One fish had a picture of Cora taped to the head, the other of him. His chest squeezed. He took the painting to where he remembered a cork board being in the kitchen. It had thumb tacks for posting notes. He took four tacks and fastened the precious painting to the board. He would show it to her when he video called her later.

Aidan began his run at the foot of the beach walk, hitting the timer on his watch. He'd never had such a wide expanse of beach to run on before. He kept to the cool, hard sand that stood stiffly between the soft, warm sand and the water. It was more compacted from the tide having gone out and had the perfect amount of give. The beach wasn't crowded due to the time of day and the fact that it wasn't yet peak tourist season. Small birds scurried as he approached, leaving their hunt for tiny mollusks and crabs until Aidan had passed. The shells crunched under his feet and his pace and breathing were smooth. He lost himself in the steady rhythm.

Alanna's stomach did a little flip when she pulled into the drive to see that Aidan had used his half of the car park to stash his borrowed truck. She opened her door and ascended the narrow stairway to her house. She cringed when she looked at the neat stacks of papers and her laptop that had been set on the desk. She knew she should work, but the day was glorious. She walked out to the deck and breathed deeply of the sea air. She was going to miss this place.

She knew after her schooling was over and her internship had ended, she was going to have to move. Her father had given her his GI Bill benefit, which had supported her during most of her undergrad studies. Her military dependent scholarships and academic scholarships, along with her small college fund, had paid up until this past semester. She'd had to work two jobs to keep up with her bills and finish her graduate degree, but graduation was only a month away.

Her internship didn't pay much, but it paid enough with the fitness classes she was teaching in order for her to squeak by. She couldn't keep sponging off Branna at this dramatically reduced rent, however. She had some job prospects, but keeping these digs on the beach was not really fair to Branna. She had kids to think about, and she could be getting way more for this place.

She'd offered it up under the guise of "managing" the other rental. Alanna knew darn well that Branna didn't really need her. She would also be free and clear to sell the property if she wasn't housing Alanna. She knew that she could live with her father. He'd offered repeatedly. She appreciated it, but at twenty-five it had to be her last resort.

She glanced over at the other side and wondered what renovations Aidan would be doing. A thought of him all sweaty and shirtless doing the handyman routine popped into her head. *Nice southern girls don't mack on their neighbors.* Just as this thought came to her, she saw him. Alanna murmured, "Baby Jesus in a manger." Then she finished in her head, *Deliver me from temptation.*

She was never going to get the image of Aidan O'Brien jogging on the beach, in shorts and a tight t-shirt, out of her brain. Ever. At ninety years old, she was going to close her eyes, and on the back of her eyelids she was going to see this man, right at this moment. His legs were muscular and powerful. He had broad shoulders, a trim waist, and a six pack showing through his unremarkable, but tight and sweaty shirt. His face was flushed with exertion, his hair short and sandy, his blue eyes intense. He stopped at the water's edge as if contemplating something. Then he darted into the water, diving under a cresting wave. He broke the surface of the water and let out a whoop. She giggled. May was relatively warm in North Carolina, but it took a while for the water temperature to catch up. She was taken back by the boyish look on his face. Unguarded and unreserved.

Aidan let the cold water settle into his hot skin, and it felt divine. He was used to cold water, living on the West coast of Ireland. Experience told him that you were better off diving right in, rather than trying to creep into the water in slow degrees. But cold was cold, and it stole his breath. It felt glorious, however, and he looked out to the vast sea with a sense of peace.

It was the same ocean, just a little further west. Its glistening beauty and smooth swells always had a way of shedding the day's stressors away. Branna had told him that it was quite common to see pods of dolphins on this beach, but he didn't see anything but a few brave swimmers, and shining waves as he stared down the long stretch of beach. He could touch the sandy bottom, and he liked the feel of it in his toes.

He turned to the shore, toward the house, when he saw her. She was like a Nordic goddess. Wheaten hair wild in the breeze, graceful limbs, bewitching eyes. *Bleeding Christ. You have no idea how beautiful you are, do you?*

He knew he couldn't get involved with her. She was Branna's best friend, more like her sister than any blood tie could be. He couldn't start an entanglement with this girl and treat her like one of his past flings. She wasn't the type you had a fling with, but more the type you loved until you drew your last breath. And wasn't that at the top of the short list of reasons why he should absolutely not get involved with her? He came out of the water, and she greeted him with a towel.

"How is the water?" She touched his forearm and made a cute little noise. "Brrrr, you must have polar bear in your DNA."

Aidan took the towel and smiled, wiping his face. "Coastal Clare rarely gets warm, but it never kept us away. The lochs are the same."

Alanna started walking back to the house. "I don't want to disturb you, I just thought you'd need a towel. The downstairs shower doesn't have hot water piped in. It's good to get the sand off, but you may want to head upwards if you have a mind to warm up."

She started the short walk up the dune when Aidan called back to her. "Are you working on your paper tonight?"

She turned, dread showing on her face. "I'm afraid so. I have to write up my sessions today. Did you make it to the store for some food?"

He nodded. "I'll leave you to it, then. Try to eat and sleep somewhere in that plan, aye?"

Aidan cooked a small dinner, using the grill under the house to grill a pork chop. As he manned the grill, Alanna emerged from her house and his jaw dropped at the sight of her. Tight yoga pants and one of those tight fitness tank tops that contained but didn't hide. She was carrying an iPod in one hand and a water bottle in the other.

She stopped short when she saw him. "Hello again. I was going to grab a quick workout before hitting the paperwork, again." She glanced around the grill and scrunched her brow together. "What are you doing to that poor pig meat, Aidan?"

He laughed. "What do you mean?"

She put a hand on her hip. "You're in the South, young man. We can't abide quickly cooked pork."

He answered her with a grin, "Ah, the famous Carolina barbecue I've been hearing tales about? Isn't this a barbecue?"

Alanna shook her head, giving him a pitying look. "You have so much to learn, grasshopper. Tomorrow night, we go out. Branna would have my head if she knew I'd not taken you to her favorite barbecue place."

Aidan cocked his head. "It's a date." Her eyes flared and she thought about saying something else but he continued. "This will set for a bit. Do you mind if I take a look in your little gym?" Aidan walked in behind her as she turned on the lights. The washer and dryer stack was in the far left corner where Branna told him it would be. There was a heavy bag in the opposite corner and his brows shot up. "Is that yours?"

She laughed, "No, I like a good Louisville Slugger, not my fists."

He shot her a glance, "Yes, I am well aware."

"It was Brian's. Then my father used it, my brother too. Sometimes men need to hit something."

He touched the bag. "Very true. I suppose this is better than a pub fight."

He looked around the room as Alanna spoke. "I have some kettle bells over there, a few hand weights, an iPod dock if you have one. The elliptical needs plugged in, but it is pretty user friendly." She turned to him. "Consider this yours while you are here. I love a good beach run, but sometimes this is quicker and I don't get distracted looking for shark's teeth."

Aidan was looking at her beautiful face when the smell hit him. "Ah Christ!" He shot out the door to the sight of his chop smoking like a warehouse fire.

He grabbed the tongs and took the blackened meat off. He closed the grill and shut the gas off. He turned around and Alanna's face was stricken. "Two meals spoiled. I'm sorry, I distracted you. I can make you something."

Aidan was touched. "This was no one's fault but mine. Being distracted by a pretty lass is the best distraction there is." His words weren't provocative. His look was gentle, not seductive.

She grabbed a sweatshirt off a hook by the door. "Come on, Aidan. It's the weekend. Time for a study break and some real barbecue."

The restaurant that Alanna took him to didn't look like much from the outside, or the inside for that matter, but experience told him that good decor didn't necessarily mean good food. They went to the counter, and Alanna started an explanation of how it worked. "You can get pork on a plate or in a bun. If you get the bun, the slaw will be on top of the meat unless you tell them otherwise. Coleslaw, I mean. It's a sort of cabbage salad. You can also get the catch of the day fish fry. You'll get hushpuppies which are like corndogs without the dog." Aidan looked at her, baffled. "They're like fried cornbread balls but a little sweeter. Really good and not friendly toward the hips."

Her heart did a little, double thump when she noticed his eyes drift to her hips. He recovered quickly, but the male appraisal had been there. "On that board right there are all of the sides you can choose," she pointed. Then she ordered first. "The okra is very good by the way."

Aidan curled a lip up in distaste. "Aye, the Iraqis eat a lot of okra. I'll pass." The slimy, oozing, green vegetable made him sick at the thought. He had a distinct aversion to okra.

Alanna smiled, "Yes, so I've heard. This will be coated in breading and fried. I'll get some and you can try it. You might change your mind." Aidan ordered the same plate with a side of sweet potato fries and green beans.

They sat down with their trays next to a fish tank that was surrounded by mesmerized toddlers. "Do you want to sit further away? Do children get on your nerves?" she asked.

He replied, "No, I'm the eldest of six and I already have four nieces and nephews. Kids don't bother me at all. Ireland lets people bring their kids into most places, even pubs." Alanna seemed pleased by his response, and that in turn pleased him. He sipped his drink and his brows shot up. "Christ, are you sure this is tea?"

She laughed as she took a sip. "Sweet tea, the house wine of the South!" She'd thickened her southern drawl and he found himself taking another sip just to keep that smile on her face.

"Aye, a little tea with the sweet."

"You get used to it. They've got other things if you prefer soda or lemonade."

Aidan declined. "No, I am going for the full experience. I don't want to look like a foreigner."

Alanna looked around the little restaurant and noticed how the women and teenage girls were sneaking glances at Aidan. It hadn't escaped her that every female employee had come to the counter to take a peek. *They won't be worried about your country of origin. That accent is half the appeal. The other half being what you look like in those shorts.* Alanna shook her head to clear those thoughts just as Aidan asked her about her thesis.

She explained it as best she could without boring him to tears. "I remember what it was like. You know by now that my father was there when Brian was killed. He took a sniper round in the shoulder. Pulled Brian clear with his one good arm." She cleared her throat and took a cleansing breath as she continued. "He came home wounded, but it wasn't so much from the bullet. I know you understand the kind of hurt I'm talking about."

Aidan's eyes were intense, his body still. *Such reserve,* she thought. Then she continued. "I had a hard time, too. My parents were divorced and we were staying with my grandparents at the time it happened. They wouldn't let me go to Germany, to the hospital. I was angry. I was old enough, but I didn't have the resources to rush a passport and get on a plane by myself. I didn't even have a credit card. Erik and I were eighteen and nineteen."

She waved her hand dismissively. "That's not important, though. Sorry for babbling."

Aidan's hand came over hers. "You don't have to go on, but I want you to know that if you want to tell it all, I want to hear it." His thumb stroked the back of her hand and it soothed her. She looked at him, his beautiful, masculine face held such tenderness.

"After the worst of it, the funeral and daddy's initial medical treatment, he had some time off for recovery. He was so silent. So distant. I was a stupid child, really. Eighteen seems all grown up, but it's not. I was going to school at the community college, starting my first degree. He started jogging on the beach. He couldn't do a lot of lifting or calisthenics. His shoulder couldn't bear weight at first. He wasn't eating or sleeping. When he did sleep, he had nightmares." Aidan fidgeted a little, picking at his food. "I'm sorry, you probably don't want to hear about this." She was backpedaling, realizing she was causing him discomfort.

"Please, don't stop," he said softly.

His eyes were a little more guarded, but she continued. "Like I said, I was having trouble, too. Kids are self-centered, especially older kids that have their own lives. I came so close to losing him. Watching Branna and Meghan grieve…" Her voice grew tight and she took a deep breath until she felt his hand again. It was big and warm and he ran it smoothly up her forearm. She closed her eyes, stilled by the contact. "I lost my way, a little. Made bad choices." She tensed slightly when she said it, and Aidan noticed that she pulled the neck of her shirt up. It wasn't low cut, and he found it an odd thing to do.

"Anyhow, one day I went running with him. We just jogged silently at first. I started going with him every night. The routine was nice. The closeness was there, even though we weren't talking or touching. We were tuned into each other. Pretty soon we were talking. It wasn't long before that familiarity was back, daddy and daughter. We found our way back to each other through a very physical means. First it was jogging, then we'd find ourselves splashing each other in the surf, or we'd race into the waves like you did today."

"You're smiling now." Aidan said.

She looked at him and giggled a little, her cheeks blushing. "I love my daddy more than anything. I am so proud of him. Not just because he's a great Marine, or because he's the type of man that would use his one good arm to try and save his friend. I love him because I saw him broken, and I watched him rise from the ashes. I look back at how far he's come, how far we've come." She shook her head. "I just want to give that to other men and women. I want to help them and their families do what we did. I think there's a very physical element to emotional healing, especially for physical people. He isn't a banker; there is a very physical aspect to being a warrior. The body heals to one degree or another. Surgery, medicine, therapy. The heart and mind? Well, that's a little harder. I've seen families break up due to PTSD. It's a silent, invisible injury, but it is real. Men come home and have blood on their hands. They have trouble reconnecting with their wives. They don't want to play with their kids. They get depressed. The suicides are rising." She put her hands flat on the table, her face intense. "Maybe I'm crazy, but I want to try and think outside the box. These guys don't like head shrinkers. There has to be a different approach."

"And that's what your thesis is about? A different approach?" Aidan asked.

"Yes, but it's a bit hard to explain," she said. Aidan stayed quiet and it gave her time to think. "I could show you, though. Would you like to see what I do?" Aidan looked surprised and she flushed with embarrassment. "You probably have a lot to do. You probably don't want to come to my work on your down time. It's okay."

Aidan interrupted her with his soft, baritone voice. "I'd be honored."

She smiled shyly, "Well, if you're sure. I could use the help, actually. On Friday afternoon if you're available. I tried to get a male therapist to assist, but haven't found one that isn't tied up. Interns don't pull much weight, and some of them think my approach is a little out there. They think my boss is too indulgent." She shrugged in a self deprecating way.

"They're jealous," he said. "They don't like someone shaking things up and finding new ways that have eluded them." Aidan said simply. "Fuck 'em. Count me in." Alanna choked on her sweet tea. "Sorry, I forget my manners sometimes," he said.

Alanna beamed. "I like it. You're genuine. So, what do you think of the barbecue?" He looked down and realized he'd barely touched his food, so engrossed was he in the woman across from him.

He took a bite of the pork and was surprised. "It's tart and a bit spicy. It's really good." He tried the sweet potato fries. "Well, those are very good. More like a dessert than chips, but good." She smiled a mischievous smile, holding up a little pinwheel of fried okra.

"You can keep the okra, lass." He shuddered.

"Chicken," she challenged. She twisted it like a wheel in her fingers and made clucking noises. He took her wrist and brought her fingers to his mouth. He took the okra straight from her hand and his lips grazed her fingers. Her eyes flared. As he chewed, his nose twitched a little. "I'll admit it's not quite as bad as the Iraqi version, and the delivery was much better," he said with a sexy smile. "Still, that slimy texture comes out at the end."

He gave a thumbs down and made a buzzer sound. Then he saw Alanna instinctively lick the fingers he'd just had his mouth on. He felt a rush of blood run straight down to his groin. He fought the urge to pull her across the table and take her mouth. The hunger he felt must have been reflected in his face, because she paused. He realized he was looking at her mouth, and he raised his eyes to hers.

She looked away first, picking up her napkin. Christ, what was he doing? This was not the right direction. "So, how was your tour of the base?" Her tone was light, but there was a charming blush to her cheeks.

Aidan tried to think back to the last actual date he'd been on. It had probably been over a year. He certainly hadn't had sex in that long and tension was tight in his body. Not that he just wanted sex. She was appealing on just about every level, and that spelled trouble. It spelled heartbreak considering their circumstances. He did admit, however, that he'd never enjoyed a woman's company this much in his thirty-one years.

Alanna pulled into the drive, parking under her side of the duplex. They got out and she walked over to the storage space that was her makeshift gym. She turned to Aidan, hand on the doorknob. "I can't skip the gym now. Not after eating all of that tasty fried okra." She giggled when Aidan made a face. "Thank you, Aidan. I've been so busy. I haven't made time for friends. And you should have let me pay. I owed you."

He shook his head. "Not going to happen." She looked at his face a little longer than was wise before going to her workout.

4

Alanna grunted in frustration as she dragged herself out of bed at two o'clock in the morning. She was sweating, not from the air temperature, but from the straining, aching heat she felt in the aftermath of her dream. She walked into the kitchen and poured a glass of water. She took it to the sliding door and walked out onto the deck in the dark. The wind was refreshing, the sound of the ocean bringing her heart rate down. In the aftermath of her dream, her nipples were taut and the breeze made them tingle against her thin t-shirt. She ran her fingers through her hair, taking deep breaths to further calm herself.

Aidan was lying on the chaise lounge when Alanna slid the door open and walked out. He should tell her he was out here, but something in him just wanted to watch her briefly. She was resplendent under the moon and stars, her hair blowing away from her face. When she slid her fingers through it and arched her back, he caught a silhouette in the small amount of light. He'd thought her more athletically built, but he could see now that the tops she usually wore were constraining. She was lushly curved on top, and the arch in her back showed off a beautiful, perfectly shaped ass. He couldn't keep his presence quiet. It was too much like spying on her. "Couldn't sleep, again?"

She jumped at the sound of his voice with a squeak. "Baby Jesus in a Manger, Aidan! You scared me!"

He was laughing lightly. "I'm sorry, darlin'. Don't hit me with your wee club."

She had her hand on her heart, a murderous look in her eye, but his laughter was contagious. She started to chuckle. She walked over and smacked his knee. "I'm not used to this neighbor thing. Why are you up? Jet lag, or are you a regular insomniac?"

He pulled the other lounger from alongside the rail and offered her a seat beside him. She took it, thanking him. "I don't sleep very well, I'm afraid. The jet lag doesn't help. So, what woke you? It wasn't me again, was it? I was extra quiet."

She shook her head, telling him a partial truth. "No, a dream. I just thought I'd come out and stargaze; listen to the water. Sometimes it helps."

Aidan just grunted in understanding. Between neighboring lights and the moon and stars, Aidan could see her pretty clearly. Her shirt was loose and thin and white and her nipples were hard.

"What kind of dream?" he asked. His voice was low and husky.

She looked at him, a little alarm showing on her face. "It was nothing. I really don't remember." She said dismissively. He noticed that when she answered him, she put a steadying hand on her belly. She was wearing loose pajama bottoms, and he wondered if she slept in them, or had put them on to come outside. The thought of her lying in her bed with cotton panties and that little t-shirt made him thicken in his trousers. He could see her, hair splayed around her, kissed by the moon coming through her window. She was so beautiful. Even more beautiful than he remembered.

"Do you still perform? In the little pub we went to last time?"

She smiled shyly, "No, I lost my band members. Honestly, I didn't have time this last semester. I had to work a lot more. Money's been..." She stopped before revealing anything.

He knew he shouldn't pry, but he didn't like the thought of her having financial stress on top of her already heavy load. "What happened to your two guitarists, then?"

She shrugged. "Well, Brent was unreliable. He liked the booze and the local women. Our music was interfering with his drinking and whoring."

Aidan sputtered out a laugh. "Aye, it often gets the best of many young men."

She smiled, "True enough. Danny, well, his departure was a mystery. He was frustrated; I don't know why. I thought we were friends. We'd rehearse; he was really talented. I thought it was working. One night in the middle of a song we were rehearsing, he just stopped playing. He was looking at me with that frustration showing on his face. I asked him if I'd missed a note." She put her hands up and then slapped them down on her lap. "He just said that he had to leave. That he wasn't getting what he needed, that it wasn't healthy for him. He just walked out. I knew he was a recovering alcoholic, so I thought maybe it was the bar scene he was talking about. It wasn't good for his sobriety. I asked him if that was it, but he just shook his head and left."

Aidan had tensed at the direction of the story, but then had realized that this beautiful, talented, smart woman was completely clueless. "He was in love with you, Alanna." He said softly. She looked at him like he had a dick on his forehead, and he laughed. "You mean to tell me that never occurred to you?"

She started shaking her head. "No, we were friends. It was never like that between us."

He continued, "Christ woman. You have a mirror. Surely you know what you look like."

She put her arms crossed around her chest. "You're wrong."

He grunted. She bristled. "I understand that I'm pretty. All I have to do is watch the women around my father and brother to understand that I have what the world considers to be good looks." She waved her hand around her face. "This and this." She picked up a strand of her blonde hair. "This is DNA. It is like a pretty flower in the garden. People walk by, admire it. Then they keep going. There's no earth shattering draw to the flower. Pretty isn't everything."

He said, "Pretty is one thing. You're more than pretty, even if you don't know it. You're so beautiful that it's downright terrifying. And you sing like the angels and you're kind and smart and ambitious. That poor sod ran off because he couldn't stand being around you anymore if he couldn't have you. And that's the most truth you are ever going to get on the matter."

What in the fecking hell has gotten into you? What are you saying? He cringed inwardly at Alanna's silence. Then he looked over at her.

Her jaw was slightly dropped, then a big smile came across her face. "I've never been called terrifyingly beautiful before. I think I need to record that so that I can replay it every weekend when I don't have a date. I like the accent, too."

He chuckled, "Don't get all fat headed about it."

She giggled. "You just sounded like Brigid."

He sharpened up. "How do you know that?"

She blushed. "I don't really. It's just, Branna has painted such a vivid picture of you all. I love hearing her stories, hearing her describe all of the O'Briens and the townsfolk. She puts on the accents and everything. I feel like I know everyone. Your hometown sounds like a little piece of heaven."

Aidan's heart squeezed. "Aye, I suppose it is. You'll have to visit when school is done."

She sighed longingly. "That is not in the budget. I don't know what's ahead. The clinic doesn't have any staff openings right now. I could try to wait it out, but this last semester put a drain on my wallet. I need to find a job and I need to let Branna get a better income out of this place. I'm afraid a plane ticket to Europe is impossible right now."

Aidan was taken back. "You'd move from here?"

She shrugged. "Time to grow up. I have to get a job. I can't keep paying this low rent. I could live with my dad in Virginia, but that doesn't appeal. He'll move in a few months and I'll be in the same boat. Honestly, I want to be independent. He's done so much for me. I didn't have to take one dime out in student loans. He gave me his GI Bill. Between that and scholarships, I have gotten a hell of an education. It is time to stand on my own two feet."

"Do you want to stay here?" Aidan asked.

She shrugged. "It's beautiful, but there are a lot of beautiful places. I want to be where I'm needed. I've moved all my life. I can move again. My grandparents and aunts and uncles are down in South Carolina. I could look there as well. I don't know what's ahead. I'll be fine though. I have a good support system. I won't be homeless."

"You're very strong, Alanna. It seems you could do anything with that attitude."

Aidan felt her hand on his and she squeezed. "Thank you, Aidan. Now, if you're done boosting my ego, I think we should both try the sleep thing again. What do you say?"

Aidan groaned internally, thinking that he would love to pick her up off that lounger and carry her off to bed. "I suppose we should."

Aidan slept late for the first time in years. After his two o'clock chat with Alanna, he'd gone to bed feeling relaxed and calm, and he hadn't even dreamed. He started the kettle and fired up his laptop. He opened up his WiFi menu to find his options. The strongest signal was Falcon's Nest and he smiled, knowing it was Anna's. There didn't appear to be any wifi for his house. "Damn," he mumbled to himself. He decided it wasn't too early to go over and bum the password. Her blinds were drawn, so he figured it was okay to go to the sliding glass.

He knocked, and she yelled from the interior that she was coming. She was in a University of North Carolina sweatshirt and a pair yoga pants. Her hair was knotted behind her neck. She let him in and he noticed she looked a little out of sorts. She walked back over to her desk.

"It can wait, lass. I didn't mean to bother you." He was stepping back when he noticed she was exiting out of something on the desktop computer and pulling something out of the printer to stuff in the desk drawer. Her hands were shaking. "No! Aidan, please. It's ok. I was just..." She paused. "I, uh, I was just cleaning out my e-mails. Please, come in. Do you want some coffee? It's fresh. I made it a half hour ago. It's Sumatra blend." She was babbling nervously.

"Alanna, what's the matter?"

She shot him a look. "Nothing. It's nothing." She came to where he stood. "Please, sit down. I was just going to have a snack. I skipped breakfast."

He noticed she locked the door again and his instincts were firing off. He came into her kitchen nook and took her by the elbows. "Jesus Christ, you're shaking." He sat her down on a stool. She wouldn't meet his eyes. "What do you want, darlin'? Coffee? Let's see what you've got in here."

"Aidan, I am fine. I just got an email I didn't care for. Someone complaining about my..." she paused, "my Zumba classes. It just ticked me off. I'm okay. Let me wait on you, please." She came around him and started pulling some things out of the fridge and pantry. She started to pour two mugs of coffee and Aidan could hear the carafe clinking against the mug as she shook.

He put his hand over hers and extracted the pot. "Caffeine might not help just now."

She looked at him, irritation flickering. "I told you..."

He cut her off. "A lie. You told me a lie. If you don't want to tell me what's wrong, that is your choice and I'll respect it. Tell me to stick to my own business. But don't lie to me, Alanna." His accent was thick and she could tell he was a little irritated himself. He put the coffee pot down. "I just wanted the WiFi password. I'm trying to video call home."

She looked at him blankly. "Oh, okay. I'm sorry. I'll write it down."

She went to the desk and opened the right drawer. Aidan noticed, along with sticky notes, that she had a pistol in there. "You keep a gun in your desk?"

She took a deep breath. "No, not normally. Normally it's in my nightstand. I have a Concealed Carry permit, so I also travel with it. I'm in here a lot and I just moved it. You aren't going to lecture me on gun control are you, Irishman?" Aidan coughed out a laugh and she looked at him. She exhaled on a grin.

"No, Yank. I was just thinking I was glad you brought the bat on my first night," he said with a teasing tone.

She raised an eyebrow. "True enough, but calling a good southern girl a yankee is a way to get smacked tush." She was teasing him, trying to lighten the mood, but he knew that something had rattled her. She wasn't going to tell him, though. He was wondering if it was something he'd done. Maybe coming outside last night to find him sitting in the dark had started to worry her. She'd seemed okay last night, but she was a woman living by herself. Maybe he was making her nervous.

She wrote down the password on a sticky note and handed it to him. He looked her in the eye as he took it. "I want you to know that you are safe around me. I hope I haven't done something to worry you."

Her face changed and she interrupted him. "Oh, Aidan! It isn't you. I know that. Don't think that for a minute. Everything is fine. It's actually comforting having someone familiar next door."

His jaw ticked, but he kept his thoughts to himself. He knew what fear looked like. Something had scared her. For some reason she kept a bat and a gun nearby. Yesterday her windows were open, but something had set her off. Made her lock down and move her pistol.

"I'll be next door if you need me. I was going to do a little exploring today, but I don't have to go."

She shrugged. "Why wouldn't you? I have to study, but it's a beautiful day. Is there anything I can help with? Do you need directions?" He shook his head. "No, I was going to head to town, try the pawn shops for a guitar. All that talk last night got my fingers twitching."

She smiled at that. "I guess you had to leave yours at home. Well, they are probably cheaper here than where you live. You should be able to pick up a used one for about a hundred dollars. Bring it over if you get one. You can tune it from my piano."

He looked around, not seeing a piano. She walked over to one of the bedrooms and opened the door. "They're being sorely neglected." He peered in to see her violin, an upright piano, and a music stand nestled into the bedroom with a daybed for guests. "The piano was Branna's. She gave it to me when she left. I heard all about her new one." She smiled, "Your brother sounds like quite the romantic."

Aidan looked at her, "I suppose he is. The right woman will do that."

"So, the piano is in tune, feel free to come over and use what you need. I have sheet music too."

Aidan turned to her, searching her face."Only if you agree to play with me," he said.

Alanna had to fight to keep her eyes open and steady. His voice was deep and playful and suddenly all of the stress streamed out of her, heat pooling in her belly. She put her hands on her hips. "Aye, laddie, 'twould be a pleasure to be sure," she said in a botched Irish accent. Aidan barked out another laugh. "Our wee raven's been giving the falcon some lessons." His accent was extra thick for effect, and it made her giggle, as he had meant it to.

She winked at him and walked back into the living room. As she swept past him he took her arm. "You'd tell me if something was amiss? Something I could help with?"

She looked at him, lifting her chin. "Everything's fine, Aidan. Right as rain."

He paused, searching her face and then nodded. "Okay. I thought I'd go to the fishmonger, get some prawns or fish. Would you like to have dinner on the deck, if you don't have plans tonight? I know my way around the kitchen, despite the three alarm fire at the grill last night."

She nodded, "I'd love that. I usually eat alone. My friends have been as neglected as my violin. I'll bring the beer. You do like beer, don't you?"

He looked scandalized. "That's like asking the vicar if he likes bread and wine." She giggled again and damn it to hell, every time she did that it made his stomach lurch. He bloody well better not burn dinner tonight!

Aidan signed on to the WiFi in the dining room. He looked at his contacts and decided to call his parents first. No one picked up on their computer, which didn't surprise him. Their computer was a little old, and they didn't keep it on all the time. He could call them on his pre-paid phone later. Next on the list was Michael and Branna. After a few seconds of ringing, Branna appeared. She was screeching to someone behind her. "It's Aidan!"

Michael's head popped in and greeted him. "Dia duit, brother. How is America treating you?" They fell into easy conversation, him telling them about the long flight, meeting Denario's family, and his tour of the base. Branna was visibly fidgeting, and he suspected she'd already had a tongue lashing from her best friend.

"So, lass. Were you going to tell me that Alanna had a bat and pistol waiting for me if I woke her up?"

Michael's eyes bugged out. "She held a pistol on you?" Aidan looked at Branna who was avoiding eye contact.

"No, she luckily went with the bat. Did Branna tell you that she neglected to tell her friend about my visit? She thought I was a bloody prowler."

Aidan didn't get the response he was expecting. Michael was grinning. "Aye, I heard. Was it fun wrestling the bat from her?"

Branna covered a laugh with her hand and Aidan rolled his eyes. "Christ, I don't know which one of you is worse." He knew that trying to make them feel guilty was a lost cause. Branna knew exactly what she was doing. *Baby brain my ass.*

"Well, I'm headed out for some exploring. Once the training starts, I'll have less free time. I was going to the pawn shops to find a cheap guitar, then I thought I'd just drive. I want to pick up some fresh catch at the fishmonger."

Branna seemed pleased at this change of subject. "Ok, well just drive down the coast once you leave the pawn shops. There are little towns just past the base that are full of fishermen and several places to get fish. Captain Sam's is cheap and their clams aren't sandy. The sign is close to the ground, but it's just over the bridge. If they are open, there will be a black lab at the driveway to meet you. It's a small place, right on the water."

Aidan talked a bit more, then he said goodbye and got ready to leave.

Aidan was cruising down Highway 24 with a used Alvarez guitar riding shotgun. After hitting a series of pawn shops within a mile of the base, Aidan had found the used guitar and had haggled the price down to eighty dollars. He drove through a small historic town which he had made a mental note of to explore later. It was at the mouth of a river and the old part of the town seemed to be built around the fishing community. It reminded him a bit of the Irish Coast.

The sun was high in the sky and the water sparkled around a series of fishing boats, which had great netting systems poking out either side. He stopped when he saw a sign for Captain Sam's Seafood and sure enough, an old, pudgy labrador along with another dog came to greet him. He walked into a rough, cinder block structure where a woman stood behind mounds of ice and shrimp.

There was an empty stroller to the left and a sign on the wall that said, "Please do not pick up the baby." He looked at her and she was rocking side to side with a baby on her hip. Fans blew all around and the smell was a bit pungent, but it smelled like fresh seafood, not anything rotten. The fans most likely worked to keep the flies at bay as well as for a cooling effect.

"How can I help you, honey?" She had a native accent and Aidan smiled as the baby babbled, drool coming down his chin. The little boy smiled, and Aidan could see the emerging teeth that were breaking the surface of the bottom and top gums. "Yes, ma'am. What do you have in the haul today?"

Her brows shot up in surprise. "Well, well. Seems you ended up on the other side of the Atlantic. Are you here on vacation?"

She was sweet and friendly. She reminded him of some of the fisher wives in his own town. "No, I'm here training on the base. My sister-in-law is American. She told me you were the lass to see about some clams and prawns?"

The woman's face lit up and a blush came across her cheeks. "Well, no one's called me lass before. I see why she fell for your brother, if he's as cute as you. Don't tell my husband I said that." She winked and he knew she was being playful, not meaning anything by it.

"Today I have three sizes of shrimp and the prices are up here." She pointed to the sign. "Also, you happen to be in luck, because the men got some beautiful clams a couple of days ago."

He scowled. "Will they still be good, two days later?"

She nodded reassuringly. "Oh, yes. The way I take care of them they will be. Do you want a dozen or so of those? I have to go to the dock if you do."

He was intrigued. "Absolutely. If you pleased Branna, you must have some sort of secret."

She stopped. "Branna? The dark haired girl? Lived here a little while back?" Aidan was surprised she knew her customers by name, and he said as much. "Not all of them, but she was sweet, and as pretty as a rose. I remember her mother." The woman's eyes grew sad. "Her mother got real sick. Branna would come get clams for her. She said her mother wouldn't eat any meat, was getting too thin, but she loved my clams."

The woman shook her head. "Losing both parents like that? She had the saddest eyes I've ever seen. I wondered what had happened to her."

Aidan's heart squeezed. "She's happy," he said softly. "She's living in Ireland with a set of beautiful, raven haired twin babies." The woman's face lit noticeably. "We're taking care of her. She's not sad anymore." He said it with a smile and the woman's eyes teared up.

She just nodded. "I'm so very glad to hear that."

Aidan picked out some shrimp and then followed the woman to the dock. She pulled up a net that was tied off and dropped over the dock into the water. "See, if you keep them in the water, they stay fresh. I hang them off the bottom by a foot or so and move them when the tide changes the water level. They work out all the sand and don't take in anymore since they're off the bottom. After a day or two, they've spit all the sand out."

Aidan laughed. "I do believe you are a genius."

She laughed, blushing as she grabbed the baby by the shorts to keep it from toddling off the dock and in the water. "Fishy!" he said with a wet grin.

"Any hope I had of this one not being a fisherman is slowly swirling the toilet bowl."

Aidan laughed again, "Aye, the sea's in his blood to be sure." Aidan knelt down to the child and the little boy grabbed his nose. "You'll not go giving your mam a fright, lad."

The baby squealed. "Fishy!"

Once back to the block structure, Aidan took his wallet out. "How much do I owe you?"

The woman smiled, her face sweaty and tired. "Five for the shrimp. The clams are on the house." Aidan shook his head and she stopped him, "For Branna. I'm glad y'all gave her a good home. Send her my good wishes. My name is Sheila."

Aidan shook her hand. "Aidan O'Brien. Thank you ma'am. I'm sure these will be lovely and I'll tell Branna that you asked after her."

5

Alanna was a lot of things. One thing she wasn't was a coward. That e-mail. That darned e-mail had come through right at the worst time. Aidan O'Brien was hands down the most polite, considerate man she'd ever met. That was including her father, and she was a daddy's girl to the core. She'd received that e-mail right before he'd come over. No sooner had she swept the drapes closed and locked the slider, than he had come knocking. He undoubtedly thought she was batshit crazy. She thought about the email and the sender. She would not let that little asshole rattle her. She was in control. Her life. Her mind. Her body.

How did she keep coming back to this? Steve Andrews was a youthful indiscretion. He was a jerk and a loser. He'd taken enough from her. She would not let this continue to affect her life. What had it been, almost seven years? He hadn't lived here in all this time. Why couldn't he just leave her alone? She'd blocked him from her social media, e-mail, and her phone. She had changed her accounts several times, changed passwords, had pseudo names. The truth was that she wasn't a kid anymore. She needed these avenues for job hunting. She had to use her real name.

He knew she wouldn't call the police. Her father didn't know anything about what had happened all those years ago. Her jackass brother thought he knew, but he didn't either. She had to keep it that way. Sgt. Major Hans Falk didn't play around when it came to his baby girl. She knew that anything he found out would end in bloody knuckles or worse. He had been through so much. Overcome so much. She would not let him throw away a stellar career on some little turd that wasn't fit to lick his boots.

She'd failed when she was eighteen. She'd made bad choices. She would not let that little swine steal one more thing from her. The fact that he'd been close friends with her brother made things worse. She didn't even want to think about the lies he'd told her brother, and that Erik had so readily believed.

The problem was, he'd never been this bold before. He'd always managed to get her information. The creepy ass postcards from different ports had been coming for years, but only since she'd been out of her father's household. Cryptic messages, short and sweet. The fact that he was so far away had been a sort of comfort. This e-mail, however, was different. He usually went old school. Yes, he'd harassed her on just about every form of social media she was on, but she'd been able to block him. The paper always came, though. Sometimes it took four months, sometimes six or longer, but it always came.

The messages were short, yet always managed to make her skin crawl. Sicken her. *I miss your scent. I still feel you. Remember, I was your first.* She shuddered. He actually thought that what had passed between them was something to treasure. She'd gotten past it. She knew her own part in the whole mess. She just wanted to forget it.

This message had been different. She knew he was overseas, or at least she thought she knew. He'd just sent a postcard from the Indian Ocean six months ago. The message she just opened in her e-mail had been clear, though. "How was the barbecue, whore?" The hair stood up on her arms and neck. Did he have someone watching her? She thought about the difference between him and her new neighbor. Aidan was everything he wasn't. The genuine concern, the gentle assurances, the quiet power and protective nature she saw in him. She'd been tempted for the first time in seven years to tell someone everything. She wanted to feel his protective arms come around her and feel truly safe. She'd held back because she'd made this mess, and it was her burden to bear. Aidan didn't need any more ugliness in his head. He didn't need one more person to rescue.

She wanted to know what it was like to be with someone who made her burn. That all consuming passion that novels waxed poetic about. Maybe it was too much to ask, but damn it, Branna had found it. Was she cursed like her father? Like Erik? Cursed to make bad choices, or worse: finding the one person she thought she could love, but knew would never love her in return? Of all the people for her to be drawn to after all this time, why did it have to be him? Aidan O'Brien didn't want a forever girl.

Could she be a "right now" girl? She wasn't sure. And although he'd been polite and gentlemanly and very kind to her, she wasn't sure the attraction was mutual. He was so reserved.

Her expertise was clinical psychology, but she couldn't get a read on him. Sometimes she thought that she saw something, like a foggy landscape or a blurry photo. She just couldn't get a clear reading on him. What did Freud say? *The Irish is one race of people for whom psychoanalysis is of no use whatsoever.* She wasn't trying to psychoanalyze him. Personally, she thought Freud was a little overrated. Not everything led back to mommy or daddy or potty training.

Sometimes things just sucked and you needed to find your way out of them. She had to find her way out of this. She had to. She was twenty-five and had honestly never had one minute of intimate fulfillment. She could not accept that she was just broken. Once she had felt that way, felt broken. But when she dreamt, she felt. And when she looked at Aidan O'Brien she felt. Maybe she wasn't completely broken?

She closed her eyes. *Don't do this to yourself. Don't get hung up on someone you know you can't have. It's just as bad as being broken. It's setting yourself up to get re-broken.*

Aidan emptied his fishy smelling parcels into the fridge along with a bottle of white wine he'd picked up at the liquor store. He needed the wine for cooking and a bottle of Jameson Reserve had caught his eye as well. He changed quickly into his running clothes and went out the back door to the deck. He looked over the sea and breathed deeply, smiling as he saw the far off shrimp boat. It had it's nets out, and they looked like wings reaching out from a great bird. He wondered if that was one of the ships that docked at Captain Sam's.

It was afternoon now, just past tea time, and the sun was lower in the sky. The breeze was cool and he walked down the beach walk and stretched on the railing and steps. It was a beautiful time for a run. His pace was so steady and the sand was so easy on his joints that he ran until he came to the end of the island. He'd seen a map and knew that he was living on the North end. The beach was narrow, and he was stunned to see that there were remnants of houses on the shore. What had once been ocean front property had become wreckage, the second row houses now taking prime billing.

By the time he returned, he slowed at the waters edge and stretched his legs a bit. Then he entered the ocean on a run and dove smoothly under a rolling swell. He could get used to this sort of exercise. The sea was salty on his lips as he bobbed on the surface, taking in the beautiful day. He floated on his back, his ears underwater as he stared up at the sky. He thought about his unlikely kinship with the fish woman and the toothy grin of the baby. It made him think of wee Colin, Brigid's son. He was younger than the little boy at the dock, but they seemed to grow in leaps and bounds. The twins and little Cora, too. They meant so much to him, even though they weren't his own children. He'd grown rather close to them once he'd returned to Ireland from Afghanistan. He was able to go home on the weekends and see everyone. It had been nice.

Brigid had birthed Cora during another deployment and he'd not been a part of her life for the first couple of years. He needed to make sure he called them tomorrow.

He showered quickly below the house and emerged from the outdoor shower with a towel around his waist, when he saw Alanna. She stopped with a swoosh of breath, and she couldn't hide the reaction to him before he saw it. Female appreciation.

The thought of her looking at his body, that she liked what she saw, made his brain take a hiatus and his blood heat up. He wanted to drag her into the gym, drop the towel and cover her with his body. "Is everything all right?" he asked. His voice was deep and slow.

No, but it will be if you drop that towel and let me lick the rest of that water off your body. "Yes, perfect. I was just running out to get some beer. Do you want Guinness or will you try some local stuff?" She was trying really hard not to ogle him, but his body was unbelievable. He wasn't overly ripped or lean. He was just big and muscular and beautifully proportioned. And he was in a towel. Talking to her. Dripping…no, glistening. *Yeah, you need to get in the car. Now.*

"Something local would be perfect. Whatever you like," he said. Alanna made a hasty exit, hopping in the car with her wallet.

Aidan climbed up to the deck from below. The breeze off the sea was washing over his wet body as he came to the top of the deck. It made his skin prickle, sensation waking him up even though the time change was still dogging him.

Her eyes. He shook his head to rid himself of the thought, but he kept coming back to those eyes combing over his body. He walked into the sliding doors and shut himself in, leaning over the counter as a wave of lust rolled through him. *Don't do this. Don't do this to either of you.*

He went to the cabinet, still in his towel and took out the good bottle of whiskey. He wasn't a big drinker. Despite what the world thought of the Irish, his da had always stressed moderation. Drink was to be savored, used perhaps in celebration or to take the edge off, but never to excess. As a youth, he'd not heeded that warning, but as a man, he did. The edge was sharp today, however, and the whetstone was blonde with green eyes and an exquisite ass. He poured the amber liquid into the glass. Only one finger that he shot back in one smack. It exploded in the back of his throat. *That'll get your mood right.*

After that he went back to the cabinet and took out a tumbler. He drank two glasses of water one right after the other. Finishing up a run with a dram of whiskey was not the best plan. He threw on his Royal Irish Regiment t-shirt and a pair of jeans, and went back into the kitchen. It was still too early to start dinner. Seafood cooked quickly. He poured himself two more fingers of Jameson, having let the quick ounce settle his heart rate. He grabbed his laptop and went outside to the deck.

He might never get tired of this view. The sky was clear and the water was calm. Waves rolled in steadily and the sound was soothing to him. Aidan sat down on the chaise lounge and opened up his laptop. His Skype account was open as usual. It was hands down the best invention in modern day. For not one single cent, he could video call his family. He noticed that he had missed two calls, one ten minutes ago. It was from Brigid. It was almost ten at night in Ireland. A little stab of panic hit him. His parents were still pretty young, but he had grandparents. He rang her, hoping he wasn't waking the whole house up.

Brigid answered the video call on the third ring. "Is everything all right, love? It must be late." Brigid was sitting at their computer, hair a mess, obviously in her pajamas.

"I'm sorry, Aidan. Everything is okay. We're having a wee problem with your niece."

No sooner had she said this then a curly haired, fair skinned, little pixie popped into view. She was wiping her eyes. "Uncle Aidan?" Her voice was strained and he could see she was put out.

"How's my little darlin'? Why aren't you in your bed?"

She put her face close to the screen. "Why is it so light there? Aren't you ready for bed, too?"

Aidan smiled. "No, love. It's only five o'clock in America. It's not even time for dinner. Tell me what's wrong darlin'. Why are you still awake? You don't want to wake your wee brother, do you?"

Cora's face scrunched up and she sniffled. "I miss you Uncle Aidan. I wanted you to come for the weekend and momma said you're too far away. Who'll sing *The Fox Song* to me?"

Aidan's heart was breaking. She had about ten other people in her life that would pluck and sing until she fell asleep, but she wanted him. "Well, we can't have you going to bed without *The Fox Song* can we?"

Cora's face lit up and she shook her head. "Mommy doesn't do it like you do."

Brigid's eyes were brimming with tears, it was blurry but he could tell. "Well, love. Good thing we've got Uncle Aidan on the line to do it properly."

Aidan started seeing the dreaded pixelating right then. *Shit shit shit,* he thought. Brigid was talking to him, obviously seeing the same thing. Her voice was cutting out as well. "Brigid, let me try to get a stronger signal." The thunk of the video hang up made Aidan curse.

Alanna didn't mean to eavesdrop, but her windows were open. After the quick run to the 24-7 store on base, she'd come home to work a little before dinner. The houses were so close, though. The decks were separated by a half partition, but shared a beach walk. She may as well have been in the next room. She'd heard little Cora on video call to Aidan and it was enough to rip your guts out.

Everything had been going well until the wireless signal had pooped out on them. The signal over there was decent, but video conferencing overseas was tough even on a hardwired internet signal. She sighed. There was no way she was letting that little girl go without her fox song, whatever that was. And she wanted it from her Uncle Aidan. Alanna couldn't fix everything, but this she could fix. She could hear Aidan swearing, trying to call them back. "Aidan," she said.

Aidan looked up in surprise. "Hello Alanna, I'm sorry. Was I disturbing you?"

She emerged from the other deck and smiled shyly. "I heard some of it, I couldn't help it. I wanted to tell you that you could call from my desk top. It's hardwired, not wireless. The signal is way better."

Aidan's face flooded with relief. "Mother Mary, you are a life saver. Let me grab my guitar, and I'll be right over."

Aidan signed into his Skype account on Alanna's desktop, and rang Brigid and Cora. They picked up on the first ring. Finn was in the back, rocking Colin. "Did I wake him?" Aidan asked.

Finn shook his head drowsily, "No, brother. It was Cora's screeching and your sister's cursing that woke him."

Aidan laughed, "Oh, aye. Colin, lad, get used to it. Our women are excitable. They'll be no rest if one of them's got her knickers in a bunch."

Cora was jumping up and down on the computer chair, curls bouncing with the effort. "Sing, Uncle Aidan!"

Brigid looked at him through the screen. "Where did you get the guitar, then?" He told her about his trip to the pawn shops.

"All right, Cora. When you get a song, you'll go to bed for your da, aye?"

Cora looked very serious, "Oh, yes. I promise. I'll go right to my bed!"

Alanna was sitting at the table pretending to work as the scene unfolded. Aidan got his guitar on his knee as the most beautiful child she'd ever seen peered at him from the computer screen. As Aidan started the song, Alanna's heart jumped into her throat. Not only could he play and sing, but his face. He looked at that little girl with such love in his eyes. Alanna couldn't imagine Erik fawning over a child of hers like that.

He sang a few verses of what was obviously a folk song about a fox getting the farmers goose to feed his family. After he was part way through the song, he stopped and to her delight, his sister started playing from the other side of the Atlantic. He had a beautiful voice. Branna had told her that the whole family was musically talented, but she'd talked more about Michael. Yes, Aidan had a fine voice.

When Brigid started playing, she had to turn around. It was a fiddle solo that had Alanna's fingers itching to play along. Then Aidan came back in again as the little girl swayed back and forth to his playing.

They finished the song and Cora clapped her little heart out. "Goodnight, a leanbh." *Beloved child.* "I love you." Aidan said softly.

"Good night, Uncle Aidan. I love you, too." At that, Cora went willingly with her father off to bed.

Brigid stayed by the computer, a sad smile on her face. "Are you well, deirfiúr? Are you settling in?"

Aidan nodded, "Aye, it's grand all together. The house is right on the beach. I actually want you to meet someone." Aidan got up and walked to the table where Alanna was studying. "Come, lass. Meet my sister."

Alanna blushed, "I don't want to intrude. Maybe I should go outside."

Brigid yelled from screen. "Alanna? Branna's best friend? Get your arse over here, girl."

Aidan rolled his eyes. Brigid was ever the blunt one, a pushy little peahen. Alanna sat in the seat, her face blushed with embarrassment. "Hello, Brigid. It's a pleasure to meet you."

Brigid gasped. "Bloody hell, you're adorable. Listen to that accent. Branna didn't tell me you were so gorgeous."

Aidan broke in on a choked laugh, "Brigid!"

Brigid smiled at her brother. "Well, she is. Maybe we need to get her over here to meet Tadgh." Aidan was behind Alanna, keeping his face even, but Brigid's comment hit its mark. She innocently babbled on, pretending that she didn't know exactly how that comment would needle Aidan. "Don't you mind me. I've been up for days. That little fiend Colin is teething and he won't sleep unless he's absolutely certain that I can't."

She turned to Alanna, "It was very nice to meet you, Alanna. What's your surname?" Alanna told her and she looked thoughtful. "Beautiful falcon, well that's fitting, isn't it? All right, off to bed.

Thank you for loaning us your computer. I am afraid Cora may abuse your good will."

Alanna laughed. "I'll tell you what. I will leave the program open and leave Aidan signed in. You call anytime you want, day or night."

After they ended the call, Aidan picked up his guitar and looked at Alanna a little shyly. "I wasn't expecting to play so quickly. It's a bit out of tune. I'm sorry about barging in here. I'm afraid that little lass has got us all on a short leash."

Alanna laughed at that. "She's a beauty and a sweetheart. No mortal man could deny her anything."

He smiled at that. "I'll go. You look like you're working. Does six o'clock work for dinner, or do you need it to be later?"

Alanna was walking with him to the door. "Six is perfect. Honestly, other than the case study findings, my thesis is done. I'm just editing and probably overthinking it."

Aidan walked out on to the deck and picked up his whisky. "Well, then. I'll leave you to it."

As he walked off, Alanna was pretty sure that him walking away in low slung jeans was not an image that was going to help her concentration. *This is not a date, this is not a date.* She called to him, "Aidan." He turned to her, his face impassive. "Your voice, it's incredible."

Impassivity was replaced with a bashful smile. "Music is in our blood. All of us. Thank you, Alanna." He paused, looking at her. "That night I heard you sing this past winter, it near stopped my heart." Then he walked into the house without a backward glance.

6

Aidan grabbed his phone on the third ring. "Hey, O'Brien. How are you settling in? The truck working okay?" It was John, and Aidan could hear chaos in the background. "Oh, aye. It's perfect. I did a bit of exploring today. Thanks for the GPS. This burner phone doesn't have it."

"Maria wanted me to call and ask you if you wanted to come to dinner. She's making ziti." Aidan liked the sound of that, but he gave his regrets. "Captain Sam's! Love that place. That's where Maria gets her shrimp, too. She likes the dog. You didn't try to pick up the baby, did you?" John said, jokingly.

Aidan laughed, "Anyway, I'm making seafood tonight."

John persisted. "Bring it over. Maria will cook it up. Then you won't be eating alone."

Aidan cringed a little. "I, uh, won't be. I invited my neighbor over."

John gave a husky laugh. "The Sgt. Major's daughter. Niiiiiiice." Aidan rolled his eyes, even though John couldn't see him. "Don't start that shite, brother. It's not a date. She's a nice girl, that's all."

John chuckled at that. "Dude, you are crazy. If it isn't a date, you should make it one. She is off the rails beautiful. She teaches yoga and Zumba at the gym. The Marines line up to take her class or watch her shake her bom bom through the glass." Aidan's hackles rose at that. *Nope, you are not jealous. Not at all.*

He heard a muffled female voice in the background and then his friend was stuttering. "No honey, I never watched. No, I never took her class. Maria, honey, she's not as pretty as you are." He mumbled in the phone, "Ah, fuck. Now I'm in for it. Hormones." Then Aidan heard some sort of thump. "Baby, don't throw high heels. They leave a mark. Throw the flip flops."

Aidan was laughing loudly now. "Listen, John. I was thinking it would be nice to have you over tomorrow night. Bring the kids. They can play on the beach." John was laughing, too. Aidan knew they adored each other, and that Maria was half kidding.

"I'll tell you what. What would you think about me bringing a few of the men from the training class over. It starts Monday, but it might be a little easier on you if you know a few faces before you walk in that first day." Aidan thought that was a great idea and he told him so. "Just a couple of officers. Maria will bring some food over, I'll have the boys bring some beer. They may want to bring girlfriends or wives, you okay with a little crowd?"

Aidan replied, "Absolutely, brother. We'll make a real night of it. Don't make Maria cook, though. Let the lass put her feet up. I'll handle the food." Aidan ended the call with Denario and decided he'd better get dinner started. He took the shellfish out of the fridge and rinsed it. He went about setting the table outside, keeping it simple. He didn't want to make Alanna uncomfortable by setting it up to look like a date.

Alanna had worked for a solid couple of hours, and had to admit to herself that her thesis paper was very good. She had no doubt it was "A" material. She'd left open ended paragraphs for the final conclusions. She had two weeks left of her alternative therapies, then a closing goodbye gathering with her patients. She thought about what Branna had said about Aidan. If he really was having issues, the fact that he didn't have the resources he deserved just made her crazy. She wanted to help him, but he wasn't a patient. He was, however, becoming a friend. She was on shaky ground. She thought back to him coming out of that shower. Heat pooled in her belly. Visions of showering with him assaulted her mind. She hopped up from the table and headed into her bedroom.

She needed to distract herself, so she began looking through her closet, trying to decide what to wear. She looked at a thin, gauzy, cotton dress she'd bought, but not worn. It was sexy. Halter top, low cut, graduating hemline. The white dress was soft and feminine and draped nicely. It was backless, dipping to her lower back. She'd loved it when she'd seen it. She just hadn't had anywhere to wear it. No one to wear it for.

It wouldn't do for tonight. This was a casual, neighborly dinner. She slipped her clothes off and pulled it over her head, then slid the closet door closed to see the mirror. It dipped low between her breasts. She touched herself on the swell, then down between them. She wondered, just to torture herself, what Aidan would think of her in this dress. She shook her head at herself in the mirror. "You are pathetic. This is not a date." She removed the dress and hung it back in place. Then she went to the bathroom to get ready.

Aidan heard a light knock on the screen frame and looked up. His breath expelled like someone had punched him in the gut. The low sun was peering around the house and it lit her up from one side, picking up the copper in her hair. "Come in."

She slid the door and stepped in, and he looked at her from head to toe. She tugged nervously. "I went casual." She had obviously mistook his appraisal.

"You're perfect. It wasn't a critical look, it was more," he paused, "appreciative."

She gave a blushing smile and then shot her chin up. "Are you that surprised to see me showered and groomed?" He knew she was joking. Compliments obviously embarrassed her. He walked over and took the beer out of her hand. "Well, I wasn't going to say anything, but..." He pinched his nose with the other hand. She dropped her jaw, feigning offense. "O'Brien, you take that back! I have never smelled in my life!"

She came into the kitchen as he was laughing, and putting the beer in the fridge. He turned and came close. He looked down, all trace of laughter gone. He leaned his face down near her ear and inhaled. "It's usually more citrusy. Tonight you smell like night Jasmine," he said softly.

Alanna's body flared to life. "You have a good nose. It's Jasmine oil from the Iraqi markets."

He smiled, but it had an edge to it. "Boyfriend?"

Her breathing was shallow. "No, daddy brought it home." He backed off slowly, but not before his eyes landed on her lips. She thought for a moment that he would kiss her, but he backed away.

Aidan had to back away from this woman before he did something stupid, like kiss her. Christ, she was shy about how she looked? She was wearing a v-neck t-shirt. It was the palest pink he'd ever seen, with the logo of her university across the chest. Pink like the inside of a shell, and it was a perfect color for her. Whatever she'd been wearing under her shirts up until this point had to have been one of those snug exercise bras, because she'd obviously been concealing what he saw now. Creamy, high, full, and a hint of cleavage showing just enough in that t-shirt to give him an idea of what she looked like. Her waist was trim, curving inward then back out to round, beautiful hips. She was wearing cut off Levis Button Fly jean shorts that showed just enough thigh to draw his eye, but not overly short. She had smooth, toned legs and she was barefoot. She looked like a sex Goddess as far as he was concerned.

She'd certainly gone casual, but the sight of her had shot straight through him. Her hair was freshly washed. She had no make-up on except for a little shimmer at her lips. Probably simple lip balm, but it played off her full lips and beautiful face. He'd noticed, now that he was close to her, that she had a light speckling of freckles on her nose and cheeks. Almost too light and small to notice, but they made her look young. She was only six years younger than him, but she looked eighteen right now.

It was only within the light green eyes that he saw the woman. They weren't the eyes of a girl. Smart, bewitching eyes that held a heat that made him ache to his bones.

"So, any luck at the fish market?" she asked. Aidan opened the fridge and showed her the marinating shrimp and bowl of clams he'd rinsed. "A man who marinates. Now I am impressed."

He grabbed two beers from the six pack and took them to the counter. Then he stopped, "I have some wine and whiskey, too. Any preference?"

She shook her head. "I might have a glass of wine when we eat, but I'll try the beer."

He opened them, took two glasses out of the cabinet and slowly poured. He handed her one, "Sláinte," he said.

She repeated the toast, clinking glasses, and took a sip. She smiled, but it was a little sad. "Brian, he used to say that when he had a beer with my dad."

She watched as he dropped the shrimp into one hot skillet, and the clams into another after melting a hunk of butter. He added garlic and wine and the steam hissed. Then he checked on some flat pasta he had boiling and turned the heat off. He covered the clams and turned to her, sipping his beer. He didn't mind the quiet, she noticed. He was okay just letting something stew.

He took another drink and looked at the amber liquid. "This is good. Duck Rabbit seems an odd name for a brewery."

She welcomed the change of subject. "Yes, it's a North Carolina beer. They have some good ales and dark beers, too. So, where did you get the shrimp and clams?" He told her about his trip to Captain Sam's. "Sheila? Perfect! Did you see the dog?" Then she put her hands on her hips, "You didn't pick up that baby, did you?"

He laughed and put his hands up, "No way. Fisher wives are a tough lot. I'm not looking to get my arse whipped."

She giggled and it lit her whole face up. He continued to steam the clams in the butter and wine, and she watched through the clear lid as they started to pop open.

He drained the pasta and then poured it into a big bowl. He turned the shrimp and then took them off the stove and poured them over the pasta. Then he took a small sauce pot of something creamy and poured it in with the pasta and shrimp. "You are quite the chef."

He shrugged shyly. "I stole this recipe from Maria, Captain Denario's wife. Don't give me too much credit." He took another big bowl and poured the clams, garlic drenched and steaming, into the dish. She put down her beer and grabbed one bowl, following him outside.

"Do you mind eating out here? It's such a gorgeous night."

She put the bowl down. "Not at all. Al fresco and oceanfront is as good as it gets." They went back inside where Aidan opened the fridge, took out a salad and a bottle of wine. She grabbed the remnants of their beers and walked back out.

She looked out at the water and sipped, waiting for him to get everything arranged. She put her phone on the nearby deck table. "I'm sorry, I need to keep it near. I'm expecting to hear from my dad. I swear I'm not one of those maniacs that keep their phone glued to them every minute."

He came over and pulled her chair out and she was shocked. She sat. "Thank you. Considering I grew up in the South, you'd think I would be used to a gentleman. It's a dying art, though."

He gave her a chiding look. "You need some lessons from my mother on how to train your men."

She put her chin on her hand. "Your family seems wonderful. Whole and wonderful." He poured a glass of wine for her and then one for himself. She noticed that he had a water jug and goblets and she in turn poured them both some ice water.

"I'm a lucky man. My family is everything to me." He paused, then asked, "What about you? Your parents are divorced, but you seem to be close to your da. How about your brother?"

She sighed, "At times. He can be a bit overbearing. Cocky like all pilots." He grunted in agreement. She continued, "My mother is kind of a fruitcake. She calls it being a free spirit. A lot of hippy talk for irresponsible, bi-polar, basket case behavior. I love her, don't get me wrong. She's just more like a weird aunt than a mom. And she hurt my dad. He tells me not to worry about it, that it takes two people to ruin a marriage. I remember, though. He loved her. He tried to be good to her. She just wasn't the marrying kind. She had no sense of loyalty to anyone but herself. She just wasn't made to stay put and think about other people."

He listened intently, not showing much of what was on his mind. "Well, I suppose you're right. Some people are better alone." Alanna wondered if he was speaking personally.

He picked up his glass and lifted it to another toast. "What shall we toast to?"

She lifted her glass. "To good neighbors," she smiled.

He clinked her glass. "Aye, I'll drink to that to be sure. My neighbor in Belfast is in his late fifties, wears a toupee, and smells like gin and cat piss." Alanna choked on her wine, sputtering as she laughed. He was grinning, "It's no laughing matter. You should get stuck in the lift with the creepy fecker!"

Her eyes sparkled with tears and mischief. "Jasmine isn't so bad, I guess."

He shook his head. "No, Jasmine is much better." His brogue was a little husky when he said it, and it made her body tingle.

They tucked into the food and Alanna moaned. She covered her mouth, embarrassed and Aidan's smile was wide. "Mmmm, those clams are perfect. That woman has some sort of magic trick with the clams. Not a speck of sand. And the wine and garlic is perfect!"

Aidan gave her a sly grin, "She didn't share her secret with you?" he asked.

Alanna popped to attention. "She did not tell you." He took a sip of wine, brows lifted with mischief. "She did!" she screamed. He laughed. She shook her head. "Well, apparently all we needed to do is send in a smoking hot guy with a sexy accent. I can't believe she told you!" Aidan stopped his fork midway to his mouth. He set it back down.

Alanna's face immediately changed to a look of horror. *You did not just say that out loud. Nope. Because then you would have to kill yourself.* His grin changed. It was too edgy to be called a smile. Alanna could have sworn there was something a little feral in his eyes. She stuttered. "Ah, I mean. I didn't…ah, crap." She put her hand over her mouth for a second, then took a deep breath. "This non-stop work and studying is grinding away at my social graces. My filter is broken."

He cocked his head. "Filter?"

She raised her brows and rubbed a non-existent spot on the table. "That filter between my head and my mouth."

Aidan felt himself harden almost instantly. He was always in a semi-state of arousal anytime he was near this woman. He'd never experienced anything like it. He hadn't had his bollocks this much in charge since he'd been seventeen. God damn. What had just come out of her mouth? And now she was blushing, her cheeks and her mouth were pink and her breath was stuttering. If he'd been smart or the least bit of a gentleman, he would have played it off. Let her off the hook and hid his reaction. His wasn't feeling very smart or very gentlemanly, however. Not.At.All.

"I'm glad you approve," he said huskily. Then a stab of conscience surfaced through the arousal and he changed the subject. He had to, really. His cock was at full salute, and if he didn't make small chatter and get back to the food, he wasn't going to be able to talk the old boy down before he had to stand up. It was pressing mercilessly against his jeans. "Apparently she ties them in a small net and hangs them off the dock for a day or two, keeping them off the bottom. They spit out all of the sand." Then he took a bite. "Christ, those are good."

She had her fork in her hand, dangling down from her fingers and she smiled into the top of her hand. "So who taught you how to cook?"

Aidan took a sip of water to clear his throat. "Ma and Gran mostly. Some of it was bachelor trial and error. Once I didn't have to live in the barracks, I had a kitchen. It's a skill that comes with old age."

Alanna rolled her eyes. "You're only six years older than me. Does that mean I'm getting old too?"

He shook his head. "Not at all. You look young. A hot woman with a sexy accent doesn't have too many worries in the world."

She threw her napkin at him. Annoyed and giving him a chiding look. "You shouldn't tease me Aidan."

He just looked at her, "Not teasing in the slightest." He tossed her napkin back. "The pasta's cooling, have a taste." She did and it was marvelous.

"So tell me about the Royal Irish Regiment. It isn't common for someone from the Republic to enlist, I'd suspect." They ate as he told her about his family. His mother Sorcha's life growing up in the North, his father Sean in the Republic. Both Catholic, with lives straddling the border.

"My grandparents are still there. All of the troubles, that was before my time. It was a terrible time, but God willing, it is over to some degree. I can't deny my Northern roots anymore than I can my father's bloodline. How do I work with the British? Truthfully, it's not my job to worry about politics. Religion tore at the region for a century. I don't give a shit if my men are Catholic or Protestant or Atheist or Hindu or any other variety. I just care that they are safe, that they're trained, and that they watch out for each other despite their differences. My duty is to them. I've worked with British, American, Iraqi, Afghani, French, German, Welsh, and Scots. It's where I belong. With that being said, if the British government ever tried to put the RIR into local troubles, I'd drop my rifle and walk over that border. There's been enough of that shit, and I'd have no part of it. They wouldn't, though. That's not our job, and it would be asking for trouble. They've got other forces that deal with any unrest that lingers."

Alanna just listened. It was so interesting to hear more about him. "I wish there were more people that thought like you do, Aidan. Some people just have no sense of duty, no honor. Our generation is full of effeminate males that don't know what it is like to believe in something enough to die for it."

Just as Aidan started to talk, her phone went off. He stopped talking. "Go ahead, I can get it later," she said.

Aidan refilled their wine glasses. "It might be your da, go ahead."

She gave him an apologetic look and leaned over to grab her phone. "Huh, it's a Virginia number. Maybe he's at work." She answered, and he could tell immediately that it wasn't her father.

"Hello, Tim. Wow, how are you?" She gave Aidan another apologetic look and stood up, walking a few feet away. "Actually, I'm having dinner with a friend. Can I call you later?" She paused, listening. "You're in town? Um, sure. Okay, I'll call you later. What was that?" She listened again then looked at Aidan. "No, it's not Izzy. It's a new friend."

Aidan wanted to know who the hell this tosser Tim was, even though it was absolutely none of his business. She continued, looking awkward. "Yes, the friend is male. Listen, I'm being rude. Just let me call you tonight, OK? Thanks. See you soon."

Alanna hung up and she was embarrassed as she looked at her dinner host. "I am so sorry. I never pick up the phone at dinner. I saw the Virginia number and thought it was daddy. I'll turn it off and call my dad later." Aidan assured her that wasn't necessary, but she did it anyway. "I don't like interruptions. My dad tried to make sure we sat down to dinner together as often as we could. No phones, no TV, just us eating and talking. That wasn't easy with two teenagers and a single dad, but he did a pretty good job."

Aidan understood that. "Aye, it was the same at our house. Meals were big family gatherings. My mother had to cook for six kids, a husband, and worked as a midwife. She made it work, though." He took a sip from his wine, "So, Tim was it? Old flame?" *Why are you asking? None of your business, asshole.*

Her cheeks flushed, "Not really." She paused, shrugging. "Well, yes. For a short time. Old flame might be a stretch. I don't know how flammable it was. We've been friends since high school and we're still friends. The other stuff was brief and didn't stick." Aidan noticed she took a bigger sip of her wine. If she didn't want to talk about Tim-the-Tosser, that was fine with him.

"So, is your father coming for your graduation?" he asked.

She exhaled, relieved at the change of subject. "He's going to try. He's put in for a long weekend of leave. Erik is close, so he may come too. My mom wants to come, but I told her she couldn't bring her latest boyfriend. So, we'll see. It doesn't matter. I already had my undergraduate cap and gown routine. This is just a small summer ceremony. No one really even needs to be there."

Aidan disagreed. "I'm sure they're proud of you. You should have them there. I know Branna wanted to be here with you. She's just tied up with the twins. They're still so small."

Alanna smiled. "I would love to have seen them christened. They're so beautiful."

He gave an indulgent smile, "They are that. The O'Brien's make some beautiful babies. That's for certain. You've seen wee Cora. Colin's just the same, but he looks more like my da than Cora. Cora has the look of Finn. Dark Irish, silkie blood."

Alanna could listen to him talk for days. "What about my coloring? Any fun Celtic myths about pale and blonde?" she asked jokingly.

Aidan looked at her, caressing her features with is eyes. "Well, Falcon's are considered bad news, but that's not what they'd be saying about you. That long, flowing hair, your athleticism, those piercing eyes. You'd be found in the Norse Legends. The Vikings invaded Ireland. I suspect they'd mistake you for a Valkyrie. Beautiful, fierce, warrior females who would swoop down on a horse from the sky and choose who lived or died in battle. You'd snatch up your chosen warrior and take him to Valhalla." *What a way to go,* he thought.

"Warrior female. I like the sound of that. It's certainly better than *she died with her nose in a school book, never did anything amazing,*" she said, picking at her food.

"Come on now, hen. Don't start the pity party. You're nearly done. You said so yourself. Then it's on you. Will you live like the bookworm or the Valkyrie?"

She raised a brow saucily. "You want another round with my bat to see which side I favor?"

Aidan's smile was blinding. "There she is. The lass who tried to take my head off on first sight," he grinned.

As they sat out on the deck, eating, drinking and talking, Aidan was struck again by how beautiful Alanna was. It wasn't just the blonde hair and the pretty face that she'd so easily dismissed. It was her spirit. She was feisty and smart, and he was able to appreciate those qualities, having grown up around like minded women. She took care of herself, didn't seem to need anyone, and she certainly seemed to be passionate about the work she was doing.

He thought back through his career. Everything he'd told her was true. His priority had always been the man to the left and the man to the right of him. He'd lived a soldier's life, though. He'd done violence, seen violence, witnessed true evil. He wondered what it would be like to be inside her head, where the world was a beautiful place and people were worth saving.

He shook that thought off as he realized the wind had picked up. Alanna looked over the water at the same time as he did. They'd been so engrossed in each other that they'd missed the squall line until it was close to the shore. Alanna started grabbing dishes and napkins. "Put the chairs up against the side of the deck." They scurried around the deck, running things into the house and on the last trip out, the downpour started. Alanna squealed and it gave Aidan a start until he realized she was jumping up and down with her arms stretched up to the sky. The rain came fast and hard, and he was stuck in place as he saw the wild and reckless joy take over her. She whipped her head around and laughed.

"Don't tell me an Irishman is bothered by a little rain." Her face was playful and he couldn't take his eyes off her. "Last one with salt between their toes has to do the dishes!" she yelled and then she darted down the beach walk.

Aidan shot after her, and just before her feet hit the water he caught her, swinging her off her feet, and running backwards into the water. She squealed. "That's cheating!" she laughed.

"Whatever works. You've been out maneuvered, lass," he chuckled in her ear. He put her down. "Christ, I was dreading doing the washing up. It's a good thing you run like a girl."

Her jaw dropped. She put her hands on her hips, walked slowly toward him, eyes sparking with something way more Valkyrie than bookworm. "I've been outrunning boys since I was knee high to a grasshopper, Captain O'Brien. How about double or nothing?" That southern accent was more pronounced and sexy as hell.

Aidan cocked his head. "Do your best, little hen." She took off toward the deck, head down, running as fast as her little pink feet would carry her, but Aidan's stride was twice hers. He caught her right before the first step of the beach walk, and threw her over his shoulder. They were soaked and sandy from their feet kicking up the sand. "No! I hate dishes!" she laughed. He put her down on the deck. The rain was starting to slow. They locked eyes, and before sound judgement took hold, Aidan swept a thumb over her face, pulling a stray clump of hair from the corner of her mouth. "Christ, you are trouble aren't you?" he said softly. Her mouth was slightly parted, and he noticed her lips got pinker right after he touched the corner of her mouth. He wanted to taste her so badly that he'd had a momentary urge to tell his conscience to go to hell, and cover that beautiful, pink mouth with his.

Then her whole body did a little shiver and he noticed she was covered with goose bumps. That cold front had certainly arrived, which was hopefully the explanation for the shiver. If she wanted him as badly as he wanted her then he was in deep shit.

He opened the door and grabbed a throw off the chair. He wrapped it around her wet shoulders, trying very hard not to look at her wet t-shirt. He pulled the ends together, "You are fast, I'll give you that. If my legs weren't twice as long, you would have beaten me for certain."

She walked in the house behind him. "Fair is fair. I'll wash up and you go get dry."

He shook his head, "No, I'll do the washing. The fun was in the chasing and the catching, not the prize."

She gave him a sideways glance. "Don't try the honeyed tongue with me, O'Brien. Once my graduation is done, I'll start training. Then I'll open up a can of whoop-ass on you."

He laughed, "Big talk, little girl. Go get some warm clothes before you catch your death."

Her face lit up. "How about letting me make dessert? It's fast. Can I use a little of your whiskey?" she asked.

Aidan watched Alanna mill around his kitchen and mentally kicked himself in the ass. That was twice in one night he'd almost kissed her. *Holy Bride, what the hell are you doing?* he asked himself. He could not go down that road. Not only was she Branna's best friend, she was most certainly not hit and run material. But as he watched her discreetly from behind, all he could think about was having his arms around her. Those squeals of joy, her wet hair in his face, her daring him to chase her.

Jesus wept. He needed to clamp down on this problem. He changed into a long shirt because it was the only way to conceal the raging, bloody hard-on he'd had ever since he'd caught her rain soaked body on the beach. He needed to find some way to deal with this attraction he was feeling, something to quell his baser urges. Out of nowhere, he thought of Michael. How in the hell had Michael stood living under the same roof and held out as long as he did? He couldn't ask. That little hellcat was scheming already. They would be greatly amused by the pain he was feeling.

What the hell was wrong with him? He wasn't a teenager. He'd never been this physically drawn to a woman. He was standing against the counter, hands on his hips, looking at the long shirt tail that was covering his dumb handle. "Do you happen to know the mass schedule at the base chapel?" Yep, he needed to church it, maybe go to confession.

Alanna flipped around and his breath caught in his throat. Her hair was damp and she'd changed into a sweatshirt and yoga pants. "Nine and noon. Are you going tomorrow?"

Aidan nodded. "Yes, I suppose I should."

She continued, "Your momma would be proud. I go to the nine o'clock, but I have to go early. You need directions?"

Aidan was surprised, "You're a Catholic?"

She turned to him and nodded. "Yes, did you think all southerners were Baptists?"

He laughed a bit nervously, "I don't know about southerners, but Scandinavians are mostly a branch of the Lutheran Church."

She laughed, "Lord, don't get my daddy started on Martin Luther. No, he's a Catholic from the Scottish side and the Swedish. Mom was Anglican, then tried on Catholic for size, then she got into some New Age hippie '*It's all about me and my journey*' church. Me? I'm a garden variety Catholic just like daddy."

Aidan should not have been as happy as he was that she was a Catholic. Nope, because why in the hell would it matter at all what religion she was? *It doesn't.* "Why do you go early?" he asked.

She smiled, "I'm in the church choir." *Of course she was.*

"Well, then. Maybe I'll see you there." *Shit. So much for getting his mind right at church.*

Alanna was busy making one of the few desserts she was proficient at that didn't involve just opening a tub of Ben and Jerry's. Aidan had gotten very quiet behind her, and it was starting to make her nervous. She whisked the cherries around in the skillet, letting the butter get them hot. She sprinkled sugar over them, then she poured whiskey into the pan and lit the flame. *Whoosh.*

Aidan jumped and she looked at him apologetically. "Sorry, I should have warned you."

He peered over her shoulder. "What sort of witchery are you up to over here? Some sort of potion?"

She let the flame burn down and poured the concoction into two bowls. Then she took out the ice cream. "If you had rum, I'd have used bananas, but since you're a whiskey man, I thought cherries would be nice. Like Cherry Bounce with some ice cream."

She handed his bowl and spoon to him and he took a bite. "Tis gorgeous all together," he said on a moan. She could tell it wasn't empty praise, because his accent got thicker.

She beamed under his praise. "I didn't want you to think I was lying about being able to cook." They went into the living room and Aidan invited her to sit on the sofa. Then he sat on the chair.

It didn't escape Alanna's notice that Aidan sat about as far away from her as he could get while still being in the same room. She wasn't sure what switch had flipped, but he'd gotten a little more serious since she'd gone and changed out of her clothes. He was cordial, eating his dessert and making small talk, but it felt a little forced.

It occurred to her that perhaps she was being less than guarded with her attraction toward him. She hadn't meant to be. She wasn't very good at the male-female thing. *It wasn't a date,* she reminded herself. She'd almost forgotten it wasn't a date. She'd really enjoyed his company and she was attracted to him. She'd let her guard down, and he'd obviously picked up on her case of the swoons. It was also becoming obvious that the feeling wasn't mutual.

She'd kind of invited herself in, afterwards, now that she thought about it. Okay, she was feeling more awkward by the minute. He was so nice, such a gentleman. She really didn't want to make an idiot out of herself. "Well, if you're sure you don't need help with the clean up, I need to head off. I have a couple of phone calls to make, and then it's time to hit the books."

Aidan got a strange look on his face that she couldn't read, but then he stood up and saw her to the door. "Thanks for the wonderful dinner, Aidan. I'll see you at church tomorrow." She gave him a little wave and made a quick exit.

Aidan was grinding his teeth as Alanna left. Left to go make some phone calls. One of them was probably to Tim the Tosser. Not that he cared. Nope, because he was keeping his distance.

7

Aidan parked at the St. Frances Xavier Catholic Chapel on Camp Lejeune and was surprised at the large number of families pouring into the church. As he locked the truck, he heard John Denario give a shout from across the lot. He was carrying the two year old girl Clara, and Maria had the hand of the little four year old boy they called Frankie, but who's name was Francis. They were dressed in their Sunday best, Clara all frills and flowers and little Frankie wearing a clip on tie and trousers that matched his father's. Maria was dressed in a linen sheath dress and pink cardigan. Her belly was pronounced, as she was due within weeks. She waddled laboriously as the four year old tried to get her to pick him up.

"Dia Duit. You're all looking rather smart this morning," Aidan said.

Little Frankie sharpened up at this. "Oh, yes. I am very smart. I can write my name. First and last with no help!"

Aidan knelt down to the lad. "Well, that's fine isn't it? Perhaps you'd like to walk with me and let your mother rest a while. I need a smart lad to help me find my way around. Do you know where I'm supposed to sit?" As the little boy gave him an indulgent look, like he was aiding a smaller child, he took Aidan by the hand. Aidan winked at Maria and she mouthed her thanks to him.

As they sat five across in a pew in the chapel, Aidan looked around the large sanctuary to see all of the different families. Young single military men sitting together, old timers who were probably veterans, young families, teenagers, high ranking uniforms who were probably working through the weekend, just stopping long enough to attend mass. There were all races, varying ages. What was most prevalent was all of the young families with toddlers, babies, primary aged kids, and a disproportionate amount of pregnant women. This was a big base and the place was packed.

They had another service later, plus one last night. This was a good sign. There were always the naysayers talking about the death of organized religion. The wise little shit birds that tried to make you feel simple for being a Christian. Not here. This place was packed to the gills with humans, all here to worship together. Kind of made him feel like all wasn't lost.

The service was a bit different, but the bones were the same. The liturgy was very similar. No Latin or Gaelic, but familiar enough that he knew all the highlights, the stand up, sit down moves. He stole a peek at the choir section on occasion. He saw the small blonde head, got a peek at a pretty face reading from her music.

Part way through the service, John leaned in and whispered. "You're lucky. Father Matthew is up on rotation today. He'll be our chaplain on the job as well. Father Matthew Callahan. Nice, white boy like you."

Aidan snickered and Maria gave them both chiding looks. Frankie was sitting next to his da, but Clara was climbing all over Maria, pulling on her hair and cheeks. Aidan reached over and got the small child's attention. He did the universal open hands sign for *Do you want to come to me?* The little girl hopped off her mother's lap and jumped on him.

"What am I, chopped liver?" John said as the child passed him on the pew, climbing over him to get to Aidan. She put a chubby arm around his neck and stood on his lap, looking over the crowd.

Maria rearranged her hair, wiped the sweat off of her cheeks, and straightened to pay attention to the service.

Aidan thought about Brigid, struggling with the wee ones while they rejected Finn's interference. Kids just loved their mothers. And new guys. They were always intrigued by fresh meat, so Aidan was able to distract her just enough to give Maria a breather. She leaned over to John and whispered. "That's it. We're adopting the Irishman."

John chuffed in response. He looked at Aidan who had a two year old trying to pull his ear off. "Kiss ass," he said jokingly.

Just as the offering plate was headed around, the familiar Latin hymn started raising up from the piano and chorus. *Veni, Lumen Cordium,* one of the Latin hymns sung during Pentecost. Translated: *Come, Light of our hearts.* It was a beautiful, classic piece of sacred music, and when the soloist stood to the front, his heart leapt in his throat.

He'd remembered her singing the bluegrass style song at the pub, but this was different. She'd obviously had some classical training. Her clear, soprano voice lifting the hymn to new heights. In the pub, the only other time he'd heard her sing, she'd spurned a sort of lust in him. Territorial and inappropriate given the fact that he'd barely spoken two sentences to the woman. This time, it was different. Her voice washed over him, giving him a bone deep peacefulness. He bowed his head and exhaled, just listening, not wanting her physical beauty to distract him. He'd longed for peace so often, and in this moment he felt it.

Her solo ended and the choir rejoined her as she stepped back into the ranks. He looked up and noticed that John and Maria were looking back and forth, between him and the choir. He looked the other way, not wanting the speculation. As his eyes skimmed over the room, they landed on another pair of familiar green eyes. Not female, but male. *Bloody hell.* Sgt. Major Hans Falk just nodded from across the room and looked back toward the front.

As the mass ended, John led the family over to Father Matthew, anxious to introduce Aidan to the battalion's Navy chaplain. Father

Matthew was fairly young, probably in his late thirties, with an easy smile and smart eyes. His coloring could have put him in any County in Ireland. "John has told me a bit about you, Captain O'Brien. It is good to have you here, and off to a good start showing up to mass."

Aidan shook his hand, "It's a pleasure, Father Callahan. Do you know where your people come from? Over the water, that is."

The priest patted his shoulder, "Oh, yes. County Meath. I'm second generation American, so I still have family over there."

As they talked, Aidan saw two blonde figures coming from the right. Father Matthew's grin widened. "Hans!" The tall, powerful man gave the priest a manly hug. Alanna was smiling at the men. She took obvious pride in her father, and that made Aidan miss his own da. They were worthy and admirable men, both of them.

He walked around the men to come next to Alanna. "I see you made it. Glad to see you this morning," she said.

Her eyes were a little wary, and he had a stab of conscience. He'd cooled toward her at the end of the night, more self preservation than anything, but it hadn't gone unnoticed. Christ, he was at such odds with himself over this girl.

"You sounded lovely, lass. Like an angel." He said gently, and she blushed.

"Thank you. Those high notes had me worried." He caressed her face with his eyes, until he noticed the two men to his left, as well as the Denario family, had all silenced.

He turned and met Alanna's father with a steady gaze. More steady than he felt. "Dia Duit, Sgt. Major Falk. It's good to see you again."

Hans met his gaze, and there was a lions share of big-daddy speculation in them. "I guess that little rescue mission this winter bore fruit in more ways than one. I hear you're doing an exchange?"

Aidan nodded, "Aye. It's a bit of a pilot program. They're testing the waters for a longer program. Trading up Royal Troops with American for an eighteen month tour. Mostly Royal Marines, but I managed to pull a few strings."

More speculation, "Really? You've got some pull for a junior Captain. Then again, four combat tours is more than any Irishman I have come across. More than most British, as a matter of fact. You must be doing something right."

Hans Falk didn't get this far in life or in his career without honing the ability to read between the lines. This Irishman was sharp. The Irish regiments were active, but he'd never known one of them that had the experience this young man had already gained. And someone must have owed him a favor to get sent on an exchange to the states instead of British special forces or Royal Marines.

He needed to dig a little, see what this man's background looked like. Not only was he living next door to his daughter for three months, but the boy had stars in his eyes. He was trying to hide it. Trying like hell to hide his attraction to Alanna behind those haunted eyes. Hans knew that look, though, and it wasn't just lust. He'd known for twenty-five years that he'd be beating the males off with a stick with that beautiful little girl of his. This was different, though. He saw something akin to pain in this man's eyes whenever he looked at Alanna. He'd seen it this past winter, and he saw it now. Pain from wanting something you didn't think you could ever deserve, someone you didn't think you had a right to. And wasn't that interesting.

As they walked out the door of the church, Aidan parted ways from the Denarios after solidifying dinner plans. He caught up to Alanna and her father before heading to the truck. "I wanted to tell you both that I am having an impromptu get together tonight. I'm sure you have plans, but in case you don't, then please come join us. John is going to bring a few of my training mates over to meet me before we start tomorrow."

Alanna blushed. "Aidan, you don't have to include us. We can stay out of your way. Feel free to use our deck to spread out. Daddy has to get up early and head back and I have to go to work."

Aidan looked at her father, cutting off her protests. He knew that his somewhat erratic behavior last night had caused this hesitation.

"I'd love to have you. I think there will be a couple of women and kids there, it'll be social and low key." He cocked an eyebrow, "And I brought cigars from duty free."

Alanna rolled her eyes and her father laughed, smacking Aidan on the back. "Now you're talking my language."

His daughter gave him a chiding look. "You said one cigar a month, daddy."

He kissed her on the top of the head with a one armed embrace. "This little girl takes good care of me. I'll have you know, Miss Priss, that I haven't had a cigar in three months. So, I think we should be neighborly and head on over."

She smiled, "All right, what can we bring?"

Aidan shook his head, "Nothing. The lads are bringing some snacks and beer and Maria's bringing a dessert. I thought I would just buy something easy. Maybe a bin of that barbecue we had the other night?"

Hans whistled, "Pig, beer, and cigars. We might make a southern gentleman out of you yet, Aidan. I think the boys will like that." The Sgt. Major continued, "Why don't you let me take care of getting the barbecue and you can take my little girl home. She's got some work to get done and I wouldn't mind a drive. I miss these little coastal towns. Virginia feels like one big interstate."

Aidan reached into his wallet, getting money to give the man. He put his hand up. "No, son. You bring the cigars and have something cold for me to drink and I'll take care of the barbecue." Aidan argued, but he knew Hans was going to get his way on this.

Alanna was stuttering, "Daddy, maybe you should just drop me off first."

Aidan pulled her by the arm toward the truck. "Christ, hen. Do you always overthink everything?" Aidan heard the Sgt. Major chuckle as they walked away from him.

Alanna was pretty sure her father had lost his damned mind. She walked briskly to Aidan's borrowed truck and was surprised when he came around to open her door. She sat in the cab and waited for him to get in and start it up. "Thank you for inviting us. I'm afraid neither pops nor I have much of a social life. This will be fun for him."

Aidan looked at her as he exited on to the road. "I like your da. He seems like a good sort and he certainly loves you."

She just smiled and gave a nod. "He's a good daddy. He's close enough to drive down for the night if he doesn't mind a lot of windshield time. I guess he was missing me. Erik is gone for the weekend, so it's just us."

Aidan drove for a few minutes in silence, then he asked, "You don't talk about your brother or mother much. Where does your mother live?"

She didn't look at him. "This year she's living in Georgia, outside of Savannah. She moves around a lot. She job hops a lot, too. It is part of her deal."

"Deal?" he asked.

She had her fingers by her mouth, looking out the window. "She job hops, man hops, state hops. Every move she makes is the best move ever. The new place and new job is her new shot at a clean start to wipe away her latest bad decisions. She gets 'laid off' a lot. It's always the boss's fault. The truth is that she's unreliable and she has no sense of duty to her employers or anyone else. She doesn't like being tied down."

Aidan listened quietly. This Felicity sounded like a piece of work. "I'm sorry, Alanna. Kids should be able to depend on their mother. Frankly, I don't know what I'd do without mine."

She smiled sadly at him. "It's ok. I had..." She paused and swallowed. "I had Meghan for a while, and I have my grandma."

He thought it was time to move on, that mother of hers was a sore spot. "What about Erik?"

She sighed. "We are close in age. He's only eighteen months older. He's a good Marine. He's nothing like my mom in that regard. He's driven, good at his job. He's got his issues, but I guess you could say that about anyone. He took it hard when my mom left. He was angry. He directed that anger at me."

Aidan stiffened and she looked at him. He was gripping the steering wheel. She corrected his line of thinking, "No, nothing like that. He never laid a hand on me. Daddy would have kicked his behind. He was never the violent type, he was just angry, and you can say a lot of unkind things when you're angry all the time." Aidan thought about that and was suddenly grateful that his parents and grandparents had stayed together.

After a stop at the commissary, they once again drove over the bridge and ICW onto the island. They pulled into the drive and Alanna hopped out of the truck, swinging her purse over her shoulder. Aidan called to her before she went through the door. "Do you mind if I call them now? On the computer? I know you have stuff to do, I'll be brief. I didn't catch them at home and we kind of set a time after church."

He could try on his laptop again, but the truth was that he didn't want to say goodbye to her yet. "Of course, any time. Come on inside, you're still signed into your account." Aidan watched her unlock the door and he held it for her as she went inside. She was wearing a modest, cotton dress and her hips swayed as she ascended the stairs. *Fucking hell,* he said to himself. Her father would slice his balls off if he knew the way Aidan was feeling his daughter. Hopefully the bastard wasn't a mind reader.

"So, did your da surprise you?" She was walking into the main living area that overlooked the sea. He took a second, again, to admire the sense of rightness her space had. What did they call it? Feng shui or some shit? Some spaces made you feel peaceful and this one did.

He noticed she took a dry erase board out of the kitchen and started hiding it behind the desk. "What's this?" He caught her hand before she slid it behind. She blushed. "It's my weekly calendar. I just, well..." She sighed. "Some kids have to hide porn or drugs. I have to hide this."

Aidan pulled it out of her hand and had a look. "Jesus Christ, Alanna. How long have you been keeping these hours?" He noticed that she basically worked full time at the clinic, had been teaching at least five fitness classes a week, and had spaced no less than three hours a night for school work. She also had entries for church and something that said SAPR Volunteer. "What's SAPR?"

She took the calendar nervously out of his hands. "Sexual Assault Prevention and Response." She didn't meet his eyes. "It's a rape crisis team. I just volunteer to work the phones a few nights a month. I can study while I man the phones. I've had to stop doing it though. I wasn't getting enough sleep. Last week was my last shift for a while."

She went to the computer and wiggled the mouse, clicking open the video conferencing link. "It's all yours." She said brightly. He noticed that she took a key from the top drawer and locked the bottom drawer. He remembered the night he'd seen her take something off the printer and put it in there, the night she'd been scared. Then he watched as she took the pistol, walked into her bedroom, and took the magazine out. He'd heard the unmistakeable sound of the mag release. Then it sounded like she put the gun away in a drawer.

She came out and wouldn't meet his gaze. He didn't call his parents, and the weight of his gaze finally got to her. "What? I'm just cleaning up a little before…"

He finished her sentence. "Before your da comes through that door? It seems like you aren't cleaning as much as putting up some sort of facade to put him at ease."

She shrugged. "And what's wrong with that? He worries too much. He has a lot on his mind and I don't need to give him an excuse to worry. Everything is fine, Aidan. He just doesn't know how much I'm working and he doesn't need to know."

Aidan shook his head. She shot her chin up, "I can take care of myself. If he sees money is tight, he will try to give me money. I'm not doing that. Just keep your gob shut, or you and I are going to tango. Don't try to tell me for one minute that you tell your parents every problem you have." She shot her hand up to stop him. "Not that there are any problems. There aren't. I am fine."

Aidan cursed under his breath. Alanna thought she heard some sort of crack about being surrounded by "pigheaded, stubborn women." She put her hands on her hips. "I'll take that as a compliment." He gave her an impatient look. She sighed. "Look, I used my dad's GI Bill for my undergraduate studies. I got scholarships that paid for grad school, but some of the scholarship funds gave less this year. This internship paid me, but not enough to cover the tuition. The last six months have been very lean. I had to use all of my extra money for rent and living expenses. It's ok. I made it all stretch. I'm fine. My dad has done enough. I just don't want him to know that I am working that many hours. He's already pushing for me to move up to Virginia with him. He needs to have his own life, and so do I."

Aidan crossed the room and stood in front of her. "You don't have to do this all yourself." He put his hand on her forearm and squeezed.

She answered him with her head high. "Just because I don't have to, doesn't mean I shouldn't." She pointed at him, "You keep a lock on it, O'Brien, or I'll think twice about that bat." She was not adorable when she threatened him. Not at all.

Sean appeared on the screen on the second ring. "Hello, son. God, it is good to see you. How are you settling in?"

Right next to him, Sorcha popped her head in. "How's my beautiful boy?" Aidan's ears reddened, and he shot a quick glance at Alanna's bedroom. She'd closed the door, giving him privacy. The smell of something spicy and floral was wafting under the door, though. He wondered if she was in the bath, but nothing could quell carnal desire like your parents on video conference.

"I'm fine, ma. The place is beautiful and I am having a few training mates over tonight. We start tomorrow."

His mother's face grew serious. "Be careful, love. You can get hurt during training, too." They made small talk, catching up, when Sean seemed to be looking behind Aidan. "Brigid said you had to use the lass's computer next door. Is that where you are now?"

Aidan nodded. "Aye, she's got a landline wire in her desktop. It's a stronger connection."

Sorcha's face brightened. "Oh, is she there? I'd love to meet her. Branna said she's practically family."

Aidan shook his head, "She's stepped into the other room to give me some privacy and to study. Maybe the next time." There was no way in hell he was going to pull her out of the bath to come say hi. Wouldn't that start his mother's tongue wagging? She'd be booking the wedding cottage for the fall.

"I'm going up to check on Gran next week. She's not feeling her best, and I'll check on the flat while I'm up there."

After a few minutes, Aidan heard the front door open and close over the video. "Seany, come say hi to your brother!" Sean Jr. bent down into view. *Christ, he's getting huge.*

Aidan's heart squeezed. The youngest of the O'Brien boys was becoming a man. He'd missed so much of his life. He wore his hair like Tadgh's, longer and tucked behind an ear. Said the girls loved it. He looked like Da, so much like Da. His face was innocent, though. It held not a trace of pain. He was a handsome lad. He had his guitar strapped to his back. "There he is! How's the young buck doing? Still making the girls swoon with that guitar?"

"You bet your arse, brother." Seany was laughing when his face changed. "Bleeding Christ, who is that?" As if on cue, Alanna walked out of the room with her hair flying loose around her shoulders. He hadn't heard a hair dryer, but he could tell she'd kept her hair up and dry. In the bath, not the shower. *Fuuuuuuuck.* She smelled fantastic and she had a pair of cotton shorts on and a pull over. As Sorcha elbowed Seany, Aidan called her over.

She walked shyly to the computer. "I want you to meet my parents and my little brother."

Seany cursed under his breath. "Not that little."

She put her face up to the screen. "Hello, everyone. I've heard so much about you from Branna. You must be Seany." She smiled at him, and he had stars in his eyes.

"Please tell me you have a younger sister."

Sorcha scolded him and pulled his ear, "Sean Jr!" Seany gave her an unrepentant wink. "She knows I'm joking," he laughed. Aidan was shaking his head. The kid was incorrigible.

Then his father spoke. "Hello dear, I'm Sean, Aidan's da. This is Sorcha."

She gave a sweet little wave. "Well, it is so nice to finally meet you. You've been like an answer to my prayers. Thank you for taking such good care of Branna. Life is hard without a good momma and daddy." She said softly.

Aidan just looked at her, then his mother. Sorcha's eyes had misted. "It's been our sincere pleasure, lass. Would you like to see the twins? They're awake." Sorcha's smile was knowing.

"Oh! Could I? I haven't seen them in a couple of months. I never seem to catch them awake!" Sean stood up and Sorcha followed him.

Seany took front and center. "So, tell me about the bikinis, Aidan." Sorcha yelled from behind him as Alanna cracked off a laugh. She covered her mouth.

Aidan was trying to suppress a laugh, "Seany, please."

The junior gave another unrepentant smile. "I'm sixteen. What do you expect me to think about?"

Sean shooed him out of the seat as Sorcha sat with one baby, and Sean with the other, in the crook of his arm. He was big like his sons, and the babies looked even tinier in comparison. They were looking at the screen with their big blue eyes and black hair. Halley had a little bow in her hair.

Aidan looked at Alanna and froze. She had her hand loosely over her lips, tears in her eyes. "Oh my, little ones, your momma is an artist." She took her hand off her mouth and touched the screen where the babies were. She stifled her tears. "I wish I could have come to the christening. Are you giving mom and dad some time off?"

Sorcha nodded. "Aye, we told Michael to take her to Dublin for the night. Twins are hard on a woman. I know from experience."

Alanna looked longingly at the babies, then cleared her throat, looking at Sean and Sorcha. "I can't thank you enough. Branna needed you. You're everything she needed," she said softly.

Sean looked at her thoughtfully, "Aye, and we needed her. She's a blessing beyond measure. She's a true mate to Michael, and that's all we ever hoped for."

Alanna smiled at that. "I'll let you get back to chatting. Tell Branna to call me day or night. I want to hear all about her romantic getaway. It was an honor to meet you both, and you too, Seany."

Seany popped his head onto the screen. "The pleasure was certainly mine, lass."

She walked out of view and Aidan heard her close the bedroom door again. "I have to go. She's got things to do, and I need to get the house ready for guests."

Sean gave him a sad smile, "Ok, son. We miss you. I'm so very proud of you, lad."

"I know, Da, and I miss you too."

Then Sean said, "Aidan, she's a lovely woman, isn't she?"

Aidan looked behind him, afraid she'd heard. "Aye, she is. Please tell Gran and Grandda I said hello."

Sean Jr. gave a final wave. "Tell Da that I'm old enough to fly alone. I want to come stay with you for a couple of weeks."

Aidan put his hands up. "You're welcome, lad. You know that. But don't put me in the middle of it. That's their call."

Seany grunted. "Then there's no hope. They think I'm still a child."

Aidan hung up the video chat and scooted the chair back. He knocked on Alanna's door and heard her yell to come in. He opened the door hesitantly, and he instantly regretted the intrusion when he saw the big bed with the soft, white bedding. Smells assaulted him. Jasmine and soap.

He looked to his left and the breath shot out of him. The floor plan was open. The bath was visible from the bed. Huge Olympic sized garden tub. It was deep and oval and had modern lines, jutting up from the floor. "Wow," was all he could manage.

Alanna stopped brushing those long silkie locks and looked at him and then at the tub. "Yes, Meghan renovated this side. She liked a good tub. No beach house stall showers for her."

Aidan's arousal stirred in his trousers as he realized that she'd, just minutes before, been lounging in that bath with herbal oils and steam and pink flesh. "I, I uh.." He took a breath and shook his head. "I'm done with the computer. I just wanted you to know. Thanks, again. I'll try not to bother you too much."

She was pulling her hair up into a high pony tail, arms above her head pulling the hair together. The motion made her back arch and her ass tipped slightly in those shorts. She finished her tie job, turned around and stopped. Clearly the lust was showing on his face. Her lids lowered just a hint, and her mouth opened just a crack. She walked toward him. He understood her, already. She had no idea that her body betrayed subtle hints of arousal. She wasn't the teasing type.

"You can use it whenever you like. Do you need anything else?"

Yep. How about you take those clothes back off, pull that tie out of your hair, and stretch out across that soft bed. I'll take it from there. "No thank you. I'll see you later, then?" She nodded, her cheeks flushed. He noticed that when he got close to her, her lips flushed more pink. Like they wanted to make sure he knew right where they were. He leaned in, smelled her ear. She smelled fantastic. Both like the oil she'd used and her own unique scent. He liked that she hadn't washed her hair again. She had an earthy, womanly smell at her hairline that mixed perfectly with what she wore on her skin.

"More Jasmine," he said huskily.

She was breathing shallowly. She turned her head and looked up at him, at his eyes and his mouth. She swallowed hard. "Yes. It's kind of my signature scent."

He smiled a wolfish smile, "Then I'll go to my grave thinking of you when I smell it." Then he turned and briskly walked out of her room and out the door.

As she heard the slider click in place she dropped limply on to her bed. "You are in such deep shit, Miss Priss."

Aidan heard a knock on his back door, which was open and a male voice call out. "Barbecue is here." He went into the living room and took the pan out of Hans's hands, stashing it in the oven on warm. "Jesus, thank you, Sgt. Major. This smells incredible."

As Alanna's father stepped into the space, he spoke. "You need to call me Hans, I insist."

Aidan stopped, nodded. "Well then, Hans. Can I offer you a beer without getting you in trouble?"

He laughed, "Absolutely. She only counts the cigars."

Aidan popped off the top, "Glass?" Hans shook his head and took the bottle. Aidan tipped his to toast. "Slàinte."

A flicker of something came over the Marine's face. Aidan understood, without him saying it, that he was thinking of his fallen comrade and best friend. "So, how's little Branna doing, and the twins?"

Aidan took a long draw of his beer before he answered. "She's an amazing woman. My brother is a lucky man. The twins are running them ragged as you can imagine. They've got a lot of help, though. My mother and da and my sister and Finn, we've got a lot of family around to help. You needn't worry over her."

Hans's face softened. "Yes, well that's like telling a dog not to bark. My girls worry me. I feel as responsible for her as my own children. I wish I could have done more. She just picked up and left for Ireland, and I wasn't here to see her off."

Aidan shrugged. "You're not in the ground yet, man. She knows she can depend on you. So does that stubborn one next door."

Hans barked out a laugh. "Well, well. I did hear about the bat. You're lucky she didn't grab the gun. She could shoot the nuts off a gnat with that aim."

Aidan spit his beer out on a laugh, just as Alanna walked through the door. They both shut up instantly. "Uh huh. What are you two up to?" Her hands were on her hips again and she had one brow up. And that was not adorable. Nope, it really wasn't.

Her father broke the silence. "Man talk. No chicks allowed."

Aidan snickered, and she eye balled him. "Choose sides wisely, Irishman. This one will get you into trouble."

Alanna's father walked over to her and kissed her on the cheek as he strolled out the door. "Thanks for the beer, Aidan. We'll see you for supper."

He walked out and Alanna's eyes followed him, her head shaking. "He must really like you. He's normally not this friendly."

Aidan shrugged, "Irishman are known for their charm, and offering a man a cold beer is rarely a bad move."

She smiled. "True enough."

Alanna was proofreading and editing her paper when her father came in from his workout. "How was the gym? Too hot?" Alanna asked.

Hans shook his head, wiping his neck with a towel. "No, not yet, but another couple of weeks you'll need that AC unit installed. I can come back down and do it. You'll want it put in before your graduation guests get here." Alanna fidgeted in her chair. "You did invite the family, right? Your mother, Erik, your grandparents?"

She sighed. "Daddy, it's a small ceremony. Summer graduation from graduate school is not high school graduation. You and Erik are all I need."

Hans stiffened. "Is your mother coming? It isn't that far of a drive from Georgia."

Alanna fiddled with her papers. "She's not sure. She, um, didn't like my terms." Her father just looked at her. They had a sort of non-verbal communication, and he was telling her to expand. "I told her she couldn't bring the flavor of the month. I'm not letting one of her creepster boyfriends stay in my house. She suggested that if I was the one with the problem, then perhaps I should pay for a hotel room for her. Then I said that maybe if she didn't date hippie losers with no gainful employment, they could pay for their own hotel room."

Silence. He was silent behind her. She peered over her shoulder, looking sheepish. "Alanna, she's your mother." He was trying to be serious, but a grin was niggling at the corners of his mouth. He admired a sharp tongued woman, even if she was his daughter.

This argument was old. "Dad, I know that. A mother who thinks I'm a prude because I don't want her latest boy toy creeping around my house." She looked at her dad. "I am not a prude."

Her dad laughed. "I didn't say you were. You're my daughter. I'm glad you're…" He stopped.

"What?" She said defensively. "Your glad I'm what? A prude?" She put her forehead on her arms.

"Honey, I don't think anything of the sort, and I'm glad you respect yourself. It just surprises me how few men you've had in your life. Tim was a while ago. Don't you ever date? I'm not saying I want you catting around town. I just don't want you to be alone."

She lifted her head, shrugging. "I'm very busy. And it's not like they're beating down the door."

Hans sat next to her at the table. "Bullshit. There's no way it's from lack of interest. You're smart, beautiful, you're an athlete, and you're the kindest woman I've ever known."

She rolled her eyes. "Daddy, stop. You're totally biased."

Her fathered sighed, "Just because your mom and I made a mess of things, doesn't mean you will. Erik made a bad move, but he got out early, before he had kids. You two haven't had the best example, but I want you to be happy. I want you to find someone to love you and take care of you." She stiffened her spine and her father put his hand up. "Don't start with that independent woman speech of yours. Just because you are strong and you can take care of yourself doesn't mean you should have to do it alone."

Alanna gave a snort. Hadn't she just had a similar conversation with Aidan? "Now you sound like that infernal Irishman."

Hans perked up at that. "Aidan? Really? Now how on earth did that conversation come about?"

Alanna was kicking herself. This is not a direction she wanted to go in and she didn't want him probing Aidan. "Nothing daddy, it was just something he said. I don't even remember how it came up," she lied. "Just don't worry about my love life or lack there of. What about you? How many dates have you been on in the last five years?" *When in doubt, launch a counter attack.*

He hopped out of the chair like someone had zapped him with a taser. "Weren't we talking about your mother and why you should be inviting her to your graduation?"

"Nice deflection. Now, as for momma, I invited her. We did our part. If she comes alone, she can stay with me and you can stay with Erik. If not, then you will stay here. As for Grandma and Grandpa, they really don't need to drive up here for this. It's not that big of a deal."

Hans came around to where she was sitting and squatted in front of her. "It is a big deal." He shook his head, breaking eye contact to collect himself. "This work you're doing is important. I couldn't be prouder. Everyday, since you were a little peanut, you have made your daddy so proud. You know that, right?"

Alanna's eyes misted. "I love you, daddy."

He squeezed her hands and stood up. "I'm going to shower. I'm a little too manly for that big tub." Alanna laughed. "Dad, men bathe. It's not a gender specific thing."

He just grunted, obviously disagreeing. Before he left the room he stopped and looked at her. "He doesn't call you Anna. He calls you Alanna. Was that your doing?"

She picked at her shirt hem and didn't make eye contact. "No, he just said it suited me." She shrugged.

"Brian and I were the only ones that ever called you that," he said softly.

She smiled sadly. "Same ilk, I suppose."

8

John and Maria were coming up the drive when Aidan yelled from the wrap around deck. He walked down, grabbing the dish out of Maria's hand and took the child from around her leg and held his hand as they ascended the stairs. John carried his daughter and a six pack of beer. "Aidan, this place is beautiful. I can't believe you are living ocean front!" Maria said.

They came up the stairs, and little Frankie ran to the edge of the deck. "Swim! I want to swim!" He was pointing and jumping the way that little children do.

"Sweetie, it's still a little cold. We'll take you down in a little while, but you might not be able to go in all the way." Aidan slid the door open and John followed him inside. Maria also followed, holding her son by the hand. "John, can you go back down and get the diaper bag and the kid's cooler?"

John's face blanched. "What cooler?"

Maria had murder in her eyes. "I told you three times to grab the diaper bag and the cooler, John." Her voice was strained with the effort of keeping her voice down.

"Oh, shit. She's talking through her teeth. I am so dead."

Aidan slapped him on the back. "Which is why you always have a man at your six." He walked over to the cabinet and took out the children's crackers that looked like fish, juice pouches, and a bunch of bananas. "I've got cheese and peanut butter, too."

Maria looked at him, then at her husband. "That's it, we're adopting him."

John looked at Aidan. "I would call you a kiss ass again, but you just saved my bacon, so I'll shut the shut."

Aidan laughed. "I have two nieces and two nephews and cousins uncounted. I found out early to keep that shit, uh, I mean stuff in the house when they come for a visit." He cleared his throat, remembering that little ears were listening. "I asked Alanna what American kids liked and this is what she said was the go-to dish of choice." He dangled the goldfish bag from two fingers.

"Crackfish. Good call," John said, and left to retrieve the diaper bag.

John came back up on the deck with four other people that Aidan assumed were two of his training mates. John started the introductions as Maria took the chips and beverages from them. "Captain Aidan O'Brien, Royal Irish Regiment, this is Major Hector Diaz and his wife Hatsu. And this is Lt. Joseph Drake and Lt. Shull. They are your intel and artillery officers." Aidan shook their hands.

"Call me Joey. Thanks for the invite."

He shook the two Lieutenants and Major's hands and then turned to his wife, a lovely Japanese woman. "Madam, it's a pleasure to meet you." He didn't call her Mrs. Diaz because not all cultures did the woman take on the last name of their husband, and he wasn't familiar with the Japanese take on that.

She took his hand lightly, and bowed ever so slightly. "Please, you can call me Hatsu."

She was very slight and elegant and Aidan's curiosity overriding his manners, had to ask. "That's a lovely name. What does it mean, if you don't mind me asking?"

She smiled, "Not at all. It means *first born*."

Aidan smiled in return. "Oh, aye. I'm the first born of six. It's a good name. Please, everyone come in and get a drink, and I'll start setting up the food." Just as they prepared to enter the house, Hans and Alanna made an appearance around the deck.

Major Diaz yelped in surprise. "Well I'll be damned. Sgt. Major Falk, I thought they sucked you down I-95 into Purgatory."

Hans laughed. "Well, they did. This here is my little girl. She lives in the adjoining house. I'm just up here for the night."

Introductions were made, but Aidan couldn't take his eyes off of Alanna. She was wearing an emerald green blouse. It was sleeveless and silky with a scoop neck. At the top of the neckline was a bow. The green made her eyes explode with color. She was wearing white shorts and strappy, flat sandals that matched her blouse. Her hair was partially down, but she had the sides braided along her head until they came together at the back. This accentuated the copper and sand and lighter sun kissed streaks that made up her unique hair color. He only looked away when he saw a subtle shift to his left. It was Lt. Joey sidling over to get closer to her, shaking her hand and smiling. On the other side was Ryan Shull, stars in his eyes as well, but being less obvious. She was smiling nervously, surprised by the attention. Aidan had to fight the urge to nudge Lieutenant Drake off the deck, and on to the dune below. "Let's all head in and grab a drink, aye?"

As they piled into the house, Hector whistled. "Boy, you weren't kidding about the digs, John. How is the Regiment putting you up here?"

Aidan came around to the refrigerator as he answered. "They're not. I'd be living in John's garage on their budget. My sister-in-law owns this place. Her father was a Marine."

Hector looked at Hans, and the wheels started turning. "Brian," he said. Not a question. "I remembered he owned a place down here. How is his daughter doing?"

As they continued to talk, Aidan walked to Alanna and leaned in, kissing her on the cheek. "Thank you for coming. I know you're busy. What would you like to drink?" He did it casually, but he noticed that Lt. Joey transferred his attention to the drink selection and left her side.

She smiled back at Aidan, and it gave him a little satisfaction that she'd not even noticed the young Lieutenants departure. "Surprise me."

He went into the kitchen and started playing the host, giving Maria leave to get the kids whatever they wanted while he handed her a Pellegrino. He open a bottle of French Rosé and poured a glass for Hatsu and Alanna, while John handed out beers to the Marines.

Hans came next to Aidan and picked up the bottle of Jameson. "No Bushmills?"

Aidan looked scandalized. "I might fight for the crown, but a man's loyalties only go so far."

Hans laughed. He picked up the bottle and two lowball glasses. "Neat?"

Aidan nodded. He poured them both a finger of whiskey. "Sláinte mhaith," Hans said. Aidan clinked his glass. "Sláinte mhaith."

Everyone filled their plates with barbecue, coleslaw, and hush-puppies. Hatsu opened a green bean dish that smelled delicious. "Hatsu, that smells gorgeous all together. What is it?"

Hector put his arm around her. "She's a genius in the kitchen. She keeps me in shape, unlike my Mexican mother who stuffs me with tamales."

Hatsu blushed. "It's called shiraae. It has crumbled tofu, miso, and sesame seeds and then some sugar and soy sauce. It's very healthy, but it has a nice flavor." Her accent was there, but her English was excellent.

"What part of Japan are you from?"

She smiled, "I am from Okinawa. That's how I met my husband. I helped my father run a shop near one of the bases." Everyone took a helping of Hatsu's beans and they reconvened on the deck. The men pulled deck chairs from Alanna's side and everyone sat and ate, making small talk. Lieutenant Shull left early, having to stand duty that evening.

Major Diaz was the first to bring up work, which was really why they were all coming together. "So Aidan, where have you been? I'll see your files tomorrow, but we don't usually get Royal Irish on exchange. What's your backstory? John told me the why of it. One parent Northern Irish, one from the Republic. Did you join as an officer after college?"

Aidan swallowed his food, cleared his throat, and spoke."No, Sir. I was part way through university. We kept hearing about the casualties the U.S. and British Forces were taking." He shook his head, "Honestly, I got tired of watching the shite on the news. I dropped out my last semester and enlisted. I didn't become an officer until later, after I finished my degree."

"A mustang. Nice. Mustangs make the best officers," Diaz said. Aidan cocked his head, confused, so Hector explained. "A mustang is an officer who was prior enlisted. My experience is that getting a little time as an enlisted grunt does you some good when it is time to be the boss. You understand your men better, because you've been in their shoes."

Aidan nodded, "I agree. So, will we all be on the same team, tomorrow?"

Hector nodded his head. "Yes, you will be my Captain alongside Denario. You'll work right under John, which is perfect because my other Captain is getting augmented out of Pendelton and we will meet him in theater. It's a fourteen man team. The Pendelton captain will be bringing a Lieutenant and Staff Sergeant with him that will act as our S-3 team. You will meet the rest of the crew tomorrow. Some good boys. We called them Military Transition Teams in Iraq and they are Embedded Training Teams in Afghanistan. What do you call them, again?"

"Operational Mentoring and Liaison Teams is what the most common term for them is," Aidan said.

"That's right. Liaison Teams, that's the NATO speak. So, how much time have you spent in theater?" Diaz asked.

The guy was a straight shooter, Aidan noticed. He liked that about him. "Three tours in Afghanistan, one in Iraq." Alanna's eyes shot to his and he looked away.

Lt. Drake whistled. "Damn, man. You've done your share, haven't you?"

Sgt. Major Falk had quietly listened up until this point, but he interrupted at this point. "The Irish Regiments haven't been deployed as much as some of the other British forces. The battalion in the North is reserves. How did you manage four tours?"

Aidan picked at the label on his beer bottle. "I went on an individual augment with the British Army during Operation Telic. I was in Basra, mostly. I was with 1st Battalion most of my career, the active duty battalion. When I finished with my last deployment, they transferred me back to the North with the 2nd to help with training, and because I asked for it. My family is closer. First Battalion is in Shropshire, England. The commute for Sunday roast was a bit far," he said with a joking grin.

"So you volunteered. You went out of your way to get to where the action was."

It was not a question, and it made Aidan look the Marine in the eye. "Aye. I didn't join up to stand on the sidelines. I didn't have a wife or kids. I could go whenever they needed me."

Hans's eyes were shrewd. He simply nodded, like he'd gotten the answers he wanted.

Maria interrupted, "Enough shop talk, boys. Who wants dessert?"

Major Diaz put his hand over his heart. "Ah, Maria, you little Italian goddess. What is it? Tiramisu?"

She grinned mischievously. "Nope. Try again."

He moaned. "Holy God, woman. Did you make cannoli?"

She smiled, "Bingo."

Alanna hopped up. "I'll help you, Maria. Everyone sit and relax. Coffee for anyone?"

Aidan got up as well. The three of them walked into the house, and Aidan noticed Maria pressing her hands to her lower back. "Are you feeling all right, lass?"

Maria patted his cheek. "Just swollen feet and back pain. Nothing out of the ordinary. My blood pressure was high at my last appointment. I just have to watch the sodium, I suppose."

Aidan looked at her ankles and they were very swollen. "Come here, lass. Sit down and I'll handle dessert."

She protested, but he stopped her. "You've got two under five years old and another on the way. You need to take a break and put your feet up."

Alanna watched as Aidan sat Maria down on the couch and propped her feet on the coffee table with a pillow. "You're going to be a good husband Aidan. I'm still pushing to adopt you."

He laughed, "My mother would never part with me." He went to the kitchen, poured a glass of ice water, and took it to her. Then he joined Alanna in the kitchen. He started working on plating the dessert when he noticed she wasn't moving. He looked up at her, and she had such a strange look on her face.

"What?" he asked.

She just looked his face over, his eyes and mouth. Then she shook herself, realizing she was staring. "So, three people want coffee. A half pot should do it."

"So, Alanna, besides having a beautiful singing voice and tempting the young Lance Coolies at the gym, what do you do with yourself?" Maria asked. Aidan sputtered out a laugh. Maria was as blunt as Brigid.

Alanna looked at her, confused. "Tempting?"

Maria put her hands out, palms up. "Really? You don't have any idea, do you? Girl, they line up at the window to take a peek at the smoking hot Zumba instructor. Didn't you notice your class is always full and half of them are men? Men in a Zumba class. That didn't make you scratch your head at all?" Aidan was suppressing laughter while he worked at the cannoli, and Alanna was blushing.

"To answer your question," she said saucily, elbowing Aidan for laughing, "I am graduating from Grad school in a couple of weeks."

Maria's eyebrows shot up. "Wow, you seem young to be finishing a Masters program. What's your field of study?"

Alanna fiddled with the coffee pot while she spoke. "I have a dual bachelors in Social Work and Psychology. My graduate study is Clinical Psychology. I'm an intern at Heroic Spirit, in the PTSD therapeutic services."

Maria looked at Aidan. "Wow, smart and gorgeous. That is amazing. I worked as a trauma nurse before I started having all of these babies. I keep my continuing ed up on-line so I keep my credentials. It's hard, though. That is amazing work, Alanna. It's important. Heroic Spirit is a wonderful clinic. They have such a whole patient approach, unlike the VA."

Alanna nodded excitedly. Aidan noticed that she was even more beautiful when she talked about her work. She got excited, passionate. "I wish there were more clinics out there. Heroic Spirit can't see retirees. They couldn't handle the patient load."

Maria smiled at her. "That's where people like you come in, isn't it? We've gotta whole lot of men and women that need just what you're doing. You are going to make the difference."

Aidan looked at Alanna who was quiet. Her eyes were misty, but she wasn't going to let herself cry. She never really did, did she? "Thank you, Maria. That's exactly what I needed to hear." She took out plates of desserts as Aidan watched her go.

"Aidan, you better get your shit together. There are plenty of young bucks on this base that would line up and cage fight each other for a crack at her."

Aidan pulled out of his daze. He shook his head. "Maria, she's just a friend. She also lives an ocean away. I can't toy with a girl like that. She's Branna's best friend."

Maria let out an exasperated breath. "You want to check the miles between Okinawa and Texas? Hatsu and Hector have been together for twenty years.They fell in love and she didn't look back. The right man is worth it. I know you are interested. Your hackles went up as soon as Joey got within five feet of her. You can try to fool yourself, Aidan, if that makes you feel better. I'm not buying it."

Aidan gave her a sideways look. "You know, woman. If it wasn't for the dark eyes and olive skin, I'd swear you and my sister were separated at birth."

Maria laughed. "She must be a smart lady, then."

Another chiding look. "Drink your water, hen. And stop makin trouble." With that, Aidan walked out with a tray of cannoli and coffee.

Aidan went out to the deck and passed out the coffee, when he noticed a few heads were missing. He looked down on the beach and saw Alanna, Hatsu, and Hans with Clara and Frankie. "The kids were getting restless, so they took them down. Where's Maria? Is she okay?" John got up with a little look of panic in his eyes.

"Her feet are swollen. I put her on the couch with a glass of water," Aidan answered.

John sighed. "Her blood pressure is high with this one. Doc said that the swelling will get worse with the heat."

Hector interrupted. "Have her talk to Hatsu. I know the Japanese women have some good homeopathic type stuff for that. You don't want her getting pre-eclamptic."

Aidan nodded his head in agreement, "Aye, he's right. I can call my mother about that, too. You need to keep her off her feet and get a BP cuff for home."

The young Lieutenant looked at all three men, baffled. "How the hell do you all know this stuff?" He looked at Aidan. "I thought you were single with no kids. Did I miss some kind of class or some shit?"

Aidan laughed. "I'm the first of six, and my mother is a midwife. You pick it up. Now, who wants a cigar?"

Aidan walked down to the beach and greeted the child minders. "Thank you. Maria needed a little rest. Hatsu, Hector seemed to think you might have some advice for Maria. Would you mind going to check on her? I'll call my mother tomorrow morning as well. She's a midwife." Hatsu nodded in her mild way and walked upstairs.

Aidan walked over to Frankie who was digging in the sand with Hans. "What are you making, lad? Is it a castle, then?"

The boy scrunched his brows. "No. It's a fort. This is where I'll put the cannons."

Aidan's brows shot up. He looked at Hans. "Cigar?"

Hans accepted the cigar and lighter. "You're not having one?"

Aidan shook his head. "Maybe later." He gestured to the sand fort. "I'll leave you to it then. Don't shoot me when I come back." He walked over to Alanna who had Clara by the hands, her feet in the surf. Clara was trying to flee into the water.

"This one is a water baby. She's dying to get in that water."

Aidan knelt down by Clara who immediately recognized him. "Swim!" she said with a burst, pointing her finger to the water.

"Well, lass. It's a bit cold. Do you want to walk a bit further?" She took his hand and began heading in. Just as a wave that would have had her wet to her waist made contact, Aidan scooped her up and swung her around, letting her feet skim the water. She squealed. "Oh, you like that, aye?" He let her stand again and she started bopping up and down as another wave approached. She put her hands up for Aidan to grab her and he swooped her up again.

Just as he put her down, he saw John and Maria walking down. "I'm missing all the fun!" Maria shouted over the surf. She stepped into the water and squeaked at the temperature. "I need a nice, cold soak. Mommy's feet look like Fred Flintstone's!"

Frankie asked, "Momma, who's Fred Flintstone?"

Hans laughed. "You just dated yourself, Maria."

She shrugged and sighed as the water came over her feet and ankles. John came behind her, drawing her into his body. His arms were around her belly. "I'll rub your back and feet tonight, baby."

She smiled and turned for a kiss. "I think this pregnancy started with one of your back rubs."

He gave a husky laugh. "Oh, yes. I remember." Then he grew serious. "You need to take it easy, okay. No lifting Clara. I'll be out in the field. You need to let some stuff go and put your feet up. You're going to make me worry. Promise me you'll take it easy."

She relaxed into his arms. "I promise."

Alanna watched the couple and something aching was settling in her chest. They seemed very happy and they had beautiful, well behaved children. "Do you know what this baby is?" she asked.

Maria shook her head. "Nope, we got a butt shot at the ultrasound. We decided to wait and let it be a surprise."

Alanna smiled at that. "Isn't that exciting. How about names?"

John rolled his eyes. "That has been a battle. All we know is that we want them to be named after Saints, just like Clara and Francis. If it's a girl, we like Cecelia, Catherine, and Teresa. The boy, we can't decide. We might just have to see the little meatball in person before we decide."

As they talked, Aidan stared out at the sea. Clearing his mind the way only the sea could do. Hatsu came next to him. "Water is very healing. It helps you find balance, yes?"

He nodded. "Yes, it does. My people, they're from the West coast. Well, my father's people. My mother's kin are from Belfast. We've grown up near the sea, though. I can't imagine going long without it."

Out of the corner of his eye, Aidan saw Hans tense. Then the glare happened. Hans pulled Alanna to him. "Daddy what's wrong?" Adrenaline spiked through Aidan as he put himself between the light and Hatsu. Then he heard Hector speak to Hans with an uncharacteristic softness.

"Stand down. It's a camera lens, my man." Aidan looked down the beach and saw the man's non-distinct form. A large camera with an even larger lens in his hands. A tourist with a camera. He looked at Hans. Alanna was rubbing his back.

"Sorry about that, baby. Old habits." He noticed Hans was sweating, flushed. Alanna grinned.

"It's okay, daddy. Glad to know those reflexes will work in my favor if I ever need them."

Aidan sighed, and he felt Hatsu squeezed his hand. "It's nice to know Hector isn't alone. We've been where you are."

Aidan didn't need her to clarify. They were all trained to look for the sun's glare off a rifle scope. And the thought that Hans had lost his best friend to a sniper? That shit didn't wipe off. Ever. Kind of made a man twitchy during his dwell time, just like seeing a bundle on the side of the road or hearing a car backfire. Little punishments.

Hector and Joey came up behind them and Aidan shook off the dark thoughts. "Do you need another beer, Major? Lieutenant?"

They shook their heads in unison. "No, we have an early morning tomorrow, but thank you. I wanted to prepare you for tomorrow. It's going to be a lot of intro stuff, explaining the training sections. With four tours under your belt, some of this may be a refresher for you. We'll get into the team stuff, though. Operating in small teams, sometimes away from a major base, sometimes on a joint installation with the natives. This isn't Iraqis we're dealing with, though. The Afghanis have more incidents of friendly fire, bad eggs slipping through the cracks and waiting for an opportunity to shoot you in the back." Maria paled and John rubbed her shoulders, whispering in her ear.

"In the Marines, we'd have a Major at the chief position, but with your time in arena, you might get the opportunity to be the boss with your own teams, even though you're a new Captain. Regardless, you'll be going back to First Battalion and training the soldiers there. Am I right to assume that your time in the North will end with this training?"

Aidan nodded his head. "Aye, they'll move me. Time to go back to Shropshire."

Hector nodded, understanding. "I'm going to give you as much opportunity as I can to take a leadership role. You don't need to sit in the back of the class if you are going to go home and enhance the training for your men. You'll be on my team, and I plan on delegating between you and John. I've done this training when we went to Iraq, and some of it is redundant. You'll be using our firearms and our comm equipment and our transport. There was no getting around that. Getting your weapons over here was a logistical can of worms that your command didn't want to deal with. I am assuming you know how to work your own shit, so just consider this a chance to play with some new toys."

Aidan clapped him on the back. "Aye, Sir. I can't wait to get my hands on some of that equipment. I might even need to pick up one of those K-bars you lot are so fond of." The four Marines in attendance let out a boisterous "ooh-rah" and Aidan laughed.

"Oh, we can certainly get you some cutlery, Irishman. Abso-fucking-lutely," Hector said.

Hatsu whispered, "Hector, language."

Hector looked at John and Maria. "Sorry, I forgot about the little ones."

Maria waved her hand in dismissal.

As everyone walked to their cars, the women hugged and said their goodbyes. While Aidan was talking to John and Lt. Drake, Hans pulled Hector discreetly out of ear shot. "If you don't mind, I'd like a little intel on the Irishman," said Hans.

"Whatever you need, Sgt. Major. Any concerns I need to know about?"

Hans shook his head, "Not in any way that involves his job. More along the lines of his back story. He's living next door to my daughter for the next three months. I just want to know more about him. Four deployments in ten years. That's no fucking joke, as you know. I mean, in the Marines? Absolutely. But he had to pull some strings to get this hook-up. I'd like to know what he's done. Any awards, medals, any details on his deployments. I know you'll have access to that. I wouldn't ask, but…."

Hector put his hand up. "I get it. He's trying like hell to hide it, but he's not immune to that daughter of yours. Who could blame him? I'll check him out, get back to you this week. Sound good?" Hans nodded as Alanna approached. Hector hugged her. "Take care, baby girl."

Hans approached Aidan and gave him a pat on the shoulder. "That was a nice thing you did tonight. I think things will be more relaxed tomorrow morning with a few friendly faces. Now, if you two don't mind handling the clean up, this old Marine needs to get on the road at four in order to make it to work tomorrow."

Alanna kissed her dad on the cheek. "Go ahead and go to bed, daddy. I'm so glad you came. I'll help Aidan, and you get some sleep."

Aidan interrupted, "You were a guest, lass. You don't need to clean up. I'll take care of everything."

"Aidan, you have fed me four times in as many days. Now, as you Irish like to say… shut your gob. I'm helping."

9

Morning came early for everyone. Alanna got up with her father, made him coffee, and took some time to get her work in order before heading to the gym. She had to be in the clinic at nine, but she was teaching a seven o'clock spinning class for the early bird gym rats. She heard Aidan milling around on the other side and thought about trying to join him for a cup of tea, but decided against it. She needed to make sure she wasn't becoming a pest, or worse, a puppy following him around. He had been so wonderful to her, but he wasn't interested in being anyone's boyfriend. She thought she sensed some attraction on his part, but if he knew about the mammoth sized crush she had on him, it would make things very awkward all summer.

She needed to get back to thinking about work. She had a fitness class every day this week, five full shifts at the clinic, and had to work on her thesis. Two weeks of sessions and she was done. She also had to get her resumes to the hospitals in the DC area, maybe in South Carolina and Texas, too. She didn't want to look any further, right now. She couldn't afford the airfare and hotels to fly out for an interview. She pushed away the stress of impending unemployment and focused on getting ready for work.

Aidan pulled into the training facility after a peaceful drive through the remote training areas. He was stoked to get started and meet the other men. He was amazed at the magnitude of this base. Already, there were aircraft flying, trucks full of men heading in different directions, and he was actually stopped at a tank crossing to let a couple of armored vehicles get through. Apparently there was beach access nearby, where they trained as well as where the families could go to swim.

He thought about Branna and Alanna growing up on bases like this. Men running in uniform, aircrafts, even hovercrafts rolling onto the shore, according to John. He'd known the U.S. military had juice, but seeing it in person was something else. The Marines being the best of the best, he noticed the hard lines of their faces. He also noticed the physical condition they were in, whether they were privates or colonels. He'd been with a reserve unit for the last several months. Men and women who had careers outside of the military, who were only part-time warriors. These were more his type of people. The ones who couldn't imagine doing any other job.

Men were piling into the training room with paper cups of coffee, rucksacks, and purposeful gaits. Aidan got more that one double take, being in a different uniform. John hollered over the din at him as soon as he entered. "Yo, Aidan. Over here!"

Aidan felt a bit like the new kid at school, even though that was ridiculous. He kept his head up and shoulders back. He was suddenly grateful for John's idea to have a get-together last night. As soon as he approached Lt. Drake and Capt. Denario, he got a whomp on the back from John. "How's my favorite Irishman?"

The men fell into talking until everyone was told to sit. At that point, an introduction to the training was given via power point. After the power point ended, the lights came on and Hector went to the front, after being prompted by the Colonel in charge.

"Good morning ladies!" The grumble of laughter went through the room. Ball breaking was a varsity sport in the Marines, and no one took offense. "The colonel has been nice enough to leave some introductions in my capable hands. Many of you have noticed the pretty boy in the beret who looks a little out of place."

Everyone looked at Aidan, and he gave a grudging smile to Hector. "Sorry, sir. You're a little hairier than I fancy." He gave the full force of his accent, just to make a point.

Hector laughed and winked at him. "Well, that aside, I thought we should give our paler brethren a proper ooh-rah welcome." The whole group gave an "ooh-rah" in unison.

"Captain Aidan O'Brien has joined us from the Royal Irish Regiment in Northern Ireland. Don't let that little feather and harp on his cap fool you. I've seen his files, and he's both experienced and decorated. Four tours in theater and some pretty nice metal on his chest. You treat him as you would any other man in this room. Those below the rank of Captain will treat him like any other superior. He is here to take back the best training material he can get his hands on. His priority is his men at home; the men to his left and right when he's in combat. He decided he should learn from the best, and we are going to do everything we can to give him what he came for. So, he'll be on my team for the duration of the summer. I have it on good authority that he's quite the musician, too. So, if you're real nice, maybe he'll sing for you." More laughter. "Anything you want to say, Captain O'Brien?"

Aidan stood. "Dia Duit, I'm glad to be here. I'll sing for no less than a bottle of Jameson. Thank you." Then he sat down, and the group started laughing and hooting.

Alanna was sitting in her cubicle when Rick came to her desk. "Hi Rick, how was your weekend?" The young counselor was handsome in an average sort of way. He was a couple of years older than Alanna and had been sort of standoffish with her. So, she was baffled that he'd initiated contact with her.

"It was good, uneventful. I slept in and did laundry. What about you?"

Alanna was astonished. He never made small talk. "Oh, you know, a lot of hitting the books, finishing my thesis."

He nodded nervously. "So, you're graduating soon. Where will you be going? Any job leads?"

Alanna sighed. "Not locally, unfortunately. I have some pending applications, but nothing concrete. I'm starting to look out of state." She couldn't figure out what his deal was. He was fiddling with her pens, not making eye contact.

"I was wondering, since your internship is almost done…" *Uh-oh.* "if you might want to go out sometime." *Shit.* He was a nice enough guy. Not particularly helpful when she needed it, but never rude or unprofessional. "I know we never interacted much. I have been hearing good things about your work. I just, um… obviously it would've been inappropriate while you were interning. I just thought since you were done, we might get to know each other, outside of the clinic."

Alanna felt like she'd walked into an alternate universe. "Um, well. I am really busy right now. My thesis takes priority. How about I give you a call after graduation? Maybe we can meet for coffee or something." *Coffee was neutral. Perfect.*

Rick smiled and took out a card from his pocket. "Here is my number. I'd like that. I really would." He left her in stunned silence. It wasn't that she'd never received male attention. She had. It just felt different. He wasn't a classmate or some skeeve at a local bar. He was a colleague of sorts. She wasn't particularly attracted to him. But he was interested, and that was something. He seemed like a nice, safe guy. He was for all intents and purposes, the complete opposite of Aidan O'Brien. She wasn't sure what had prompted the comparison, but there it was.

The thought of him made her tummy flip flop. *But he isn't interested, and the guy in front of her was.* "Okay, then. We'll keep in touch." He smiled warmly and walked away.

Alanna's first appointment was with a Sergeant who was having trouble acclimating after his latest deployment. He had a wife and two children, and was a less than cooperative participant with regard to therapy. It was determined that he had a minor TBI (traumatic brain injury), nothing that would medical board him, but enough to pull him from his next mission in order to go through the concussion recovery clinic. His marriage was suffering due to his inability to face his combat related stress and was compounded by having two small children. He was self medicating with alcohol which had done nothing but intensify his problems. As she stared across the room at him, she gave an internal sigh. His body language was all, *I don't want to be here.* His wife, seated next to him, looked tired and fed up. Dr. Jennings sat off to the side, observing.

"So, Sergeant. How was your week?" He plucked at his trousers, then looked up.

"Well, they started the transition team training today, and I'm not there, so how do you think it was?" His wife said nothing.

"Okay, I understand how that is hard for you. It must be difficult for you to see your unit preparing for a mission without you. If you want to talk about it, we can."

He shrugged. "What's the point. I got yanked because some doc thinks my headaches are a big deal, and my wife can't seem to understand that not listening isn't the same as not remembering."

The Sergeant's wife stiffened and turned to him. "Right, because everything is someone's fault. It can't be that there's actually something legitimately wrong with you. It must be the doctor and wife are just hysterical ball breakers? Sound about right?"

The Marine just got handed the excuse he needed and shot out of the chair. "This is bullshit. I'm out of here."

Alanna needed to get a handle on this before it escalated, or she lost her patient out the front door. "Sergeant Jones, please. I know you are frustrated. Please don't leave. The more we all cooperate, the sooner you are back where you want to be." That got his attention. He knew this recovery program wasn't optional. He sat back down, refusing to look at his wife.

"What I meant to ask was about this past week, at work and at home? Did you work on any of the things we talked about?" Silence. Alanna withheld the sigh she wanted to let out, keeping her tone even. "Sergeant, I understand a bit about what you are feeling and what Jessica is feeling."

He looked at her. "Really, you know that from your school books, do you?"

Alanna didn't flinch at his tone. She stayed completely calm and met his gaze. "No, I know because my father was wounded. He took sniper fire during the Battle of Fallujah." Brows raised. That got his attention. "I was a young adult when he went through his recovery. It was a long road and it was hard for him and his family. He lost his best friend, who died in his arms. He wanted to be back with his men. So, you see, I'm trying to help your family because I care. Please, I know this is difficult. Just give this a chance."

By the end of the session, Sergeant Jones and his wife had agreed to come to the family sessions on Wednesdays and the couple's sessions on Fridays. Dr. Jennings had been sitting quietly in the corner, observing and taking notes. When the couple left, Alanna walked back to the desk, sat and put her head down. "That man is so stubborn."

The doctor laughed. "Well, that won't be your first or last. You know how they are. Don't like to admit any perceived weakness, the memory issues, especially. The wife gets the brunt of it. They say she never told them; she must have moved their keys; she gave them the wrong time. Whatever can make it not about the fact that their brain isn't retaining memories. You handled him very well, Alanna. I honestly thought he was going to leave. He walked out on his last therapist. You subtly reminded him that he wouldn't go back to his unit without this program, and you also related to him on a personal level."

Alanna blushed. "I wouldn't normally share personal information. I don't want to take the focus off the patient. Marines aren't typical, though. They don't live ordinary lives, so they think some shrink in a starchy button down isn't going to be able to help them. I just thought maybe if he knew I was in the family, so to speak, that he would be a little more receptive."

The doctor nodded, "Your instincts were right. He seemed to change his attitude after the show and tell. You did well. I am really going to miss working with you."

Alanna smiled. "Well, you can come take Zumba or spinning at the gym and see me. That's where I will be working until I find a position."

The doctor clapped her hands together. "Oh, thank you for reminding me. I got an e-mail today from my friend at Walter Reed. They'd love to have your resume."

Alanna's spine straightened. "Really? Oh, thank you. I will get it to them today! I know that doesn't guarantee anything, but I really appreciate the help."

By the end of the day, Aidan was exhausted. Not from any physical taxing activity. The exhaustion was from the all too familiar "hurry up and wait" game that the military was famous for. Standing in line after line to be issued different gear for the training sessions. He'd also met the men that would make up his team. Besides Hector, John, and Joey, there were two more Lieutenants. Shull, the quiet one from last night who was the artillery officer, and Lt. Saxton who was the communications officer.

There were also the enlisted men, including one corpsman. The Navy Independent Corpsman's name was Mike O'Malley from New York, who everyone called Doc. Then there was Staff Sergeant Christopher Williams from Idaho who was the s-4 logistics guy, Corporal Eddie Washington from New Orleans who was the other artillery guy, Sgt. James Porter from Montana who was the intelligence man working under Lt. Drake, and Sgt. Nick Polaski from Chicago who was the other comm guy that worked with Lt. Saxton.

Apparently the Gunnery Sergeant in charge of logistics had gone through the previous class, because his wife was due this month and living off station. He would duplicate training with them as needed, but he'd be in and out depending on his wife's status. John hadn't been so lucky. Maria was ready to pop, and he was going to be smack in the middle of training. It happened, and it was far preferable to being in Afghanistan for the big event. So there were twelve including Aidan, fourteen would go, Aidan would return to Belfast having trained with eleven of them, but not going with them. That felt oddly disheartening. He watched the men getting to know one another, feeling each other out, and that itch to go with them, to see this through, was already starting to nag at him.

They all seemed to be good, solid men. Despite the accents and cultural differences, they fell in tune with each other almost immediately. The Staff Sergeant seemed to keep them somewhat under control, as senior enlisted tended to do. The jokers were Corporal Washington and Sgt. Polaski. The corporal was a handsome, athletically built African American man from New Orleans, which caused an immediate debate about the Braves and the Cubs, which then brought Doc into the argument with the declaration that no one was going to beat the Yankees this year. Americans loved their baseball.

"What about you, Captain?" Washington asked. "You get baseball over there across the ocean?"

Aidan put his hands up. "Leave me out of this one, lads. I'm a rugby man. When it comes to baseball, I don't get off the pub stool unless it's the Red Sox."

The men all bellowed. "No! Ah, shit. Not another one."

Hector laughed, "Niiiiice."

Aidan looked at him. "I thought you were from Texas?"

He smiled, and there was a hint of sadness. "Brian O'Mara converted me as a boot lieutenant. Never went back."

Aidan looked thoughtful. "Were you with them? Hans and Brian, when it happened?"

Hector's eyes were stoic. "Yes, I was. Worst day of my life." Aidan just nodded, because what else do you say to that?

Aidan was leaving the parking lot when a thought occurred to him. He rolled the window down to speak to Lt. Drake. "Hey, Lieutenant. Where is the gym?"

Joey approached the truck. "Which one? There are several."

Aidan thought about it. "My neighbor, she teaches yoga and some other classes."

Drake gave him a knowing look. "The new one, middle of base. Follow me. I could use a work out after standing and sitting all day."

As the two men went into the gym, Aidan's jaw almost hit the floor. There was a huge rock wall, racquetball courts, cardio, state of the art machines, and several rooms for classes. He could smell chlorine, too, so they obviously had a pool on the premises. "Bleeding Christ. Maybe I will let the Denario's adopt me."

Joey laughed. "Yes, it is impressive. You don't have a gym like this in Belfast?"

Aidan snorted. "They don't have a feckin gym like this at Buckingham Palace."

Joey considered him for a moment. "Your neighbor probably teaches over in one of those rooms." He pointed. "So, are you two a thing?"

Aidan looked at him sharply. "No, not at all. We're just friendly. She's my sister-in-law's best friend."

Joey nodded. "Do you want to be a thing?"

Aidan shrugged uncomfortably. "She's a nice girl, but I'm not here for long. Best not to go that route."

The Lieutenant shook his head. "Good luck with that. She's gorgeous and she's next door. That is temptation and proximity. You're a better man than me."

They walked over to the classrooms and he spotted the yoga class. People were starting to pile in, mostly young men. Not a surprise. He saw her just as she bent in those little pants and tight tank top for a stretch. "Fucking hell," he muttered under his breath just as Joey let out an appreciative "God damn." Aidan gave him a sideways glance.

"Don't worry, Captain. I'm just looking."

Alanna spotted them through the window. She waved and ran to the door. Her heavy braid was swinging as she came to a halt and swung the door open. "Are you coming to my class?"

Aidan groaned inwardly. He hadn't planned on it, but she looked like a kid whose parents came to see their art show at school. "Actually, I hadn't planned on it. I'm not one for yoga."

Her face fell a bit. "Oh, okay. Well, have a good work out."

The lieutenant stopped her. "I love yoga, count me in." Aidan almost growled when he saw the smug look on Joey's face and the smile from Alanna.

She turned to him, brow raised. "Are you sure? The class gets filled up within minutes. I promise not to go too hard on you." There was challenge in her gaze.

Joey broke in, "Give it as hard as you like, I can take it. Maybe the captain can take the senior citizen class." And he walked through the door toward the mats.

Aidan sighed, "Bloody hell, I'm not going to live this down if I bow out, am I?"

Alanna giggled and turned her back, and Aidan could have sworn there was a little more sway in her hips when she did. He bit back another growl, walked through the door, and grabbed a mat.

Aidan rolled out his mat next to the lieutenant while cursing under his breath. "Holy shit, is that Gaelic? Are you actually cursing me in another tongue?" Aidan looked at him sideways and he laughed. The cocky fucker actually laughed. "You're not really mad. You just needed a little incentive to walk through that door. Now you have a front row seat, and you can make sure she doesn't fall in love with me right under your nose." He rubbed his hands down his abs. "This shit is powerful. The women can't resist me."

Aidan snorted a laugh. "Cocky bastard. You might be lean, and you can probably run very fast, but when I catch you I will eat your feckin lunch, brother. Women like strong, brawny lads like myself." He put his accent on thick for affect.

Before he knew what was happening, he had gained the attention of the several surrounding yoga enthusiasts. "Oh my God. Are you Irish, like from Ireland?" The leggy redhead wasn't hiding her appraisal.

Her friend, a caramel skinned, very fit Asian woman, got within inches of Aidan. "So, are you stationed here? You are gorgeous. No ring either," she commented as she looked at his ring hand.

Aidan was starting to blush, but held his own. "Hello ladies. Aye, just for the summer. Captain Aidan O'Brien."

Both the women were struck stupid. "Okay, it isn't possible for you to be any more adorable." This came from a third woman, a beautiful african-american woman with biceps that even Aidan envied, and an outfit that was leaving little to the imagination.

Joey was shaking his head, laughing to himself when a whistle broke through the chatter. "If everyone is done running their jibs, let's line up and start class. Shall we?" Aidan looked up and was shocked to see a bit of irritation on Alanna's face. One hand on her hip, unamused brow lifted. Everyone scurried to their mats.

Joey hissed under his breath. "Uh-oh. Teach is eyeballing us. Did you see that look?"

Aidan shrugged. "Yes, she's pissed everyone's talking during her class. I don't blame her."

Joey snorted a laugh. "You are blind, Irish. That was pure female jealousy. I thought she was going to hiss at those girls."

"Shut your gob and do your down faced dog or whatever the feck she said."

By the end of the class, Aidan was laying on his mat covered in sweat. "Holy God, I think the little vixen broke me."

Joey was next to him in a similar position. "Fuck me, we are going to be screwed tomorrow."

Aidan lifted a head. "Why tomorrow?"

Joey whimpered. "PT at seven."

Aidan groaned, "Now you tell me, you rotten fucker." Both men started laughing, holding their stomachs as their muscles trembled. Aidan opened his eyes and Alanna was standing over him.

"You dead, O'Brien?"

He smiled. "You're a little she-devil. What the hell do you call this class? I thought we were going to be meditating or some shit."

She smiled, "Power Yoga. You need a wheelchair old man?"

Aidan popped up and had her over his shoulder before she could blink. The class had emptied, and she let out a squeal as her braid flew over her face. "What was that, hen?"

She smacked his butt. "You were sand bagging, O'Brien. I'm not going easy on you next class!"

The lieutenant jumped to his feet. "I'm headed out. You better put him in the front row like the naughty kids next time. That accent was causing a wave of female hysteria back here."

Aidan put her down and she swept her hair off her face. "Really? I didn't notice. I was wondering what all the noise was." Then she spun around and started rolling up her mat.

Aidan walked Alanna to her car. It had turned dark. "So, you taught a spinning class this morning, worked all day, then came here to teach another class?"

Alanna was putting her bag in the hatch of her car. "Yes, I teach anywhere from five to seven classes a week, depending on if I cover for another instructor." Aidan was suprised. "Christ, no wonder that fried okra and ice cream doesn't catch up with you."

She smiled, "Well, it's a two for one. I get paid to work out. It supplements my income."

Aidan took a sip out of his water bottle. "Well, you beat my ass. I'll admit it. That burst of energy at the end was purely ego driven."

She gave a charming little laugh. "I'll see you back home, Aidan. I've got some work to do from my sessions today, and then I'm off to bed."

He nodded. "Aye, apparently we have early morning PT tomorrow. I'll eat and go to bed."

She paused before getting in the car. "Do you know how to get home from here?"

He looked around. "Well, I've got the GPS if I get turned around."

She hopped in the front seat. "You can follow me. The GPS won't take you through the training areas. It'll take you the long way."

As they pulled into the beach house, Aidan parked and got out. He grabbed his ruck, his gym bag, and his water bottle. "Alanna, I was meaning to ask you. Would you make up a list for me of repairs or jobs that need done on the other side? I want to get started next weekend. Just when you get time."

Alanna nodded. "There isn't much. My dad and I have done a few things, but there are some little jobs that need done. If you are going to do the deck on the other side, you're probably going to want to do both sides. I can help. Maybe my dad or Erik can come and help too."

Aidan shook his head. "No need. This is part of my agreement with Branna. Your schedule doesn't have any room for handyman chores. Just make the list."

Alanna conceded. "You have a point about the schedule. Come mid-June I may be singing for my supper, though."

Aidan stopped. "I'd feed you every night for a song."

Alanna blushed, "I might have to stand in line behind half the girls in my yoga class."

He grinned, "I thought you didn't notice?"

She turned with a swing of her hair. "Oh my God, are you Irish? Like from Ireland?" she said in her ditziest voice, and walked to her door.

As Aidan watched her enter the house, he put the key in his dead bolt and froze. It was unlocked. That was strange, because he was positive he'd locked it. Maybe Alanna had come in, needing something. He ascended the stairs and looked around. Nothing was out of place that he could see, so he went to his room. His nightstand drawer was open just an inch. He checked his room and everything seemed fine. He was being paranoid. He'd obviously just left the door unlocked. He was pretty tired when he left.

10

The next two days flew by in a flurry of activity. The training had begun in earnest. It was Wednesday afternoon before Aidan was able to call home. Brigid hadn't answered, and neither had his parents. On a whim, he tried Patrick. "Hello, brother! About feckin' time you got around to calling me!"

Christ, Aidan missed his family. He'd gotten used to seeing them in the long respite he had after Afghanistan. The reserve unit had an easier work week, and often he'd found himself jumping in the car and headed west to see his parents and siblings. "How's Caitlyn? Is she settling into the city?"

Patrick yelled behind him. "You can ask her yourself. She's just done the washing up."

Caitlyn came to the screen with her bright eyes and easy smile. "Hello, gorgeous. How's America?"

Patrick looked scandalized. "Gorgeous, is he?"

Aidan laughed. The two of them had such a light hearted way about them. "I miss you, brother," he said softly. Aidan said it before he thought about it and Patrick stopped suddenly, looking serious.

"I miss you too, brother. I sort of got used to having you around again."

Aidan shrugged. "Shropshire is not so very far. How's mam? Did she get her tests back?"

Patrick nodded reassuringly, "Yes, brother. They meant to call you tomorrow. She's all clear. Nothing to worry over."

Aidan exhaled in relief. "Thank the Holy Virgin," and he crossed himself. They chatted a while longer and Aidan let them go. It was getting late in Ireland. He poured himself a whiskey and walked out onto the deck, looking out at the sea. He was bringing the glass to his lips when the loud boom of artillery went off, shaking the air around him. His glass shattered on the deck as the second explosion went off.

"Aidan, it's me. Sweetheart, look at me."

Aidan was leaning on the rail of the deck when the voice penetrated his brain. He looked at the figure in front of him. Green eyes. The most beautiful green eyes he'd ever seen.

"Alanna, what is it? Is something amiss?"

She looked hard at him. "Aidan, your foot is bleeding." Another explosion and he tensed. "We're close to the training areas. It is artillery training. Do you understand? It's the Marines. They're training."

Aidan shook himself. "Aye, I understand. I'm not daft. There's not a problem," he said angrily. He walked away from her, and she noticed he was sweating. It wasn't that warm out. There was a nice breeze coming off the water.

"Aidan, your foot. It's bleeding. You broke your glass."

He shrugged her off as she touched his arm. "I'm fine, it's nothing serious. I'll get a broom."

She pulled back at his tone. "I'm sorry. I shouldn't have touched you. Some people don't like to be touched when…" she trailed off.

He looked sharply at her. "When what? I'm fine, Alanna. I don't know what you think happened here, but I'm fine, and I don't like the head shrinker routine. I'm not one of your case studies." He spat the words, and her jaw tensed. Her back straightening.

He walked into the house and grabbed a rag for his foot. Whatever had cut him was not stuck in the skin, so he grabbed the broom, and came back outside to find Alanna gone.

"Bloody hell," he cursed to himself, cleaning up the glass. The artillery was still going off from the training areas further inland, but now that he knew what it was, his heart rate started to ease. He put the glass in the bin and put the broom away. He also had to walk under the deck to grab a huge shard of whiskey glass that had fallen on the dune. Then came back up to the deck and looked at the water. He took a few deep breaths. "Fucking hell," he hissed under his breath.

He wasn't pissed at Alanna. He was pissed at himself. He'd bitten her head off, and she didn't deserve it. She was used to working with broken men all day. She'd read more into the situation than was accurate. He knew that he had his moments, but he was handling everything fine. Who wouldn't be a little jumpy after four combat tours? But he hadn't ever been wounded. Not like her father, not like other men he knew. She didn't understand that he was fine. Still, he'd been rude to her, and he needed to apologize.

He walked over to her slider and knocked. No answer. He knocked again. *Christ, are you in there pouting?* He sighed and walked through his own side of the house to see if her car was there. As he approached the stairway to the front door, he heard the music. She was down in her little gym. *Jesus, like she doesn't get enough exercise.* As he descended the stairs, he heard the booming base of something familiar.

He chuckled to himself. *Sabotage* by the Beastie Boys was roaring through the walls. He didn't bother knocking. She'd never hear him over the music. He walked in and froze. She was swinging, balls to the wall, on the punching bag. With every ounce of energy that little firm body could put forth, she fisted that thing like she wanted it dead. It occurred to him that he may have underestimated how pissed off she was at him.

She was mumbling too, and he could make out a few words between the whoop ass she was throwing and the loud music. He made out three words over the din. Stubborn, jackass, and kick.

He was used to feisty women. God knew his family had enough of them. He watched her for a few seconds. *Christ, she's beautiful,* he thought. She was grimacing, sweating, and breathing heavy, and she couldn't have been more beautiful. He came up behind her and she saw the motion. She turned and swung a back fist before she could stop herself. Aidan caught it easily, however, like he'd expected it.

Alanna saw the motion out of the corner of her eye and just reacted. She was in a sort of zone with the ass beating she was giving the heavy bag, and she just reacted. After she'd been caught by a firm hand, Aidan's face came into focus. She jumped back. "Jesus, Joseph, and Mary! I almost knocked your block off, Aidan! Don't sneak up on me!" She pulled her gloves off and threw them.

Aidan walked over to the iPod dock and paused it. "I'm sorry, lass. You had the music so loud, you didn't hear me."

She had her hands on her hips, breathing hard. "Do you need something?"

Alanna shot her chin up and met his gaze. She was not going to ask him how he was doing. She was going to keep her distance. He obviously didn't want or need anything from her.

He had the good sense to look contrite. "I'm sorry I snapped at you. I know you were trying to help or something."

She snorted. "Or something?"

He sighed impatiently. "You misunderstood. Everything is fine. Maybe due to your line of work, you…"

She interrupted him, putting her hand up. "Aidan, I obviously overstepped. You are right. You aren't one of my case studies. Since I am a lowly intern, they aren't even really my patients. You were absolutely right. I need to butt out."

He growled, "I didn't say that. Don't put words in my mouth."

She flipped her hair over her shoulder and turned her back, retrieving her water bottle. "My mistake. Now if you don't mind, I was working out."

She grabbed her gloves and put one on. Aidan cursed under his breath. She began struggling to get the second one on when he stepped in, taking the glove. He held it up for her to put her hand in. She met his eyes briefly and slid her hand into the glove.

"You're doing it wrong. You're going to strain your shoulder or a wrist," he said, feeling the need to change the subject, but not willing to leave things as they were.

He got behind her, turning her to the bag. She stiffened under his hands at first, then settled. He positioned her shoulders as he shadowed her from behind. "Don't bring your arm around. Lean in and jab." He showed her and she repeated the motion. He put his hands on her abdomen. "Use your center of gravity, here and here, to keep your balance on impact." He put his hands on her hips.

Aidan should not be touching her, he knew it. They were both a little raw. He needed to touch her, though. He wasn't sure why, but the fact that he'd obviously hurt her really got under his skin. He needed some tangible way to reconnect with her. He thought about what she'd said about her work, her father's recovery. There was a physical element to psychological healing.

He straightened her wrist. "Ok, hit it." She punched. "Harder." He said next to her ear. His mouth grazed the top of her ear. He heard her breath catch, but she did it harder. "Again." She punched, harder and harder. He didn't move. She brushed him with her body on the recoil. She exhausted herself until she couldn't punch anymore. Her hands dropped with her head.

Aidan's hands went back to her hips and Alanna felt his forehead rest on her shoulder. "I'm sorry, lass."

She absorbed the contact for a moment, then she spoke. "I'm sorry, too."

He brought his head up. "You have nothing to be sorry for, Alanna, nothing."

He could hear the smile in her voice, as well as the sadness. "I'm sorry for imagining the punching bag was your face."

Aidan tried not to laugh, tried hard. Alanna felt the tremble of his laughter, which spurned her own. Soon she was laughing so hard that her stomach hurt, and she dropped down to the mat at nearly the same time as Aidan. He put his head back and laughed like she'd never seen before. A free, loud, belly laugh with tears coming out of the corners of his eyes. It was a beautiful, contagious laugh that fed her own mirth. They lay on the mat exhausted.

She swung one more punch at him and he caught her wrist. He pulled her over him, and continued rolling until she was under him. She was panting, eyes sparkling with mischief. "I like it when you really laugh, Aidan." He had her right hand pinned to the ground, and he slid his hand up from her wrist to slide her glove off. Their palms came together and she gasped a little at the contact. Aidan slid the other glove off and their fingers interlaced. He had a thigh between her legs and his arousal was undeniable as it pressed into her hip. Her breathing was shallow and her lips and cheeks were pink. Her eyes were sparking, searching his face.

Aidan was mindless with need. He was keeping himself somewhat under control, but he was ready to crack. She was exquisite; hair wild across the mat, eyes fiery, mouth pink and tempting. He could tell she was as aroused as he was, and it was screwing with his self control.

He'd sworn he wouldn't do this. Yet, even with that mental reminder, all he could think about was kissing her. Just a kiss. God, he wanted to taste her mouth more than he'd ever wanted anything. His saving mercy was a simple, well timed chime of the doorbell. Then a knock.

Alanna heard the doorbell and knock just as she was sure that Aidan O'Brien was going to kiss her. He stiffened, and she knew it hadn't been her imagination.

"Alanna! You home?" She heard a male voice. Aidan jumped to his feet and pulled her up with him. She smoothed her hair back and walked out the gym door. "I'm in here, Erik."

Erik, the brother, Aidan thought. He looked down and realized that he was in his bare feet, camouflage pants, and his undershirt. He tucked his erection against his stomach, folded under his waistband. It was as close to concealment as he was going to get. Then he heard Alanna squeal. "Tim! Oh my God!" Aidan growled under his breath. The brother had shown up with Tim the Tosser, the ex-boyfriend. Fucking perfect.

Aidan walked out to the car park from the gym shortly after Alanna. Erik gave him a once over. He was the spitting image of his father, except he was a little slimmer. "You must be the RIR Captain I've been hearing about; Branna's brother-in-law. Lieutenant Erik Falk, nice to meet you." He put out his hand, and Aidan couldn't find fault with his manners.

It was his tone and look of speculation that was giving Aidan the scratch. Erik was looking at his attire. "Working out, were you? Interesting choice of PT gear. Do you work out with my sister often?" Aidan didn't dignify it with a response, but turned his attention to the other gentleman who was currently enveloping Alanna in a bear hug.

Tim put her down, and that's when Aidan noticed the prosthetic leg. She turned to him. "Aidan, this is one of my very best friends in the world. Tim, this is Aidan." Her smile was genuine, and she had pride in her voice. "Tim was a Marine as well. We went to high school together."

The tall, dark and handsome Tim the Tosser gave a self deprecating grin. "Medically retired," he said, and gave his stump cuff a knock. He had long hair that was back in a short ponytail. The sides of his hair tucked behind his ears. His face was friendly, and didn't that make Aidan feel like the tosser.

"It's good to meet you. I'll let you all catch up. I've got to get a run in and a shower before supper." He nodded to Erik who still had the look of speculation in his eyes, and walked up the back stairs to his deck.

"I don't like him," was all Erik said, once they'd gone upstairs.

Alanna looked at him in between sips of water. "You don't know him, Erik. And what was with the big brother stare down. It's not like you've ever had any kind of protective instinct before, so save it. I can take care of myself."

He looked at her with a snide expression. "Yes, we all know how good your judgement and restraint is, don't we?" Alanna stiffened and she saw Tim do the same. Erik looked at Tim. "No offense. You tried to make an honest woman out of her."

Tim put his own drink down. "What the hell did you just say?"

Alanna broke in. "Tim, don't bother. I don't have to explain myself to him."

Her brother shrugged, "Whatever. I just don't like him. He's only here for the summer and he's looking for some easy action. I know the type."

She put her hand on her hip. "Takes one to know one, eh? How are those divorce lawyer bills coming, did you pay those fees off yet?"

Tim stepped between them. "Enough. Both of you. I'm here to visit, not referee." He pointed to Erik. "You're being a dick. I don't know where you got your ideas about your sister, but you are dead wrong about her. Just because Leah was a slut, and you have shit to sort out with your mom, don't take it out on your sister. She's a good girl."

Erik shook his head. "If you say so. So, what's on the itinerary? You have anything to eat around here or should we go out?"

Alanna sighed. "I'll make something. Just give me a few minutes. We need to eat outside. My homework is spread out in here."

Erik got a beer out of the fridge. "Duck Rabbit. Nice. What's the occasion?"

Alanna was milling around in the kitchen. "Aidan made me dinner and I bought some beer. Plus, Daddy was here."

He stopped, "When did Dad come?"

She shrugged. "He came Sunday morning and surprised me at mass. He spent one night. You were boating in the islands."

He changed subjects abruptly. "So, the Irishman made you dinner, huh? Did Dad meet him?"

She smiled. "Yes, Daddy met him this fall, when they came for Branna. Then, again this time. They got along great. Aidan had some of the men from his training team over, Daddy sprung for barbecue. They ate, drank, talked infantry, smoked cigars. He, unlike you, is a good judge of character." Erik grunted and left it at that, retreating to the living room.

Alanna cooked some chicken in a skillet while Tim kept her company, chopping lemons and garlic. "Nothing is going on between Aidan and me. I just didn't think I needed to explain myself to that oaf."

Tim put his arm around her. "Why don't you tell him, Anna? He should know what really happened with Steve."

She looked behind her nervously, to make sure her brother was out of ear shot. "No. I tried when it first happened. He didn't listen then, he won't listen now. Especially after all this time. I just want to forget the whole thing. Okay? You promised." Her look was intense and held a bit of pleading that cut Tim to the bone.

Tim was silent for a moment, then he spoke softly. "It was a stupid promise. I shouldn't have made it."

She looked at him sharply. "But you did, and I trusted you. I trusted you with everything. Don't let me down, now."

His stare was hard. "You make me crazy, you know that?"

She exhaled, changing the subject swiftly. "So, how's the love life?"

He laughed. "Non-existent. Yours?"

She smiled, "Ditto. Yours can't be from lack of opportunity, Tim. I've seen the women look at you. Especially in the gym when you go all wounded warrior bad-ass caveman with those weights."

He just shrugged. "Maybe you've ruined me. My standards are too high, now."

She beamed, "Awe, that's the nicest thing anyone's ever said to me."

He laughed. "You are totally discounting my broken heart!"

She smacked him. "You don't love me that way, Tim. You thought you did for a while, but you didn't. You know that deep down."

He shrugged. "Yeah, the snoring thing was kind of a bummer."

Her mouth dropped. "I did not!" and she snapped him with a dishtowel.

"You know I'm kidding, right? I know we're better off friends," he said as he bumped hips with her.

She smiled sadly. "I know. We are a pathetic pair, aren't we?"

He leaned back, running his fingers through his long hair. "Speak for yourself. I'm turning them down left and right."

She handed him two beers. "Make yourself useful, Romeo. Go give one of these to Aidan and invite him to dinner. And be ready to elbow that brother of mine in the nose if he says anything stupid."

He paused, holding the beers. "You want him. I can tell."

She blushed. "He's only here for the summer, and he doesn't feel that way about me."

Tim smirked. "We'll agree to disagree on that."

Aidan was running up the beach when he saw Alanna's friend Tim standing on the deck. He walked up the beach walk as the man walked closer. Aidan approached and was handed a cold beer. "Sláinte," Aidan said, and they drank. "Any reason for the deluxe treatment?" Aidan slid the door open to his house and motioned for Tim to come in. He dipped his sandy feet in a bucket by the door and dried them as Tim pulled up a stool.

"Anna has invited you to dinner."

Aidan looked at him, pausing as if to choose his words carefully. "I'm not sure that's wise."

Tim smiled, "Now why is that?"

Aidan took another towel and began drying his face, neck and shoulders. "I didn't get a particularly warm vibe from the brother. I'm also not sure of my ability to hold my tongue if he turns that attitude on his sister."

Tim folded his arms over his chest. "You're a quick study. What conclusions did you draw about me, in that short meeting?"

Aidan met his gaze. "You're a good sort, and you care for Alanna. That's enough."

"Well, then. The attitude coming at Anna has already been addressed. Erik's a friend, but I don't tolerate him being a dick to his sister. If I promise to keep him in line, you can promise to put a smile back on Anna's face and come over for some chicken."

Aidan didn't meet his eye as he busied himself with filling a glass of ice water. "She seemed happy enough to see you. I don't think you need me for that."

Silence. Long enough to make Aidan meet his gaze. "She doesn't smile at me the way she smiles at you. As a matter of fact, she's never looked at anyone the way she looks at you, and I've known her since she was fourteen. How about you come to dinner?"

Aidan looked at him, sharply. "Why do you care?"

Tim gave him a wry grin. "Because I'm a good sort, and I care for Anna. Isn't that enough?"

Aidan snorted a laugh, impressed that the bastard had thrown his words back at him. He was actually starting to like Tim the Tosser. "You've got the wrong idea, mo cara. I can see that. But since you brought me a cold beer, I'll come to dinner. Just let me shower."

Aidan reflected, part way through dinner, that Tim the Tosser was indeed not a tosser. He was a pretty fucking inspiring lad, as a matter of fact. Wounded at twenty, medically retired against his wishes at twenty-one. He'd actually tried to prove he could still deploy by taking the physical fitness tests with his prosthetic. The problem had been the hearing loss from the explosion coupled with a minor TBI. Once the hearing loss reached a certain level, they were considered too impaired for duty, and he didn't want to push a desk in DC. Aidan hadn't even noticed the small hearing aid in the right ear, but he supposed that might be partially responsible for the flowing locks of brown hair he was sporting. The hearing thing must be working, because he didn't seem to miss a thing. He also had to admit that once he'd gotten past the dickhead defensiveness, Erik wasn't a bad guy either. He was as cocky as most pilots he'd met, but not a bad guy.

"Al Anbar Province, patrolling. Hostile fire exchange, then ka-fuckin-boom. I was lucky. That damned corpsman saved my life. So did my buddies. And it's below the knee. Whole different ballgame when you take the knee out. Luckily, the rest of the men were okay."

Aidan was impressed. This guy's attitude was pretty spectacular, considering the shit he'd gone through. "Ruined my favorite boots, though. Fuckers. You know that pair you get broken in just right? Covered in blood. That shit doesn't wipe off, you feel me?"

Aidan laughed, "Aye, just throw 'em in the wash. They'll be grand."

Even Erik had to chuckle begrudgingly. "Amen to that, Irishman."

Alanna just shook her head. "It's slightly demented that you three boys find this funny."

Aidan smiled over the rim of his beer bottle. "Yes, I suppose it is."

Tim interrupted. "It's nice, though. You might not understand because you've never been in combat. Sometimes you get tired of the pitying looks and chats about your feelings. Plus there is the upside that this thing is a chick magnet," he raised his prosthetic foot for show.

Erik snorted. "Right, it's not the Fabio hair and the six pack. It's the stump. Gotcha." Aidan spit some beer through his lips at that, and soon all three of them were laughing again.

Alanna got up and started clearing the table. "Sickos. All three of you."

Aidan followed Alanna in the kitchen with dirty dishes and immediately started rinsing. "You get along well with them. It's nice to see," Alanna said.

"Don't look so surprised. I'm not that hard to get a long with, am I?"

She gave him a sideways look. "No, you're lovely. My brother on the other hand." She didn't need to finish the thought.

"Aye, well maybe Tim's a good influence. He seems to be minding his manners. Speaking of which, I'm sorry about downstairs. I was a little out of line."

She looked at him curiously. "Which part? The apology or pinning me to the mat?"

He barked out a laugh. "You're not going to make this easy, are you?"

She looked him dead in the eye and just did a slow back and forth with her head. "Easy is overrated."

Aidan heard the slider open and turned back to the dishes. "We've got to head off. I have a long drive, and I have early training flights."

Aidan grabbed a towel and dried his hands, walking back out to the deck. "I'm headed back over as well. It was good to meet you, both of you." He shook hands with the two and Tim held his for a moment. "I'll be around for the weekend. Maybe I'll buy you a beer before I leave."

Aidan nodded. "I'd like that. I'll be doing some repairs to the house, but I can take a break." With that, the two left as Alanna walked them to their car.

"He calls you Alanna, not Anna," Erik said. Alanna didn't comment, so he continued. "I guess he's all right. I still think he wants in your pants, though, so be careful."

She growled and smacked his arm. "Would you shut it. He's not like that. He's a perfect gentleman. You could use a lesson or two in that regard."

Erik smiled, "But you still love me, right?"

She sighed and hugged him. "Yes, Erik. I still love you. You big jerk."

Aidan woke at about two thirty in the morning when the artillery started again. He'd been dreaming, and it was a strange feeling realizing he wasn't in some barracks in the Middle East, given the background music. He looked around the dark room, disoriented. Not in his flat in Belfast, either. It was with the sound of the waves coming in on the breeze through the window that full awareness eased into his mind. He was in North Carolina. He rubbed his face, shaking the dream away as his mind drifted to another time. Earlier this afternoon, downstairs. The feel of Alanna's shallow breaths underneath him, his erection pressed into her hip, begging for attention.

Her eyes had sparked with arousal, and her mouth had visibly flushed. He looked down the sheet to his hard arousal and knew there was no way he was going to get back to sleep with his dumb handle ringing the five alarm. He got up and pulled some shorts on, walking out to the kitchen. He took a sip of water and turned to the back of the house that overlooked the beach. He saw a light coming from the deck.

Aidan slid the door open and walked out to the sound of waves hitting the shore. The air was inviting and cool on his skin. He walked past the divider between the two decks, and his heart squeezed. Alanna was sound asleep on the deck table, laptop and notebook abandoned to slumber. Her hair was pulled off her face in a tousled bun on the top of her head. She had a throw around her shoulders.

You work too hard, mo chroí, he thought. He lifted her laptop and notebook and took it inside. Then, ever so gently, he picked her up and carried her into her house. She stirred a little and seemed to look at him briefly, then she drifted back to sleep with a small smile curving her lips. He put her down on her bed and pulled the blanket over her. "Sleep well, a rúnsearc." *Secret love.* Then he kissed her forehead.

He left quickly, so as not to wake her, throwing the latch on the sliding door as he went. It wasn't until he was almost back on his side that he noticed she'd put the bat under the table at her feet.

11

Alanna woke to her alarm at five in the morning with a feeling of disorientation. She sat up in bed and realized that she was laying on top of her comforter with the other half pulled over her. She also had the throw from the living room under her shoulders. She didn't remember going to bed. She got up and walked into the living room, where she saw her laptop and notebook on the end table. She checked the back slider, and it was locked. She closed her eyes, trying to recall the last thing she'd been doing. She was working on her laptop out on the deck. She'd had to stay up late to make up the time from Erik and Tim's visit. She opened the slider to see the dawn's light coming over the water, just before sunrise. Aidan was sipping from a cup by the railing.

"You put me to bed last night," she said. He looked at her briefly, his eyes sparking at her small t-shirt and sleeping shorts. He hadn't noticed them the night before. Her nipples were visible and he had to quickly avert his gaze.

"You sleep like the dead, darlin. You need to get more rest."

She came beside him and looked in his cup. "I thought you Irish liked tea?"

He smiled. "Aye, but coffee gets the job done if you need a kick in the arse. Sip?"

She took the cup from him and sipped. "Mmm, nice and strong. Just how I like it." She looked out over the water and took another sip, then handed it back. "Thank you. I don't normally fall asleep outside. I'm just burning the candle at both ends right now, and my visitors threw off my schedule. I had some extra stuff to write up, some problems with a patient."

Aidan watched her profile, and his heart broke a little at how tired she looked. Beautiful, but tired. "What sort of problem? Can you tell me?"

She shrugged, "He was supposed to bring his family to the Dance with Daddy session I had scheduled." She swallowed, "He's a bit of a pill. Self medicating with alcohol, not connecting with the family, his marriage is suffering. He had to stay sober for this event and he didn't. It gave him the out he needed not to show up. His little girl and his toddler boy showed up with momma and he was a no show. It was kind of sad. I'll see him today, try again. It just pissed me off and I have to get my mind right before I talk to him. I'm not a doctor and this wasn't mandatory treatment. I just thought it would do them some good, but the stubborn jackass let everyone down."

Aidan wasn't sure how to respond. This wasn't her fault, but it was weighing on her and it was important that he found some way to encourage her. "I know you're frustrated. I'm sure the family is, too. Don't give up on him, though. It's difficult. When you come home, you've got this stuff in your head. Shite you wish wasn't in there, but it is. It's there for good. You don't want it to touch your family. You don't want those burdens that you're carrying around in your mind to infect them. But you get lost in your head about it sometimes and they don't understand. Just…just don't give up on him. You're doing the best you can, and that'll matter to him in the end."

Aidan wasn't looking at her, so she put her hand on his arm, compelling him to turn. When he did, she kissed him on the cheek. "Thank you. God, thank you. I think I'm ready to talk to him now."

He searched her face, taking in her features. He smiled, "You are a beauty in the morning, lass." He held her gaze for a few moments, then shook himself, backing away a bit. "So, will I be going to the family session on Friday?"

Her smile was blinding. "You can make it?"

He nodded. "Aye, I'll be done by the start of it. I'll be there."

"It won't be a family session. It will be couples," she answered. One masculine brow rose. She laughed. "Don't give me that look, O'Brien. It's not an orgy. It's going to deal with nightmares, sleep disturbances. A lot of the men come home and have sleep trouble, night terrors. The wives have asked for some support with how to handle them in the middle of the night. Some of the men are agitated when they wake. So, I have a little couples therapy going in the yoga room. I need a role playing partner if you are willing to help. It's better when I can do an actual demonstration."

He gave her a wolfish smile. "Count me in. This should be interesting."

Aidan had done a lot of physical training during his time in the army. He'd also played rugby on and off throughout his life. He considered himself an athlete. These Marines were bloodthirsty animals, however, and it occurred to him after dry heaving next to Denario, that his instructors were sadistic sociopaths.

Burpees. The devil's favorite exercise. This is what they did in hell. Millions and millions of burpees. He'd held his own, however. He hadn't fallen out, even though the day was humid and warm and the water they were drinking was tepid. They were training for a combat fitness test next week, and he was not going to be the only pussy to fail, and put up with jibes about how much tougher the Marines were. His unit's good name rested solely on his shoulders.

The first half of the day had been spent in a weapons simulator, which was all fine and good, but didn't replace actual weapons training. These yanks had some expensive toys, however.

He groaned to himself as the instructor went over the next physical exercise. Some sort of mutant tires off of a large vehicle. The instructor, who had mostly watched and not broken a sweat, deftly hopped up on the stack of two tires with no effort. Hector swore in Spanish, and the men grunted their agreement. This was going to suck.

Alanna came home from the gym exhausted. A morning spinning class, a full day at work, and then a Zumba class. She couldn't do school work. She really couldn't. The thought of opening her mouth to chew a meal was more than she could muster. She grabbed her romance novel off the lip of the tub and walked outside into the fresh air. As she walked to the edge of the deck, she looked over and was startled to see Aidan sprawled out on the chaise lounge.

She covered her mouth on a giggle as she took in the sight of him. He was passed out cold still in his uniform. She tip toed over and sat on the lounger next to him, taking in his face. He looked younger when he slept. More like a young boy and less like a hard ass. His face was peaceful and beautiful. She settled back in her chair and read in silence, enjoying the idea of him sleeping next to her, even if it was in a pair of lawn chairs.

Aidan came awake to the sound of birds and waves and the smell of Jasmine oil. It was an ethereal awakening, perfect in its simplicity. When he opened his eyes, he was looking at Alanna's lovely profile, engrossed in reading. He stretched, and she looked over at him. She quickly stowed her book under the cushion, and he wondered what she'd been reading.

"Morning, sunshine. Did they put the hurtin' on you today?"

He groaned as he stretched. "Fecking burpees, hundreds of 'em."

She hissed. "Agh, burpees are the worst!"

He looked just past her arm and froze. "Hold still, there's a bug." He reached past her and snatched her book from underneath the pillow. She grabbed for it, but he was too fast. "What is this? Christ, you little vixen. *The Saxon's Bride.*This doesn't look very scholarly."

He held it away as she laughed and tried to steal it back. "Give it over! That book is the only action I'm getting!" Aidan froze and so did she. She was half over his lap, body over his chair, one knee over his leg, the other leg still draped on her chair. He'd been holding the book away, forcing her to reach for it. She blushed and started to scurry off him when he grabbed her mid thigh; book dropped and forgotten.

"Is that so?" he said softly.

Alanna was completely paralyzed except for shallow breaths and a thumping heart. She'd managed to dive for her novel, only to end up half straddling her neighbor in his lawn chair. He had one hand on her hip, right where it met her thigh. The other hand was on her bare leg, just past the hem of her shorts. Her skin burned with heat where he touched her. Her arousal was instant and fierce. His thumb stroked her bare skin, making her wish like hell that he would slip that hand into the leg of her shorts and put her out of her misery.

Aidan's cock went instantly hard under her, and he felt her hips jerk in response. Her palms were on his chest and her eyes were dazed. He surged his upper body up to meet hers, ready to take her mouth. He hovered, like a coward, just a breath away from her lips and his hands still possessive on her hips. Searching her face, he thought, *This is where you need to stop me.* He didn't want her to, though. He wanted to slide his hand up her thigh. He wanted to touch her and taste her, lose himself in Jasmine and smooth skin and silky hair.

The sound of a screeching child on the beach jolted him back to reality. He became instantly aware, as she did, of where they were. On an open deck in full daylight, beachfront on a public beach. She jerked her legs off him. "I'm sorry. I didn't mean to sit on you! God, um, let me just get my book. I'm sorry I woke you." She snatched up her book and began a quick retreat to her side of the deck.

Aidan jumped up and pursued her. "Alanna, wait. Christ, I'm sorry."

She spun around, flushed with embarrassment. "No. Don't be. It was my fault. I should have stayed over here on my side. I know you don't..." she swallowed. "I know you don't feel that way about me. I didn't mean to jump on you like that." She hurried through the slider, but there was no way he wasn't following up on that comment.

He followed her through the door. "Alanna!" he said, with a little more force than he should have. He was edgy and aroused and pissed off at himself. She was in the kitchen fiddling with a water glass, trying to look busy. "Look at me," he said.

Her eyes shot to his. "It's okay Aidan. It won't happen again."

He shook his head. "Are you feckin' kidding me? You think it's from lack of interest? Jaysus Christ, woman. You can't be that daft!"

She shot her chin up. "I know what that word means, and I assure you I am not. You don't need to explain any further."

Aidan sighed, scrubbing his face with his hands. "I do. I do need to explain. I shouldn't have put my hands on you like that. It wasn't your doing. I just..." he growled. "I'm lacking in self control when it comes to you."

He looked at her, and he was taken back by the look of confusion on her face. "Holy God, Alanna. Do you think I'm made of stone? You're gorgeous, smart, kind. You're pretty much perfect. I'm only feckin human!" He ran his hand through his short hair. "You're also Branna's best friend. I'm not here for long. Three months and I'm gone, and this is not a complication that I need. I'm not going to take advantage of her hospitality or yours by trying to get in your knickers, only to leave here at the end of the summer." He sighed. "It's not that I don't think about it every single day, but I won't. I won't do that to Branna, and I won't put you in that position. I'm sorry, I know I was out of line out there. It won't happen again."

Alanna was trying to concentrate on his words, but damn it that accent got thicker the more upset he got, and it was hot as hell. She also burned between her legs where she'd felt him stiffen underneath her. It had been so long since she'd been that close to a man, and it had never felt like that. She came around the counter, closer to Aidan. He was staring at his boots, hand on his hips. "Look at me, Aidan." He did, and the fire in those blue eyes almost stopped her heart. He was always so reserved, almost stoic. Not now, though. His eyes burned. "I'm a big girl, and that wasn't one sided out there."

He exhaled. "Aye, and it would be much easier if it were. This can't happen, though. I can't let it. You shouldn't want any part of this, of me. Nothing good can come from giving in to this attraction," he ground his teeth and exhaled.

Alanna cringed inwardly, feeling a little rejected. She stepped back a little from him. He was clear enough about what he did and didn't want.

"Okay, Aidan. It doesn't mean we can't be friends. You've proven you can control yourself, and I can do the same. Branna is like family to me, I want things to be comfortable between us." She put out her hand to shake. "Friends?"

He took her hand and squeezed. "You're too good to be true, you know that?" He said softly. He let go of her hand. "I've got some washing, eating, and sleeping to do. Enjoy your book." He gestured with his eyes to the novel she'd forgotten about.

"Don't worry, I will."

12

Aidan's head was pounding by the time work was done. He'd spent hours in the classroom with a Middle Eastern Culture specialist and some other experts from the US Government. Much of it had been a review about the tribal systems in Afghanistan, regional disputes, language nuances, and cultural differences. They'd gone over the roles of the translators and what they could expect when mixing day to day with the Afghani troops.

The headache had come during the section on the human rights atrocities that were ceaseless in the country. They discussed the murdering of young men and boys, the kidnapping of young girls, and the defiling of both. It wasn't like he didn't know this stuff went on. He knew first hand. It was just something he'd managed to lock away in that part of his mind that he kept sealed. He knew the training was necessary, but by the end of the day his head was throbbing, his brow was sweaty, and his lunch had soured in his gut. He sat in the truck, in the lot of the Heroic Spirit Clinic, and wondered if he should just text Alanna and tell her he couldn't make it.

He sighed, placing his forehead on his hands that were at the top of the steering wheel. She'd seemed genuinely thrilled that he'd taken an interest in her work, and hadn't she also mentioned that none of her male co-workers had offered to step in and help her?

He climbed out of the truck, put his uniform hat on, and headed toward the main entrance.

The clinic was impressive. Soft spoken staff received Aidan at the desk, surrounded by relaxing music, aromatherapy, and live plants scattering the sunny lobby. He thought he'd walked into the wrong building and had stumbled into a day spa. "I'm here to see Alanna Falk?"

The lobby assistant smiled radiantly. "My, my. You are a long way from home. Let me try her extension."

While Aidan waited, a middle aged female in a lab coat approached him. "Dr. Alexandra Jennings. You must be Captain O'Brien."

Aidan shook the woman's hand. "Yes, ma'am. It's a pleasure to meet you."

The doctor's smile was genuine. "What do you think of our clinic, Captain?"

He answered, "It's amazing. Alanna has told me a lot about what you do here. Honestly, I wish we had these sort of resources in Ireland and the UK."

The doctor seemed pleased by the praise. "This is run through a non-profit. I would love to see our model reproduced in the UK as well. Any advice you want to throw our way about a sister charity overseas, I'm all ears."

Aidan nodded. "That's a bit above my pay grade, but I will keep it in mind."

Alanna approached, and Aidan's heart jumped in his chest. She was wearing a button down blouse and pencil skirt. Her hair was pulled back in a bun. She looked professional and very beautiful.

"I see you two have met."

Dr. Jennings gave her a sly grin. "Yes, where have you been hiding him? Is he here to help with your couples session?"

Alanna blushed. "Ah, yes. I didn't have much luck scrounging up any help. Memorial Day weekend… everyone has left town early or couldn't help. Aidan has agreed to be my guinea pig."

The doctor put her hand out to Aidan. "It was a pleasure, Aidan. Thank you for helping my favorite intern. I will try to poke my head into the session, but I have the misfortune of a last minute board meeting. I need to hunt down some caffeine so they don't bore me to death." Aidan laughed as the doctor walked away.

"She seems a good sort," he said.

"She really is. She's actually found a job lead for me up north in Virginia. Two of the big military hospitals have these clinics. There's a position in Northern Virginia and the Naval hospital also has an opening for a licensed counselor. I sent resumes, after a personal introduction from her, so we'll see if something comes of it."

Aidan couldn't explain the flare of panic in his chest, but he couldn't deny it. It has something to do with him leaving in three months and her going to Virginia to live her life, and them never being neighbors again. He'd only been here a week, and the feeling made no sense. "That is great news. Really. Job hunting is stressful, especially in these financial times. Having her in your corner is a huge edge. You must have impressed her."

Alanna shrugged. "I am pretty darn impressive."

"Aye, and humble," he laughed. "So, what are we up to tonight? I didn't have time to change, but I have gym clothes if that's better."

She shook her head. "No, just remove the camouflage blouse and work in your t-shirt for comfort sake. Most of these guys will be coming from work and will do the same. I, on the other hand, need to get out of these clothes. Come sit at my desk while I change."

Alanna walked Aidan to her little intern cubicle. He sat down and looked at her neat space. She had a picture of Halley and Brian clipped to her message board. There was a framed picture of Alanna and her da. He was in his dress blues, and she was in a ball gown. Her father had obviously taken her to a Marine Corps Ball instead of a date. That made Aidan smile. She had a good father.

"Are you waiting for someone?" The male voice came from behind Aidan and he bristled a bit at the condescending tone. He turned in the chair to meet the eye of a twenty something employee. The name tag read Richard Rheinhart, LCMHC.

Aidan stood, towering over the man. "Yes, sir. I'm assisting Ms. Falk in her session today. She's just gone to change." The man looked at Aidan and he swore he could see a bit of irritation in the man's face. "That's a lot of letters after your name? What exactly is that particular credential? Are you an intern as well?" Aidan knew he wasn't an intern, but for some reason he felt like needling the guy. Probably for the same reason he was getting the once over from Richard the LCMHC. This was a territory dispute.

"I'm a licensed clinical mental health counselor. Royal Irish Regiment? We don't see that uniform very often." The man was polite enough, but Aidan wasn't impressed. This guy had time to stand around and give him the third degree, but obviously didn't pitch in to help Alanna when she needed help in her therapy session.

"Yes, here on exchange. Alanna and I are friends and neighbors. Apparently she couldn't round up any help internally, so here I am."

Richard, with the long job title, stiffened a bit. "Yes, well I was going to be tied up, but I've had a schedule change. I can assist, if you need to get back to work."

Aidan smiled, "No, don't bother yourself. Ah, here she is." Alanna approached in yoga pants and a golf shirt with the clinic logo on the breast.

"I see you two have met. Aidan, are you ready to get briefed? The session starts in fifteen minutes."

Aidan smiled. "Absolutely, lead the way." They walked off to the therapy room as Alanna waved farewell to Richard.

"So, is Richard a friend?" Aidan said lightly.

Alanna shrugged. "He goes by Rick. And no. Funny you should ask."

Aidan perked up, "Why do you say that?"

She was rolling out yoga mats. "Well, he hasn't really paid me much mind over the last four months. Then all of the sudden he's at my desk, telling me he wants to get to know me better. I think he figured it would be inappropriate, dating an intern. He said as much. Now that I'm almost done, he said there's no conflict, and he'd like to take me out."

Alanna was talking absently, preparing the room for her class when the silence became noticeable. She looked at Aidan and he was poised over a yoga mat, deep in thought. "Earth to Aidan." He shook himself and when he looked up, she saw a flicker of something like irritation on his face. "What's wrong? Did Rick say something to you?"

He shook his head. "No, not at all. He was a bit cool, but the fact that he's interested in you would explain that. He actually offered to let me get back to work. Said he would help you. Would you rather have him here?"

She looked at him, not sure how to respond. "Do you want to go?" His eyes were intense. He shook his head once in negation. "Then I want you here. Rick had his chance. With this, I mean. I'm still not sure about the date thing."

Aidan snorted. She bristled, "What was that for? Are you that surprised someone likes me enough to actually follow through with a date?"

Aidan shot up from the floor and grabbed another mat from the rack. "Of course not. He just doesn't seem your type."

She laughed. "How do you know what my type is?"

He gave her a direct look, grinning. "Well, I've met your ex for a start. Tim's a bit more of a meat eater than Richard the LCLAM."

She sputtered out a laugh. "It's LCMHC."

He muttered, "Aye, whatever. And let's not forget that the first time you met me, you slammed the door in my face. The second time, you came at me with a bat. Little Richard the counselor wouldn't know the first thing about taking on a woman like you." It was Alanna's turn to fall silent.

He looked at her, and she was grinning. "I'm not sure you meant that as a compliment, but I'll take it as one." Then she shrugged. "Regardless, it was nice to be asked."

Aidan closed his eyes, willing his mouth shut. Thankfully, she moved on. "So, this is what's going to happen. The couples will trickle in, usually the wives first since the men are working. Some of the women work, too, but they always manage to get here on time. These feel good sessions have a tendency to put off the men-folk."

Aidan chuffed in agreement and mumbled something about scab picking. She ignored him and continued. "Interrupted sleep patterns, insomnia, nightmares, it's all a part of the challenges of coming home from a combat situation." As she was talking, she noticed Aidan was sweating and rubbing his temples. "Does your head hurt?"

He squinted up. "Aye, it started a couple of hours ago. I'll do. Go on."

She came over to him and took his head in her hands. "Where does it hurt?" He pointed out the area around his temples, reaching back to his neck. "It's a tension headache. What were you doing today?" She pressed his scalp and he moaned, his eyes closing.

"Just the culture classes. Ah, God woman. That feels fantastic."

She giggled, "And what were you talking about when the tightening started in your head?"

His eyes popped open. "Nothing in particular. Your people are going to start coming in, finish telling me what I need to know." He stepped away from her.

Alanna felt the wall slam up like a physical blow. She wasn't going to push, given the time restraint, but what had started out as an easy conversation had suddenly halted with an unspoken door slam. She suspected something in the training session had triggered a headache. The fact that he'd shut down at the mention of it made her suspicions even stronger. *God, deliver me from tough guys.* She quickly explained the progression of the session when the men and women starting showing up to the class.

Aidan stepped off to the side of the room as Alanna addressed the group. There were five couples in the room, and from what she told him, it looked like she had one hundred percent attendance.

He wondered, as he looked around the room, which one was the man that had left his wife and kids without a dance partner. He found him easily enough. He'd heard the wife call him Luke and another man call him Jonesy. He was glad that the guy had shown up. He didn't look particularly pleased to be there, but he'd shown up, and that was something.

"Now let's get started by introducing my assistant and friend." Aidan took his back from the wall and walked to the front with Alanna. She'd put a small bag of objects by her mat and actually had two mats and two pillows displayed up front, where she stood. "This is Captain Aidan O'Brien from the Royal Irish Regiment. He is here on loan from Northern Ireland, for the summer, to train with the infantry Marines. Since he's my neighbor and sort of family, I coaxed him into being my guinea pig today." The group grumbled with laughter.

"We've talked about different nighttime issues that have come up during your dwell time. So, if you'll humor me, I'd like to share some of my ideas. I know you all have your own coping methods and comfort levels, and I want you to know that it means a lot to me that y'all are willing to have this session with me. I think, together, we can work on some new tactics. You can keep what you like and dispose of what doesn't suit you. Does that sound all right with everyone?"

Aidan watched her easy demeanor. She was so genuine, and she was at ease in front of a group. His chest swelled with a bit a pride as he watched her. She had a good soul, and she put people at ease. "Now, there are two ways we can do this. We can just lay y'all down and get to it, or I can show you some of my ideas via demonstration with my Irish hostage over here." She pointed a thumb at Aidan as the group chuckled with laughter.

"Get up there, Irishman. If we have to do this, so do you," one of the men from the group said with a joking tone.

Aidan came to stand beside Alanna as she spoke. "Consider me at your disposal, military allies and all that." The men grumbled appreciation, with one man giving a little ooh-rah in a deep voice.

"If you'd like to get in a circle around us and have a seat, you can be close enough to watch and ask questions." Alanna said.

As they did, the joker said in a falsetto voice. "Dear Fantasy Forum, I never thought I'd be writing to you…" but his sentence was interrupted by a jab in the ribs with his wife's elbow, and snickers from the other men.

Aidan looked at Alanna, confused. She was rolling her eyes. "I'll explain later. Rogers, don't make me get the muzzle."

She said it with affection, as his wife answered, "Please do."

Aidan felt like a zoo animal in a glass enclosure, being stared at fixedly by the group. Alanna and he reclined down on to the mats, heads on pillows. His head was still pounding, even though the brief rub she'd given him had been a temporary ease. He closed his eyes, and was with great effort, pushing the subject matter out of his mind that had caused his temples to burn. Alanna was talking to the group and he followed a bit of what she was saying, but more importantly was the sound of her voice. It soothed him, whether she sang or spoke. The combination of pitch, cadence and her sweet southern accent was like a balm to him.

"I know that each of you wake up from your dreams in a different way. Not everyone shouts or even jerks, physically. Your wives know, though. They are familiar with your sleep patterns and your bodies. They feel you wake. I think there's something soothing about that, and I want you to feel that way when your wife tries to help you."

Aidan looked at Alanna as he felt her lay back down and turn to him. Her face was gentle, her body turned and curled like she was sleeping on her side, next to him. Their eyes met and she touched his arm gently at the inside of his elbow. She gently rubbed his bicep, then smoothed her hand down to take his. Their fingers intwined, palms flushed to each others. "I'm here, Aidan. Are you okay?"

Aidan looked at her, lost in her eyes. "Aye, I feel you."

Alanna smiled. "I'm not going anywhere." He squeezed her hand. "Does your head still hurt?"

He swallowed. "A bit." She put her hands in his hair, kneading his scalp with her fingers. He shut his eyes. He'd almost forgotten where they were when she sat up gently, a minute later.

"You can talk to each other, figure out what you want to hear. Maybe you want to hear that you're home, if you wake disoriented. It's normal to wake up and not know where you are. It can happen for months or even years after you've been in theater. Ladies, maybe you can ask your husband if he needs something. Maybe you don't have to say anything. Maybe you just hold each other. Maybe you do more than hold each other," she said with a shy smile. "This is your journey, and you can figure it out together."

Aidan was surprised at her candor. She hadn't come out and talked about sex, but the implication was clear. Sometimes they might need a deeper connection, making love to bring him back to her. He couldn't argue the logic. Many nights he'd woken from a nasty dream, or not been able to settle, not able to put his demons to rest. His solitude had been a choice, but sometimes he ached to lose himself in a woman. To feel something soft and sweet and real. To smother his pain with pleasure. Somehow she knew that some men needed that, although he suspected her experience with men had been limited.

A stab of jealousy nagged at him. The thought that perhaps she'd learned that particular bit of knowledge from Tim. Had Tim reached for her in the desperate hours of the night? Had she soothed him with her caresses, her body?

One of the wives in the group asked a question. It was the wife of the Staff Sergeant they called Jonesy. He stiffened when she talked. "What about light? Sometimes I think it would help to turn a light on, but the jostling around, the sudden brightness, sometimes it makes it worse. I just think maybe if we could see each other…." She shrugged, trailing off.

Alanna nodded. "That's a very good question, Jessica. It's actually something I have been thinking about." She shuffled around in her bag. By this time Aidan was sitting up as well, watching her. She took out a few objects. One was a small lantern, something a backpacker would use. She squeezed it and the lantern emitted a soft glow. The other item was a clicking LED light attached to a lanyard.

"Some of you may want to invest in a touch lamp. They usually have a dimmer setting. If you don't want to do that, then hanging something like these items off of the bed post near each of your heads might be a good solution. They aren't overly intrusive as far as brightness, but you'll be able to see each other. They sell both of these at the Military Exchange and they're not expensive. That was a really good question, Jessica, thank you."

Aidan watched as Alanna went to each couple, sprawled out on the mats with the pillows they'd brought from home. She'd dimmed the lights and was taking time with each couple. When she came to the joker, who Aidan learned was named Mike Rogers, they started talking about their baby. The man was laughing, sharing that their baby often slept between them. "He's a grunting, scratching, little titty hog that stole my wife from me!" This caused a roll of laughter and sympathetic grunts from the other men.

Alanna hopped up and went to her bag. "I thought of that, Mike!" and she pulled out a baby doll the size of a real infant. She plopped the doll between the grinning couple. Aidan watched as they grew serious, looking at each other. The wife reached across the distance and put her fingers in her husbands hair, and it was such an intimate moment that Aidan looked away.

He saw another couple, younger and more quiet. The Marine couldn't have been more than twenty-three or twenty-four. They were facing each other. She had a pillow between her knees and she was pregnant. Their hands were clasped together, resting on her belly.

He looked at the other couple, Luke and Jessica. Her eyes were sad, like she was mourning him for dead. He was on his back, looking at the ceiling. Alanna was kneeling near the woman. "Jessica, maybe Luke would feel more connected if you put your hand on his arm." The woman did it and Aidan saw the man shudder slightly and close his eyes. She moved her hand slowly, placing it on his chest, over his heart. He grabbed her suddenly, pressing her hand to him. His breathing settled and he opened his eyes. He never turned to her, not with his body. But he gradually tilted his head, meeting her eyes, and Aidan saw him squeeze her hand. Then he looked away again.

Christ, he hadn't expected this. When she told him what they were doing, he'd smiled indulgently, but he'd secretly doubted the effectiveness. It seemed so strange, laying on yoga mats being told to touch each other. He thought about Alanna's hands on him. Her voice. He also realized that in the midst of this unlikely group therapy, his headache had disappeared.

"She's wonderful, isn't she?" The voice had come from behind him. At some point Alanna's overseeing doctor had entered to observe.

He met her gaze, then looked back at Alanna. "Aye, she is. She has a way with them, hasn't she?"

Dr. Jennings sighed. "I wish I could keep her. My staff is full. I'm going to lose her to some other clinic and that big brain and huge heart are going to be working for someone else." Aidan didn't say anything. There wasn't anything to say. He knew how she felt. Aidan would leave at the end of the summer and she would move on. She'd get married, have children, and that big brain and huge heart would belong to someone else.

He'd never know what it was like to roll over into her arms at night, seeking succor. No matter how much a part of him wanted it, he knew that. He'd felt it instantly, though, the connection. The moment she'd opened the door on that autumn day and mistaken him for Michael. The sight of her had shot straight through him. *Mine.*

He'd heard his grandda and da wax poetic about the O'Briens and their mates. His da had fallen in love with his mother on first sight, and they still loved each other with a deep passion that made their children both squeamish and grateful. He'd watched Brigid fall in love with Finn, and the truth was that the two of them were a goddamn inspiration. Where she was the scorching sun, he was the cool rain. They complimented each other on every level, and their children were an extension of that perfect union.

And Michael…Bitter, heartbroken Michael had collided with Branna, forever altered by the dark haired, fiery beauty. It wasn't that he'd doubted his ability to fall in love. He just knew that his life was not his own, and his soul was too darkened to mate itself to some unsuspecting woman. Lost in his thoughts, he barely noticed that the lights had been turned back up and that the couples were helping Alanna roll up the mats. He snapped to attention and began helping.

"Have you been over there? To the sandbox?" Aidan turned to the voice. It was Luke. He met the man's haunted eyes.

"Yes, I have. Three in Afghanistan, one in Iraq."

The man nodded. "I thought so. It's in the eyes." His wife came up next to him and took his hand. He smiled weakly at her and they walked away, the man saying nothing else to Aidan.

Aidan was listening to Alanna talk to the pregnant couple about aromatherapy for both of their headaches, then the room was finally empty but for the two of them. Aidan slid his uniform blouse back on, buttoning it as he headed for the exit. Alanna approached him, two pillows under her arms and her bag thrown over one shoulder and her purse over the other.

"Let me take something for you, lass. You look like a wee pack mule."

She smiled, "My father would say I was as stubborn as one, too."

Aidan took the bag and one pillow from her. "I suspect he gives as good as he gets."

She forged ahead, "Amen. He gives me the third degree about not dating, and the man hasn't had a date since Nirvana was still together!"

Alanna went to her cubicle, signed out of her desktop, and led Aidan to the exit. "I'm headed to the commissary. Do you need anything?" she asked.

"Actually, maybe I'll follow you over. I need several things, and I want to look at the hardware section in the exchange."

Alanna pulled out and began driving, trying not to think about what it had felt like to lay next to Aidan and put her hands on his smooth skin.

Aidan pulled into the shopping center of the base, right behind Alanna. He was ready to park when he noticed that Alanna had stopped in front of a van that had the hatch up. She threw the car in park and hopped out, and that's when Aidan noticed Maria. He swung into a parking spot and jumped out.

"Maria, honey are you okay?" Maria was rubbing her head, sitting on the tailgate. "My head hurts. Jesus, it really hurts. I just came here to see my doctor." Alanna looked at Aidan, alarmed.

Aidan knelt down to her. "Darlin', you aren't at the hospital. Do you need an ambulance? Where are Clara and Frankie?" Maria looked at him through squinted eyes. Aidan noticed the edema in her hands and face.

"I thought…" She looked around her. "I guess I went the wrong way. I left the kids at my friend's house."

Aidan looked at Alanna. "It's gotta be her blood pressure. How far? How far is it?"

"It's just past my clinic, about four minutes from here," she said.

Aidan looked at Maria's feet. The ankles and feet were swollen worse than before. Aidan picked Maria up, carrying her to the truck. "I can beat an ambulance. Call John's cell. If you can't get him, call Hector's. They're together. " He handed her his phone and she immediately started thumbing through the contacts.

She gave him her phone. "Go, take her. I'll call you on my phone when I get him."

Aidan pulled out of the commissary, heading back toward the hospital. "Maria, did you take your blood pressure reading today?"

She shook her head. "No, Frankie had a play date. I was running around taking care of the kids. I forgot. Aidan, I'm scared. My feet are really swollen." Aidan looked at her and saw the tears welling up. "My head really hurts, too. I'm worried about the baby!" Her voice was starting to raise.

He stopped at a red light and took her hand. "Ok, darlin'. You and I are going to breathe together, aye. Long and deep." He rubbed her inner forearm, just as Alanna had done to him in the therapy session. "I'm right here with you. Breathe, lass. That's it. Long and deep and calm." His voice was soothing, and he could see that she was getting calmer. "You are going to stay calm for me, and I'll sing that little babe a tune until we get there. How about that?"

Maria closed her eyes, breathing deeply and nodding. Aidan started to sing a sweet, soothing Irish lullaby and the corners of her mouth turned up. He held her hand as he sang and out of the corner of his eye, he saw her massive belly move like something out of a sci-fi movie. Her other hand went to her tummy. "The baby likes it. Keep singing."

Aidan did, and she took his hand and put it on her belly. Aidan could feel a foot kicking rapidly. He laughed as he sang, "She might be a dancer." Before he knew it, they were making the turn at the blue H and he followed the signs past the clinic. He pulled into the main hospital and up to the Emergency room chute, just as the phone began to ring.

"They're not picking up! Where the hell are they?" Alanna said.

Aidan cursed. "They're mapping out a hike for Monday. For feck sake, that whole area is a cellphone dead-zone. You need to go get him, mo chroí. They're parked near that C-store just past the beach, in Training Area C. Keep calling them, too. Try texting. You don't need as strong of a signal for that." Aidan hung up the phone just as a nurse was loading Maria into a wheelchair.

"Don't leave me. Please, don't you dare leave me until she gets him here." Maria had a vice grip on his forearm. He looked at the nurse.

"She's the boss. If she wants you with her, you can come."

13

Alanna was frantic. She had no cell signal as she roared down the main road of the training area. "Please don't let me hit a tank, Please don't let me hit a tank." She mumbled this prayer as she sped twenty miles over the speed limit. At this point, she wished an MP would pull her over. He could help her find Hector and John, and didn't they have loud speakers on their cars? She passed the beach access road and knew she was close. The C-store was next. Then she sighed with relief as she saw the Harley and Hector's SUV.

She pulled next to them and hopped out. She started leaning on her horn repeatedly. Then with everything she had, she screamed John's name, then Hector's. She repeated the ritual two more times when she saw Hector, then John come barreling out of the woods. They saw her and ran as she waved her arms like a lunatic. "It's Maria. Aidan took her to the hospital. You need to come now."

John went apeshit. "Holy shit, what's wrong? Is she in labor?"

Alanna shook her head, "No, she isn't."

John's face blanched. "Jesus Christ."

He started to hop on his bike, but Hector stopped him. "No fucking way, Gus. Let her drive you. I'll take care of the bike. You don't need to get on that death machine while you're upset."

John threw his keys to him and didn't argue. He hopped in Alanna's car and she headed back, leaving Hector in a cloud of dust.

"We found her in the lot of the commissary. She was sitting on her tailgate. She was confused and her head hurt. John, she was really swollen at her face, hands and feet. I'm no expert, but it may have been her blood pressure."

John was running his hands through his hair. "I told her to relax, put her feet up, take a bubble bath. Christ, she's so stubborn! She let the kids have a play date today. She probably overdid it! Fuck!" He slammed his fist down on the door's armrest.

"John, I know you're upset. You vent all you like while we're in this car." She paused. "Look at me." He did. "Curse, yell, punch something, whatever you need. But when we get to that hospital, you shut the shut. You hear me? She needs you cool as a cucumber. She needs support and kind words. She doesn't need to hear that she over did it and put the baby in danger. Do you understand? If you start giving her a lecture, she's going to knock you into the middle of next week, and I will help her."

John closed his eyes, stifling a half sob, half laugh. "She really would. She would kick my ass."

Alanna smiled. "You aren't the first man to fall for a feisty lady. Buyer beware." She checked Aidan's phone. "I have a signal! Call the first number. It's Aidan."

John hit redial, and Aidan answered on the second ring. "Aidan, holy fuck. What's going on? Is she at the hospital? Wait, is that her yelling at someone?"

Aidan was yelling over the noise. "Aye, let me step out."

John heard him shifting and leaving the room. "Shit, is she in labor? Why is she screaming?"

Aidan sighed. "They tried to give her blood pressure meds, and she went full berserker on them. Apparently she feels the meds are risky for the baby. Where the hell are you, brother?"

John cursed under his breath. "We're ten minutes out. Tell them to keep her calm, and don't give her anything but saline until I get there. She's a nurse, Aidan. If she doesn't want the meds, there's a reason. Can you put her on the phone?"

Aidan went back in the room and interrupted the row. "Excuse me, it's her husband. How about you ease off the lass for a bit and let her husband talk to her. He's ten minutes away. Just bide a minute and let him get here."

The doctor flung his hands up. "Who the hell is the doctor here?"

Aidan gave him a pointed look. "You said yourself her pressure was coming down. Don't go spinning her up again." He handed the phone to Maria and turned back to the doctor. "Did you get ahold of her midwife?"

The doctor looked at the nurse, "I'll be back in ten minutes. You try to talk some sense into them." Then he walked out.

The nurse looked at Aidan. "I'm sorry. He lost two patients today. There was motorcycle crash with a young marine and his girlfriend." Aidan closed his eyes, sorry and sad. "He lost them both. Such a pity. They come home, and the behavior can be reckless and erratic. It happens more than you'd wish to know. The doctor is stressed out and frustrated, so you aren't catching him on his best day. He's just worried about her. We did get ahold of her midwife."

On cue, the midwife walked in, all business. He was struck instantly by her resemblance to his mother. She had auburn hair, was about fifty, and she looked like a little hard ass. "How's my girl doing?"

Aidan took the phone from Maria who had disconnected with John. "Better than my husband and his driver. They just got pulled over for speeding."

Aidan cursed. "For the love of Christ, what next?" The midwife took his measure, looking at his uniform. "Are you the stand in?"

Maria laughed shakily. "He is. He stays until John gets here."

The nurse spoke then. "Her blood pressure was through the roof when she got here, but it has come down significantly. He, um, sings to the baby. It seems to calm them both," she said with a grin.

The midwife gave a grin. "I can't wait to hear it. We're moving her to the labor and delivery wing. I'm admitting her. I hope you don't have dinner plans." A corpsman came in and the three of them moved Maria to a gurney. They hooked her saline bag to the gurney and wheeled the monitor and Maria out of the ER.

"Please, sir. I know I was speeding. His wife is pregnant and had to be rushed to the ER. I promise you can give me as many tickets as you like if we can just get him to the hospital. I had to go find him in the training areas, and it's been almost thirty minutes." Alanna knew she sounded hysterical, but she was not going to be responsible for Maria sitting in that hospital by herself.

The young Marine looked at her military ID. "Who's your father? Is he on the base?"

She sighed, "No, he's in Virginia. He's still active duty, though, and I work on the base. I'm a counselor at Heroic Spirit."

John spoke up, "Please, devil dog. She was frantic on the phone. I need to be there, yesterday."

The Marine handed the ID back to Alanna. "Follow me."

He got back in his car and activated the lights and siren. He didn't go overly fast, but after about five minutes of driving, Alanna noticed the police cars holding up traffic at the main intersection. They strolled right through the light. Then one more light, there were two more police holding up traffic. Her eyes started to water. "Where else on earth would you see this, John?" She looked at him briefly and noticed his eyes were misty.

"Ooh-fuckin-rah" he mumbled. The MP took them all the way to the hospital. Alanna parked close to the ER gate, stopped, hugged the MP on impulse, and ran after Denario into the hospital.

"Labor and delivery? Holy shit, is she in labor?" Alanna came up to John as he was raising his voice by the desk.

"I don't know exactly what her status is, sir, but I can give you directions and a room number and you can see for yourself, sound good?" They hurried through the hospital until they arrived at the labor and delivery wing.

The midwife met them at the desk. "They called me from downstairs and said you were coming. Calm down, she and the baby are fine."

John collapsed his upper body, bending at the waist and leaning his hands on his knees. He took a few deep breaths. Alanna rubbed his back. "See, she's fine. They're fine, John."

He stood erect. "Tell me."

She walked him to the room, explaining the progression of her condition. "I suspect that her blood pressure was even higher when they found her in the parking lot. She was disoriented; she really shouldn't have been driving. It was 180 over 85 when they took it here." John swore under his breath. "It's a lot lower, though. It's 150 over 70 now. She's had a good helper." They came to the open hospital room and the midwife put a finger to her lips. "Listen." They all listened at the door, and Alanna stifled a sob as she heard a sweet baritone voice. Then she listened harder.

And now for the future I mean to be wise,
And I'll send for the women that acted so kind,
I'd marry them all on the morrow by and by,
If the clergy'd agree to the bargain

"What in the hell is he singing?" John looked at Alanna who was now stifling a giggle.

"*The Limerick Rake*," she whispered. They walked in quietly. John and Alanna both stopped, amazed at the scene before them. Aidan was sitting bedside and was holding Maria's hand. He was singing softly to her belly, bent gently over the side of the bed. Maria was sound asleep. He looked up when he noticed them. He eased his hand out of hers and stood. "Tag, brother. You're it." He smiled.

John was just looking at him hard. Then he grabbed Aidan in a bear hug. "Thank you. Jesus, thank you."

Then he turned to Alanna and grabbed her. "I'll never forget this. You've got a set of lungs on you, little sister. I think they heard you in Wilmington," he joked on a sob. Then he went to his wife. It was the midwife's turn to speak.

"You're going to be an amazing husband and father, Captain. You've got half the staff in the ER and this floor swooning in their scrubs.Thank you for staying. You've managed to get her pressure and the baby's heart rate down with that Irish baritone." Then she walked into the room.

Aidan was blushing as he looked at Alanna. Her smile was radiant. "You did good, Aidan. Although...*The Limerick Rake*?"

He coughed out a laugh. "I only know a couple of lullabies, and I was running short of material."

Alanna put her hand on his face. "You have quite the touch with the ladies. That baby's probably a girl."

He shrugged. "I only had one sister, but she's deirfiúr mo chroí. The sister of my heart. She's a handful like that one," he said, gesturing to the room, "but I cut my teeth on learning how to handle her." He smiled at the thought of Brigid, the longing acute in his chest.

"You miss her, your sister," she said. Not a question, but he answered.

"Yes, I do. I miss them all. Now, speaking of crazy women, did you get a ticket for your dodgy driving?"

She put her hands on her hips. "I am an amazing driver. And no, I got an escort. He was bewitched by my feminine wiles and my southern manners." She paused for emphasis. "And he was cute, too. Might have to bake him some cookies."

Aidan squinted his eyes. "Feminine wiles, eh? Whatever gets the job done, I suppose." They began walking toward the lobby, and he bumped her hip with his. "Smart arse. You haven't baked me cookies."

As they walked to the cars, Aidan took Alanna's arm. "It's too late to worry over shopping. Let me take you out."

She smiled as she took in the sight of him. "You'll have to change. No cammies out the gate."

He looked down at himself. "Christ, I didn't think of that."

She walked to the car. "We'll eat on the island. You like seafood?"

Aidan lay in bed, unable to settle. He'd heard from John. The midwife had convinced Maria that the blood pressure medicine they had chosen was safe for the baby. She was also convinced that the best option was to schedule a c-section for the morning when the obstetrician was there. According to John, Maria had argued against it, but had seen reason when the midwife assured her that this was the best bet for a healthy, problem free delivery. He also thought about Alanna. John had told him that she'd leaned on the car horn, screaming like a banshee until they'd heard her from the woods.

She'd been the first to notice Maria in the parking lot, too. He shuddered to think of them missing her all together. Alanna called the chaplain while they waited for a table. The wait was long, as tourist season had started, so they opted for take-away and had eaten together on the loungers on his deck. "Best seat in the house, and always ocean front," she'd said. She pulled a strand of hair away from her mouth. The breeze was lovely and the weather was mild. He had to agree.

As sleep was eluding him, he decided to go back outside. The sea had a calming affect on him. It was starting to get warmer and he slid a pair of shorts on, forgoing a shirt. As he slid the door open, he found Alanna on her deck, reading with the little lantern that she had used for her class. She looked up and set her book aside. "Couldn't sleep either?"

He shook his head, then grinned. "You've got your book, I see. I don't want to disturb you if you're getting a little action."

She put her hand over her face. "I'm not going to live that one down, am I?" she giggled. He pulled his lounger over next to her.

"I'm afraid not, love. So, did he get the girl?"

She grinned widely. "Oh, he got her all right. Multiple times and in multiple venues."

Aidan barked out a laugh. "You are a surprising woman. Bent over your school books like a good lass. Then I catch you reading these naughty books and have to reshape my opinion a bit."

She waved her hand. "It's escapism. Studying, working, my volunteer work. It's all a bit stressful. You can't deny me a little romance and a literary romp, can you?"

His eyes held a bit of curiosity. "Aye, I suppose not. I just can't fathom why you don't have a man in your life. I'm sure you'd agree that books are good, but the real thing is better."

She put her head back, looking thoughtfully at the sky. "I'm not good at the real thing. Books are easier, safer."

Aidan thought about that. "So you're hiding in your novels, is that it?"

She looked at him sharply. "No. Not exactly. I just…" She fidgeted. "Look, I have my reasons. It's not like you bare your soul to me, so I'm not talking. Let's just leave it at that. I have my reasons."

Aidan looked down below her chair. He picked up the object beneath it. "Aye, fair enough. How about we start with why you're afraid to fall asleep out here without a bat?"

She jerked and sat up, taking the bat from him. "Seagulls. Mutant, vampire seagulls that only hunt at night." She stood up, walking to her door.

"Don't leave. Christ, I'm sorry. Don't leave angry," he said. She propped the bat against the slider and walked back over with her chin up.

She sat and gave him a piercing look. "Fine, but remember this. You don't show me yours, I don't show you mine."

He put his hands up in defense. "Understood. You could give my mother a run for her money with that gimlet eye." Aidan surprised her by completely changing the subject. "Your boss watched part of your therapy session. You may not have noticed. She came in and spoke with me a bit while you were tending to the couples."

Alanna's eyes shot to his. "What did she say?" Aidan looked at her thoughtfully, and seemed to take in her face with his eyes. She felt almost caressed by the look. She had been trying not to ogle him, but her body was thrumming from his proximity and the fact that he had nothing but a loose pair of shorts on. They were low slung on his hips. His chest was a wide expanse of muscle and smooth, flawless skin dusted with light hair. His abs and hips were toned and tight with that trail of hair disappearing down into his waistline. He was beautiful. Trying to have a serious conversation with him after he'd caught her reading a steamy novel was difficult enough. All of the skin that Aidan was showing was ringing her bell, big time. She cleared her throat. "Did she seem to approve?"

He nodded. "She was impressed. She doesn't want to lose you. She seems to feel you won't have an issue finding a job if you are willing to leave the area."

Alanna gave a sigh of relief. "Well, that's something. I have to drive to Northern Virginia for an interview next week. I'll miss work on Monday and Tuesday, but maybe it'll be worth it."

"You were good with them. I have to admit, I thought it sounded a bit strange when you explained what you were doing. They listened to you, though. They respected your advice. I could see the connections they were making when you dimmed the light. I've never been a big believer in therapy, but I was proud of you, Alanna. You are good at what you do."

She smiled at him and he could tell that she was basking in the approval. Then she gave him a cheeky grin."Now, that surprises me. I thought you'd be the type to sign right up for some feel good, get in touch with your feelings type of action. I know how much you love to share," she said, giving him a sideways glance.

"You're being a smart arse, again," he said.

She shook her head mockingly. "Oh, no. I was thinking you and my father could start a support group. Get all those feelings out in the open in a big circle, invite some more bad-asses."

He snatched her book away from her. "You shouldn't mock broken men, lass. It isn't nice. Now, let's see what we have here." Her face blanched. "This page looks well worn. Have you read it more than once?" She hissed, trying to grab the book. He started reading out loud then stopped, silencing. His eyes widened, and still he read. And read. Then his jaw opened a bit. Alanna suddenly liked the idea of him reading it. Mister stoic, *I don't need a woman, I will control myself.* Let him get a dose of her suffering.

His eyes were fixed, then he turned the page. She leaned over and whispered in his ear. "Are you seeing the appeal?"

He snapped the book closed, looked at her. Then at her mouth. "The stable door, eh? Never thought that would be sexy, but bloody hell."

She smiled, removing the book from his fingers. She got up slowly and Aidan noticed she was wearing a long sleeping t-shirt, that came mid-thigh, and nothing else. She swayed to the door and looked over her shoulder. "Goodnight. Sweet dreams," and the torturous woman walked into her house and shut the door.

14

Alanna woke to spraying. Loud spraying. "What on earth?" She mumbled as she pulled some sweats on and looked out the window. Aidan was power washing both decks. The furniture was missing. "Need any help?"

He looked up, shutting off the sprayer. "No, sorry I woke you. I wanted to get an early start."

Alanna came from her bedroom and exited the back door. "I have a Zumba class at ten. It's okay. I can't sleep in, anyway. I have work to do beforehand, then I have a yoga class at eleven thirty."

He shook his head. "You work too much." Just as he said this, they both heard the computer. The distinct ring of the video call was coming through the window.

Alanna ran inside. "That's gotta be for you, Aidan."

She answered as he turned off the power washer, dried his hands and walked inside. "Hello! Oh my God! You're both there!" Branna was squealing with excitement.

Alanna was hopping up and down. "How was Dublin? Oh, God! I saw the twins. Sorcha showed me them. They're so big. Oh, God I miss you! I wish I could hug you!" The two women chatted excitedly and Alanna told the story of their eventful evening. By the time she got to the scene in the hospital, Branna was starting to sniffle.

"So, she's having it today? How wonderful!"

Aidan put his head next to Alanna's. "Are you two hens done?"

Alanna swatted his cheek. "Shut your gob, O'Brien. We need some girl time."

Branna laughed, "I miss you, too, dearthair. Give us a kiss." She was putting on her best Irish accent which always amused everyone.

Aidan blew a kiss at her through the screen. "I miss you, too, sister. Where's that fat headed brother of mine?"

Michael appeared behind her, cradling a baby. "Aye, you're one to talk. How's the training going?"

Alanna excused herself for the shower and Aidan waited until she was out of earshot to speak plainly. "Look, Branna. I wanted to talk with you about Alanna. She'd tan my hide if she knew. She's working about sixty hours a week and barely paying her bills. She's out of scholarship money. She's paying her way for this last bit of school and her regular bills."

Branna's face was intense. "She's stubborn. She won't ask her dad for money. That brother of hers takes every opportunity to point out that she's getting a free ride from her dad's benefits. It's a pride thing for her at this point. Should I talk to Hans?"

Aidan shook his head. "She'd kick my arse. I was thinking I could pay her rent. You don't have to tell her. She did some work since you were here. She's put flooring in the living room, painted, done some other small work with her da. You can tell her that you wanted to reimburse her and comp the rent this month. Just let me do this."

Branna looked at him curiously. "That's a very nice gesture, Aidan. Too nice. You should let me do it. If she did work, I'll waive her rent this month. She's not your responsibility."

He shook his head. "You and I both know that you could be getting holiday rates for both of these places all summer. You're losing money on both of us. You need to let me do this. Please."

She cocked her head. "She's a wonderful girl, isn't she? I was starting to think you were immune."

He sighed. "Don't go getting those wheels spinning, hen. Just take the money and lie like a good girl. She's looking for a job out of state. I think things will stabilize for her soon." Aidan heard the shower turn off. "She's out of the bath. Just do as I say. Call her next week and tell her. I'll put double rent in your account on Monday. Whatever you do, don't tell her what I did."

Branna was staring at the screen, Michael was behind her with Halley. They'd disconnected from the video call. She stood up and turned, smiling at her handsome husband holding their beautiful daughter. "I don't like lying to her, Michael."

He shrugged. "You started this, mo chroí. You need to let it play out. Aidan's a good soul, but this isn't some random gesture. He's not comfortable with it, but he's got feelings for this girl. He's being protective, feeling the urge to take care of her. That is a bit more than neighborly. Surely you sense it. You sensed it back in the fall." Branna smiled at that.

She took Halley from his arms and put her in her Moses basket. Then she wrapped her arms around Michael. "You O'Brien men make falling in love look like a boxing match."

Michael threw his head back and laughed. "Who are you kidding? You American girls give as good as you get."

She pulled his head down for a kiss, sucking his bottom lip. "And you love it, don't you?"

He took her mouth, hard, pulling her whole body into him. "Aye, I do." Then he picked her up by the thighs, wrapping her legs around his waist. "To bed with ye' woman. Those little fiends will be awake before ye know it."

Alanna came out of her bedroom with fresh workout clothes and her hair braided down her back. Aidan was leaving through the back door, to continue his work, when she shouted to him. "Do you need some sweet tea? It's already getting hot outside."

He smiled, "That sounds lovely, thank you."

He started working and she brought him the glass. "I'm going to work for a couple of hours, then head to the gym. If you need anything from the store, text me. I'll be home at one, otherwise." She looked at his work. "Did you get the paint yet?"

Aidan was sipping his tea and shook his head. "No. I'll go this afternoon. Don't worry about the store. I'll stop on my way home. Painting is tomorrow after the water dries. It's not supposed to rain and it's not windy. This is the perfect weekend. I'll stay out of your hair as long as you don't mind the noise."

She looked at him, brows drawn together. "I feel bad that you are doing all of this. Maybe I can help?"

He shook his head. "No, lass. What you can do is pick up a bouquet of flowers if you get a chance. I want to go see how Maria and John are doing, and I think they'd like you to come as well, if you can. He won't tell me if it was a lad or lass. Said I have to come see for myself."

She clapped excitedly. "I love babies! I'll be ready by three."

At three o'clock sharp, Alanna was knocking on Aidan's glass door. His breath caught in his throat at the sight of her. She was wearing a pale yellow dress that was short and flowing. Her hair was down around her shoulders except for two small braids at her temples. She had on cowboy boots and a jean jacket and she looked good enough to eat. The light breeze was blowing her skirt to the side and he saw a splendid amount of leg. She stepped inside, wearing a beautiful smile and no makeup. She didn't need it, he thought. She was fresh faced and naturally beautiful.

She had an air of innocence about her. She had moments where he could see the fire in her, but she stifled it. He had a feeling that if she let herself go, she'd be more Valkyrie than bookworm. He tried to imagine this sweet little southern belle, with her books and good manners, coming completely undone in bed. Smooth, firm, feminine curves, mouth open on a gasp, that little dress rucked up around her waist, boot clad ankles over his shoulders as he put his mouth on her.

He shook himself, and she had a questioning look. Her head was cocked a bit and there was a flare in her eyes. "You look…" he paused, treading carefully.

She looked down at herself. "What?"

He gave another slight shake of the head. "You look beautiful."

She raised her brows. "Thank you. It's not too 'giddy-up' for the hospital?" She said with a grin. He shook his head, afraid of what would come out of his mouth if he spoke. "Well, O'Brien, are you ready to go give that baby an encore?"

Alanna and Aidan walked down the labor and delivery hallway to Maria's room. The door was open, but Alanna gave a knock anyway. She was glad she did, because John was coming up for air from a languorous kiss. Her heart squeezed in her chest. The baby was in the crook of Maria's arm. She had an IV in her hand, and her hair was gathered in a bun on the top of her head. She looked pale and tired, but she looked happy. Especially after that kiss.

"Here they are! Our heroes!" Maria said brightly.

John turned to them and hugged Alanna. Then he looked at Aidan. "Flowers? You shouldn't have. Give me a kiss."

Aidan dodged him. "They're not for you, ye tosser. They're for this beauty." He bent down and kissed Maria on the head. "How are you feeling, darlin?"

John scoffed at that. "I'll have you know I am an amazing kisser. Now quit flirting with my wife."

Aidan smiled at Maria. "So, enough with the suspense. Is it a boy or a girl? And which Saint did you name it for?"

Maria smiled beatifically. "See for yourself, you can hold….it."

Aidan laughed, "Reveal nothing, girl. All right, hand it over." He gently took the baby from the crook of her arm. "Surely you aren't going to make me look in the nappy?"

She laughed. "Look at the arm bracelet."

He did, and he froze. Then he read it out loud. "Baby Boy Aidan Alann Denario," He looked up at John, then at Alanna.

"You two earned the honor. God knows what would have happened if she'd gotten back behind the wheel. We owe you this much at least. It's an added bonus that you're named after a saint," John said, trying to sound lighthearted but failing. He turned to Alanna. "Since it's a boy, we changed yours to the masculine. Hope you don't mind."

Alanna's eyes were welling with tears. "Oh, Maria." She went to her new friend and hugged her. "I don't know what to say." Then she looked at the bundle in Aidan's arms. The baby turned to her voice, blinking at her the way that newborns do. "He's beautiful. God, look at that hair and those eyes. He's just beautiful."

Aidan handed him over. She slipped off her jean jacket, afraid the buttons would scratch him. Then she took him in her arms, sighing and cooing as she held him gently. "He can't take his eyes off you. He must like the ladies, already."

"We'd like you both to be his godparents. For Frankie we had my sister and her husband, but they are in New Jersey. For Clara, we had Hector and Hatsu, but Hatsu isn't a Catholic. What do you think? You want to stand up for our boy?" John asked.

Aidan was looking hard at Alanna. She looked so natural holding the baby. Her body swayed back and forth with that instinctual rocking rhythm that all mothers seemed to have. The baby rooted at the top of her dress, searching for something to suckle. She laughed, "Sorry, my man. Those are decorative."

John barked out a laugh. "Atta boy."

Maria rolled her eyes at her husband. "You are such a pig."

Aidan couldn't take his eyes off of them, though. He could with little effort see her sitting in a rocker, a child at her breast. A fair haired baby with a small fist reaching up to her hair. The thought made his chest ache. She looked up from the baby and saw his internal struggle, puzzled by it. "What do you think, Aidan? It's your call," she said.

Aidan nodded. "Aye, it would be an honor. We'll do it."

After the visit to the hospital, Aidan and Alanna retired to their separate houses. Aidan cooked a light dinner, cleaned, did a little laundry, and settled down with a book. It occurred to him that Alanna's graduation was rapidly approaching. He'd brought a small gift for her from Ireland. He'd had to order it, so Branna was mailing it along with her gift. He needed one more thing, however. Something that had occurred to him as he'd gone back through their conversations in his mind. He smiled at the thought of it and had to remember to stop by the local bookstore to pick it up. He suddenly remembered that he hadn't checked the mail, so he went downstairs, slipped some shoes on, and went outside. There was a crappy Toyota driving slowly past the house, but then it sped up as he came down the drive.

Aidan checked his mailbox to find a small package sent international mail. Bingo. Branna had sent her gift. He didn't know what it was, but she'd seemed insistent he keep an eye out for it. He didn't receive bills or any other mail at this address, so he was surprised to see an envelope in the box as well. It was a thick envelope that had been opened. He flipped it over to see the recipient, and it was Alanna's. He headed back to the house and rang her doorbell. He thought back to their first meeting and her slamming the door in his face. They'd come to collect Branna, with marching orders from his da that if they had to tie the wee hellcat to a row boat and row her back to Ireland, they'd better not come home without her. He could see that same fire in Alanna, though she was better at hiding it. That little shit, Richard the Counselor, would never be a match for her. The thought of her on a date with him made Aidan's teeth grind.

Thumping footsteps sounded her approach and she peered through the curtain with a puzzled look on her face. "Why are you coming to this door?" she asked upon opening the door, looking at the envelope in his hand. "Is that my cell phone bill?"

He handed it to her. "Yes, it was in the wrong post box, and it was opened. You may want to make sure it's all there. Maybe they just didn't seal it well, but you never know."

Alanna shrugged, “I should go paperless. That would solve the issue, I suppose. You headed to bed?”

“Aye, in a bit. I’ll be up early to put the first coat on the deck, then to mass. You?” She nodded, “I’ll be there. As for bed, I’m still working. I have to get my interview clothes ready and get a bag packed.”

Aidan walked toward his door, “Good night, then. Don’t stay up too late,” and he walked back into his house.

15

Mass ended and Aidan walked out with John and Hector and Doc O'Malley, the team Corpsman. "Are you headed back to the hospital, John?" Hector asked.

"Yep, I need to pick the little ones up and take them. They slept with me last night. They miss their mom, I guess. Maria's mom flies in tonight, so then we'll have help. Oh, hey, tell Hatsu thanks for dinner. The kids loved it."

Aidan said his goodbyes and drove the long drive through the base to the bridge that led to the island. He needed to get another coat on the deck, and he was looking forward to seeing Alanna before she left. He changed out of his church clothes and went right to work. He put on his iPod and worked for about an hour before the heat started to get to him. The beach was more crowded, since the tourist season was upon them. He'd run down to the public beach access a mile down the road and was thankful that he had a semi-private beach. He thought about going down a few miles to Surf City to see the pier and social scene. He considered calling Joey, since he was single, and seeing if he wanted to be a wing man and get a drink and a bite to eat.

Alanna came home after going to the base gas station to fill the tank and wash her car. She wanted to top the fluids off before she headed up to Virginia. She was excited, thinking about the job interviews. She was a little sad, too. She loved the beach and loved North Carolina, but Virginia had more job opportunities. It was important that she keep her momentum going from a successful internship. She pulled the blinds from the glass slider and the air shot out of her lungs as she looked at the vision on the deck. Aidan was rolling paint on the deck with no shirt on. He was sweaty and his shorts were slung low on his hips. She didn't want to get busted gawking at him, so she slid the door. "You've gotten really far. You're on the second deck already."

Aidan turned to her, popping an ear bud out of his ear. "I'm sorry, I only caught about half of that."

Alanna blushed. "Sorry, I didn't see the headphones." Then she looked closer. "Good God Aidan, your back is getting pink. Do you have sunscreen on?"

He peered at his shoulders. "I put it on my arms and legs and face when I started, but I forgot when I took my shirt off."

Alanna gave him a chiding look. "Where's the bottle? You need to towel off and put some sunblock on, white boy. Have you ever seen a melanoma?"

Aidan gave her a sideways grin. "You're a pushy little hen. Hold on, I'll get it." He slipped through the door and came back out with a towel and a bottle of sunblock. He toweled off the sweat and then attempted to cover his exposed areas.

"Give me that." She said, not leaving room for debate. He handed the towel and the bottle to her. She rubbed the towel down the smooth length of his back. "You've got skin that any woman would envy, Aidan. You need to take care of it."

Alanna was talking, or chastising was more accurate. Aidan didn't hear a word once she started toweling him off. Then he felt her hands. She smoothed the lotion over his shoulder blades, then down his back. It felt so good that goosebumps broke out all over him, despite the afternoon sun."

She stopped. "Are you chilled?"

He shook his head. "No lass, you've got a good touch is all."

She said nothing to that, not sure what she'd say even if she'd found the courage. But she continued. She warmed the lotion with her hands and then touched him. She traveled over his muscled back, his broad shoulders, his trim waist where his shorts met skin. He was still beneath her hands, quiet as the dead. She stopped her hands, leaving them on his back for just a moment, then she stepped away. "I think you can reach the rest," she said weakly.

He turned, then, and she was taken back by his face. Hunger. It was plain on his face. It made a thrill go through her, the power of her touch. But he didn't act on it. He wouldn't. She knew that. He had needs like any man, but he wasn't willing to risk her getting all moony over him and then having to explain to Branna why a couple of months of sex was all he was willing to give. So he gave her nothing.

She looked away, suddenly sad at the thought of having nothing. As if from some divine providence, her phone went off in her pocket. She didn't recognize the number. "Hello? Oh, hello Rick. No, I'm not busy. How can I help you?" She waved a quick goodbye to Aidan and went back into her house.

Aidan finished up the painting in record time. He'd rolled with a vengeance, throwing all of his frustration into hard work. *Christ, I can still feel your hands on me, a rúnsearc.* Her touch had been exquisite. Smoothing her hands up and down his back, he was assaulted with the thought of her hands curled around him, running along his muscles as he stretched above her, filling her up. Did she dig her nails in at the end? Would she pull his ass to her and dig her nails in, begging him to go deeper? Or was she quiet when she made love? *No feckin way. Not with me, she wouldn't be. I'd make sure of it.*

He swore under his breath. This was not the way he should be thinking considering he'd actually been stupid enough to tell her he would keep his hands off her. Damn it! She'd gotten a call from that sensitive little counselor. He washed his hands in the sink, then his face. He toweled himself off and put his shirt back on. He needed a shower, but he needed to see her for just a minute.

Alanna heard the doorbell and knew it must be Aidan. Rick wasn't due for another half hour. She'd hidden in here after the phone call, getting work done. Her thesis was done, but she had her certification test to take next month. She wasn't worried about it. She'd aced the last level she'd taken and had always been a good test taker. She scored an 1870 on her SATs. The problem wasn't going to be the test to be a licensed counselor, the problem was going to be the job market.

She closed her eyes as she thought about how far she might have to travel to find a job. She knew some companies did Skype interviews, so she was hoping that if Virginia was a bust and nothing showed up in Georgia or South Carolina, that video conferencing was a viable option.

She'd also taken the time to clean herself up, put some make-up on, and change into a cute outfit. She had a date. Holy shit. When was the last time she'd been on a date? There had been a couple after Tim, but it had been…what…two years? She wasn't really attracted to Rick, but he was nice, and he was interested. He was also a southern boy. Born and raised in North Carolina. She needed to give this a chance. So, why the hell was going out with him depressing her instead of making her happy? *Because he's not Aidan.* She shook that thought from her head.

Alanna answered the door and Aidan's face darkened. She was dressed up. She had a denim skirt on that came just above her knee and a loose peasant blouse that came down to a key hole neckline between her breasts. She'd even painted her toenails. "Going somewhere?" he said, dryly.

She gave a tense smile. "Yes, I am. I actually have a date. A short one. I have to get up early, but Rick is taking me to dinner."

Aidan clenched his jaw and his fists before he caught himself. He cleared his throat. "Well, I just wanted to tell you not to use the deck. It should be dry by morning, but check it before you step out. Have fun on your date."

He turned and walked away. "Aidan!" she said, and ran outside in her bare feet. He turned back to her, a look of complete calm on his face. Maybe she'd misread the tension. *More like wishful thinking.*

"If I don't see you before I leave in the morning, I wanted to say goodbye."

His face softened. "Good luck on your interviews, Alanna. I hope you get everything you want. And have fun on your date with Richard the CLMAF or whatever the fuck his title is."

She cocked her head. "Why don't you like him? You barely spoke with him for two minutes."

Aidan shrugged. "I didn't say I didn't like him. It's just a feeling. I don't trust him. Why would he ignore you the last few months and then just suddenly ask you out?"

She stiffened. "He said it would be unprofessional while I was still interning. Why does he have to have a reason? You can't believe that he might just want to see me socially, that he might be attracted to me?" Her chin was up and her tone was defensive.

Aidan shook his head fiercely. "You know that's not what I meant."

She talked over him. "You say I am terrifyingly beautiful, yet my social life is in the crapper. Personally, it's refreshing to see a man who has the stones to go after what he wants."

Aidan's nostrils flared a bit. "Stones?"

She leaned in. "Yes, stones, balls, bollocks. Goodbye, Aidan, I'll see you Wednesday." She swung her head around and marched back to her door, leaving Aidan with his mouth agape.

Aidan growled when he heard the car pull up. Then he heard the door bell ring next door. Stones? She thought Mr. Sensitive Counselor Boy had stones? What the bloody hell did that mean? He'd patrolled the streets of Basra, he'd cleared houses in Kabul. He knew about big stones, and he had them in spades. He picked up his phone, calling Lt. Drake. He needed a drink.

Alanna got out of Rick's car at nine o'clock, shooting for a swift departure. The date had gone well for a while, but by the end, Aidan's words were replaying like a broken record in her head. *I don't trust him. Why would he ignore you the last few months and then just suddenly ask you out?* She was such an idiot. Oh, Rick was interested. That wasn't in question. But as much as he showed an interest in the hint of cleavage she was showing and the freshly shaved legs, he had equal or more interest in her upcoming job interviews.

He hadn't been interested enough to ask her out until he figured out that he could get some intel from her. The added bonus of getting in her pants was a distant second. Just as she was dodging a kiss from him, headlights shined on them both, and a Mustang pulled in the drive. Aidan got out of the passenger side. He stopped, looking at them both for an awkward moment. "Sorry to interrupt."

That was all the infernal man said, and then he walked into the house. Alanna looked at the Mustang. Lt. Drake from the barbecue was driving, and he had two women hanging over the seat from the back. "Hi again, sorry to interrupt." Then he pulled out, leaving her standing there with Rick, and feeling like an idiot.

"Ok, well thank you Rick. I have to get packing, so I'll probably see you on Wednesday."

Rick stuttered over his reply. "Oh, so early? Well, I don't want to keep you. We'll have to do this again when you get back. I want to hear all about your interviews." She smiled frostily. *I'll just bet you do.*

Aidan couldn't sleep. He was lying in bed, stifled by the closed window. He'd shut the windows and turned on the AC to avoid paint fumes. He counted the hours since he'd finished. The paint had to be dry. It had been finished by mid afternoon and had several hours of sun beating down on it. He got out of bed, putting on some clean shorts. He walked through the house into the kitchen, where he poured a glass of water. He'd only had two beers, tonight, but he needed the fluids. What a night it had been. Joey had taken him to a local pub for dinner, drinks and music. It was a decent enough place.

They'd gained the attention of two women who were on the island for the week. College girls, as a matter of fact. They were cute, too. They were young, randy, and looking for a little no-strings attention. Most men would have thought they'd hit the jackpot, but they put him off. He couldn't quit thinking about Alanna being out on a date. About those smooth legs and painted pink toes, and her beautiful, pink mouth on someone else's face. "Feckin hell," he hissed. He walked over to the slider, needing some fresh air.

The drapes were pulled, but he could see that her light was on. Had she kissed him? Did he touch her? The thought made him mental. *You've got no right to feel this way.* The wood was dry, so he was standing at the railing, looking out over the sea. He looked back at the light that was still on in her house and had to fight the impulse to knock. *Time to take a walk.*

Aidan walked along the beach with nothing but the moon to guide him. The moon and the stars were bright, even with the light pollution. He needed to go to sleep. He had training in the morning. They had a big hike at 0800. He walked for a few minutes, seeing the shadows of ghost crabs scurrying along the sand. He felt shells under his feet. It was soothing, walking along this vast shoreline. When he finally circled around and found his way back to the house, he heard her. More specifically, he heard her violin. It was faint, but he heard it as he walked up the beach walk.

He followed the sound to her deck and around the side of the house. There she was with her little lantern. He'd never seen this area until he'd painted. She had a hammock hanging on the side of the house that was hidden from view, along the side deck with bamboo shades enclosing it on two sides. She was lightly playing, so faint that a neighbor wouldn't even hear her.

"I thought the deck was still drying?" she said drowsily.

He gave a quiet laugh. "It's dry enough. How did you get out here?"

She used her bow to point to the window. "Climbed out, right on to the hammock. Where there's a will, there's a way."

"What were you playing just now?" Aidan asked.

She put her violin on her lap. "It's called *Swanee River,* an old southern song."

Aidan leaned against the house. "How did your date go, then?"

Alanna looked at him intensely, trying to figure out how to respond to the question. She swung herself out of the hammock, deciding she didn't owe him an answer. "Not as exciting as your night out, I'd wager." She breezed by him.

"What's that supposed to mean? The girls in the car?" he asked, irritated.

She shrugged. "It's none of my business. Military boys have been heading to saloons to get some grind for hundreds of years. Hell, probably thousands of years."

Aidan shook his head. "Did you happen to notice I got out of the car alone? Drake might be tag teaming the two of them, for all I know or care, but I left alone. They're not of interest to me other than to share a pint. Now, you didn't answer my question. How was the date? You don't seem to be in a particularly good mood, considering you had your hands full when we pulled up. Did he get that kiss he was going for, after I left?"

Alanna stiffened, then she slid her violin into the doorway. "Good night, Aidan," she said as she retreated into the house.

He closed in on her before she was totally through the door. "What? You can make assumptions about me, but I can't ask you how your date went?" His voice was getting an edge to it, and didn't that just jack her up.

"Why do you care whether I kissed him or not? You took a pass, remember? You should be happy I was on a date! You won't have to explain yourself to Branna, right? I'm just the sort of complication you don't need."

She swung around, going back for the door. "You still haven't answered the question," he said softly.

She growled. "Ok, fine. You want to know how my date went? He spent half the time looking down my shirt and the other half pumping me for information on my interviews. He actually wanted me to inquire about any openings in Virginia for him. He probed into who was hiring, what the salary was, if I knew how many were interviewing for each job. He's looking to get out of North Carolina. You were right. Bravo, Aidan. You totally nailed it. He only asked me out to get information, with the added bonus of hoping to get in my pants on his way out of town!"

"Well, things looked cozy when we pulled up. It couldn't have gone that badly. Did you let him kiss you? It's a simple enough question." He said it calmly, which pissed her off.

She shouted, "No! I didn't!"

He pressed her. "Why not? He obviously wanted to."

She ground her teeth, lips tight with anger. "Because I didn't want his mouth on me." Her eyes shot to Aidan's mouth. He took a step toward her. "You don't have the right to ask me these questions," she said with a thick voice, not meeting his gaze.

"I know," he said.

Her eyes shot up to his. "I don't understand you! Why do you care?" she hissed. Then she shoved her palms into his chest. "I don't know what you want from me! What do you want?" She shoved him again, and he grabbed her wrists with his hands. As she resisted, he pulled them around his neck, pulling her face to face with him. Their breath intermingled. "What do you want?" She said on a choked sob.

Aidan's faced hovered over her, his hands pulling her closer. "Your mouth," he whispered. "I want your mouth." And he covered her mouth with his.

Alanna felt her brain short circuit when Aidan kissed her. He moaned as he took her mouth. He let go of her wrists and pulled her body to his. His kiss was expert. There was no hesitation. He didn't even use his tongue at first. Long sweeping kisses with firm, sure lips. Like he was drinking her in.

Then small sips as he buried his hands in her hair. She was panting by the time he broke that first contact. He looked at her with hooded eyes. He must have liked what he saw, because he went in again, and suddenly her back was to the sliding glass door. Then he deepened the kiss and she whimpered as his tongue touched hers.

"Christ, lass. You taste incredible." He kissed her again and pressed into her, and she kissed him back with everything she had. She ran her fingers in his short hair as he took her hips in his hands, pressing his arousal into her. Then he started kissing her neck. She moaned as she grazed his scalp with her nails.

Aidan was assaulted with sensation. He smelled Jasmine and supple skin and silky hair. He tasted pink lips. He felt heat and need. He heard the ache in his own voice and in hers. He heard her soft pants and her breath catch when he pressed into her. The thought of her out with another man had made him lose all sense. He needed more. More of her mouth, more of her hands on him. He was shirtless, and she had one hand in his hair, the other on his shoulder.

The glass door gave a squeak and it occurred to him where they were. Under the porch light on her deck. He'd all but shoved her up against the door. *What the fuck are you doing?* He blocked the voice out. *Just a little more.* He nibbled her chin as she tilted her head back. Then he threaded his fingers in her hair and took her mouth again. He knew he needed to stop, but her mouth was so sweet, her body melting into his.

No, no, no. Don't stop now! Alanna could feel him pulling back. His kisses became more shallow, pulling back in a slow retreat. They became small, nibbling kisses that spoke of an ending, not a beginning. He finally rested, and she met his eyes. He was breathing as heavy as she was. His arousal was pressed to her, and she realized, to her horror, that she'd arched her back to press further into him. She relaxed her back and felt her bottom touch glass. She'd been robbed of speech, however. Not happening.

"What are ye thinking, a mhuirnín? Don't think about your answer, just tell me," Aidan said, concern marring his beautiful face.

Alanna took a steadying breath. "I'm thinking that a four year dry spell might have been worth that kiss."

Aidan's smile was blinding, and she knew instinctually that it was a rare sight. Men like Aidan wore their feelings quietly. Then the smile was gone. He brushed her bottom lip with his thumb. "Four years? That's a long time for such a beautiful woman." He backed up and took her hand, pulling her from the glass as he slid the door open and guided them both inside. "Now, I'm sure that's a long story, and when you return, I'll need to hear it." He turned and faced her, taking her other hand. "But for now, you need your sleep, love. You've got a long drive tomorrow."

Alanna lifted a brow. "What makes you think I'll tell you that long story? I'm more of a quid pro quo kind of girl than an over-sharer." Aidan stiffened visibly. "Not in the mood for a little tit for tat?" she said, shaking her head. "That kiss didn't change a thing, did it? So, why did you bother? Were you taking pity on me because of the date from hell? You can save it next time."

Aidan's face twisted with irritation. His eyes narrowed and he pulled her to him, covering her mouth in a rough kiss. He had one hand in her hair and one on her tailbone and he pulled her body into his hard erection. He kissed her deeply and possessively. When he let her mouth go, she let out a little sigh. "Does this feel like pity?" he hissed. He kissed her again, erasing any doubt in her mind about how he felt on the matter. When he stopped, she was panting against his lips. "Now, you're going to go to bed like a good lass, and I'm going to go take a cold shower." Then he kissed the tip of her nose. "Good night, a mhuirnín," and he left without another word.

16

Alanna woke up bright and early, needing to be on the road by six to time the Virginia traffic. The five hours of sleep she'd gotten had been surprisingly restful. Nothing like having the shit kissed out of you to work the edge off. As painfully aroused as they'd both been when they'd parted, there was a peacefulness that came from it as well. A soothing peace that came from contact, from affection, from human touch. She'd thought herself immune to it, looking back on her two failures. She'd never burned to her core from a man's touch, from his kiss. Not until now. When Aidan had finally let her come up for air, she had to fight the impulse to check her body for burns. Good Lord above. That kiss.

Aidan hadn't slept more than an hour or two, total. He'd taken that cold shower, but it didn't stop his mind from playing that kiss over and over again. She'd responded to him with every bit of the passion he'd thought she would. When he'd let himself fantasize about kissing her, it had been good. But nothing had prepared him for the real thing. Her taste, the feel of her, the little sounds she made when she was aroused, when she wanted more. They'd kissed like it was the only thing keeping them both alive, and stopping had almost killed him. It was a stupid thing to do, of course. This wasn't headed anywhere but toward a whole lot of heartbreak.

The problem was that he hadn't thought about the possibility of her dating someone during his stay. He'd felt a connection with her almost instantly, but being the type of man that was able to exercise some discipline, he'd never questioned his ability to resist the temptation. What he hadn't considered was how intimate living next door to her was going to be. Then that little prick from her work had come calling, and that territorial instinct that the O'Brien men were so famous for had reared it's ugly head.

When he'd pulled in the driveway to see her co-worker going in for a kiss, he'd had murder on his mind. *Mine.* He'd kissed her because he'd had to. Like a barbarian that wanted the beta males to know that she was his, and he was hers. And he needed to stop that line of thinking. Right now.

Even with the lack of sleep, he felt somewhat calm as he lay in the early morning dawn. She soothed him. Her voice, her smell, the feel of her hands on him, it was like a balm for his soul. As painful as the arousal had been, there was a magic in it as well. *You can't have her. You can never really have her.* He closed his eyes, understanding that fact. She wasn't the sort to leave things be. She wanted to crack into his head, not just his heart. She wanted to see him naked, exposing his inner demons. He couldn't do it, though. Sometimes the best thing you can do for your loved ones is to keep them out of your head and thus out of your hell.

"Hey Hector, my man! How the hell are you?" Hans said when he picked up the phone on a oner.

"Great, Sergeant Major. Perfect. Just getting ready for a hike. I know it's early, but I also knew you'd be up." Hans had him on speaker phone, and was dealing with morning rush hour by easing forward at a snail's pace.

"What can I do for you?"

Hector answered, "It's more like what I can do for you. I got some interesting information on the Irishman staying next door to your daughter."

Hans perked up at this. "Shoot. Give me everything."

"Well, I did some digging. That's why it took me a bit longer to get back to you. He has some pretty impressive stuff in his records, but you know as well as I do that the back story is what tells the tale. Did he change some general's tire in a combat zone, or did he get serious with the enemy? Besides the regular good boy medals and campaign medals you would get for not being a screw up and doing your job, he has two that stick out. One being The Distinguished Service Order which is only given when the service member engaged in actual combat with the enemy and only during acts of exemplary leadership."

He continued, "We're talking enemy fire exchange and the DSO is rarely given to anyone under the rank of Major. He got that in Sangin, Helmand Province, Afghanistan in 2006. Heavy fighting with the Taliban. He must have done some pretty fancy moves to get that award. They took casualties in his regiment. He was put in for the Victoria Cross by his commanding officer. That's like our Medal of Honor and damned near impossible to get, so he got the DSO instead. Still an extremely hard medal to get, especially as young as he was. He couldn't have been more than a first lieutenant."

Hector paused. "You still there, brother?"

Hans grunted a yes, "And what was the second one?"

Hector continued, "This one I was a little confused about it. The Conspicuous Gallantry Cross which was awarded after a tour in Kabul. According to the current CO who pulled his paper, he had something to do with the capture of some high ranking Tangos, but there was something else. Something about gallantry in the face of human rights atrocities. It worked in somewhere with the capture of the rebels, but there weren't anymore details. The man who put him in for the award has since retired. Other than the two I just mentioned, he got some lower level ribbons in Iraq when he was enlisted. He was there in 2004. He spent most of his time in Basra, some in Baghdad, and as you know, that shit got critical on those patrols. I do know this. He's seen some genuine action. His last tour was Camp Bastion; the third of his tours in Afghanistan. Any medals he has coming from there are still pending. All the guy could tell me was that there were definitely some pending."

Hector sighed. "I'll be honest, Hans. When I saw this guy was coming and he wasn't a Royal Marine, I figured he had to be some parliament member's kid or some shit. That he'd pulled political strings to get the assignment, but when I saw he'd deployed four times, and then I met him, my preconception wasn't jiving with the reality. The dude's a damn good soldier. I'd take that Irish bastard off their hands any day of the week if I could have him on my team. He's here for training, and the UK has all but pulled out of most of the conflicts, but I'm going to hate to lose him at the end of the summer. He's already proven he can hold his own with the Marines."

Hans was silent a moment, not sure how to process what he'd been told. When he looked at the young captain, he saw a lot of things. He saw intelligence, discipline, he saw a family man. He'd seen a picture displayed proudly from his niece. One of those hand drawn, childish pictures that he'd obviously treasured enough to travel with and put in his new home. He saw ghosts, too. The kind you get when your hands are bloody. Maybe from the enemy, maybe from watching your buddy bleed out, but he had that air about him, no doubt. Like recognizes like. He also saw very clearly that this dark horse from the Emerald Isle was falling in love with his only daughter. The connection had been obvious, even during their short meeting in the fall. And who could blame him? He may be biased when it came to his daughter, but he knew quality. Alanna was amazing on just about every level.

"I can hear the wheels turning in your head, Hans. Tell me where you're at." Hans looked at the line of traffic ahead of him. He was leaving DC for good, somewhere around the New Year. He couldn't get North Carolina. No one with his rank or job was moving yet. He also hated DC. It was time to go. The job in Europe was a dream job. His twilight tour could be spent running between Spain and Italy and helping command Marines who guarded their assets in Europe and Africa. He wanted the job and the only hesitation had been his daughter. Could he leave her during one of the biggest transitions of her life? She was actually interviewing up here in Virginia, for Christ's sake. She wouldn't hesitate to tell him to grab the dream job with both hands. She was like that.

He answered Hector, "I'm thinking that he sounds like a good man, a really extraordinary man. The type of man you would love to call friend."

Major Diaz finished the thought, "Or son. Any man would be proud to call him son. You think it's headed that way?"

Hans gave a weary sigh. "She's a tough nut to crack, but let's just say that if it is headed in that direction, I've decided not to get in the way."

Hector laughed. "God deliver us from daughters. I tell you what, my old friend. I plucked a beautiful woman out from the clutches of an overprotective daddy over twenty years ago. Swept her off to a distant land, and to hell with anyone who didn't like it. Her father came around after a while, but it sure as shit would have been easier if he'd been on board from the start. Your girl, she's a rare one. Smart, beautiful, and she's got a good head on her shoulders. You can't expect her to lead an ordinary life. She was raised in the duffle bag, just like my kids. She's got the military in her blood and all of the wanderlust that comes with this life. I think I like the idea of the two of them. And the irony that Brian's little girl will watch her six in that family? Shit, sign me up. I'll play cupid all day long."

Hans laughed. "Not necessary, Hector. We'll just let this play out. From the way they look at each other, I don't think they'll need the help."

On mile seven of the hike, it occurred to Aidan that he should have gone to bed earlier. *But if you had, you wouldn't have gotten that kiss.* He closed his eyes briefly at the thought, until he tripped on another infernal vine. The terrain was full of them, and Staff Sgt. Williams had accurately referred to them as *catch-me-fuck-me vines.* Lt. Drake snickered behind him. "Your mind is wandering, Irish. Did things heat up after I dropped you off?"

Aidan grumbled an expletive which made the men around him chuckle. "Crossing ahead!" The group stopped at the dirt crossing as a Marine guarded the path, letting an MRAP go by.

Major Diaz came along side Aidan as they continued. "Have you ever played with an MRAP?"

Aidan laughed. "Of a sort. We've got the Mastiffs, Ridgebacks, and the Wolfhounds. They take a fecking hit better than the stuff we had in the beginning. I'm sure I don't have to tell you that."

Hector nodded, "Hell yeah, I remember. These MRAPs have cut the casualties down like crazy. They're fun to drive, too." Then he yelled to the group, "We're coming up on mile eight, ladies! Two more miles to go before you get your chow!" A mixture of relief and dread rumbled through the group of eleven men.

They sat in clearing at the end of their hike, sweating, dirty, and tired. The supply truck was replenishing their fresh water, and they were each given an MRE. "Ah, shit. I got potatoes and ham, who wants to trade? I hate this shit," said Sgt. Porter.

Corporal Washington piped up, "No way, my man. I got jambalaya. Just like momma makes."

Aidan doubted that, unless his mother was a horrible cook. He looked at his own. "Chicken and rice?" he offered.

Sergeant Porter grabbed the pouch. "Now you're talking! Thanks, Sir."

Aidan didn't think you could screw up potatoes and ham, in his experience, but mystery chicken dishes could be unsavory. He'd eaten worse, and when you were hungry enough, dirty socks smothered in toe jam would be good. He opened up the meal and started spreading it out. "Ah, shit. You got M&Ms! You want my Skittles, sir?"

"Christ, what you must have been like as a lad. Just eat yer fecking lunch, Sergeant," Aidan said.

Washington choked on his Jambalaya and broke out in laughter until he was beaned in the head with some Skittles. Aidan smiled. They were young and full of easy laughter. He tossed his M&Ms to the young sergeant.

Doc O'Malley, the corpsman, got up and addressed the group as they ate. He briefed them on hydration, and talked briefly of foot and jock fungus and how to remove ticks. Aidan looked around, then leaned over to Denario. "Are ticks really that much of an issue?"

Denario started to answer, but it was Staff Sgt. Polaski that responded first. "Yes, sir. You just wait till you get home and out of these clothes. Intrusive little bastards. No respect for a man's privacy."

O'Malley added to the sentiment. "He's right. Besides your head, check your sock line, between your toes, between your butt cheeks, in the crease of your thighs, armpits, testicles. The sweatier the crevice, the better they like it. If you have a lady friend, maybe she'd like to help," he said with a wink.

The men chuckled at that. "You got a lady friend, Captain?" Lt Drake asked him with a mischievous grin.

"No, Lieutenant. Why? You're not offering to check my sweaty ass crack for ticks, now are you?"

Hector barked out a laugh as Lieutenant Drake waved his hands. "God, no! You're going to give me nightmares!"

"Did anyone talk to Captain Denario? When is he coming back to training?" Lt. Drake asked. "We got the play by play of the whole night, starting with you carrying Maria to the truck and the captain and your lovely neighbor getting a police escort," he said to Aidan.

Hector answered. "The mother-in-law came in last night. He'll be back tomorrow."

As the men piled out of the truck at the training building, Aidan thought about going back to the house without Alanna there, and it left an empty spot in his gut. "So, why did you take off so early last night? Brittany and Ashley were ready to party," Joey said, sidling up to Aidan. "Were you going to check on your roommate?"

Aidan stiffened. "She's not my roommate. She lives in a completely different house. And no, I wasn't checking on her," he said, pissily. "Brittany was a fine bit of stuff, but she was a bit young for my taste, and she was half in her cups. Drunk and fresh out of grade school is not my idea of a dream date."

Joey shrugged. "I just dropped them off at their condo rental. I went home, too. Probably best. This hike sucked, big time. So, what's up with your neighbor? Did she get a boyfriend while you were hanging back, not making your move?"

Aidan nudged him, "Shut your gob. She's a good girl. What do you expect me to do? Use her for a few months and toss her aside when I leave?"

The young Lieutenant looked at him like he was crazy. "Hell, no. A girl like that? You sweep her off to Vegas, and you marry her before she wises up. Take her back to the motherland. She's a keeper." Aidan gave a non-committal grunt and grabbed his gear. Home. He needed to go back home, shower, and take a long nap.

"Hello, baby! How's my little girl?" Alanna walked into her father's embrace.

"Hi daddy. I'm fine. I'm tired, but fine." He kissed her cheek.

"Well, is this bag it?" he said, grabbing her backpack. She nodded. "All right, come in and we'll scrounge up some dinner." She laughed to herself. He didn't really cook. He grilled and he ate stuff out of a can. That was it.

As they sat at the table eating Dinty Moore beef stew and a tin of ready to bake biscuits, Alanna was unusually quiet. "Something's on your mind, Miss Priss. How was your interview today? This was the one at Heroic Spirit Clinic at Walter Reed, right?"

She nodded. "I think it went really well, actually. The one with Bethesda Hospital is tomorrow."

He looked at her, curiously. "Which one suits you?"

She shrugged. "The job at the hospital pays better. I have a lead at the VA, too."

He smiled. "They'd all three be damned lucky to have you, but you didn't answer the question."

She picked at her stew. "I think I'd like to stay with the non-profit. Less bureaucracy. The clinic at Lejeune has been good to me. I like their mission. It doesn't have to be the same non-profit. I just want to branch out. The VA is so broken. I think I would die a little trying to fix it. I need a job, though. I may have to take something I don't want, at first. I'm prepared for that reality."

Hans picked up his glass of sweet tea. "To getting our dream jobs," he said. Then they clinked glasses.

"I love you, daddy. I want you to be happy, too," she said.

He just smiled at that. "I am happy, baby. As long as my children are happy, so am I."

She smiled, mischievously. "Erik doesn't seem to be that happy."

He snorted, dismissively. "He's happy. He's just kind of a dick." Alanna shot her tea through her nose. He looked at her innocently. "What? I love my son as much as my daughter. Don't mistake me. I was kind of a dick at his age, too."

She held up the tea for another toast. "Here's to outgrowing your dick-itude." It was her father's turn to laugh.

Aidan pulled into the beach house to a strange car in the driveway. As he pulled in and parked, he noticed the disabled veteran license plate from Virginia. *Tim the Tosser?* As if summoned from his thoughts, Tim emerged from the stairs leading up to Alanna's deck. He noticed that he had to be careful when maneuvering the stairs but was very nimble considering his missing limb. "I told you I'd see you again before I left." Tim was smiling and put a hand out as Aidan approached him.

"Aye, you did. Alanna's gone up for her interviews. She won't be back until Wednesday."

Tim took in his appearance. "Did you lose a fight?" Aidan was opening his front door with the key.

"Hump, ten miles. You'll need to drink a beer while I shower and de-tick myself."

Tim made a distasteful scowl. "I did my training in the winter. Thank God."

Aidan led him up the stairs and they came to the main living area. He pulled a beer out of the fridge and handed it to Tim. "I'll only be a few minutes. Sit outside if you like."

After a shower, Aidan walked out on the deck and sat in the chair next to Tim. "So, what brings you here? I know it's not just my company."

Tim laughed, taking a sip of beer. "I wanted to check on Anna, actually. She's under a lot of stress. I don't get down here that often, but she's one of my best friends. I'm sorry I missed her."

Aidan looked out over the water. "Well, surely you can see her in Virginia tomorrow, right?"

He shook his head. "I live in the Norfolk area. Not up in DC. It's not far, though. I'll catch her later."

Aidan wanted to ask him something. It had been pressing on his mind, but he didn't know how to bring it up. "You're curious about something. I can almost hear you thinking about it. What's on your mind? I may not answer, but if I can, I will."

Aidan sighed. "It's not right. I shouldn't go nosing about behind her back."

Tim put his prosthetic foot up on the ottoman. "She and I have been friends since we were teenagers. We were together for a very short time. It was a mistake. A very pleasant, beautiful mistake. We needed each other. We were both in a rough patch. There's nothing but friendship there now. Is that your concern?"

Aidan's body was tense. Christ, the guy was a straight shooter. That couldn't have been easy. "I appreciate your honesty. There's nothing like that happening with us. I don't know what's happening. I'm kind of screwed up about it, actually, but don't tell her I said that. I'm a short timer and I don't want to toy with her. I'm not what she needs." He shook his head, clearing it. "Anyway, that's not what I was wondering about."

Tim met his eye, "Then what?"

Aidan picked at his beer label. "Can you think of any reason she'd be afraid?"

Tim sat up. "What do you mean?"

Aidan met his eye. "I mean, she won't stay out here at night without a bat. Keeps the gun close when she's not in her bedroom. I mean afraid." He cursed under his breath. "I know the difference between cautious and scared."

Tim's eyes were unfocused, as if he was searching his mind.

"Does she have something in her past that would make her paranoid?" Tim's expression was all he needed to see. "What?"

Tim shook his head back and forth. "You need to talk to her about this. Seriously, bro. I like you. I think you are good for her. This is territory we can't cover, though. I can talk to her, see if she's got something she wants to tell me, but I think you should just come out with it."

Aidan scrubbed his face with his palm. "I tried. She's a tit for tat kind of girl, as she calls it."

Tim put his head back and laughed. "Yes she is. She's probably dying to crack into that head of yours. Well, my man, maybe you should let her. She's a good listener."

Aidan gave him a sideways glance. "I'm sure she is. Maybe I don't have anything to tell," Aidan said dismissively.

"Bullshit. She can sniff that shit out like a blood hound. Time to ante up." Tim got up slowly, finishing the rest of his beer. "You look like you need a nap, my friend. It was good to see you again. You tell Anna I asked after her, will you? And you are wrong."

Aidan stood up, too. "Oh, yeah? What exactly is it I'm wrong about, then?"

Tim put his bottle down. "I think you are exactly what she needs."

Aidan woke to his cell phone ringing. He'd squeezed in an hour nap. "O'Brien." He mumbled.

"Hello, son. How are you?"

Aidan sat up. "Da? Christ, it's good to hear your voice. Should I call you on the computer?"

Sean said, "No, lad. I hardly know how to work the damned thing. I just missed ye. Tell me how your training is going."

Aidan sat reclined in the living room and talked to his da for a long time. They talked about the training, the men. His da had been an inspector by the time he'd retired from An Garda Síochána. It had been a long, hard career. One that had led him to his mate and Aidan's mother. He was brave and strong, and knew the price that was called due for those traits. Strength and bravery often called a man to serve.

His knew about leading men as well. Now, he was reserve Garda. Only there if the need arises, but he understood Aidan like no other. Michael, too. Then there were Patrick and Tadgh, gone off to answer the call. That nagging call to serve, to guard, to protect. His heart squeezed tight at the thought of home and of his brothers.

He must have paused noticeably, because his da got right to the point. "Something is ailing you, lad. I can feel it. Tell me. Is it your woman?" Aidan shut his eyes and gripped the phone.

"She's not mine, Da." He was put out that his da could read him so well.

"Aye, I understand that. It's because you haven't made it so. But she's yours nonetheless. Ye've just not come to terms with it."

Aidan took a deep breath. "It's not that. She's just a friend. But she's dear to me, and I can't figure out what's amiss." Aidan told him. About the gun, the bat, the locked drawer in her desk. He told him about the feeling, deep in his bones. About the fierce independence, the things she kept from her father. Then he told him about the work she did. The men she helped and their families. He talked for a long time, painting a picture of this girl he'd become so entangled with.

"She's not one for theatrics, Da. She's more one to stifle it all. She reminds me of Branna in that regard. She hides her pain and her fear. I feel it though. I see it as plain as day."

Sean was silent for a time. Aidan knew his da. It was the sure sign that he needed a moment to think. "Ye need to gain her trust, yes? If you invade her privacy or push her, it will come to no good. She could turn on you for the betrayal. She must come to you on her own. She's got to trust you with the secrets she's gotten so good at keeping. I don't want to scare you lad, or upset you. It's just…" he paused.

"What, da?"

Sean sighed. "It's just that there are certain things that shame a woman. Shame her into silence. I'm not saying that's the case. It's just, I know from experience. It's certain things that make a woman pull back, hide things. Especially from the men in her life. You need to be careful. Do you understand what I'm saying?"

Aidan was gripping the phone, his throat thick with emotion. "I understand, da. It's what I've feared. I just, Christ…" his voice broke. "I don't want to make a mess of it. I want her to tell me, but I don't want to make a cock-up of this."

His father said nothing for a while. Finally he said, "The words will come to you, son. Whatever the case may be. It might not be all that you fear. You're a good lad, the best. You'll handle it well, whatever it is. I swear it. You're strong, and she'll find a way to tell you if you open the door."

Sean hung up with his eldest son, and he sat at the table in the kitchen, his mind busy with his thoughts.

"She's the one, isn't she?"

He looked up and his beautiful Sorcha was there in the doorway in her nightgown. She walked into the kitchen and went to him. "I don't know, mo chroí. I think she could be." He rubbed his neck.

"I didn't hear much, but the end. She's got some troubles, then? Is it the girl next door, wee Branna's friend?" she asked.

Sean shook his head. "Christ, Sorcha. She sounds too good to be true. She's working with the military men, helping them after the war. You know, with their mind. She's working in a PTSD clinic."

Sorcha put her hand to her mouth. "My beautiful, baby boy." She swallowed hard. "You all think I'm blind to it, and him my first born? He's come back time after time, more withdrawn than the last. He's hurting, and I can't do anything to ease him. If this girl's the answer, then by God, we need to push him along!"

Sean pulled her to him, opening his legs to pull her into the space between. "It's never easy for us is it? The O'Brien men just never come to it easy."

Sorcha smoothed back his sandy hair, peppered with silver. Even seated, he was big and she was small. "No, you don't. But you don't choose ordinary women."

He squeezed her hips. "True enough. I want it for them, though. All of them. I want this." Sorcha knew him so well, could read his body as well as her own. She bent down to his mouth and gave him what he needed. "I love you, a chuisle," he whispered against her mouth. "I love you."

17

Alanna was traveling from her second interview when her phone rang through the speaker system. "Hi Aidan, how's my beach?"

"It's grand all together. Clear and sunny. How were your interviews?"

She smiled. "They both went well. I may be cocky, but I think I have a shot. How's training?"

He laughed. "Well, I've become intimately acquainted with a family of ticks that seem to like the waistband of my knickers."

Alanna burst out laughing. "Welcome to the South. How's Maria and little Aidan Alann?"

"Oh, they're doing great. They came home last evening. I wanted to tell you that Tim stopped by to see you. I told him you'd be back Wednesday, so you may want to call him."

"Oh, really. Did you two hang out?" she said with a smile that he could hear.

"We had a beer, chatted a bit. I'm going to need in your house this week to do a little work. I want to get it done before your graduation."

"Awe, Aidan. Thanks. My mom is coming. She decided to leave the boyfriend at home. Daddy will stay with Erik."

Aidan thought about that. "That's a far drive from Cherry Point to Wilmington for the graduation. I've got a spare room if your da wants to stay with me."

Alanna paused, "That's very nice. I'll tell him you offered. I'm done with my interviews, so I may actually try to drive back tonight. I haven't decided yet."

"Don't drive if you're too tired, lass," Aidan said.

"I won't. I just have to work tomorrow. I have the last Daddy and Me class, and I don't want to be rushing tomorrow. I'll text you if I leave this evening, deal? I just want to avoid rush hour, so it might be a little later tonight."

As Aidan ended the call, his chest felt lighter. *Because ye missed her,* he thought to himself. And he had. Two days has seemed an eternity sitting on the deck, looking out at the sea. As hard as his training was, he'd busied himself with running on the beach, doing odd jobs in the evening, and reading. The little vixen had left her copy of *The Saxon's Bride* on his lounger with a note. *You know you're dying to read the rest. The good parts are marked.* So, God help him, he had read it. A completely historically inaccurate, predictable bodice ripper. But holy hell, the parts she'd marked. He did get the girl. Numerous times, in numerous places, and in great detail.

Aidan heard the car door close at ten o'clock. Alanna had texted him, telling him when she left Virginia. He walked down the stairs of the deck into the carpark. She was pulling her bag out of the back when she saw him. A smile broke out on her face. He was dressed in a loose hoodie and shorts and he looked just as beautiful as she remembered.

"Hello, neighbor." He took her bag from her and carried it to the door behind her. "I was worried, I wanted to see you home safe before I went to bed," he said simply.

"That's nice. I'm not used to having someone here to greet me." They went up the stairs to her living room where she threw her keys on the counter.

"I got your post, like you asked." Aidan pulled out a stack of mail from his hoodie pouch. He tossed it next to her keys and she saw the paperback.

She grinned and picked it up. "So, did you read the whole thing or just the juicy parts?"

He raised a brow. "How do you know I read it at all?"

She snorted. "I saw your face while you read the stable scene. You'd never be able to resist," she mocked.

"You are pure trouble, woman," he said.

She shrugged. "I'm just doing my part to support the troops. You might be missing some lady friend in Belfast. I'm willing to share my literary booty call."

He smiled, but it was calculating. "There's no one," he said simply.

She tried to keep it light. "That's right, you're the self-imposed bachelor. I know the type." He cocked his head, so she continued. "If the army wanted me to have a woman and children, they'd have issued me some." She said it in the same husky, mocking voice Maria had.

"You sound like Maria. You two don't know as much as you think." Alanna looked at him. His tone was stiffer.

"I'm sorry, Aidan. I shouldn't tease you. We all have our reasons for the way we live. It's none of my business." Her tone was apologetic, and he knew she meant it.

"Aye, I suppose if anyone understood, it would be you. You live the same way, don't you?"

She gave a noncommittal shrug. "No, not really. I'm not taking some bachelorette vow. I just..." she paused.

"You just what?"

She shook herself. "So, tell me about your training. What did you guys do this week?" He didn't answer her, so she met his gaze.

She growled under her breath. “We all have ghosts, Aidan. It isn’t important. Do you want something to drink?”

Aidan cleared his throat. “No, lass. Thank you. We’ve both got an early morning. I’ll leave you to your unpacking.”

Alanna gave him a casual smile, fiddling with her mail. “Ok, well, thank you for waiting up. Good night.”

He nodded and spoke softly. “Oíche mhaith, Alanna.”

Alanna woke with a gasp. She sat up in bed and her body was humming. She was flushed, her breath coming in short bursts. Another dream. It had been a couple of weeks since she’d had one, but that kiss had finally seeped into her subconscious mind. “Damn you, Aidan.” He hadn’t tried to kiss her again. That thought had plagued her as she’d tried to drift off. Obviously he’d had two days to regret it and rethink his actions. She sat on the edge of her bed, her body thrumming with arousal. She left her bedroom on shaky, bare feet and went to the kitchen for a drink.

The sound of the ocean called to her through the dark, and she went out, palming her bat on the way. She put it against the wall, near the sliding door as she walked to the deck. The night was warm, but there was a gorgeous breeze that cooled her flushed skin. She breathed deep, tilting her head to look at the stars.

“I missed you the most at this time of night.” Alanna started at the voice. “I’m sorry. I was just sitting here enjoying the stars and the night wind,” he said.

She turned to Aidan.”It’s okay. I just thought I was alone. You didn’t have the light on.”

He smiled in the moonlight. “Ye can’t see the stars as well.” He got up and came near her. She could see his face clearly now, with the stars and moon and light pollution from an overpopulated beach. His eyes narrowed. “Look at me.”

She did, and his body roared to life. Her eyes were hooded and her mouth was pink, the bright pink that he'd come to know.

"What are you looking at?" She said defensively, turning her eyes from his. He walked purposefully to the door and flipped the light on. He came back to her slowly, taking in her face and body.

"What woke you?" His eyes bore into hers, and she could not hold his gaze. *I will not have this conversation.*

"I don't know," she said.

He replied, "Try again, and the truth this time."

Her eyes darted to his. "Are you calling me a liar? Those are fighting words in the South," she said icily.

"Yes, I am. So fight me," he goaded.

She shrugged him off. "Don't be ridiculous."

He came closer and put his hand on her upper arm, squeezing intimately. She shuddered and pulled away from him. "You are very antsy, tonight. Anything in particular have you on edge?"

Yes, I had a steamy dream about you and woke up hovering on the edge of orgasm. Again. "No, I'm fine. What is this, twenty questions?"

"Was it a dream, or were you reading one of those books of yours?"

Her back stiffened and she met his eyes. "What are you talking about?" she snapped.

He stepped toward her again and this time he took her face in his hands. "Because you're aroused."

The breath shot out of her. She wriggled under his gaze. "You can't possibly know that!" she spat, a little too vehemently.

"Aye, I can. I've seen it before, and well you know it. Your cheeks are pink and your lips," he paused a moment, collecting himself. "They blush deep pink, like they're trying to draw my eye."

Her breaths started to come closer together. "I'm not talking about this with you," she said. She pulled away, irritated. Then she turned on him. "Do you get some sort of sick pleasure from teasing me? From knowing you can walk away without a second glance and leave me all breathless and glassy eyed? Well guess what, you cocky, smug, control freak! I choose! I choose who I let into my head. And until you walk it like you talk it, you don't get to hear any of it! Not my dreams, not what wakes me up all hot and bothered, and you don't get to kiss me like you did and act like it was nothing! You may have had a couple of days to think about what a mistake it was, rationalize it all as a lapse in discipline, but I'm on to you!" she hissed the last.

Then she marched up to him. "You want me! The only thing that allows my ego to get up in the morning is that you want me, too. I hope it makes you miserable. I hope you're sick with it!" She poked him in the chest when she said it. Then she spun around and retreated with Aidan sputtering on her heels.

He put a palm up as she attempted to slide the door shut. "God dammit, Alanna. Wait!"

She turned on him. Her eyes were blazing green, her face at a high flush, and he was on her before she could say another word. He towered over her as he pulled her to him. "You're right. I want you so badly it's driving me fucking crazy!" He kissed her, and when they came together they both cried out. He picked her up by the waist and walked to the counter, seating her face to face with him. "Tell me. Tell me what that dream was about."

She whimpered as he kissed her again. "You know," she croaked. She pulled at his shirt, first pushing him away, then pulling him closer. "Damn you," she whispered against his mouth. She closed her eyes and dropped her head. He leaned his mouth against the crown of her head as she spoke.

"This is a bad idea, Aidan. I shouldn't have said anything. You shouldn't have asked. We need to stop this before you find yourself tangled in a situation you don't want to be in. The initial thrill will be gone, and you'll be looking at your feet wondering where the exit is. I don't want to go through that." She slid off the counter, inching around him.

"It may be a bad idea, lass, but we seem to be failing at staying away from each other." He took her wrist and pulled her to him. He brushed her lip with his other thumb. "You make me lose all sense, mo chroi." Then he kissed her soft and sweet. She moaned lightly, and he deepened the kiss, molding her to his body. He broke the kiss, his voice guttural. "I can't get the taste of you out of my mind. Christ, I need this."

Alanna broke at the tone in Aidan's voice. The desperation, the pleading in his voice, it emboldened her. She went up on her toes and buried her hands in his hair, kissing him with all the desperation she felt herself, feeding off his own. He smoothed his hands down her body and cupped her ass, pulling her to him. He teased her mouth, pulling away, nibbling her lips until she was out of her mind, digging her nails into one shoulder. Then she felt his hand, bare skin to bare skin on her waist. Then to her back, beneath her shirt. She jerked at the contact.

"We need to go outside, lass." He practically growled it. She looked at him, her eyes unfocused and hooded.

"Outside?" she asked incredulously.

He swung her up into his arms. "If we don't go outside, I'm going to drag you in that bedroom. I can't be this close to a bed right now." He carried her out the sliding door, to the side of the house. He put her down, but he couldn't quit kissing her. "Hammock," was all he said. Then he laid down and pulled her to him.

Alanna squealed as she was pulled onto the hammock. All at once, she was touching Aidan everywhere. They were pressed together, her palms on his chest, his knee between her legs. She wasn't wearing much. A thin t-shirt and a pair of sleeping shorts that were loose and soft. He was dressed similarly. His legs had a dusting of sandy hair, and they were long and muscular. She could feel his erection against her hip and stomach. She hadn't had a lot of experience with men, but she knew he was big. The thought of it made her shiver.

"Are you cold?" he asked.

She shook her head. "No, it's just the feel of you."

He put his hands on her back, sliding them on her skin as he explored under the back of her shirt. "You're so beautiful, mo mhuirnín. Give me your mouth." She lowered herself slowly and hovered over his lips. She brushed hers lightly over his, and he shuddered. When he felt the brush of her tongue, he reared up and took her mouth hard, sliding his tongue deep. He pressed his knee up into the V of her thighs. She gasped, bucking against the invasion.

They were lost in each other, hands running over each other, deep kisses, desperate noises and warm skin. Aidan gathered her hair in his hands and titled her head back to meet her eyes. "I need to touch you. Let me finish you, darlin. I want to feel you finish. I won't ask for anything else."

He was looking her in the eye, so sure he could do what he offered. Willing to walk away with nothing for himself. She smoothed her hand over his face. "That's a generous offer, but I'm afraid I'd disappoint." She swallowed hard and pushed herself up.

Aidan sat up with her, holding her. "What do you mean, lass? Why would you think that?"

She blushed. "I don't..." she paused. "It doesn't matter." She put her head on his chest. "This is wonderful. You don't have to."

Aidan was still, too still. "Alanna, are you a virgin?" She shook her head and was silent. Then he heard a sniff.

"Please look at me. Why must you always hide your tears? I didn't mean to push you." She lifted her head and his heart broke. She was so composed. She could control everything but the tears that gathered and fell. "Please talk to me." His lust was corralled and the fire in his eyes had turned to tenderness. She pushed off him and sat up, hanging her legs over the edge. Then she hopped off the hammock.

"I'm sorry. I ruined this. It was perfect and I ruined it."

He took her wrist. "No, you're wrong. We're finally getting somewhere. Come sit with me. Sit with me and talk to me, please."

She lifted her chin. "Because you are so willing to share with me?"

He sighed. "It's not a competition."

She shrugged, "You're right. It's about trusting each other."

He removed himself from the hammock. He approached her and put his hand out. When she took it, he said, "I trust you, darlin'. I vow that I do. Come with me, please."

Aidan slid his glass door open and he walked Alanna through the house to his couch. "I swear, I'm not gonna jump on ye. I promise you can trust me."

She smiled at him sadly. "I never doubted that, Aidan."

He sat, hooking a leg in and letting the other hang. She sat next to him, tucking her feet under her body. Aidan pulled a stray wisp of hair from her face and smoothed it back. "So, that baseball bat that you brought outside with you tonight, it wasn't for me?"

Her brow furrowed. "No, God, no. I just..." she paused. "I like to have it nearby, when I'm alone at night."

Aidan adjusted himself, then he took her hand, bringing it up to his lips and kissing the back of it. Then he just held it, looking at her. "You say you're not a virgin, but you seem to..." he stuttered over his words. "You seem to pull back. To stifle yourself, to avoid men."

She sighed, blushing but fortifying herself for the conversation. "I know, Aidan. I'm afraid my comfort zone with this sort of stuff is rather narrow. I've only been intimate twice."

He cocked a brow. "You mean you've had two lovers?"

She nodded. "Yes, but that's not what I meant. I've known that level of intimacy with two men, but I also said what I meant. Two times. When I told you that I didn't want to disappoint, it was first hand knowledge. I've been with two men, and neither went well. There wasn't a repeat performance. I just steer clear now."

Aidan propped himself up on one hand. "I'm not trying to pry, lass. Well, aye, I suppose I am, but..."

She cut him off with a hand to his mouth. "The first time, I was eighteen. He was a little older. He pursued me when I was younger, and I didn't respond to him. I was sixteen and he was twenty, so I didn't take it seriously. Then, a couple of years later..." she swallowed hard, "my dad got shot and Brian died. I was sort of messed up. I wanted to feel something other than scared and sad. He paid attention to me. I thought he cared. I shouldn't have been with him. I was self absorbed and stupid."

Aidan stopped her. "You were young and in pain. Don't be so hard on yourself. It sounds like he took advantage of you at a weak moment," Aidan said with an edge to his voice.

She nodded, "I suppose that was part of it. Anyway, I let him take me out a couple of times. He was very charismatic. I…" she paused.

"Take your time, Alanna. You can tell me what you are ready to share." Aidan said softly.

"I gave him my virginity. I'd known him a while and thought he was something he wasn't. Let's just say it didn't go well." She exhaled.

"What do you mean? The first time for a woman is a bit rough."

She shook her head. "It wasn't that." She stiffened. "To put it plainly, he wasn't particularly gentle. He wasn't gentle at all, as a matter of fact, or patient. He barreled ahead despite my inexperience, and it was extremely unpleasant."

Aidan went still as the grave. His body strung tight as he spoke. "Did he rape you?"

She shook her head. "No, no Aidan. I consented. I swear it. He was just a bit brutal with the delivery. He wasn't careful or concerned that I might need something from him, a little tender guidance or understanding. It actually seemed to please him when I was in pain. When it was over, I cried. He told me that it wasn't his fault that I was uptight and frigid and didn't enjoy it. Then he drove me home, and I got out of the car and that was the end of the night."

She swallowed hard and was afraid to meet his gaze. She felt his finger under her chin. "That wasn't your fault, sweetheart. You know that, right? He was no man, and he took a gift and trampled it. The fault wasn't yours."

She smiled through unshed tears. "Thank you, Aidan. You're right. He was a grade-A asshole. He didn't deserve what I gave him, and I was stupid to think he did."

Aidan touched her face. "So, you never saw him again?"

Her jaw stiffened under his hand. "I did, once more. He showed up to my school the next week. I had an evening class at the community college. He was in his car and he pulled up as I came out from class. He begged me to let him apologize. He swore that he just wanted to talk and that he wanted to be friends. He said he was embarrassed about how he'd treated me. So, I got in the car with him. It wasn't until he pulled away that I smelled the alcohol on his breath."

Aidan's eyes were burning now, his body still. "I told him to let me out of the car, that he was scaring me, that he was drunk and shouldn't be driving. He wouldn't, and I couldn't figure out where he was going. He turned into an empty lot, behind a closed business. He started trying to kiss me. When I resisted, he got angry." She was shaking now, and Aidan squeezed her hand. "This time it wasn't consensual. He called me a whore and a tease and started tearing at my clothes. He busted my lip with his teeth." She closed her eyes.

"Did he rape you, Alanna?"

She opened her eyes. "He tried. I broke the prick's nose. I slammed the heel of my palm in his face and broke his nose. Then I grabbed my purse and ran out of the car. There were woods that skirted the empty lot. I ran into the woods, took my mace and my phone out of my purse and screamed that if he didn't leave, I would call the police." Her face was fierce. Aidan almost broke down with the sight of her. She exhaled. "He left. I called Branna. She came and got me. I hid until she came."

Aidan pulled her to him. "You're a strong, brave woman. If I could kill the bastard a thousand times over, I would. You got away, though. Jesus, what did your father do?" Her head was turned sideways, her face against his chest. She didn't answer. He exhaled on a curse. "Oh God, you never told him."

She croaked out her words. "I only told two people. I told Branna that night, and then a couple of years later I told Tim."

He rubbed her back. "And now me."

She stifled a sob. "Yes, and now you." She bore into his chest with her face.

They lay together for a long time, her settling as he petted her. "Tim, he was your second." It wasn't a question, because he knew she'd had some sort of connection to the man.

She pushed away from him so she could see his face. "Yes. He was my second. It was only once. He'd been recovering from being wounded. It had been a little over a year since he'd come home. We got together for a visit and started seeing more of each other. I told him what happened. We'd always been close. He was my best friend next to Branna. We turned to each other. Do you understand? And I don't regret it. It was a mistake because we were friends, but I don't regret it."

She searched her mind for the words to explain. Then she just smiled and her eyes misted. "He showed me that it didn't have to hurt. He was everything that Steve wasn't. He was tender and patient and loving. It just wasn't supposed to be that way with us, so it was the only time, and we were both okay with not going there again." She sighed. "So, now you know."

Aidan took her face in his hands and kissed her lightly on the mouth. "Thank you for trusting me."

She laughed a little, then. A nervous reflex. "I just didn't want you to think it was you. It's me that has the problem."

Aidan looked at her confused. "You've got no problem, girl."

She sat up and crossed her legs. "I do, Aidan. Steve might have been an asshole, but he was right about one thing. I can't…" She blushed.

He sat up. "What?"

She started to get up. "It's not important."

Aidan pulled her arm gently, keeping her in place. His voice was firm. "You are not a whore, or a tease, or frigid."

She closed her eyes. "You're wrong about one of those."

He ran his hand up her arm. "What are you saying? That you think you're frigid? Have you ever climaxed?"

She looked at him, defensiveness on her face. "Not with a man."

His brow went up. "With a woman, then?"

She choked on a laugh. "No!" Then her face turned as red as a tomato. "I mean, Aidan, that at twenty-five, I've learned to figure it out on my own."

He coughed, stifling a laugh. Then he fell back on the couch. "Holy God, woman. You want me to have a serious conversation with you and now all I can think about is you doing….that, and my mind's gone out the window!"

She slapped his chest. "I'm serious, Aidan. Oh, just forget I said anything." She pulled away from him and he caught her.

"Don't leave," he whispered behind her ear. His arms came around her waist. "Don't leave me," he said again. "Not yet." Then he turned her and kissed her. Her body came alive again. He kissed down her neck. She moaned his name.

"Christ, look at you. Within seconds you're right back to where I want you. There's not a fucking thing wrong with you, Alanna. I feel the heat in you, feel you rouse to me."

She met his eyes, arousal and need warring with the desire to flee. He took her hand and put it on his chest. "Feel me. Feel my heart. Feel what you do to me."

She stood silent for a moment, just feeling his heartbeat. "You make me feel things I didn't think I was capable of, Aidan. Things that make me feel like I may not be broken."

He pressed her into the wall. He had one palm laid flat above her head, one weaved into her hair and around the base of her head. "I need your mouth. Please, give me your mouth." She arched her neck and gave it to him, and his whole body shuddered as he kissed her slow and deep. Then he moved his hips and she felt the other things she did to him, a hard ridge against her hip. He lifted her, wrapping her legs around his waist. He rotated his hips, mimicking sex. Then she felt his hand on her bare thigh, inching closer to the leg of her shorts. She arched against him. She breathed against his mouth, looking at him as he slid his hand inward. When his thumb touch her panties, her hips jerked against him.

"Tell me to stop. If you don't, I won't stop until you're finished." She answered him with her mouth. She pulled his head to her and kissed him, pushing her hips to meet his. She wanted this. She wanted to see where he could take her, to see if there really was nothing wrong with her.

That's when he slipped his thumb beneath the cotton to touch her. Aidan groaned. "You're wet." He found the top of her sex, and her head fell back against the wall. Then he bent his head to her nipple. He suckled her through her shirt, and she whimpered as her hips started to move. He met her rocking with his own gentle grind, adding to his thumb's intensity as he glided it over her sensitive flesh. Her breaths became more ragged and shallow, her hips finding their own rhythm. His cock was pounding with need, but this was about her. Not him. He wouldn't leave this room until he'd made her come.

He changed to the other breast, so easy to feel her through the thin fabric of her night shirt. He lifted her knee, tilting her hips and then he slid his finger inside her, still working the top of her with his thumb. "Aidan!" She was out of her head. She was so close. He pulled up from her breasts and met her eyes. She stilled and concentrated on his face, his hand, her flesh.

"I dreamt of you, too. During the worst of my nightmares you came to me. Sweet and soft and wet, like you are now. And when you came for me, it was like heaven." He kissed her again as he explored her and he broke away and moaned. "Nothing prepared me for the real thing, though. You are utterly perfect."

Her eyes were hazy and hooded, and he slid his finger deep and worked her sensitive flesh intensely. He spoke to her as he looked deep in her eyes. "Let go, darlin'. I need you to let go." Her breath stuttered, and he felt her body grip him. The pleasure on her face nearly undid him as he saw her peak, the unfocused bliss as she moaned. He closed his mouth on her nipple again and she screamed, bucking against his hand and his hips. He eased in and out of her with a slow glide, letting her ride it out to completion as he whispered in her ear.

Alanna couldn't understand Aidan's words, but the guttural tone, the intensity, they were words of passion and praise. She rode out her climax until she was limp and exhausted. Then she felt his hand pull away and he hooked her legs tighter around his waist. She put her head against his chest and he rocked her as he whispered. She started to come to herself in slow degrees. She felt like someone had removed her bones, but she finally found the strength to lift her head. His face was sweet and his eyes were triumphant. "You did it, Aidan," she said, smiling.

"We did it," was all he said, then he closed his mouth over hers, giving her another skillful, lingering kiss. She uncurled herself as he walked into the bedroom and sat her on the bed.

"Stay with me. I'll not let you oversleep. Just stay with me, tonight." She answered by getting under the covers. He did the same on the other side.

"There'll be no living with you after this," she said with a wry look.

He laughed. "It's not about competition, it's about trust. Isn't that what you said?"

She shrugged, "Not in that context, but I suppose it fits just the same. And what about you? Do you trust me?"

He kissed her, sweetly. "I do. But that's for another night, a stór."

She nuzzled him. "You're never going to be able to sleep with that little problem you have under the covers." He caught her bottom lip, and a sigh escaped her.

"I'm fine, lass. And for future reference, never use the word little when you're talking about a man's cock."

She raised a brow, "Oh, I felt it well enough.You are right on that account."

Then he looked at her, his face serious. "Watching you come for me, feeling you let go, it was better than any orgasm I've ever had." Then his kiss was light and soft. "You need your sleep."

He felt her hands on him as she confidently pushed his words aside. She pulled his t-shirt over his head. Then her mouth was on his. He groaned against her mouth. Then she put her palm against his groin and his hips rolled, his cock hard against her hand. "I want to touch you," she whispered against his mouth. "Are you going to tell me no?" He hissed as she closed her hand through the fabric. "Little was definitely the wrong word. Let me see you, Aidan. Let me touch you like you did me. I want to watch you."

His feet kicked ferociously at the covers until they were at his feet. He looked at her, and she was smiling. "You like turning the tables, don't you," he said.

Her face was mild and sweet. "I like that I can make you feel so good. It's a powerful thing, watching you." She sat up and looked him over. "You're beautiful, Aidan," and then her hands were on him. She smoothed them over the wide expanse of his chest, then she grazed his nipple with her nail. He bowed off the bed. Her eyes flared. She bent down and ran a circle around his nipple with her tongue and he moaned. "Your hair, it's all around me. You smell like Jasmine." She flicked her tongue on his nipple just as she slid her hands inside his shorts, palming his erection. His whole body jerked. "Give me your mouth, lass. I need your mouth!" He pulled her up and took her mouth. She gave him her tongue just as she started moving her hand up and down his shaft. She broke the kiss and looked down, and a little moan escaped from her.

She sat up again, pulling the waist of his shorts down so that she could see the length of him. Then she started again. She looked at his body, straining. His abs were tight, his jaw clenched. "Am I doing this right? It's been a while. Tell me what you like."

He looked at her and his face was helpless. "You're doing just fine," he choked out. She felt emboldened. It had never been like this the other times. She loved his response, loved watching him. He was letting her be in complete control. She looked down and took her bottom lip in her teeth. Then she slid her hand down and cupped his testicles, gently palming them. She looked at his face again, curious to see the response. His neck was arched and his eyes were shut. "Alanna, I can't…" He moaned as she palmed him, then swept the length of him again, all the way to the tip. "I'm going to…" the next sounds were gurgled.

"Do it, Aidan. Let go." She whispered as she leaned in to kiss him. She intensified her stroking. He grabbed the back of her head and looked into her green eyes, and that did it. He barked out a shout as he pumped himself in her hand. She watched him in the thrall of his climax and it was exquisite. His orgasm spurting against his hard stomach, his magnificent erection kicking in her hand, it made her heart race. She kissed him as he rode out the final spasms.

Aidan felt like someone had pumped him full of paralytics. He couldn't even lift his head. "Holy God, woman. What have you done to me? First power yoga and now this. You'll be the death of me!" he said on a laugh.

She beamed. "We did it again."

He pulled her down for a kiss. "Aye, and I've made a mess."

She hopped up and went to the bathroom. He could hear her at the sink, readying a washcloth. She came back into the bedroom and sat next to him. She started to wipe his chest, his abs, and then his cock. He hissed at the contact. "Does this guy ever go down?" She joked.

He looked at her curiously. "I haven't had a lass do that to me since I was in school."

She smiled. "I suppose you're used to moving a little faster, going right for the gold."

He took her wrist. "It was amazing. Watching you explore my body, seeing your face as you watched me. It's one of the most erotic things I've ever experienced. Don't sell it short."

She blushed and went back to the bathroom, rinsing the cloth and then returning. "Now we'll both sleep," she said. Then she curled next to him. "Thank you, Aidan."

He stroked her hair. "For what?"

She looked up at him. "For showing me that I wasn't broken."

He kissed her head. "You were never broken. When you were with Tim..." he swallowed, surprised that he was willing to talk about her ex while she lay in his arms. "It was tender and it was loving. He was your friend. This..." he motioned between them. "This was passion. It's a different thing all together. I'm honored that you trusted me like this. That you gave yourself over to me and let me do the same."

She kissed his chest. "I don't expect anything from you, Aidan. Don't worry about that, okay?" He tried to speak and she stopped him, propping up on an elbow. "I know you're leaving. I won't expect anything other than the right now, however long that is. Our lives will separate in two months. It's the reality. Let's just enjoy our time now. If you want tonight to be the end of the hanky panky, I'll understand."

Aidan laughed, "Hanky panky?"

She smiled. "You have your dialects, we have ours."

He touched her cheek, then he ran a thumb over her mouth. "I couldn't bear it if this was the last time I touched you or kissed you." He covered her mouth and they both melted. He rolled her on her back and she slid her hands in his hair.

He broke the kiss. "We can't. We can't start this again. It's already four o'clock."

She was panting. "I know."

He pulled her over his chest, nestling her under his chin. "You'll be the death of me. Jesus Christ, ye'll be the death of me."

18

Aidan slowly came awake as the sun came through the window. His nose was filled with Jasmine and the delicate, feminine scent that was uniquely Alanna. "Beautiful falcon," he whispered in her hair. She was spooned against him, wrapped in his arms. His hands moved over her as he smelled her hair, kissed her temple. She stirred as he slipped his hand into her bottoms, touching her where he'd been last night. She arched and her bottom eased against him.

"Aidan, oh God." He soothed her with his soft tones, murmuring Gaelic endearments as he skillfully brought her to the ceiling. The sounds she was making were making him crazed. He wanted desperately to push inside her from behind, come deep inside her. "Come for me, mo rúnsearc. Come for me, again." He closed his teeth on the tendon that ran from her neck, just enough to taste her. She cried out, quaking and spasming against his hand. He tended to her until she had nothing left to give. She was shaking and panting.

Her voice was strained. "That's quite an alarm clock." He barked out a laugh. Then she stretched herself in his arms. "Did you sleep okay?" She said.

He kissed her hair. "Aye, I did. I slept peacefully, which isn't usual."

She turned in his arms. "So did I. No steamy dreams."

She was grinning, and he laughed again with mischief in his eyes. He rolled on top of her. "Aye, that's because you got the real thing." Then with a crooked grin he said, "It might not have been the stable door, but it was flesh and blood."

She looked up at him, her bright green eyes sparkling. "It was better than the stable door."

He leaned down and kissed her, feeling the need coil between them again. Then he rested his forehead to hers. "We've got to go to work, love," he said.

She groaned. "I know. It's my last group session this afternoon." Aidan was kissing her neck, starting to press against her.

"Do you think Luke will show?"

She popped her head up. "I never told you it was Luke who was the problem child."

He shrugged. "It wasn't that hard to figure it out."

She sighed. "He said he would stay sober and come, but he's said it before."

Aidan nodded, "I understand. Do you want me to try and make it, in case the mum has two babes and no partner?"

She brightened. "Would you?"

He thought about it. "I can try. I'm not sure how late we'll go today, but I promise to try. If he comes, I'll just duck out."

"Thank you for offering, even if you don't end up being able to come. It means a lot that you'll try." Aidan was nuzzling her cleavage, not helping the situation at all. He came up to her and took her mouth again, pinning her hands as he intertwined their fingers. She wrapped her legs around him instinctively. The alarm clock started blaring, and it shook them out of the direction that they'd been heading. "I'll get ready next door at my own place," she said, smiling against his mouth.

"Aye, smart girl."

"Why do we have to take all of these stupid classes? I'd rather just do it. Can't we go in the field?" Aidan laughed to himself. Sergeant Porter, or Jimmy to his peers, put him in mind of Liam. He liked to have fun, was a more hands on guy. Liam was smart enough to go to med school, but wanted to skip the books and go right to the scalpel and gore. Porter wasn't stupid, either. He was their comm guy and was damn handy with electronics. He just didn't like to be inactive. He was young and had the attention span of a twelve year old when it came to long spans in the classroom. He was like an older puppy that had grown into a big, adult body, but still wanted to play all the time.

Hector had a paternal tone with him. "First we read, write, and discuss. We learn, then we practice the shit in the field. Pay attention. This shit could save your life. We also have to teach this shit to the Afghanis." *Shit* being Major Diaz's preferred noun for any situation.

Their week was filled with training, maneuvers, and IED avoidance and detection. EOD expert Master Gunnery Sergeant Stowe had come in to lecture them on detection, the *keep your fucking hands off* and *get your ass clear until we get there* being stressed repeatedly. Then the horror flick started. IED aftermath footage, wounded men, blood splatter, civilian casualties. By the end of the happy little powerpoint, Aidan had broken out in a sweat and his head was throbbing.

They were released for lunch and Hector came beside him, throwing an arm over his shoulder. "How you holdin' up, Irish?"

Aidan shrugged. "Just fine, sir. Why do you ask?"

Hector looked like he was about to say something, then bit it back, then he stopped in his tracks and looked at Aidan. "I've read your file. All of the highlights. I also spoke to your CO."

Aidan stopped with him. He didn't look at him at first. "Aye," then he made eye contact. "Your point, sir?"

Hector shook his head. "Yeah, I get it. You wanna play hard ass with me, I get it. I can tell you that watching this shit gets under my skin. A lot. I've learned to deal with it, do what needs doing, but I ain't gonna say it doesn't get to me. You see as much combat as we have, it starts to take a toll." Aidan stiffened. "Yeah, yeah. I know. You're fine. I'm just saying I get it. I watched one friend get shot and pull another friend out of the shit. Watched him rock him in his arms while he died. That shit doesn't wipe off all the way. It leaves a big, fucking stain as a matter of fact. You need someone to talk to, I got you, brother." He patted Aidan on the back. "Now, all this feel good is making me hungry. How about we go see my bride about some lunch?"

Aidan drove in Hector's SUV and was impressed as he pulled up to an old breakfront colonial with a view of the river. "Well, this is grand enough, isn't it Major? I thought Denario's place was nice, but this view is gorgeous all together." Hector smiled.

"Yeah, your view ain't so bad either, Captain. How are the beach renovations going? You need any help?"

Aidan shook his head. "No, it's not so bad. I did the deck this past weekend. That was the big outdoor job. Both sides. Now it's just the interior in my place and a bit of work on Alanna's side, leaky faucets and the like." Hector was taking his boots off in the doorway and Aidan did the same. There were slippers by the door and they both put them on.

"Sorry, Japanese household. No shoes allowed." Hector said.

"Not at all. I think I like it. I may have to get some guest slippers and try this in my flat." Then Aidan stopped. "Good Christ, what smells so bloody good?" As they walked into the kitchen, Hatsu was busy with a small table top charcoal grill type contraption. She was putting paper thin pieces of marinated beef on the grate that was set over the coals. The meat sizzled. She also had a broth and noodle pot with vegetables simmering. A knock from behind them had Hatsu bowing her head slightly and going past them to the door. Hector assumed the grill duties until she returned, and she wasn't alone.

"Maria, baby! How are you? How's our little devil pup?" Maria kissed him and then turned to Aidan.

"Hello, handsome. How is training going?" Aidan took her diaper bag and made small talk until she sat down, obviously exhausted. There was an island with stools in the middle of the kitchen. There was also a window that overlooked the backyard.

The baby started to fuss as soon as Maria sat down. "Give me the lad and take your rest. Where are the others?"

Maria sighed as she sat unencumbered. "They're with my mom. She's been a Godsend."

Aidan walked around the kitchen, mumbling to baby Aidan as he investigated the contents of Hatsu's pots. "Do you cook like this all the time, Hatsu? It smells heavenly."

Hatsu gave a meek smile. "I am better with Japanese food. My mother taught me many years ago. I try to bring back Japanese cooking tools every time I visit my parents."

The baby let out a big yawn and started trying to kick out of it's swaddling. "He's strong. I think he will be brave and worry his mother." Hatsu was looking from the baby to Aidan. "And he has a strong name. You are good with children, Aidan. I think you will be a very good father." Aidan wasn't sure what to say to that, so he said nothing.

Hector watched Aidan interact with the women and hold the baby that was named for him. He was one of them, already. He just was. It was going to be hard to let him go. A little part of Hector wanted to see the guy with Hans's daughter. She was a beautiful soul, and God knows, it would do Aidan some good to have the love of a good woman. Out of the blue he asked, "Maria, John never told me how you two met. What's the story?"

Maria grinned. "On the subway from Newark to Manhattan. He was there for Fleet Week. I worked downtown at a big metro hospital." Everyone stopped to listen. Even Hatsu had an ear perked over her cooking. "Some jackass was giving me a hard time on the train. You know the type. Standing too close, leering looks, innuendo. So, I told him to piss off."

Aidan choked on the tea Hatsu had poured for him. "What? You think I was always this sweet? Anyway, I'm hanging on to the overhead bar, keeping my pocketbook tucked in, and here comes John. Fresh out of training and looking all hard-ass fine in his uniform."

Her New Jersey accent got thicker as she talked. "He came over, asked the guy sitting on the bench near me if he could make room for one more. The guy scoots over, and John motions for me to sit. I give him my best prickly look, like I can take care of myself. He gives me one back that says, *don't be a pain in the ass.* So, I sat," she shrugged. "Like I said, he was looking fine. Then he takes my spot on the bar and faces the creep. Stares at him. You know, like he wants to eat his lunch. The guy's all *what's your problem bro? You think that uniform makes you tough?* and John is still staring. Not a word. So finally the guy shoves him. Bingo. He pops the guy in the mouth right at my stop, and waltzes off the train behind me.The dude is screaming like a girl as the doors shut. Then he just nods and tells me to have a good day. Calls me ma'am, for God's sake."

Hector's shaking his head laughing. "And did you? Have a good day?"

She laughs. "Oh, yeah. Very good. I offered to buy him a coffee, which he ended up paying for. We get to talking and figure out we grew up two neighborhoods away from each other. Coffee turned into dinner after work, and that turned into three kids and a house on base. What about you and Hatsu? She said you met in Oki, but she was light on the details," Maria said with a mischievous look at Hatsu.

"Well, she probably told you that her father ran a shop outside the base. Tailoring and seamstress work. I needed some patches sewn on, and everyone said that was the best place to go," Hector explained.

Aidan interrupted. "Are you a seamstress, Hatsu?"

She shook her head. "No. I was the bookkeeper. I have an affinity for numbers. I rarely came from the office to the front of the shop. I parked behind the shop. My father liked it that way. He didn't want the sailors and Marines that came into our shop to see me."

Hector laughed huskily. "Smart man. You should have seen her. She had this polka dot dress on, a little pink sweater, strappy sandals. Her hair was longer, almost to her waist and she had these little clips in her hair. I was struck stupid as soon as I saw her."

Hatsu laughed lightly. "He kept coming into the shop, needing buttons sewn, repairs."

She gave her husband a knowing look, then Maria broke in. "Let me guess, you were pulling buttons off and tearing your shirts just for an excuse to go back in."

Hector pointed at her. "Exactly. I had a signal, you see, since she worked in the back." Then he whistled the first bar of Dixieland. He went behind his wife, putting his hands on her waist. He kissed her temple.

"Then I stole her out from under her daddy's watchful eye, and we eloped." He looked at Aidan. "Kind of a dick move, but I was young. Some asshole does that with my daughter, I'll whoop his ass."

Aidan lifted a brow, "And did her da forgive you?"

Hector shrugged. "Yes, her mother smoothed the ruffled feathers, got us all on speaking terms, then you add a grandkid and all was forgiven."

"So what about you, Irishman? How did you come to be living next door to the Sergeant Major's daughter?" Hector wiggled his brows.

Aidan saw where this was going. "Oh, we're not. I mean, she's not..."

Hector held up a hand. "Maybe not, but you don't have a wife and I see the way you look at her, so tell us a story."

Hatsu took the lunch to the table in the dining room and they all sat, serving each other and eating as Aidan told the story. Not his, but the story of Branna and Michael. By the end, the women were swooning. "That is the most romantic story I've ever heard," Hatsu said softly.

Maria had known part of it, but never the whole story. "Wow, that is something special. That's a love that will last. And that's how you met Alanna? She slammed the door in your face, huh? Sounds like you like 'em feisty."

Aidan gave her a chiding look. "Don't start, hen."

She shrugged innocently. "I'm just saying, she's quite a girl. You say that the O'Brien men have one mate. Did you ever think…"

He cut her off. "I'm leaving, Maria. She's got some great career opportunities ahead. We're just friends."

She let out a hard breath. "Party pooper."

The food was amazing. Simple, light, and flavorful. As they were headed back to work, Aidan remembered what he needed to ask Hector. "What time are we done today?"

Hector shrugged. "We won't go late today, you got plans?"

Aidan felt a blush coming on him. He explained about Alanna's family session. "You go on ahead. If you cut out at 15:45 you should make it. We're not doing anything ground breaking in that last hour."

"Thank you sir. It's her last one and I'd like to be there in case she has a no show."

Hector thought about it. "She sounds like she's doing some good work. Lotta young guys coming home with those kind of issues. Hans must be really proud."

"I'd imagine he is," Aidan answered. Then they drove to the training area to resume the classwork.

Alanna was watching the clock, preparing the therapy room for the party. She'd gone to a dollar store and bought them out of fairy wings and knight helmets. She had her iPod dock set up with the usual play list. Jack Johnson, Kidz Bop, and her personal favorite that was the final song. She borrowed a disco light from the Morale, Welfare, and Recreation department on base. Just as she finished setting up, the families started pouring in. One man was in a wheel chair, one had a prosthetic below the knee. The rest were TBI patients. Her heart sank when she saw Jessica come in with their two little ones and no Luke. She gave Alanna a sad smile and a shrug. Alanna walked over to them and gave Jessica a hug. "I'm sorry, sweetie. We tried." She whispered it so that the children didn't hear it. They started running around with the other kids, just happy to be there.

Alanna texted Aidan. *Luke is a no show.* Aidan returned her text. *I just pulled into the car lot. Be right in.* She exhaled. "Jessica, if you don't mind, my friend Aidan is going to fill in and help you with the kids."

Jessica smiled, "He doesn't have to do that. They know the difference."

Alanna rubbed her back. "But it will help you, and that's why he's doing it. You can take your son, and he will take your daughter. Then you aren't trying to juggle them both."

The woman shook her head. "Thank you. I'm not sure how much longer I can take this, Anna." Just then Aidan approached, looking handsome and smiling. Jessica continued, "He made it to the parking lot. He just picked a fight with me on the way here over nothing, said his head hurt, and stayed in the car. He's on his phone. Honestly, I'm not sure the texting isn't to another woman. I just don't know anymore. You'd think he'd do it for the kids, but he just shut down and stared out the window."

At this point, Aidan interrupted. "What does your car look like?"

Jessica answered, "Red Jeep Liberty. We're parked on the south side."

Aidan nodded. "Okay. I'll be right back." Aidan walked out with both women calling after him. He just waved dismissively and walked out.

"Okay! Looks like everyone is here! How about we get this party started. You daddies haven't forgotten how to have a good time have you?"

All the kids yelled "YES!"

Alanna put her hands on her hips. "What? You mean to tell me that they've lost their dance moves?" All the kids yelled again. "Yes!" while the dad's yelled, "NO WAY!"

Rogers was the loudest. He started doing the cabbage patch. "I got my eighties moves!" Which made everyone start laughing and his wife and kids hide their faces.

"Ok dads. I understand that some of you have some physical challenges, but where there's a will, there's a way! Right?" Alanna watched as the staff sergeant in the wheel chair lifted his toddler in the air. The other child stood on his foot rests while mom steered from behind. She started the music and picked up Luke and Jessica's little girl to dance.

Aidan saw the Jeep and headed over to the passenger window. Luke Jones was looking at his phone, a sullen expression on his face. He looked up as Aidan approached. "You're late for your date, brother." He leaned on the door. "Need an escort?"

The Marine bristled. "I'm not going. It's a stupid waste of time. How the fuck is dancing going to help me?"

Aidan leaned in. "It's not just for you, Sergeant. It's for your children. They want you to play with them. Your wife wants you to have fun with the family that you've made together. Surely that's not too much to ask."

The guy gave him a shitty look. "Do you have kids? I don't see a ring. Are you even married?" Aidan shook his head, slowly. "Well, then don't lecture me, Paddy! You don't know shit."

Aidan ground his teeth. This guy was pissing him off. He spoke steadily, keeping his temper in check. "I don't need to have a wife and kids to see when someone is fucking it up, Jonesy. How about you just come in, humor your kids, make them smile. What are you losing by doing that?" The man ignored him. "Fine, you know what, forget it. Just remember this warning. You opt out on the wife and kids, she will eventually find someone who will take care of them. So, you sit here and pout like a little bitch. I'll go play with your kids. That's why I'm here. I was the stand by in case you didn't show up. Tis a pity they had to make arrangements ahead of time, aye? Maybe I'll swing your wife around the dance floor, while I'm at it. The lass seems a bit lonely."

Aidan turned his back just as the car door came open. Bingo. He turned back quickly as the guy got in his face. "You don't fucking touch her, you got it?"

Aidan smiled. "You don't like that idea do you? Well, maybe you need to nut up and show your wife she still has a partner." Then he walked back in the building without a second glance.

Alanna saw Aidan walk in alone and wanted to cry. He jumped into the fray and played with the little girl's pigtail. "What's your name, love?"

She smiled. "Kylie. I'm four!"

Aidan gave a surprised look. "Only four? I thought you were five! Aren't you a pretty thing? Would you like to be my partner, Kylie?" She nodded and Alanna handed her over.

"Thank you," she mouthed. "Okay everyone, wave your wands, and boys, wave your swords!" The kids all obeyed as a Disney song came on. Some of the little girls were singing along. She looked at Aidan, and the little girl was standing on his feet, holding hands with him. He was smiling down at her and singing to her. She noticed that Jessica was watching them too, with tears in her eyes. Then the door opened and they all looked to see who it was.

Aidan swept the little girl into his arms so she could pretend she was flying to her daddy. Luke caught her and she squeezed his neck with her chubby little arms. "Daddy!".

Alanna put her hand over her mouth and she looked at Jessica who was smiling through unshed tears. Jessica walked over with their son and joined them. Luke was awkward at first. He was obviously out of practice. Aidan came up to her and she asked, "What did you say to him?"

He shrugged. "Man talk. I just reminded him of what he had to lose. I didn't think it helped."

She rubbed his arm. "Obviously it did."

Behind them, the doctor's voice interrupted. "You two are quite a team. Glad to see that everyone is here."

Alanna was radiant. "Me too. I'm going to miss this place."

The doctor looked at her sadly. "We'll miss you. I do have some good news. Our Virginia office just advised me that they are calling you for a second interview. You made the first cut."

Alanna squealed, "That's great news!" She looked at Aidan. "A second interview."

"I never doubted it, lass. They'd be lucky to have you."

The doctor agreed, "Now, why don't you take my intern out on the dance floor and show them how it's done?" Aidan took Alanna's hand and pulled her into the group of kids and parents.

Two Disney songs, one chicken dance, and three Kidz Bops songs later, Aidan had two kids clinging to his legs and one on his shoulders. Alanna was laughing as she took the one off his neck and handed him back to his dad. "Do you rent him out for parties?" one mom asked.

Alanna laughed. "He sings too. You might be on to something." Alanna was dancing with Rachel and Mike's eleven month old, as he swung his wife around the room. His older daughter danced with their other daughter.

Aidan watched from across the room as she swayed with the baby on her hip. Then he looked at the Jones family. They each had a kid on their hip. Their spare arms were entwined and their foreheads were pressed together. It made him happy to see.

Alanna started jumping up and down at the last song. So did all of the kids. *Happy* by Pharrell Williams was playing and she started marching around, singing to all of the kids and dancing with them all. Even the little baby that belonged to Mike Rogers and his wife was touching her face and hair as she sang to it, giving her a toothy grin. Everyone was smiling and happy.

Christ, woman. You're a saint, Aidan thought, as he watched her, witnessed her unique way of connecting with these wounded vets and the families. His heart broke a little as he watched the man with a prosthetic awkwardly dance with his kids. The wheelchair bound man was spinning his chair in circles with a squealing child on his lap. He was having fun, so were the kids.

"You need to practice what you preach, Irish." Aidan turned to find Luke watching him. "You like her, our therapist."

Aidan shrugged. "I'm gone in two months. It's the reality."

Luke paused, choosing his words. "She's a good girl. She tries real hard. She doesn't know how to give up on people." Aidan just nodded. "I, uh, wanted to say thanks for lighting a fire under my ass out there. I was on a self pity roll. You didn't coddle me. As much as I hated it, I like it better than the coddling." He motioned to his wife. "She's too good for me. She tolerates a lot of bullshit, and I'm honestly not sure why she even bothers."

Aidan looked at her and then at him. "Because she loves you, ye daft jackass. She loves you."

Luke snorted. "She shouldn't. She'd be better off with someone who handles shit better. Someone like you."

Aidan lifted a shoulder. "I don't always. Sometimes it backs up on me. I just don't have a family to burden with what's in my head. Maybe that makes me a coward."

Luke thought about that. "Maybe. I just..." he paused. "I just wanted to say thanks. This made my kids happy, and I haven't been real good at that lately. I'm glad we had this." He left without another word.

Aidan helped Alanna clean up. "I have to stay and write up some stuff. Then I'll be home. I turn my thesis in tomorrow afternoon, so I'll be finishing up the conclusions tonight."

Aidan smoothed his hand over her hair. "I'll stay out of your hair tonight and let you work. You just let me know if you need me, aye?"

"Aye," she said with a smile. Just as Aidan was about to kiss her, the door opened.

"Hey Alanna, Captain O'Brien. How did the session go?"

Alanna stiffened. "Hello Rick. Very well, actually." Aidan was also tense, giving Richard the Counselor the once over.

He leaned in and kissed her head. "I'll see you at home." Then he walked past Richard without acknowledging him. Rick's brows shot up. He stuttered over his words. "I was wondering how the interviews went. You free tonight? Or do you need to get home?"

Alanna cringed internally, the unasked question sitting between them. "I have to finish my thesis tonight. I'm not free. As for the interviews, they went well." She didn't expand, even though she knew he wanted her to. "Okay, I'm all done here. I have some work to do at my desk and then I'm headed out. Nice to see you Rick." She led him out the door of the therapy room and shut the light off.

19

Alanna woke up stiff and exhausted. She worked until two o'clock. Her thesis and case studies were done. *Holy shit, Falk. You are done. You are actually done.* She poured herself a cup of coffee and walked out on the deck to find Aidan sipping tea and looking out at the water. He turned and set his tea down. Then he took her coffee and set it next to his cup. He gathered her in his arms. "You're done. You did it," he whispered.

"I did it. Seven years, and I'm done. All I have to do is send in the paper electronically and take the certification test next month. I'm really done." The relief in her voice was palpable.

Aidan pulled away from her just enough to look at her face. "Graduation on Monday?"

She nodded. "Yep, my parents come in Sunday evening. I'm making dinner. I'd like you to come over. I know you can't come to the ceremony, but come over after, okay?"

Aidan kissed her then. Long and slow. It spiraled into heat and lust as he put one arm around her waist, one hand at the back of her head. He pulled her off her feet, desperate to bring them closer, to feel her whole body. "I missed you last night." He said, breaking the kiss for a moment.

"I missed you, too, Aidan. God, I missed you." Aidan set her down, but his mouth was relentless. He ran his hand up her side, from her waist to her ribs, stroking her with his thumb. She moaned when his thumb stroked the under side of her breast.

"I want to see you tonight," he said against her mouth. Then he pulled away. He looked at her mouth. "Pink, your lips get deep pink. That's when I know I'm getting to you."

Alanna looked down at the heavy bulge in his shorts. "You're a little easier to read." She had a brow up, and he pulled her to him.

"You are a naughty, little bookworm." His tone was playful and his accent was heavy. She could feel the heat and the hardness of him. "Have a good day, love."

"What are you doing today?"

Aidan pulled away and handed her coffee back to her. "Convoy training. Yesterday was classroom stuff. The rest of this week and next week is in the field. Once at night, which should be fun."

"Okay, then. Just be careful. Training accidents happen all the time."

He picked up his tea. "I always am."

Aidan and his ten teammates had a grand time tearing through the training area, learning the finer nuances of operating the MRAP. The area they focused on all day was passing under and over bridges. The training areas were superb. Aidan was thoroughly impressed with the mock up scenarios and physical areas they'd built up for training with different vehicles. He knew there was an area called Combat Town that they would train in later. Convoys, yes, but also urban warfare, clearing buildings.

He loved this shit. He was good at it too. He was hot, though. It was June in the South, and the heat was starting to climb everyday. The equipment was heavy and cumbersome, and he was soaked to his knickers in sweat. All he could think about was getting in that cool ocean when he got back to the house. When he said so, his lieutenant perked up. "That's right, sir. You have a beach house. When's the team party?"

Aidan laughed. "I can definitely do that. The water's getting warmer, the tourists are starting to show up. You can bikini watch from my deck."

Porter let out a whoop. "Now yer talkin'!"

Aidan was sitting on a picnic table outside one of the training buildings, hydrating and covering the next day's schedule with his team when his phone rang. He looked at the number and didn't recognize it. "Captain O'Brien," he said.

"Christ, thank God you picked up."

Aidan stood. "Hans? What's wrong?"

Hector and John stood as well. "You need to go to Alanna. As soon as you can. Her office called me. One of the Marines from her therapy sessions shot himself in the middle of the night."

Aidan cursed. "Jesus Christ. Is she still at the clinic? Which man? Do you know who?" But Aidan already knew. In his gut he knew. He thought of that sad woman, the two small children, and the bile rose up in his throat.

"I don't know. They wouldn't say. All I know is that this is going to hit her hard. She left the clinic. They said she was pale but calm. That is not good news, Aidan. Do you understand me?"

Aidan did. "The calm before the storm blows in, aye. It's not good."

Hans sighed heavily over the phone. "I can't get there for several hours. Optimistically, I can be there by two in the morning. I need you, Aidan. I can't get ahold of her brother. He's in the air and honestly, he's not Mr. Sensitive. Her friend Izzy is deployed, and Tim is up here doing some Wounded Warrior run. He's no closer. You are my boots on the ground. Can you go to her? Now?"

Aidan looked at Hector. "Whatever you need to do, brother. We're done here for the day."

After Aidan hung up, he filled Diaz, Drake and Denario in on the situation. The rest of the men were either inside or headed home.

"Any idea who it is?" John said.

"I don't know for sure, so I hate to speculate. I'll have more details tomorrow," Aidan answered. He got in the truck with his gear and put his phone on speaker, calling Alanna's cell. It went straight to voice mail. Aidan disconnected and banged the steering wheel, cursing every obscenity he knew in Gaelic and English.

Aidan pulled into the beach house, relieved to see Alanna's vehicle. He rang the doorbell, but she didn't come to the door. He tried it and it was locked. He ran up the deck on her side, past the hammock to come to the beach side of the house. That's when he heard the smashing. He also heard angry sobs, like a wounded animal. He checked the slider, glad to find it unlocked. He stopped in his tracks at the scene before him. Piles of ripped notebooks, text books. She had something framed lifted over her head. She smashed it to the floor, glass cracking and bits of frame splitting. He quickly went to her, holding her arms to her sides.

"Let me go!" Her voice was shrill with anger and sorrow.

"Please, darlin. Oh, Christ. I'm so sorry, lass. Please, let me hold you. Shhh." He spoke in gentle tones, his mouth to her ear.

"All this work meant nothing! You don't understand!" Aidan eased them away from the broken glass, sitting on the couch and bringing her with him. She was hyperventilating, wracked with sobs. She struggled against him, growling like an angry child. "It was all for nothing! Seven years of nothing! I'm nothing!" All he could do was hold her. Let her scream her head off, struggle, and exhaust herself, as she railed against his efforts to soothe her.

He whispered to her, both in Gaelic and in English until she began to settle. It was inevitable. The level of fury and anguish couldn't be maintained and would sap her strength as surely as a sedative. Soon enough she began to tremble, hiccuping and whimpering in his arms. He finally loosened his grip, turning her around to cradle in his lap. He rocked her, covering her head and temple with soft kisses, murmuring to her. She put her arms around his neck and wept.

It took a long time before Aidan felt comfortable talking to her. She was raw and angry and sad. She was also riddled with misplaced guilt. Finally he asked. "Was it Luke?" She said nothing, only nodded. "I'm so sorry. Sweetheart, you did everything you could. He was happy when he left. I saw it. He was as happy as a man like him was capable of."

She sniffled. "He was taken off of training and out of a deployment cycle because of his minor TBI. He had to go through the program before they let him join his unit again. He got replaced on a transition team. He wasn't handling it well. He felt guilty. He had nightmares, terrible nightmares. Headaches, insomnia, combat stress. He was Dr. Jennings' patient, but he was mine, too. We failed him. We failed his family." Her voice broke, and she put her hand over her eyes.

"Don't hide your tears, darlin'." He took her hand away and tilted her head up to meet his gaze. "You did everything you could. He was in pain, and he was pushing his family away. You did everything you could. Sometimes it's not enough, no matter how much you try. What he did was selfish, and his family will suffer in his absence. This was not your fault."

Her eyes overflowed with tears, her cheeks flushed and wet. "He wouldn't talk to her, to me, or to his doctor. He wouldn't get it out. It was poisoning him, and I couldn't figure out how to get it out of him. Seven years of study, and I couldn't get him to talk to me."

Aidan hugged her, not sure what to say. She got up from his lap, wiping her face. She looked at the mess she'd made. "I suppose I should get a broom."

"Make some tea, love. Let me do it," Aidan said as he stood up from the couch. Alanna went to the kitchen, grabbed the broom and dust pan and the trash bin and handed it over. Then she started the kettle. Aidan looked at what she had destroyed. School books on counseling, her notebooks, her framed diploma when she'd received her bachelor degree. He salvaged what he could and put the rest in the bin.

Alanna looked out over the setting sun, tea cup in her hand. "I'm sorry, Aidan." He looked up from his laptop. He was sitting on a lounger, reclined in the evening sun. He had decided to give her some physical space while staying within reach.

"For what?"

She took a sip, not meeting his eye. "I'm sorry you had to deal with that display. You didn't sign up for babysitting when you rented the house. I'm sorry you had to see me like that."

Aidan got up and walked to the deck rail, closing in behind her. "You're more than a neighbor to me. You know that. Your father knows it too. It's why he called me."

She leaned back against him. "I figured that's how you found out. He's on his way," she said.

"I'll stay with you until he's here, if that's all right with you."

She gave him a sideways glance. "Afraid I'll destroy some more property?"

He pressed his cheek to hers. "No. I just want to hold you. I want to help."

She turned her head and accepted a lingering kiss. "I'd like that." Then she looked back over the water.

"He went to some woods behind the house. He didn't want the kids or Jessica to find him. He called the Provost Marshall's Office. He calmly told them where to find him, and he just hung up and did it. Took a pillow to muffle the sound, left his house while they all slept and shot himself. The MPs were too late, even though they were there within minutes. It wasn't a cry for help, he'd decided. He calmly called and told the dispatcher that he was an organ donor, and that he'd be dead before they got there. He told her to tell the

MPs not to let his kids see him. Jesus Christ, what a phone call to take." She put her head in her hands. "The first responders, the doctors at the ER, his collateral damage is uncountable. They'll send a CACO Officer to his parents, the Marines that do the death notifications along with a chaplain, most likely. You shouldn't hear that news over the phone. The wife and kids will lose their housing in a month or so, have to find somewhere to go. Jessica must be a mess."

She looked at her hands, as if some answer was held there. "He left a note. Said that he'd been planning it for a while. He knew that if the doctor put him on anti-depressants or considered him a suicide risk, that his career was over. He'd lose his security clearance and that would be it. Damaged goods was how he referred to himself. He also talked about the war. His convoy was hit with an IED. He saw a young lance corporal bleed to death. He would never talk about what happened. It poisoned him slowly." Her jaw was tight. "He's a war casualty as much as any other. The suicide rates for veterans just keep rising, Aidan. I'm trying. With my little corner of this whole shit storm, I'm trying. And it's breaking my heart." Her voice was tight with the effort of holding it together. She put her head down on her clasped hands and let out a shuttering breath, and Aidan held her.

Hans came into the house at about two o'clock, tired and wired from too much coffee. He walked through the small house and didn't find his daughter. Aidan had texted him when he'd calmed her enough to divert his attention. *Calm before the storm rolls in.* Yep. That was his girl. She swallowed her pain until her head popped off.

He slid open the glass to check over at Aidan's house. Then he froze. There they were, the two of them. The two deck loungers were reclined back until they were flat. They had pushed them together. The arm rests came up between them, but they were holding hands. Aidan had his arm stretched over to clasps hers. Their faces were turned to each other in quiet repose. They had pillows and blankets and their phones nearby, but they were turned into each other like they were in their own private world.

Aidan stirred, sensing Hans even though he hadn't made a sound. He turned and looked behind him, easing his hand out of hers. "She said it was too close inside, she needed the air," he said simply. Aidan got up and walked on to the other side of the deck, sitting at the table with Hans.

"Thank you for staying with her."

Aidan said nothing at first. "She had a hard time of it. She went apeshit, to be honest, but I think the worst is over."

Hans nodded. "I can get the details later. We should get her in bed." Hans stood up and walked over to where she lay. He scooped her up into his arms with little effort. Aidan's throat tightened. He reminded him a lot of his own father. Smart, strong, brave, and such a dedicated family man.

Alanna stirred in his arms. "Daddy?"

He spoke in soothing tones. "It's all right, baby. Daddy's here."

She croaked as she put her hands around his neck, "Oh, daddy. I'm so sad."

He looked at Aidan, "I know baby. You can tell me later. I'm here now, so you can sleep." Hans mouthed another *Thank You* and walked into the house, Aidan sliding the door shut behind them.

Aidan woke with a stiff neck. He was exhausted. He'd slept a little outside with Alanna, but the rest of the night was plagued with nightmares. He was clearing buildings in Kabul. When they came around the corner, Sergeant Luke Jones was slumped in a corner with his head blown off. His wife and children enslaved by the enemy. He couldn't find them. On every street in every building he looked, but he couldn't find them.

He was running late, having set his alarm later than usual. He threw on his uniform and went outside to see if anyone next door was stirring. Hans came out on to the deck as he appeared. "She's still asleep. She woke up a couple of times last night, crying in her sleep. She's settled now, though. I'm going to let her sleep. She'll probably go to the clinic when she gets up." Then he looked Aidan over. "You look like shit, Captain." Aidan snorted a laugh. "Did you get any sleep?"

Aidan spoke over a yawn. "A little, bad dreams." Then he looked like he woke a bit and regretted the admission. "I mean…"

Hans held up a hand. "I get what you mean. Have you talked to anyone about those dreams?" Aidan gave him a look. Hans put his hands up. "All right, that's your call. Take a cup of coffee with you. I make it strong." Hans ducked into the house and came out with a hot cup of coffee. "I'll stay until her graduation. I got ahold of Erik. He's going to come over tonight. I told him not to say anything stupid. Just get some food in her and listen if she wants to talk. I should head to his apartment and try to get some sleep. I grabbed my charlies for the graduation and some extra clothes before I headed here. There's no reason to drive all the way back if I was going to be here on Sunday anyway." Aidan nodded, then looked at his watch. "Go, I got this. You saved my bacon last night, Aidan. I won't forget it."

Aidan looked at the door. "Let me know how she's getting along at lunch time?"

"Will do," Hans said.

Aidan paused before leaving. "I know her mother comes to town on Sunday. I wanted to offer my spare room. You don't have to drive all the way to Cherry Point. Honestly, she might need you again. Erik is welcome as well."

Hans considered that. "It's a kind offer. I'll talk to them both and get back to you tonight. Fair enough?"

20

Captain Denario met Aidan in the parking lot of the training facility. "I wanted to grab you before you go in. Luke Jones, is that who it was?"

Aidan was surprised. "You knew him?"

John answered, "Not really, just in passing. He was supposed to train with us. Sergeant Porter was good friends with him. He replaced him when he got pulled. He's not taking it well. It made the rounds through the gossip mill last night, and he found out. He spent last evening trying to deal with Luke's wife and the kids. He's too young to be dealing with this kind of shit!"

Aidan swore to himself. "We're all too young to deal with this shit, but here we are. I'll talk to him. I'll keep an eye on him today."

Aidan looked across the MRAP at Sergeant Porter and felt old and tired. The kid obviously hadn't slept. He wasn't much older than Liam, probably younger than Patrick. The young man was usually full of easy laughter and joking with the other men. He was quiet and serious. "Sergeant, how are ye holding up this mornin?"

The young Marine looked at him. "I'm fine. Why?"

Aidan cleared is throat. "Because you lost a friend last night, and that had to be a shit time. How is Jessica holding up?"

Porter's eye shot to his. "You knew them?"

Aidan shook his head. "Not really, I just met him a couple of times."

The young sergeant looked out the window. "I'm sitting in his chair, did you know that? He got pulled and he recommended me for his spot. Said he was glad I got the opportunity, since he didn't get to go."

Aidan thought that was odd, but at the same time he understood. Military Transition Teams or Embedded Training Teams, depending on which sandbox you got dropped, were dangerous gigs. You lived among the natives, trained them, and mentored them for the inevitable turn over. It was a great job if you were one of those guys that didn't like to push a desk on some base in Fallujah or Camp Leatherneck. It's the kind of fighting you dreamed about when you looked at recruiting pamphlets as a lad.

"I should have known. They say there are signs. I didn't catch them if there were. Too busy or too stupid or popping shit instead of listening."

Aidan sighed. "No one knew. He had doctors. Trained professionals, a family, friends. Everyone was doing what they could for him. It was his choice. You can't take this on as your damage, lad. Do you understand?"

He just looked at Aidan and nodded once. Aidan saw the guilt and pain and betrayal warring on his boyish face. But that was suicide for you. The blast radius was wide.

21

"You didn't have to come in today, Alanna. We could have postponed the closing session," Dr. Jennings said. "Did you get any sleep?"

Alanna nodded. "A little, after a dramatic melt down that undoubtedly scared my neighbor back to Ireland."

Dr Jennings smiled knowingly. "He didn't look like the type that scared so easily. So, what did you take it out on? The dinnerware?"

Alanna blushed. "Textbooks, journals, and a framed copy of my diploma."

The doctor cocked her head. "Interesting choice. I guess I don't need to psychoanalyze that."

Alanna shrugged. "I'm okay now. I need to figure out how the hell I am going to contain the damage with the rest of the group. If they don't know yet, they will find out this afternoon."

"I've been thinking about that as well. As you know, it can be contagious. He made friends in my support group, and those are the same men in your couple and family groups. They're going to take it hard. They're going to be mad as hell, too. I guess the answer is that they are entitled to those feelings and so are we. We will take it as it comes." The doctor rubbed her temples, shutting her eyes briefly. "They're transporting the remains on Saturday. I talked to Jessica. She'll head to their home in Indiana on Sunday morning. The CACO Officer has already notified the parents."

Alanna exhaled, feeling a heaviness in her chest. "Farm boys aren't supposed to kill themselves. They're supposed to get on the tractor or the horse or the porch swing and ride it out. They're supposed to be the stable ones."

Dr. Jennings nodded. "He doesn't fit the stereotypical suicide, but war changes the playing field. None of them are immune."

Alanna shook herself, wanting to change the subject. "I turned in my thesis. There's a copy in your inbox."

The doctor took her hand and squeezed it. "I read it last night when I couldn't sleep. You've done a beautiful job. I'd give you an A+ if I was your professor. You are an extraordinary counselor. Not everyone is cut out for treating military men and women. I think the Virginia office would be crazy to pass up an opportunity to hire you. Did you get the invitation for the second interview?"

Alanna cracked her neck, feeling nervous. "I'll check my email today."

The group came in slowly. Most of the families were on time. The adults were childless. One of the other therapists had taken the kids to a separate room, not wanting them to be there for the discussion that was to come. This was supposed to be a goodbye session, a closing to the work they had done together. Now it was a critical incident debriefing.

Alanna could tell by the looks on their faces that every single one of them knew of Luke's suicide. They came into the room couple by couple, and to her relief, the tragedy had seemed to fortify their relationships. They were holding hands, hugging each other, the wives stroking their men with reassurance. This was going to be hard, but they were all going to get through it.

After fifty minutes, the group had run the gauntlet of invading emotions. Anger, despair, confusion, pity, back to anger. It was only when the door to the room cracked, and they all looked up, that all of the sound was sucked from the room. It was Jessica. She looked tired, so very tired and fragile. But she was there, and Alanna felt a giant flood of relief as she greeted her at the door and took her in her arms. A shudder rippled through Jessica's weary body and then Alanna felt the tremors, felt the wet tears on the shoulder of her blouse. That's when her own tears started.

They stood there, weeping silently for minutes uncounted, until Alanna felt another set of arms. It was Rachel Rogers, Mike's wife. One by one the women came, huddled like footballers, joined in the sisterhood that was as old as war itself. These were the women who were left behind. Either for duty or unto death, they stayed behind. But they shared the weight of wartime in equal measure to their husbands. They were the shield that protected the children. They were the rock foundation that held it all together.

Sometimes, they held each other up. The men came and went with the tides of war. The women, often separated by geography from extended family, learned to lean on one another. They cried together, laughed together, they delivered each others babies, they scolded each other's children, pitching in as a second set of eyes and ears and hands when another parent was needed. They drank coffee and wine and said prayers together. And God forbid the time came, they mourned together, the wound of one sister slaying them all anew. It was the endless reminder that war was the great thief, and no one was safe.

And it wasn't always wives. The women who served in the military had their husbands who were always at odds with their position. Never truly fitting in with the men or the spouses, it had its own set of challenges. But the men managed, forged friendships with the other spouses, found their niche in this strange life, and sent their wives off to war.

When the women finally parted, they looked at their husbands, who had been silent witnesses to this inner sanctum. Even Mike Rogers was uncharacteristically stoic. Then the first of them stood. The youngest going to his pregnant wife and taking hold of her, their unborn child nestled between them. "I love you. We're in this together. I promise. Always together," he whispered.

The rest of the men followed suit, coming to first hold their wives, wipe their tear stained faces. Then one at a time, they went to Jessica to offer their condolences. At the end of the hour, everyone was calm and drained and ready to part. Everyone who left that room was marked by the time they'd spent together, and now by a mutual loss. Luke had marked them with his death, but Alanna hoped that there was also resolve.

Resolve to heal and communicate and gut out the hard patches. Jessica's weary face had marked them as well, and it was good for the men to see the aftermath of what such a decision wrought. There was an unspoken promise on all of their faces, a promise to their wives. *Never. I will never choose to do this to you.* Perhaps one good thing had come from Luke's terrible act.

Aidan came home from training and jumped right into his swim trunks. He needed the water. He needed it to wake him up and renew him. Water had always done both. He dove into a cresting wave, loving the silence it offered before his inevitable ascent. He breathed deeply of the ocean air, feeling the soft sand under his feet. The salt tasted good on his lips. He swam past the sand bar into deeper water, leaving some lingering tourists in his wake. He stared out across the ocean, pretending that he could see the rocky coast of Clare if he squinted. *I miss you, mom. God, I could really use you right now.*

It hadn't escaped him that in the midst of the crisis last night, it never even occurred to anyone to call Alanna's mother. She and Erik depended on their da. They tolerated their mother. That was sad. It was, however, all too typical. Divorce was like that. Except for the rare exception, one parent ended up carrying the bulk of the load. One parent was the pilot, one was the tourist.

Aidan looked out over the water and something caught his eye. At first his heart jolted a bit, seeing the fin. It wasn't a shark, though, and it wasn't alone. About fifty yards out from where he treaded water, a pod of dolphins swam together. That sight more than anything made him think of his beloved home. Dolphins and seals speckled the shores of coastal Ireland. He wouldn't hear seals barking or see them gliding through the water, nor would he turn to the shore and see cliffs and rocky coves. It was the same ocean, though, and he took solace in that.

The thought of moving to England again made him slightly melancholy. He'd enjoyed it when he was younger. Had traveled all over the UK and France during his free time. The thought of going back alone nagged at him more than it excited him. He would be apart from any family. The bachelor life was his choice, but sometimes it was damned lonely. He thought about what the doctor had said to Alanna after the family therapy session. He knew that she was going to get that job in Virginia. If she did, she might move before his training was even done. He closed his eyes as he fought the sickening sorrow that had nothing to do with Luke Jones and everything to do with being marked to his soul by a woman he didn't deserve.

Hans leaned against the deck rail with his son at his side. "Don't say anything stupid. Please. Set that sibling rivalry that you love to feed so much aside. Do this for me. She was a mess. Aidan handled the worst of it, and I think she's past the initial shock and grief, but you need to tread carefully."

Erik rolled his eyes. "Jesus, dad. I'm not going to say anything insensitive. Chill out. She's a big girl." Hans just grunted. He looked out over the water at the man swimming with the dolphins. *Wake up, my friend. You're the one,* he thought. That Irishman had taken the worst of it and never left her side.

Aidan walked out of the water, grabbing his towel as he looked up at the house. Hans and Erik were both watching him from the deck. He waved and Hans gave a shout. "How's the water?"

He toweled off his face and neck as he approached. "It's a grand, soft day. Not too warm, not too much surge." He walked up the beach walk and Hans handed him a beer. "Dia duit, Erik. How's life on the air side?"

Erik shrugged. "Sweet as always. How's the training going? You keeping up with our ground boys?"

Aidan laughed. "Aye, well enough. They're running me ragged. I'm loving every minute, though. Good toys, too." Both men grunted in reply. "MRAPs and convoy training this week."

Hans smiled. "MRAPS are very fun toys. Not so good for us tall guys, but still fun. I swear half the TBI injuries could be avoided with about six more inches of head room."

Aidan lifted his bottle. "A-feckin-men to that, Sergeant Major." He took a sip, then asked, "How was she today?"

"Quiet. She was really quiet," Hans answered.

"She's tough. She's angry, but she'll get back on the horse. Did she tell you she had a second interview?"

Hans perked up. "In Virginia? Which one?"

Aidan smiled, "The one she wants."

Erik watched the two men with the back and forth and was starting to get irritated. "You two want to let me in on the gouge?"

Hans looked at him with a sideways glance. "If you did a little more asking and a little less nut busting, your sister might talk to you more."

He bristled. "Right, because I point out the obvious?"

Aidan stiffened. He turned to him, "And that means what, exactly?"

He shrugged, prickishly, if you could call a shrug prickish. Alanna walked up the deck stairs right at that moment. Erik didn't see her. "I mean she's done nothing but teach aerobics and freeload off my dad's career for the last seven years. It's about time she got a job."

Aidan swore under his breath as he saw Alanna come around the deck. By the look on her face, she'd heard her brother's callous remark. Erik stiffened and turned around in sync with his father. "Talking shit about me as usual, Erik? Thanks for that. Perfect ending to a shitty day." She walked past them into the house.

"You don't know shit, asshole. Mind yer feckin' manners while you're in her house drinking her beer." Aidan went in behind Alanna. The two men followed. Hans was hissing something under his breath.

Erik came in, trying to ignore his father. "Anna, I'm sorry. I shouldn't have said that today."

She looked at him sharply. "It doesn't matter. It doesn't sting any more today than any other day. Today, I'm just too tired and preoccupied to think of a pithy comeback. You can feel free to fill in the blanks."

Hans wasn't watching Alanna. He was watching Aidan. He was close to losing his shit all over Erik, and maybe Erik deserved it, but it wouldn't help Alanna.

"Tell them, Alanna. Tell them or I will," Aidan said. Then he glanced over at the desk. Hans looked at his daughter.

"This isn't your business, Aidan. Just don't," she warned.

Aidan ran his fingers through his hair and swore under his breath. Hans walked over to the desk. There was no clue as to what he referred, until he saw something wedged between the desk and the wall.

"Damn it, Aidan. You had no right!" she said as her father pulled out her calendar. He was quiet for a long time. Erik was over his shoulder looking, too. Her father's voice was calm, but there was a demanding tone. "Jesus Christ, Alanna. How long have you been keeping these hours? This is a fifty hour work week on top of your studies. Why are you teaching all of these classes on top of the internship? You've barely had a day off in the last two months." She wouldn't look at him. "Why, Alanna? You have a full ride."

She exhaled, sending Aidan a vitriolic look. "The two military dependent scholarship foundations cut their numbers this year. One cut graduate students all together. Apparently the charitable donations have been down, and they had to make sacrifices. I paid last semester almost entirely out of pocket. The internship was all out of pocket as well. Your GI Bill benefits ran out eighteen months ago."

Hans was speechless. So was Erik for once. "I would like to point out that those scholarships were earned because of my grades. They weren't complete charity, Erik." She looked at her father, blushing. "I also turned twenty-five, so I don't have your medical insurance coverage as of two months ago. I couldn't afford the premiums. I have minimal coverage through the college up until I graduate, which is Monday." Aidan and Hans both cursed.

She had her chin up, attempting to keep her dignity. "I'm okay. Branna credited me a months rent because of the work we did. I didn't go in debt. I just dwindled my savings to nothing and had to work extra hours. I did it. I'm done. I have a second interview in Virginia. I'm fine, Daddy."

Alanna was caught between tears and anger. She was pissed at Aidan, but she understood why he had pushed her. Honestly, it wasn't anything she hadn't been tempted to do every time Erik started calling her a princess and reminding her that she was freeloading off of their father. Reminding her that he'd gone to the Naval Academy, paid nothing, and earned his own GI Bill, not using their father's education benefits. She was tired of hearing it, even though it was true. She'd done it though. She'd gotten through the last six months on her own, even working slave wages.

"Why didn't you tell me?" Her father's look was direct. It made her squirm. She felt fifteen again.

"It wasn't your problem to deal with, Daddy. I'm a grown woman."

Erik started to make a comment and Hans cut him off with a slash of the hand. "You are going to want to shut the fucking shut right now."

He looked at Alanna. "My insurance will put you back on the policy if I pay the premium. That starts tomorrow. No," he cut her off, "you will not be without medical insurance. Period. As for the rest, I wish you would have told me. I would have helped. I will help until you find a job. Once Branna can find another renter, you can live up in Virginia with me. I have a two bedroom. Just until you get on your feet. You can teach yoga and Zumba up there just as easily as here."

Alanna bristled. "I am more than a fitness teacher. I'm good at what I do. I will get a job. I don't need hand outs at my age. I will find a job, and I will support myself. My work is important. Someone will notice, and someone will hire me."

Her father looked at her patiently. "I know that, baby. I'm glad you know it, too. Family supports each other, though. I've got your six, Miss Priss. Until you find that job or until I relocate. I've got your six."

Alanna smiled. "I know daddy. I've always known." She straightened her spine then looked at Aidan. "Now, as for you," she pointed at him. Erik and Hans both took a step back, not wanting in the strike zone. Aidan was undaunted. He met her eye to eye and folded his arms over his chest. She bit back a few caustic comments, ground her jaw. Then she took a deep breath. "I'm in the mood for some fresh seafood. You feel like taking me to Captain Sam's?"

Aidan's smile was slow. "Not at all, darlin'. Just let me shower and I'll be over in ten." He walked out the back door without a backward glance.

Erik came into the kitchen as Alanna rinsed her lunch cooler. "I'm sorry. It was a stupid thing to say. Especially today..." he took a breath, "but I shouldn't have said it at all. I was being a dick. I do that."

She gave him a sideways glance. "I've grown accustomed to it. It doesn't matter."

He sighed, "It does. We don't talk. Adult stuff, your job, your school, my life, we don't talk. My marriage was falling apart, and we didn't talk. I needed you, and I didn't ask. I'm starting to realize that I'm to blame for this division between us. I'm sorry. I don't really know why I act like I do."

She gave him a sad smile. "It started when mom left. We never really found each other again after that."

Erik pulled her to him. "I'm sorry. I'll do better. I will really try to do better," he said into her hair. "I'll start by making sure I'm at your graduation on Monday. That is, if I am still invited?"

She squeezed him. "Always. You're always invited."

Her voice broke and he pulled her tighter. "I'm so sorry about your patient."

She sniffed against his shoulder. "Me too. I'm sorry and sad, and I feel like I failed him."

Erik separated them, looking down at her. He wiped her tears away. "Sometimes it's not enough, Anna-Banana. You understand that, deep down. We just had a suicide at Cherry Point. Last month one of my Naval Academy classmates killed himself. He'd been in theater three times. It's a problem. It's a real fucking problem. I'm proud of you for trying to help. I should have told you that a long time ago."

Aidan came back over to find Alanna on the couch with her brother. They had their feet tangled and were looking at his phone, watching silly cat videos and laughing. They reminded him of Brigid and Michael. Alanna looked up. "That was fast. You ready?" Alanna untangled herself from her brother and slid some flip flops on in lieu of the heels she'd worn to work. "Let's go."

Aidan was watching Alanna from the passenger seat. "You don't have to look so satisfied with yourself, you know," she said.

"I didn't say a word. I'm just glad you didn't come after me with your bat," he said.

She leaned over and gave him the gimlet eye. "I was feeling generous. Don't push it."

Aidan laughed. "You're a good girl. You have a good heart. You forgave your brother without hesitation."

She shrugged. "He's my brother."

Aidan understood that. He treasured his siblings above all others. His mother always reminded them that they would be together long after she was gone. That they should take care of each other.

"You're staring," she said, chiding him.

"Am I?" he answered.

"Stop," she said.

"I like looking at you," he crooned.

She tried to suppress her grin. "You're thinking about Tuesday night. You're making me blush."

He laughed. "Aye, I see that. I like when you blush. I like when your lips are pink and your cheeks get flushed." She stopped at a red light, and Aidan tickled her thigh with the back of his knuckle.

She sucked in a breath. "You are the devil," she said.

"I think you should let me drive on the way home. You look tired."

She looked sideways at him as she started forward again. "What are you up to, O'Brien?" Her text went off but she couldn't look. "What does it say?"

Aidan took her phone. "Erik is headed home. Your dad is going to dinner with Father Matthew. He'll be home around seven thirty or eight."

"Good evening Sheila! My God that baby has grown!" Alanna said as they exited the car, greeted by several dogs.

"Well, hello there Anna! I see you've met my new Irish friend!" Alanna walked into the concrete building and scooped the baby up out of the pack and play. Aidan looked at the sign on the wall that strictly forbade picking up the baby.

Alanna snorted. "That doesn't include me, does it Sheila?"

The woman smiled, "Absolutely not. You can pick up the little fiend anytime you'd like." Alanna gave Aidan a self satisfied look.

Aidan walked out onto the dock with the women to get a bundle of clams. "No shrimp today; just the clams."

Aidan looked out at the barrier island in view of the dock. "That is a small island. No houses?"

Sheila shook her head in negation. "No, the tide takes most of it under water. Just that boat that docks there everyday. He keeps to himself, mostly. You'd like him. He's an old sailor, retired Navy. He doesn't really talk about what he did, but I think he must have some stories. He's got one of those trident things tattooed on his arm." *A retired SEAL,* Aidan thought. A lot of men made the claim only to find out they were swabbing the deck during their short stint in the Navy. He found himself curious about the guy. Maybe he would rent a kayak one day and do a drive by.

Aidan drove and let Alanna rest. What had been innuendo on the way to the shrimper's home had swiftly become a reality. She was tired. She leaned her head against the window and was asleep within minutes. Aidan took his time, driving through a side gate, through the main base and entering into the training areas in order to exit out the back. Cutting through the base was far preferable to skirting around it. He knew that there were closer fish mongers, but he liked Sheila. He and Alanna had needed the down time and a scenic drive was a perfect distraction.

It was when he came to the training areas, wooded and abandoned for the most part in the evening hours, that she began to stir. Not awake, but with the shallow breaths and twitching eyes that meant she was dreaming. He watched her, looking between her face and the road. She was in her work clothes. A button down blouse and a knee length skirt. Her skirt was riding up, her legs scissoring a bit in her restlessness. She whimpered, and it occurred to him that she was having a nightmare. Her lips parted slightly and a little moan escaped her. He touched her arm to gently wake her.

She opened her eyes and looked at him, confused in her drowsy state. He felt his cock stir in his pants at the sight of her. She sat up, lips and cheeks pink, eyes glazed with arousal. She shook herself, running her hands through her hair. When she lifted her arms, her full breasts swayed and stretched against the cotton shirt. She met his eyes, speaking to him wordlessly. *You woke me up too soon.* He put his hand on her knee and she sucked in a breath, closing her eyes. "Show me, show me what you want." That was all he could manage.

She looked at him, all playfulness gone. He felt her open her knees as her hand went over his. "Please."

She was breathless. Her neck arched. She didn't need to ask twice. "Look at me. I want to see you when I touch you." She looked at him as he slid his hand under her skirt.

"I don't want to think about anything but your hands on me," she said. He touched her over the lace of her panties, going right to the heart of her. She put one hand in her hair and arched, pressing into his hand. He started stroking her as her breathing became labored. He took his hand away and she gasped. "Aidan!" she snapped, testily.

He gave a husky laugh. "I need to touch you. Undo your top buttons." He struggled to watch her face and the road, arousal and pleasure fighting with frustration. She unbuttoned the top two buttons, then did a bonus move when she unclasped the front of her bra. Aidan swore under his breath as he slid his hand to cover the well of flesh she'd unbound. When he touched her bare nipple they both cried out. "Fuck! Why did I start this now? I need both hands. I'm going to wreck the fucking car!" he hissed. Then he circled her nipple, adding pressure until she was out of her head. Her hair was coming unbound, she was looking at Aidan like he was the only thing keeping her breathing. Then he made his final error. He slid his fingers in the leg of her panties and she was drenched. She moaned, and he felt his own orgasm dying to break free. Just the feel of her, the sight of her completely sexed up, it was bringing him to the brink.

He was breathing hard, cursing in his native tongue, and she was a hair's breadth from coming against his hand. Then he saw the empty lot near the wooded training areas. He yanked the wheel over. It was full dusk now, no cars in sight. He pulled her out of the car half dazed and adjusting her clothes. She didn't even question him. He picked her up as soon as they penetrated the forest, avoiding the catch-me-fuck-me vines in her sandals. He stopped at a big oak tree and pulled her behind it. Then he took her mouth and pressed her against the tree.

"Christ. You'll be the death of me, woman." Then he kissed down her neck and shoulder, opening her blouse to get a better look at her. "You're so beautiful." He ran his thumbs over her nipples. "One of these days I'm going to get to see all of you at once." She choked on a laugh.

"I need to taste you. I want my mouth on you." She closed her eyes and ran a hand through his hair. She pulled him to her breast and moaned when he drew her nipple into his mouth.

"Ah, God. Aidan, don't stop." Her hips bowed off the tree trunk as he pulled her to him, his warm mouth and hand kneading her flesh, flicking her nipples with his tongue. He licked and took deep pulls until she was hovering close to orgasm, then he dropped to his knees. He looked up at her as he slid his hands up her legs. Her eyes widened, fear mixed with desire.

"Tell me now if you want me to stop, or I won't stop until you're coming against my mouth." The baseness of his words deepened her blush, but her body knew what it wanted. Her hips jerked in response. "I don't know what to do."

He smiled wolfishly. "Just let me worry about that. Just feel me. Feel my mouth on you." Then he slid her panties down.

He rucked her skirt up around her waist and started kissing her hips, moaning in Gaelic. She couldn't understand him, but knew they were lover's words. Then she felt his mouth close over her, and she groaned. She looked down and he was all over her, exploring her with his lips and tongue. She put a hand in his hair as he started an intense rhythm, right where she needed him. She rocked her hips, moaning unashamed to the woods around them. He stopped suddenly and she met his gaze. "Come for me. I want to feel it."

Then he slid a finger inside her and covered her with his mouth, blue eyes bore into hers as his finger went deep inside her. She did what he told her to do. She just felt, and she found her own rhythm, rocking her hips and clenching her muscles against him as he spread her thighs with his free hand. "Don't stop, Aidan!" She reached up and touched her own nipple, circling it as he had done, and he groaned against her at the sight.

She came with a fury, screaming and bucking and clenching. He never relented. She felt her orgasm double back and re-crest when he slid a second finger inside her and sucked her flesh into his mouth. He pinned her to the tree as she lost complete control of herself. All of her stress and pain and anger pouring out of her as he knelt in front of her, taking it all away, pleasuring her to the point of complete and utter surrender.

Alanna was completely blitzed out as Aidan tended to her. She felt the soft kisses on her legs and as he turned her to face the tree, he placed tender kisses all over her bottom, her legs, the backs of her knees. Then he helped her slip back into her panties and adjusted her skirt. He was so gentle with her, such a contradiction to the man that had pulled her from the car, pinned her to the tree and driven her wild to the point of screaming. He was never too rough, he was just big and dominant and hungry and it made what he did to her so much more pleasurable.

"Aidan," she said weakly.

He turned her to face him, fastening her bra after lightly kissing her breasts, stroking them with utter reverence, then buttoning her blouse. "I'm afraid there is no fixing your hair. You'll have to pull it down and tame it before we take you home." She heard the smile in his voice. Then he kissed her eyes, her nose, her mouth. "Thank you, love," he whispered against her hair.

She laughed weakly. "You're thanking me?"

He took her face in his hands. "You let me explore the most intimate parts of you. You let me drag you out of the car like a barbarian and jump you in the woods. Yes, I'm thanking you."

She ran her fingers over his mouth. "You couldn't have gotten much out of that."

His look was feral. "You have no idea how much I got out of that."

She started to say more, looking down at his obvious arousal and instinctually wetting her lips. "No, lass. We need to get back. If you go there, I'll have your bum pressed up against that tree for another hour. Don't worry about that." He took a finger and put it under her chin, forcing her to look up at him. "This was beautiful. It was exactly what I needed from you. Now we need to get you home. You're exhausted and your father is probably home already." Then he picked her up and carried her through the bush, back to the path. She was limp in his arms, her head on his shoulder.

As they drove over the bridge to their island, Alanna spoke. "I never get tired of this drive. I love the wetlands. I'll have to take you on a kayak through them. It's so peaceful."

"I'd like that. I'd like it a lot," he said.

She took her head off the window and looked at him. "The things you make me feel." She closed her eyes. "I didn't realize it could be like that. I didn't know that another person could sweep me away like that. I want it to be good for you, too. I want to give you what you give to me."

Aidan squeezed her knee. "It doesn't have to be the same. Christ, I can hardly explain it." He looked ahead. "Ye had a difficult start to…" He paused, finding the right words. "intimacy. Feeling you come alive, blossom under my hands, my mouth. The trust you give me. I feel you respond to me, I hear you cry out. I see your hunger, and I know you hunger for me."

He worked his jaw, overcome. His accent was thick, his voice husky. "It's the most perfection I've ever known. It feeds my own hunger, and at the same time, you give me a peace that I've done so long without, I can scarcely remember having it."

When he looked at her, she saw pain. "Don't think for one minute that this is one sided. You heal me lass, whenever you let me touch you. When you touch me, run your hands o'er my body. When I hear your voice, singing like an angel or speaking in that sweet, southern way. When I feel your breath on my face, you soothe me. Do you understand?"

Alanna was watching his profile, his beautiful face, barely breathing. "Yes, Aidan. I think I do."

Aidan looked at her hair, then he reached over and pulled a leaf out of her crown. "A souvenir."

She smiled dreamily. "I don't need a souvenir. I'll remember those woods for the rest of my life."

They pulled into the empty drive at just after eight and Aidan was surprised. "Your Da's still out."

She gave a snort. "He's with Matthew. It could be a while. They like to hit the pub afterward."

Aidan laughed. "Aye, well he is an Irish priest."

She pointed a finger at him, "Exactly. I've had to pick them up a time or two, drunk and singing. He's a pool shark, too." Aidan was starting to like Father Matthew more and more. "He doesn't gamble for money. He tells them to put a donation in the alms box."

22

Aidan knew on some level that he was dreaming, but it never made the experience less intense when he was in the throes of the nightmare. He was in Kabul. That cursed housing complex in Kabul. They'd been through there a few days earlier, spoken to an elder in the community. He hadn't given them anything other than tea. No information, only alluded to things in the way that this culture did. He was protecting his family from retaliation, refusing to give information on Taliban hiding in the area or about a stash of weapons.

Aidan's dream took him back to that apartment; back to the little girl in the corner. She was probably about thirteen or fourteen. She had a doll propped up against the wall. Tea set for two. He hadn't even realized that he'd absorbed the girl on any level until he'd returned several days later, in the aftermath. The girl, now huddled on a pallet on the floor, febrile, blank stare, clutching the dirty doll.

There are no men in our family left to do it. Just her little brother and her cousin. They are young; they won't. They can't. Please, it is honorable. Take her away and do it. She's too sick to do it herself, and I am too old. The other men in the village, they wouldn't be quick. It should be quick. She shouldn't suffer. You have kind eyes. You will not make her suffer. Take her before they come for her.

As Aidan and the other men filled the small apartment, interviewing the grandmother in the aftermath, the words of the Afghani translator filled Aidan's ears, his head. The bile rose in his throat. He shot out of bed, not knowing where the hell he was. He looked around as he stumbled. *The beach. You're on the beach.*

He went to the sliding door, suffocating, needing the sea air. He stumbled onto the deck and to the railing just as his dinner made the exit. He retched for a minute or so and then the shaking and sweating started. He felt her before he saw her.

"Aidan? Sweetie, are you okay?" He was crouched on the deck, and the feel of her jolted him. He shot up to his feet and backed away from her.

He looked at her face. Concern and sadness, which he really couldn't handle right now. "I'm fine, lass. Just go back to bed." He shook himself, the remnants of the dream still swirling in his head. His temples were pounding, the headache cresting over his scalp to land like a burning coal in the base of his skull. He gripped his head, rubbing his scalp. Alanna tried to touch him again and he jerked back.

She pulled her hand back. "I'm sorry. I won't touch you. I can help, though. Please, Aidan."

He looked at her, shook his head. "Get that feckin' shrink look off your face, hen. I'm fine. I just need a walk. This isn't a problem." Then he turned and padded down the beach walk into the night.

Alanna had been half awake, lying in bed when she heard Aidan stumble out of his door. He was usually quiet, but there was an urgency in his footsteps this time. Then she heard him retch. She knew instinctually that it had been a dream. This wasn't food poisoning or illness. She'd seen him, the frantic look on his face, the barely contained violence, the eyes filled with darkness. He was sweating, shaking, and agitated. It wasn't like before, with the artillery. This was something else. This was horror revisited.

His rebuff stung, she couldn't deny that to herself. Every time she thought they'd become closer, that she was getting to the heart of him, he gave her a shove. *Intimacy isn't love.* She watched him fade into the night and ground her teeth. She kept forgetting herself. He was leaving. He'd been clear about where he stood. It was she who kept forgetting.

"You need to let him walk it off. He's all up in his head, and he doesn't want an audience."

She stiffened at her father's voice behind her. "I do this for a living, daddy. I understand the dynamic." She looked at him, brows tight.

His stare was equally direct. "Yes, but he's not a patient and you're not his therapist. Your romantic entanglement is going to muddy the waters. He's not ready."

She exhaled. "How do you know so much?" He had the good sense to look contrite. "Oh my God, you've been checking up on him, haven't you?" she said.

Hans shrugged. "He lives next door to my daughter. You bet your ass I did, and I won't apologize."

She walked into the house, huffing all the way. "Hector?" she snapped. He gave a single nod. She looked at him a bit sheepishly. "You going to tell me what you know?" She was rubbing her fingers along the counter, not keeping eye contact. He was quiet, which made her look up. "What?" she snapped.

He sighed. "He's decorated. Big time. He had a very active few deployments. I don't have the details, and even if I did I wouldn't tell you. That's on him. It's not my place."

She growled as she stalked by him. "You men all stick together. Too tough to talk. It's infuriating." Just as she started in on the rant, she heard Aidan knock. She looked at her dad, "Speak of the devil. Come in!"

Aidan made an appearance through the sliding door and looked at Hans. "I can see you tomorrow. I just…" He swallowed. "I'm okay. I'm back. I'm headed back to bed."

She threw her hands in the air. "Of course you are! Everyone is fine!"

Hans walked past her to the door. "I'm next for a walk. You two go ahead and talk." Then he exited. Aidan heard Alanna mumble under her breath, "Chicken."

"You need to relax. There's nothing to fix here. I woke up, got sick, went for a walk. End of story. I'll see you in the morning."

She swore under breath. "You know what? Fine. If you want to act like you got a bad clam, far be it for me to interfere with your cover story."

Aidan stiffened. "Leave it, hen."

She gave a bitter laugh. "Right. Because that worked wonders for Luke! We all just needed to give him space, right? He didn't want to talk about it. Everything was fine! He was coping!" She was screaming now.

"I am not Luke and you are not my goddamn therapist!"

She flinched. Then her face hardened. "You're right. I'm not your therapist or your girlfriend. Since you are leaving and don't need any complications, I'm just a neighbor and a…." She threw her arms up. "I don't know what the hell I am. What I am not is an idiot. I know combat stress when I see it. I don't know what is going on behind those baby blues, Captain O'Brien, but I know a ticking time bomb when I see it. If you want me to butt out, fine. I don't need to be in the blast radius when you finally explode. I can't do this!" She motioned between them. "Whatever this is. I can't. We're not good for each other. I can't let you into my heart and my head if you are going to chew me up and spit me out. This was a mistake. It ends tonight. Goodnight, Aidan." She swung around and went to her bedroom, slamming the door as he sputtered indignantly.

Hans sat across from his daughter in the morning light, sipping his coffee. She'd made him breakfast. She was cool as a cucumber. Calm and collected. Not good. Not good at all. "You need to talk to him after you both have calmed down. I don't know what went on last night, but you can't leave it like this."

Alanna picked at her food. "We just clarified a few things. He's leaving in two months. Whatever I thought was starting between us has stopped. This is a bad idea. He's a short timer, and he's got problems. I don't need this in my life right now." She took a sip of her coffee.

"You sure that's what you want?" her father said.

Her eyes shot to his. "Since when is it ever about what I want? Nothing is ever that simple. He has a say in this, too. He doesn't want a relationship. He's a perma-bachelor. No wife, no kids, no life other than the military."

Hans shook his head. "You're so wrong, I don't even know where to start."

She shot her chin up. "How is that? What exactly was wrong about what I said? I think it's clear enough. Me getting all moony over him is just the path to hurt and humiliation. This needs to end."

He pushed his plate away. "Christ, deliver me from Falk pride. It's the one thing I wish you hadn't inherited. You think you know what's going on in that boy's head? Well, let me tell you what I see. I see a man eaten up by the shit in his head. I see darkness. I see scar tissue. He thinks he's damaged. He thinks he's protecting you. You think he's some swinging bachelor with commitment issues? You don't know shit, Miss Priss. Look harder." He slapped the table, and she jumped. "Look harder."

"He's got the same do-gooder streak you do. He thinks he's got something to pay for, some sort of amends to make. You think he doesn't care, but what I see is hurt and bone deep wanting, and a man who thinks he doesn't deserve to live the kind of life he wants. You have no fucking idea the shit we see in those third world shit holes, the damage it does, the chunk it takes out of your soul, of your humanity. He thinks it's better if he's alone. It doesn't mean he wants to be alone," Hans said.

Her father got up, pacing around the kitchen. "I never understood why you didn't date, why you closed yourself up with your books and your jobs and your ambition. Now you have a man right within your reach that needs you, that adores you, and you are going to get pissy and toss him aside because he's challenging you? Work at it. Pull yourself back a bit and see what he needs, not what you think he needs." He picked up his plate, rinsed it off, and looked at his daughter. She was stunned into silence. *Good, Miss Priss. Chew on that for a while.* "I'm going for a run," he said. "Thanks for the breakfast."

Aidan got up early and left. He just grabbed a map, the GPS, and he left. He needed out of that house, away from that infuriating woman. He'd finally fallen asleep, but dreams had plagued him all night. Not the nightmares. Nope. That would have been too easy. Holy shit, the dreams. In living color and stereo surround sound. The taste of her. Her fingers in his hair as she bucked against his mouth, screaming in the forest. Her short breaths, her gasps, her own finger stroking her nipple. Every exquisite detail.

He'd taken it further in his dream, however. Bloody hell, had he ever. He'd stood up and picked her off the ground. Split her thighs and thrusted inside her. He'd fucked her for hours in his dreams, her wet sex gripping him, her flushed cheeks, her pink mouth, her beautiful breasts. He woke climaxing, covered in sweat, hips jerking. He hadn't had a wet dream since he was a teenager. He'd just not been able to contain it anymore. He'd had her over and over again in his dreams and his helpless, sleeping body hadn't been able to withstand it.

He showered, dressed, grabbed his keys and fled. She'd dumped his ass hard last night. Not that they'd really even been together. They'd been intimate to a point, but he hadn't taken her fully. He'd convinced himself that it was due to her history, that he needed to take it slow. He'd also not had a condom either time they'd been together.

He hadn't been prepared for the overcoming need that swept him away. But that was what it was like with Alanna. Zero to ten in one second. The need came over him, and he lost all sense, had to have her in some way. To taste and kiss and touch her. He knew she'd have let him have her completely. She was so open and trusting, and she'd been his for the taking.

The hard truth was that he'd held back for an entirely different reason. If he made love to her, he'd never get over it. How the hell would he ever leave her? Last night, she'd been livid. Her eyes flaring, fists clenched, she'd looked like she was ready to do battle with him. When she'd so easily dismissed him and turned her back on him, it had taken every bit of discipline he possessed not to push her into that bedroom, slam the door, and throw her on the bed. He wanted nothing more than to push inside her, make sure that she remembered what he could do to her. That not so long ago she'd been begging him not to stop.

Her fury had only fed his hunger. *Mine.* He found himself thanking God that her father was there. He'd gone back over to his house in an awful temper. He was pissed at her, yes. She was pushy and wasn't able to separate her professional life from her private life. When he calmed, he heard her words over and over again in his mind. *We're not good for each other. I can't let you into my heart or my head if you are going to chew me up and spit me out. This was a mistake. It ends tonight.*

He was leaving. He was leaving her in two months. She was right to end it before it went any further. She needed a different kind of man. She was right. They weren't good for each other. She didn't need to work with head cases like Luke everyday and then come home to another. Nightmares, "episodes", headaches, a sucking black hole in his head. She needed someone loving and stable; someone that let her come home to peace and strength and support. He wasn't good for her, and he didn't deserve her. So, he got in the truck and drove.

Alanna was in one of the blackest moods that Hans had ever witnessed. She paced, walked out on the deck, mumbled, checked her phone. He'd gone for a run, needing to clear his head and calm his temper. His baby girl was making him crazy. Not only had she been putting up some sort of front while she financially struggled through the last six months, but she was nursing some pretty serious wounds. That suicide had taken a hunk out of her, and she was stifling that pain like she always did. She was also in love with her neighbor. Her neighbor was in love with her. And those two stubborn goats were fighting it tooth and nail.

If Meghan O'Mara hadn't taught him anything else, she'd taught him to fight. He'd lost her before he'd ever really told her how much he loved her. He'd given her space, let her grieve for years, let that grief steal her from the world, from her daughter, from him and his two children that needed a real mother. He was certain that no one got three chances at love. Two? Maybe, but in the long term, he was fucked. He'd blown it. Twice. Once by choosing poorly, once by holding back. Alanna, however, was young and smart and beautiful. She was the light. She deserved a life full of love and passion and family. He just didn't know how to help her. He sucked at this. He really did.

Alanna checked her phone again. Nothing. That stubborn, jackass was ignoring her texts. She was fighting the temptation to toss her phone in the drink when she heard the skype firing off from inside the house. She sprinted to the computer. "Hello?" The face that appeared never ceased to shock her. This could be Aidan, twenty-five years from now. Blue eyes, sandy hair mixed with silver, strong features, and so handsome.

"Hello, lass. How are you? Is my son around?" Sean was taking up most of the screen, but Alanna could see others milling around behind him. She cleared her throat. "I'm afraid not. He took out of here early this morning and he, um..." She took a deep breath. "He's not answering my texts, so I'm not sure when he will be home."

Sean O'Brien was a smart man. He was good at reading people, even via the internet. There was a tone of discomfort in this girl's voice that had not been there before. Something tired and sad drifted in her eyes. Something was wrong. "Are ye all right, love? Is anything amiss?"

Alanna smiled sadly. "I'm sure everything is okay. Do you have his cell phone number?"

Sean paused, "Yes, I do. I'll try that next. But what about you, girl? Ye seem a bit out of sorts. Is everything okay?"

Alanna's bottom lip started to tremble, her eyes misting. She swallowed hard, gaining her composure before she tried to speak. "It's been a hard week. I'm fine. Thank you." Alanna heard some whispering and shuffling and saw a dark mane of hair spill down over Sean's shoulder. He nodded and looked at her through the screen.

"All right, then. I'll leave him a voicemail, darlin. There's someone here who'd like to speak with you. Bye for now." He stood up, and in his place Branna's sweet face appeared. Alanna choked on a sob, covering her mouth.

"Thank you, Sean. I'll be out in a minute," Branna said. Then a door shut. "Tell me. Tell me everything," Branna said.

She told her best friend everything. Well, almost everything. She skimmed on the details about the oak tree. She'd also neglected to mention the biggest secret, the only thing she'd never told anyone. The one thing she'd kept from her best friend. The letters, the postcards, the emails, the years of looking over her shoulder. She shoved that thought to the back of her mind. Steve was far away and had nothing to do with this.

Branna's look was tender, sympathetic. "I'm so sorry about your patient, Alanna." She touched the screen. "I wish I could be there to hug you. I really do. And right before your graduation." She shook her head. "I'm glad Aidan was there for you. He's a beautiful man in every way. I'm not surprised you're in love with him."

Alanna sat up straighter, opened her mouth to argue. Her old friend threw up a hand. "Save it. Been there, remember? Just save it, sister."

Alanna squeezed her mouth shut and closed her eyes. "Don't tell him," she said weakly. "Promise me you won't tell him. He doesn't want that. He doesn't want me that way. He's attracted to me, yes, and we're having a little trouble staying away from each other. It's not the same as it was with you and Michael, though. Don't make that mistake. He's leaving and I need to protect myself. He might desire me, but he's not going to ride in on a white horse at the end and sweep me off to Ireland. I know where I'm at with him, little sister. Please understand that. I just..." her voice broke. "I wasn't very understanding. The stress, the suicide, I just snapped. I was harsh, and he was in pain, and I didn't handle him well. He doesn't want me poking around in his head, and I need to respect his boundaries. He won't answer my texts. I think I really blew it. I think I blew the friendship."

They talked for a long time, and by the end, Alanna felt a lot better. "He doesn't have it in him to hold a grudge. He's a good man, Anna. He probably just needed some air and some time to think. He'll be back."

Alanna nodded. "I'm sure you're right."

"Anna..." Branna paused. "I'm glad you told him about Steve."

Alanna exhaled. "Me too. I've learned a lot about myself in the last few weeks. He's a big part of that. If nothing else, I'm grateful for that. Plus the fact that we're little Aidan Denario's Godparents. He's going to have to talk to me sooner or later."

Branna laughed, "Ah, just play a song for him. Sing him a pretty little tune and he'll be like putty in your hands." Alanna cocked her head, thinking about his guitar. Thinking about him saying he wanted her to play with him. They'd been so busy. They hadn't made time for music. It was a thought.

Branna disconnected the video chat and walked out of the home office where Sean and Sorcha kept the computer. The room fell silent. The entire local bunch was there. Michael, Sean, Sorcha, Grandda David, Grandma Aiofe, Brigid, Finn, Cora, Colin, Seany. Even Tadgh and Liam were in town. The only ones missing were Caitlyn and Patrick.

"Well, what has that fat headed lout done now?" They could always depend on Brigid to come right out with it.

Branna sighed. "I can't talk about everything. It's private and she wouldn't want me too. I can tell you that she lost a patient this week. I told you about the work she does, with the military members suffering from PTSD. One of her patients shot himself. Left a wife and two small children."

The room was filled with sighs and curses. Michael spoke. "Christ, the poor lass. What does that have to do with Aidan?"

Branna shrugged. "He was helping her in her sessions. He'd met the guy. I don't have all of the details." She looked at her hands, not meeting their eyes. She did have most of the details, but it wasn't her place to provide them.

"She's in love with him, isn't she?" Branna looked at Brigid. She said nothing. She couldn't. She'd promised.

"She's a good person. She's had her own challenges. I'm not sure what else I can say. I just don't want Aidan to make a mistake. I think she could be the one." They all stood quietly, absorbing that. The one, his mate.

"Well, who's going?" Tadgh said easily. "I would, but I can't. I don't have enough time off during my probationary period, or I would go." He looked around the room. "You know the stubborn fecker isn't going to make this easy. He's worse than that one." He motioned to Michael. "Who's going to fly across that ocean and give him a good kick in the arse?" The group grumbled with laughter.

Aidan skimmed across the water, letting the warm sun soothe him, and the sea air renew him. He drove until he found himself at the kayak rental, just beyond Captain Sam's. He alternated the two sides of the oar, his strokes smooth and purposeful. He explored the mouth of the river and the barrier islands where the river met the ICW. It was gorgeous and brimming with life. Boats, fish, birds, plants. Beautiful wetlands that were guarded by the soaring osprey and the dragonflies that skimmed the water's surface. He came around the island that could be seen from Sheila's dock. There it was. The bright turquoise boat was lilting to one side, the tide being low. The beach was decorated with lights and tiki lamps. The back of the boat had the name painted in simple lettering. "Tired of Tangos" Aidan read aloud. He laughed quietly. Tangos were radio code for terrorists. Sheila must be right. Retired military.

As Aidan gave the boat a wide berth, he saw a head pop up on deck. The man was about his father's age. It was hard to tell with the harsh face that had seen a lot of sun over the years. His hair was white, but he was strongly built, and it was cut short like Aidan's. He had a full white and copper beard.

"Ahoy. How's the water?" the man yelled.

Aidan came about. "It's grand, all together. Good for the soul."

The man perked up. "Royal Marine?" Aidan wasn't surprised. Like recognizes like.

"No, not so fancy as all that. Royal Irish Regiment, Captain Aidan O'Brien."

"Well, what do you know. An Irishman. Senior Chief Don Montgomery, retired U.S. Navy."

The old sailor put a hand out, "Throw me your line. I've got a Guinness that's feeling a little homesick in my galley."

Aidan laughed and tossed the line. "We can't have that, now can we?" Three beers and a bag of Doritos later, the men were like old friends.

"It's like the lady says," he pointed to the stern. "I got tired of tangos. I could have taken that last rank, milked another three or four years as a Master Chief. The knees were giving me trouble, though. The head, too." He said, pointing to his temple. "Cost me two wives. The shit up here. They could have taken the separations. They couldn't take my own personal brand of head-fuck. Not that I can blame them."

Aidan nodded, understanding all too well. "Aye, I've dodged that bullet. No woman needs to swim in this sewer with me."

The man stopped his beer halfway to his mouth. "Well, now. That's no way to think. No way to live, either. You young guys need to learn from our mistakes. Women are tough as shit. They can handle just about anything, if you pick a good one. Don't piss away a good thing when you find it. You got any prospects?" he asked, giving Aidan a sideways glance. Aidan's silence spoke volumes. "Ah, that would be the part where you are out here on the water alone, trying to clear your head. Well, you need to get your ass back in that boat and go fix whatever you screwed up. Life's too short not to love a good woman."

Aidan barked out a laugh. "You sound like my father."

The man looked at him. "I ain't that old. Not quite. Your pops sounds like a smart man though."

Aidan smiled at the thought of his father. "He is. He's the smartest man I know. Twenty-five years in the Garda. Good cop, good husband, good father."

The man's brows shot up. "Man, I wish my kids talked about me like that. They think I've gone off the reservation, living out here on a sand bar."

Aidan laughed. "Nah, I think you've got the right idea. You'll go back when you've sorted it all out. Or when you run out of beer, which ever comes first."

Aidan was pulling out of the kayak shop when his phone started ringing. "Where the hell have you been, O'Brien?" Hector's voice was salty and gruff.

"Sorry, sir. I was out on a kayak. Is something wrong?"

Hector let out a loud exhale. "No, nothing's wrong. Hatsu invited John and Maria over, I thought you'd like to join us. I called Lieutenant Drake as well. We were thinking about five o'clock if you're available."

Aidan was speaking loudly over speaker phone. "Sounds perfect. Can I bring anything?"

"Just yourself, per the wife," Hector replied.

Aidan stopped by the base liquor store, searching for something nice to bring to Hatsu. He looked at the sake selection, which was grim. She liked to cook, so he decided on a good ruby port. Perfect for drinking, but you could cook with it as well. When he checked out and showed his ID and paperwork, the cashier raised a brow. "You're far from home." She had long red hair and a tattoo on her arm that he immediately recognized as Pictish art.

"Do you have Scots blood, then?"

She smiled. "Cute and smart. Who's the port for? No offense, but you look like a whiskey man."

He laughed then leaned in. "Boss's wife."

She nodded, turning up the bottle to see the label. "Good choice. Let me know if you need anything else."

She took a blank receipt and wrote some numbers on the back. "In case you need someone to show you around town." She didn't hide her approval as she looked him over in his shorts and RIR shirt. Aidan had to admit to himself, she was beautiful. Young, too. Probably about twenty two. Tall, lean, amber eyes and long auburn hair. Too young, though. Not for a tussle in the sheets, but he was past the whoring phase of his youth. He took the number, not wanting to hurt her feelings.

"Thanks, Keiley. I'll keep that in mind."

"There he is!" Joey answered the door at the Diaz household like he owned the place. "How's life on the beach?"

Aidan stepped in, taking in the crowd. "God bless all here," he said and walked to Hatsu. "For you, ma'am. Thank you for having me, again."

Hatsu looked at the bottle. "Port. My goodness, we'll have to open this after dinner. Thank you, Aidan."

He shook hands with Hector, then was man-hugged off the floor by John. "Christ, did ye miss me?"

Maria laughed. "Come see your godson Aidan." Aidan walked across the living room and sat beside Maria. The boy was swaddled up in a blue blanket, but trying like hell to kick his way out of it. Underneath, he had a cotton one piece on with sea creatures adorning the front and little blue socks that kicked out from chubby legs. "Well, he's filling out, isn't he."

She gave him a sideways look. "Yes, I've become a human pacifier. Just call me Bessie."

Aidan smiled as he took the baby from Maria. He was already rooting and fussing. "No, no lad. Let her have a rest. The men have business." The baby looked at him, blinking hard and pursing his lips the way that newborns did. "How are ye liking the outside world, little man? Have ye taken a wife, yet?"

Maria giggled at the sight of her newborn son kicking and flailing his fists at the sound of Aidan's voice. "I think he recognizes your voice."

Aidan looked curiously at the pudgy little creature. "Do you think? I suppose it's fortunate I didn't sing some of the more bawdy tunes I know."

Lieutenant Drake interrupted their chat. "So, when do we get a concert?"

Aidan was letting the baby grip his fingers, making faces at him. "Do ye have that bottle of Jameson?"

Drake groaned. "Come on, that shit is expensive."

Aidan shook his head. "Then ye'll hear none of it." The young lieutenant went into the kitchen where the other men had gathered around the beverage selection, bored with babies and domestic talk.

"The baptism is coming up. You still up for it?" Maria said.

"Oh, yes. Of course." Aidan knew where this was headed, having a nosey, matchmaking, peahen of a sister.

"And Anna? How is she?" Aidan looked sideways at her.

"She's fine. The end of the week went sour pretty fast, as I'm sure you heard."

Maria crossed herself. "Yes, I heard. What a pity. What an awful, awful pity. He had a lot to live for if he'd just looked ahead and not back." Aidan nodded, not knowing what to say.

"She's a wonderful girl. You made any progress on that front?" Aidan played with the baby, ignoring the question. "Oh my God, you have!" she screeched. Aidan looked at the kitchen, shushing her and attempting to silence her with the evil eye.

"Holy shit, Aidan. Are you hitting it with the Sergeant Major's daughter?" she said in a frantic whisper.

"No! Christ, woman, have you no sense of a man's privacy? This isn't cocktail party talk."

She gave a husky laugh. "You can get all offended if you like, but you are holding out on me, brother. You've got something going."

He sighed with frustration. "Listen, there may have been some activity," he said, treading carefully. "It's done, though. She wised up early. It's ended before it even started. She's smart."

Maria looked at him, eyes narrowed. "What did you do?"

He sputtered. "Why do you assume I did something wrong?"

She pointed at him. "There's no way in hell that a healthy, twenty-five year old, single woman would put the brakes on it with someone like you unless there was a reason. You had every nurse and female doctor in that hospital going into heat after two hours. That poor girl is living next door to you. She didn't stand a chance. You must've really pissed her off to get her to slam on the brakes."

Aidan was quiet. Maria nudged him."Fix it. Go home and fix it, Aidan."

He sighed. "You are the second person today to tell me that. Did you ever consider the fact that maybe she's right? Maybe this whole thing was a bad idea?"

Maria's face softened. "Why, Aidan? Why do you think that?"

He handed her back the baby, then he rubbed his hand over his face. "Maybe she knows that she deserves better."

Maria took his hand and he looked at her. "Not a chance, big man. Not a chance."

"Yo, Sergeant Major." Hans answered on the second ring.

"Hector, what's the word?"

"I only have a second. He is here, Hans. He was kayaking, but I finally got through on the cell. I wanted you to know that he's here, and he is fine." A loud exhale came over the phone. "Talk to me Hans. Do I need to worry?" Hector was hiding in the garage, talking in hushed tones.

"No, Jesus. No. He's completely okay on the job. He and Alanna, they had a fight. He doesn't like being psychoanalyzed."

Hector gave a snorting laugh. "None of us do. That shit gives me the scratch."

Hans continued. "She couldn't get ahold of him. I guess I overreacted. I just didn't like the thought of him being so far from home, feeling like he had nowhere to go."

"You sound like you like the guy, and I can't blame you. He's good people. You heard what he did for Captain Denario's wife."

Hans stopped him. "No, I didn't. What happened?"

Hector told him the whole story. Hans was silent for a long time. "He's a stand up guy, all the way. Listen, my man. I'm sorry about Anna. She's had a rough week. That shit catches up with you. I'll tell you what. I'll talk to him. I won't tell him you called, I'll just feel him out. Then I'll send him home."

Hans hung up with his old friend and thought about what he'd told him. Jesus Christ. He was everything good about young military men. He thought back to the scene on the deck. He'd been a mess. Shaking, puking, and the look on his face was ruined. Fucking ruined. He didn't know what Aidan O'Brien had seen in his life, but that shit was coming home to roost. He remembered the previous conversation. What had Hector said? *Gallantry in the face of human rights atrocities.*

23

Aidan drove through the dark training areas with the windows down, letting the night air wash over him. Dinner had been wonderful and had lingered for hours as he and the other men and their wives talked. Hector was by far the most experienced in combat. As Aidan knew, he'd been there when Brian O'Mara had been killed, and when Hans had been shot. He'd been a 1st lieutenant at the time, just like Joey was now. Since that tour, he'd been to Iraq two more times. This would be his first Afghanistan tour. Joey had done one tour in Iraq as a boot. John had done one tour in Iraq and one in Afghanistan.

They'd all seen combat to one degree or another. Joey had been lucky. There had been no casualties in his unit, although there had been some while he was there. There were always some casualties, every month. It never ended. British, Australian, American. There were others, too, but those three countries did the bulk of the fighting and took the bulk of the losses. Camp Bastion was broken up into several pieces. Americans, Brits, and the section called Camp Viking. which housed the troops from Denmark. Aidan had made a lot of friends there, and he kept in touch with all of them, thanks to the internet.

Aidan sometimes had trouble remembering what he had for breakfast if his mind was scattered, but he could pull up so many faces. He remembered vividly getting invited over to the American chow hall, by John, on the Marine Corps birthday. The U.S. military was overly uptight about alcohol, but on the USMC birthday all of the Marines got two beers. They had a choice between Bud Light and Guinness, so John was thrilled to take two of the stouts and share one with him.

Marines were like that. They took care of each other, and for some reason, he and John had hit it off. One Italian American from the dodgy part of New Jersey and one eldest son of an Irish cop, plucked out of a small town in County Clare, had crossed paths and become friends. That friendship solidified by another unlikely meeting, all due to a dark haired beauty who'd bewitched his brother.

He'd sat at the dinner party, watching Hector relive the scene in living color: the day Branna's father had been killed. He remembered his words.

As long as I live, I'll never forget the sound of those rounds hitting Brian's flack jacket, the thud it makes. Then the blood, the fucking blood spurting out of his neck as he held his hand over it. Hans ran right into the shit to pull him up, took a hit in the shoulder. He barely flinched. It was pure adrenalin. He pulled Brian into the building while we secured it. Our comm guy was on the radio, the corpsman was working on Brian.

Then he paused, needing to take a minute. They weren't talking about the weather, and honestly, Aidan didn't know how the guy was doing it. How the hell he was talking about it so openly? Hector looked up and met his eye.

I'll never get the voices out of my head. Hans was screaming. "Don't you fucking die on me! You are not going to die in this shit hole, you hear me!" Brian was calm. He just squeezed Hans at the arm. He spoke fast, like he knew he didn't have time. The bleeding started affecting his speech.

"Take care of my girls. Please. We don't have any family. Promise me." I was watching over them, securing the perimeter until we could get a medivac rolling. It all happened so fast, but I swear it took a year for that bus to get there. It didn't matter. Hans's wound was bad, but not fatal. Brian bled

out in probably a minute. Christ, she looks just like him. Branna, she looks just like him. It is like looking at a ghost."

Aidan had watched Hatsu during this little reveal. She rubbed his back, didn't make eye contact with anyone. Maria was in a bedroom, nursing the baby, and Aidan wondered if Hector had waited until she was out of earshot. He'd spoken openly in front of his wife, though. She never flinched. She'd obviously relived it with him before, and as was her way, she sat quietly. Comforting him with her physical presence, but not saying a word. It made him think of Alanna. *There's a very physical element to emotional healing.*

He walked up the side stairway, directly onto the deck, and he heard her. She was playing her piano. He peered around the deck, saw into her house. She'd moved the piano. Her desk had been banished to the guest room and in its place was her piano. He smiled, pleased that she was playing. At first it was some classical piano. Then she started another song, and he closed his eyes as he recognized it. A Fiona Apple song, without the sultry, smokiness of the original artist. This sweet soprano, with a charm that was pure American south, was its own brand of lovely. He'd thought about her singing for months, tried to remember every nuance, back in his Belfast apartment. When sleep evaded him, and he needed soothed to sleep, it was this voice he heard.

Aidan exhaled a shuttering breath. This was going to kill him. Not physically, but it would be the death of him otherwise. After all the shit he'd seen and done, he wasn't capable of giving this woman the whole of him. It wouldn't be fair to her. She had a bright future and was on the cusp of starting a promising career.

Part of him just wanted to surrender to his need, wanted to take everything she would give him, so that he could save it up for dark days. So that he could say that for a little while, he'd loved someone and let them love him. He couldn't do it, though. If he did, she'd be a wound that slowly bled him to death over the course of the rest of his life. He didn't notice when the piano stopped.

"Are you okay? Did you have a good day?" Her voice was hesitant. Her eyes guilty. She knelt next to him. When she spoke again, her voice broke. "I'm so sorry, Aidan."

He took her in his arms. "You've got nothing to be sorry about. You were right. Everything you said was right."

She pulled her head up. "No! Don't say that. You're nothing like Luke. It was an awful thing to say. You're one of the strongest men I've ever known." She threw her arms around his neck. "I was hurting. I was messed up, and I lashed out at you right when you needed me to be understanding. I'm so sorry, Aidan."

He rubbed her back. "Shhh, it's all right, love. I'm okay. We're okay." He held her for several minutes, just letting her calm down. "You were right about a lot, darling. Even if I'm not like Luke, I'm not good for you. You know that. You were right to send me away."

She wiped her tears, shaking her head. "No, no!"

He took her face in his hands, wiping away more tears as they fell. His face was so tender. "We both know you've got better things ahead." Her face was sad, so sad. Aidan fought the impulse to kiss her. That wouldn't get them anywhere they needed to be.

"Promise me two things?" she said. Her voice was strained and trembling. He nodded, not waiting to hear what the two things were. Whatever they were, he'd give them to her. He owed her some trust. "First, don't ever turn your phone off like that again. I'm not in a good place in my head right now. I know you're not like Luke, that's my damage, not yours. It just scared me."

He smiled, "Deal. I'm sorry. I just went for a long kayak ride. I needed to clear my head. I promise, I won't go silent unless I tell you where I am. Now, what's number two?"

She exhaled. Then she stood up. "Wait here a minute." She walked into her house and came out with a pad of paper and a pen. She placed it on the deck chair. "I understand that you can't talk to me. I know that I shouldn't have pushed you. I also know there's something up here…" She pointed to his temple. "And there's something in here…" and she pressed her palm to his chest, "that you think is too awful to let out. I think it is causing your headaches, your stress episodes, and I think it's causing your nightmares."

She put her hands up, stopping him. "I get it. You barely know me. You also have a chivalrous streak a mile long. I understand you aren't going to let me poke around in that head of yours. Just do this, for me. Write down the first five names that come to mind when you think about what happened. Five people that you feel like you could tell, that you could talk to. You can't stop until you have five people. Okay? Don't worry, I'm not going to make you call all of them. Just write them down. I'm going to leave you alone while you do it."

Aidan rubbed his chin, feeling the stubble from not shaving this morning. "Please, it's just a piece of paper. Will you do this for me? You don't even have to show me the names." Aidan looked at her for a long moment. Then he stood up, took the pad and pen and reclined in the deck lounger. Alanna squeezed his shoulder, planting a chaste kiss on the top of his head. Then she went back inside.

Aidan stared at the pad of paper for a while. He didn't know why he was resisting such an easy task. He opened his mind, staring out over the dark sea. He let himself think about the engagement they'd been in, while patrolling in Sangin. The young corporal's face was crystal clear.

He was so fucking young. He had that lanky build of late puberty, not done growing at the age of twenty. He had brown hair, dusty blue eyes, a carefree smile. He'd been so excited to finally get in on some action. They'd been in two groups, so Aidan and his men were patrolling nearby when they'd heard the explosion, then the distress call came in. In what seemed like a single heartbeat, that young soldier was on the ground, gasping, spitting blood. Shrapnel had hit an artery, and there was a spatter where his leg used to be.

Aidan squeezed his eyes closed. He'd been like a man possessed. Like a switch had flipped in him. They all had, but he'd led the charge, thrown himself into the assault; to hell with his own safety. By the end, the enemy casualties were huge and the rest were running. But the lad was still dead. He'd received a medal and that kid got shite. Aidan remembered the picture inside his helmet. Not a wife and kids. Nope, he never got to do that. It was his parents. He looked like his mother. His parents and a little brother. They were smiling on the front stoop of what must have been his home.

Aidan sat there for a long time, cleaning the slate of his mind. Locking away those memories where he kept them safe. That trip down memory lane had been a cake walk compared to Kabul, compared to that little girl, her cousin, and her grandmother. He didn't need to relive that. It was fresh in his brain from the night before. He looked down at the pad of paper, the pen hooked into the binding. He took the pen out, writing a list of one to five. *The first five names that come to mind when you think about what happened. Five people you feel like you could tell.* His father's strong face replaced the bad memories, washing his mind clean with those knowing, wise, blue eyes.

It didn't take him long, once he'd started the task. He could never tell Brigid. She was sheltered on that coast with her dark, handsome husband and her beautiful children. No, not Brigid. Sean Jr. was a boy and Liam still young enough to believe that the world was grand and fun and one big feckin party. They needed to stay that way as long as they could. His other brothers were older, more experienced, and had seen a bit of the world. Patrick in the Garda, Michael in the Coast Guard. They'd seen death. Aidan sighed. He hated this assignment. He should have never agreed to it. He didn't need this. As much as he protested to himself, the pen moved along the paper.

1. Da
2. Michael
3. Patrick

His pen hovered over the page. He could never tell his mother. She had lived in a war zone, seen awful crimes done in the name of religion and patriotism. She'd seen enough for two lifetimes. She'd begged him not to enlist. No, he couldn't tell his mother. Tadgh. His chest ached when he thought about Tadgh. He'd lost his da as a boy. He was like another brother to all of them. He was the best of men. He was smart, too. He'd graduated from the academy right after Aidan had left for this training. Top of his class. He got top pick for his first assignment. Tadgh was good at figuring things out, of seeing to the heart of things. Yeah, he could talk to Tadgh. He put his name in the fourth space.

That last spot stayed empty, but he had to fill it. He'd promised. He thought about his comrades, the men in his unit. He thought about the relationships he'd forged through the years. He loved his men. He'd die for each and every one of them. It wasn't them that came to him with perfect clarity. When he opened his mind, he was back in Camp Leatherneck, having gone to the American side with John as an escort. He was sitting at the table, surrounded by young men eating birthday cake and drinking beer. Two cans of Guinness in a seven month time period, and John slid one over to him without hesitation.

5. John

Aidan exhaled. Why had that been so hard? He sat for several minutes, then stood up with the pad in his hand and went to Alanna's door. She was reading, sitting on her couch. She looked up, motioning for him to come in. He sat next to her on the couch.

"That was difficult." He met her eye, but a slight blush started on his face.

"I'm sure it was, Aidan. Thank you for doing it."

He shrugged, "So, what now?"

She took his hand, interlacing their fingers. "That's up to you. The one that's the most significant is number one. That's the person you feel like you can trust more than anyone. It's also the person that you feel is strong enough to take on the burden of what you have to say. The other four are for you to remember that you aren't alone. That you have at least four other people besides #1 that you can turn to, talk to, when your father is not an option. You have people who love you."

Aidan raised a brow. "I didn't show you my list. How did you know my father was #1?"

She smiled. "Because I see his strength. I see his love for you. And he's who I would have chosen for you. He's a first responder. He would understand about critical incidents."

Aidan tapped the pen on the notebook cover. "So, you think I should call him?"

"If you are asking, then yes. It is ultimately up to you, but yes." She turned to him, smoothing her hand over his handsome face. "You hurt. Deep in your bones. I can't help you. I know that. As much as I hate it, I'm not your therapist and I'm not on that list. If I had to guess, I'd say that every person on that list is male. You protect the women in your life. You wouldn't put this on them. I just..." her voice broke. "I just want to try and give you something. Some way to lighten this burden, whatever it is."

Aidan's face was sad as his eyes roamed over her face. He took her hand in his and kissed it. That's when he heard her father coming up the front stairs. "Your da is home. I better head back over."

He stood as Hans walked through the doorway. "I see you two are on speaking terms again. That's good to see. With Felicity headed this way, I don't need any additional drama in my life."

Alanna giggled. "Don't worry daddy, I'll protect you." He grunted. She whispered to Aidan. "She didn't care for being his wife, liked to cat around. It doesn't stop her from drinking too much wine and trying to have a go, for old time sake."

Aidan choked, surprised at her candor. Her father said, "I can hear you. Please stop talking about my sex life, Miss Priss. It gives me the willies."

She laughed, "It's only a sex life if you're actually getting some, daddy."

He plugged his ears, "I'm not having this conversation with you!" She gave an evil chuckle.

"You shouldn't mock your da, lass," Aidan chided.

Hans pointed to him. "See, I knew he was smart. Don't mock your daddy. And you have no room to talk..."

She cut him off. "Okay, I'm done mocking. Totally done mocking, Daddy. You can stop now!"

Hans wiggled his eyebrows. "You can dish it, but you can't take it." He got a pint of ice-cream out of the fridge and tucked in with a spoon. Aidan marveled at how incongruous the sight was. This big, hard ass Marine with his cropped blonde hair, huge arms, and ice green eyes, was standing in his stocking feet, a Ramones t-shirt, and a pint of Cherry Garcia. "Aidan, I was thinking. If your offer is still open, I'd like to use your spare bedroom Sunday and Monday. I can move my stuff over after mass."

Aidan stood up. "Aye, the offer still stands. Of course. I've got plenty of room." He smoothed a hand over Alanna's hair. "I'm off to bed, mo chroí. Sleep well." He nodded, "Hans, I'll see you at mass."

Aidan slept well for the first time in a long time. He'd decided that Alanna was one of the smartest women he'd ever known. The comfort that she offered, the peace they'd made, and the comfort of his list of five. He slept without nightmares, stirring awake only occasionally to grab a sip of water or open a window. He looked out over the morning surf. It was misting, but rain had never bothered him. There were sandpipers scurrying across the beach, grabbing small mollusks to break their fast.

He heard the slider open. "Last one with salt water on their feet has to make coffee." Aidan had barely processed what she'd said before a blur of blonde hair and limbs whipped past him. He sprinted, needing to make up the lead she'd shamelessly stolen. She was almost to the water, head down, and he could just imagine the determination on her brow.

Just before she hit the water, he caught her, swinging her around and off her feet. He did his classic move, running backwards to let his feet touch first. "No!!! Dagnabbit, O'Brien. That's not fair!" She was giggling through her protests.

Aidan whispered in her ear. "You want to be wet? I think we both know I can arrange that." His tone was husky and she froze, stopping the struggle, then he tucked her under one arm like he would a small child and sprinted into the water. A wave crested and soaked them both. He held on to her, drenched like a wet cat in her pajamas and robe.

She turned on him and tried to dunk him. He stood like a tree trunk, immovable. "Do you really think you can best me in a water fight, lass? I'm twice your size and a rugby player. You couldn't take me down if your sweet, little ass depended on it," he mocked.

She stood there, soaked, with hair in her face. "You're going down, O'Brien." Then she leapt on him like a little monkey. She pushed and twisted and grunted, and he didn't move. The waves kept coming and one knocked her off her feet, only to add to her humiliation. Doubled by the fact that Aidan had to help her up with all of her wet, heavy clothes on.

"Are you done, hen?"

She was going to wipe that smirk off his face. She cocked her head, thinking of a tactic that would work. Then she did something unexpected. She closed in on him, slowly, seductively. "Maybe I'm a lover, not a fighter. What was it you said about getting me wet?" His eyes flared. She put her hand on his hips, leaning in. Then she seized his ribs, and he yelped. Her face was triumphant. "Holy crap. The tough guy is ticklish." She leapt on him, grabbing him at the ribs as he started to laugh and squirm. He was so busy, trying to clasp her hands, that he didn't see the wave. But she did. Right as it hit, she swept his leg out from under him, and he went down.

Aidan came up out of the water just in time for Alanna's triumphant scream. "Yes!" She started climbing out of the surf, swinging her arms and smiling like she'd just conquered Rome. Then Aidan had to laugh as she raised her arms above her head and did a little side to side dance, like Rocky. Then she started shadowboxing."Woohoo! Taken out by a wee lassie!" she pointed at him, reveling in her little victory. It was right at that moment that Aidan knew he would love her until the day he died.

"You got honey trapped, Aidan. Oldest trick in the book!" Hans yelled from the deck, laughing just as hard as his daughter. Aidan came out of the water, smiling at the sight of Alanna. Her hair was in a wet tangle, half in her face. Her clothes were wet, sandy and dragging the ground. She was still dancing. He scooped her over his shoulder in one swift move, walking up to the house. She was hanging upside down, and still she gloated. He smacked her rump. "If you're done popping shit, lass, I need to make some coffee." He put her down and she giggled, hysterically.

He watched her walk over to her father and slap a high five. "All weapons are good weapons. Isn't that what you taught me, daddy?"

Her father hugged her. Water, sand and all, he hugged her. "It's good to see you laugh, baby." Then he looked over her shoulder at Aidan. "It makes me happy to hear you laugh. It's been too long."

Mass was less crowded this week. Aidan suspected that the summer months were like that. School was out, families were moving, they were road tripping it to see extended family. He shook hands with Father Matthew. "I didn't see you up at the communion table. How have you been, Captain O'Brien?"

Aidan smiled, embarrassed. "I didn't make time for confession, I'm afraid."

Matthew looked at him, speculatively. "I can make time if you can."

Aidan laughed. "I suppose there's no need for a confessional, the accent would give me away, aye?"

The priest laughed, eyes sparkling. "How about a beer instead?"

Aidan's grin broadened. "That sounds perfect."

Matthew put a hand on his shoulder. "I'll need about twenty minutes."

"Damn shame about that young man. It really was. He didn't attend mass, I asked around. He hadn't been in touch with the chaplain, but he was a Catholic," Father Matthew said.

Aidan shook his head. "Father, I don't mean to question the Canon…" Matthew sighed. "About suicide? I understand. I struggle with it myself." Aidan's brows shot up.

"What? You think priests don't have doubts? I work with veterans every day. Active, retired, reserve. The fact that the suicide rates keep climbing, that I could lose one of them any day. The argument for their salvation nags me daily. How do I help? How can I stand at a widow's side and tell her that her husband might be doomed? All I know, Aidan, is that we have to do more. We all need to be more like Anna. Figure out a better way." Aidan's eyes flared at the sound of her name. "That's right, I've followed her work. She's spoken to me about all of this and more." Matthew said.

Aidan couldn't meet his eyes. "Would you like a confession for the books?" Aidan said. He picked at his beer label. "I can't stop thinking about her. I met her seven months ago, briefly. Then I went back to Ireland. The sight of her…" He paused, shrugging with a crooked grin. "It shot straight through me. Something in my soul, not my eyes. A connection. I never stopped thinking about her. Now we're neighbors."

Matthew looked up at him, willing Aidan to meet his eyes. "That doesn't sound like chance. That sounds like you had a few reasons for taking this exchange."

Aidan closed his eyes. "I've no right to her. I never intended on marrying or having children. This isn't a life that is cohesive to family and marriage."

Father Matthew barked out a laugh, "Bullshit." Aidan's jaw dropped. "Sorry, that's not very priestly but it's true. Have you looked around you, Aidan? This is all about family. You aren't going to meet a better bunch of family oriented people than on a military base. The spouses are like something out of a superhero comic. The kids are worldly, smart, well traveled, interesting, and fiercely patriotic. You go around the family housing areas when they play *Colors* and watch the kids on the playgrounds. As soon as that bugle starts over the speakers, those kids stop what they are doing and stand at attention. Go into the movie theater and you won't hear a pin drop when they play that national anthem. This is God's country, Aidan. And God created marriage and love and the creation of children to be a holy sacrament. If you are holding back, that's up here." He pointed to his own temple.

"Now, I'm not going to lecture you about impure thoughts. I've worked with young, healthy males too long to fight that battle. Plus, I've seen Anna, and no one could blame you. I'm going to talk to you about right and wrong. The biggest sacrifice I make everyday is not having a wife in my bed and a child in my arms. I do that for God and for God's people, and I do it for the U.S. military. It's hard, though. Some days it's almost unbearable, but I chose this life. You? You chose the life of a soldier. You don't have to give up the rest. You are choosing to do that for some reason. You are choosing to deny yourself, not because of the laws of the church or the military, but because for some reason you feel like you shouldn't have it."

Aidan ran his hand through is shorn off hair. "Maybe I shouldn't."

Matthew looked at him sadly. "I don't believe that, Captain. I can't believe that. It doesn't matter what I believe, though, does it?" the priest asked.

Aidan came into his house to find Hans sitting on his couch. "Glad to see you're still in one piece. Matthew doesn't pull any punches."

Aidan snorted a laugh, "I noticed. He's good at what he does, though. I can't imagine having the same conversation with my parish priest at home. Not without the wall of the confessional hiding my face."

Hans smiled, staring off at nothing. "I think I'd like to see your country. I did a tour in Japan, but I never made it to Europe. I might have to do a trip between my next assignments."

Aidan cocked his head, "Alanna said you might be up for rotation. Any good prospects?"

Hans paused, thinking, then he came out with it. "Can you keep a secret?"

Aidan sat across from him in the old upholstered chair. "Aye, I can."

Hans sat straighter. "There's an infantry Sergeant Major position with a FAST Company. It's in Spain." Aidan whistled. He'd heard about the FAST Marines from Hector. Fleet Anti-terrorism Security Team. He was looking at a similar job as Commanding Officer.

"Same as Major Diaz?"

Hans shook his head. "No, his is in Bahrain."

Aidan nodded. "I see. So, why is that a secret? Are you worried ye won't get the job?" Aidan asked.

"No, it's mine if I want it."

"You're thinking about Alanna," Aidan said.

Hans nodded. "She's going through a big transition right now. I'm not sure I feel right about leaving her." Aidan understood. "It's a good job. A perfect twilight tour. I'd be stationed in Europe, could do some traveling. Maybe even go see Branna and the new babies. And the job is outstanding."

Aidan shook his head. "You deserve this job, Hans. Alanna would want you to take it."

Hans sighed, "You're right, she would. I just haven't told her."

"She's a strong woman. She'll find a job, and she'll be fine. She wants to make her own way. I won't tell her, but you should," Aidan said.

Hans nodded, "I know. I have a little time before they need an answer. I just want to see how this next interview goes."

"So, you want to tell me why you're hiding out over here? Is her mother here?"

Hans laughed. "Smart man. Yes, but I'll take you over now. Erik is here, too." Hans got up, slipped his shoes on, and walked out the door in front of Aidan.

Felicity Richards was a beautiful woman. She was a little younger than Aidan's mother. She had a few more age lines from too much sun, but she was beautiful. She had hair that came down to the middle of her back, but unlike Alanna's thick tresses, it was thinner and very straight. It was darker blonde, and she'd put a large blue streak in it that seemed slightly childish for her age. She wore a flouncy, bohemian looking skirt and a halter top that showed off more of her chest than Aidan would be comfortable with, were she his mother. She had about ten bracelets of various colors and textures on her wrists. She was loud, too.

"This must be the Irish Marine I've heard about!"

Aidan shook her hand, "Army, actually. Nice to meet you, ma'am."

She waved a hand dismissively. "Army, Marines, I can never tell. Call me Felicity."

Erik rolled his eyes. "You know the difference. You just pretend not to know the difference in front of your hippie friends, and now it's a habit."

She turned, looking pouty. "You don't have to be so rude, Erik. What happened to those southern manners your daddy is so proud of?"

At this point Aidan broke in, derailing the petty argument. "So, you've come to see Alanna graduate. You must be very proud." She turned back to Aidan, gave him a head to toe appraisal.

"Yes, I am. So, little Branna married your brother. What a wonderful girl she is. How is she?"

Aidan smiled, "She's grand all together. Twin babies, a few months old. Brian and Halley, beautiful just like their mother."

Felicity clasped her hands together. "Married with twins, good for her. Marriage suits some women. She was always a serious child, talented too. Just like my Anna. They used to spend hours at the piano and violin, making up songs, playing Brian's old sheet music." She looked at Alanna. "You'll have to play for us while I'm here."

Alanna had been uncommonly quiet, Aidan had noticed. "Maybe, if we have time. You're only here two nights, though. We'll see. So about tonight, I wanted to make everyone dinner. Tomorrow will be an early morning since we have to head to Wilmington for my graduation. I bought some steaks..."

Felicity interrupted, "I'm a vegetarian. I thought you knew." Hans and Erik snorted in unison.

"Since when?" Alanna asked.

Felicity smiled, "For about three months."

Erik interrupted. "Let me guess, right after you met Logan?"

Felicity gave him a sideways stare, "It's Hunter."

He laughed, "Of course it is. His name is Hunter, and he doesn't eat meat. And what grade is he in?"

"Enough, Erik." Hans finally spoke up. "I'm sure we can accommodate you, Felicity. If I need to run to the store, I can."

Alanna sighed. "It's okay, daddy." She looked at her mother. "I have a grill. Will you eat fish?"

Felicity nodded, "Yes, I will. Do you have halibut?" At this point, Erik walked away.

"No, mom. I buy local fish. This isn't California. I have snapper and flounder in the freezer."

Her mother shrugged. "Snapper will do. Thank you, baby."

Aidan walked into the spare bedroom where he found Erik pecking on the piano. He handed him a beer. "You look like you could use a drink."

Erik took the bottle. "Yes, thank you. Anna tells me you are a musician, too. What do you play?"

Aidan took a sip of his beer. "We all started out on the piano. My grandma Aoife taught us. Then we chose what else we wanted to play later. My mother taught Brigid to play the violin. Da taught the boys the guitar and mandolin, a little on the bodhrán," Aidan said.

"Wow, y'all must have some fun parties."

Aidan smiled, "Oh, aye. It's quite something when we all get together. Branna fit right in."

Erik smiled as much as he ever did. "She's an amazing woman. I'm not surprised." He looked at Aidan. "I offered to marry her when she showed up pregnant. After she left Ireland." Aidan's face showed some surprise. "I guess you didn't know. Yeah, I offered for her. She turned me down, of course, as gently as she could."

Aidan thought about that. "That was good of you. It was an honorable thing."

Erik shrugged. "Honor might have been part of it. Honestly, I would have given my left nut for a shot at a girl like her. Pregnant or not," he said unapologetically.

Aidan laughed, "Well then, it's good she turned you down. My brother wouldn't have taken kindly to the idea. O'Brien men don't share."

Erik's face darkened. "No man should have to."

Aidan saw him visibly cringe as Felicity's loud cackle came through the house. "The Falks have a problem with being unlucky in love. They choose unwisely."

Aidan looked out at the three in the living room. He hoped not. He wanted nothing but happiness for Alanna. He saw what the fuss was about. Tim had walked in. Aidan flinched as Tim picked Alanna up and twirled her. He watched from the bedroom door, willing himself to stay in place.

Hans was starting to get a headache. The side effect of too much time playing nice with the ex-wife. He looked over to see where Erik was hiding when he saw Aidan. Stoic, still, restrained. But he was staring. He followed his eyes. Tim was spinning Alanna around by the waist and kissing her on the cheek. He'd have laughed if the look on Aidan's face hadn't been so serious. He was jealous. He was keeping it hidden, probably because the rational part of his brain liked Tim and knew there was nothing going on. But he was jealous. He didn't like some other man's hands on his woman. He'd never admit that in a thousand years, but Aidan thought of Alanna as his.

"How have you been Tim? I haven't seen you since Anna graduated from high school!" Felicity said.

Alanna blushed, feeling uncomfortable with the way her mother always ogled her male friends. Right now, she was actually doing the "hang on too long after the hug" move, clasping him at the elbow, leaning back to look at him. She didn't really even know him, and she was acting like they were old friends.

Alanna was trying to figure out a way to extricate him from her clutches when Aidan came forward. "Tim, how are ye, man?" Tim made a quick retreat, meeting Aidan across the floor. Alanna shot her father a look. He was rubbing his temples. This was going to be a long two days.

"So, how has she been?" Tim asked. He'd retreated to the deck with Aidan and Hans. Erik had gone on a beer run, clearly an excuse to get out of there, considering they didn't need beer.

Hans answered first. "She's been quiet. She's better if she's busy."

"What a mess, and the worst possible timing," Tim said.

Aidan nodded, agreeing. "She came home, and I heard screaming. It was bloody mayhem. She'd started shredding her notes, her text books, smashed her diploma. It took a bit of effort to calm her. Then she just cried it out. Women are like that. They're better at getting it out."

The men grunted in agreement. "She's always taken on too much responsibility. She's the first to blame herself. She works too hard, pushes herself too much. It's like she's trying to prove something or trying to make up for something. I never understood it." Hans said, shaking his head. "They really don't come any better than her."

Aidan lifted his beer bottle. "Amen to that." And they all clinked bottles.

By the end of the meal, everyone was rubbing their temples but Felicity. She'd insisted on overseeing the grill, afraid Alanna wouldn't cook her fish the way she liked it. Then she'd made some vegetarian atrocity with tofu, sweet potatoes, and vegan cheese that everyone had to choke down.

Alanna pulled out something that smelled heavenly from the oven. "Who wants dessert?"

The men all raised a hand. "What is it?" Felicity said, picking at her plate.

"They're slutty brownies."

Erik choked on a laugh. Aidan smiled, "Oh, aye. And how did they sink to such a lowly reputation?"

Alanna straightened her spine, looking very serious. "It's a sinful concoction. Cookie dough at the bottom, a layer of oreos, and then covered in brownie batter. Then you bake it, and it gets all warm and gooey."

Aidan took a bite and his eyes rolled back. "Bleeding Christ, these are good. You've been holding out on me, hen." He gave her a mischievous grin, his eyes sparkling. Alanna felt herself glowing a little from the praise.

"You know, Anna, you shouldn't be eating this. It's full of gluten and sugar and not very figure friendly. You've always had to be active to keep the weight off, and you've gained a little since I saw you last. Maybe you should try the vegetarian diet I've been following."

Alanna's face grew tight, but she played it off. Hans stiffened. Tim looked at his plate. Erik's fist tightened around his fork, knuckles white.

"I think they are perfect with all that gluten and sugar. Don't change a thing," Aidan said. "I also think Alanna's perfect."

Aidan directed that comment to Felicity. "She's got those perfect Scandinavian genetics and good southern manners from her da. Considering she's opened up her home to everyone and made us a lovely meal, you should keep your criticisms to yourself." Aidan said this in a cool, calm tone.

Felicity's jaw dropped. "I didn't mean…"

At this point Hans cut her off. "Actually, you did. You've never been very good at seeing another woman get attention. Now, we're going to clear the table, do the dishes, and Aidan is going to take our lovely daughter for a walk on the beach."

Felicity was sputtering. Aidan took Alanna's hand, her face stunned, and drew her toward the beach walk. Aidan heard chuckling from Tim and Erik.

"You didn't have to do that." Alanna said. Her tone was even, but she was still blushing.

Aidan took her hand. "Aye, I did. As much for myself as for you. She needed someone other than your father or Erik to say it. Maybe this time it will sink in. I'm guessing this isn't the first time she's taken an opportunity to belittle you."

Alanna shrugged. "She seems to like to do it around my male friends. I think she gets jealous, as awful as that sounds. My teenage years were very awkward."

Aidan understood. He'd seen the type. "Aye, well she seems to want to stay a teenager. Younger men, no responsibilities, can't admit she's old enough to have a grown daughter."

Alanna looked at him as they walked. "You see a lot, that's exactly it. I think it also bugs her that we both look so much like my dad. There's none of her in us that you can see."

Aidan put his arm around her, giving her a squeeze. "You're right. God knows you didn't get your culinary skills from her." Then he took a napkin out of his pocket, unwrapped it, and there was a huge glob of Felicity's sweet potato, tofu casserole. He threw it to a group of seagulls. Alanna burst out laughing as Aidan lifted one shoulder. "That is singly the worst shite I've ever had on a plate."

Alanna was laughing so hard, she fell on her butt, into the sand. Aidan plopped down beside her, grinning. "I love seeing you laugh, girl."

She put her head on his shoulder. "You make me laugh. I don't think anyone has ever made me laugh like you do, except maybe Branna." She swallowed hard. "I miss her. God, I miss her."

Aidan kissed the top of her head. "You need to make the time, darlin'. Make the time for a visit."

She sighed wistfully. "Maybe if I get this job, I'll be able to afford it. My second interview is Friday. I take the licensure test the day before."

Aidan was surprised. "I thought you had a couple of weeks at least?"

She shook her head. "That was for the North Carolina license. I need to get licensed in Virginia."

Aidan was quiet for a few minutes, soaking that in. "You'll get it."

She took her head off his shoulder, "How do you know?"

He smiled gently at her, "Because they aren't foolish enough to let you get away."

24

Aidan was distracted the next morning, filled with thoughts of Alanna's graduation. It was a small ceremony, given in a small lecture hall for the summer graduates. She'd assured him it would be short and sweet, and that he wasn't missing much, but he still felt like he should be there. As it stood, he was here to train. He couldn't just take leave whenever he felt like it. They were working out in the field again. There would be a mock convoy, men on the ground, and they'd be clearing buildings in combat town. He needed to be with his team, even if they didn't stay together.

The thought chaffed. He found himself itching to follow through, to go with these men he'd come to know, fight with them, train with them. The thought that they would go on to Afghanistan without him made him feel almost panicky, like he was abandoning them when they needed him.

Part way through the day, Aidan had cleared his mind of everything but the men to his front and rear. "Wolfhounds, the wolves are howling." It was Hector over the radio in Aidan's ear. He led into the next room, keeping low and quiet, clearing each room one square foot at a time. They took the stairs in line, moving like one being instead of separate people. Aidan did a quick peek around the corner, then signaled. As they entered the room, all hell broke loose. There was another room, the doorway barely noticeable. A room or a closet that had been deliberately designed to be missed. They designed the scenarios to make conflict inevitable, stacking the odds against the men who were training. They wanted to see them in action. Two tangos came out firing, and the team of men lit them up. They were down in seconds.

"I got one hit!" Corporal Washington yelled. "Corpsman!"

Aidan turned to see Staff Sergeant Polaski on the ground. He had a paintball smear on his forearm. Doc O'Malley was already on it. Washington and Porter covering him as he worked. Aidan's stomach flipped as he remembered the young Lance Corporal from the fight in Sangin.

God, keep them safe without me, he thought as he looked at the young men. "It's a flesh wound. It wouldn't have been fatal."

The mock tangos got up, pulling their helmets off. "Nice shooting, boys. That shit is going to bruise," the one man said as he rubbed his chest where three paintballs had hit him.

"Nice work, ladies. Fall in for chow," Hector came over the radio.

They all sat on the ground, eating their MREs. "How did you guys do?" Lieutenant Drake was talking to Aidan.

"Don't tell him, Captain. We switch buildings after lunch, and they'll run your scenario. You guys get to come with me and clear building two," Hector said.

Aidan swallowed his food. "Sorry, lad. Mums the word." Joey cursed under his breath.

Aidan noticed Porter sitting off by himself. He got up and walked over, plopping down with his lunch. "You did well in there, Sergeant." Then he handed the young man his M&Ms.

"Thanks," the Sergeant shrugged.

"How are you feeling, lad? Have you been keeping in touch with Jessica?"

He concentrated on opening the bag. "Nah. She's got her family and his. She doesn't need me bugging her."

Aidan nodded, "Aye, you can't very well leave in the middle of training. Did you hold vigil for him? You are a Catholic? I've seen you at mass."

Porter scrunched his brow together. "I didn't think of it. Do you think it would help? I mean, if he's stuck or something?"

Aidan cocked his head. "I don't claim to know everything, but I know it's a good way to mindfully pray for someone who might need it. It helps the living, too, I suppose. Since we can't go to the funeral, I think it'd be a nice way to send him off. Would you like me to arrange something with Father Matthew?"

Sergeant Porter thought about it, looking down at the candy in his hand. "I think I'd like that. Would you be there?"

Aidan smiled. "Of course. I'll be there the whole time. We've got night ops tomorrow. I'll try to arrange the chapel for tonight at midnight. Once we're done, we can sleep in a bit before work." Aidan slapped him on the back. "Why don't you join your teammates, ask anyone who knew him if they'd like to come?"

As Aidan got up, he noticed Hector and John watching him. He approached the two men. "That was good of you, Captain. I think it's just what he needs. He's been in a funk. He needs to say goodbye, feel like he did something for him. I wouldn't have even thought of it," Hector said.

"Yes, he needs to put him to rest. The funeral is tomorrow. The timing worked out for us to stay up all night. That is, if the Father agrees."

"Oh, he'll agree. Matthew would do anything for these boys. You let me know if you get any push back, but I don't think you will."

As Aidan walked away, Hector cursed under his breath. "God damn, I am going to miss that Irish bastard."

John's arms were folded over his chest. "I hear you, Major. I hear you."

Aidan came home in the afternoon to find several cars in the drive. Felicity had parked her beat up Subaru in his carport. He parked behind her and went up to take a shower. Then he went over to congratulate the graduate. "Aidan! Come in. You're home early." Alanna went to him and he hugged her, lifting her off the ground. He noticed Felicity's speculating gaze on them.

"Are you joining us this evening, Aidan? Anna would love to have you."

Alanna squeezed his hand. "Yes, you have to. We are going to dinner and then out for karaoke!" Her face was radiant. He couldn't deny her.

"I suppose so, if that's what you want. I can't stay out late, though. Sergeant Porter and Father Matthew and I are going to hold vigil overnight for Luke."

Alanna's face changed. "The young Sergeant that you told me about? That replaced Luke in the training?" He nodded. "Jesus, Aidan. Was that your idea?"

He shrugged. "I've done it at home before. We did it with my father when we lost my uncle. It helps, I think. He can't go to the funeral. This is a way for him to put it to rest."

Alanna smiled, her eyes misting. "I would like to come, once everyone goes to bed. I won't drink tonight."

Aidan's face shifted. "This is your day, lass. You shouldn't stop celebrating for this."

She rubbed his arm, taking in his face. "I won't let it affect my night. I'll have my party, then I'll join you. I want to be there."

Aidan said, "All right, then. Come whenever you're done. We'll be in the smaller chapel at midnight."

Hans had reserved a waterfront table at an Italian restaurant for the occasion. The whole family was there as well as Aidan and Tim. To Aidan's amusement, Felicity had ordered Proscuitto wrapped melon and Veal Piccata. "Thank God they had that vegan ham and veal on the menu," Erik teased.

Felicity waved a dismissive hand. "It's a special occasion. My only daughter has her Master's Degree." The table was rumbling with suppressed laughter.

The waiter came with the dessert tray. "Oh, she doesn't like all that gluten and sugar, just skip her order," Hans said to a puzzled waiter. "But I'll have the cannoli." More giggles.

Felicity smirked at him. "You always could eat whatever you wanted and still stay looking fine." Felicity said in her best southern drawl. Aidan noticed the provocative once over she was giving her ex-husband.

"So, Mom, tell us about Logan." Erik's brows were up, perkily waiting for an answer. Aidan smiled over the rim of his wine glass.

Felicity straightened. "It's Hunter, sweetie. Hunter. He's wonderful. He's introduced me to yoga, actually. Have y'all ever done yoga? Anna, I think you would like it." The entire group looked at her, amazed.

"Um, yes. I actually have tried yoga." Alanna said, trying to keep a straight face. She was trying hard, but it started with Tim. The snickering was like a contagion sweeping through the group until they were all laughing. All but a very confused Felicity.

"What did I miss?"

"Nothing, Mom. Nothing at all." Alanna said.

After dessert and coffee, Hans ordered everyone a glass of prosecco. He clinked his glass with a fork and everyone sat at attention. "I'd like to make a toast to the most beautiful, smart, compassionate woman I've ever had the pleasure of knowing. My daughter, Alanna. Congratulations baby, I'm so proud of you." Everyone raised their glasses and Alanna hugged her father. "Now, for the gifts!"

Alanna blushed. "Daddy, you didn't have to get me anything. This dinner is enough."

Felicity pulled out the first gift. "Mine first." She gave a conspiratory glance to Erik and Hans.

"Thanks Momma. It's big." She unwrapped the box and pulled out what looked like an Irish fisherman's sweater. "Wow! Mom, did you knit this?"

Felicity preened. "Yes, Branna sent me the pattern. It's the O'Brien weave, but she said you had permission to wear it."

Aidan spoke, his voice thick. "Aye, it is. It'll look lovely on you, lass. That cocoa wool will bring out you're eyes." Felicity clapped, as if she couldn't contain her pride or excitement.

Alanna kissed her. "I love you Mom. I'm glad you're here."

Next was her father. He pulled out a small package. "Erik and I did this together along with your grandparents."

Alanna opened it and it was a guidebook. She looked at him strangely. "Ireland? That's very nice, Daddy. Thank you. I can't wait to read it. Maybe once I get a good job, I can go."

Her father just smiled indulgently, "Open it."

She did and she gasped. It was an airline voucher for a round trip ticket to Dublin. We locked in a good fare and you pick the dates."

She leapt out of her chair and threw her arms around her father's neck. He hugged her back as she squealed with happiness. Then she threw an arm out and grabbed Erik, pulling him into the love. "You need to go see your best friend, and those babies. You earned a vacation, baby."

Alanna pulled away, looking at them. "This is too much."

Erik smirked, "That's what I told him." She punched his arm. "I'm kidding! You do deserve it. I am just jealous. Dad got me a knife when I graduated!"

Hans feigned offense, "It's a good knife!" They all laughed.

Alanna looked shyly at Aidan. "Guess I'll get to meet your family." His look was unfathomable. He swallowed hard and nodded once.

Tim was next. "Damn. After all that, my gift is kind of weak!" As Alanna opened his gift, Aidan pulled out the package from Branna. He waited patiently as Alanna looked through a digital photo album of Erik, herself, and Tim when they were younger, all the way to present day. There were even some pictures of Branna in the mix.

When they'd finished, he gave her the package. "Branna mailed it. She was sorry she couldn't be here."

Alanna opened the package. On top were pamphlets from sites around County Clare, then some for other parts of Ireland. There was also a travel agent voucher for her to hire a car, book excursions, what ever she wanted to use it for. When she reached into the bottom, there was something heavy. She pulled it out and choked on a sob. It was a framed picture of the twins. Brian and Halley were smiling with toothless grins, wearing matching onesies that said *tis himself* and *tis herself* across the chest. Branna had captioned the photo. *Come see us Auntie Anna!*

Felicity groaned. "Oh, God. Look at them. They're beautiful!" She put her arm around her daughter. "Now all you need is a tour guide." She looked pointedly at Aidan. "Someone to show her around, keep her safe."

Alanna blushed. "Mom, stop. He doesn't need to do that. He's going to be moving anyway, right? To England?"

Aidan's eyes burned with emotion. The thought of Alanna traveling around his country, wearing his family weave, holding his niece and nephew, stirred something all together primitive in him. "I'd make the time." His voice was labored, husky. He shook himself, breaking the stare.

He cleared his throat. "I've a little something for you, too. It's nothing as grand as all this, but it made me think of you, so..." He pulled out a beautifully wrapped package. One smaller box attached to a bigger item. Alanna took it from him, her cheeks in high color. She was wondering what a man like Aidan O'Brien chose as a gift. She opened the first one. It was a pendant on a chain. It looked like a henge stone with slashes and marks on it. "It's Irish Ogham, a sort of Medieval hieroglyphics, like runes. It's your name, Alanna. It's silver because the Ancient Celts believed silver was for protection."

Alanna looked up from the gift and a single tear came down her face. She handed it to him. "Would you help me?" and she stood up. She pulled her hair off her neck and she could feel his breath on her, soft fingers, then a silky brush of his thumb before he backed away. "It's beautiful."

Then she opened the next one, some sort of book, by the feel of it. She pulled the wrapping paper aside to reveal the cover and title. *Valkyries in Art.* She stared at it for a long minute, then opened the inside. He'd written an inscription on the inside panel. *Now you don't have to choose, little bookworm. Love, Aidan.* She put her fingers over her lips, stifling her emotion. His words came back to her. *Will you live like the bookworm or the Valkyrie?* The book was filled with beautiful paintings, poetry, sketches, all different variations on the myth of the Valkyrie.

She shook her head, speechless for a moment. It wasn't the most valuable gift she'd received, but both of the gifts were so precious and perfect. He'd obviously had the pendant made for her, and she wondered if he'd done it before he came. *I dreamt of you, too.*

"It's perfect," she said simply, caressing his face with her eyes. Then she decided to live like the Valkyrie, and took his face in her hands, planting a sweeping, mind stealing kiss on him. Then she looked in his eyes, the knowing between them. It was Erik who cleared his throat. She stiffened and pulled away. Aidan's gaze was tender and a little bit ruined.

"So, where to next?" Erik said to no one in particular.

25

Aidan hadn't been karaoke singing since he'd been stationed in England. He'd been extremely drunk at the time, but he vaguely remembered a particularly harrowing version of *Wind beneath my Wings* performed by a completely, piss drunk lieutenant colonel who was pretending to serenade his executive officer. They'd been entertaining some Japanese troops, and those bastards were small, but they could drink like Irishman. They also liked to gamble. They'd been taking wagers about whether he would fall off the stage before the song was finished.

This, however, was a different crowd all together. No one was particularly drunk. Although he had no doubt Erik would be sleeping in his bed tonight, and suspected the alcohol intake was to ease the stress of spending this much time around his mother. And how sad was that. Erik and Tim were in the middle of a Hank Williams Jr. song. Tim couldn't sing for shit, but he was up there for moral support. Erik was actually pretty good. Aidan laughed, watching them lose their place on the lyric screen, then punching one another, each blaming the other.

Alanna nudged him. "Country music isn't your thing, I suppose?"

He shook his head. "I'll have to admit, I don't see the appeal. I like the bluegrass, but this modern country? No feeling. Music should be sad or sexy or the type that makes you want to get up and swing your girl around."

Alanna perked up. "You don't think country music can be sexy?" Aidan looked at their fellow companions just as Tim missed a low note, as if to stress his point.

Alanna narrowed her eyes."Hmph. I think you just threw down a challenge, Irishman."

Felicity laughed. "Oh, Aidan, you have no idea. Hans, cover your eyes. This is about to get real."

Hans chuckled. "She's all grown up. As long as it's not a strip-tease, I can take it."

Alanna took the stage as the boys finished. The bar was almost empty, it being a Monday night, but Aidan noticed every man there moved in closer as soon as they saw who was on the stage. The mere presence of Alanna, both classically beautiful and other worldly at the same time, drew a man's gaze like a moth to a torch. The music started, thumping percussion followed closely by heavy acoustic guitar. The screen said *Tornado* by Little Big Town. The beat was intense, driving, and Aidan knew just by looking at Alanna, tapping one sandal slightly and gripping the mic, eyes flaring, that she was about to make him eat his words.

Holy God. The bar was mesmerized. She was the sexiest thing Aidan had ever seen take the stage. Hair flipping, eyes intense, she looked like she could eat you alive and you'd relish the death. She was, quite literally, a tornado. Her voice was perfection, as always, and Aidan couldn't have looked away from her to save his own life.

She pointed a finger straight at Aidan and cocked a brow. Aidan heard the men all chuckling behind him. Tim slapped him on the shoulder with a palm. Felicity had enjoyed telling them about the little can of whoop ass Anna was getting ready to serve up. "What was that you were saying?" Tim asked, but Aidan's brain had checked out. He didn't hear or see anything but that blonde firecracker with the come hither eyes singing to him from the stage.

Memories stormed his mind. Her skirt rucked up to her waist, Aidan on his knees. When she finished, everyone went crazy. Even the cooks from the kitchen had come out to watch her. Aidan shook himself, stood, meeting her as she left the performance area. He bowed deeply to her. "My liege." She put her hand out and he kissed it, making her giggle in that sweet way he loved so much.

Felicity was laughing. "That's my girl." Alanna sat, face not hiding the triumph.

"So when do we get to hear you, Irish? Branna said that all of you O'Briens could sing," Erik asked.

"I'm more of a player than a singer," Aidan said.

Hans spoke up. "That's not what I heard. I heard you were killing it on the labor and delivery floor."

Aidan cursed. "Give me the list."

Alanna snatched it first. "No Irish songs, it's too easy."

He gave her a sideways glance. "You're gonna get it, peahen."

She leaned in, "Do your worst." She handed him the book of songs.

He glanced through it. "Jesus, you call this shite music?" He finally settled on one and walked up with a swagger that had Felicity and Alanna cat calling. He took the mic and addressed the small crowd.

"The lovely lass who's just performed, wasn't she gorgeous all together?" All the men hooted and clapped. Alanna was covering her mouth, suppressing the never ending stream of giggles. He was putting his accent on in full force, and suddenly she could imagine him up on stage with his family, playing to the crowded pub of tourists and villagers.

"Now, my American friends have asked for a song. Being a guest in this fine country, I can hardly decline. I have one condition. I want some dancing if I'm gonna stand up here like an eejit. I've got three single men here with me tonight. Who's going to dance with them?" He gave Hans and Erik a look that said *gotcha*, wiggling his eyebrows.

Alanna squealed, clapping her hands. When the song came up on the screen, Erik barked out a laugh. The mariachi music started, and Aidan began singing. It wasn't a Mexican song, but *Ring of Fire* by Johnny Cash. The cocky bastard nailed it, even with a hint of a brogue, rolling the r's when he sang *burn burn burn.*

The women that were at the bar were a little edgy looking, and had been drinking, so it wasn't hard to get them to play along. Three tattooed, denim-clad women pulled the men out on the dance floor, and they swung the ladies around to the cheers of the other patrons. By the end, the bartender had walked around from behind the bar and given Aidan a shot of Jameson, which he gladly accepted.

He sat, smiling and rubbing his tummy from the burn of the whiskey. "You did not just get people to dance during a karaoke song." Alanna said, a little miffed.

"Aye, I did. Do ye need an encore? I'm sure the other lasses would like a shot at your brother."

Felicity was smiling at the exchange. "Aidan, I thought you were the stuffy military type, but you're actually living up to your bloodline tonight. What can I get you to drink?"

Aidan shook his head. "I can't, but thank you. I've had enough. I have to drive, and I have something at the chapel tonight."

Hans said, "Alanna told me about that. It's a good thing you're doing for that young man."

Three more drinks appeared for Hans, Tim, and Erik, and the older blonde that had danced with Hans gave him a little wave. "Dad, you are a lady killer!" Erik said, taking a sip of the beer. Felicity squirmed in her seat.

Aidan watched Alanna nudge her with her arm. "What about a duet, mom? You still got some stuff?"

Felicity's smile was beaming at the thought of being included. They opened the booklet to choose their song. After a spectacular rendition of *Nine to Five* with her mother, Alanna walked over to Hans. "Nah, you go ahead baby."

She put her arms around his neck. "Come on daddy, remember when you and Brian used to sing with us? It's my party. Come sing with me."

Aidan's eyebrows shot up. He leaned into Felicity's air space. "Can he sing, then?"

She smiled, "Oh yes. He doesn't do it very often. He used to get drunk with Brian and they'd come home arm and arm, singing one thing or another." She looked at Aidan, more seriously. "I know I'm the family joke, and the family failure. I did love him, though. We were happy for a little while. Losing both Brian and Meghan almost killed him. I was already gone. It was easy to block it out." She swallowed hard, "He's a good man. A good father, too. A better parent then I'll ever be."

Aidan suspected the two drinks had loosened her tongue a bit. He also noticed that Erik was listening, trying to pretend he wasn't. "Well, it's never too late to start. Just be her mother, don't try to be one of her girlfriends."

Felicity rubbed her upper lip nervously. "I don't know why I say the things I do, sometimes. I guess it's jealousy. Not like you think. Not of Anna. The cooking? I didn't teach her that. Neither did Hans. Meghan taught her. Meghan taught her a lot in those tender years, when I took off. It's ludicrous, of course, being jealous of a dead woman."

Aidan was taken aback by that little reveal. According to Branna, Hans had been in love with Meghan. Not while Brian was alive. The love grew from the tragedy later. "The only mother you should be competing with is yourself, Felicity. Be a better one than you were the day before."

She smiled, "Good strategy. I'll keep that in mind."

The conversation was interrupted by Tim hooting loudly as Hans and Alanna took the stage. They walked up together and took the mics, the women catcalling Hans from the bar. Alanna started singing, and Aidan shut his eyes, her voice washing over him as it always did. Any guitar player worth his salt had a few James Taylor songs under his belt. Then his eyes shot open when her father joined in, and just like that, he could see Brigid and his own da, voices blending to the delight of everyone within earshot.

In my mind I'm goin' to Carolina
Can't you see the sunshine
Can't you just feel the moonshine
Ain't it just like a friend of mine
To hit me from behind
Yes I'm goin' to Carolina in my mind

He missed his family, missed home, but he would miss this place as well. The sweet, slow way of the south. The wetlands and the surf, the osprey and dolphins. He'd miss the Marines, Sheila the shrimp lady, the old SEAL that lived in his boat, and he'd miss this family. This coastal stretch had its own rhythm, just like Doolin did.

The thought of leaving Alanna was a constant ache, always creeping in the back of his mind. The thought that she would visit, with those travel accommodations she'd been gifted, both elated and saddened him. He would love to be the one to show her Ireland, to show her where the Vikings invaded, and the Valkyries swarmed the sky.

"Oh, my. You've got it bad don't you?" Felicity really needed to get some tact.

"Don't start, mom," Erik chided.

"What? It's obvious enough," She said, innocently.

Tim scooted a chair out. "Aidan, how about you join me up at the bar? I need a freshie."

Aidan looked at him, relief flooding his face. Alanna and Hans were returning to the table. He kissed Alanna's forehead, cradling her skull with his hand. "Ye cut me to ribbons, a mhuirnín." Then he went to the bar with Tim.

"Nothing for me, just a soda water." The bartender gave them both their drinks.

"Are you really going to do this? You're just going to leave in August?" Tim never liked to beat around the bush.

Aidan gave him an impatient look. "I thought this was a rescue from Felicity pecking at me. Are you going to start?"

Tim shook his head slowly back and forth, "Wrong move, my man."

Aidan slammed his glass down. "You think I don't get that? Do you think I won't pine for her until I'm in my grave? This isn't about me. She's got a good job offer coming, and I am not what she needs. She doesn't need one more broken fucker to come home to. She needs better. Surely you understand that?"

Tim gave a shrug. "You're right. She's in a great position to get some do-gooder job. She's also gorgeous, smart, sexy. It's only a matter of time before some dapper young lieutenant in Quantico snatches her up and marries her. She'll have her pick up in DC."

Aidan ground his teeth. "Is this supposed to be helping?"

Tim looked at him, plainly. "No," and he walked back to the table.

The chapel had an eerie quiet to it, only the emergency exit signs glowing. The crucifix hung over the altar, silent and watchful. Alanna and Aidan had driven together, the night winding down early. As they walked in, Father Matthew stirred from behind the pulpit. He approached them. "Thank you for coming. This was a great idea, Aidan. I understand that the young man had drifted away from the church, but this will be good for his friends and for you," he motioned to Alanna. "It's a way to say goodbye and pray for his soul. I'm so grateful you included me. I've been looking for a way to connect with these boys. I don't know if anyone but your young Sergeant will come." As he said it, Sergeant Porter walked in with two young Marines, heads shaved to the quick, collared shirts and khakis. They quietly sat down in the pews of the small chapel. Then two more came in.

Aidan went to Porter and shook his hand. "I hope it's okay. The guys from his unit, they wanted to come too. The word got out around the barracks." Aidan saw three more come in, two females and one male, all bowing and crossing themselves at the holy water font. His throat tightened.

Matthew's hand came on his shoulder. "God is here with us, friend. Can you feel it?" Aidan nodded, not trusting himself to speak. He looked at Alanna, her eyes traveling over the young men and women. This was them. This is who she wanted to reach, to save, to lift up and heal. Then Aidan noticed two couples came in from the therapy sessions she'd hosted. She went to them and hugged them all in turn. John and Hector were the final people. At final count, fifteen people had shown up and Father Matthew was glowing beatifically. He walked to the pulpit and began.

"It's been a while since I held an overnight vigil, so you'll all bear with me as I take a bit of an informal approach to this evening. First, I want to thank you all for coming. It warms my heart in this day and age to see so many young, strong faces following the word of God."

The priest fiddled with some papers on his pulpit, then looked up at them all. "Suicide is a tough subject. We were all taught by stern nuns and hellfire priests at one time or another that it is a mortal sin, capable of robbing someone of their salvation. I've been thinking a lot about that since I joined the Navy, especially over the last few years. The suicides are climbing. It's a problem I can no longer watch from the sidelines." Aidan was tense, listening to the priest's words. But he didn't condemn Luke.

"The truth is that no one knows another's soul, to the depth that God knows it. Suicide is never condoned, but culpability is diminished in many instances. Psychological difficulties, anguish, grave fear, many other things can cause a person to take their own life, but they are not doomed to Hell. Luke was in pain. All of you who knew him understood that he was being treated for both a brain injury and other things."

The other things being psychological, but Matthew didn't need to say it. "In his final words, he asked his family to forgive him. He also asked God to forgive him." Father Matthew swallowed a sip of water, struggling as he saw the sad faces of the men and women before him. "I can tell you that none of us knows what was in Luke's deepest mind and heart, only God knew. All we can do is help Luke on his way by praying the Divine Mercy Chaplet, Prayers to St. Michael the Archangel who watches over all warriors, and to seek the words of the scripture in order to better serve Luke and his family. We will start with the Chaplet that you'll find in your leaflet. If you don't have your rosary, we have a basket that Aidan will pass around containing some lenders." Aidan walked around the room, offering the prayer beads to anyone who didn't have a set. Then they began.

At the end of the five hours, everyone was numb. At first there had been tears, then silent obedience as Father Matthew took them through the prayers. He had each person read from some selected passages in the bible dealing with death, eternal life, salvation, and grieving. At one point when everyone started getting bleary eyed, he had a few of the young men come up and tell some stories about Luke. Not sad ones, but good stories about what he'd been like before his decline.

Before they knew it, their time was over. The sun was coming up and Luke would be buried today. They all gathered together holding hands. "Lord, lift up these young people in the work they do. Reward them for their faith and for the sacrifice they made this evening to ensure intercession for their friend Sergeant Luke Jones. Give them the strength to use this loss to minister to others. Ease their hearts and help them to seek comfort in you, oh Lord, and in each other." At this Alanna squeezed Aidan's hand and he looked at her, a slight smile on his face.

When they all parted, the men shook hands with each other. The women hugged. "Thank you Captain. I've never had a superior do something like this for me, ever. I wish you were going with us," Sergeant Porter said, "as crazy as that sounds."

Aidan clapped him on the back, "Not at all, lad. I wish I was going with you, too." As the young man walked away, Aidan turned and got enveloped in a man hug by none other than the hard assed Major Diaz.

He pulled away and met Aidan's eyes. "You are good people, amigo. Thanks for doing this. I think this helped him a lot. He needed to get his mind right about this. Especially before we head to the sandbox. Your men back home are lucky to have you." Aidan was embarrassed by the praise, so he said nothing. John and Hector left for home, and Aidan and Alanna began the drive back to the beach house.

"I'm proud of you Aidan. This was a good thing. I know it helped me, and it seemed to help the others," Alanna said.

Aidan shrugged, "I just made a phone call. Father Matthew handled it all. Sgt. Porter got all the others there."

She rubbed his arm. "But you thought of it. You were worried about him, and you figured out what he needed. That's a gift not everyone has. Face it Aidan. You are a good Catholic boy at heart."

He gave her a sideways glance. "I think we both know I'm no saint."

She smiled, "Well, that's true. I have first hand knowledge on that account. Hey!" She pointed out the window. "Isn't that our oak tree?"

Aidan barked out a laugh. "You are shameless. And you having come right out of mass. Don't go reminding me about that when I'm tired and my defenses are down."

She put her head on his shoulder. "I'm just teasing. I'm sorry." Then she fiddled with her necklace. "I love my gifts. They're special. You thought about it when you chose them."

He kissed her head where it laid. "You're never far from my mind, girl. I may be keeping my distance, but you're never far from my mind."

Aidan walked into his house and found Erik passed out on his pull-out couch and Tim in his bed. He was glad they had been sensible enough not to drive. He took a blanket and walked outside, running into Alanna. She was drinking some water and staring out at the water. "Let me guess, no bed?"

He laughed, "No, I'm afraid not. I'm headed for the hammock until someone wakes. It's shaded. Do you mind?"

She shook her head. "No, not at all. I'd offer to let you snuggle up in my bed, but that always gets us in trouble."

Aidan gave a grunt. He'd love nothing more that to sleep with her spread across his chest again. That one night they'd shared a bed was burned in his memory. Not the hanky-panky, as she called it, but the feel of her. Her breathing, the smell of her hair, the softness of her legs tangled with his.

"I think about it, too." She said sadly, reading his mind.

He took her hand, removing the bottle of water from her grip. "Just a little while. Please. I need you just for a little while." He took her under the covered deck area and laid on the hammock. She went with him, settling between his legs. The ropes squeaked, but the padded area enveloped them both. Alanna sighed as she spread across his chest and felt the light blanket come over her.

"We shouldn't be doing this," she said softly.

Aidan ran his fingers gently through her hair, grazing her scalp. "I know. I just need it. I need it for just a while. I promise, I'll behave."

She looked at him, propping her chin on his chest. "And who says I will?"

He pushed her head back down on his chest. "Behave ye little vixen. We've just come from church." She giggled and settled down into his body. They were both asleep within seconds.

Tim woke them two hours later, and Aidan crawled into bed after a shower. The temperature had risen, and he and Alanna had been sweaty upon waking. He almost hated to wash her off of him. He carried the scent of her skin and hair and clean sweat. He'd put the A/C on and draped a blanket over the window for a darker room. He fell into a deep, restful sleep. By the time he woke up, Erik, Felicity, and Tim had all gone, and Hans was getting ready to head back to Virginia.

"Thank you." Hans seemed to utter those words without reason or preamble.

Aidan cocked his head, stirring honey into his steaming cup of tea. "For what?"

Hans looked at him as if he were a child, or daft. "For taking care of her."

Aidan looked away. "I don't do anything an honest neighbor wouldn't do."

Hans coughed out a laugh. Aidan met his gaze, a bit of challenge creeping into the exchange. "If that's all she is to you, Captain, then you best make it clear. Real clear." He shoved something in his bag with a little more force than was warranted.

Aidan cursed under his breath. He stepped away from the tea, running his hand through his tightly cut hair. Hans softened a bit. "Just don't toy with her. She's a good girl. The best. She deserves something real."

Aidan clenched his jaw, taking a breath before he spoke. "Don't you think I know that she deserves better? It's why I've been keeping my distance."

Hans looked taken back. "That's not what I meant at all. I think you are good for her. I think a lot of things. But if you won't give her all of you, if you won't love her, then what I think doesn't matter."

I already love her. With every breath of my body, I love her. "Aye, I understand."

26

Night training had been an outstanding bit of fun. Night vision, signal flares, sneaky sneaky in the dark. The only downside had been the bugs. Mosquitos, ticks, and even fleas. Aidan spent the morning shower time de-ticking himself around his ankles. He fell asleep instantly until his nightmares had awakened him. He got out of bed and walked into the kitchen, needing a cup of tea. As he waited for the kettle, he looked at the tablet on the counter. His list of five. He looked at the clock on the stove. It was tea time in Ireland, five hours ahead. Shit. Was he really going to do this?

Alanna had just gotten out of the shower after teaching back to back yoga and Zumba classes. She heard a tapping on her door and pulled back the blinds to see Aidan standing there. The only word she could think of was nervous. He looked nervous. "Come in. Are you okay? How was work?" Then she looked in his hand. He was holding the writing tablet she'd given him. She softened, running her hand over the back of his head, putting their foreheads together. "I'll go outside." She kissed his mouth softly and started toward the door.

"Wait, I wanted to show you that I added someone." He showed her the list. He'd put a sixth name at the bottom. *Alanna.* Her breathing was shaky and she covered her mouth. "Just go in your bedroom, leave the door open. I can't..." he paused. "I can't see you. I won't get through it if I can see you." She nodded, her eyes welled with unshed tears. Aidan sat at the computer. He'd texted his father a few minutes ago to see if he was home. He could do this. Alanna went into her room, leaving the door ajar.

"Hello son. It's good to see you." His father's gaze was speculative. He knew something was up.

"Is Ma around?"

Sean looked behind him. "I've gone in the other room, like you asked. Did you want me to get her?"

Aidan shook his head. "No, Da, I just need you for now." Then he began. He started with the nightmares, the headaches, the flashbacks. His father's face was sad, but not particularly surprised. As Aidan went through the details, he eventually began to unwind, his joints loosening a bit. Then he told him about the list of five and what Alanna had been doing to help him.

That's when his father's face registered the first glimmer of pain. "I've always been at the top of your list, boy. Always. You tell me. Tell me whatever you are ready to share."

Aidan cleared his throat, trying to ready himself. "We were patrolling in Sangin. We knew there'd been Taliban activity in the area. There was a young corporal. It was his first deployment. Christ, Da. He was so excited. Nervous, but excited. You know how it is, when you're new and untried?"

His father nodded, "Aye, I do. Not like what you did, but I get it."

Aidan continued, "It was an IED, followed by an exchange of fire. The boy, he was the first casualty. His leg..." Aidan swallowed. "It was gone. Shrapnel in a few places. It severed an artery. He was gone so fast."

He looked at his da, intensely. "We made them pay. It's when I got the Distinguished Service Order. I was like a robot. I shut down my grief, disengaged every emotion but stone cold fury. I fought like a demon. I avenged him." His voice broke. "Then I helped put him in the vehicle, even part of his leg. It was too late, but we got him home. I picked up his helmet, and there was a picture of his parents in the lining. His parents and his little brother. They were from Antrim County. He looked just like his mother. We got him home to her." Aidan looked at his father and immediately second guessed this decision. Tears were coming down his face, silent tears. "Da, I should stop," he said, quickly.

"No! No, son. You don't quit. I'm okay. I just mourn for you and for the lad's family. Don't you worry about me, Aidan. You've done that enough. You keep going. Please, we need this."

Aidan sighed. "I dream about him sometimes. I see his face in my men, especially the young ones. He was a good kid. He was funny, happy. He was about Liam's age. He'd barely lived at all. He had a sweetheart back at home. He met her on leave, wanted to marry her. I got a medal for that day, and he went home in pieces." Aidan's throat was thick and tight.

"I'm so sorry. Christ, I'm so sorry, Aidan."

Aidan shut his eyes. "I'd give it back. I'd give the medal back, all of the medals and awards. I'd give it all back if he could just be alive. If all of them could just be alive. I'd change places with him if I could. He was twenty years old. He should have been able to come home, get married to that girl he fancied, have children. He should have had all of that. I should have watched him more carefully. When we split up, I should have taken him with me."

Sean's face changed. "Jesus, Aidan. It wasn't your fault." Aidan ground his teeth, saying nothing. "The only people at fault were those bastards that set off that mine. You hear me? They robbed him of those things. You made it as right as you could. Ye did your duty." Then something occurred to him. "Ah, God." His voice broke. "Is that why you haven't married? Because he didn't get to? Is that what you've been making yourself pay for?"

Aidan squirmed under his intense gaze. "I don't know what you mean, Da. I told you why..."

Sean cut him off. "Maybe you don't see it, but I do. I see everything. You love children. The way you are with little Cora, with the twins and Colin. I see the longing. You want your own, but you haven't let yourself have them, or a woman. Not for real. That young man would not have wanted you to give it up. He'd have wanted you to treasure the opportunity to live a full life, like he didn't. You deserve to be happy, Aidan. God, you're the best man I've ever known. My beautiful sons, so brave and smart and good. I want you all to have what your mother and I have. You don't deserve to be alone."

Aidan slapped the desk. "You don't understand. It's not just the fighting. It's not just losing men. Christ, the stuff in my head, Da! The shit in my head!" He pounded his finger to his temple.

Alanna was sitting on the floor of her bedroom, her back against the door jam. She put her head in her hands and wept, silently. She wept for Aidan, for the young man that died that day, for his family. She wept for the sweetheart that he never got to marry. She wept for Sean. The pain was straining his voice, pain for his son.

"You've been over there four times, Aidan. More than anyone I know. You just keep volunteering. Is that the only incident? There's more. I can tell by your face that there's more."

Aidan put his hand over his brows. "I don't know if I can, Da."

Sean touched the screen. "I wish I could reach through this screen. I wish I could hold ye like I did when you were young. I wish I could touch you, and tell you to your face, that whatever it is, I can handle it. Let me bear some of this for you. Please, Aidan."

His voice was trembling now. "Do you think I don't understand? I haven't been to war, but I've seen my own share of depravity. The worst scum of humanity, child abusers and rapists and murderers. I didn't always work in the country and villages, Aidan. That's all you remember, aye, but I worked in the city earlier in my career. Babies goin' hungry to feed their mother's needle. Cigarettes put out on the skin of children. Bodies thrown in the bin for the rats to chew."

Aidan blinked, speechless. "You never told me any of that. You never talked about it."

Sean sighed, "No. I didn't. I didn't want to put that on you. You're my child. Maybe I should have, when you got older. I just tried to put it behind me."

Aidan swallowed hard. "And who was on your list of five, back when it was happening?"

Sean smiled, "Good question. Well, let's see. I suppose my brother, until he died. Yeah. He was on there. Father Christopher, the Garda Chaplain. I talked to him sometimes. My da." Then he shrugged, "And your ma, of course."

Aidan stopped him. "You told Ma?"

Sean snorted. "Oh, I tried to keep it in. I thought I was protecting her. Nose like a bloodhound, that one. She always knew. When I'd had a rough night, she knew. Said she could read it in the lines of my face, the set of my body. That little hellcat wouldn't let me sleep until I'd spilled my guts. Said it wasn't good for me to go to bed with it weighing on me. She'd likely have beat it out of me, if I'd been stubborn about it."

Aidan laughed, so did Sean. "She's tough, Aidan. We love that, the O'Brien men. We like our women strong. It's a blessing and a curse. Your ma is my best friend, though. I tell her everything."

Aidan thought about that, and about Alanna in the next room. He could feel her, the essence of her as if she was seated beside him. He'd only had the courage to do this because of her. He couldn't tell his father that, though. "I miss you, Da. I miss you all," Aidan said.

"We miss you too, a mhic. Now, you've got more to tell me. Am I right? Don't be afraid. You can tell me anything."

Aidan slowed his breathing and opened his mind, unlocking the box that he kept shut so tightly. The place in his mind where he choked down the memories that only crept out in his nightmares. He remembered it all.

The platoon had been conducting searches and interviews for days. The intelligence they'd been given said that there was a group of rebels in the area, somewhere on the east end of Kabul. More intel about a stash of weapons. Aidan took his helmet off, wiping his brow with the bandana Brigid had sent him. The tribal elder sat across from him as his wife poured the tea. Aidan had men guarding the entrance to the rundown building, the hallway exits, and the door to the apartment. He sat there with his interpreter and two other men from his unit.

Artillery was going off in the distance, in another part of the city. The air was thick with dust and the stink of poor plumbing and decaying building. Aidan thanked them in their native tongue and sipped the tea. Strong and sweet, at odds with the dull and tired surroundings. The man's sons were scattered throughout the room, and a little girl played in the corner with a doll at her grandmother's feet. She was old enough to have her head covered but still young enough to play with dolls.

"Tell him we need the location of those men, and the guns. It's safer for everyone if we find them. They are attacking the people, stealing food, starting fires. It is best if he just helps us. It will be better for his family."

The interpreter talked to the man. He shook his head and spoke. "He says he doesn't know anything. He says he will keep his family safe. He can't be caught helping us, even if he did know something." They spent the next hour trying to persuade him to talk. Aidan could tell that his older son wanted to say something, but when they spoke with him, his father snapped at him. The boy dropped his eyes and fell silent. In the end they got nothing. These people were just too scared.

Aidan looked up at his da. "In the end someone did talk. Later that day, the Americans got some information on the guns, they seized part of their weapons stash, but still no men. I didn't find out about the attack until several days later."

Aidan walked through the same building with his men, and his guts were rolling. The smell of dried blood was thick in the air. Patterned splatters on walls and steps. Spent casings outside the building. This was a murder scene, plain and simple. He came to the door of the apartment where he'd interviewed the community elder the week before. The door had been kicked in, the lock portion splintered, along with the door jam. He took a deep breath and knocked. The interpreter called out the greeting. They stood ready, hoping a fight wasn't coming. A young boy came to the door, one of the younger sons, Abdul. He was about eight or nine years old. Behind him was another boy, about ten, a cousin from a few apartments over.

"The armed men had shown up after the weapons seizure. Word had gotten out that we'd been there." Aidan rubbed his eyes, tired and trying to scrub some image from them. "The menfolk were dead, all of them. The older sons as well. The cousin, Sharif, was there because they'd killed his father as well, and his older brother. Both the wives, too, after they'd raped them." Aidan's voice was quiet, strained. He closed his eyes, remembering as he kept talking.

Aidan sat before the grandmother, the only adult left in the house. Her eyes were ruined, tired, angry. "She says that they tried to tell them that we'd given you no information. They didn't care to hear it. They were sending a message to the rest of the people. They killed her sons and her grandsons. They defiled their wives, and then killed them when they were done. The only one they left alive was..." The interpreter motioned with his head to the bundle of blankets in the corner. The young girl, huddled, eyes blank, clutching her doll. The old woman kept talking and the translator made a sound, coming from his gut.

"What? What did she say?" asked Aidan.

The men had used the girl, but they left her alive. Threatened to come back. The interpreter spoke her words, sweat coming down his face, voice shaking as he translated. "There are no men in our family left to do it, just her little brother and her cousin. They are young, they won't. They can't. Please, it is honorable. Take her away and do it. She's too sick to do it herself, and I am too old. The other men in the village, they wouldn't be quick. It should be quick. She shouldn't suffer. You have kind eyes. You will not make her suffer. Take her before they come for her."

Aidan looked at his father, one tear coming between his eye and nose. "She was hurt inside, badly." He choked on the words. "And she had a high fever. She needed a doctor, but the old woman wanted me to put her down like a dog," he said bitterly. "In the end, we took the girl. It was against the rules, but I knew of a Doctor's

Without Borders clinic not too far from the complex. Her cousin was the oldest boy. He acted as her chaperone. They found someone to transport them behind us in an old truck. I carried her, laid her across the flat bed, protecting her with pillows and coverings."

Aidan met his father's eyes. He was like stone, jaw tense with stifled emotion. He wanted to keep it together, not wanting his son to feel like he had to stop. "They took her into the clinic. I waited there with the boy. He thanked me for not doing what his grandmother had asked of me," His voice stuttered as he continued.

The interpreter sat next to the boy as he ate an MRE from Aidan's pack. The boy was starving, but he spoke to Aidan as he ate. "He says that if they hurt the boys, no one does anything. When they hurt the girls, she is supposed to go away. She is shamed. He said he doesn't want them to make his cousin go away. He wants the Americans to help her. He said he will join and fight with you if you help her."

Aidan pointed to his patch. "Irish," was all he said. Then he addressed the interpreter. "Tell him that he doesn't have to fight. I will do what I can."

The doctor came out then, a woman doctor wearing a hijab and a lab coat. Aidan stood, telling the interpreter what to say. "I speak English, Lieutenant. You may speak to me directly." Her accent was heavy, but her English was very good.

"How is the girl?" The doctor looked at the boy. "He has no English. You can speak freely. We will tell him what we think he can handle."

She smiled at that. "He's a child of war, which means he is no child. He's not had the luxury. Go ahead and translate for him. It is his right. As for the girl, she's not well. She is septic. The internal wounds have festered, her bowel is perforated as well. The infection has spread to her blood. Her internal injuries are numerous. She also has several broken bones. She hasn't had food or even water for days. I'd imagine they were hoping she'd slip away, quietly. We are doing what we can for her, but this is a clinic. Getting her to the main hospital would be dangerous, they are watching it. I'm not sure, even if she was strong enough for surgery, that the doctors would help. They are local doctors. They would give her back to her family and then they would wait to bury her."

Aidan cursed, "How can they be so cruel? She's a child!" He was raising his voice.

The doctor's face was sad. "What did her grandmother say?"

He clenched his jaw. "She told me to do it quick, make sure she didn't suffer."

The doctor nodded. "She's from a different generation. That's perhaps what her family would have done, or tried to marry her off to someone who would accept her impurity."

Aidan was sweating, the room closing in. "She's not impure. She's the victim. She's a goddamn baby!"

The doctor stopped short, "Do not lecture to me, Lieutenant. I'm giving you the reality, not the fairytale. In this country, she's of marriageable age. You think it doesn't make me sick? I grew up here. My parents tried to marry me off to some man old enough to be my grandfather when I was fifteen, because he was wealthy! I got out. I had an aunt that lived in the West, in England. She bribed and schemed, and she got me out."

Aidan was breathing hard. He wasn't mad at this woman. She was trying to help. Then he felt his interpreter's steadying arm on him. "They are not all like that. Perhaps if her father had lived…but now she is seen as damaged. It is cruel, but you have done what you can. You need to go back to the base. This isn't a secure place."

Aidan's other men were within ear shot. He looked at them. "Aye, I know."

The doctor spoke again. "There are underground networks. The infrastructure of the country is gone, so it is more difficult, but they still exist. I can try to place her if she lives. I'll keep the boy here, and I'll try to place her. Then he can go back and take care of the grandmother and smaller child."

Aidan looked at her sharply. "He's ten."

She shrugged. "If he was a full grown man, he'd be dead with the others. He knows his duty." She turned to the boy and spoke in his language. The interpreter translated for Aidan. "You are a brave boy. You help these men anyway you can. Then you take your place as the head of the household." The boy nodded solemnly.

Aidan said,"Can I see her? Before I go? I just want to make sure she's ok, that she feels safe."

Aidan followed the doctor with the interpreter and his fellow Lieutenant, along with the young boy. The others stayed back to watch the exits. They weaved through the building, passing rooms with too many beds and not enough staff. There were people stacked in the hallways as well. It was clean. As clean as they could make such humble circumstances. The equipment was old and looked outdated. "I'm sorry. I shouldn't have turned my anger on you."

She smiled as they walked. "You're a good man, Lieutenant O'Brien. I understand about anger. Some days, I think have enough anger to burn this city to the ground."

"Why did you come back? You escaped," Aidan said.

The doctor shrugged, answering his question with another question. "Why did you bring this girl to me? She is nothing to you. You could have walked away," she said.

Aidan nodded, understanding. She took him into what looked like a children's area. The clinic was small, but they managed to keep the kids together, away from the others. She led him to the girls bed. She had an IV, clean linen and a hospital gown. Her hair was uncovered now, because their was a bandage on her forehead and they had forgone the hijab. She had long, glossy hair that curled at the ends. Child's hair, lovely and unrestrained like Brigid's used to be as a girl.

She looked at him weakly, her big brown eyes scared and sad. "Tell her I hope she's feeling better, that she should eat and rest." The interpreter told her. She cleared her throat. Aidan didn't understand what she said, but he caught one word. "Papa".

"She wants to know if you have children back at home."

Aidan shook his head. She pulled her covers in closer. Aidan sat down in a small chair, next to her as the tears welled in her eyes. "I have a niece. She's just a baby, but she likes it when I sing to her. Would you like me to sing something for you?" She listened as the interpreter talked, then she nodded. So, Aidan sang. A lullaby, soft and sweet, as the girl drifted to sleep.

Aidan came awake, outside of his head, and looked up, surprised to see his father still there on the screen. His father had his hand over his mouth, tears breaking the surface and rolling. "She died the next day. I checked on her. The boy gave us the information his father and uncle had kept a secret. There was an old cafe. It was boarded up, connected to another office building. They were hiding there, living off the dry goods. It was a good location, a couple of exits, food, water, centrally located."

His face tightened with fury. "We hit it the next day, with the Afghani forces. The leader was on one of the most wanted lists. A heavy hitter, a well earned reputation for being a horrible fuck. I looked around at all of their faces. The boy told me about one in particular. The one that had done the worst to the women, especially the girl. He said he had one eye like habib…milk. One milky eye and a scar from his ear to his collar bone."

Aidan's hands were clenched. "I grabbed the bastard, started to beat the hell out of him. I wanted him dead, Da. I wanted him dead, and I wanted it to take days for him to die, like it did for her."

His face was hard. "Aye, son. I understand. You didn't kill him, though?" His eyes were wary, the unsure set of a man's face when he wasn't sure he really wanted to know.

Aidan shook his head. "No, we needed to question them. Two died in the raid, but we needed the rest alive. My captain put an arm on me, or I may well have beat the wee mongrel to death. Then we talked to the Afghani troops that were with us. I told them what they had done, what he had done. They said the milky eyed man was of no consequence, a low ranking soldier. They said they would make sure he got what was coming to him, after the interrogation was finished." He looked at his father, "Whatever they did, it wasn't enough. We brought those men to her house. They let us into their home, gave us tea. Then we left and the retaliation happened. We didn't protect them. We couldn't protect any of them. Maybe if I'd checked on them sooner."

"Aidan, look at me. Look at me, boy." Aidan looked at the screen. "I'm sorry for it. Christ, if I could take that memory from you I would. It's scars you to your soul, things like that. The worst part of humanity would harm a child. But you did everything you could for that girl."

Aidan put his hand over his face. "I got the Gallantry Cross for it. For catching one of the leaders and for gallantry in the face of human rights atrocities." He laughed bitterly. "Only in such a fucked up world would I be considered gallant for taking a sick, brutalized girl to the hospital!" His chin was trembling. "I wake up, and I can still smell the dirt and the crumbling concrete and the musty walls of that building. I see that little girl playing tea party in the corner. This shit is in my head. It's there for good." His tears were silent.

The strength of his son both made him proud and made him want to scream. "I wish I was there with you, son. I wish I could put my arms around you." Sean was weeping now, with that same silent way about him. His throat ached with the effort.

"I'm here." The voice was soft behind Aidan. Sean watched as the girl came on shaky legs. "I'm hear, Sean. I'll hold him," her voice stuttered as she knelt down next to Aidan and took him in her arms.

Aidan gripped her tight. "I'm sorry, lass. Christ, don't cry. I'm sorry. I shouldn't have let you hear."

She pulled away from him. "No, Aidan. This is not about me." She kissed his face, his eyes, she wiped his tears. "Let someone else comfort you. I'm here. Let me soothe you." She ran her palm along his face. He shut his eyes, soaking in the contact. She looked at Sean. "I'm here. I'll be here as long as he needs me."

Sean smiled sadly. "Thank you, girl."

Sean finally ended the call and stayed there for a moment, not ready to face his wife. He sat staring at the blank screen, hand over his mouth. Then the stuttering sobs started to finally escape. "Oh, God. My boy." He had always known that the war brought harsh memories for his eldest son. He knew about the nightmares, the jumpiness that would come from loud noises, crowds. He hadn't suspected the depth of his experiences. The true horror of the war, and the toll it had taken on Aidan. He closed his eyes, remembering the telling. When he'd talked about the little girl, it had been necessary to shut off his emotions to do it. It was almost like he'd been reading an article in the paper or speaking from a far off place. Detached. It was the only way, Sean suspected, that he'd been able to get through it.

Then wee Alanna had come to him. She was breathtaking in her beauty. Every bit as lovely as Branna, but another side of the coin. Where her hair was raven, Alanna's was sun and copper. He saw the blue depths of the ocean in Branna's eyes, but in Alanna's eyes he saw the green of new spring grass, still cold and fragile, so brightly green as to hurt your eyes with its beauty.

Aidan was in love with her. He'd never seen his son react to a woman in such a way. Christ, the way they'd held on to each other. Like he was the sun and the moon and the earth beneath her feet, like she was the air that kept him breathing. He knew he had to talk to Sorcha about this, all of it. What he didn't know was how much to tell her.

Then he heard her. He turned to see the door, once closed, cracked open. He heard his wife's muffled sobs. He got up and opened the door. She was sitting on the floor, right by the door. Her head was on her knees and she was weeping. "No! Oh God, Sorcha. Why did you disobey me?" He sunk down on his knees. "He didn't want you to hear this, darling. Why?"

Her face was soaked, her eyes fierce. She grabbed him by the shirt. "He's my baby! My beautiful baby boy." She choked on another sob. "I need him, Sean. I need my baby. He needs us." She was hysterical now.

He held her, choking on his own sobs. "I'll make it happen, love. I'll call Miriam in the morning. We'll go to him, darling. As soon as we can get to him, I swear it."

Alanna took Aidan into her bedroom and they curled together under the covers. She cradled his head against her breast, rubbing his head and mumbling soothing words to him. "You're the bravest man I've ever known, Aidan."

He snorted a bit. "You're a bit biased."

She grazed his scalp with her nails. "You're wrong. I see you perfectly. You're brave and you have a pure heart. What you did for that girl, as hard as it was to hear, I see to the heart of you now. You can't hide from me anymore."

He sighed, quiet for a while. "When I carried her to the truck, she was so small. Small for her age. I tried to be careful. She was bundled and that was good. She was delirious, beaten, utterly broken." His breath stuttered as he let it out, heavy and tired. "I went back, after I'd been to the base. We gathered as many rations as we could, stuff they could eat. Some water purifying tablets, blankets, some fresh water. The boys were grateful. The grandmother told them to hide it all. When I asked the boy about it, he told me. If others knew they had it, they'd accuse them of taking bribes for information, then they'd steal it all. They'd steal the only food an old woman and two small boys had in the world."

Alanna tightened her grip on him, let him feel the reality of her as he continued. "I went back. This last time I deployed, I went back. The two boys were older, o'course, and the grandmother was dead a couple of years. They'd stayed in the apartment. They were almost men, starting to get a bit of chin hair, taller, wider in the shoulders, but I'd seen their faces so many times in my dreams. They remembered me, too. My new interpreter was confused. He said that they had a nickname for me."

She pulled his head to meet his eyes. "What was your nickname?"

He looked away from her, focusing on nothing "Mikail, from the Quran, one of their archangels. He is said to provide nourishment for body and soul, and he was their angel of mercy." He put his forehead against her chest. "I was there with a gun and my men and our aircraft and tanks. We brought war to these boys, but they thought I was an archangel. I'm not. I couldn't save them anymore than I could save their sister."

"Oh, Aidan. Don't you see? Michael was a warrior angel, but he was a guardian, too. You put down your sword and you tended to that sick child. She died in a clean bed, with food, medicine, and the sound of your singing in her head." Her voice was strained, cracking as her tears started again. "You fed an old woman and two small boys. You might not be an archangel, but you are pretty damn close." She kissed him between the eyes, and he pulled in closer to her, their limbs entangling. He fell asleep after a few minutes, and she turned the light off.

Later, he woke with a jerk, not knowing where he was. "It's ok. It's me. You're in my room," she whispered. Then she leaned over and clicked on the small lantern she'd used in her class. She turned her face to his, sliding her hand down to clasp his. "I'm here." Aidan kissed her mouth softly, then he closed his eyes and went back to sleep. The next time he woke, it was morning, and Alanna was out of the bed.

Alanna was taking a sip of coffee when Aidan walked out of her room. A thrill ran through her that would make a southern girl blush. Low slung shorts and a splendid amount of one hundred percent Irish eye-candy. He'd shed his shirt in the middle of the night. She looked him up and down, and suddenly she was right back in his bed, stroking him, abs flexing, hips rolling. His face and body had been resplendent as she'd brought him over the edge.

Aidan noticed her appraisal, as if he could read her thoughts, and she darted her eyes away. He'd been clear about what he wanted. Yet, his eyes had flared. Of course they did. He never said he wasn't attracted to you. He just said it was a bad idea.

Alanna took a cup out of the cabinet. "You like cream in yours, right?" She turned and ran into his big body. He took the cup, set it down and pulled her close. She melted into the hug, breathing in his earthy, sleepy scent. "Thank you."

27

Alanna left for Virginia with a spruced up resume, transcripts, and a copy of her thesis paper in her briefcase. The feel and the scent of Aidan was still with her. There had been no hanky panky last night, but the intimacy was potent. He'd flayed himself open to her and his father. She smiled sadly to herself as she drove the long stretch of highway, up to Northern Virginia. He'd seemed tired, but something about him was lighter this morning. A burden shared between three was lighter. Her phone was binging one right after the other. Whoever was texting her had sent several, consecutively. Either that, or she was on some dreaded group text.

She pulled over at a rest area, parked, and grabbed her phone. When she opened the messages, her gaze was fixed, not completely registering what she was seeing, then the words. *You've been busy. Does your father know what a whore you are?*

She screamed and dropped her phone. Her breathing was shallow, her vision started to dim. Panic attack. Breathe. The pictures scrolled through her head. Standing on the deck with Aidan, sharing a cup of coffee, then her date with Rick, one of her and Tim out to dinner, more with Aidan, reclining on the loungers. How in the hell did that bastard have her cell phone number? She'd put it in her father's name, on a family plan, to avoid it. Then the memory of her cell phone bill ripped open came back to her. Someone had been in her mailbox.

Between the studying, the death of Luke, and her newfound friendship with her neighbor, she'd let herself forget about Steve. It was easy to do. His communications were sporadic. He'd go months without contact. Mainly because she'd moved around, changed her numbers, used altered names on social media. The only site that had her real name was a professional site. She'd upped her security as high as she could. He'd gotten her e-mail though. That was the last time she'd heard from him.

He was supposed to be in Asia somewhere, but he was obviously having her followed. Either that, or he was nearby. The last postcard had been from Thailand, but that was months ago. The mere thought made her look around, look in the back seat. She was wishing, now, that she'd brought her gun.

It wasn't until she felt dampness on her wrist that she realized she was crying. Tears soaked her face, her nose running, and she was shaking. She picked up the phone. She saved the pictures to her email, in case she lost her phone. She had to put them in the file she kept. She'd spoken to the police in Virginia, when the unwanted contact had first started happening. The fact that he was a previous intimate partner made them turn the tables a bit, thinking she was a jilted girlfriend looking to get back at him.

Regardless, they had told her bluntly that stalking was hard to prove. The fact that he was stalking her from overseas made it more difficult to prosecute, and really "It's not like he's threatened you." She'd left the police station mortified and defeated. One thing she did take from it was that she should document everything. So, she had. Locked in the bottom drawer of her desk, every contact, every postcard, every email.

This was the first time he'd ever sent pictures. The contact seemed to be getting more aggressive, more angry. Like he was a jealous lover. The thought made the bile rise in her throat. The memory of his breath assaulted her. Rum or something similar, angry words, his teeth smashing her lip. She opened the glove box to stow her phone. She didn't want it near her. That's when she saw it. A red carnation. Only one man had ever given her red carnations. She hated the flower because of that.

She fumbled for the door of her car. She exited it with a fury, running to the grassy part of the rest stop to empty her coffee and oatmeal onto the grass.

28

The week went by swiftly. Aidan trained every day. Mostly in the field, but some in the classroom. He'd gained a new appreciation for the plight of a dog as he picked the ticks from his sock line. He'd yet to find any in his more intimate areas, and made sure to use the citronella oil generously on his more vulnerable spots.

He missed Alanna with a constant aching, wishing she would hurry back from those interviews. She'd texted him yesterday, reminding him that he could use her computer and to make sure he used the key to lock the door. Once, he'd gone in and called Brigid. She and Cora had talked his ear off about everything. He'd been able to catch wee Colin awake and chatty, chewing on a stuffed bear.

Even Finn had been home, his quiet strength soothing Aidan as it always did. He'd thought, more than once, that Finn would have been a fine soldier or some sort of spy. Strong, big, and muscular like the O'Brien men. A sharp, tangible intelligence. He was great with computers or any electronics, and he was patient. He found himself missing his brother-in-law as much as his blood brothers. That was the way of family and marriage, though. It forged unbreakable bonds, binding two families together as one.

It made him think of Erik and of Hans. He pushed that thought away. Alanna was certainly going to come home with a job offer soundly in her pocket. *But you've thought about it. Thought about asking her to leave it all. Leave it all for you.* He shut his eyes. *Stop it. She'll find someone else, and you will go back to work and survive her.* He couldn't deny that he wanted her. He wanted her so badly, it was a sort of injury that he suspected would never heal.

The idea of letting her go, leaving her to her new opportunities, her new job, her new life, it would be hell for him. It was the best thing for her, though, and he had to put her happiness first. The beauty of these summer months could give him a little taste of happiness. The hard part was going to be keeping his hands off her. They'd slept as lovers last night. Entwined, mixing their breath, sharing the warmth and feel of each other. He smelled like her that whole next day, and showering had been a painful thing, losing the smell of her on his skin.

When he'd gone in to her house to call Brigid, he'd looked at the drawer that she kept locked in her desk. He didn't even check to see if she'd locked it. He couldn't betray her trust and invade her privacy, but he couldn't say that he hadn't been tempted.

Alanna drove several hours through east coast traffic to get home. After three days away, she wanted to spend the weekend on the beach. Other than a few fitness classes over the weekend, she had the weekend free and clear. For once, she was going to veg on the beach and swim in the ocean, without worrying about homework deadlines or case studies. She'd be moving soon, and she certainly wouldn't be oceanfront in Northern Virginia.

She got out of her car in the driveway, looking around her for any strange people lurking around. It was hard. Tourist season was in full swing. There were lots of unfamiliar people. She locked her car and entered the house through the main entrance, flipping the deadbolt before ascending to the main floor. She turned on all of the lights and dropped her bag in her bedroom. She looked through the whole house, checking the closets and spare rooms. Aidan had left a note on her computer keyboard.

> *Thanks for the key. I got to talk to family. Come see me when you get home. Aidan*

She went to the slider and listened, hearing the sound of a strumming guitar. She didn't recognize the tune. She slid open the door and peered around the partition. Aidan had a foot propped up on a deck chair, seated with his guitar. He looked up and her stomach flipped. Blue eyes, skin blushed from the sun, pink lips smiling in greeting. "Hello, darlin. How was your trip?" She walked over and he set his guitar aside, offering her the second chair. "Tell me."

"I got the job. They want me to start the second week in August," she said as she gave a shy shrug.

Aidan said, "I never had a doubt. Congratulations. You're father must be thrilled."

She got a funny look. "He seemed happy, though not as happy as I thought he would be. He seemed to have something on his mind. He said it was nothing, but I know him."

Aidan wondered if it had to do with the job he wanted in Spain, but he kept that to himself. "We should celebrate. I want to take you out. Unless you've been in the car too long."

Alanna beamed. "I would love that. I'm tired, so I'll let you drive. Where to?"

Aidan thought about it. "Maybe that new tapas place?"

She clapped, "I've been wanting to try that. It's pretty fancy. Are you sure you don't want to..."

He cut her off. "Nope, I'll hear none of it. Just let me change."

She got out of her chair. "Me to. I'll need a half hour."

Alanna stood looking in her closet. That white dress was calling her. Did she dare? *Go big or go home, Miss Priss.* Nope, she was not channeling her father for dating advice. Not happening. She ran her hand over the gauzy slip of a dress.

Aidan slapped some aftershave on his face and looked in the mirror. He didn't have much in the way of dress clothes, but he had a pair of summer weight dress slacks, dress loafers, and a button down shirt. He thought briefly about a tie, but this was an island town so he decided against it. He adjusted his belt, smoothing his shirt tail where it was tucked, and decided that was as good as it was going to get. He walked over and gave a knock, hearing Alanna's high, sweet voice telling him to come in. When he did, he was struck stupid at the sight of her.

Holy God. Her hair was brushed to a sheen and cascading down her bare back. The dress she was wearing was loose and flowing and cut low in the back, showing her skin all the way down to the small of her back. When she turned around, his breath caught in his throat. The top was halter style and deeply cut. The swell of her breasts were exposed. She usually dressed casual and relatively conservative. This was a whole new look, and it was drop dead gorgeous.

She had high heel wedges on, making her look taller than her 5ft.4in. He swallowed hard. "Christ, woman. You're stunning." She smiled, her cheeks blushing to a high color. He approached her, not hiding his appraisal. He put a hand on her waist, smoothing it down her hip just an inch. Her breathing sped up. "This dress was made for you. Is it new?"

She shook her head. "I was just waiting for someone…" She coughed, "somewhere, I mean. I was waiting for somewhere nice to wear it."

Aidan wasn't saying anything. He knew it was rude, but he couldn't stop looking at her. He was trying like hell to control his lust. He shut his eyes. "You'll be the death of me, girl."

Aidan had been sitting across the table from Alanna, nibbling on tapas for hours. The little restaurant was intimate, candlelit, elegant and quiet. His focus had been absolute. They'd started with sangria, but had switched to water as the night progressed. Neither of them drank heavily, and honestly, they didn't need it. This was a new Alanna, another layer to a complex and fascinating woman. This was the Alanna that was unencumbered by school work or money problems or tragedy. They talked non-stop. She wanted to know all about his family. He told her stories of them as young boys, the trouble they'd been in and the tricks they liked to play on their only sister.

She told him about growing up in the military, all the places she'd lived. She talked about her father's parents in historic Charleston and her other grandparents in Georgia. She talked about hurricanes and summers on the beach and her first kiss, standing on a Japanese Bridge. They'd been on a school field trip, and the young man had stolen it while the teacher was distracted.

They nibbled on seafood, meats, cheeses and roasted vegetable dishes, all in small portions, all shared between them. He never wanted the night to end. But closing time inevitably came, and they finally noticed that they were the only ones left in the place besides staff. Aidan drove home, feeling deliriously happy. Alanna's hair spun around her face, the window open to catch the night air. They arrived back at the house and walked right up to the open deck.

"Thank you, Aidan. I think that might be the best date I've ever been on." He stood next to her, loving the night air. The stars and the moon were out, and he could make out the moving shapes of people walking along the beach. Lovers on holiday, old married couples, even children chasing crabs with flashlights.

"The pleasure was mine. I know it's the best date I've ever been on."

She looked out at the water. "I have an early class tomorrow, but then I am coming home and playing on the beach all day," she said with a determined tone.

"Sounds wonderful. I may have to join you. Do you have any more of those bodice rippers for me to read?" he wiggled his brows at her.

She giggled. "Oh, I've got a really good one. Not a bodice ripper. A kilt lifter." He thought about that for a minute, understanding coming across his face.

He barked out a laugh. "Kilt lifter, indeed. What is it with you American girls and the Scots."

She gave him a look that was pure mischief. "It must be that rumor about what they wear or don't wear under them."

Aidan shook his head. "Naughty bookworm."

Alanna looked behind her, eying his guitar through the window. He'd put it in the living room, abandoning his playing when she'd interrupted him. "What were you playing earlier, when I came out?" Aidan rubbed the back of his neck, blushing a bit.

"That was my failed attempt at picking up a tune by ear. It's from a CD my brother sent me. I just liked the song and the guitar. It's a Dublin artist. He hasn't released internationally yet, but he will. His stuff is amazing, really unique."

Alanna took his hand. "Let's hear it."

They walked into the house, both buzzing with nervous energy and expectation. Something was different tonight, for both of them. Aidan slid the CD into his laptop drive as Alanna picked up the case. "Hozier. Is he Irish?"

"Yes, he is. He's a Trinity College drop out who plays the pubs in Dublin. Liam thinks he's up and coming, and he knew I'd like the guitar."

The music started and Alanna immediately recognized the tune of the plucking guitar at the beginning. "Sounds like you were picking it up just fine."

Aidan pulled her to him, a gentle hand on her wrist, then one on her waist. "Dance with me," he said against her hair, and she let herself be enveloped in his arms. He sang in her ear, just for her, and the goosebumps rose on her whole body as she listened to the words.

I had a thought, dear.
However scary
About that night
The bugs and the dirt
Why were you digging?
What did you bury
Before those hands pulled me
From the earth?

She let out a little sigh as he rubbed a hand down her back to her tail bone. She felt herself arch into him, a reflexive curve in her back. Her chest pressed to his, and her heart was pounding, and still he sang. She felt safe and cared for and desired. She was dizzy with it.

His other hand weaved into her hair, sliding fingers at the base of her skull. She looked up at him, his eyes, then his mouth. She felt his hand at her lower back as he pulled her closer, so she could feel the length of him, feeling what she did to him.

Aidan knew this was a bad idea. He also didn't care. He might have been able to resist if it weren't for the dress, the beautiful night, the music, and the pink lips tilted up to him, ripe for the taking. He covered her mouth as he pulled her body into his. There was no hiding his arousal. She felt it, and her hips jerked in that involuntary way they always did.

She moaned sweetly against his mouth. He deepened the kiss, intensifying everything about it. His hand in her hair, the one at her back, his lips, his tongue going deep. She pressed against him, circling his neck with her arms. Then he got serious.

He backed her to the wall and she pulled him tight to her body, rolling and arching as his hands roamed over her body. He wanted to see her, wanted to taste and lick and touch her. He wanted nothing between them. He broke the kiss. "Oh, God lass. You need to tell me to stop." Then he kissed the hell out of her. "Tell me to stop," he whispered against her mouth.

She pulled away a few inches, looking at him with tenderness. This is where she would stop him. She smoothed a hand over his face. "Is that what you want, Aidan? Do you want to stop?" He rubbed his lips along her neck and a little sigh escaped her.

"No, you know I don't, but…"

"Then tell me, Aidan," she interrupted. "Don't worry about what you think you should do. Tell me what you want."

He showed her with his body, lifted her, rubbed his erection right at the heart of her. "I want inside you." He groaned as he worked her, his hands on her bare legs.

"Then no. I won't tell you to stop. That's right where I want you," she whispered. He rolled his hips, mimicking sex. "Inside me. I want you in me, Aidan." She whimpered as his mouth moved down her neck and he pulled the deep neckline of her dress aside.

"You're so beautiful." He thumbed the underside of her breast as he took her in his mouth. Her hips started moving as she dug her fingers in his hair. She rode the ridge of him, pulling them both along to an inevitable joining.

"Aidan, bedroom. I need you." He secured her legs around his waist and closed the distance in long strides, taking her down on his bed within seconds.

He sat up, between her legs. He ran a finger from her neck, down between her breasts. "I want to see all of you." She sat up, coming to her knees in front of him. He untied the halter fastened behind her neck. The slips of fabric fell, pooling around her waist. Aidan pulled the dress down past her bottom and she sat, letting him pull it off her smooth legs.

She was wearing white lace panties. He just stopped, taking in the sight of her in nothing but that scrap of lacy fabric. Her breasts were full, perfectly proportioned for her body. Her skin was pale and soft and smooth. She was athletic, but there was a feminine curviness to her that had his groin pounding to get at her. Round, lush hips and tone limbs. "You're…" He stuttered over his words, not knowing what to say that would be sufficient. "I'm speechless.

You're exquisite." He watched her face as he ran his hands up the inside of her thighs. Her head went back, neck arched as he brushed a thumb over her panties, finding the center of her.

Then he slid her panties off. She heard him hiss as he uncovered her completely. She glowed and blushed under his touch. He touched her nipples, hard and ready. Then he glided a knuckle over her wet flesh, and she opened herself. He hovered over her, kissing her as he touched her. "No, Aidan. Not yet. I want to wait for you."

He gave a husky laugh. "Once more with feeling."

She was whipping her head back and forth now, and that's when he closed his teeth lightly on her nipple. An orgasm ripped through her as he worked her, a flood of new moisture and heat against his hand. "That's it, love," he whispered.

She was loud and wanton, arching up and jerking her hips as she rode out the climax. "I want you. Aidan, I want to come with you inside me, please." But even as she said it, she moaned and slid herself on his hand, unable to stop the momentum.

She popped off the bed and grabbed his belt before he could argue, undoing his trousers. "I need to see you." She took her time, undoing his buttons, smoothing her hands over his chest, his arms, his back. She was trembling from the aftershocks, but she explored him thoroughly. Only his boxers remained, and her eyes roamed over his body.

She stood up, getting off the bed to stand in front of him. Then in one motion, she pulled his boxers down as she got on her knees. He stepped out of them, and before he could pull her up, she was palming him. His head fell back. Then he felt her lips nuzzling him. "Alanna, you don't…" and then he was robbed of speech as she touched her tongue to the head of him.

"You're going to be a reasonable man and let me do what I've been wanting to do for weeks." The air shot out of his lungs as her mouth closed over him. His hands went to her head, cradling it as he looked down, watching her take him in her mouth. It was almost over in a flash until he pulled her up, tossing her on her back.

She looked him up and down and Aidan saw a flicker of panic. "What's wrong, Alanna?"

She shook her head slowly back and forth. "Nothing is wrong. You're perfect. A little too perfect," she said, taking in the size of him. "I haven't done this in a long time."

He stretched out alongside her. "I don't want to hurt you, darlin," he said, starting to mirror her concern.

"You won't hurt me Aidan. I've been hurt. Nothing about you could hurt me. We just need to take it slow. Let me get used to you."

He rolled his hips and she was hot and slick. "I've wanted to do this since I first saw you. Your green eyes flaring, pink lips. I wanted to fill you up. Come inside you. Do you want that? Do you want all of me?"

She reached between them, positioning him. "Yes," she said, but it came out more like a moan. He nudged against her, parting her flesh. He hissed as he pressed, "Ah, God. You're tight."

He tried to retreat, but she cupped his chin. "It's okay, I'm okay." He looked in her eyes and pressed, her flesh yielding to him a little at time. She closed her eyes. "Look at me, mo chuisle. Let me see your eyes." She met his gaze with those ice green eyes, a storm brewing in them. He slid into her, slowly, watching her face to make sure she was okay. Finally he was in her to the hilt. She was clenched around him, her body almost fighting the invasion, but her eyes. Her eyes told a different story. Ecstasy at being completely possessed.

His breath came out in a stuttering spurt and he moaned a little. "Oh, God. I'm in you." She touched her palm to his face. He was utterly destroyed by their joining, his throat tight, his eyes taking her in.

"You feel incredible." She ran a hand down to his ass and jerked involuntarily, her muscles begging. Aidan started moving and her breasts came up. He felt her body respond, warm and inviting at her center. Her eyes became unfocused, raising her hips to his. He pinned her hands above her head and she rolled her hips in rhythm with is. He was big and broad, and his hips pressed her legs wide as he pumped inside her. She could feel the skin and hair of his abdomen rubbing the top of her sex as he filled her, so deep he couldn't go any further. Her nipples grazed against his soft dusting of chest hair as he surged and retreated, and she felt every ridge and texture of him deep within her.

She felt the climb as he went even deeper, pushing past what she thought was physically possible. "I feel you, lass. I feel the start of it. "She moaned as she began to peak, and he intensified his movements, faster, harder. "Yes, harder. Ah, God!" His hips were pistoning, relentlessly filling her. She gripped him with her muscles as he pushed and retreated, taking her higher and higher. The sounds he was making told her how close he was. A thrill went through her at the thought of how turned on he was, how much pleasure he was feeling, and that final thought dropped her off the edge. She came violently, a whole other type of orgasm with him inside her. It was catastrophic.

That's when he let go. His words were guttural, nothing she could understand. She felt him come, warm inside her, and her body gripped him, milking him as she took all of him. He covered her mouth with his, climaxing inside her with a pace that had the bed frame slamming against the wall. He threw his head back and growled, shoving and jerking.

Aidan was out of his head. It occurred to him, fleetingly, that they weren't using a condom. He didn't care. A reckless part of him didn't care if he got her pregnant. And how fucked up was that? It would solve the issue of leaving her. He'd throw her over his shoulder and drag her over the ocean if she were pregnant, just like Michael did Branna. He jerked and growled like a beast as he came deep inside her. She was wild under him, bucking and gripping him. She took all of him, her strong body meeting him blow for blow. When he'd finally wrung the last of his climax out of himself, he opened his eyes and looked down at her. She was completely blitzed out. Lips glossy from his kisses, eyes dazed, flush all over her, a smile appearing as she came back to herself. He covered her mouth with small kisses, over her face, rubbing his lips lightly over her skin. They trembled in each other's arms.

He rolled them, still joined, and she sprawled on him. He stroked her back, her hair, her beautiful bottom. She rested her chin on her hands, perched on his chest. She looked like she wanted to say something. "What's on your mind, little hen?"

She blushed. "I just wanted to tell you that I am on birth control, in case you were worried."

He sighed, "I should have asked. It was careless." Then a confusion came over him. "Why?"

She shrugged, her face registering some uncomfortable answer. "I take a shot every three months. I started after the..."

She paused, not wanting to take up any airtime talking about unpleasant things. "I just do it to protect myself. When I have children, they will be wanted." Aidan smoothed her hair back. The thought that she'd been taking birth control for years, out of fear of being attacked, made him sad and angry. The thought that she had a barrier between them, that she had protected them from pregnancy should make him happy. For some reason it didn't.

"You don't have to take anything. I'd use a condom if you wanted to go off the shot." She put her cheek to his chest. "It's okay. I'm not due for another two months. I have the control. I know that's not very Catholic of me, but it just seemed the safer route."

Aidan stroked her. "You're a strong woman." He took her hair, pulling her face up to meet his eyes. "I hope it was as beautiful for you as it was for me.'

She smiled. "It seems stupid when I say it, but I feel like I finally lost my virginity."

He grinned, glowing from his feelings. "Aye, I suppose you did." He closed his eyes, "You don't get many perfect moments in your life, but this was one of them. For me, this was one of them."

Alanna pulled up and kissed him. Soft at first, then deep and passionate. He felt himself thicken inside her and she raised a brow.

"Again? Already?"

He cocked his own brow. "Did you think I was an old man?"

She blushed, "Of course not. I just didn't know you could..." She covered her face. "I'm a little ignorant on the subject."

"Give me your mouth, hen," he said huskily. She did, and he kissed her soundly, rolling his hips under her. Then he pushed her gently upward until she was straddling him like a saddle. She put her hands on his chest. "I've never been like this, I don't know what to do."

He chuckled. "I've seen you shake that beautiful arse in your Zumba classes. Just do what feels good." She took her lip in her teeth. Then she moved, experimentally. He palmed her inner thigh, putting the pad of his thumb right where she needed him. As he rubbed her, she started to find her rhythm. Her lips parted on a sigh, and she rocked her hips, impaling herself on his hard length. Her breasts were heavy as she rocked herself on him. He was mesmerized, watching her.

"That's it, take me. Show me what you want." She gasped as he pressed harder with his thumb, gliding over her raw flesh. She started rolling her pelvis, her round hips straining to get closer, get more. He'd dreamed of her, just like this. She arched, throwing her head back and Aidan groaned, sweating with the effort of not finishing before she was done.

He felt the shudder go through her as she peaked. He raised up, taking a nipple in his mouth and he drew it in deep, the way she liked it. Her hips went wild, riding him, her hair flying as she strained to get him deeper.

He held back. He wasn't done. She settled against him, limp from her efforts, and he flipped her over, before she could register what he was doing. She was on her stomach, her beautiful ass tipped up in invitation. He pushed one knee up, exposing the heart of her. Then he slid into her from behind. She gasped, raising her hips.

"Are you okay?" he said tightly.

She looked over her shoulder. "Don't stop," was all she could choke out. He started thrusting, shoving into her until his hips were locked against hers, a deep invasion that had her contracting, residual quakes from her last orgasm. He entwined their fingers and whispered in her ear, relentless stroking as deep as he could go. Her face was tilted to the side, and he brought her mouth to his, kissing her from behind, penetrating her twice.

Alanna felt the moment Aidan let go. She rode the waves of his release. She gripped him, taking everything, committing it to memory. She felt him trembling behind her, his breath on her neck.

Aidan's throat was tight, his body trembling. The intensity of his orgasm was catastrophic. It had more to do with the woman pulled tight against his chest. *Oh God, what have I done? What have I done to myself?*

"Why did you wait til now?" she asked. "Why have you been holding back?" He exhaled against her hair. "Did you think you were protecting me?" she asked.

He pulled her closer, burying his nose in her hair. He inhaled, not wanting to think, not wanting to answer. "Did you ever think I might be protecting myself?"

She burrowed in closer. "Don't think about it. I know where we are in all of this. I know you'll leave. Just be here with me now. No holding back."

He exhaled shakily. "Okay. You have me. All of me."

After throwing on some clothes and darting next door, Aidan lingered languorously in the deep, warm tub with Alanna nestled into him. She was warm and slippery and he washed her thoroughly, leaving no part of her body unexplored, as he tended to her. "I could get used to this," she said as he toweled off her body, kissing her everywhere he went. Then he took her to the closet, her nude body flushed and supple from the bath and his attentions. Her closet door was a full mirror. He was huge behind her, wearing only a towel, and she looked at him through the mirror, feeling shy at her nudity.

He drew her to the edge of the bed, bidding her to sit. He knelt down before her, spreading her legs. "I need you," he whispered against her mouth as he pulled her toward him for a kiss. She started to understand just as he dipped his head between her legs.

She was propped on her arms and he pulled her hips to the edge. He wanted her to watch herself in the mirror, watch him doing this thing to her that made her wild. And she did. Peripherally at first, and then greedily as she felt his mouth on her, looked in the mirror at his broad shoulders, his sandy hair, his hands on her thighs, big and rough. She put a hand in his hair, urging him as he drank deeply of her. "Aidan, don't stop." She saw the flush in her cheeks, her nipples were hard and pink, and she was clenching his hair as she watched herself slide off the edge. It was the most erotic moment of her life. Then his towel was gone and he was inside her again, and all she saw was him.

They slept together, their nude bodies entwined. He would periodically stir, get the feel of her and the smell of her in his nose, and he'd take her again. She welcomed him, letting him inside. He never tired, never rushed. The night went on like that. He'd go get them a snack or some tea, then he'd start again, then they'd fall limp and exhausted into a short sleep, then he'd come to her again. He couldn't get enough, he was insatiable. Like a starving man, he feasted.

The next morning, after they'd slept in, she stood at the counter, cutting fruit. She was wearing his shirt, and the sight of her went straight through him. She ate a berry, looking at him with a mix of embarrassment and curiosity. "I didn't know it could be like this. I didn't know my body could..." she blushed. He got up from the table and came to her, holding her from behind.

"What?" he asked.

"I didn't think it was possible to do it that many times and you know...every time."

He pulled her to him. "It's not like this with everyone. It's never been like this. The way you rouse to me. It's a gift between us."

She smiled against his mouth, turning for a kiss. "A gift. I like that." He gave her another lingering kiss, feeling the urgency start between them again. "Oh, no you don't. I'm too sore. How am I going to teach spinning tomorrow if we keep at this?"

He laughed against her mouth. "I'm sorry. I could kiss it and make it better."

She eased away from him. "I've got to go get dressed. I have a yoga class. I'll be back, then we'll play on the beach."

He watched her like a lion watches a gazelle. "I like the look of you in the morning."

They relaxed on the beach, reading, snacking, and intermittently swimming. Alanna would send him steamy looks over the top of her novel. He'd decided that if he only had two months, he wouldn't waste a minute of it. He would imprint himself on her in every way possible. By the time he left, she would be forever branded by him. Her sexual awakening at his hands would stay with her until she was an old woman. He'd give himself that one thing.

"You keep looking at me like that, and I'm going to get arrested for shagging you on that lawn chair, hen."

She looked innocently. "What? How am I looking at you?"

He put down his book. "Like you're remembering the mirror."

She blushed, swallowed hard. "Yes, I liked the mirror. I really liked the mirror. And that fluttering thing you do." A few scurrying steps, and they were back in the house. A few flicks of the wrist and the suits were off, her sandy ass pressed against the cold mirror. They were never going to get any sleep.

They'd finally stopped, both too sore to continue at the zealous pace. "I'm sorry if I hurt you," he said as he washed her. He was never a tub guy, but a tub for two was seriously growing on him.

"You didn't hurt me. We just need a breather."

For once, he wasn't aroused, not in the physical sense. He liked washing her, taking care of her."Should I sleep next door?" he said, a bit of vulnerability in his voice.

"No. We'll be separated soon enough. You can stay or I can come to you. I just want this time together." She felt his smile against her temple.

"I can't..." He paused. She sat up and turned around.

"What is it?" He looked at her, uncertainty mixed with a stubborn set of his jaw.

"I can't share you. While I'm here, I can't share you. If you were to go out with Rick or someone else, I'm not sure I could handle it. I know this is temporary, but I'm not wired that way. I couldn't share you."

She kissed his mouth softly. "I don't share either." She said it with a quiet, forceful tone that confused him.

"You won't have to worry on that account," he said. She looked down, not meeting his eye. He took her chin. "What is going through that head of yours?"

She stiffened. "Who is Keiley?" He burst out laughing. She pulled back.

"How did you know about Keiley?" Her eyes flared. "No! I never took her up on the offer. How did you know?" She was wiggling, trying to pull away, which for some reason, delighted him.

"It's not funny. You saved a receipt with her name and number on it. It was in plain view on your dresser top!"

He stopped, thinking about that. "It was a bit of trash out of my pocket, lass. There was a receipt from Subway in there as well, but I'm not trying to shag the lad that made my sandwich."

She stopped, shoving him in the chest. "You took it, and you kept it!"

His eyes narrowed. Her jealousy was juicing him up. She was feeling possessive and angry and he snatched her forward, sliding inside her with one slick, shove. She gasped.

"Maybe you need a reminder. I've got no time or desire for Keiley or anyone who isn't you," he said fiercely as he moved her buoyant body up and down. His accent was thick, and she was dizzy with the storm he whipped up inside her. Her whimpering took on an edge. She took him hard, digging her nails in his shoulders, water splashing out of the tub. He felt her close her teeth on the tendon between his neck and shoulder. He shouted as he came. "Only you," he growled as he climaxed. She looked down right wicked as she rode him, and she came in waves, a triumphant smile as she jerked and slid against him.

She grabbed his hair, pulling his head back. "Burn that receipt."

He laughed huskily, cupping her ass with his hands and piercing her nice and deep as she spasmed. "You'll be the death of me, but I suspect I'll die satisfied."

29

Hector grinned to himself as the men cleaned their weapons. Captain O'Brien was humming to himself, and the fucker was glowing, actually glowing. John came into the room to join the cleaning party, took one look at Aidan, and started chuckling with a deep, husky knowing.

Aidan looked up. "What?"

John shook his head. "Don't even, brother." Aidan creased his brows.

"Don't tease him, Captain," said Major Diaz.

The other, younger men were listening. "What did I miss?" Lieutenant Drake asked.

It was Washington that spoke up, "Damn, sir. Who's the lucky lady? You are glowin' whiter than usual."

Aidan kept cleaning his weapon, "Would you hens quit your speculating. I don't know what the hell you're on about."

Porter was next. "Jesus, that blonde from the gym? The one who sings at mass? Holy shit, sir. You're a legend!"

Hector derailed the conversation. "If you ladies want to keep gossiping, I can have you transferred to the supply room to hand out maxi pads." They all shut up, but they kept sneaking glances at each other.

Aidan shot them a look. "Gentlemen don't discuss their women. What is or isn't going on with me and some hypothetical woman is not fodder for gossip. It's disrespectful." His tone was serious.

"Ooh, that's love, right there. That's what that is. That's a gawt damn inspiration."

Hector barked out an admonishment, barely concealing a laugh. "Washington! Enough." He looked at Aidan who was trying like hell to suppress a grin.

Alanna was sweaty and exhausted. She'd taught two classes again today. She had two every day this week due to instructor shortages. She'd forgotten her phone as well. She drove up the street to her house, seeing Aidan on the deck in the distance. As she walked through her house, her phone was blinking with unchecked messages. She'd blocked the number that had sent the last messages from Steve, so she grabbed the phone, not as wary as she should be. She opened the messages and screamed.

Aidan came storming in the house. Alanna put her phone in the drawer and faced him. She was shaking. "Jesus Christ, what's the matter?"

She wiped the tears away. "I'm fine. It was a spider."

He looked at her with incredulity marring his beautiful face. "Don't lie to me lass! You're scared half out of your wits!" She steeled her jaw. He went to the desk and opened the top drawer. "When did you move the gun again? Why?" She closed her eyes. "This is not about something that happened seven years ago. You are scared. I've sensed it from the beginning." Nothing. He slammed the drawer shut. "Let me see your phone."

She stifled the panic, but she didn't give him the phone. "I'm fine. It was a big spider. It went under the fridge."

He shook his head. "So this is about trust, aye? I trusted you with everything. I opened a vein and bled out in front of you the other night. But it doesn't go both ways, I suppose." He walked out and she called after him, choking on a sob. Before she could collect herself and go after him, he was back. He slammed something down on the counter beside her. A pen and the tablet she had given him. Challenge in his gaze. "It might not be me, but you need to write them down. Five. Don't stop until you have five." Then he walked out, slamming the sliding door.

Aidan took a while to settle. He could have forced her to give him the phone. He could have pried that feckin drawer in her desk open, but that would get them only so far. She was hiding something, something beyond the attack seven years ago. She needed to come clean, and the only way he was going to get her to do that was to put forth the same challenge she had given him. So, he waited. He'd just about given up when she knocked. She came in, face puffy from crying. Her legs were shaky.

His anger deflated at the sight of her. "Oh, God, Alanna. Please." He took her in his arms. She cried. She cried so hard she shook with it.

"I need help. I thought I could do this on my own, but I can't. Oh, God. I shouldn't have let it go on this long!" She shoved the pad in his hand and he read her list. He was at the top. There were others. Tim, Branna, her friend Izzy that he hadn't met. But he was at the top.

"I'm ready," her voice was bordering on hysterical. "I'm ready to tell you." He held her, and she was racked with tremors as she wept. He soothed her, stroking her hair.

"Nothing you tell me is going to change what I think of you. Nothing." She took his hand led him into her house and took the key from her desk. She unlocked the drawer and took out a file. She pushed it across the table and he sat, accepting it. There was a note on the file. *IN CASE SOMETHING HAPPENS TO ME.* The hair on the back of Aidan's neck stood up and he opened the file.

At first, it didn't register what he was looking at. Then he started to understand. Postcards, emails, some of them with thinly veiled innuendo causing the bile to rise in his throat, and the most recent, threats. He read one. *How was the barbecue, whore?*

Then finally the photos. Alanna with him, with Tim, with Rick. One photo was taken the day on the beach when he'd had the officers over for dinner. *The camera lens incident. When Hans thought it was a rifle scope. Fucking hell.* "Jesus Christ. Is this the same prick that..." She nodded before he finished. "How long has this been going on?" She wouldn't look at him. "How long, Alanna?" His tone was rougher than he meant it to be, and he saw a flicker of doubt come across her face, doubt and shame.

He stood up. "I'm sorry. Jesus, this isn't your fault." He picked her up, cradling her like a child and took her away from the table and that God forsaken file. He sat on the couch and held her. "Tell me, tell me everything. Then we'll figure out what to do. I'm here with you now. You aren't alone in this."

She sniffed, wiping her nose. "I don't know where to start. It has been going on for so long. I tried reporting it in Virginia, when it started. The police wouldn't help me. He wouldn't stop. I tried to get him to stop, I changed my phone, my email, I used other names on the internet." Her voice was getting hysterical.

"It's not your fault. We will fix this, love," he said. She burrowed into his chest. *I need my Da. He'd know how to handle this.* He would call him later, after they'd talked and he had more information. They had to call the police.

"What was the last message? What came in on your phone?" He felt her start to shake again. She got up and took the phone out of the drawer. She handed it to him. "Jesus Christ," he hissed. A picture of a woman. She was beat up, a fist in her hair as the sick fucker snapped the picture. And then there was the message. *She didn't taste as sweet as you, but she'll tide me over until I come for you.*

He looked at Alanna and saw a side of her he never wanted to see again. She was hugging her knees, rocking. She was terrified. He was going to kill that bastard with his bare hands. The doorbell went off and they both jumped. She shot off the couch, scrambling to hide the contents of the file. He grabbed her from behind. "Easy, love. Be easy. I'll get it." If he'd been given a hundred chances to guess, he would have never guessed who was at the door.

Sean looked at Sorcha, a little worry on his brow. "I hope we aren't disturbing the lass. Maybe we should call him again. Maybe we shouldn't have surprised him." Just then the door opened and Aidan stood for a moment, not believing his eyes. Then he lurched forward and grabbed his father.

"Holy God, Da. I swear the almighty must have heard me, but I didn't think he worked so bloody fast!"

Sean laughed, being squeezed to the point of discomfort by his son. Then Aidan let go. "Ma, Seany, it's good to see you."

Seany took out a little horn and blew it. "Happy Birthday!"

Aidan looked at him, confused. "Jesus, Da. He's forgotten his own birthday."

Sean was looking at his son, reading the stress and panic and relief all warring for top billing on his face.

"Something's happened," he said.

"Come in. Please. Leave your bags, and we can get them later. I need you right now. Sorry to dive right into it, but you have no bloody idea how much I need you right this minute."

Alanna heard voices, but she was too numb or too shocked to make sense of it. She kept looking at that file on the table, the carnation that she'd ziplocked. She couldn't believe she'd told him. Then the next shock came. Aidan walked upstairs, and behind him were Sean, Sorcha, and his little brother Seany. She put her hand over her mouth, stifling a sob. What would they think of her?

Before she could even speak, Sorcha marched over to her and took her in her arms. "There there, love. I don't know what's amiss, but you look like you could use another woman in the house." She melted into her. Tears soaking Sorcha's blouse. She was small, but she was soft and smelled like fresh soap and something all together motherly. She'd never felt like this when her own mother held her. She shuddered in her arms. "There, there," Sorcha said, stroking her hair.

Tears pricked Aidan's eyes as he watched his mother holding Alanna. This is what they needed. He was in over his head. He needed his da, and she needed a mother. She'd never told her own mother about this whole mess. That made him sad. So very sad for her.

He looked at Sean and his little brother. "Come over to my house, we'll talk there. Mam, will ye care for her?"

Sorcha nodded, "I'll put the kettle on and we'll have a nice long chat."

30

The longer Sean listened, the more pissed he got. He could feel the rage rolling off his son. O'Brien men protected their women. He might not know it yet, but that beautiful, sweet woman next door with his wife was Aidan's mate. They'd tried to send Seany away, but he had adamantly refused to be sent away like a child. "If you can hold your tongue and learn something, you can stay. Just watch what you say, especially in front of the lass." Sean's stomach churned at the details Aidan had given him.

When he was done, Aidan said, "I wouldn't normally invade her privacy like this, Da, but given your background, she's going to have to trust me on this. I need your guidance."

Sean rubbed his eyes. "You need to call in the locals. It's way past time for it."

Aidan nodded. "She tried to report it, years back. The police in Virginia didn't help, and I think they made the situation worse. I think they thought she was some scorned girlfriend or something. The actual attack happened when she lived here, so they wouldn't take the report for that. She wouldn't tell her Da. She's ashamed. She's got nothing to be ashamed of. Nothing. He took advantage of her, he hurt her, and ever since then, he's stalked her. She's scared, but she's strong, and now she has me. I will take his fucking scalp before he harms one hair on her head."

Sean was very impressed with the officer that was helping take the report. She was young, sharp, professional. She'd put Alanna at ease as soon as she came into the house and introduced herself. Just who you needed on a case like this. She was a rookie, though. Her training officer was a great deal less impressive. "So, you just kept all of these mementos in your desk for years, and now you want to report it? It seems to me that this is an old boyfriend keeping in touch. There's no direct threat here."

The female officer bristled, and Aidan stiffened. Sean stepped in. "I don't mean to tell you your job, officer, but I think she explained the brush off she got from the police in Virginia. I am sure it also hasn't escaped your keen eye that the contact has become more aggressive. He's agitated. And it appears he's now in the area. This is escalating. He broke into her car, for Christ sake."

The officer sniffed, pulled his belt. "Of course I understand that. I was getting to that." Sean bit his tongue. This guy was such a dickhead. He'd sent Sorcha and Sean away, giving Alanna as much privacy as he could. Her phone started buzzing. They all looked at her.

"It's my father." She picked up, leaving the table.

Aidan could hear half of the conversation. "Nothing. No, Daddy. Please don't do that."

Aidan approached her. "You need to tell him, sweetheart. He needs to know so that he can protect you, be aware when you are in Virginia. It's time." She shut her eyes, tears starting fresh. "Let me talk to him. We'll get him here, tell him together," he said. Relief flooded her eyes.

"Hans, aye. It's Aidan. Look, can you take a day of leave? This isn't phone business. Can you come? No, don't send Erik just yet.

Have him come with you. I won't leave her alone. My family is here. Don't worry. She's safe." He ended the call and she looked at him, slightly panicked at the though of telling him and Erik. "A neighbor called him. Another Marine.They keep an eye on the place and they saw the police car." She nodded. That was so like her dad to have people watching over her.

The female officer was talking directly to Sean, now. Trying to ignore her supervisor. "I think you're right, this is definitely escalating. The language is more direct. And the pictures would indicate that he's either having her followed, or he's not in Asia anymore. A lot of the stickiness to this is that we have overseas, internet, and mail contact. We also have no solid proof that these are from him, yet." She emphasized. "We probably need to get some guidance from the feds. You said he's in the Merchant Marines. If we can contact the higher ups, track his activity with the ships these were mailed from, that could help build a case against him and also locate him. He could be anywhere if he's on shore leave. Getting back to the initial sexual assault, I have to check, but I don't think there's a statute of limitation on that. She could file charges even now. Alone, I doubt a prosecutor would touch it, but coupled with all of this other behavior, I think we should try it. It happened in the neighboring town, but I can get in touch with Onslow County sheriff, and they can combine efforts with us."

Sean narrowed his eyes. "You're pretty sharp for a new officer."

She looked over at her partner who was smoking on the deck. "I'm a transplant. I moved from Wilmington for better pay. I lost my seniority and gained the bozo standing over my shoulder." Sean barked out a laugh, and it even got a smile from Alanna.

Alanna spoke then. "I know I should have tried the police again. I just thought I could handle it since he was so far away. I don't know what escalated this."

Sean said, "It could be a few things. He could have lost his job, could have moved back to the area, could have ended a real life relationship causing him to focus solely on this imaginary one he has going in his head with you. It could be that he couldn't find you, with all the precautions you've been taking. Honestly, the presence of another man could set him off as well. He thinks of you…" Sean stopped, not finishing.

"As his. He thinks I'm his," Alanna said. Then a chill ran through her.

Aidan said, "You belong to yourself. Don't let that bastard put one more bad thought in your head. We won't stop until you are safe." Aidan kissed her head.

The officer smiled at him. "You need to change the locks. Both sides, immediately." Then she looked at Alanna, "I'm glad you told someone. You have the power now, Miss Falk. You took back the power." Alanna lifted her chin, nodding.

The officers left, leaving contact information and a promise that they would regularly patrol the area surrounding her house. They would also contact PMO and let them know about the report, allowing them to have the suspect information as well as her schedule at the gym.

"I'll head over. Your ma and brother are knackered, headed to bed. The time difference and all." Sean hugged him. "Stay here with her, lad. She shouldn't be alone tonight," he whispered.

"Thank you, Da. I don't know how you knew I needed you, but I did. This is singly the best birthday present you could have given me."

Sean hugged him again. "I love you," Sean said.

"I love you, too."

Sean looked at Alanna, and her face was stricken. "It's your birthday? Why didn't you tell me?" She gave Aidan a hard shove.

Sean laughed. Damn, how he loved a feisty woman. "Don't be too hard on him, girl. I think he forgot himself. And his birthday is actually Friday. This was the cheapest flight we could get." Sean kissed her on the forehead and started to leave.

She grabbed his hand. "I'm sorry."

He crinkled his brow. "Whatever for, darlin?"

She teared up. "You came to surprise him, and I ruined it."

A soft feminine voice came from the sliding door. "Now, now. You did no such thing. We have eight days to catch up. Besides, he has his training. I'll need a local tour guide. I can't wait to have you show me around town." She hugged her and pushed her hair off her face, like a mother would. "Branna is near beside herself with envy. It'll all be grand. You'll see. Nothing but sun and fun and family."

From behind them was another voice. "And bikinis."

Sorcha sighed. "God, deliver me from testosterone. Get to bed, Seany!"

He waltzed in, ignoring her command. "I haven't even said a proper hello to the girl." He scooped her up and swung her around. She giggled. He looked at his brother. "If you don't keep her, I'm going to sell her on the benefits of younger men."

He winked at her as Aidan put him in a headlock. "Mind your manners," Aidan said, laughing. Then he pulled him in for another hug. "I missed you, brother. I'm glad you're here. I've got a guitar next door, if you get homesick for Dana."

Alanna laughed, "You name your guitars? What did you name this one?"

He cocked a brow. "I haven't named her yet. She won't come home with me, so maybe you should name her."

"Does it have to be a woman's name?" she asked, brow cocked.

"Yes," said all three O'Brien men.

"Sorry," she put her hands up in defense. "What's your guitar at home named?"

Aidan smiled,"Ah, that's my Tessa. She's a good girl." They all laughed in unison.

"What will your parents think, you staying over here?" Alanna asked as she watched Aidan brush his teeth. He rinsed and turned to her, pulling her close.

"My da's idea. He told me not to leave you. He wants you to feel safe."

She blushed. "And your mother?"

He laughed. "My mother has a story or two of her own. You won't get anything but hugs, cookies, and good advice from that woman. She's pretty much seen it all."

Alanna was delirious as Aidan surged inside her. Slow, tender, lots of eye contact. He whispered to her. It was all in Gaelic, but the tone was like a vow. He took his time, stroked her arms, ran his hand up her ribcage, feeling every inch of her. Whatever he was saying, it wove a web around her, deep rolling R's and husky, long vowels. The shuddering started and he smiled. "Come to me, a rúnsearc. Let go." She did let go, pulling him along with her. It rolled through him in waves, their eyes never leaving each other. Tears pooled at the corners, rolling through her temples into her hair line.

He knew how she felt. The tenderness, the slow, deliberate lovemaking had been more shattering than all the wild, marathon sex they'd had over the weekend. *My beloved. My secret love.* He translated in his head as he spilled himself inside her.

"I'll protect you," he said in her ear as they lay spooned together.

"I know you will, Aidan, but I have to take care of myself, longterm. My father needs to move on, and so do you. This is on me." Aidan closed his eyes, pulling her in closer. "It's okay, Aidan. We knew that when we started. I'll be okay. This doesn't change anything."

It did, though. The thought of that bastard out there, watching her, scaring her, worse. It brought forth every protective instinct and territorial response he had in him. The thought of the coming confrontation with Hans and Erik weighed on them both.

Aidan heard the chain lock clatter as he jumped awake. It had to be Hans. They didn't usually use the chain and Hans had a key. The sun was coming through the window. Aidan jumped out of bed. He'd slept in his clothes and had put a bag in the spare room. He'd also messed up the bed. It made him feel like a teenager, covering his ass.

Alanna was fragile right now, though. Her privacy had been invaded out of necessity, but she was feeling exposed enough. He had to protect her dignity as much as he could. "Stand by, Hans!" he yelled as he made his way to the downstairs door. Alanna had jumped out of bed as well, trying to wash her face and collect herself.

He unlatched the door and Hans barreled in with Erik on his tail. "Where is she? Alanna!" He was as frantic as a man like him got. He grabbed Alanna, hugging her. Her tears were inevitable. "What is it, baby? Tell me what happened."

Erik was pacing. "I'm okay Daddy. It's okay." Alanna looked at Aidan, so unsure of herself.

"Why don't we sit down. Get a cup of coffee. It's kind of a long story and she has had a long night."

Part way through the explanation of what had brought the police here last night, Aidan started watching Hans for signs of a meltdown. His fists were clenched, his eyes burning, his jaw tight. Alanna talked, and Aidan elaborated when necessary. Erik sat with his arms crossed, stoic and still. Unreadable.

"I reported it in Virginia, but it's complicated because he's out to sea, and I have moved around. The mailed stuff, the phone texts, the emails, he's never been in the area since it started. I got the brush off from the police, even after I told them everything."

Hans exhaled, "But you haven't told me everything. Have you? You have been avoiding the obvious details about how you knew this man and what his name is." Alanna's bottom lip started to tremble.

"Jesus Christ. We know him. That's why you've kept this quiet," Hans said.

Erik sat up ramrod straight. "You said he was out to sea. Is he a fucking sailor? Is he Navy?" She shook her head.

"You didn't tell me they knew him, Alanna," Aidan said. He reached across the table and took her hand. "It's all right, lass. You'll feel better, I swear it. Tell it all."

She put her chin up, wiped her tears, and looked at her father and brother. "He's in the Merchant Marines. It was Steve Andrews." It took a moment for the name to register with Hans, but Erik's eyes popped up.

"Steve? My buddy from high school? Anna, come on." Aidan was across the table before anyone could act. He had Erik by the shirt, pulling him out of his seat.

"You brought that fucking animal around your sister?" Erik was ready to fight, the instincts of two alphas colliding. But he was also warring between insult, defensiveness, and confusion.

Hans was immediately between them, and Alanna was screaming for them to stop. "What the hell is your problem O'Brien!" Erik yelled. "She went out with one of my best friends behind my back, screwed him, and now this?"

Hans pointed at his son, dead serious. "Shut it. Not now. Not after this. You shut it." He turned around to address Aidan and froze. "Where is she?" Aidan looked behind him and she was gone.

Alanna couldn't deal with this. The anger, the shame, her brother's doubting face. She ran out the slider before she had time to think about it, tears blurring her eyes. She went for the boardwalk only to run smack into a giant. Sean steadied her on her feet, and she broke out in a sob. He just pulled her to him. "Don't pay them any mind. Men are downright stupid when it comes to their women. Don't cry, lass."

Aidan shot out the door with Hans and Erik behind him. He stopped short, causing a domino effect. She was crying in his father's arms, and Seany was standing behind them, arms crossed, no trace of boyhood in his face. He looked, to Aidan, like a warrior angel. Long hair, big body, handsome, youthful face, and a quiet strength that was at odds with his normal boyish charm. This was the man he would be.

Aidan exhaled. "Christ, Alanna. I'm sorry."

Erik just couldn't keep his gob shut. "Why the hell are you apologizing to her? And who the hell are these two?" Aidan knew the look on his father's face well. Bridled strength and the patience that came from raising five, unruly sons.

"I am Sean O'Brien. This is my youngest, Sean Jr. You must be Erik and Hans. It's a pleasure. Now, that said, how about you keep a civil tongue with your sister before you have three men that want to throttle you," he said calmly.

"Four." That was all Seany said, but both Aidan and his da fought a prideful grin.

Hans stepped forward and took Alanna from Sean's arms gently. "I'm sorry, baby. Please, don't run from this. Come tell me the rest. I swear to you that whatever you say, I will take it as gospel. And so will that idiot brother of yours." He shot Erik a look that would cut flesh off of bone. She was shaking in her father's arms and silent tears fell down her cheeks. Erik's face softened, anger replaced by pain. He nodded.

"When did you go out with this Steve? I remember him from the school when Erik was younger, but I don't remember you going anywhere with him." Hans said. They were back in her house, gathered around the table. Aidan's family was back on the other side, with assurances that they were all going to behave.

Alanna cleared her throat. "It was when you were recovering. I made some bad decisions. He was older. I was selfish and feeling awful after you were hurt and Brian…" her voice broke, not finishing the thought. "I'm ashamed, Daddy. I went out with him. He was nice to me. And," she swallowed and closed her eyes, "I gave him my virginity." Tears started again.

"Alanna, baby. Look at me." She did, and the sight of her gutted him. "Sweetie, you're a grown woman. You're twenty-five years old. I didn't think you were still a virgin."

She let out a little half laugh, half sob. "That wasn't the worst of it."

She looked at Aidan, and he squeezed her hand. "It was once. Only once. He hurt me."

Erik interrupted. "What do you mean? It hurt? Christ, I can't believe I am having this conversation with my sister."

She lifted her chin, trying to hold on to as much dignity as she could muster. "I mean he hurt me on purpose," she paused, barely keeping the bile down, "He was rough, he held me down and just did it. He didn't care if he hurt me. It was awful. Then he called me names, told me I was a lousy lay and frigid. Then he dropped me off, bruised and bleeding and crying."

Aidan actually pitied Erik to the depths of his soul right now. He couldn't imagine if this had been Brigid, and the asshole responsible had been his friend. Both he and Hans were dead silent, barely restraining their fury. "I saw him one other time, a few days later. He came to the college. Tried to apologize. He begged me to let him explain. When I got in his car, I smelled booze. He was drunk. I tried to get him to let me out, but he wouldn't take me back. He took me to an empty lot, isolated. Behind that old fabric store that had closed down."

Erik groaned. "Oh, God. No, God." His fingers were in his hair and the tears started.

Hans's voice made the hair stand up on Aidan's arms. "Did he rape you?"

She looked him right in the eye, showing a strength that had been lacking during the rest of the story. "He tried," she said.

"What happened?" he asked.

"I broke his fucking nose." All three brows went up. Alanna never used that kind of language. "I hit him with the heel of my palm, just like you showed me, daddy. I fought like hell, kicked the son of a bitch across the seat, grabbed my purse, and ran out of the car. I hid in the woods with my mace. I told him I was calling the police. He left, and I called Branna."

Hans was shaking. "The weekend you came to visit me, before I got released from rehab. You had a busted lip. You said you tripped and hit your mouth at the gym." Her face was like concrete, except for a single tear. "His teeth."

Erik cursed. "Why didn't you tell me?"

She looked at him. "I was ashamed. Then he got to you within hours, told you that he took me out, and how sorry he was that he did it behind your back. How he thought I was a nice girl, but that I'd thrown myself at him. That he found out that I'd been with a few of your friends, that I'd happily let them pass me around. All lies, but you confronted me nonetheless. I tried to explain, but you didn't believe me. *What kind of daughter are you, that our father is lying in some recovery unit, a wounded hero, and you are out spreading your legs for everyone?* Did I get that right, Erik? Isn't that what you said?" It had been seven years, but the resentment boiled up in Alanna like a cancer.

"You say one more fucking word that I don't like, and I will choke you, son." Hans was fury incarnate. At the world, at his son, and the bastard that dared to harm one hair on his daughter, at himself. "Did your mother know?" Alanna shook her head. "How about your grandma? She was staying with you during all of this. It was right before we moved to Virginia."

She shook her head. "No one knew but Branna, then I told Tim a couple of years later. He wanted to tell Erik, but I begged him not to." She looked at her brother. "I knew you wouldn't believe me." A ripple of emotion ran through Erik's face. He got up out of his seat, towering over her, and dropped to his knees. His face was destroyed.

"I know I don't deserve to be forgiven, but I am so sorry. I was an angry asshole. I took that anger out on you. All of it. Mom leaving, Dad getting hurt, losing Brian and Meghan." He choked on his words. "I remember when it happened. I came home on liberty from the academy for the specific purpose of giving you hell about Steve. I didn't even give you a chance to tell me what happened. You needed me, and I was a prick and a horrible brother to you. I'm so sorry." He lay his head in her lap and she felt the tremors. Her anger seeped out of her. She cried with him, cradling his head. Aidan and Hans sat silently, bearing witness to the whole thing.

Finally, Erik looked up, his face tear stained and red with fury. "I swear to you, I will spend the rest of my life making this up to you. And I will get that fucker if it's the last thing I do. I will check every street in Wilmington if I have to."

Alanna paled. "Wilmington?"

He nodded. "He left the Merchant Marines six months ago. He was dismissed, actually. Something to do with a female on the ship. I heard it through the grapevine. I haven't actually heard from him in five years."

Aidan sighed. "That would explain a lot. Why the situation has escalated."

Hans's eyes shot to his. "What do you mean escalated? What brought the police out here tonight?" That's when Alanna finished telling the story. The reason she kept the bat nearby, the gun, why she'd changed phone numbers so often. Then she finally told them about the pictures. He was watching her, stalking her every move, taking pictures with some disposable phone, stealing her new number from the mail.

After seven years, he might have changed enough to where he could easily escape her notice. And then there was the woman. That final picture, that final threat, the poor, beaten woman with green eyes and blonde hair. She showed the phone to Hans and Erik.

That final bit of the story made her father go mental. "That's it! You're moving up to Virginia tomorrow. I will extend my tour there, or find another job in DC."

Alanna stood up, irate. "I will not. I am not giving up my summer here, my final days in North Carolina. My last two months..." she paused, closing her eyes. "My last two months with Aidan. I will not let that maniac take one more thing from me or you, do you understand me?" She pointed to her father. "You are taking that job in Spain."

Hans looked at Aidan. She growled, "He didn't tell me, although I will kick his butt later, because he obviously knew. Father Matthew let it slip. He thought I knew, and I didn't tell him otherwise."

Erik looked from one face to the other. "What job in Spain? What is she talking about, Dad?"

Hans stood up, meeting her glare. "You, Miss Priss, will not worry about Spain. You will let me protect you. You will let your brother protect you, like we both should have done seven years ago. I will not go off to Spain and fail you again." His voice broke with emotion.

Alanna covered her mouth. "Daddy, don't say that." She came around the table and hugged him fiercely. "This had nothing to do with you. This was not your fault."

He gripped her. "It was. I was gone too much, too worried about my career."

Erik interrupted. "No. You're the best dad we could have ever asked for, it was me who screwed up. He was my friend. I brought him into our house."

Alanna pulled Erik in to the hug. "No," she whispered. "I should have told. I should have been brave. I'm sorry about all of this. I tried. I tried to make up for it, Daddy." She was sobbing now. "I tried to make you proud. To be the good girl you thought I was."

Hans pulled away, "You always made me proud. Jesus, is that why you didn't date? Why you worked so hard? Why you never asked for help? You listen to me, Alanna Falk. You and Erik are the best part of my life. My babies. There is nothing you could tell me that would change that. I trust you and I love you."

She kissed his face. "I love you too, daddy. Now, please understand. I won't leave my home." He sighed, pressing his forehead to hers. "And you are going to take that job in Spain."

He ground his jaw. "Forget about that for now. I have a couple of months to decide. Maybe they'll have caught him by then. What are they doing? What did the police say?"

They talked for another half hour until Sorcha came knocking. "You've all interrogated the lass long enough. Time for breakfast." They all made their way over to Aidan's side of the duplex.

"So, I am sorry to meet under such unfortunate circumstances, but I am damned happy to meet you all." Hans said with a smile. He shook hands again with Sean and Seany, then Sorcha hugged him. His ears turned red.

"My father is blushing." Alanna said under her breath. Sorcha was beautiful and charming. She also had that spark that drew men like flies to honey. "Ye've had a rough night and morning, I suspect. Sit down and have some rashers, a bit of tea. I've got scones in the oven."

Hans rubbed his hands together. "Sean, I don't have to tell you that beauty and baking are the best combination in the world."

Sean laughed. "Aye, though she didn't bake so well those first couple of years. I married her for her moxie."

Sorcha gave him a smack. "Mind your manners."

Erik hung back. He looked, Aidan reflected, like a penitent dog. Alanna walked over and hooked her arm in his. "I'll give you the crispy part of my bacon."

He smiled at that, obviously remembering simpler times. "I love you, Anna Banana."

She gave him a bump. "I know that. I really do know that."

The two families ate and talked and laughed. "I've been wanting to go to Ireland since I was a young man. Now that little Branna is settled over there with a new family, I might have to make it happen." Hans said.

"Once you're in Spain, it will be a short trip." Alanna said, daring him to argue.

"Oh, aye. Take the train through France, and you could hop a flight or a ferry to Dublin out of England. She'd be delighted. We've got room for you all if it comes to that," Sean said.

"Daddy, maybe we can go together!" Alanna said, her mood brightened.

Aidan was smiling stupidly as he watched the two families intermingle. Sean Jr. was plucking on the guitar, talking to Erik, the parents were talking like old friends. He looked over at Alanna and she wore the same smile. She looked at him, then, with knowing in her eyes. Knowing and relief. The relief of a burden shared. And didn't he know all about that? He'd shared his burdens, too. They'd both helped one another. What a gift that was. Everything was different.

He could easily see her in County Clare, joking with his sister, playing with Cora, dancing with little Colin on her hip, and singing with his mother and Branna at Gus's. He closed his eyes as a wave of longing came over him. She had a whole new life starting, right when he could think of nothing else other than whisking her away to Ireland, and then to England. He was in love with her. Finally, he'd let himself love someone.

She needed to see this through, though. Her purpose was bigger than being his wife. The thought was as clear as it was startling. He'd marry her without a doubt, and love her until he was in his grave, if things were different. They'd marry in the family parish, he'd dance the O'Brien set with her. That wasn't going to happen, though. She'd studied seven years to get that job. He could not, would not, muddy the waters. Make her choose. All those men she could help, the amazing career she would have. O'Briens had one true mate, but she was a Falk. She'd fall in love again. He couldn't be selfish.

"Is your head hurting?" Alanna's voice was soft and sweet, and he leaned into her hands as she touched him.

"No, a mhuirnín. I'm just tired. I might need a date in the hammock, later. I've got to go to work, though. I texted Hector, told him it was an emergency, that I'd be in late. I've got to go, though."

She rubbed his scalp. "Later then." Aidan stood and noticed that everyone was quiet and staring.

He cleared his throat. "I've got to go. I'm late."

Hans stood as well. "Tell Hector to call me during the break. I have to head out, too. So does Erik."

He looked at Alanna, worry etching his face. "She's in good hands, mo cara. I promise you." Sean stood and put his hand on his shoulder. "I'll protect her like my own."

Hans exhaled. "Are you sure you don't want to come with me, Miss Priss? I can move you in the spare room."

She smiled. "I will be there in August when my job starts. Don't worry Daddy. We know he's local, now. I'll keep the gun on me."

Sorcha crossed herself and Seany's jaw dropped. "Christ, Aidan, your woman is a bad ass." They all started laughing. Sean Jr. had that disarming way about him. But all Alanna could think was, *I'm not his woman. Not really.* But she wished with all her heart that she was.

31

Aidan was distracted, but he got through the day. At some point, he could feel Hector's eyes on him. He knew it all. Well, the important stuff, not some of the more intimate details to be sure. No way he or Hans would share the most gory details. Just that he'd hurt her, tried to rape her, and had been stalking her. That the fucker had been on the beach by her house, out in public where she'd been with friends, with Aidan. The rage thrummed in his ears, when he dwelled too long on it. The men could sense something was up, but they didn't pry. Probably on Hector's orders. Alanna had told him he could confide in John. He had, during lunch. Again, light on the nitty gritty, but he got his point across.

"We need to find that rat bastard," John said.

"Aye." Some things were too personal to leave completely up to the police. Even his father knew that.

"We are here for you. No matter what you need, you feel me? I'll bring the fucking shovel." Aidan was soothed by John's anger. It was right, and it was genuine.

As he left, John ran up to the truck. "I know you have a lot going on right now, but about Sunday. Maria said I should remind you."

Aidan smacked his head, "The christening, aye. Jesus. I'm glad you did. My mother will be beside herself at the notion."

John laughed, "That's because she's hoping that baby thing will rub off. She wants more grandkids."

Aidan rolled his eyes, "She's not as bad as my Gran. The dear woman is relentless."

John cocked his head. "You sure you don't have any prospects. You can deny it all you want, brother, but Alanna is the one. You gonna just walk away from that?" His Jersey was coming out in full force, which meant the boy was serious.

"She got that job, the job she really wanted in Virginia," Aidan said.

"Shit," was all John could say.

Alanna decided, about thirty seconds after her father, brother, and Aidan left, that she owed the O'Brien family a southern-style day on the town. She had completely ruined their surprise, kept them up late, and the woman had made her breakfast instead of vacationing and going to a restaurant. She took them all around the island, promising they would see the base, where Aidan trained, tomorrow.

She took them in silly souvenir shops where they picked out gifts for everyone. Her favorite shop had a huge shark in the front, and you had to walk through its open jaws to get to the front door. She took photos of Sean Jr and his father pretending to get eaten by the shark. They bought extra beach items and towels, planning to let Seany take the towels to University.

Then they lunched at her favorite crab shack that had a gallery attached to it. It was full of beach themed paintings, photographs, and sculptures from local artists. Sorcha loved it. She bought a pottery platter with a fishnet pattern covering it and ornate sea creatures around the edges. She bought a small painting for the twins' room and a pewter mermaid hair clip for little Cora.

For dessert, Alanna took them to the hands down local favorite. Island Delights was a hot dog and ice cream parlor done up like a fifties diner. It was a hole in the wall, and was always packed with tourists and locals alike.

They played on the beach, and she promised to walk everyone to the end of the island after dinner. When Aidan came home, he noticed that his father had changed the locks. He went up through the ocean side, up to the deck and in through the slider. Alanna was in the kitchen with Sorcha, frying hush puppies and steaming shrimp and clams. "Did you go see Sheila?" he asked.

Alanna shook her head. "No, don't tell. She's too far, and we were much too busy today." She gave Sorcha a satisfied look, and Sorcha put her arm around the girl.

"It was a gorgeous day, all together," Sorcha said.

Aidan's chest squeezed at the sight of them. "I'll go get cleaned up." Then he yelled, "Da!" Sean was out on the deck. "I've got some cold local beer!" Sean and the junior both hopped up and came in.

"Don't even start about the drinking age in America, Ma. I'm on vacation," her younger son said with a hand up.

She gave him a smirk. "Don't drink more than two. I'm still young enough to box your ears."

Seany kissed her cheek. "Don't I know it." He shuddered with fear, winking at Alanna. Then he took two beers from the fridge and handed one to his da.

They walked out on the deck and Alanna followed them, while Aidan retreated to the shower. They relaxed in each other's company, getting to know one another.

"It's gorgeous all together. I can't believe Branna owns these places. My brother married well," Seany said.

"That he did, and it's got nothing to do with these beach cottages. So tell me, Alanna." He paused. "Do you prefer Alanna or Anna?"

She smiled. "Well, Aidan calls me Alanna. So does my father."

Sean nodded. "Well, then, wee Alanna. Has my son been earning his keep?" asked Sean with a wink.

Alanna was next to him with her hands on the deck railing. "Oh, yes, he has. He's done some work out here on the deck, worked on some small plumbing issues. I think his next job is the carpeting on his side. He needs to rip it out and have someone come and lay new carpeting."

Sean waved a hand. "There's no need to hire anyone. We can help him as long as I can rent the tools. I've put down carpeting in my house, Brigid's, and my mother's house. My da showed me how to do it years ago. It would be good for both the boys to learn."

Sean Jr. took a sip of his beer. "I keep telling my da that Aidan could use my help all summer. I don't start school until September."

Alanna raised a brow and looked at Sean. "And what does your daddy think about that?" Sean shrugged, not commenting.

"My mother is the hard nugget. You can work on her for me." Alanna saw the elder Sean hide a grin under the rim of his bottle.

"I think it's a fine idea. I like the idea of having two big, handsome O'Brien men protecting me all summer. I'll see what I can do. If it's okay with Aidan, that is." Seany put his beer down and grabbed her in a big bear hug.

"Are you making a play for my neighbor?" Aidan said from behind them. He was freshly showered and had his own beer.

"Oh, aye. We've decided to elope. Unless you've got some eligible young ladies on board to distract me."

Aidan took Alanna's wrist and pulled her to him, eyeballing his younger brother. "Do you need a drink, darlin?"

She looked up at him. "I'll have something with dinner. I picked up a bottle of white wine." Aidan looked at her mouth, resisting the urge to pull her over to her side of the duplex and not come out until dinner.

"I'll go help your mother," she said, sliding away from him. As he watched her go, he noticed that both his father and his brother were watching him.

"What?" he said defensively.

Seany snorted. "What, he says. Why do the men in this family make everything so hard?" Seany asked.

Sean laughed and messed up his hair. "You just wait, lad. You're half O'Brien and half Mullen. You'll eat those words. I'll wager on it. "

Seany took a sip of his beer. "I can't wait. All that fighting and making-up looks fun." Aidan and Sean both laughed.

Sean slapped his youngest on the back. "Aye, I suppose it is." Aidan's smile held a little something like doubt. His father could see it, plain as day. "What is it, Aidan? Why do you hold back from her?"

Aidan sighed. He never could fool his da. "She's got a very good job offer. Exactly what she wanted."

Sean's face grew serious. "In Virginia? I heard her mention moving to her da." Aidan nodded.

Seany said. "They've got jobs in England, too, brother. Convince her."

"It's not that simple," he said quietly.

Sean had gone in to help Sorcha, leaving Aidan and Sean Jr. alone on the deck. "How are you, brother?" Seany asked. There was concern in his voice and a maturity that Aidan hadn't noticed before.

"I'm fine, why do you ask?" Seany didn't answer him. "Why did they come, really? It wasn't for my birthday, was it?"

Seany met his eyes. "I don't know all of it, but I heard most of it. It happened after you called Da. He went in the bedroom and told Ma and me that you two needed some privacy. You know Ma. She's as bad as Brigid."

Aidan rubbed his face with his palm. "Aye, who do you think taught Brigid how to be a nosey peahen? Go on."

Seany shrugged. "Whatever you were talking about, she heard it all. Something about the war, I'm guessing." He shook his head. "She was crying. So was Da. They booked the tickets the next day. What did you tell Da?"

Aidan looked hard at him. "It's nothing you need to hear about, lad."

Seany straightened his spine. "I'm not a child. Another year or so, it could be me going off to war. You've been gone for most of my life, Aidan. In and out for visits, but we never got the chance to be brothers the way you are with Michael and Patrick, even with Tadgh and Liam. I just want in. I'm not a boy anymore."

Aidan's eyes were burning with emotion. He was right. Their's was the biggest age gap. He'd missed so much of Seany's life. He was practically a man. "Ma mentioned that you wanted to stay for the summer."

Seany perked up at that. "She keeps saying no. I think she fears I'd be in the way. I can help though. I can help with the repairs and help watch over Alanna."

Aidan grabbed his brother, holding him close. *I just want in. I'm not a child anymore.* "I'll talk to Ma," he said into Seany's shoulder. "I'd like it if you stayed." His voice was heavy with emotion, and Seany squeezed him tighter.

"Thank you."

"Ma, have I told you how much I miss your cooking?" Aidan said, licking his fingers.

"Only about five times since I got here." She threw an extra napkin at him.

"Mrs. O'Brien, I love these potatoes. You are going to have to tell me your secret."

Sorcha smiled at her. "You really need to call me Sorcha, sweetheart. I'll be sure to write it down for you. The secret is lots of cream and butter."

Sean and Alanna started clearing plates. "So tell me again what this dessert consists of?" Sean asked.

Alanna rubbed her hands together. "They're called s'mores. We'll need to start a fire first. The tide is low, so it shouldn't be too hard."

Aidan hopped up. "I'll start digging the pit. Seany, come with me and carry some wood."

Alanna took the sponge from Sean's hand. "Go take your wife on a romantic beach walk. I will wash up. Scoot, now!"

Sean pulled Sorcha out of her chair. "You heard the girl. Romance. Now, woman."

Alanna blushed at the way they were looking at each other. "It's nice to see a marriage last. You two are an inspiration."

Sorcha smiled at that notion. "O'Brien men love fiercely. It's not something that fades away. When they love for real, they love forever." She seemed to be relaying a message with her eyes, and Alanna looked down. She played back the scene on the deck. Aidan had referred to her as his neighbor. Not his girlfriend, not his woman, even though everyone had quickly caught on to the growing relationship, if you could call it that. His neighbor. Right. *It's better than calling you a convenient piece of ass or friend with benefits.* That's all she really was, though. He'd given into his attraction to her, but he was still gone in two months. They were friends that were sleeping together.

She cleared her throat. "Have fun on your walk."

Alanna was finishing up the dishes when her phone rang. It was an international number. She answered it and got nothing but a squeal from the other end. "I am so freaking jealous! Do you love Sean and Sorcha? Couldn't you just eat little Seany up! I'm so jealous I could spit!"

Alanna was laughing, though in the back of her mind it occurred to her that Branna was going to hear about everything. It was better that it came from her.

After about ten minutes of Alanna talking non-stop, she finally took a breath. That's when she heard the sniffling. "It's ok, Branna. I should have told you sooner."

Branna was trying to speak, stifling sobs in the process. "I should have told someone when it happened. I should have made you tell your mother. We should have told my mother."

Alanna said, "Branna, it was my choice. I was never close with my mom, and you had just lost your father. I should have never burdened you with such a serious thing. That bastard is not worth one more tear." She said this, of course, in between her own sobs.

"I wish I was there. I wish I could hug you. But honestly, Sean and Sorcha are the best possible people for you to have right now. Sorcha has a way of making everything better. Sean, well, he was a cop for twenty-five years. He knows his stuff." She exhaled, finally done crying. "I'm glad Aidan was there for you, and I'm glad you told your dad and Erik. I'm sorry you had to go through all of that, but at least you know you're not alone."

Alanna laughed a little. "No, we have a full house, and they are all up in my sordid past."

"Tell me about Aidan," Branna said simply.

Alanna felt herself blush, even though Branna couldn't see her. "Well, let's just say I'm going to need a Gaelic phrase book."

Branna said, "Gaelic? Why is he speaking…Oh!" Understanding her husbands propensity toward Gaelic endearments when they made love, she understood exactly what Alanna meant. "You and he? Oh my God, Anna! Tell me everything!"

Alanna shushed her. "I am not going to tell you everything."

Branna begged. "Come on, I tell you everything."

Alanna scoffed at that. "That is a shameless lie. You showed up on my doorstep knocked up with twins, and as tight lipped as a nun."

Branna said, "I don't know why I am best friends with you. You suck."

Alanna giggled. "Ok, little sister, I'll tell you this. He's the most amazing man I've ever known. In every way. He's just…" she searched for some way to explain.

Branna said, "It's all right, I understand. These O'Brien men are like something out of a fairy tale."

Alanna mumbled under her breath, "A really hot, horny fairy tale." Cue another squeal. "Would you control yourself, Branna. They can hear you in Wilmington!"

Branna gave a husky chuckle. "If he's anything like Michael, you're not going to be able to walk by the end of the summer."

Alanna came back over to Aidan's side of the house, just in time to see the fire start up. Seany was doing some sort of fire dance around the pit. Alanna grabbed the roasting sticks and all of the supplies, and Sean carried down a small table. They'd set up beach chairs around the fire, and Sorcha was sitting with a glass of wine. "How is Branna?"

Alanna plopped down next to her. "She's jealous."

Sorcha giggled. "Well, we'll just have to take plenty of pictures to tide her over, until you visit. When will you come?"

Alanna thought about that. "Well, I have to go up to Virginia in a couple of weeks to meet the staff and do a little training. I'm going to talk to them about taking some time off. I'd like to come before the winter. Given my recent graduation, I doubt they will deny me a well earned break, even if it is unpaid. Maybe September?"

Sorcha patted her hand. "Oh, that's a fine time to come. It's cool, but not too cold. The heather won't be in bloom, but the fall is lovely in Ireland.You might get some rain, though."

Alanna waved a hand. "I love rain. It keeps everything alive. Two years in the desert cured me of wanting sun every day."

Sorcha said, "While you're in town, I insist you stay with us. Michael and Branna have a lovely cottage, but you'd be sleeping on the couch. They've only got two bedrooms. Brigid's got a little more room, but Sean and I have two empty bedrooms to choose from. You can stay as long as you like."

Alanna looked at Aidan and found that he was watching them, listening. She blushed, wondering if he would be comfortable with her integrating herself so intimately in his family, after they had parted ways. Still, she could hardly say no. "I think that would be lovely. I want to travel a bit. I'd like to see Dublin, and go up to the North, where you're from as well. You'll have to tell me all about Belfast while you're here."

Aidan's heart did a jump at the thought of Alanna coming to him in Belfast. He'd be leaving for England in the winter, but he would be there if she came in the autumn. He pictured her in the city park, a sweater, boots, her coppery blonde hair against the autumn foliage. Her hair splayed across the pillow in his bed. The thought of her staying in his childhood bedroom gave him another thrill. What would teenage Aidan have thought of this beauty, sleeping in his bed? He watched her with Seany as they toasted marshmallows, and his throat was suddenly tight, thick with longing.

"You've got heavy thoughts swirling around in that brain, lad," Sean said.

He looked at his father and gave him a crooked smile. "More like fairy tales, Da. Never mind that. Just pass me one of those sticks and the bag of marshmallows."

Aidan sat on the outside deck, watching the stars and moon glimmer over the ocean. Alanna was sleeping, the day's events finally taking a toll. She'd cancelled her exercise classes today but she had to be up early tomorrow. The fact that she felt safe with Aidan and his family there made him happy. Seany was strumming on Aidan's Alvarez, and Sean and Sorcha were quietly seated as well. "Aidan, why don't you take a walk with your mother. You haven't had a single moment to catch up with her," Sean said.

Aidan knew this was coming. He loved the idea and hated it. His mother had listened to his confessions, and heard things he would have never readily shared with her. Not because he didn't trust her, but because he wanted to protect her. Maybe to protect himself as well. No one could see into his heart more easily than his mother. He stood and put his hand out, his mother taking it without a word.

"I like her. She's a good girl. Smart, too." Sorcha said. They walked along the warm surf, the moon and lights from the beach houses paving their way.

"She is. She's a wonderful girl. The work she does is important. She's got a way with the men, and the families. I've never met anyone like her." Aidan said.

The pride he showed, when he spoke of her, warmed Sorcha's heart. "Well, she got you talking didn't she? She must be a miracle worker."

Aidan gave his mother a sideways glance. "Aye, I suppose she did. I know you were listening. Seany told me. Is that what prompted this visit? You came to make sure I hadn't gone off the deep end?"

Sorcha stopped, hands on her hips. "Yes, I did listen. And yes, that's why we came. And no, we weren't afraid o' you goin' off the deep end." His mother's Irish was thick when she was emotional, which normally amused him.

"I'm sorry I didn't talk to you, Ma. I just couldn't tell you or Brigid. Alanna says it's because I protect my women, that I didn't want this stuff in your head, and yes, that was part of it. It was certainly the why of it with Brigid. She's got a good, blessed life. She doesn't need to hear about what it's like in a war zone."

Sorcha nodded, "I understand. But me? Christ, Aidan. I grew up in a war zone. I lived it every day."

Aidan picked up a shell and tossed it into the surf. "I know that, Ma. I just didn't..." He stopped, wiping the sand off his fingers on to the leg of his shorts.

"What, Aidan? Finish that sentence." He looked at her and she was taken back by his expression. She put a hand on him."What is it, mo chroí?"

He exhaled. "I didn't want to disappoint you. You told me not to go. You begged me not to enlist. I know you didn't like me joining with the crown, that you didn't understand. Then I'm over there getting medals while other people are dying and…"

Sorcha lurched forward and put her hand to his lips. "Stop! Please, Aidan." To his horror, she was starting to cry.

"I'm sorry, Ma." She shook her head violently in negation. "Don't cry," he said as he took her in his arms.

She could barely speak. "Is that what you think? That I'm ashamed of your service? Oh, Aidan. My beautiful boy, please forgive me." She was hiccuping, and Aidan was confused and devastated that he'd upset his mother so much. What would his father say?

He took her over to the dune and sat her down next to him. "How can I help, Ma? I didn't mean to upset you."

Sorcha was sniffling, trying to compose herself. "Aidan, I have always prided myself on being good at three things. I'm a good wife, a good mother, and a good nurse. I thought after six children, I'd finally perfected my mothering skills to an expert level. It's not your fault that I just got a good lesson in humility."

Aidan's brows were drawn together. "What are ye talking about, woman? You're the best mother in the world. There's no better."

She looked at him sadly. "You've gone off to battle four times, thinking that you didn't have my blessing. When I think back to the time when you enlisted, I'm ashamed of the way I acted. I thought I showed you that I supported you, after it happened. I welcomed you home, and I did my best to say all the right things. I didn't say what you needed to hear, though. Did I?" Her voice broke as she said, "You've made me so proud. You are brave and loyal, and as this war has progressed, I've learned to understand the reasons you felt you needed to do this. I was wrong when I tried to keep you from going. You've done such good in the world, and you still come home, and are able to be kind and gentle. I know you've had a hard time, love. I know you've seen things that have scarred you inside. But you've handled it better than most men, and you're worthy of every medal on your chest. The fact that you were in such danger, that you could have been killed over there like that boy you talked about." She shook her head, hiccuping as the tears fell. "You would have died thinking that I didn't approve. The thought of it threatens to bring up my dinner."

Aidan sighed. "Don't think like that, Ma. I did come home. I just didn't know how to talk to you about what it was like. I joined a division of the British Army. After what happened during The Troubles, how could you not resent it?"

She swallowed, breathing deeply, choosing her words. "The Troubles, back in my day, that was our war. A battle for my generation and many generations before mine. That's not your war. Your generation has worked to heal that rift. You've always been my child of two worlds. One foot in the North and one in the Republic. You love the city I grew up in, and you have lived there during a time of re-birth and forgiveness. The fact that you can find common ground with the other side of those segregation walls makes me think that maybe all of that suffering and fighting and negotiating might have finally worked itself out. I'm sorry I never told you that, Aidan. When you joined up, it was right at the end of the cancer. I wasn't myself. Pain, illness, fear…it changes you. That is no excuse, though. So I'm going to tell you now. You make me prouder than I ever thought was possible. You've got the mind of a warrior and the heart of a priest. What you did for that little girl," she stifled a sob, "Oh, Aidan. You're the best man I've ever known. You've sheltered everyone from your pain, but you've kept us away in the process. Please, no more. Let your family help you. And for the love of God don't go making a cock-up of this thing you have going with Alanna."

Aidan barked out a laugh. "You did not just say cock-up, Ma."

She nudged him, "Aye, I did. I meant it, too. She's been hand-picked by the Almighty just for you. Don't doubt it."

Aidan dug in the sand, not meeting her eyes. "She's got a good job offer. She's got great things coming, and I can't put her in the position where she has to choose."

Sorcha looked at him like he was daft. "A job? What's a job when love is at stake? And don't you doubt it for a minute. She is so in love with you she's sick with it. A woman knows these things. I see the way you look at each other. Like a pair of tea kettles ready to boil over."

Aidan blushed. "I'm not having this conversation with my mother."

She snorted. "Aye, well then have it with your father. That is a man who knows how to get the girl."

32

The next morning, Sean the senior and Sorcha heard Alanna in the other room trying to wake up their youngest. Aidan was with her. "Get up ye lazy bugger. You said you wanted to go to the gym."

Seany had expressed interest in going to Alanna's exercise classes. Aidan tried to warn him, but the cockiness of youth was ever a worthy adversary. "You're just old and arthritic. I can handle a bit of yoga and riding a wee bicycle." Aidan had just shaken his head. In the morning light, in the clutches of jet lag, Seany was a little less enthusiastic.

"Get up and get some breakfast. You're going to need it, lad. I need to go to work and so does she."

As they left Seany's room, Aidan pulled Alanna in for a quick kiss. "I'll see you at lunch. You'll bring my parents?"

She nodded. "Are you sure I can't bring anything?"

He shrugged, "Hatsu said no." His mother came out of the bedroom dressed in a pair of pajama bottoms and a Garda t-shirt that was about a hundred sizes too big for her, followed by Sean who was rubbing his hair, one brow cocked. Aidan kissed his mother on the way out the door.

"Good morning, lass. Did you get the wee mongrel out of bed?"

She giggled. "I think so. I'll head back over and let you two enjoy some peace and quiet."

Seany stumbled out of his room wearing what appeared to be very wrinkled exercise attire. "Mornin' Ma, Da." He plopped down on a stool.

"Stay for breakfast, Alanna. I'll start some eggs and sausages, and you can put on the coffee."

Aidan checked his trauma kit against the list he'd been given. Once he determined that everything was there, he put it in his pack, and joined the group. They rode out to the field and the young men were chatting.

Hector jumped in the back of the truck. "Attention ladies! It has come to my attention that we have a birthday boy this week."

Aidan put his head down, covering his eyes with his hand. "Jesus wept," he muttered.

"He thought he would slip this one by us, but his lady friend was kind enough to invite the entire team over for a little beach party. That said, if one of you little assholes gets it in your head to get a stripper, let me warn you that his parents and his little brother have flown across the ocean to see him, and it would be ill advised."

The men gave a collective whine. "Ah, man. I had the perfect dancer, too. He's identifying as a woman this week."

The truck rumbled with laughter. "Quiet, now. I will e-mail the particulars. Be polite, be on time, and bring your swim gear if you want to swim. Our lovely hostess is a sergeant major's daughter, so I feel compelled to warn you that if you don't mind your manners, you will be shitting in a bag when he's done with you."

Aidan rode with Hector and John to the Diaz home for lunch. As they pulled in, he saw his family getting out of Alanna's car. He looked at his brother and started to laugh. "Is that your little brother?" John asked. Aidan nodded. "Jesus, you didn't tell me he was handicapped."

Aidan smiled as he approached them. "He wasn't until he took two of Alanna's classes back to back." Aidan thumped him on the back. "Kicked your arse, did she? Did you make it through both?"

Seany nodded, looking exhausted. "Oh, aye. I vomited in the trash can outside the spinning room, though."

John laughed. "Ah, the PT pukes. Gotta love them. You should come do Crossfit with us next week. You'll love it."

Seany smiled weakly at Aidan. "You've got yourself a she-devil. She's ruthless. She makes my rugby coach look like a dandy."

"I tried to tell you not to take both. You wouldn't listen," Aidan said. He mussed Seany's hair, still wet from the gym shower.

Aidan looked in the kitchen where Hatsu, Alanna, Maria, and his mother were cleaning up and passing around the baby. "Your son is quick on his feet, I'll give him that. And he never left my side, not until my husband was there. He also tangoed with my doctor until the midwife showed up."

Sorcha was rocking the baby, making cooing noises at him. "Well, little Aidan Alann. It sounds like you were ready to come. Aye, that's a fine strong lad." She turned to Maria, "I'd suggest if you have another, you talk to a dietician and an herbalist to control that blood pressure from the start."

Maria exhaled. "Yes, we want at least one or two more. Aidan told me you are a midwife. I was a nurse before all of these little guys showed up. I worked trauma. Do you still practice?"

Sorcha handed the fussing boy to her. "I haven't, not since the breast cancer. I've started taking classes, though. I'm going to go back part-time with a new practice in Ennis. I miss it. I miss the mums and the babies. It was a good calling," she said. "Sean and

I made an agreement. If I hit the ten year anniversary and was cancer free, I could try to go back to work. So, it is well past time."

"Doing what you love is important. Has Anna told you about her work?" Maria said.

"Oh, yes. Aidan has as well. It's wonderful. They'll be lucky to have her at her new position," Sorcha said lightly, carefully watching Alanna.

Maria's brows went up. "Virginia?" she asked. Alanna nodded. "Wow, so are you happy about the move?"

Alanna shrugged. "The job is good. Really good, actually. The DC area has a lot of high profile medical facilities. I think it's a good place to jump start a career."

Maria smiled, and there seemed to be a question in her eyes. Then she looked over at Aidan and realized he'd been listening. He met her eyes briefly and then he looked away.

The night and next day sped by with Alanna teaching classes, showing Aidan's family around, and enjoying nights around the table with conversation, music, and laughter. "I think Aidan would love to have him, Sorcha. Ask him before you make your mind up. He'd probably even pay to have the ticket changed."

Seany butted in at that point. "I have the money. Tadgh helped me get a job at the ferry as a captain's mate. I can pay for the fare change."

Sorcha swatted at him. "Go get your father and Aidan. They need to pick the food up." Seany waited, giving her his saddest little pout.

"Oh, how can you say no to that sweet poopy face?" Alanna said, taking his chin in her hand and putting her head next to his. She put her bottom lip out in a pout. "Please, momma."

Sorcha rolled her eyes. "I'll talk to Aidan." Seany kissed Alanna on the cheek and ran outside. "That's not a yes, Sean Jr.!" Sorcha yelled.

Alanna laughed. "You little softy," she teased.

Sorcha said. "He's my last. He walks all over me."

Alanna snorted, "And you a Mullen woman? I don't believe it for a minute."

Sorcha grinned, "You've been hearing tales from my son?"

Alanna shook her head back and forth. "Branna. She's got some serious hero worship going on where you are concerned. She said you know how to handle your men."

Sorcha waved a hand dismissively. "They're all teddy bears deep down. Every last one. You'll never find a more passionate bunch of men, though, or protective. They are as wonderful as they are beautiful."

Just then, the three men came into the house. Alanna's breath shot out of her in a burst. They were beautiful. Just like Michael. Just like she suspected Liam, Patrick, and Tadgh were. Aidan would make beautiful sons, she thought. She shook her head, as if to erase that thought.

She pranced up to him with the catering list, a mix of southern delicacies. "Don't forget, baby. Extra okra."

Aidan made a gagging face. "What's okra, then?" Seany asked.

"Honey, you'll love it. Aidan just can't appreciate the finer nuances."

The men started piling in by two's and three's. John, Hector, Staff Sergeants Williams and Polanski all brought their wives. The three Lieutenants were all single, and Saxton and Shull had come together from the office. Clara and Frankie chased the Williams's little boy around, playing pirates in the sand. Lieutenant Drake was the last to show up and he had a gift bag. "We decided to pool our money for a gift."

Aidan blushed. "I said no gifts."

Then Joey got a mischievous grin on his face. "Oh, but we had motivation." Aidan pulled a bottle of Jameson Reserve Black Barrel out of the bag and all the men started hooting.

"Ah, shit," Aidan said.

"What did we miss?" asked his father.

"Aidan informed us on his first day that he would sing for no less than a bottle of Ireland's finest," Joey gloated.

Sean laughed, taking the bottle. "Oh, aye. For Black Barrel, I'll join him."

"Just try it. Don't listen to him," Alanna said. Seany scrunched his nose, sniffing it.

"Don't do it, lad. It tastes like snotty pinwheels of death."

Washington grabbed his chest. "Now, them's fightin' words, Sir. You're in the South. We were weaned off our momma's teet with okra."

Alanna put her hand up and gave him a high five. "You tell him, Corporal."

Washington sat down next to Seany. "Now, what you need is some of this good Louisiana hot sauce. Dash a little of that on there, and you'll be ready for me to fix you up with a nice Creole girl." Seany just shrugged and popped one in his mouth. He looked at Aidan, not understanding the big deal.

"Just start chewing," Aidan said.

Seany did, and his face started to subtly twitch. A look of displeasure moving into a strained swallow. "What in the fecking hell was that? It's like slimy frog eggs with cornmeal coated over it." He shuddered. "The seeds were squirming around in the slime. That shite is worse than Ma's tripe soup, and that's sayin somethin."

Sorcha interrupted, "I'll have you know that your Da loves my tripe soup."

Meanwhile, Aidan and John were shooting Alanna and Washington smug looks. Alanna laughed as she retreated into the house.

"We tried to tell you, man. They've been brain washed to like it from birth. You won't catch any self respecting Jersey boy eating those little snot rockets," said John.

There was a disturbance at the door, then the men parted to show Alanna walking with a cake.

"Holy shit, sir. That's a lot of candles!" Porter jibed. Alanna started singing and everyone joined in. Aidan looked at his parents. They were smiling as they sang. He couldn't remember the last birthday party he'd had. He'd probably been about ten years old. Alanna set the cake in front of him. "Make a wish." Before he could think about it, he pulled her mouth to his and the boys went wild. "Ooh-rah!"

Once the cake was demolished, the entertainment couldn't be put off any longer. They all piled into Alanna's house. Seany brought over the guitar, the piano was tuned and ready, and Alanna brought out her violin. Instead of readying herself to play, she handed it to Sorcha with a deep bow. "I insist," she said, and Sorcha took it from her with a smile.

Aidan sat with his pawn shop special, and they began. They started with some classics, Whiskey in the Jar, Rocky Road to Dublin. The men were stomping their feet and at one point Porter and Washington were swinging around like school aged square dancers.

Sorcha started the warm up to a familiar song on the violin, then Sean joined her on Aidan's guitar. Sorcha nodded at Alanna who's face brightened in recognition. Aidan closed his eyes, swaying at the sound of her as she began to sing.

You walk unscathed through musket fire,
no ploughman's blade will cut thee down.
No cutless wound will mark thy face.
And you will be my ain true love.

The men and the wives were as still as stone as Aidan joined her, taking the harmony in a deep, melancholy blending. Even the small children stood silent as they listened to them wrap one another in their voices, eyes joining in silent communion.

And as you walk through death's dark veil,
the cannon's thunder can't prevail.
And those who hunt thee down will fail,
and you will be my ain true love.

It was a lover's tune, hitting every person in the room in its own special way. Lovers separated by war. When they finished, Sorcha dragging the final note on the violin, everyone cheered. John took Maria in his arms and kissed her, the same with every married man in the room. After that, the three men did a few bawdy tunes and drinking songs. The house was filled with music and laughter.

The women were busy in the kitchen while the men and children went down to the beach for some volleyball. There wasn't much daylight left. Alanna had shown Seany how to use a skim board, and he was trying to teach the little ones. Maria sat contently on the couch, nursing little Aidan. "It's nice to see a family that can work together like you do. Even your youngest is talented. Are all of your sons big and gorgeous?" Maria asked.

Sorcha threw a dish towel over her shoulder as she spoke. "Oh, aye. They've all got their father's size, length of bone. Brigid's the only one that's built like me. Some got my eyes, some his, and Michael got a mix of both. Patrick and Brigid got the red hues in their hair. Seany, Liam, Michael and Aidan all got the sandy hair like their da. All are musical and all have a lion's share of temper."

Hatsu was listening, silent as usual. Then she spoke in her mild, unassuming way. "Your son was telling us about his brother Michael, and Brian's daughter, Branna. He told us the story about the O'Brien men. Is it true? That they have a fated mate?"

Sorcha sat on a stool, her face drifting to a place within her memory. "I didn't always believe in such things. But, yes. I think so. They don't seem to come to their mates easily. Lord knows Sean and I didn't. It was like…two storms colliding. As beautiful as it was devastating. Sean is the love of my life."

Maria shot a look at Alanna who was not making eye contact with anyone. "I guess a love like that would be worth giving up anything and everything, writing a new story."

Sorcha nodded. "Oh, yes. I was bound and determined to make a life in the North. I'd fought my way into a midwife nursing program, which was no easy thing for a catholic at the Queen's university. The main university was protestant, you see. I swore to the Almighty that I wouldn't let thugs or militants or the church wars drive me out of that city. Then Sean came along. Challenged everything I had set for myself. Yanked me out of the blood and smoke and chaos, and he dragged me over that border screeching like a wee hellcat."

The women giggled, both from Sorcha's accent and her way with words. She shrugged and said, "Then….well… then he set to convincing me. The type of convincing O'Brien men do best. Then I saw only him. Everything else fell in place behind him."

Alanna hung onto her every word. What would it be like to have a man love you the way that Sean loved Sorcha? The way Michael loved Branna? "You're a lucky woman, Sorcha. It's the kind of love most women only dream of. I think I'd love to hear that story in its entirety someday."

Everyone was gone, and Sorcha stood on the deck, looking out at the ocean. "I see why Branna loves this place. She's a child of the sea," she said.

Aidan was drinking a glass of tea, watching the moon glide over the waves. "Yes, it's a good place to spend the summer. Especially if you're young," Aidan said, giving her a sideways glance.

Sorcha sighed. "Are you sure it's a good idea? He doesn't drive. He'll have no friends. What if I leave him and he gets homesick?"

Aidan tried to hide the smile under the rim of his glass. "He's not a child, Ma. He's nearly a man." Then his tone was more serious, "He's practically grown, and I've missed it."

Sorcha looked at him, her eyes showing some understanding. "Aye, I suppose you did."

Aidan said, "He wants to be included. He's the youngest, and that's a hard spot to be in when all of your older brothers are so close in age. Michael and I had each other and Tadgh. Liam and Patrick were close. Now Liam's off at school, and Patrick and Michael are married. Seany feels left behind. I think this would be good for both of us. I feel like I barely know the boy. I want to, though. I want to know him. Instead of chasing girls and hanging with his mates this summer, he wants to be with me."

That was singly the best speech he could have given to sway his mother. "How about a compromise? He has obligations this summer; the job at the ferry and some other things. Another two weeks. He's old enough to fly back on his own, so I'll allow him to stay two more weeks."

"Yes!" Aidan and his mother jumped at the booming voice behind them.

"Sean Jr. it is impolite to eavesdrop!"

Seany grabbed his mother and swung her around. "I promise, Ma. I'll be a good help to Aidan. And I'll only let two girls sleep over at a time." Sorcha swatted at him and he dodged. "Just kidding." He darted in to kiss her on the cheek. "Don't worry, Ma. I'll be a good boy. Mass on Sunday." Then he practically skipped as he went to tell Alanna.

"He likes her, your Alanna," Sorcha said.

Aidan sighed, "She's not mine, Ma. This isn't permanent."

Sorcha looked at him, and her hard gaze made him squirm a bit. "Sometimes you have to ask for what you want, Aidan. And to have the courage to do that, you have to first understand that you deserve it." She kissed her eldest son on the forehead as he bent down to her. "You're the child of my heart, Aidan. My first born. I wish I could help you, but sometimes it's not a mother's place. Sometimes it takes another woman to come in and set everything to rights. If she does that for you, makes everything right, then you can't let her go." Then she left him to go to bed.

Alanna was arranging her sheet music and putting her violin in the case when Aidan came in. "Did you have a good birthday? I noticed you didn't drink after the cake."

He nodded. "I don't like feeling witless. I wanted to be a good example in front of the younger men, too. They'd follow my lead, and we've been given a three drink limit during three months of training."

Alanna walked past him. "I've got a pot of tea in here, peppermint. Would you like a cup?" Aidan's eyes lingered over her. She'd worn the yellow dress he liked and he could see her ass moving under the light fabric.

"No, it's not tea I want." He came up behind her, pressing his hips against her bottom. She pressed back, feeling his hardness. "Do you want me?" His tone was edgy.

"Yes, always. I always want you." She sounded almost miffed about it. The need shot through him, his breathing speeding up. He reached down her belly to her white cotton panties, exploring under the skirt of her dress. She put her hand over his and moaned when he touched her. Her arousal made him snap. He fumbled with his trousers as she felt a rip. He tore her panties, bent her over the counter, and thrust himself into her.

"I'm sorry," Aidan whispered as he stroked Alanna's forehead with his fingers. She was sprawled across his chest, lying in her bed. "About the kitchen," he said.

"Why would you be sorry?"

Aidan swallowed hard, she felt it roll through his chest. "I lost control a bit. I was probably too rough." Alanna propped up on his chest and met his eyes. "I like that you can't always control yourself. You aren't any more demanding than I. You'd never hurt me. If anything, my response to you worries me more."

He furrowed his brow, but she continued. "There's a hunger in me that I never thought was possible." She shook her head. "It's powerful, consuming. It scares me sometimes. Sometimes I think I'll go up in flames from it." Her blush was deep and she wouldn't meet his eye. She was sitting up now.

"Don't ever hold back from me, girl. Seeing you wild, feeling your need. Feeling your nails and your teeth and hearing the ache in your voice," His breath was labored and she knew that if she moved an inch or two to the left, she'd find he was hard again. "The more I have ye, the more I want you. That will be my hell in the end."

Aidan woke with a start, gasping and sweating. He'd been dreaming again, a strange dream that mixed past and present. He was in Kabul again, in that dank apartment. But this time, when he looked in the corner, it wasn't the child. It was Alanna. *You said you'd protect me,* she'd said to him. Suddenly she was on the ground, her hands bound. They were surrounded by scrub and sounds of the sea. It wasn't anywhere he recognized. There seemed to be artillery going off in the background, lighting up the night sky, and her terrified face. *You said you'd protect me,* she repeated.

"Aidan, sweetie. It's okay. I'm right here." The lantern turned on, and he saw her. A harsh breath escaped him as he saw that she was safe and beside him. Her green eyes holding a compassion that undid him. "Tell me what you need. Do you want to talk? Do you need some water?"

Christ, she was trying to take care of him. That wasn't the way it was supposed to be. He was supposed to protect her. He pulled her over his chest and she went willing, her legs splitting over his hips. "Tell me what you need," she said.

He raised his mouth to hers. "I need you. I need all of you." He heard the desperation in his own voice. He didn't care. All he cared about was being in the moment with her, knowing exactly where she was and that she was whole and safe. That she was his. She didn't hesitate. She pulled her t-shirt off. Then off went the panties. She drew his shorts off his legs.

Then she was on top of him, positioned at the ready. "Take me. Please, just take me." His voice was demanding, and she wasted no time. He watched her in the glow of their little lantern as she slid herself down on his arousal and her eyes rolled back, her body shuddering as they joined. She rolled her hips and suddenly nothing of the dream remained. Just her nude, straining body, green eyes flaring, blonde hair falling in silky tangles on his chest. "I'm here, Aidan. I'm right here with you," and she covered his mouth with hers. *Oh, God. How am I going to leave you,* he thought.

33

Saturday started bright and early. Sean and his two sons ripped out the carpeting in the vacation rental and left with Aidan's borrowed truck to find some decent carpet remnants. By suppertime, the job was done and they had Branna on the computer giving her all of the details.

"You are supposed to be on vacation, Sean! You shouldn't be working," she said.

"Oh, don't worry, darlin. With three of us working, it only took a few hours. It was fast and cheap labor. It's good for them to learn," Sean said. "Now, how are those grandchildren of mine?"

Branna talked to all of them in turn, as did Michael. "I can't wait to see you," Alanna said. "I can't believe I'm really coming."

Branna bopped up and down in her seat. "You can visit us, then with Patrick and Caitlyn, then Aidan in the North. Maybe he'll take the trip with you!"

Alanna's eyes darted around. "I don't want to put him in that position. We'll see. I'll be okay on my own."

After the call, Branna put her head down on the table in front of her computer. "Deliver me from O'Brien men."

Michael choked on his tea. "Excuse me, hellcat. I don't think the men are the problem. Deliver us from stubborn, pig-headed, independent American lasses."

She looked at him with a sideways grin. "Touché. Now, what the hell are we going to do?"

Michael shook his head. "You won't have to do anything. Believe me, I know from which I speak. He thinks he's doing her a favor by not making her choose. Stepping back and letting her go for the sake of her career. But he's O'Brien through and through. That martyr tendency only goes so far. He won't be able to live without her anymore than I could live without you."

Branna walked toward her husband who was leaning against the butcher block. She slid her arms around his waist, looking up at him. "You chased me down. That was different. She's not the one running across the Atlantic. If he wants her, he's going to have to take her."

34

The church was full for summertime. Many of the non-catholic Marines that were known to the Denario family were in attendance with their families. Aidan's palms were sweating. He rubbed them on his pants. He'd seen several christenings, but this was the first time he'd be the godparent. His parents were chatting under their breaths at the sizable base chapel and the huge number of families pouring through the doors. Maria, always beautiful, was glowing. Dressed in a long, lavender dress, her hair was long and dark and wavy. John was in a suit. Clara and Frankie were dressed in their finery as well. All bow ties and sundresses. Aidan looked over at Alanna in the choir. She was wearing a white choir robe and she looked like an angel.

The part of the mass where the child would be christened approached, and the choir stood to sing. Alanna stepped forward, and she looked at John and Maria. That's when they started *Make me a Channel of Your Peace.* She took lead vocals, and Aidan could see her eyes misting as she looked down at the child that had been named for both of them. Maria put her head on John's shoulder, and they listened. "She's got a voice like the angels," Sean said quietly. "She is a rare beauty, isn't she?"

As they stood up with the priest, Father Matthew asked, "What name do you give this child?"

John and Maria answered. "Aidan Alann." Aidan's chest tightened and he looked at Alanna who stood next to him. She wept big tears, falling silently down her face as they continued. He looked down at the baby in his arms. Maria had insisted that he hold the boy.

He was awake, but quiet, looking at Aidan with wonder, his brows twitching, mouth working, his little fists batting Aidan's chest. Then it was their turn. Father Matthew turned to them. "Are you ready to help the parents of this child in their duty as Christian parents?" They answered together. "We are." The father continued, addressing the congregation, but all Aidan could see was Alanna, and all he could feel was the child in his arms. The ache in his chest was almost enough to undo him.

What it would be like to have this? What John and Maria have? What Brigid and Finn and Michael and Branna and his parents have? To stand up and baptize their child. He met Alanna's eyes, and he swore he saw the same questions in her eyes.

The priest took the holy water from the font and traced the cross on little Aidan's forehead. After a passage from the book of Mark and a prayer of intercession for the child, the ceremony concluded. Aidan handed the child to John, then took his seat by his parents as Alanna went back up with the choir.

The brunch afterwards was at the Officer's Club. Mimosas, food, and photographs by the river. Aidan and his parents were a novelty of sorts, with high ranking Marines coming over to meet them. Hector approached Alanna and asked to speak with her in private, then he nodded to Aidan and Sean to join them. They went into one of the private rooms, leaving the din of the brunch behind them.

"I talked to your father," was all he said. Alanna, blushed, swallowing hard. "Don't you feel bad for one minute, sweetheart. We've got your back on this. As few people as possible know what's going on, and they don't know all of the details. The reason I needed to talk to you is that we have some security measures to set up."

Alanna frowned. “At the house?”

He shook his head. “On you. GPS trackers to be specific. He’s always had one on your phone; you know that.” She nodded. “But a phone can be left behind, taken from you. I’m installing something under your front seat. The other one will be on this.” He held out a bracelet. It was a knock-off Tiffany bracelet. The one with the toggle clasp and silver heart. The heart pried open, however.

“This is very high tech, and a bit dear.” Sean said.

Hector replied, “Yep, it didn’t come cheap. We have friends, though. He worked it out. Your dad insisted.”

Alanna looked at the bracelet, then both of the men. Aidan saw the goosebumps on her arms. “Is all of this really necessary?”

Hector nodded. “We think so, and we’re not taking any risks with you. Your dad pulled a lot of strings, but he got in touch with the right people in the Merchant Marines. The incident that caused him to be relieved of duty was involving a woman on the ship. Apparently it was pretty ugly. It happened in international waters. The investigation is ongoing. The woman,” he paused, looking like he wasn’t sure how much to say, “She’s accusing him of kidnapping, felony assault and battery, and aggravated rape.”

Alanna made a gagging noise. She swayed and Aidan grabbed her. Sean pulled a chair out and they sat her down. Hector knelt down. “I’m sorry, baby, but you need to hear this.”

She collected herself, taking a breath. “Go ahead. Tell me it all.”

Hector continued. “He forced her into another part of the ship, attacked her. That’s all I know.”

Sean was rubbing his jaw, thoughtfully. “Do you know anything about the girl? Age? Physical description? Was it the girl from the phone text?”

Hector shook his head, “No. It wasn’t the same girl. Hans was sure about that, but…” Hector paused.

Alanna sat up, stiffened her spine. “What did she look like?”

Hector sighed, resolutely continuing. “Blonde, petite, fair skinned, mid-twenties.” Aidan cursed under his breath. “I don’t want to upset you, but we need you to understand what you are dealing with. You need to keep the bracelet on. Have your phone with you at all times in case…"

"In case he comes for me," Alanna said with a deadened tone.

When they finally made their way back to the beach, they were all ready for a nap. Seany passed out on a lounger while Sean and Sorcha went in out of the heat. The day was overcast but very warm. After they'd changed clothes, Aidan took her hand and walked around the deck to the hammock. The waves were steady, the birds calling to one another, the sea air sharp with impending rain. He pulled her into the hammock with him, and they drifted off to sleep.

Alanna woke in slow degrees, as if her body knew that Aidan was awake. She opened her eyes to find him looking at her. "The rain is starting. Seany went in."

She wiggled around to get a better view of the sea. The white caps churned as the sea took on shades of blue and grey. The sea oats slanted in the wind as it swept over the dune. The front was moving fast. She pulled her unruly hair over her shoulder, out of Aidan's face. "Sorry," she giggled.

"Leave it," he said. "I like the feel of it." The rain started in big, lazy drops. As it picked up momentum, it tapped on the extended roofing that went over the side of the deck.

Alanna stretched, getting up lazily. Aidan wasn't fooled, though. He could read the lines of her body, preparing for flight. She looked over her shoulder at him. "First one with salt water in their toes gets to be on top," she said with a sultry smile. Then she took off. Aidan was out of the hammock in an instant, regardless of her shameless cheating. He was gaining on her, and she was squealing. When her feet finally hit the water, she turned, stunned at her victory. Aidan was standing just at the edge of the foam. "You let me win," she said, hands on her hips.

He came toward her and dipped his face down to hers. "I like you on top," he said. Then he kissed her like the world was ending.

Sean was looking out the window when his wife approached from behind. "Are you watching the storm come in?"

He chuckled. "That's a new name for it, but aye." Then he gestured to the beach. Sorcha looked where he was pointing and her brows shot up. Her son was kissing the hell out of that beautiful girl next door. Then Aidan threw her over his shoulder like a barbarian raider, her giggles coming on the wind as the rain whipped her face.

"Well, now. I'd call that progress," she said in her sweetest Irish lilt. Sean threw his head back and laughed.

The next days flew by quickly. Too quickly. Days of long dinners on the deck. Wine and easy laughter, and even music when the mood struck them. "Promise you'll be careful, lass. Don't drop your guard when you're alone. Keep your eyes alert," Sean said.

"I'll be careful. Please don't worry," Alanna said.

Sean tucked her hair behind her ear. "I'll worry until he's locked up or dead. We all will." She hugged him tightly. "Thank you for a lovely week, and thank you for taking care of my boy," Sean whispered. Then he walked to the car with their luggage.

Next it was Sorcha's turn. "Take care of my boys, sweet girl. You'll be in my prayers."

Sorcha hugged Alanna and suddenly she heard sniffling. "What is it child?"

Alanna wiped her eyes. "I'm going to miss you. I haven't had someone around like you since Meghan."

Sorcha's face softened. "Branna's mother? Oh, dear. I suppose you lost her as well." She took her hand. "Tell me, love. How is it with your own mother? Are things difficult?"

Alanna shrugged. "She enjoys being a woman but not really being a mother, if that makes sense. She's just never put me first. I don't think she has it in her to be a real mother. I love her, but she's always been more like a flaky aunt or older sister. Now that I'm grown, she wants to be pals. I don't need that, though. I need a momma."

Sorcha patted her hand. "Well, then. Now you have me." Alanna's sad eyes shot to Aidan and then back. "I don't know about that, but thank you. It was nice for a little while."

Sorcha squeezed. "I haven't seen my son this happy since, well, actually I've never seen him this happy. You are good for him. You soothe him, heal him like nothing else has. I love you, Alanna. And I thank you for all the love you've given my son. Even if it's for this short time, I'm grateful for you."

Alanna stifled a sob and pulled her in for another hug. "I love you, too," she whispered.

35

It had been a long day at work. The entire week was a difficult one. They'd been doing live tissue training. First aid on live subjects of the hoof and snout variety. Aidan couldn't even look at bacon or pork chops. He'd also hated saying goodbye to his parents, but the time he'd spent with his brother was a time he'd never forget.

They took long walks together, Seany telling him about school, his teachers, his girlfriends. He was currently taking a break, he assured Aidan. The lasses were a drain on him. Some were moody, others aloof, and others were clingy and needy. "Truth be told, brother, I don't understand the females at all. Do they get better? More sane at least?"

Aidan laughed uproariously. "You'll be happy to know that most of them grow out of the moodiness. You might be looking after the wrong type. You've got a full life. Sports, music, family, friends. You're not going to mesh well with the type of lass that wants your undivided attention. My experience is that those sort do not grow out of it."

Seany nodded. "So, look for a girl like Alanna." Aidan's head popped up at that. Seany continued, "Well, she's certainly got a lot going on. She's got her music, the church, her work, she's just finished school. Is that why you love her? Because she's not overly needy?"

Aidan stuttered, not sure what to do with such a blunt question. Seany furrowed his brow. "Oh, I mean, I guess I assumed. When I see you together, you seem like you love her. You take care of her like Da does for Ma, even though she doesn't seem to expect it." He paused, collecting his thoughts. "So, if you don't love her, is it just that you like being with her? I mean, is it all physical then?"

Aidan jumped on that. "No! Christ, that is far from all of it." He rubbed his palm over his short hair. "How exactly did we start talking about me?"

Seany shrugged. "I'm just trying to understand. I can't talk to my mates like this. They'd either lie their asses off, or they don't know anymore than I do."

Aidan cocked his head. "So you're still a virgin, then?" Seany blushed. "No, don't be embarrassed, brother. It's a good thing. You should wait. Wait until you find someone that's really worth it, and not just physically. Someone you feel a true connection with."

Seany picked up a shell and threw it into the surf. "How will I know what to do? I mean, I know the basics. I've done some stuff. I just, you know, I hear things...about the woman needing certain things from you. That they like certain things."

It was Aidan's turn to blush. "Maybe you should be asking..."

Seany interrupted. "Who? Liam? Right, and get my nuts busted for my trouble? Michael's so busy with the twins and work and his new wife, Patrick and Tadgh are off working for the Garda. It's not like I can ask Da!"

Aidan stopped, turning to him. "It's all right. I understand. Listen, all women are different. You have to pay attention. She'll tell you what she likes. She might not come right out with it, but you'll feel it. Listen to her body, the way it moves, the sounds she makes. A woman's body is like a very beautiful puzzle. Take your time, explore, don't push for more than she's comfortable with. If you do all of that, she'll trust you enough to relax, to really be with you."

Seany was mentally taking notes, which both amused and worried Aidan. "Listen, you need to be careful. You know about condoms, aye?"

Seany rolled his eyes. "You have met our mother, right?" He put his hands on his hips and started pointing a finger. In a falsetto voice he imitated Sorcha. "If I could count the number of women who I helped bring a child into this world and had no da to claim it! If you're not careful, you will go straight to the vicar and marry the lass! So you best just keep your britches zipped!"

Aidan laughed. She'd given them all the same lecture. "Christ, it's scary how well you've got her down." He nudged him and they started walking again. "Just take care, not just because of disease and pregnancy. It's more than that. Sex complicates things. Sometimes those complications are worth it. The experience is beautiful and it's worth the pain you'll feel later. Just choose wisely. Don't be in a hurry."

Seany took what he had to say to heart. "So that's it, then? That's how it is with Alanna. You do love her, but you know you'll still be leaving her. She knows it too. You just decided it was worth the pain?" Aidan shut his eyes. Not wanting to answer.

Alanna was standing on the deck when they approached from the beach. "What do you say we go out to eat? Burgers? Pizza? Chinese? Seany's been wanting to go to the Exchange on base. Let's go get some junk food and rent a movie!"

After a binge of soda, burgers and slices of pizza, Alanna was driving back through the base, headed back home. "Stop the car!" Seany yelled. Alanna slammed on the breaks just in time to see them. A young woman, maybe about sixteen and a smaller girl that looked to be about four or five years old. Then she saw the vehicle.

Aidan and Seany jumped out before she could say a word, and she pulled off the road. When she approached them, the teenage girl was crying. "Please, help us. My dad, he went off the road! I don't know what's wrong with him."

Alanna took a good look at the children. “Maureen? Maureen Rogers?”

The girl looked at her, startled. “Yes. Wait, you’re that counselor. Oh God, you have to help him!” Alanna followed the girl to the driver’s side and so did Aidan and Seany. “He started shaking, his eyes went funny. He lost control of the car.” Aidan was calling the base Provost Marshall on 911 as Alanna knelt down to look at the Marine behind the wheel.

“Mike, it’s me, Alanna.” He was disoriented, but she kept saying his name. “Mike, it’s okay. The kids are okay. Can I call your wife?” At this point, the young girl Maureen spoke, “She went to see my aunt in Michigan. She’s got the baby with her, but she left us with dad. What’s wrong with him? Should I call her?”

Alanna took Mike’s hand, then she answered. “We can call your mother in a few minutes. Sweetie, it sounds like he had a seizure. Did he complain of a headache or anything?”

The girl started to cry. “He had a headache. I made him come out. I needed to get something for the show this weekend. This is my fault.” Then she looked around panicked. “Where is my sister? Oh, Jesus!”

Then her eyes landed on Seany, holding her sister on his hip. She was stunned for a moment. “Who are you?” Then she looked at Aidan. “Who are they?”

Alanna came to her and rubbed her upper arms. The girl’s tone was a bit panicked. “They’re very good friends of mine. You actually met Aidan at one of my sessions. That handsome devil holding your sister is Seany, his little brother.”

“Don’t worry lass. There’s an ambulance on it’s way and the MPs,” Aidan said.

Seany approached her. “Do you want yer sissy, then?” he said to the child. The four year old shook her head, refusing to let go of Seany.

“I can take her. I’m sorry. She’s just really friendly.”

Seany put up a hand. "Go talk to yer Da, Maureen. I'll keep her busy."

The girl nodded. "Her name is Emily." She walked over to comfort her father.

The doctor decided to keep Mike for at least one night. Alanna called his wife, who was in Michigan visiting family. "It's ok Rachel. The kids are fine. You shouldn't drive this late. Get on a flight tomorrow morning. You know I'm right. Now, about the children, I have plenty of room. You said yourself that a bunch of the families you know are gone on vacation with the Fourth of July coming up. I promise you that I will take care of them. We'll swing by the house and get some clothes for them. I'll grab the dog and check on the cat as well. Honestly, I think what they need right now is some sleep."

Rachel sighed. "Can you have Maureen check on the horses before you leave the base? I'll call the stables in the morning, have them feed them and muck. I just need her to touch base. Sassy can get antsy without some face time."

"Whatever you need, Rachel. I've got your back on this. Just get some sleep and know that everyone is safe."

Alanna pulled into the driveway of the beach houses with five humans and a golden retriever crammed into her small vehicle. They all exited, Seany and Aidan grabbing the backpacks from the back. Alanna said, "You'll stay on this side with me. I have a spare room. Aidan and Seany will stay on the other side. Let's go get you settled, and we can meet on the deck for some tea or cocoa."

Seany handed the girl her backpack, feeling shyer than he'd ever felt in his life. She was beautiful. Tall and lithe with long legs.

She had chestnut hair that fell to the middle of her back. She had serious grey eyes that showed no signs of her earlier tears. She didn't wear any make-up, which was uncommon for their peer group, but she had clear, pale skin that was dappled with small freckles at the nose and cheeks. She had a sharp, intelligent look about her.

Alanna brought the girls into her home and the little one was delighted. All she needed to hear was that they were having a sleep over on the beach, and that they would dance like in Miss Anna's therapy room. "You and Emily can stay in here. There's a lock on the door if you feel more comfortable. There's a trundle under the day bed that pulls out. The sheets are fresh." She flipped on the light for the room and the bathroom. "You two can use this bathroom. Now, it's been a rough day. Would you like to call your mommy?"

Emily wasn't listening. She was jumping on the bed. "Emily, no jumping," her sister said. "No, we don't need to call her. She needs to get the baby to bed, and I think it would probably upset everyone more. We'll see her tomorrow."

Alanna thought about it. "Do you want to go chase crabs on the beach? I bet Seany and Aidan would go with us."

Emily didn't need to be asked twice. "Oh, do they pinch?"

Alanna answered, "Oh, no. They scurry away. They walk very funny. I think you'll like it. The moon is out, and I bet Captain Aidan has some chem lights."

Alanna had to smile a little at the nervous energy going on between Sean Jr. and Maureen. "So, how has your show been going? Is this weekend your opening night?" Alanna asked. They were walking out the sliding doors onto the deck as they talked.

"Yes, it's finally here. The theater group has been wonderful. It's one step above high school, but they have good sound equipment."

Alanna walked them around the partition to find Seany and Aidan sitting on the loungers. "You know, Seany is a musician. He'll be in town another two weeks if you ever want someone to practice with."

Seany got up out of his chair and leaned against the railing. "Yes, I play quite a bit."

This got the girls attention. "Really? What do you play?"

Seany ticked off on his fingers. "Piano, of course, guitar, the bodhrán, and I've started the mandolin this year."

The girls brows raised. "Wow, that's a lot. How are your vocals?"

Seany looked at her like he was scandalized that she would ask such a thing. "Christ, I'm an O'Brien. We cut our teeth on a microphone."

The girl gave him a smirk. "Hmm. Modest, too. Well, the show starts Friday. You all should try to come by. They're letting us use the base theater, so there's no way we will sell out."

While they'd been talking, Aidan had rummaged through his gear and found little Emily a glow stick. "I want to find crabs!" she yelled.

Seany knelt down to her. "Oh, crabs is it? Well, just be glad we're not on my island. The silkie king would come to shore, looking to find a wife. They might take a liking to your sister with all that long, dark hair."

The child's eyes grew wide. "What's a silkie? Is it like a mermaid?" And that's how it started. They went off to the beach, Emily taking Seany's hand as he told her the legend of the silkies. She'd forgotten all about the crabs for a while.

"He has a little niece about her age. Two nieces and two nephews, actually." Aidan supplied. Maureen nodded, not saying anything. She was quiet by nature, Aidan noticed. She was socially aware enough to converse with others, but she was an introvert. Seany was different. He was talkative and funny and not at all serious. Then he heard them talking.

"My daddy hurt his head when he was away from us. He got blowed up by some bad guys, but I'm not supposed to know that." Alanna and Maureen both froze.

"Is that so? Well, I think your da's just trying to keep you from worrying. You were very brave tonight. Your da would be very proud of you. You and your sister, both. Would you like to find a shell for him? We can go out in the morning, and you can find a perfect one to take to the hospital."

Emily jumped up and down. "Oh, yes. Um, Seany, how old are you?"

He said, "Sixteen, why do you ask?"

She sighed. "Well, I was thinking that you could be my husband. I like how you talk. But you'll have to wait til I'm older. You're my sister's age, but she's not as fun. She said she likes horses better than humans."

Alanna stifled a laugh. Seany turned an eye over his shoulder. "Well now, she's had a hard day. We won't be too hard on her."

After a long walk and some crab chasing, everyone started to wind down. Aidan was carrying Emily by the time they got to the house. She was yawning. "I want Momma."

The mood was changing, and Maureen took her from Aidan. "It's okay, little bear. You're going to sleep with me, tonight. You can bring your glow stick under the covers and we'll sing some songs."

The little girl whined. "Can it be Disney songs?"

"Of course. I'll sing anything you want. You just have to brush your teeth and wash your bear paws. We don't want sand in the bed. Then we'll brush your bear fur and get in our cave."

Maureen turned to Aidan and Seany. "Thank you, for taking her mind off of everything. She's too young to know what all of this means." Then she turned and went into the house. Alanna watched her go, pain in her eyes.

"What did she mean by that?" Aidan asked.

Alanna looked at the two men. "Her father has been fighting getting medical boarded. He wants to stay active duty. Seizures may be the game ender. He'll get a combat related medical retirement, but..."

Aidan finished for her. "He'll never fight again. He won't be with his men." She nodded. Aidan thought about Mike Rogers. He was funny, kind of a jokester. It would be a tragedy to see such a vibrant man slip into depression. He suspected that a lot of men hid PTSD and less obvious mental difficulties for that very reason. Even Luke Jones had said that he knew he'd lose his security clearance if they thought he was suicidal.

Christ, there must be a better way to help these men. And that's where Alanna came into the picture. The thought made him as proud as it made him sad. *She needs to be with them more than she needs me.*

The next morning was full of activity. Two teenagers, a dog, and a small child all vying for the hoecakes and bacon. "Not in the mood for some bacon?" Alanna teased.

Aidan laughed. "It won't do much for my bedside manner with the pig if I smell like his kin." Aidan came into the kitchen and caught Alanna against the counter. He leaned in and whispered. "I missed you, girl. Will you welcome my attentions tonight?" She blushed as she saw Seany and Maureen watching them. He kissed her temple. "Tonight, then." She nodded. Then he left for work.

Alanna noticed Maureen fiddling with her plant. "I'm afraid my green thumb is rather pale. Branna left it when she moved, and it doesn't like me."

Maureen smiled in her mild way. "It's an umbrella plant. It needs to be moved to a bigger pot. See the roots coming over the surface? And it likes a lot of sun. Move it by the window and get a bigger pot and it will forgive you."

Seany was puzzled by the young woman across the table from him. She was quiet. Not shy so much as withdrawn. She seemed to live in her head. She had an understated beauty and she seemed very smart. "Horses, children, plants. You have a way with living things. And an artist. Your talents are many. What part will you have in this production you told me about?"

She shrugged. "Plants and animals are easy. And no Texan worth his salt can't figure out his way around a horse. My dad loves those horses. He has to be careful, with the head injury, but he raised us in the saddle." Then she said, " As for the production, it's my creation. I put the music pieces and the choreography together. I had help with the slide show and lighting, of course. I'm not as good at the technical end."

Seany's eyes flared. "Is it your music? Did you write a musical?"

She cocked her head. "No, not really. It's hard to explain. It's sort of a mash up, multi-media, interpretive dance collaboration. You'll have to see for yourself."

She got up matter of factly and took her sisters hand. "Listen, little bear. Mommy is flying in with Mikey today. Miss Anna is going to drive us home, and you're going to help me clean up to surprise her, okay? Now let's go check and make sure we packed everything."

Alanna smiled as they walked into the bedroom. She raised a brow at Seany. "She's really got a good head on her shoulders. She's like having another adult in the house, I suspect."

Seany said, "She's more serious then most girls our age. That's not a bad thing, I just wonder why."

Alanna said, "Military kids can be like that. They're often well traveled, very culturally aware, and in her case, she helps her mother a lot when it comes to the smaller kids and her father. His TBI affects his memory, he gets confused, he gets migraines. Couple that with PTSD and sleep disturbances, she's had to grow up fast."

Seany listened intently, looking toward the bedroom. "Does she have a boyfriend?" he asked.

Alanna answered, "Well, I don't know. Not that I know of, but we can call her in here and ask her."

Seany lurched off his stool. "Christ, no. Don't you dare. Can't ye be a little more discreet about it? Gather some intelligence?"

Alanna laughed. "Intelligence? Well, I suppose I can. I'll start by getting tickets to her show."

It was nighttime and Alanna had her A/C going full blast. Summer was here and so were the tourists, so the noise of the AC served two purposes. She couldn't settle, not while Aidan was next door. The one night they'd spent apart had been torture. *Better prepare yourself, sister. Come August, he's gone for good.* She thought about her visit in the fall. Wondering if they'd spend some time together. Was it wise? To prolong the inevitable seemed like its own torture.

She thought about Mike Rogers, about his wife and children, and him leaving the military community. If he was medically retired, they'd leave base, leave the school during his daughter's final year. The whole thing was sad.

The job in Virginia was good. Really good. That would have to be enough for her. She could build a life for herself in Virginia, away from her father, brother, and Aidan. It was sad to think about, but that's what she had to work with, a good job. Love would have to take a back burner. The thought of that almost undid her. She couldn't imagine feeling about anyone the way she felt about Aidan. But she'd have to eventually move on. He would. He had no doubts about his path. He was smack in the middle of a great career. He would go back and survive their separation, like he'd survived everything else.

The tears were slow, but they came. She didn't even hear Aidan use his key. Then she heard his voice, a whisper. He appeared in the doorway as she was wiping her face. He could see her in the moonlight. "What is it?"

She shook her head. "It's nothing. Please, just come lie down." He sat on the edge of the bed, looking over her face. She said nothing. She just pulled up and kissed him. That's when he realized she had nothing on. He pulled her on to his lap and she pulled his shirt off. "I need you." Her voice was achy and raw. He fumbled with the waist of his shorts, and she was on him in an instant, wrapping her legs around his waist.

He saw her fighting the tears. "No, God. Don't think about it." He knew the why, and he pulled her to him, entering her in one thrust. "Don't think about it," he said, desperate and breathless. He pulled her back and forth, thrusting as they faced each other. He took her mouth, slow and deep. He felt her climbing, felt the tension build in her body. Then her breath stuttered and she moaned. *Yes, you're mine.*

He went wild, plunging into her as he grasped her hips. His Gaelic was harsh, demanding. He flipped her on her back and took her hard, and she loved it. She bucked against him, screaming. He fumbled with one hand and turned on their little lantern. "Look at me," he choked out. And when she did, delirious and out of her head, those green eyes stole his last bit of control. He cried out like he was wounded. And he was wounded, ripped open and bleeding to death.

Alanna was without sense. The tears wouldn't stop. Aidan was whispering, his voice breaking. "Mianach, A chuisle." He kissed her face, her eyes, rocking his hips, still inside her.

She said, "I'm sorry. I don't know what's wrong with me."

He soothed her, "Shhh, mo chroí. Don't cry. Please, don't cry." He had her wrists in his hands, could feel the bracelet she wore that had the GPS device in it. The thought of something happening to her, of that bastard putting his hands on her, made him mental. He was supposed to protect her. She was his to protect.

Aidan woke to the sound of Alanna on the phone. "I understand. Yes, I'll be here for another month or so. Really, so long? Well, I suppose so. Let me check my calendar and I will get back to you. OK, thank you Special Agent Clark. Goodbye." Alanna ended the call and looked up to find Aidan in the doorway of her bedroom.

"Was that the FBI?"

She gave him a weary look. "Yes, they're in Raleigh. It's about 3 1/2 hours away."

Aidan came forward, wearing only a pair of loose, low slung shorts. He took her by the elbows. "What did they say?"

She sighed. "The Special Agent that was assigned my case is apparently very busy working on a human trafficking case. She can't come for another three weeks. She's spoken with the local police. They are going to do drive-bys more often. She told me to document everything."

Aidan shook his head, disgusted. "What about filing the sexual assault report in Jacksonville?"

Alanna said, "I'm going to do that today. I have an appointment with a deputy. They weren't optimistic, though. They said that rape is hard enough to prove. Attempted rape and assault seven years later, no DA would touch it. It's all about documenting at this point."

Aidan swore under his breath. "This is horse shit."

Alanna wrapped her arms around herself. "I should have reported it when it happened. Maybe if I had, that girl on the ship wouldn't have gone through what she did."

"You cannot blame yourself for that," Aidan said. Alanna wasn't so sure.

They both turned at the sound of a knock. "Come in, Seany!"

Sean Jr. poked his head into the house. "So, what do we need to do to get ready for these fireworks you yanks are so fond of?"

Alanna looked at him, baffled. Then she remembered. She slapped her forehead. "This weekend is Independence Day. I almost forgot." She looked at Aidan. "What's your schedule? Do you have a 96?"

Aidan looked at his watch. "Aye, it starts tomorrow. I need to go. It's our last day at live tissue training. I'm going to need four days off after this."

"Seany, you and I will make a list. The stores will be crazy this weekend. I'll go into Jacksonville this morning, if you don't mind waiting with me at the sheriff's office. Then we'll get everything we need. Aidan, do you need anything besides extra okra?" Aidan made a gagging noise on the way out the door.

They pulled out of the sheriff's office. Alanna's head was pounding. "That must have been hard. I'm sorry. I don't know what else to say besides that." Seany said.

"Thank you for being here with me, Seany. You remind me a lot of your brother and your father. You put me at ease."

Seany looked out the window. "Women never seem to have an easy time of it. It makes me glad I'm a man. I worry, though. I worry what kind of world little Cora and Haley will grow up in."

Alanna took his hand as they drove. "Haley and Cora are lucky enough to have a wonderful family. They've got strong men and women who will watch over them and teach them to be strong. Like my daddy did for me, only with lots of back up. I envy you. You've got a tribe, and a lot of the world has gotten away from that system."

Seany just smiled, but what he wanted to do was beg her not to take that job in Virginia. To move to Ireland and marry Aidan. He'd never seen his brother so happy, or so open. *You belong with us. You belong to our tribe, my sister.* "Tomorrow night is Maureen's show," he stopped, blushing. "It'd be nice to get her some flowers. Do you have a florist nearby?"

Alanna's heart melted. "I think that would be nice, Seany."

His blush deepened. "You can tell her they are from you. It's just, you know…opening night and all. Her parents have their hands full. They may not think of it." He looked out the window. The silence finally got to him and he looked at Alanna. She was all weepy, girly faced. "Don't start, woman."

36

The base theater was very full, considering it was a live theater event and not a re-run of a box office movie. Alanna, Aidan, and Seany were seated front and center, next to the Rogers family. Aidan looked down at the program. *The Sound of Freedom.* The program had many names, dancers, sound people, technicians, choreographers, set builders. It was broken down into three sections, or acts. The Early Years, The Best Generation, and Living History.

The lights dimmed. He looked over at his brother who was completely enthralled. On the edge of his seat kind of enthralled. He'd seen the way his brother looked at the young Maureen. Trouble. He was only here for another week and half. That Rod Stewart song was no lie. The first cut was definitely the deepest. It might not actually be, but it sure as shit felt like it at sixteen.

Maureen walked out on stage, dressed simply in a black skirt and blouse, her hair done in a vintage style up-do. She looked so grown up. She looked out at the audience and said one thing. "I'd like to dedicate tonight's show to my father." Then she stepped behind the curtain. Aidan looked over at Mike Rogers, and the man was stunned.

The curtains opened, and it looked like an encampment. Colonial years, most likely. Fife and drum music played and it was regulators and lobsterbacks facing off with wooden guns. Then the music picked up, a mash-up of the original music with an edgier metal. The soldiers leapt up, dancing around each other as the smoke from the musket fire clouded around them. Buckskin and homespun vs. dress military men and powdered wigs. Then they all lay, slain, and the music dimmed, the lights going dim as well.

Then the background changed. Everything was electronic. You could see the dancers rolling low and off the stage, as the next scene scrolled down the backdrop. New dancers emerged. There were ships and water. The War of 1812 with men still in tricorn hats and stockings.

As the next scene started, new uniforms were worn, the big dresses of the ladies of the Civil war. The hair rose up on Aidan's arms as the mash up music began. The song *Scarlet Tide*, a Civil War lament, merged with the same artist singing *My Ain' True Love.* On the stage, a woman searched through the piles of fallen bodies that were writhing in an interpretive dance of suffering and death. On the other side of the stage, the soldier was staggering, trying to get back home. They came together and fell into each other's arms.

Seany was completely captivated. The mash-ups were as amazing as they were intense. All electronic tweaking and layering to find the perfect blend. He'd played around acoustically with the idea, but this was really well done. The lights dimmed, the curtain fell, and the crowd went temporarily crazy. Everyone, including him, was anxiously waiting for the next scene.

The men were impeccably dressed, as were the women. The beginning of the twentieth century. Phonograph music played, and couples danced. Then the back drop changed and the women whisked away.

The men took off behind a partition and ran out wearing helmets and uniforms that had obviously been under their suit coats. *Over There* came blaring through the auditorium and the scene on the screen was the brutal trench fighting of WWI. One man held his friend, blood on his hands. Seany looked over at his brother, more to see if he was okay. His brother was as transfixed as everyone else.

Then, by far, the strangest mash-up started. Rammstein's *Du Hast* roared through the theater, the screen showed the Nazi's marching in Berlin. The music halted abruptly and the pinging sweet sound of the Japanese shamisen took its place. The movie screen showed clips of the kamikaze fighters, the bombing of Pearl Harbor. Then mixed in with the Japanese music, the distinct chirp of the French music of Josephine Baker was the delicate background music for President Roosevelt's speech. Then more Rammstein with shots of Mussolini, Stalin, and Hitler. The dancers were in various uniforms, and a large wooden tank came rolling out, pushed by more soldiers.

The three types of music would never seem to work together, but she pulled it off. Suddenly the backdrop was vintage New York City. Crowds of people in forties dress were walking by each other. Then the radio announcement played. *The war has ended.* Two dancers appear from the crowd. One sailor, one girl with dark hair and a nurses uniform. Seany almost jumped out of his seat. Maureen danced alongside the sailor, their legs flying, hips popping. Then their hands came together and boom. The kiss seen around the world. The kiss that was still famous. The sailor dipping the nurse in the middle of Time Square. The crowd went wild. Then the curtains closed.

Aidan and Seany exhaled at the same time. They looked at each other and then at Alanna, who was crying like a girl. "Wow," was all she could say. The theater lights stayed dim. No one was getting up. Obviously, unlike a play, they didn't want to lose the momentum. The performance wasn't that long, and it didn't really need a break. Everyone was too ready for the next scene.

The curtains opened and the screen had whipping snow, enough to make you pull your collar up. Something was being blown across the stage. Seany grabbed a piece of paper that flew down off the stage. "Tootsie rolls?"

Alanna whispered, "The Chosin Reservoir, Korean War."

Seany didn't know the music, but the program said Bob Hope, USO concert. Then the music stopped, and only whipping wind remained. A soldier was slumped against a fence, covered in snow. Another soldier came along. "Billy, wake up. Oh, Christ. Wake up, Billy!" the face was done in blue hues, eyes still. On the screen, it gave statistics of the men that died in the battle and then in particular, how many froze to death.

Alanna wasn't sure which show was better. The one on stage or watching Aidan, Seany, and the Rogers family react. Maureen's mother was sobbing silently. Mike was controlled, which was not like him. He soaked in everything, never looked away. There was pride in his eyes, however. Pride, amazement, pain. He wore it quietly, which was not the Mike she knew. The Mike she knew was a joker, but there was nothing funny and something all together moving about the show his daughter had put together. The edges were rough. It was a small time theater group, amateur dancers, but the overall affect was a stunner.

The whirling snow and wind faded, and the sound of bugs, rain, and helicopter thumping in the background gave way to jungle camouflage, a cardboard prop made to look like the side of a jeep, men in sweaty, ripped uniforms, painted faces. The marching beat of Jefferson Airplane's *White Rabbit* thrummed through the building as The Rolling Stones *Painted Black* was mashed with it in a psychedelic mixture of sixties drug culture. A higher leveled platform had protestors in sixties attire holding signs and swaying to the music, while the men in uniforms crawled on their bellies, sniper fire snapping in the background. Then the lights dimmed.

Aidan leaned over as the stage was dark and the sounds of the set shifting was clattering. "She really wrote this? She put this together?"

Alanna nodded. "Yes, I mean obviously she had a lot of help. The set, the choreography, but this is her baby. She's pretty good with the software you need for mash-ups. She gets help when she needs it, but the creation is definitely hers."

Aidan shook his head. Then he turned to Mike. "That's one hell of a girl you've got, brother."

Mike nodded. "I never thought she paid attention, when I'd babble on about history or about the wars. I never really knew if it got through to her." He shook his head, looking up at the stage. "Goddamn. It's seldom I'm at a loss for words."

Then the crowd hushed for the final scene played out. The crowd gasped as the twin towers showed on the screen. The set was mostly sandy coated cardboard. Aidan and Seany looked at each other as the music started. It was the beginning dialogue of *Tubthumping* by Chumbawamba.

Truth is I thought it mattered. I thought that music mattered. But does it? Bollocks! Not compared to how people matter.

Dancers dressed as modern day New Yorkers walking through the city. When the planes hit the twin towers on the screen, the people on stage stared up at the buildings. Then the towers came down and panic ensued, and the music was blaring. The Pentagon, the United flight 93, all in rapid succession on the screen. Then the music halted. Dead quiet.

It resumed at ground zero and light beams lasered up to take the place of the towers, and the music roared. *I get knocked down, but I get up again.* The dancers were now police and fire and medics. The video footage of the US President shouting to the workers on ground zero had the Marines hooting and hollering in the audience.

As the first responders all filed off the stage, they were replaced with modern US Military. The screen changed to bombing, urban warfare, the Sadam statue getting pulled down, rows of boots and rifles and helmets.

Don't cry for me, next door neighbor… I get knocked down, but I get up again, you're never going to keep me down…

The flags of allied forces started popping up on the screen. Britain, Australia, Japan, Germany, France, several others. The obvious finale was when performers wearing Marine uniforms from every time period in American military history came out, marching in lines, crossing each other. The final music mash up is Metallica's *Don't Tread on Me* and Kid Rock's *Warrior,* having no mercy for the devil's eardrums.

Every jarhead in the theater was up on his feet, banging heads and pumping fists as the screen showed door kicking and ass whooping in Fallujah, Bagdad, Kabul, and the cave bombing in Tora Bora.

Then came the amputees in physical therapy, running marathons, holding their children. Then the intense music cut out as the uniformed dancers snapped to attention and Taps hummed over the audience. The last scene was of a little boy being handed a folded flag. The screen went black and one rolling phrase scrolls across. *Semper Fidelis.*

When the music faded, the audience raised the roof off of the theater. They went honest to goodness apeshit. Row by row of the dancers and actors took their bows. Then the final person, Maureen Rogers, walked on stage and took her bow.

As the audience exited the theater, all a buzz about the performance, they stayed in their seats. Alanna said, "That was completely amazing. Maureen is truly talented. What vision she has. And the mash-ups, I can't even begin to imagine how she does it."

Her mother laughed. "Endless hours with a laptop and headphones and ignoring her mother."

Mike shook his head. "Last year, she asked for the sound equipment she needed to mix her own music. I thought she was crazy, but you know, most girls want a car or a trip to Cancun, so I figured this was better. At least I knew where she was, held up in her room mixing her magic."

Alanna said, "Oh, I am rude. I know you've met Aidan, but this is Seany. He's Aidan's brother. He's about Maureen's age."

Mike rolled his eyes. "So this is the one that my Emily thinks she's going to marry? Well, hello Irishman. I'm sorry to tell you she will be staying single for another twenty years."

Seany laughed. "Understood, sir."

Rachel Rogers stepped forward. "All kidding aside, thank you. All of you. But especially you, for Emily's sake. Moe told us how you were with her. Telling her stories, holding her at the scene, the crab hunting, everything. You kept her mind off of everything, and you let her talk when she needed to. You're a remarkable young man."

She hugged Seany just as Maureen emerged from the backstage. "It was nothing. Really. If anything, you should be commending your daughter. She was pretty remarkable as well. Your wee ones are lucky to have her as a sister." His back was to Maureen, so the only hint that she'd just heard what he said was on the mother's face. He closed his eyes. *Breathe.*

He turned to see her, and the only hint of her discomfort was a slight blush. Those serious gray eyes giving away nothing. Her father lurched forward and grabbed her. That's when her control slipped as well as his. "I'm so proud of you, baby. Oh, God. It was wonderful. You are so talented. I had no idea." Her father was fully crying now.

The girl squeezed her eyes shut. "It was for you, Daddy. It was all for you. I'm so proud of you, too."

The tears were plentiful, not only with her, but the other women. Seany felt a tug on his shirt. He knelt down to Emily. "Why is everyone crying?" she asked. He laughed, a little choked up himself.

He picked her up. "Well, your sissy was wonderful, wasn't she? Everyone's happy. Did you like the show, darlin'?"

She nodded her head, but her brow held a slight bit of disapproval. "Oh yes, but I didn't like that sailor boy kissing Moe."

That makes two of us, he thought. Aidan gave him a knowing look. "Well, I think it's all right. I don't think she's ready to marry just yet. She was a good dancer, aye?" He stopped, looking at everyone. There was a tension that had nothing to do with the show.

"Well now, I guess we should let you take your sister home." He put the girl down.

Alanna said, "Wait, Maureen. We have something for you." Alanna pulled the flowers out from under the seat.

Maureen took them, swallowing hard. "Thank you. I don't think I've ever gotten flowers before. They're such a vibrant green. What kind are they?"

Alanna's jaw opened, cocking her head. "I don't know. I didn't choose them." She looked at Seany. *Busted.*

He cleared his throat. "They're Bells of Ireland," he said. Then he nodded at them all and walked toward the exit. Maureen's parents looked at her, then at Alanna and Aidan. "Well, um. Good night?" the mother said awkwardly.

Aidan took Alanna's keys and they all piled in her car. They sat in the lot, trying to figure out where to go for supper, when the Roger's family walked to their car, minus one. Seany's gaze was fixed on the door, waiting for her to come out. "She must have driven herself," Alanna said.

Then there she was, walking to a different vehicle. Seany looked like he was ready to pop his top, deciding whether to act. Aidan coughed a word under his breath. *Cough, cough,* "coward" *cough, cough.*"

Seany's eyes shot to his. "Fuck it," he said, and launched out the back seat. Alanna gave a chiding look.

"Dirty pool, Aidan."

He shrugged. "Its better than watching him mope around. He's young. Let him have his summer romance."

She smiled, "Yes, but then it will end, won't it?" And didn't that just hang between them.

"Maureen, wait!" Seany called as she closed her car door. She opened it back up and got out. She said nothing, which made Seany nervous. He wasn't used to someone who gave so little away. "I was wondering what you were doing on your Independence Day? Are you going to the fireworks?"

She folded her arms around her chest. "Uh, no. They kind of bother my dad, so we don't go."

Seany's face softened. "I see. Well, it just so happens that there will be some on the island. We'll be able to see them from the house. I was wondering if you'd like to come over. I…" He exhaled. Her face was passive. "Christ, you don't make this easy. I don't have a phone that works here. I'm also not legally allowed to drive. I just thought you'd like to come over. If not, we could go somewhere."

Something shifted in her face. "Ah." That's all she gave him.

"Pardon?" he said, confused.

"I was wondering why someone like you would be paying any mind to someone like me. It makes sense now."

He was starting to get irritated. "I'm sorry, maybe I'm a bit slow. What exactly does that mean?"

She shrugged. "It's ok. You don't want to be housebound for two weeks, I get it. But guys like you don't usually go for girls like me. I just want you to be honest. If you need to get out, I can probably give you a ride. I'm busy, but…"

Seany cut her off. "What in the bloody hell are you talking about?" She stopped short. He put his hands on his hips. "Guys like me? And exactly what kind of guy am I, lass? Enlighten me."

She straightened her spine. "I'm not trying to be rude. I just meant that guys that look like you don't normally…I mean," she grunted.

"Don't normally what? Go for girls with brains? Girls with talent? You think I'm some sort of shallow eejit that goes for what, exactly? Some empty headed tart with big boobs?"

She put her hands on her hips. "You're putting words in my mouth. That's not what I said."

Seany put a hand up. "You know what, nevermind. You obviously aren't interested in getting together. I won't bother you again." He started walking away.

She closed her eyes. "Stop!" It was the loudest he'd ever heard her. She took a deep breath, and there was a hint of emotion in her eyes that looked a little like contrition. That was something. "I'm sorry, okay? You've been really nice and you were super sweet to my sister. I don't know what's wrong with me. I'm not good at this, okay?" He stopped, raising his brows for her to continue. "Guys don't look at me. They don't see me. I have a lot on my plate. I have a lot of responsibilities. I don't make time for this." She motioned back and forth between them.

He walked toward her. "I'm here for another eleven days and I've got nothing but time. I just like you, Maureen. I like your family. This isn't about being bored. It's about not wasting time when I see something that interests me. How about we start with you deciding you could squeeze me in as a temporary friend?"

She smiled. It was small, a Mona Lisa smile. "I'd like that. I'll ask my parents. They'll be shocked. I really don't have a life outside of family and school and this." She motioned behind her to the theater.

"All right, why don't you give me your phone number and I'll ring you tomorrow."

Alanna was glued to the window. "Are they fighting? How can they be fighting already?"

Aidan gave a husky laugh. "Yes, well, he is half Mullen and half O'Brien. We tend to get a woman's blood up pretty early on in the relationship."

Alanna looked at him, eyes narrowed. "Yes, I suppose I did slam the door in your face," she said.

"Don't forget the bat," he jibed.

She giggled. "I'm not going to live that down, am I?" she said.

"Not til you're an old woman. Sorry."

Maureen handed the paper to Seany. "I go by Moe. Well, the family calls me Moe." He took the paper and kept her hand in his.

He dipped his eyes to meet hers. "Moe it is." His eyes went to her mouth.

She stepped back a step. "Thank you for the flowers," she said and got in her car.

Seany walked back to a gaping Alanna and grinning Aidan. "Thanks. We just needed a minute to get on the same page." Aidan held his fist up and Seany fist bumped him.

"Just mind your manners, lad. She's a nice girl and you're leaving."

Seany snorted, giving Aidan a look that said, *Pot, you're calling the kettle black.* "Oh, and brother. Don't bother sneaking over after you think I've gone to bed. I'm not a child or an idiot," Seany said.

Aidan gave him a sideways look. "Don't be so cheeky."

37

Aidan and Seany were quiet in the car as Alanna drove them to the gym. "I told you it was early. You two sure you're up for this?" Aidan raised a brow over his coffee cup. "What? I'm just saying. There's a sauna. A lot of the old timers come to the gym and just sit in the sauna." Aidan snatched her knee to tickle her.

"Old timer?" Seany was chuckling in back, nursing a cup of strong tea.

The class was brutal. Seany had taken her spinning class another time, but Aidan had not had the pleasure until today. They were drenched with sweat by the end. "How is it that you two look better when your sweaty? It's not fair," Alanna said, a bit miffed at the attention the two were drawing from the women at the gym. Seany looked older than sixteen, and some of the female Marines were ogling him as much as his brother. The shoulder length hair tucked behind his ears and his massive O'Brien build didn't hurt.

Seany looked around. "Maybe she got hung up," Alanna said.

He was looking for Moe, of course, who said she'd be working out around this time. Then his eyes fixed on her. She wasn't facing him, but her body language was defensive. He came behind her as she talked to two petite, perky teenage girls who were wearing entirely too much make-up for a work out. "We heard all about the show, Moe. Had to write yourself in the script to get a guy to kiss you, huh?"

Seany didn't give her a chance to respond. He approached from behind and the jaws dropped on both the girls. "Excuse me, girls. I don't mean to interrupt." He put on his thickest brogue and his biggest smile.

One of the bitchy girls gave him the once over, her eyes flaring. "Oh my God. Are you Australian?" *Idiot.*

"Irish, lass. It's a bit to the northwest of Australia. Google it, aye?" She nodded, then got a look on her face like she wasn't sure if he'd just insulted her. Moe struggled with a smile. "I just need to talk to Moe for a moment." He turned to her. "Do ye need my address, darlin? I wanted to make sure you knew how to get to the beach house. The party starts at six."

The girls perked up at that. The head mean girl sidled up to Moe. "Party? We were just wondering what our friend Moe, here, was doing tomorrow night. We wanted to hang out." The girl's face was all sincerity, and it made Seany want to barf.

Moe extracted herself from the girls arm as Seany replied. "Its invite only. Sorry, girls," he said dismissively. "Now, how about some breakfast, love? I'm starved." He put her hair behind her ear, his tone doting. Then he looked at her mouth, and she knew deep down that this wasn't just an act to get the twin bitches off her back. She blushed.

"Well, I'm free for the morning, but then I've got things to do." He looked at the other two as if to say, *Oh, you're still here?* "I'll take what I can get. Just let me get washed up." He walked away as the two girls stood gaping.

He walked by Alanna and she grabbed him and hugged him. She whispered,"You're my freakin hero!" He laughed and went to change.

When he came out of the locker room, Moe was standing there, waiting nervously. "Listen, I know you just did that for show. I appreciate it, although I learned to handle that particular brand of mean girl a while ago. I don't expect you to take me to breakfast."

Seany reared back. "You're not bailing on me now. You agreed to go to breakfast with me, and it most certainly wasn't for show." She cocked a brow, hands on her hips. "Okay, maybe I rolled my r's a little more than usual. You American girls go all weak in the knees with a good brogue," he said cockily.

She raised a brow. "Do we, now?"

He smiled mischievously. "Well, most American girls. You seem immune to my charms. Anyhow, I know the sort. Ireland has mean girls as well. There's also not a party. It's just us and my brother and Alanna, maybe her Da and another friend. Other than that, I was completely genuine." He put his hand over his heart, to emphasize his sincerity.

Another Mona Lisa smile, and didn't that warm Seany down to his toes. Aidan and Alanna exited the locker rooms at the same time. "Mike's Place it is. Breakfast all day."

"So, is it like porridge?" Seany picked at the white, gritty paste. Moe was giving one of her rare, big smiles.

"Stir the cheese in, let it melt," Alanna said. "It's bad enough you two don't appreciate the finer qualities of okra. If you won't eat grits, we're going to have to deport your asses."

Moe giggled and put her hand on his arm. "Watch me." She took the tabasco and dotted a couple of drops on her eggs. Then she took her toast, pushed some egg, then some grits on her fork and ate. Then she dipped her toast into the runny egg and took another bite. "Right tasty!" she said with a southern drawl.

Seany laughed. "Good God, woman. You do have a sense of humor." She blushed and nudged him.

Alanna gave Aidan a secret smile. Moe's attention was drawn to Alanna's bracelet. "I like your bracelet, Alanna. It's a little different then some of the ones I've seen. Does it open?" Alanna took her arm off the table, waving the hand and bracelet. "Yes, I just haven't put anything in it yet. I guess I need a sweetheart." Aidan pinched her under the table and she squeaked, but his gaze held something deeper, so did Sean Jr.'s, and she took a sip of her juice, trying to block out the wave of fear that lay just beneath the surface of her joking demeanor.

"My dad texted me. He's on his way. So is Tim. He has the weekend off. I told him we would make room." Aidan looked at her from the driver's seat. "You know, I never asked him what he does for a living." Alanna looked surprised. "He didn't tell you? He went to college after he got hurt. Used his GI Bill and scholarships. He's an occupational therapist."

Aidan's brows shot up. "For wounded veterans?"

She shook her head. "No, actually he works with kids, mostly. He loves kids."

Aidan thought hard about that. He'd never given much thought to what he would do once he was out of the military. His brothers all had their own paths after school. One in the Garda, one Coast Guard, one in pre-Med. Brigid had wanted to be a music teacher, but she stayed home with her children and ended up only working one year at the Catholic school in the district.

"Seany, what do you want to be? What do you want to go to school for? Have you thought about it?" Aidan asked.

Seany shrugged. "Not sure yet. Sometimes I think about the Garda. I think about medicine, too. I just can't imagine all that time at school. I like music, love it. I just don't think I want that to be a career. Christ, I don't know."

Aidan batted a hand. "You don't have to know. I just wondered. You're a big lad, strong. I think you'd be a good Garda officer. You're smart, though, Seany. You could do well in medicine or anything you wanted."

Alanna interrupted. "What about a fireman and EMT? Then you get the adventure of a first responder and the medical training."

Aidan cocked his head. “Yes, I could see that.”

Seany smiled, “Great idea. Chicks love fireman.” Aidan snorted.

The sun came through the window on Alanna’s face, and she opened her eyes to find Aidan watching her. “Good morning,” she said, stretching like a little yellow kitten.

“You’re beautiful when you sleep. Ye look so peaceful.” She smiled up at him, touching his face with her fingers. She memorized the lines of his face, the sunny highlights of his hair, the blue depths of his eyes. He kissed her then, soft and sweet. Just a brief brush of her lips, but it warmed her. He hadn’t showered this morning, so he smelled of himself, his unique and intoxicating male smell. He’d slept away from her last night, since her father was in the house. She raised her mouth to him as she pulled his head down. He chuckled against her mouth. “Your da is in the next room, you little vixen. You shouldn’t tease me. Two can play at that.” He pulled the neck of her t-shirt open and took her breast in his mouth.

She bit her lip. “Okay, okay. No more teasing!” she gasped. He hopped off her bed, grinning. “I’ve made some coffee. Seany should be up soon, and Tim as well.” She nodded, not able to speak. She could still feel his mouth on her skin.

Hans came out of the bedroom stretching like a big bear. “How’s my girl this morning?” He kissed his daughter on the cheek.

“Tea or coffee, sir?” Seany said.

His brows shot up. “Good morning. I’m glad your mother let you stay a while. I heard you have a hot date already,” he wiggled his brows over a cup of coffee after Seany handed it to him.

“Aye, no time to lose. Fate favors the bold,” Seany said, grinning.

Hans threw his head back and laughed. "Hot damn, to be young again."

Alanna looked at him with narrowed eyes. "Lose your nerve in your old age, Daddy? I see women drooling over you all the time. I never took you for a chicken."

Tim whistled. "Ouch, Hans. I think she just threw down a challenge."

Hans gave her a little shove. "Ungrateful children are my curse in life."

She hugged his shoulders. "Oh, Daddy. I appreciate you. I just think you need to get back on the horse," she said.

"Or mare, in this case," Seany added, and everyone burst out laughing. Sean Jr. always had a way with words.

"Well, maybe you're right. I'll let you know when someone piques my interest Seany. You can give this old man some pointers."

Hans watched as Aidan put some breakfast in front of his daughter. Things had progressed. He was keeping a respectful distance, but Hans was no dummy. They couldn't hide how close they were. He'd been watching them off and on for a few weeks, now. Aidan was so good to her. Bringing her a sweater when the night chill came, or tea when she was seated on the deck. Helping her clean up, being there for her when he couldn't be. *Don't blow this. Don't let her take that job.*

He respected Alanna's work. He really did. He just knew how rare and precious this type of connection was. Surely the UK had some sort of work in her field. If only Aidan was brave enough to ask. "He's good to her, isn't he?" Tim said on a whisper.

Hans nodded. "Yes, he is."

Seany ran to the front door as soon as he saw Moe pull into the drive. He opened the door as he saw her pulling a dish out of her backseat. "From my mother," she said as he took it from her.

"Well, tell her thank you. What is it?"

She smiled, "It's her brisket. Her family is from Texas. It's a thing. My father is from another part of Texas. They met in college."

Seany liked the sound of her voice. It was mild and it was neither high pitched or deep. It was just right. "You don't have much of an accent."

She shrugged. "I've lived alot of places. Nothing ever stuck."

They walked into the kitchen, and Alanna hugged her. "What have you brought?" She peeked under the foil. "Good God in heaven. Is that brisket?" The men were huddled around, stealing a strip as she tried, but failed, to swat them away.

"Holy Bride. This is gorgeous all together," Aidan said as he hung a piece mid air and nibbled the end.

Seany nudged Moe. "Would you like a soda or some of that sweet tea that Alanna favors?"

She settled on tea, and the two of them went out to the deck. "The traffic is really starting to back up. I think the island will be packed in another hour."

Seany smiled nervously. "Well, we won't need to go out. I'm glad you are here, Moe."

She looked at him seriously. "This whole thing isn't wise."

He scrunched his brows together. "Why would you think that?"

She shrugged. "You're leaving. We need to be sensible."

He turned to her, putting a big hand on her wrist where she leaned into the deck railing. "Probably, but I'm not feeling particularly sensible at the moment." She exhaled, frustrated. He pulled back. "Do ye have a boyfriend? Maybe the lad in the sailor suit?"

She looked at him and chuckled. "The dancer in the sailor suit is twenty-one and gay. That is not the issue."

"Then why?" he asked.

She looked at him like he was stupid. "Maybe you're not used to losing people. You've lived in the same town your whole life. That's good. I won't be the one to teach you, though. Unless..." She stopped.

"Go ahead. Unless what?" he said.

She looked thoughtfully at him. "Unless a few days and an easy mark are all you had in mind."

He stepped back. "Christ, woman. Who in the bloody hell gave you such a poor opinion of males?"

She wrapped her arms around herself. "No one."

He ran his fingers through his hair. "So it's just me you're suspicious of? That is such a relief."

She shook her head, closing her eyes. "That's not what I meant. I just don't know what you expect of me."

He cocked his head. "I expect you to give me a bloody chance. I expect you to get to know me before you accuse me of wicked intentions! Yer smilin'. What the hell are ye smiling about? I don't find this at all amusing."

She covered her mouth. "I'm sorry. It's just your accent gets really thick when you're irritated."

He tried to stay mad at her, but the sudden thaw and that Mona Lisa smile undid him. He took her by the elbows, pulling her in close. "Christ, girl. Tell me ye don't feel it." He rested his forehead on hers. "I felt it the minute I saw you. If you tell me you don't feel it, I'll not bother you again."

She exhaled, and her breath on his face was sweet and clean. "I can't tell you that," she said.

"Then why do you fight it? Yes, I'll leave, but at least we'll have a little time to enjoy something good and sweet."

She closed her eyes. "I've never done this." He pulled back and looked at her. "I've never been this close to a boy unless it was on stage. I don't know what I'm doing. I'm in over my head. Surely you can see that."

He sighed. "I won't ask anything of you. We'll just…be together. I just want to spend time with you. I'm no' gonna jump on you, girl. It just feels nice, being close. Aye?"

She straightened her spine, her chin up. Those serious gray eyes drew him into their depths. "I don't understand you," she said.

"Yes, but you'll stay. I've piqued your interest enough for that, right?" he asked. She nodded stiffly. He took her hand. "Then let's walk a bit, away from the crowd. Walk with me." He walked backwards, not breaking eye contact with her.

Alanna was snooping, and she knew it was wrong. "You are shameless, woman," Aidan said.

She shook her head. "They're fighting again. He looks kind of mad at her."

Aidan laughed. "Don't worry, he won't be able to keep away from her." Alanna turned back to the open blinds, watching. Then Seany took her by the arms, put his forehead to hers. "And there he goes," Aidan said.

Hans laughed. "The kid's got some moves."

Aidan cocked his head. "He just knows quality when he sees it. Sometimes the one's that are hard won are the most worth the trouble." He looked at Alanna, taking in her face with a touch of sadness in his eyes.

"Very true," said Hans.

Tim snorted. "This is depressing the shit out of me. Let's change the subject. Anna, what's doing with the new job? When do you move to Virginia?"

Aidan stiffened. Alanna cleared her throat. "I go up for training in a couple of days. They want me as soon as they can get me, but I have things I need to do here. I have to pack, put stuff in storage, find a new renter unless Branna decides to sell the place."

Tim's eyebrows went up. "She'd sell? Both sides?"

She shrugged. "I don't think it's out of the question. It's a good time to sell, and Aidan's been doing some work on it. I'll live with my dad until he goes to Spain." Her father gave her a look. "Don't start dad. You're taking the job. I'll be fine."

Tim went over to her and took her hands. He put his forehead on hers. "We're all worried. You have to understand this. Not to mention the fact that I should have told someone. I shouldn't have made that promise."

She looked up at him. "That's on me, Tim. Don't even start with that. I will be okay. I'm going to be alone, eventually. The when and why is irrelevant." She pulled away from him and he cursed. Then he looked at Aidan. The unspoken challenge was in his eyes.

The teenagers were back and they sat on the deck nibbling on brisket and potato salad. Alanna had sliced up a watermelon for dessert and some vanilla wafer pudding. The fireworks started and they were all silent except for the oohs and ahs. The occasional burst of firecrackers had started to put Aidan on edge, but these big fireworks were different. The visual stimuli brought him out of his head and he could watch and enjoy, despite the explosions. As the fireworks ended and the cars started leaving the island, Moe stood, looking at her phone. "It's late. I should go."

Seany stood up. "Aye, you shouldn't drive tired. It looks like the worst of it is over on the road."

She turned to Alanna. "Thank you for having me. It was a nice night. I haven't had a break in a while."

Alanna rubbed her arm. "School, the theater, helping your mom with Emily. You've got a lot on your plate. You call me if you need to talk, okay?"

The ladies hugged and then Seany walked her down to her car. "Thank you, Seany. This was nice." She gave a small smile. Her face was lit by the moon.

"Christ, your face is glowing in the moonlight, especially against all of this hair." He smoothed a hand over her long dark hair. "The boys at your school must be daft."

She looked away. "You must see something that is escaping the rest of the world."

He put his hands on her face. "Then all the better for me." She looked up at him, grey eyes unfathomable. "I want to kiss you, lass.

Are you going to let me, although it's not very sensible?" Her eyes flared just a hint, and she looked at his mouth. He closed the distance, light at first. The feel of her shot through him. He looked at her. "Tell me you felt that."

She nodded, swallowing hard. He went in again, and this time he kissed her deep. He pulled away. "Come here," he said huskily. He took her under the pylons, then he kissed her all he wanted. She kissed him back, gaining confidence, putting her hands in his hair. He didn't push for more. He controlled his body, kept his distance where it counted, but he kissed her and kissed her until they were both breathless. Then he pulled away and looked at her. "Can you tell me that a few days of this isn't worth what comes after?" Then he kissed her softly, sweetly. He pulled her hand and led her to her car. Those serious grey eyes were sparking with energy, curiosity.

She stopped before she got in her car. "As first kisses go, I'm not sure it gets any better."

Seany's face beamed. "I'll call you, Moe." She nodded silently and got in her car.

Tim and Aidan were sitting on the deck when Seany walked up. "Damn, brother. That must have been some kiss," Tim teased.

Seany smiled, saying nothing. Aidan gave him a look. "What? I was a total gentleman."

Aidan took a sip of his beer. "Good, just keep it that way."

Seany looked around. "Where's Alanna and Hans?"

"They turned in early. He has to drive back, and she has to teach a class in the morning." Aidan said.

Seany left the two men on the deck and retreated to the house. "What are you doing, Aidan? Are you really going to just leave?" Tim said quietly, given the proximity to Hans and Alanna.

Aidan sighed. "You know the why of it. That job means everything to her. I've got at least ten more years until retirement. This is not a decision. It's a fact."

Tim shook his head. "You sure about that? Because if you are, someone else is going to have to take care of her. Maybe I can transfer my practice. Hell, maybe she and I can give it another shot. God knows, I love her like family." Aidan sat up, glaring at him. "What? You don't like that idea? Tough shit. You won't be here to do anything about it. At least I love her enough to fight for her. It might not be the passionate love that every woman wants, but at least I would love her, be faithful, protect her. You'll head back to the UK and start with the bachelor life again. Fuck some randoms while she's here picking up the pieces and watching her back all the time," he whispered with a hiss.

"That's not it at all. You think this is easy for me?"Aidan hissed back.

"Yes. I think you've got it damned easy. You can come here, get a piece of ass for the summer, and leave with a clear conscience, because she has a good job offer. I thought at first that you were falling in love with her, but obviously I was wrong. The only thing you love is your freedom."

Aidan pointed at him. "Watch it. You have no idea what you are talking about."

Tim put his hands outstretched. "I'm not so sure about that. I see you here playing house, with one eye on the exit. Obviously, you liked the chase but your curiosity has been sated."

Aidan grabbed him by the shirt. "Shut the fuck up, Tim. You have no idea what this is doing to me. She's everything to me," he growled. "I will be a walking dead man when I leave her!"

He shoved off Tim and walked down the beach walk. Tim came behind him. "I know. I just wanted you to say it out loud."

Aidan turned on him. "It doesn't change anything."

Tim smiled sadly. "You're wrong. It changes everything. Do you really think she'd choose this job over you? She can't hide her feelings. She loves you, Aidan."

Aidan closed his eyes. "It's not enough. I can't make her happy. I'm fucked up, more than you know. I'm a mess in my head."

Aidan felt Tim's hand on his shoulder. "You're wrong. I've seen fucked up. You're not. You've got some demons, but you are good for her and she's good for you. She is your ticket out of that hell hole in your head. You think I don't know what it's like to reach and reach for home, and never quite get back there? She is your way home. You need to see it before it's too late."

38

Aidan came into the house midway through the work day. Alanna was stretched across the couch, asleep. She was so beautiful. Her hair was bundled on the top of her head. She had cut off shorts and a bikini top on, with an unbuttoned cotton camp shirt opened just enough to show her beautiful tummy, the swell of her breasts. Aidan only had a few minutes. He wanted to see her before she left for Virginia, just once more before she left for a couple of days. He bent over the end of the couch and touched her lips with his. She inhaled, rousing. She smiled against his mouth. "You're here," she said.

He kissed her again and her body rose. His cock thickened in his uniform pants. She was showing a splendid amount of skin. He deepened the kiss, sliding two fingers into her bikini top, pulling it aside. "Aidan," she moaned as her hips rolled. Then he took her nipple in his mouth. She ran a hand in his hair. "I need you," she said. He slid his hand down her abdomen and plucked the top button of her jeans shorts open. Her breath started coming short. He worked her nipple with his mouth, his tongue, his teeth. Then he slid his hand inside her shorts and touched her warm, wet center. She gasped and arched and he drew her nipple deep.

"Aidan, please. Come to me."

He smiled and came up to her mouth. "I only have a few minutes. I just want this. I want to feel you. I love to watch you come, mo mhuirnín." He loved the feel of her straining against his hand, but he needed more. Then he was up, sliding her shorts off. "Just let me taste you before I go." He splayed his palms on her thighs, opening them. Then he closed his mouth on her, nuzzling her as he settled to his task. It was seconds before she exploded. He moaned as she orgasmed.

Aidan stared up at his beautiful Alanna as he pleasured her. Her taught stomach arching, her hips straining to meet his mouth, her beautiful breast spilling out of her top where he'd pulled it aside to suckle her. He barely contained his own release as her orgasm rolled through her body. This is what he needed, to see her peak, to watch her surrender. He'd rushed home for this, anxious not to miss her before she started for Virginia.

He'd been insatiable, even more than usual. He made love to her at bedtime, then sometimes again in the middle of the night, then once quickly before work, then again in the evening, sometimes more than once. The little chat he'd had with Tim was on repeat in his head. He needed this, all of her. Her mouth, her skin, her hair tickling his face. Everything. When he rose from her, she was breathing hard. "Thank you. Christ, I needed that," he said as he wiped his mouth on his hand.

She looked at him like he was insane. "You don't think you are leaving yet?" She raised a brow.

"I only had a few minutes. I wanted to give you something to tide ye over, lass," he said with a grin. When he backed away, she sailed off the couch, shoving him into the wall. Her mouth was on his, and she was fumbling with his buckle as he chuckled. "You're going to make me late," he teased.

But she was having none of it. She shoved her hand down his pants and wrapped her hand around him. "Then you take me fast and hard, right here."

His face registered shock. She'd never said something so base and raw. He hissed when she made contact with his cock, ready to blow the top off of it. Then his eyes narrowed and he grabbed her head, kissing her hard. He flipped her around and she was facing the wall. He clasped her hands above her head with one hand on her wrists. Her head fell back loose on his shoulders as he pushed inside her with no preamble. His hips were locked tight up against her ass as she arched. She was moaning as he took her. "Is this what you want?"

Her neck was arched and she choked on her words. "Yes, don't stop!"

He started a pounding rhythm, deep and fast, and she screamed as she came again, gripping him from the inside. He flipped her around to face him and hooked her legs around his forearms as he lifted her. Then he started a slow, deep grind and she was whimpering. His eyes said everything. *I wish you weren't going. I wish I wasn't going. I wish I could stay inside you like this forever.* "Come back to me. As soon as you can, come back to me." He was a breath from her lips, his face desperate. Then he came, the pleasure rolling through him as he shuddered. She held his face in her hands, watching his eyes, hers dazed with arousal. "That's it, Aidan. This is what I wanted. Come inside me."

Aidan wasn't late, but it was close. He came into the training area with his tires kicking up dust.

"Nooner," Polaski said under his breath. Williams shushed him.

Corporal Washington wasn't so discreet. "How was your lunch, sir? Did you have enough time to enjoy it?"

The men chuckled. "Washington, stand down," Williams warned.

Aidan was fixing his cover, hiding his blush as he approached Hector and John. "Well, well. Glad you made it back in time. Your belt is askew, FYI," John whispered. Aidan straightened it discreetly, hiding a grin.

They had chow delivered to the field, MREs. The young Porter was eating Aidan's M&Ms and Washington was popping shit with the Corpsman. "O'Malley, when are you gonna quit pussy footing around and marry that girl? She's gonna dump your ass for a Marine if you keep bringing her up here every weekend." The men laughed.

"What about him? Sir, you're not married. Why not?" O'Malley asked.

Aidan cleared his throat. "How did I get dragged into this?"

Lieutenant Drake waved a hand. "Nah, he's too busy with the Sergeant Major's daughter." Cue the hoots and whistles.

"Enough, lads. Don't start talking about her. She's not up for discussion."

Washington looked at him, cocking his head. "So why aren't you married? You're obviously a one woman man. Shit, we know you come from a long line of Irish white bread and good Catholics. Whatchu waitin' on sir?" Washington had that thick Louisiana accent and warm smile that disarmed whoever he was talking too.

"He doesn't want to drag a woman into this life." Porter said it so matter of factly, that Aidan was taken back. "Given what Luke put his family through, he's probably right. Maybe we shouldn't get both. I think he's got the right idea. I wouldn't want to worry about screwing up a wife and kids after I come home from war. Seems easier to just stay alone. Get a little recreational sex on occasion and stay single."

Washington put a hand up. "Damn Sergeant Porter, that is some cynical shit. Don't ever get a job writing greeting cards, mother fucker, cuz you'd suck at it."

Aidan broke in. "Don't think like that, Sergeant. You can have both. Look at the Major, Captain Denario, Williams and Polanski, they're all happily married. Don't let Luke's decisions color how you live your life."

Porter shrugged. "Well, then why aren't you married? Why do you stay alone?"

Hector's boom voice interrupted. "Line up, ladies. Lunch is over!"

The next few days of training were intense. They were back in combat town, but this time the lessons were combined. Working with an interpreter, clearing buildings, dealing with vehicle malfunctions, administering first aid, mock IEDs. The time flew by, and Aidan was actually worried that Seany was home alone too much. Yet every time he came in, the boy was just getting home. He was out seeing the neighboring towns, going to the movies. He and Moe weren't wasting a minute.

He'd told Aidan that he'd had a candid talk with Moe's parents. They'd made both of them promise that they would not come back to the beach house if no adults were there. "We made our own rule as well. The stand up rule."

Aidan raised a brow. "What's that?"

Seany reddened a bit. "No kissing unless we're standing. It'll keep us from taking it too far."

Aidan had a flash of shoving Alanna against the wall, taking her from behind. He thought it best not to inform his little brother just how far you could take it while you were both still standing.

"She's never really been physical with a guy. I was her first kiss. We just don't want to get carried away, considering how little time I have here. I respect her. I don't want to hurt her. You probably think that sounds pretty juvenile."

Aidan's eyes were gentle. "No, Seany. Not at all. I think it's amazing that you show that kind of restraint. She's very beautiful. Most lads would push as far as they could. You're a good man."

Seany smiled, warming under his brother's approval. "God, I do love kissing her, though. She is beautiful. She really doesn't understand that she is, though. She thinks she's plain, but she doesn't see what I see."

Aidan asked, "And what do you see?"

Seany exhaled. “I see old eyes. They’re so grey, so serious, but they are beautiful. They just draw me in. And skin like silk. She’s so fair and so soft. It’s hard not to get carried away touching her. Her skin is amazing, and she smells good and she’s got all that dark hair. I love the feel of it. It’s her smile, though. That’s what really gets me. It’s not big. Its like she’s letting you in on a secret, and you feel like you got to see something that not everyone gets to see. She’s got a kind of Mona Lisa smile, do you understand?”

Aidan nodded. “Yes, I think I do. I think she’s lucky to have someone in her life who sees all of that.”

Aidan laid in bed, thinking about what Porter had said. It sounded so cynical when the kid had said it, but isn’t that exactly the excuse he’d been using for years? He closed his eyes and Alanna’s face came to him. Her face when he was inside her. Her face when she was angry with him. Her face when she’d swept his leg and put him under the water, shadow boxing and dancing around the surf. As if she could read his thoughts, she called. His phone lit up in the dark room. “Were you sleeping?” she asked.

“No, I couldn’t go to sleep. I miss you.” Jesus wept. He was such a sap.

“I miss you too. I’ll head out in the morning. Things went late today. I was too tired to fight the traffic and make the long drive. I’ll be home before you.” Aidan was so glad to hear her voice.

“It’ll be nice to come home to you, love. I’ve been wanting to talk to you.”

She paused. “Okay, is everything all right?”

He said, “Yes, everything’s fine. Oh, and Seany won’t be here. He and Moe will be touring that ship in Wilmington tomorrow. He’ll get home around the same time I do.”

Alanna crooned. “Really? So they are still seeing each other?”

Aidan answered, "Every day." Then he told her about the ground rules they'd set up.

"Wow, that's really mature of them. The stand up rule, huh? Well, we certainly found a way around that, didn't we?" Her tone was teasing.

"Aye, we did. I can't stop thinking about it."

She let out a soft sigh. "You're making me want to start driving now," she said.

"No, get some rest. I'll see you tomorrow. Text me when you leave."

39

The next morning was hectic. Alanna shoved a cup of coffee at her father. "Call me when you get to Lejeune. Don't forget." He kissed her on the forehead. "Thanks for the breakfast, Miss Priss. I love you." Then he was gone.

Alanna was singing at the top of her lungs as she drove. She'd made good time. She wanted to beat Seany and Aidan home and make a nice dinner. Seany was leaving in a couple of days. Maybe she would invite Moe over for a very sweet, chaperoned double date.

She pulled into the beach house and parked under the house like she always did. When she opened the back seat to get her bag out, that's when he spoke. "Finally, a few minutes alone." Fear spiked through her, but before she could utter a solitary shriek, she felt the jolt of electricity go through her, and the world blurred in a blinding heat.

The sun was low in the sky. Aidan was later than he'd wanted to be, but he was headed home now. He pulled out of the base gate and headed for the beach house. At the stop sign turning on to New River Inlet, he looked right and noticed that there was a beat up car off to the side of the road. Something niggled at him. Something about that car.

He shook it off and thought about Alanna. She'd texted him this morning, but he hadn't been able to get ahold of her since. It wasn't like her to let her phone die and an uneasiness hovered over him. When he pulled into the house, her car was not there. He ran up the deck, taking the stairs two and three at a time. His phone was ringing and he picked it up. "Hans, what's wrong?"

Alanna's father paused. "Why are you asking that? Where is she?" Seany came in the room and looked at him oddly. "Hold on, Hans. Seany, has she been home?"

Seany shook his head. "I've been home for two hours. She's not been here. It's locked up next door." Panic struck Aidan. With perfect clarity, he saw the car again. Not at the side of the road. He saw it pulling away, the night he'd found Alanna's opened mail in his mailbox. "Jesus Christ, Hans."

Aidan sat across from the police officer barely able to control his breathing. "She's only been gone a couple of hours."

Aidan snapped at the prick. "She should have been here by noon. She left at six o'clock this morning. It's seven o'clock. Don't fucking patronize me. You know the history."

The female officer that had taken the report knelt beside him. "Look at me. Don't worry about him," she said lightly. "I got you. I'm on the same page."

Seany was on the phone with Hans, pulling up the GPS website and getting the passcodes. Then the officer's walkie talkie went off. It was another officer who was checking out the abandoned car. "Yeah, the plates and the VIN don't match. Something stinks. The owner of the plates is eighty years old and the vehicle comes back to a woman. This isn't our guy or he's using someone else's ride. I've got a tow truck on the way."

Another officer called from downstairs. "I've got a phone!" They brought it upstairs and Aidan cursed. "It was smashed and thrown in the bushes. I'll bag it for prints."

Aidan looked at the older, useless officer that had been nothing but a hinderance to his younger trainee. "Is that enough to convince you that she didn't stop for tea?" he spat the words at the male officer.

"Okay, calm down. Let's see what your brother has going on over here," said the woman.

Seany had Hans on speaker phone. "Hans, did you hear any of that?"

Hans's voice was strained. "Yes, I copied. I'm still about four hours away. Call Hector. Do you copy me? You call Hector. Do you understand what I'm telling you?"

Aidan did. *Go get our girl.* Hans didn't have to say it. "What does the GPS say? There are two besides the phone. He obviously took her car. Where is her car?" Hans asked impatiently.

The officer looked over the map. "Okay, this is weird, I am getting her car by a community dock on the mainland. It's not mobile, but…" She looked at the map, clicking the coordinates for the last GPS signal. "This other one seems to be in the water."

There was silence on the phone and in the room. "Holy God, what the fuck are you saying? That's the one on her wrist. What the hell do you mean, in the water?" said Aidan, creeping up on hysteria.

She grabbed his elbows. "Stop, don't even go there. She could be on a boat. The car is by a day slip. It's in disrepair, no one uses it because the tide gets too low. If he had a flat bottomed, boat, he could have done it. Let me zoom in. I don't know this area."

Seany got up and gave her his seat, and he grabbed his brothers face. "She's alive. She's strong. You know how strong she is."

The officer yelled, "Bingo, mother fucker!" She caught herself. "God, sorry. That was really unprofessional, but look." She turned the screen. Zooming in, they could see a series of small barrier islands. "This is further into Onslow County. I need to call the locals in that area. This is a small town here, I don't know who has jurisdiction on these islands. They aren't inhabited. They are literally mounds of scrub that shrink with the tide."

Aidan looked closer. "Jesus, I know this area. Is that Captain Sams? And the kayak shop? This is the mouth of the White Oak River, aye? Where it spills into the ocean?"

She looked harder. "Yes, exactly. Now I will call Onslow County and the Coast Guard and the local PD. I really don't know who in the hell polices those islands." She looked up and Aidan was ignoring her and making a phone call. "Hector. I need you. I need you and every man you can get. And I need a boat."

Aidan was packing his rucksack as the police officer was dressing him down. "You can't go off half cocked with a bunch of jarheads! Listen to me, goddamn it! You can't just storm out on that water."

He looked at her, piercing her with a look. "Fucking watch me." Little did she know he also had Alanna's pistol in the bottom of the bag.

"I'm going too." Seany had changed into dark pants and shirt.

"The hell you are."

Seany cocked his head. "Fucking watch me," he said, throwing Aidan's own words back at him. "I can drive a boat. I work at the ferry. You won't have to leave a man behind with the boat. I am going, brother. It's not up for discussion."

Aidan hesitated, then nodded. He turned to the officer. "You check out the car, let me know if there's anything we need to know. If you manage to get some help out there by the time we are ready to roll, then by all means, send them. I will not sit on my ass waiting for that violent rapist to get bored and start in on my girlfriend."

The officer growled. She looked at her superior. He shook his head. "That is so far out of our jurisdiction it may as well be China. No way, rookie. We go check out the car."

Captain Sam's driveway was packed with vehicles just outside the chain that had a closed sign hanging over it. Sheila was in her robe. "He's out to sea. They're not due back till tomorrow afternoon. I've got a smaller boat, but you gotta promise me you'll be careful. My husband would flip out if you crashed his fun boat." Aidan grabbed her and kissed her forehead. She took his hand. "You go get her. I called Don on the CB. He's waiting for you."

Aidan's body was strung tight. He looked at the men on the boat. Corporal Washington, Staff Sergeants Williams and Polaski, Doc O'Malley, Sergeant Porter, Joey Drake, Hector and John. Those were the only men they could get ahold of, but it was enough. "I'll never be able to repay you for this. Never."

Seany was driving the borrowed vessel as they pulled up alongside the boat, *Tired of Tangos*. Retired Senior Chief Montgomery was waiting on the deck as Seany cut the engine and glided alongside him. Introductions and explanations were brief. Hector's large screened phone held the map of the GPS coordinates. The island that was showing a beacon was as small as this one he was docked at, and uninhabited.

The retired SEAL looked at the men. "Where's our corpsman?" O'Malley raised a hand. "You got what you need if someone gets hurt, or if she's in a bad way?"

Aidan made a choking sound and Hector put a steadying hand on him. "Okay, who's the best shot? I have three guns." Hector, John, and Aidan were already armed with personal pistols and knives.

The two staff sergeants and Lt. Drake took the pistols. All of them had their fighting knives. "We should have grabbed our gear from the training area," Porter mumbled.

Hector said, "Not unless you want a court marshal. That is not our gear. It belongs to the U.S. Government. Now, I am going to say it one more time. This is not a military mission. You do not have to be here. This is off the books. You get hurt, it is not a combat mission. If you want out, do it now. No one will say shit to you. I mean it."

The original plan had been for the officers to do this alone. A couple of them were out of town, the Gunny assigned to the team was taking paternity leave. The rest of the team was there, however. Drake had called the corpsman to be on stand by, and the word had spread to the team. Staff Sergeant Polaski spoke then. "No offense sir, but cut the shit. We're a team. You go, we go." The men rumbled with a quiet ooh-rah. "The Captain needs his boys. We are not leaving him or her."

That's when the retired senior chief smacked his leg. "Hot damn, I love a good team."

Aidan cursed when the fireworks started. "Jesus, what next."

"Some asshole got the clearance sale fireworks," said Hector. Roman candles and firecrackers and an occasional bigger firework were spraying through the air as they made their way through the water at a snails pace, the inflatable life boats tethered to either side.

Aidan's face was tight with worry. "All we have is a GPS signal, we don't know where he is." He swallowed. "He could have dumped her. Jesus, John, what if…"

John grabbed him. "No!" he hissed. "You don't think like that. This asshole didn't drag this out for seven years just to grab her and boom, it's over. She's alive. He would keep her alive. You know that. I know you feel it. She's alive." The other men were all exchanging glances, like it had never occurred to them that this could be a recovery and not a rescue.

Sean looked at Sorcha and was ready to pop his top. "I shouldn't have left. I should have sent you home with the boy and stayed there and watched over her while Aidan was working."

Maria had followed Aidan's instructions. She'd called the family in Ireland, given them the details, and told them to pray like they'd never prayed before.

"Those fat headed sons of mine are going to put me in an early grave!" Sorcha screeched.

Michael took her in his arms. "What if it were Brigid, Ma? Or Caitlyn? Or Branna? He can't sit by and wait. God knows what's happening to her."

Branna was rocking on the sofa, Brigid's arms wrapped around her. "I should have told. Back when it happened, I should have told someone."

Brigid shushed her, soothing her with her voice. "No one is to blame but that feckin animal who's got her. You said she's strong. She'll do what she has to in order to stay alive."

"Why is everyone upset?" Cora appeared rubbing her eyes.

"It's all right, darlin'. Let's get you back to bed."

Finn picked his daughter up, and she stopped him with a shove at his chest. "No, I need to call Uncle Aidan. I had a dream about him and the girl. The blonde girl on the computer." They all froze. Cora was only five and a half, but they'd learned to take her dreams to heart.

"What did you need to tell him, love?" Brigid asked as she rubbed her daughter's back.

"He's got to protect her. She's got tape on her. There's a bad man, and there's a storm coming. I saw lightning."

Seany interrupted. "I've got a call coming in on your phone, brother! It's from overseas."

Aidan grabbed the phone. "Brigid? What the hell? I can't talk right now."

Brigid said, "It's Cora. She's dreamed of the girl. She said she saw the girl. She had tape on her hands and feet. She said she was dirty and that there were a lot of bushes around. She said there was lightning in the sky. She's alive, Aidan." The flesh rose on Aidan's arms. "Aidan, did you hear me? You know Cora's sensitive about this sort of stuff. She had no way of knowing. We never told her anything. Is it storming there?"

Aidan looked at the sky. "Fireworks. Jesus, it's fireworks. I dreamt this too. I thought it was artillery."

Seany drove the boat for a few more minutes when Aidan said, "Okay, stop here. He's on the other side of the island with her, according to this map, but we can't get any closer to shore. We row in from here." They piled into the two boats and each had a pair of men on the small paddles. Seany anchored and cut the engine. The hair raised up on his nape as he watched the men row into the dark water.

40

Alanna was very still, hoping that if she just stayed that way, he would forget she was there. He'd been rambling for hours. She was cramped, bound at her hands and feet. He'd cut her feet loose long enough to get her on shore and into the bush, then rebound her. The boat he'd brought her on was no bigger than a bass boat, one of those Zodiacs. Her side stung, feeling the burn mark he'd made with the taser.

When she'd come out of her stupor, he had pulled her into the little gym she'd made under the house. He was taping her up when she started to fight. That's when he'd punched her. Her eye was throbbing. He'd looked at her mockingly and said, "Payback for the nose."

He'd turned her car around so that the trunk came right up to the gym door. Then he loaded her in after laying a large seabag flat and open. "I'll leave your face out, but if you make a sound I will zip it and drop you in the fucking marsh."

Tears blurred her vision. Tears of terror and anger. Anger not just at him, but at herself. She'd let her guard down. The next time the trunk was open, they were isolated in an overgrown area off the ICW. Terror struck her at the thought that he might very well drop her in the sea, bound in this bag. Then he zipped it and pulled the bag out of the trunk. He was lean and long, but he was strong.

Probably from working at sea for the last seven years. She felt herself hoisted into a boat. *He won't kill you. He won't kill you. He's not done playing with you yet. He will not kill you.* She thought about the bracelet. The only way they would track her once the car was left behind them. He'd taken her phone and thrown it in the scrub beyond the pilings.

Now she was on the ground, sitting against a fallen tree. The shells were digging into her butt, and the bugs were biting her. She stole glances at him. The years had not been kind. He was thinner, lanky. His skin was sun damaged. He also had the smell of a long term drinker and sour sweat. He smelled, she reflected, like madness.

He'd shed his ball cap, and his hair stuck to his head. He'd exerted himself dragging her in and out of the boat. Apparently kidnapping was physically taxing work. Once he'd taken her off the boat, she'd started to struggle again. He looked at her with complete sincerity. "That teenage boy will be home alone. If you don't shut the fuck up, I will drive over there and kill him before his brother gets home. Maybe he'll have that pretty little girl with him, too. I think I could teach her a few things, just like I taught you."

There was pure insanity in his eyes at that moment. He'd also pulled out a slip of paper from his wallet. He read off Erik's address. The threats did their job. He could leave her here to rot and go after the people she loved. They were watching her back, not their own.

Now he was completely different. He was calm, almost chipper as he rolled out a blanket and pulled out some water and other provisions. He looked at her. "Now listen, sweetheart. We got off to an awkward start. I know it's been a while. We just need to get used to each other again. I'm going to take the mouth tape off and we can eat. Remember when we used to eat together? I took you to that little Mexican place outside the base."

She closed her eyes as a wave of nausea almost overtook her. That was the night he'd brutally taken her virginity, but he was talking like they were in love. Like they were an old married couple thinking about their first date. He put a hand up to her face and she jerked. "Now, don't be jumpy. I know I was a little rough with you, but you gave me no choice. We're going to start over. Let me take the tape off." He pulled it and she winced, feeling her skin pull.

He had her hands taped in front of her, so he handed her a water bottle. She drank greedily, then she spoke, "Please, Steve. Just take me to shore. I won't tell anyone. You know that. You know I can keep a secret. Please, just let me go."

He was opening some beef jerky and he shook his head. "You don't get it, do you? Your life here is over. You and I are going to start our life together. It is long past time we reconciled." He looked at her, a steely expression on his face. "I am willing to forgive you for the other men. I wasn't always faithful. We were separated a long time. That starts to take a toll on couples, even if they love each other."

She instinctually knew that spewing the venom that was on the tip of her tongue would get her nothing but trouble, so she said nothing. She had to think before she talked. "It was immature of me to send you that picture of the other woman. She was a sorry substitute. I was just pissed off, you see. That Irishman was staying next door. I saw you with him, and I lashed out. She was nothing compared to you. Just some cheap whore. They've got nothing to do with us. I'm home now, baby. Everything will be just perfect now."

Alanna cleared her throat. Her initial attempts to fight and scream had left her hoarse, coupled by dehydration. Her side was killing her, the electrical burn a constant ache. He'd also most likely broken her wrist when he'd bound her. She hadn't made it easy and he'd wrenched her wrist after punching her in the face.

"I'm hurt, Steve. I think my wrist is broken, and my side is burned. We can't live here, surely you know that, and I need a doctor." He looked at her and smiled. He handed her some beef jerky and she declined. Her throat was raw, and she wasn't sure she could swallow it.

"We aren't staying here. I've got friends on the way. I met them in the Merchant Marines. They run drugs up from Florida by boat." Alanna's face registered horror. He got to his feet and walked to her. "No, no. Don't be scared. They know you're mine. They just want to get paid. They'll get us over the border into Mexico. Then I'll take you to a doctor. We'll find a place to live, find a priest to marry us."

This was the last straw. "For God's sake, Steve. Have you really lost all touch with reality? I will never marry you. I do not belong to you!" She regretted the outburst when he backhanded her. She fell to the side, her hair going over her face.

Then he was pulling her up. "Jesus, I'm sorry baby. I didn't want to do that." He was smoothing her hair off her face and she tried to turn away from him. He yanked her hair, pulling her face up to his. "You will learn to play nice."

Then he got a good look at her. "Christ, you are so beautiful. You're even more beautiful now." His look was hungry. "I never stopped thinking about you, Anna. That night with you, it was perfection. The night I made you a woman." His breath was hot on her face, and she moaned and fought the urge to be sick. "I won't take you now. I made one mistake last time. The backseat was crude and hasty. I'm a man now, sweet darlin. We'll spend our first night together in a bed. You'll forget all about that Irishman once I'm inside you." She tried to inch away from him and he tightened the grip on her hair. Then he kissed her, a hard, punishing kiss. "Yes, you will definitely learn to play nice."

Then he was on his feet again. He went through his backpack and then threw it down, as if some sort of frustration was tormenting him, and he had to say his piece. "Did you really think I would just let you leave with him? Leave the country to be his whore?"

The men moved with quiet, slow precision. Aidan took point, motioning to the men when he saw the LED light coming from the bush. A lantern in the dark, guiding him toward his Alanna. He thought about the lantern she kept on the bedpost for him, so that he could see her face when he woke from a nightmare. But this was no nightmare. This was real, and fear spiked through him at the though of what he might find in the glow of that light.

The scrub was near impossible to maneuver, but they were trained and they were patient. They couldn't risk him hearing their approach. Occasional fireworks would go off, and Aidan started to realize that the noise might work in their favor. As he approached, he heard the angry male voice. He put a hand up and they stopped. The moon was out and they needed no light as long as they were careful. They wore dark clothing and dark paint on their faces and hands. They had the advantage on just about every fucking level. He listened. As he heard the words, he began a steady tremble, the rage boiling up in him. Then he felt a steadying hand on his shoulder. John was at his six.

Aidan was close enough to hear the man ranting. "Did you really think I would just let you leave with him? Leave the country to be his whore?"

Alanna's jaw stiffened. "I am not a whore. I was never a whore."

She wasn't sure when he'd taken the knife out of his bag, but he pointed in at her like a finger. "You weren't when I had you. You were innocent, and what we shared was like a sacrament. Now you've soiled yourself with that fucking soldier and that peg legged Marine. You let them use you like some barracks whore."

She lurched forward. "They never used me. You are a brute and a rapist. I was lucky to get away, but how many women have you violated since then, you sick fuck! That poor girl on the ship!"

He charged her then, putting the knife at her cheek. "That bitch on the ship was a tease. She was walking around like a queen, flipping that blonde hair around, giving out orders. She got what was coming to her." He pressed the tip and she felt her skin give, a small scratch just to rattle her. She knew this.

She met his eye. "You can carve me up like a turkey, but I will never be yours." She said it with a steady tone, her ice green eyes never looking away. She was so busy focusing on the knife, that she hadn't been watching his other hand. He punched her in the mouth again, her body flying to the sand and shells.

He stood, shaking his head. "I think I made a mistake letting that soldier live. He's obviously got some sort of hold on you. He won't have you, though. You won't be going anywhere with him. When we get settled over the border, I will take my time with your re-education." His look was overly familiar, raking her body with his eyes. "Before I leave, I will go back to that house and kill him and his little brother." She swallowed hard. She'd lost her temper, she had to get back the upper hand with him. The only way to do that was to appease his wounded pride.

"I'm sorry," she choked on a sob. "I don't know why I say the things I do. I think it is jealousy."

His face changed, a smile playing at his lips. "You don't have to be jealous, baby. I told you, those other girls meant nothing. Just like that big fucker next door to you means nothing. They've got nothing to do with us now."

She smiled at him then, trying to look sweet and docile. "You don't have to worry about him. I was lonely. You were gone so long. I was nothing to him. A summer fling. He would never take me back home with him."

He made fists at his sides, stiffening his body. "Don't lie to me!" he yelled.

"I'm not lying. I am sorry I was unfaithful to you. It was a fling. I promise you, he never loved me. He never said it. Not once. I was never his."

Aidan's stomach rolled. He knew what she was trying to do. That knife in the man's hand was the only thing keeping him in place. He could see her now, but barely. She'd been beaten. She was on the ground, her hands and feet bound. The words had stung. *He never loved me. He never said it. Not once.* There were fireworks lighting up behind her. *This was my dream. I'm supposed to protect her.* Then he saw them, Hector and the Senior Chief with Porter and Washington. They were at the flank.

Hans was losing his fucking mind. He was at the shoreline, standing with the sheriff's deputies. "Don't you guys have a fucking boat? Who the hell is in charge of those islands?"

The deputy's tone was even. He was after all, a father of four. "They're protected by the Parks and Recreations officers. The Coast Guard station at Emerald Isle is deploying as we speak. They'll be the quickest. You're lucky your son has a buddy over there. I know you're upset, Sergeant Major, but you need to let them do their job."

He looked at his phone. No text from Erik. Had they even left the station yet? He cursed under his breath. "I should have made her move up there with me when I found out. I told her I'd protect her." His voice broke. "I feel so fucking helpless. Can't we commandeer a jet ski or some shit?" The deputy didn't know what to say, so he said nothing.

Steve was calming down. She could tell by his body language. "Please forgive me," Alanna said. She didn't have to try to feign tears. Her eyes were thick with them, her voice straining. She was scared, hurt, and praying to God that his friends didn't show up before someone came for her. They would come. Aidan, Erik, her daddy. They would come. She wiped her eyes on her good arm, wincing with the pain in her other wrist. It was swelling against the tape and her hand was tingling and off color. When her eyes were clear, that's when she saw the movement. She was careful not to show anything in her demeanor.

He was kneeling in front of her. He lifted her chin. "You're right. You were never his. You're mine. Don't forget that or I'll change my mind about waiting for a bed. That blanket will do just fine if you need a reminder. My mouth is watering at the thought of it, as a matter of fact." His voice was husky. She could feel the arousal rolling off of him. It was less about sex and more about the violence. It had aroused him. The thought made her sick, but she stifled the urge to pull her chin away.

"I think I could eat now, if you have some left. I haven't eaten since this morning. That is, if you don't need it for yourself. I'd understand if you didn't bring enough for me."

He smiled indulgently at her. "Of course I brought enough. What kind of husband would I be if I couldn't feed my wife?" Then he put his face close. "It will cost you a kiss. I want you to put some effort into it this time, or I'll doubt your sincerity."

She started to tremble. She took her bound hands and touched his face. Then she kissed him. It almost killed her, but she did it. He moaned and plunged his tongue in her mouth. She fought the gag reflex, indulging him until he was finished. He sucked her lip where he'd punched her and split her lip. "I've got some beef jerky and some red bull."

She nodded. "That sounds perfect." She fought the urge to wipe her mouth, knowing that would only agitate the situation.

Then he got up, walked to his pack, and set the knife down, plundering for the food. That's when all hell broke loose. Men broke out of the bush on two sides, pistols raised. She felt arms under her armpits, dragging her backward. Aidan had his knee in Steve's back, a pistol at his head.

"It's me, ma'am. Doc O'Malley!" He was talking in her ear. "Are there any more?" She looked up and saw the other men. Some with weapons on Steve, some facing outward, guarding Aidan. Some had knives, some guns. It was his team of Marines.

She choked on a sob. "No, he said he had friends coming, but they aren't here yet. It's just him."

Doc called out. "He's alone! He's got a boat coming, but he's alone." The men relaxed a bit, and Aidan holstered his weapon.

"Call my brother. We need to get this piece of shit to the shore." Aidan yanked him up by his hair. "You sneeze and these nice lads will put a window in the back of your head. Got it, shitbird?"

Steve laughed. "She will never be yours. I had her first. When I get out, I will slit her throat before I let you have her," he hissed.

Aidan's anger went from a boil to a flash of white, hot metal. He beat the man with a fury. Fists, boots, two hundred plus pounds of Irish whoop ass and O'Brien temper unleashed in an unholy wave of violence. Four men, combining efforts, finally managed to get him off of the prick. "You keep your mouth shut, or I will gut you, and leave you for the fucking buzzards!" he said.

Alanna came across the distance, her voice calm. "Aidan, it's okay. He can't hurt me anymore. I'm okay." As she went toward him, Steve pushed himself up. He'd grabbed a smaller knife out of his boot and swiped at Aidan, catching the front of his shirt. Alanna moved like bird of prey, swooping down on him with all the fury of a valkyrie. She was in the line of fire, and no one could shoot the bastard until they got her clear. She screamed as she tackled him and they went down, his head smashing into a loblolly stump that was protruding from the ground. The men scrambled, O'Malley pulling her up and away. "Get the knife!" Aidan yelled. It wasn't a problem, though. The bastard was out cold, bleeding freely from his head.

Aidan grabbed her up in his arms. "Are ye okay? Did he cut you? Jesus Christ, is everyone all right?" Aidan looked around frantically. O'Malley immediately started with the life saving routine, because no one wanted the bastard to expire before he got arrested.

"Jesus Christ, woman. Are you out of your mind?" Then he pulled her to him. "I knew you'd stay alive! I knew it!" Aidan was sobbing, now. Blubbering like a teenage girl. He was completely unconcerned that he was looking like a stone cold pussy in front of his men. They didn't care. The relief was palpable.

His men. They were his men They might be from different sides of the Atlantic, but these were his men and he was theirs. They all moved with purpose, calling Seany further inland as they loaded the piece of shit on the life boat. O'Malley and Montgomery took him across the water as Aidan and Hector took Alanna in the other lifeboat boat. That's when the Coast Guard showed up. Big lights, loud speaker, then Erik. "Don't fucking shoot them! They're Marines!"

The men piled onto *Tired of Tangos* to collect themselves before the inevitable waves of law enforcement started questioning them on shore. All but Aidan and O'Malley. They rode in the Coast Guard ship with Alanna. Their medics had taken over treating Alanna's attacker. O'Malley was treating Alanna, splinting her wrist, trying to clean the worst of her cuts. She looked over at Steve, so still, bloody bandages rolled around his head, immobilized on a backboard.

"Don't watch, love." He began rocking her, humming next to her ear. He soothed her, even though she knew she was shutting down. Aidan shouted to O'Malley as her world went black.

41

Alanna came fully awake to the sounds of a hospital floor that was bustling with activity. She looked around the room and saw a nurse changing her IV bag. She fumbled with the oxygen tube around her cheeks and ears.

"Hello there. It is good to see you awake." The nurse was smiling gently. Aidan stirred in the chair beside her. Then he popped awake. Her father was on the other side, asleep. Erik was propped up on the floor, also asleep.

"What time is it?" Her voice was hoarse, "What happened?" Aidan took her hand as Hans and Erik came awake. Soon they were all standing around her bed. "How long have I been out? What happened? Why am I here?" She was starting to get agitated.

Aidan sat on her bed. "Look at me, a mhuirnín. Take it easy, okay? You' tove only been out for a couple of hours."

The nurse came back in with what must be her doctor. "How are you feeling, Miss Falk? How is your pain level?" the doctor asked.

She swallowed and her throat hurt. "I need some water." Aidan poured a cup from a pitcher on her roll away table.

The doctor continued, "I'm not surprised. You were very dehydrated and you are pretty banged up. Your body finally gave out and your blood pressure dropped. That's why you lost consciousness. How much do you remember?"

She closed her eyes. "I remember everything. I remember the taser. I remember being stuffed in a hot trunk. I remember fighting as he restrained me with tape." She looked at her wrist. It was splinted, and there were raw torn patches of skin from the tape he'd used.

"It's fractured, I'm afraid. It's too swollen to cast, especially with the tape burns. We'll have to do that tomorrow. It's a hairline, you won't be casted more than 4-6 weeks. You are getting anti-inflammatories along with your pain meds through your IV. Keep the hand elevated, and the nurse will be bringing cold packs," said the doctor.

He checked her face, his hands gentle. "Your facial damage is soft tissue only. No fractures. You have one stitch at your cheek. You had some shell imbedded in there. You have two stitches above your eye. I think you have a mild concussion, and we treated the electrical burn from the taser he used on you. The rest of your injuries were cleaned, but you should heal completely. You're very lucky. You're a very strong woman."

She looked at Aidan and her eyes blurred with tears. "Is he alive?"

Aidan squeezed her hand gently. "Aye, lass. He's alive, and he's in police custody. They took him to a different hospital, and he's guarded. He's got a pretty serious head injury thanks to that ninja tackle you pulled."

She smiled, but it didn't reach her eyes. "That can of whoop ass you opened probably didn't hurt either."

He met her gaze. "I'm deciding whether I am relieved that I didn't kill him, or angry." He shook off that thought. "The FBI will most likely take it from there. They found the other woman, the one from the photo. She's in a hospital in Wilmington. She's in pretty bad shape. He's going to go away for a long time."

The doctor cleared his throat, nervous. "Perhaps you would like your family to step out while we discuss some other things."

Aidan stiffened, as did her brother and father. Hans stood up. "Yes, we will go get some coffee and call your mom," he said, keeping his tone light.

Alanna sat up straighter. “They don’t have to leave. He didn’t rape me. He fully intended to, but he didn’t. He told me in great detail what his plans were, but he had more pressing concerns.” She spoke with a tight jaw, not making eye contact with anyone.

Her father spoke then, and she was grateful for the change in subject. “They’ll need a statement. For now the Sheriff’s Department will handle that.” Then sadness came over his face. “You are the bravest woman I’ve ever known. I am so sorry I didn’t protect you, my angel. I will go to my grave with nightmares about what could have happened to you.” Tears were falling silently down his face now.

“It’s okay, Daddy. You taught me to fight. You taught me to be brave and use my head. Those were the weapons I needed, and I had them because of you.” She hugged him. “I’m okay, Daddy. Aidan got to me in time. I’m going to be okay. That GPS bracelet saved my life.”

Erik was there, wrapping his long arms around both of them. “I love you, Anna Banana. I’m so proud of you and I am so sorry for everything.” Aidan started to slip out with the doctor, feeling like an intruder.

“Aidan, get back in here, son.” Aidan turned to find Hans standing in front of him, just outside the hospital room. He grabbed Aidan, squeezing the hell out of him. “You saved my baby. You and that group of knuckleheads risked everything for her, for us. I will never be able to repay this debt.”

Aidan whispered over his shoulder. “She’s the beating heart in my chest, Hans. You owe me nothing.”

Hans pulled back, a hand wrapped around Aidan’s skull. “Then you make it right. You take a leap of faith, son. She’s too fragile to do it. If you want her, you will have to step up.”

Alanna walked into her home, the late morning sun shining through the glass doors. She walked over to the piano, tapping with her good hand. Then she picked up her violin bow.

"You'll be playing again before you know it." Aidan came up behind her, resting his hands on her shoulders.

She said, "I guess I'll have to hire movers. This can't wait six weeks." She looked sad, looking around at all of her things that would be packed away.

Aidan took a deep breath. It was now or never. "I heard you, Alanna. When you were trying to talk him down. You tried to tell him…" Aidan's voice caught, "that I never loved you. That you were just a fling."

She turned to him, her eyes welling up. "I didn't mean for you to hear that. I just…" she closed her eyes. "It doesn't matter. I would have said anything to get the bastard to quit hitting me. I needed to keep him away from the house, from Seany. You can pretend you never heard it."

She was talking fast, walking away from him. He took her elbow gently. "Don't. Don't leave me, please." He pressed his forehead to her temple. "Can I hold you? Please, I need you." She sank into him.

He brushed the hair from her face, kissing her tears away. "You were wrong, you know. I do love you."

She tensed. "You don't have to say that."

He kissed her mouth, softly, avoiding the cuts. "Shh, love. Please let me finish, or I'll lose my courage. It's what I wanted to talk to you about. Do you remember? On the phone I told you that I had something to tell you."

He moved his lips over her face. "I love you. I didn't think I could. I wasn't sure I could love anyone, or that they could love me. I'd shut myself off from that possibility. But you did. You loved me and you let me love you, and I'm so grateful for that." Alanna was crying hard now, and she kissed Aidan's face softly, as he did hers. "I didn't come here for the bloody training. I came here for you. It was always you."

She touched his face. "I love you too, Aidan. I love you so much."

He put his forehead to hers. "I swore to myself I wouldn't get in the way of your new career, that I wouldn't ask you to choose, but bugger it all. I'm asking." He pulled her closer, raising her up to him. She furrowed her brow, not sure what she was hearing. "Choose me. Come with me. Tell that clinic in Virginia that they can't have you. Choose me, Alanna." His throat ached with emotion, his eyes were fierce.

Alanna leaned her head back to look at him, her eyes questioning. "I don't understand you. What are you asking me?"

He kissed her then, soft and sweet. "I'm asking you to marry me. Come back to Ireland with me. Move to England with me this winter. We can find a job for you. There are a lot of military men and women in the UK that need what you offer. You can continue your work." He stumbled over his words, arguing his case. "You'd be closer to Branna and your father. Spain would be a train ride from England."

She laughed, incredulously. "Aidan, are you sure this is really what you want? This isn't because of..."

He cut her off by taking her mouth.

The kiss was long, languorous, like he was drinking her in. He was careful, given how banged up her face was. He broke the kiss and whispered to her, just beneath her ear. "I love you. I've loved you since I met you. A rúnsearc, secret love." Alanna's breath stuttered and she took his kiss again, desperate to stay connected to him.

Aidan soothed her, stroking her back, her hair, whispering his endearments against her mouth. "You're more than I ever hoped for, Aidan," she finally said.

He smiled against her mouth. "Does that mean we'll be shipping your stuff overseas, then?"

She laughed, "I don't give a damn what comes overseas as long as you don't forget me." She wrapped her arms around his neck. The weight of her cast against his head brought him to heel.

"It's too soon for this. You need to heal. Let's just go lie in the loungers, watch the tide go out." She brushed her mouth against his neck.

"Is that a yes?" he asked. "Is it to the altar, then?"

She kissed him, her body rousing to his, even in her battered condition. "Yes, Aidan. I'll marry you."

Alanna slept for most of the morning, slipping in and out as Aidan brought her food, fed her from his hands, brought her sweet tea and water with lemon and anything else she wanted. Seany and Moe had been out during the morning, but they were home now.

Alanna pulled at Aidan's hand, needing his attention. "I'd like to see the men, could you call them? I'd like to see them all together before Seany leaves."

Seany blushed and Moe squeezed his hand. Alanna smiled at the young man. "I don't know how to thank you Seany. You're young, but you are such a strong, brave man, just like your brothers and your father. When Aidan told me you refused to be left behind…" her voice was shakey. Seany knelt beside her, where she lay on the deck chair.

"O'Briens protect each other, and their women. You belong with us, now. Everything is as it should be." She grabbed him and hugged him. "Don't cry, mo deirfiúr."

She wiped her eyes. "What does that mean?"

Seany smiled, chucking her under the chin playfully. "My sister."

"I'm so glad you're okay, Anna. That was like something out of a nightmare. I'm almost glad I didn't know until afterward," Moe said softly.

Alanna was serious when she answered the young girl. "It's something I wish you never had to hear about, Moe. It was an ugly business, and it all started when I wasn't much older than you. The only advice I will ever give you on the matter is that you can't be afraid to tell. You can't let anyone scare or shame you into keeping a secret like I did. Do you understand?"

Moe nodded. "I do."

Within two hours, the men were at the beach house. The only heroes missing out of the group were Don and Sheila, but she would get to them as well. She was going to give that old chief petty officer a thank you hug if she had to swim out to his boat from Sheila's dock.

Maria and Hatsu were there as well. The two women could throw together food like nothing Alanna had seen before. Maria sat next to Alanna on the couch, the baby nursing under a blanket. "We're so glad you are okay. I don't have to tell you that you had me shitting egg rolls for the better part of ten hours."

Alanna put her head on Maria's shoulder. "I'm going to miss you, Maria. And that little boy is going to haunt my hormonal dreams."

Maria laughed, "You'll have your own someday. Any news on that front?" Alanna just gave her a sly smile. "What? Don't you dare hold out on me! I need the deets!"

Just then, Aidan approached, taking Alanna by the hand. "Time for a speech, darlin'. Are ye ready?"

Alanna stood before the men in her house, and suddenly her throat was so tight that she could barely speak. "Some people would think that an experience like mine would make a woman wary of men, and I suppose they would have their reasons." She cleared her throat, trying to steady herself and get the words just right. "But when I think about yesterday, I won't think about Steve Andrews, or at least I'll try not to. He might never totally go away, but he won't color the rest of my life with fear or with suspicion of men. What I will remember," her voice broke on a sob. She took a few breaths as Aidan squeezed her shoulders. "What I will remember is the sight of you all coming through the scrub. My rescuers. I'll remember Doc O'Malley pulling me out of harm's way. I'll remember Hector and Aidan leading you all out of the bush to save me. I'll remember it all, and I'll never forget your faces. I love you guys. I owe you everything."

One of the men gave a whoop, and they all yelled. She went around to each of them and hugged and kissed them. Hector held on to her, then he looked at her cast. "I wish you didn't have this all in your head, but you were so brave, baby girl. You were brave and strong, and when I talk to my girls about all of this stuff, I am going to remember your flying tackle on that son of a bitch." He lifted her cast, touched her stitches on her face. "We all have battle wounds, bebita. And now you have yours."

Aidan walked over to Alanna and put his arm around her. He turned to the group and cleared his throat. "We have one more bit of news, and we thought you should be the first to know. This beautiful lass has agreed to bugger the whole deal with her new job in Virginia and be my wife instead."

The men went ballistic and the women burst into tears.

"When's the wedding? Is it here or back home?" John asked.

Aidan's face drew a blank. "I, uh, well that's a good question. We haven't..."

Alanna cut him off. "The wedding will be in Ireland, in Aidan's home town."

His face was radiant and he kissed her without apology. "Thank you, mo chroí. My mother will be beside herself."

Everyone left, and Moe and Seany helped Aidan clean up the kitchen. Then they went next door to say their goodbyes. Aidan decided to give them their privacy, given the fact that Seany would fly back to Ireland tomorrow. "This is a hard lesson. They're so young. He adores her, though. The depth of his feelings is so much more than I was capable of at his age," Aidan said.

Alanna sighed. "They're both remarkable people. I feel awful for them. It's out of their control, the leaving."

Seany slid a cup of tea in front of Moe, her serious grey eyes not meeting his. "Maybe you could come to see me," Seany said.

She looked up from her tea, a small smile turning up. "My parents would never agree to that. I'd have to wait until I was eighteen, and still they wouldn't like it."

Seany nodded, "I understand. I do."

He came around the counter and stood beside her. "Aren't you going to have any tea?" Moe said. Her tone was even, but Seany felt the same nervous energy thrumming through her.

"I don't want any tea just now." Then he lifted her face to his and kissed her. It was so familiar, the feel of each other, the taste of their kisses. Kissing was all they had done, but they'd done it a lot, savoring the one thing that they'd allowed themselves.

Moe came up on her toes, emboldened by their raw feelings. She wrapped her arms around his neck and pulled him into her. He felt her body shudder and he pulled her closer. The contact causing a jolt through both of them. "Just once, Seany. Lie down with me. I need to feel you. Please."

Seany growled into her neck. "Jesus girl, you're playing with fire."

She took his hand. "I won't let it go too far, neither will you. I just want something more. Just a little more for our last night."

He was, of course, completely helpless to deny her. He wanted something more, too. Just to touch her. To lie with her and feel what it was like to press himself against her. So, he went.

42

After talking to her parents and brother, Alanna was emotionally exhausted. Everyone was thrilled. Even her mother, who had sworn that she was *against the institution of marriage because it stifled the woman,* was ecstatic.

Aidan watched her now, sleeping soundly on their bed. They needed to call his family, but it could wait for a couple of hours, until she got some more rest. He checked the time and knew that it was time for Moe to get home. She had a curfew.

He walked next door, and he didn't find them in the living room. The door to Seany's room was cracked, so he listened. Then he eased it open. There they were, both asleep and holding each other. The clothes were askew, but they were on. Thank God.

He closed the door back and knocked. They both woke instantly, jumping out of bed. They came out. Moe, never one for big emotions, was blushing. "I don't want you to miss your curfew. I'm sorry. I know this is hard."

Moe smiled sadly. "I'm a military kid. Hard goodbyes are my specialty."

She swallowed, fighting tears, and turned to Seany. "Walk me to the car?" Then she turned to Aidan. "I'm glad about you and Miss Anna. You two are meant to be together. I wish I could come to the wedding, but I will look for pictures." Then she hugged him and walked out of the house, with Seany trailing behind her.

Ten minutes later Sean Jr. came upstairs and Aidan's heart broke for him. He hugged his brother.

"It was worth it. The time we got was worth the pain that will come now," Seany said in his shoulder.

Aidan pulled back and looked at him, marveling at what a remarkable young man he was turning out to be. He nodded. "Then I'm glad for you, brother."

Alanna was struggling in her sleep, Aidan woke to her noises, fear and panic in the soft, unintelligible sounds. She woke with a jolt, her whole body flailing. Aidan reached above him to the small lantern she kept on the bed post. The lantern she used when he had nightmares. He turned on the dim light, but it was enough to see her face, and for her to see him. "I'm here, my love. It's me. You're okay." She was sweating, panting, but the panic gave way to relief.

She clung to him. "Did I dream the rest? Are you really taking me with you?" Her voice was strained, tears at the corners of her eyes.

Aidan spoke in soothing tones. "It wasn't a dream. I won't let you go. I'm yours, darlin'. I'm yours and you are mine, a chuisle." He kissed her then. There was no heat in it. Only comfort. That's what she needed.

"I know it's the middle of the night, but I was thinking," she said.

"You want to call Ireland?" he said, smiling.

She nodded. "I need something good right now. Then we can go back to sleep."

Aidan grabbed his phone. "I'll text them and give them an hour to get everyone together. Then we'll video call them." As he did that, Alanna rested her head on his chest. "I can't believe I am going to live in Belfast. Then in England. I can't believe this is real."

Aidan put his phone down and rubbed his hand over her smooth hair. "I can't believe you'd give up your job for me."

She raised up taking his head in her hands. "Nothing is more important to me then being with you. I can find a job in the UK. I know that Dr. Jennings would love to help me. She'll understand about the Virginia job. Maybe that jerk Rick can take my job," she joked.

Aidan laughed, "Well, he's not invited to the wedding. That's for feckin sure. You need to call Tim, though."

Alanna cocked her head. "You like him, don't you?"

Aidan nodded. "He's been pushing me this way all along. He's a good friend to you. To me too, I suppose. It would be nice if he could come. He'd like my brothers."

Alanna rolled over, running her fingers through her hair. "I just want my dad and brother there. My best friend already conveniently lives there. My grandparents may or may not be able to make it. They are getting old and they don't travel much. My dad's parents are old southern high society, however. We can expect a nice gift."

Aidan perked up. "Really? I'm marrying a rich spinster, then? That is a bonus." She smacked him and he rolled over on her. "You're fun to tease, hen. I think I'll not give it up until we are old and gray."

She smiled. "I hope not even then." Then she kissed him, raising up to him to give him her mouth. He melted into her, taking the kiss, slow and soft. "Is this okay? I don't want you to rush it. You've been through a lot."

She answered him with another kiss. "You're mine, Irishman. We need to seal the deal."

He laughed, loving that sweet, high, southern drawl of hers. "So we do." Then he took her hand. "I'll get you a ring. I promise. I wanted to wait until we got to Ireland, if that's okay. I can try to find something here if you don't want to wait."

Alanna shook her head. "I don't need a ring to bind me to you, Aidan."

He kissed her then, a little more purpose behind it now. "Aye. You're my mate. I wasn't sure I believed in all of that before, but I knew it as soon as I saw you." His voice was desperate as he removed her t-shirt, then slid her panties off. Then he was touching her, tasting her skin, slipping inside her. He rolled over, putting her above him. She put her hands on his chest, her cast rough against his skin. He touched it.

"Don't think about it Aidan. Look at me." Her eyes pulled him in, and then all he saw was her.

Brigid was pacing the floor. "Has it been an hour? Let's just call!"

Sorcha gave her a chiding look. "We need to wait for Branna. She'll be here…ah there she is!" Branna walked in with one twin and Michael the other. She hugged Caitlyn and Patrick who were visiting for the weekend.

"Do you know what it's about? Is it something about Anna? I thought she was released? What if she's hurt worse than they thought!" she said.

Patrick took Brian out of her arms. "Don't borrow trouble, lass. We'll find out soon enough." As soon as the words were out of his mouth, the video call came through.

Brigid lurched toward the computer. Aidan and Alanna were both on the screen and Brigid squealed. Branna shoved her butt over and sat on the chair with her. "Are you okay? Oh my God, is that a cast? Are those stitches?" Branna immediately started crying, which got Brigid and Caitlyn going.

Sorcha was shaking with fury as Sean put his arm around her. He felt the same way. "She's home and she's safe. The rest will heal, Sorcha. We'll make sure of it." Sean said.

Alanna nodded. "Yes, I'm okay. Aidan's been taking good care of me." Sorcha stifled a sob, and now all of the women were crying. "Please don't cry. I'm okay."

Patrick spoke then. "I've not had the pleasure, darlin. But this is my Caitlyn and we're awfully glad to hear you're okay. You're a brave, fierce woman. We're looking forward to your visit."

Caitlyn chimed in. "You can stay with us if you come to Dublin. Then you can meet Tadgh and Liam as well." Alanna was beaming, looking at this big family.

It was Brigid who got to the point. "It must be the middle of the night there. Is everything okay?"

Aidan smiled. "Yes, Alanna was having trouble sleeping so we wanted to call. We've got some news we thought you'd want to hear."

Aidan could see everyone lean in closer to the screen. "Well, it appears her trip to Ireland will be sooner than she'd planned. Since the job in Virginia didn't work out, she'll be coming earlier."

The faces fell. "Oh, well I'm sorry about the job. I thought you had it for sure?" Branna said awkwardly.

Alanna nudged Aidan. "Don't tease them."

He laughed. "Aye well, seeing how she'll be marrying me, she decided to turn the job down." Dead silence. Then Brigid and Branna squealed so loud the speakers on the computer vibrated. Then O'Brien men were hooting and fist bumping in the background.

Then Sorcha was pushing Brigid off the chair, right onto the floor. "My sweet baby boy! Thank the Lord. Oh, Alanna. My dear, sweet girl. Another daughter." Then she put her hands over her face, overcome with emotion.

Branna hugged her. Her own face tear stained. "Oh my God. I prayed for this. All of my scheming and plotting actually worked!" Everyone started laughing.

"Yer a wee, scheming little hellcat, deirfiúr, but considering how well this all worked out in my favor, I'll let it slide," Aidan said.

Aidan came back from the airport with a long face. He missed his brother already. Something else was wrong, though. Alanna could sense it. "Something is up. I can tell. Something you don't want to tell me."

Aidan sighed. "Christ, girl. You're going to fit right in with that peahen sister of mine. Nose like a bloodhound." He sat next to her on the deck. "It's Hector. He's under investigation."

She sucked in a breath. "Because of me?"

"Because he took the men on a mission that wasn't approved. They would have never let him do it. He didn't care. Said he'd do it all over again."

She shook her head. "If you had waited even an hour I would be beaten more, maybe raped, maybe on my way to Mexico with a bunch of drug dealers. We have to do something!"

Aidan nodded. "Yes, you're right."

Alanna stood with purpose. "I'll be ready in twenty minutes."

Alanna and Aidan walked into the Division headquarters. They weaved down a hallway to the Commanding Officer's office. To their amazement, the female police officer from the island was walking out of the office. She winked at them both and took her leave.

"I'll go in alone," she said. When the duty officer took her into the office, the colonel behind the desk jerked visibly at the sight of her. She'd deliberately worn no makeup, pulled her hair back so that he got a good look at her battered face. She had on a pink sundress, probably the most girlish thing she owned. It showed the cuts and scrapes on her legs, showed the abrasions and tearing around her one wrist from the tape, and the cast on the other side, the ligature marks around her neck and finger bruises on her arms. *Take a good look, Colonel.*

He came around the desk. She put her hand out. "Good morning, sir. Thank you for seeing me so quickly." His face was stiff, but his eyes were ruined. She saw the photos, a picture of his daughter on her graduation day, another one of his other daughter posing with a soccer ball.

"Please, Miss Falk. Sit down. I can't even tell you how sorry I am that this all happened to you."

She looked at the photos, then at him. "Yes, I suppose you can at least attempt to put yourself in my father's shoes."

She smiled, wincing at her busted lip and putting a finger to it. Then she took a hanky out of her purse and dabbed. "You'll have to excuse my appearance. Now, about this investigation involving your Marines."

He put a hand up. "Sweetheart, you shouldn't worry yourself about that."

She interrupted. "I beg to differ. I was at the mercy of two entities, lying there in the dirt, bound and beaten. Local law enforcement red tape and a brutal sex offender. A sex offender that spent his time telling me all the things he was going to do to me once the boat showed up to take us to Mexico." The Colonel's face blanched. "You didn't know about that, I'll guess. Well, let me enlighten you."

The high ranking Marine sat and listened, respectful and quiet. He could no more deny her a say then he could have denied his own wife or daughters. He was pale, his mouth twisted with anger as she explained not only what had happened, but the turf disputes of the law enforcement involved. The longer she'd been on that island, the more injuries she'd sustained. As for the serious injuries sustained by Steve. She'd done that, not the men. They'd saved her.

According to the Coast Guard, they'd intercepted the drug boat a few miles away. The men had confessed that they'd been hired to take her and her attacker into international waters and eventually to Mexico. If they'd waited for the local police or the FBI, they wouldn't have come in time. "If Major Diaz and his Marines hadn't come for me, I'd be in Mexico being raped, tortured, and eventually murdered. My father might not have even had a body to bury." The Colonel was rubbing his brow, obviously distressed.

"The men had their personal weapons. They were not in uniform. They did not use any government equipment or water crafts. They came for me because they care about me, and they were helping my fiancé and my father. They saved me, Colonel. You should be giving them an award, not looking for a way to punish them. If it had been your own daughter, or the woman you loved, what would you have done? If you knew where they were, would you have waited?" The Colonel's face hardened. "Right. You'd have done whatever you had to in order to get them back," she said.

She put her hands flat on her knees. "The man that did this to me is up on charges from other women as well. He won't be causing any trouble. He'll be lucky if he doesn't die in prison. Your men did that. All I want is for you to do right by them. If you don't, then it's all but saying that my life wasn't worth putting their bacon on the line."

The Colonel smiled. "Well, you aren't the first one in my office this morning, or on the phone, that is singing the praises of those Marines. I can tell you, however, that your visit has been the most compelling. The mere sight of you makes me want to go kill that bastard myself, if you'll pardon my candor. I heard every word you said, Miss Falk. I swear to you that I will do right by Major Diaz and the other men. Can you trust me to do that?"

She nodded, getting up from the chair. He followed her out of the office. "And congratulations to you both. I've heard some pretty remarkable things about you as well, Captain O'Brien. You might have some recognition coming your way as well. I'll be contacting your superiors in Northern Ireland," he said, nodding at Aidan.

"Thank you, sir," Aidan said, shaking his hand. "It's been an honor training with your men, Sir. Even the young ones. I wouldn't hesitate to fight alongside any of them. And that corpsman did some fancy work at the scene. He treated Alanna's injuries and her attacker."

The Colonel gave a brisk nod, "I will keep that in mind, Captain."

Aidan was making a sandwich in the kitchen when he looked at Alanna's dry erase calendar. Since he had spilled the beans, she kept it in plain view. She'd had to cancel her fitness classes. "I paid your rent. I put the money in Branna's account," he said.

Alanna bristled. "You didn't have to do that."

Aidan looked at her plainly. "You're going to be my wife. And you're injured. You're also going to have to go through some expense to move. Please don't be a pill about this."

She folded her arms, cocking her head. "You paid my rent last month didn't you?" He said nothing. "Aidan. Didn't you?"

He didn't look up from the pastrami on rye he was making. "I did." He braced himself for an argument.

She approached him. "Thank you," she said, putting her hand on his arm. He stopped what he was doing and his brows were up. "Don't look so surprised. It would be ridiculous for me to chastise you, considering I don't have a job yet."

Aidan pulled her in for a kiss. "I can take care of you. I have a sizable savings. If you can't find a job when we move, don't feel pressured. You can volunteer, you can travel back and forth to Ireland, you can…" he paused.

"Finish what you were going to say," she said.

He shrugged. "Nothing, all I'm getting at is that there's no pressure. We're financially comfortable. You've been under a lot of stress these last six months. I don't want you to worry about money."

She exhaled. "My instinct is to resist. You know that about me."

He pulled her in closer. "Aye, but you've never had a partner before. I'm not your da. I'll be your husband. We're a team."

Her smile was radiant. She pulled away and bumped him over, away from the counter. "Let me make your sandwich. You can start boxing up my books."

He laughed. "Oh, yes. We can't leave all of those kilt-lifters and panty droppers and bodice rippers behind."

She giggled, "No way. We might find a country house with a stable door. We want to do our homework."

43

Aidan came home from the field, tired and muddy. He stripped under the house and put his uniform right in the wash. He showered in the outdoor shower, not wanting to foul up the house or the indoor shower with mud. He went up the side stairway to the deck. When he slid the door open, he heard her. She was on a video chat in the bedroom.

Alanna was convinced that little Cora was hands down the cutest little girl she'd ever seen. "I'm sorry little darlin'. You're uncle Aidan isn't home yet. Can I help you?"

Cora smiled at her in a uniquely childlike way. Sweetness mixed with mischief. "Mama said you sing, too. She said you're going to marry uncle Aidan. Can I be in your wedding?"

Brigid yelled in the back ground. "Cora! That is not polite."

Alanna giggled. "Why of course. You're going to be my right hand girl. You need to make sure that your momma and granny and Auntie Branna are doing everything just right. Can you do that?"

Cora nodded seriously. "I dreamed of you, Auntie Alanna. I saw you all banged up on the ground. I'm sorry you got hurt, but you're going to be okay. You'll come live near us, and we've got all sorts of big men to protect you. Uncle Aidan is very strong."

Alanna fought for composure. The little girl was so beautiful, her voice like a song with rolling r's and a childish lilt. "You're right, baby. Uncle Aidan is my hero. He'll always take care of me. Now, about that bedtime. Tell me what I can do."

Cora cocked one eye, concentrating. "I think I'll need a song, please."

"Okay, I might not know the songs you're used to but I think I can handle a bedtime song. Do you like Disney movies?"

Cora clapped, "Oh yes."

She waved her cast in the air. "I'm going to have to do this without the piano or violin for now."

Aidan kept in the shadows, listening to Alanna with Cora. He could tell that she loved children. She'd been so good with the children of those military men, and she was a natural with babies. Now she was singing to Cora, and a bone deep longing washed over him.

> *Far away, long ago, glowing dim as an ember.*
> *Things my heart used to know, things it yearns to remember...*

He looked closer, seeing Cora on the screen. She threw her arms out and started to sing along. He could barely contain a laugh, the whole scene was so sweet.

> *Someone holds me safe and warm, horses prance through a silver storm...*

Then his sister was there, singing at the top of her lungs, they all were. *Girls and their Disney songs,* he thought. They ended on a high note, all of them arms stretched wide.

Aidan started clapping and Alanna yipped like a puppy, startled at his appearance.

Cora squealed with laughter. "Uncle Aidan, Mammy said it's rude to lurk in corners and listen!" Her hands were on her hips, but she couldn't hide her delight.

"Yes, well I was waiting for the part where the prince comes in." Alanna was in the same exact position as little Cora. Face red, hands on her hips. He grabbed her and dipped her. She squeaked and then she laughed. "Kiss her Uncle Aidan! Kiss her like Prince Charming!"

Aidan cocked a brow. "That's my cue." Then he dipped his head and kissed her. Brigid and Cora were clapping and cheering. Alanna laughed under his mouth. Her blush tripled when Finn popped his head on to the screen. "Now that's how it's done, brother. By the way, you realize you've got nothin' but a towel on?"

The next month went by fast. Alanna spent her spare time getting her household together. She let Erik, her father, and Tim pick from her furniture. They came in and out, mostly on weekends, wanting to spend as much time as they could with her. She actually enjoyed the downtime. She put a plastic bag over her cast and played on the beach, she cooked big, extravagant meals that she hadn't had time for in a long time. She cleaned and packed up as much as she could. She'd contacted a realtor for Branna and they'd even started the process of putting the houses on the market.

Aidan came in and out, helping with the packing, spending the evenings telling Alanna about Ireland and England. One afternoon he came in early to find Alanna surrounded by clothes. They'd all been pulled out of her drawers and closet. She was muttering, throwing jeans across the room. He stood in the doorway of her bedroom both baffled and amused. "What's all this?" She looked at him and he took a step back. He had a sister, he knew this was some form of estrogen induced fury. "Lass, you look like a prickly porcupine. What's the matter?"

She tossed jeans at him and they bounced off his chest. "That's what's the matter. They're too tight! All that studying, this stupid cast, too much fried okra! I look like a doughy sow!"

He laughed and then immediately knew that was a mistake. "It's not funny! I'm going to go to Ireland and have to squeeze these sweaty ham hocks into some sort of clothing to meet your family. Walk down the aisle," she pointed at him, "No! Hoof it down the aisle into the arms of some hot Irishman who thought he was getting a firm, sexy yoga instructor. I have scars on my face. I'm a mess!"

Aidan grabbed her up in his arms. "Bloody hell, woman. Are you listening to yourself?" Then he shrugged, "Besides, I love ham." There was humor in is voice, but she growled. He was trying not to laugh, but she was adorable when she was pissed. She was being ridiculous, of course. He turned her in his arms, taking her face in his hands. "You're so beautiful it near stops my heart to look at you."

"You're just saying that. You have to say that!"

He couldn't think of what else to do, so he threw her down on the bed, right on top of the pile of clothes. Words of appeasement were not going to help. He put her arms above her head, her breasts rising high under her t-shirt. He growled and buried his face in them. He pressed his arousal into her hips. "Feel what you do to me, little hammy."

Her face was murderous. He laughed and pressed his hips into her again. He covered her mouth and moaned as he moved his hips. Then he drew his hands down, sliding her shirt up and over her head. He smothered her breasts with hot kisses. "Christ, you're so beautiful. You are perfection." There was nothing patronizing about his tone, which is what finally got through to her. He kissed down her tummy, lean and soft at the same time.

He yanked her shorts off. "Aidan, you're cheating me out of my meltdown!" She tried to sound stern, but the sentence ended on a squeak as he nipped her thigh.

"Shut yer gob, ye wee, daft harpy. I've got business down here, and you're wrecking the mood." He covered her thighs, her stomach, where her leg met her bottom with hot, suckling kisses. She was panting. "I'm going to kiss every beautiful inch of you, until you get my meaning, hen." Then he dipped his head down, all she could do was gasp.

After he'd improved her disposition, they lay together, covered in the scent of each other. The piles of clothing had been pushed to the floor and he stroked her and kissed her all over, then flipped her on her stomach. He went under the covers, and suddenly she was wiggling and screeching. "What are you doing? Aidan! Stop looking at my butt!"

He was laughing, a husky, playful laugh. "I'm checking you for ticks."

She tried to roll over, swatting at him with her good hand. "I do not have ticks. Ah! Aidan! I definitely don't have them in there!"

He popped out from under the covers. "Doc O'Malley said you can't be too careful. You have to look in all the nooks and crannies." His smile was devilish. He shot back under the covers, and her squeals rang through the house.

Aidan came home the next evening and went right to the computer. "Something's up. I need to call home." His father appeared on the screen.

"It's your Gran. She's taken a spill. She broke her ankle."

Aidan cursed. "That house is getting too much for them."

Sean nodded, agreeing. "We are going to put a rented bed downstairs."

Aidan shook his head. "No, just go to my flat. I've got the spare room. Take that bed."

Sean's face brightened. "Aye, good thinking. We'll do that. She's fine, though. That ankle is just going to need time. They don't heal so well at her age."

Aidan got to thinking about that. "Do ye think they'd be interested in going back to the flat? After we move to England."

Sean cocked a brow. "Well, it's got a lift. It might be something to think about. Try to call your Gran. She's beside herself that you've found a wife."

That warmed Aidan. "I'll do that. I've missed her. Now she can quit trying to marry me off to the bank clerk."

A few days later, Branna called to talk to Aidan. "I was thinking. I need to roll this money into a new investment once I sell the island houses. What do you think about me buying Gran and Grandad's house in the North? Your ma said it's dated, but in good shape. I could turn it into a vacation rental. They could take Sorcha's flat and the money would give them a big nest egg for their retirement."

So it was done. Once Aidan and Alanna moved out of the North, his mother's parents would move back into the flat they'd left almost forty years ago. They'd keep their house just outside of Belfast in the family. It was the perfect solution.

Training had been brutal this week. It was hot as hell. Aidan was exhausted and sweating, pouring water into his mouth from his water bladder. "Christ, it's hot. Don't ye get a breeze, being this close to the ocean?"

John was next to him, sprawled on the ground. "Not with all of the trees for cover. Fuck me. I think something is crawling in my pants! Ow!" He jumped up, yanking his pant leg up. "Fucking ants! Ah! I hate fire ants!"

Aidan shook his head. "Ye feckin think ye'd learn, brother. Doc! Get over here with that magic stick. The Captain sat down in another feckin ant hill." The rumble of laughter traveled through the men.

Sergeant Porter plopped down beside Aidan as Doc went after Denario with his bug bite remedy. "Sir, we're going to miss your Irish ass. Now the most interesting accent is going to be Washington over there with his Cajun accent.

"That's Creole, mother fucker. Get it right! This is pure plantation bred!"

Sergeant Williams gave him a shove. "Bullshit," he laughed. "Says the little rich boy that went to the private high school."

Washington was cackling. "All right. You got me there. My granddaddy was a foreman in the sugar factory, and my daddy is an accountant. What does your daddy do, Captain?"

Aidan took another long draw on his water, then cleared his throat. "Garda, twenty-five years."

Washington whistled. "That's like federal police, right? Not bad, not bad. No wonder you're such a boy scout. Daddy didn't play."

Aidan laughed, "No, he didn't. My mother, though. She's a wee thing, but God almighty, don't piss her off." He shuddered to get his point across.

Washington laughed at that. "Brother, you don't have to tell me. My momma whooped my ass ten times more than my daddy ever did. I got caught vandalizing train cars when I was about thirteen. Hot damn, she kicked my ass down the street, and all the way to the church. Put me down in front of that altar and told me to beg for mercy from the good Lawd, cuz I wasn't getting any from her!" Corporal Washington was an animated young man, and the men all chuckled as his voice escalated. "Ah, but she's a good woman. She took good care of us, kept us out of trouble. Put us in good schools."

Williams broke into the conversation. "Speaking of good women, when is the wedding, Sir? Are you gonna drag your feet on this?"

Aidan shook his head. "Hell no, brother. I've got to get her in front of the priest before she has the chance to change her mind."

Williams put his fist up. "Amen to that, Captain."

Aidan fist bumped him. "I'm going to miss you lads, too." He slapped Porter on the back. "If you're ever over on my side of the ocean, you make sure to see me. It goes without saying that you're all invited to the wedding."

44

Hector and John sat with Aidan on the deck of the beach house, a beer in their fists. The women were down on the beach, playing with the children. Aidan watched Alanna sitting in the sand, the baby in her lap. She kissed little Aidan, lifted him and blew raspberries on his tummy. They could see his toothless grin from thirty feet away. "Hard to believe the three months went by so fast," Hector said. "It feels like yesterday we were meeting on this deck."

John nodded. "So, Aidan. Maria's mother said she'd keep Frankie and Clara. We'll be at the wedding next month."

Aidan popped up in his chair. "Holy shit, no kidding. That is outstanding! I suppose you'll be bringing the little one?"

"Yeah, he's still on the tit. Won't even take a bottle. Not that I can blame him." John wiggled his eyebrows and Hector snorted.

"Ah, little ones like that are easy. They sleep on the plane as long as momma is right nearby. It's the toddlers that kick your ass."

John pointed a finger. "Exactly, which is why those two little hell raisers are staying back."

"I wish Hatsu and I could go, I really do. We've had this trip to Japan planned for a year," Hector said.

Aidan waved a dismissive hand. "Not at all, brother. I know you'll be thinking about us. Guess who else is coming?" They stopped the beers going to their mouths in sync, and turned expectantly. "Doc O'Malley and Sergeant Porter."

Hector's brows went up. "Really? Damn, that's some extravagant living for young guys. Then again, Porter has some serious hero worship going on with you."

John said, "Total man-crush. You took those boys on some high adventure. They aren't likely to forget you."

Aidan said, "I'll not forget them, either. They'll stay in a hostel for the wedding, but then they're going to spend a few days in Dublin with my brother Liam. He and Tadgh will most likely get them drunk and laid."

Hector smacked his thigh, "Good for them! It is good to have connections."

Aidan turned to John, "You and Maria will stay with Brigid. She's got two children as well, so you won't be hurting for help with wee Aidan. Cora has designated herself the child minder at the ripe old age of five. My parents and Aunt Katie and my Da's parents will put up everyone else. It'll be an intimate affair. Just close friends and family and the village people."

John said, "Well, tell your sister we appreciate that. Maria will want to call her."

Aidan nodded absently, but his eyes were back on Alanna. She was curled on her side now, the baby curled into her, sleeping on a blanket. His heart squeezed.

"You're getting old, my friend. You best get started ASAP if you want to catch up to me. Oh, and I told you so. Just wanted to point that out."

Aidan looked at John, rolling his eyes. "Christ, I suppose you did, didn't you."

Jacksonville Airport, NC

Alanna hugged her father with all of her might. "I'll see you in a month, right?" Hans cradled her head in his big palm, looking over her face.

"My baby girl. It seems like yesterday that I could cradle you in one arm. One month, Miss Priss. Then I'll be in Spain by Christmas. Once you two get settled, you can expect a visit in England."

Alanna's tears were starting. She grabbed him again, tight around his neck like she did when she was small. "I love you. You're the best daddy in the world." She was crying now, talking in a whisper. She wiped her eyes and went to her brother.

He scooped her up. "Everything is different now, Anna Banana. Things will be different. I promise. I love you."

She kissed his cheek. "I love you, too. Erik. I'll see you soon." She moved on to Tim. "You're coming, right? Promise me?"

He pulled her to him. "I wouldn't miss it." He kissed her between the eyes. "Maybe you can fix me up with some little Irish honey who doesn't mind the stump." He was kidding, of course, but she saw something in his face that looked like loneliness, like an acknowledgement of a door closed, forever.

Alanna smiled a crooked smile and shrugged. "Well, I don't know anyone that isn't married, but I think we can arrange some wife hunting for you."

Aidan watched Alanna say goodbye to her men, and a pang of guilt hit him. As if he'd read his mind, Hans spoke. "Don't you worry about us. We'll never be far, Aidan. All I ever wanted at this phase in my life is to see my daughter with a good man. I've known it from the beginning. You two are good for each other. I'll never be able to repay you for being there when I couldn't be. I will meet my maker and still be in your debt."

Aidan hugged Hans, thumping him on the back. "I'll take care of her. I swear it."

They sat at the gate, waiting to board when Aidan got a text. He chuckled.

"Brigid again?" she asked.

He smiled, "Aye, she is fit to be tied."

Alanna nudged him. "You know, we could have flown into Dublin."

He looked out the window, lost in his thoughts for a moment. "I want to show you my flat, our flat. I want to show you where I work. I guess I'm being selfish. I need a few days with you, just us. It's a simple place in the city. It's not like what you're used to. You might see it and change your mind, hop back on the first plane you can find."

His tone was teasing, but she sensed a vulnerability in him. "I'm not going anywhere, Aidan."

He squeezed her hand. "I want to go see Gran as well. Poor thing just wants to do so much and her body doesn't always keep up with her spirit." Alanna understood that. "I'm sorry I didn't get to meet your grandparents," Aidan said.

Alanna shrugged. "There's time. We've got longevity on both sides." She shrugged. "If Steve doesn't plead guilty outright, we may have to come home for the trial. Are you going to be able to do that?"

Aidan nodded. "I'd never let you go through that alone. They deposed all of us, the whole team. They won't be able to pull the others out of a combat zone. Honestly, he's a fool if he doesn't take some sort of plea. We're talking about three women in three different jurisdictions, but if the feds take over, he'll be lucky if he doesn't die in prison. Don't think about it, darlin. Maybe we won't have to come back."

Alanna rubbed her wrist, her cast freshly off. "I won't. I won't think about it anymore. I just want to look ahead. I want to think about being your wife."

He kissed her, just a touch of his mouth to hers. "I love you, mo ghrá."

Aidan opened the door to his flat, weighed down with luggage. They walked in, flipping light switches as they entered. He dropped his bags and helped Alanna with hers. Then he looked around. He was used to this, the strange feeling of getting reacquainted with his home after a long absence. He wasn't used to having someone next to him, however. This was going to be their home until they moved. Then they would look for a home to rent in England, together.

"Does it feel strange? Having me here, I mean? It must." Aidan turned to her, and there was a hint of insecurity in her eyes.

"It's strange, but in a good way." He looked down, rubbing his hand on the counter. "I never thought I'd be this happy." She put her hand over his and squeezed. Something occurred to him. "When you talked to Branna, you said you needed an appointment with Doc Mary. Is everything okay?"

Alanna blushed. "Yes, totally fine. It's just, I am due for another shot. I should have done it last week, but we've been so busy. I just kind of forgot. Do you mind using condoms for a week? I picked some up at the drugstore before we left." Her face was flushed, mainly because Aidan was so quiet. "I'm sorry. I don't like the idea of using them either. If you want to just wait…"

Aidan cut her off with a kiss. "Whatever you need. It's your body, darlin."

She smiled, but it didn't quite reach her eyes.

They had dinner in the city, not far from the flat. They talked for hours, walking around the neighborhood. Aidan showed her interesting buildings, the bakery where he bought his bread when his Gran hadn't had time to bring some to him. "Wow, you are a spoiled little boy. I guess I'm going to have to learn how to bake something other than my slutty brownies." She was grinning, her whole face was lit up with joy and excitement.

"We'll go see them tomorrow, if that's okay."

She nodded, "I want to stop and get her flowers. Is there a florist?"

Aidan's heart was about to burst. She loved his city. He had been worried. Living oceanfront could make your expectations high.

"England will be a lot different. The shire where the base is located is not so fast as all this."

She took his hands, walking backwards. "I know, I've been googling like crazy." Her face was flushed, her eyes sparkling.

He stopped, just taking in the sight of her. Then he pulled her into him, burying his face in her hair. "I swear to you, I will make you happy. I'll do everything I can to make you happy."

She leaned back, looking up at him. She smoothed her hand over his face. "I'm already happy, Aidan. Anywhere we go, I'll be happy as long as I'm with you. You don't have to worry. I grew up in this life. I will bloom wherever you plant me." Then she kissed him and the emotion that washed over him was a sort of pain.

"Let's go back home." His voice was hoarse, edgy. "I need you, mo chuisle. I need ye so badly, I feel like I'll burst from it."

Aidan hastily opened the door to their apartment, and then he had Alanna up against it, kissing her with everything he had. He made short work of her clothing as she fumbled with his trousers. He was hard, jutting out of his pants like he was trying to get at her. His desperation fed her own need. She understood it. He'd brought her into his life. They'd left their little sanctuary, the bubble they'd been living in. She was in his home, her home, now. He needed to make it real. He need to make love to her here, make her a part of this place. Bind her to him. She pulled his shirt over his head, running her hands down his muscled chest. He lifted her and pushed inside. He moaned. He was hard and she was hot and slick, gripping him. God, she didn't want to stop this, but she needed to.

"Aidan, condom." She choked it out as he surged inside her. He froze, panting against her ear. He was trembling with the effort of stopping. "I'm sorry. They're in the bedroom," she said.

He exhaled harshly and carried her into their bedroom. He laid her across the bed and she was under him, shaking with her own desire. It almost killed him, but he pulled out of her. He'd seen her put them in the nightstand. He'd not wanted the damn things anywhere near them. He didn't want anything between them. Not latex, not chemicals. "Aidan, what are you thinking right now?" He shook himself, realizing that he'd been hovering over her, looking at the condom still in its wrapper.

He rolled over on his back. "Nothing, love. Would ye like to help me with this?" He was trying to be playful, wiggling his brows, but she knew him. She took it from his hand, looked at it. "It's only a week. Then I can see Mary and we won't have to fuss with them anymore."

He touched her face. "Whatever you want, darlin'." She scrunched her brow. She laid over his chest, kissing his warm skin. "Please tell me what's on your mind. I can't read you right now. It seems like you're conflicted about something, like about using birth control. Is that it?"

His smile was contrived. He took the condom out of her hand, "I can do it. I just need you. Come to me, please. I just want to feel you." He pulled her to his mouth, then tore the wrapper open. She pushed his wrist to the bed, keeping him from putting it on himself. She took his mouth deeply, moving her body all over his as she took the condom out of his hand. His chest was pumping, his mouth urgent. He rolled her on her back. She raised up, giving him her mouth. "Tell me, Aidan. Say it." She moaned as she whispered against his mouth. "Tell me what you want."

He was poised at her entrance. "I want you. That's all I need."

She knew he was holding back. "You're allowed to want things. Tell me." His defenses were slipping, especially with the way she was moving against him. Her legs were wrapped around him, so warm and inviting.

He put his forehead to hers. "I want a child." His body shuddered, overcome by his own words. He pulled back from her, fighting the urge to plunge inside her. He sat on the edge of the bed, eyes shut tight. "We never talked about it. I'm sorry. It's too soon. I know I'm older than you. I've got my career started. I haven't even given you a ring yet. I don't know what the fuck I'm saying."

He wasn't looking at her, so she guided his face to hers with a palm. She was smiling. "So, you want a child. Just one?"

Her grin was disarming. He laughed, "No, not just one. Christ, girl. I don't know what I'm saying. If you wanted this now, you wouldn't be holding that condom. We've got time. Please don't feel like…" She cut him off by straddling him where he sat. Her body, so smooth and lithe, pressed against his. His breath stuttered and he grasped her hips. "I want to keep you in this bed until you forget what it was like without me inside you." He took her nipple in his mouth and he felt her heat up, felt her wetness.

She rolled her hips. "Aidan, don't stop. Please."

He broke away from her breast. "Look at me." He rolled her on her back, never breaking eye contact. He pressed, so slowly. Tears welled up in her eyes, tears of happiness. She was smiling. "I want this too. I wasn't sure you did, but I don't want to wait either. I want to start a big family with you." His smile was so sweet, so unguarded. So unlike him.

Then they were joined. Nothing between them. His hand slid from her wrist to her palm, sliding the condom out of her hand and onto the floor as he began to slide deep, grinding his hips. "Alanna, I don't think I can hold on. This is too…Jesus, I want this. I want to come inside you. I want to leave something inside you."

The scream started deep in her belly and peaked. It was his words. As much as his body brought her pleasure, his words were what brought her swiftly to climax. She wanted this. Her body arched under his, contracting inside, her hips straining to take all of him. Then he joined her, a guttural scream ripped from his throat.

They were silent for a bit, still joined, both ruined. He spoke, his voice shaking, "I shouldn't have put you in this position, I know that. I just can't bring myself to regret it."

She smiled, rolling on top of him. She propped her chin up on his chest. "I want this too, Aidan."

He exhaled. "Aye, but perhaps not so soon? You'll want to start your career. I won't hinder you. We'll make it work. We'll get a nanny if you find a job that pleases you. The base has some good resources. Are you sure?"

She sat up straddling him. "I am completely sure. To be honest, it might not happen for a few months. The medication I was on, sometimes it takes a while to clean out of your system."

Aidan brushed her nipple with his thumb. "So you're telling me it might take several months of persistent love making to get a child on you?" He chuckled. "I think I can suffer through that task."

Her eyes flared as he thickened underneath her. His eyes connected with hers and his voice held an ache. "When I saw you holding wee Aidan, that's when I knew. I knew I wanted to see my child grow inside you. I wanted to see my son or daughter at your breast. I wanted as many children as you'd give me." Then he kissed her, and didn't finish kissing her until the early morning light.

45

"Gran, you're as stubborn as Ma. Would ye sit and let me get the tea? Grandad, talk some sense into this woman, please."

Aidan's grandfather, Michael, just shook his head. "She's a Mullen by marriage, but that stubborn streak rubbed off. Edith, love. Sit down before you give the lad a stroke." Aidan carried the tray over to Alanna who was ordered to sit and be waited on. She was a guest, after all, and Aidan's new bride to be.

Granny Edith sat next to her. "They're pushy, aren't they?"

Alanna laughed. "They're right. I just got my cast off as well. It takes time. I know it's hard."

Edith's face was thoughtful. She put her hand gently over Alanna's healing wrist. It was thinner and pail. "You're a brave girl. I heard all about your trouble, my dear. You've the heart of a lion. You'll suit each other well."

She looked at Aidan. "He's the child of my heart. My first grandchild. I've prayed so long for him to find you."

Tears came to her eyes. Aidan poured her tea. "Now, Gran. Don't go getting all weepy on me, this is a joyous day. What do you think about the plan to move back into the city?"

She sighed, "I will miss my garden, but it will be fun to be back in the old place. We were young like you when we lived there.

Sorcha and her brother had to share a room. He complained, o'course. We had to put a curtain up, then we put him in the dining room when they got too big to share. We partitioned it off. It was terribly cramped. One bathroom for the four of us. By the time we could afford to buy this place, Sorcha was starting university."

"Michael, would you like to show Alanna the garden?" He gave her a knowing look.

"That would be lovely, dear. Alanna, come lass. My Edith has a way with the roses."

When they walked outside Aidan looked at his Gran. "What is it? Is everything okay?"

She patted his hand. She pulled a box out of her jumper pocket and laid it on the table. Aidan swallowed. "Gran, you don't…"

She put a hand up. "I've saved it for you. It was your Granddad's mother's ring. I wore it for years, but it is time. I thought about giving it to one of your brothers. I just couldn't do it. I knew who it belonged to. I've known since the day Sorcha put you in my arms. I noticed she hasn't got a ring yet. Please, Aidan. I want it to stay in the family."

He took the box and opened it. He exhaled on a shudder, putting his hand over his grandmother's frail, aging one. "It's beautiful, Gran. It's perfect. She'll love it."

The ring was white gold, art deco style from the thirties. The center stone was an emerald in the traditional square cut. The scroll and structured edges were typical of the art deco architecture and artwork of that time. It was genuinely unique and the emerald sparkled like green ice. "It is like her eyes."

His grandmother nodded. "Aye, I noticed that right away. She was meant to have it, and she was meant to be yours. You did well, boy. She'll make you very happy."

Alanna was looking up at Belfast castle and her smile was beatific. "This is so beautiful. It feels like a dream." She looked at him. "The last few days have been like a dream, Aidan. I can't wait to go see Branna, see your home town."

He took her in his arms. "Aye, it's time. I am being stalked by my entire family, asking when we are coming."

She smiled. "I bet they didn't expect you to come back engaged. Do you think they'll all be happy? I think your mom's parents liked me. Don't you?"

Aidan reached in his pocket. "Oh, I know they did. Everyone will love you. They'll be overjoyed to have another wedding. But first, we've got to make it official."

Alanna's eyes widened at the box in his hand. "When did you have time to get a ring?"

He shrugged, "I had help." He opened it toward her and she gasped.

"Oh my God, Aidan. This is an antique. It is exquisite." She put her hand over her mouth, stifling a sob. "It's the most perfect ring you could have ever chosen."

His voice was husky with emotion. "Gran gave it to us. It was hers, and my Grandad's mother before that. She said she's been waiting. That it's to be yours now."

Alanna burst into tears. "Oh, Aidan. It's perfect. I'll save it for our first son. I'll take good care of it."

He knelt on one knee at the foot of the castle. "I didn't do it properly the first time." He had the ring in his fingers. She put her hand out and he slid it on. A perfect fit. They were staring at each other, lost in the moment, when they heard the clapping and the hoots. Tourists, police, on-lookers all clapping for them. Aidan barked out a laugh.

"Give us a kiss then, lad!" An old man yelled from the bench in the castle gardens. So he stood up and kissed the hell out of her.

Branna yelled through the house as she saw Aidan's car pull into the drive. "They're here!" The whole family came piling into the kitchen and out the door. Alanna was opening the car door when the stampede happened. She was immediately pulled out of the car by her best friend. The tears flowed, freely. "You're here. You're really here!" Branna was sobbing and so was Alanna.

"Yes, sister. I'm here. I love you. I missed you something awful!"

Alanna was completely overwhelmed with the size of the O'Brien clan. Everyone was there. All of Aidan's siblings, their spouses, the children, Sean's parents, David and Aoife, Tadgh, his mother Katie. They all welcomed her with hugs and kisses and tears and laughter. They shoved food at her constantly. Seany smiled from across the room and she waved him over. "I missed you, little brother. How are you?"

He shrugged. "I'm okay. I'm glad to see you, Alanna. You belong here with us."

She hugged him, then whispered, "I have a letter for you. She brought it over to the house before I left."

Soon dinner was served. There wasn't room for everyone around the table, so they wandered through the house with plates, chatting, holding babies. Alanna sat on the sofa between Branna and Brigid, cradling little Haley in her arms. The baby yanked at her hair, putting a fist full of it in her mouth. Alanna looked up to find Aidan watching her. She blushed, thinking about that night in their apartment. He kept her up all night, taking her over and over again. She wondered, with a start, whether she could already be pregnant. She kissed Haley's head, smelling her black, curly hair. "She's so beautiful. You do make beautiful babies, Branna."

Brigid nudged her. "I saw that look. What's going on?"

Alanna blushed. "He's just so wonderful. I'm afraid I'll wake up and this won't be real."

Brigid smiled. "It is real, and down the road, you'll be holding your own children."

Alanna exhaled with a giggle. "I don't doubt it. He doesn't want to wait. He said he wants as many as I'll give him."

Brigid was silent, and Alanna worried she'd shared too much. She looked at her and her eyes were filled with tears. She hugged Alanna, putting their foreheads together. "Oh, Alanna. Thank you. I wanted this for him. I prayed for it. He'll be such a good father. I prayed for you, sister. Every night I prayed for him to find you."

Tadgh handed Aidan a beer and clinked their bottles together. "She's lovely, brother. She is absolutely stunning. You're a lucky bastard, and I am not ashamed to admit that I am envious as shit, right now." Aidan watched Alanna with his sisters and Branna and the baby in her lap.

"Your time is coming Tadgh. She's out there."

Tadgh shrugged. "Well, apparently I need to look in America."

Aidan laughed. "Not necessarily. Look at Patrick." They looked over at Patrick who was nuzzling his wife's neck.

"Yep, you and Liam are next. Hell, even Sean Jr. got the jump on you."

Tadgh gave him a sideways glance. "Aye, I heard. He's been trying to hide it, but that lass is on his mind. She must have been something."

Aidan smiled, nodding. "She was. She's a wonderful girl."

Liam approached and Tadgh switched his attention. "What about you, brother? Any prospects in that sea of young women at Trinity? Or are your teachers driving you too hard? Maybe a nurse or another pre-med student?" Liam was uncharacteristically quiet. This didn't go unnoticed. "Wait, there is someone, you sneaky fucker. Who is it?" Tadgh and Aidan both closed in on him. "Don't tell me the Trinity rake has found a woman."

Liam shrugged. "I might have met someone."

Brigid was walking by and zeroed in on them. "What? Who? Tell me!"

Liam rolled his eyes. "Oh God, don't get her started."

Branna was sitting, cuddled with Alanna. Haley was asleep on Alanna's chest. "It doesn't seem possible to have this many beautiful men in one room." Alanna shook her head. Patrick was big, but not so big as Aidan. He and Brigid had some auburn in their hair and they had green eyes like Sorcha. Aidan, Seany, and Liam all had Sean's coloring. Beautiful blue eyes, fair skin, sandy hair. Michael, too, except for that ring of green at the center. Tadgh was the wild card. His coloring was similar, but the eyes were all his mother. Amber, the color of whiskey, and he dripped with sex appeal. They were all drop dead gorgeous. Finn wasn't an O'Brien, but he had those dark Irish genes with long, dark hair and warm dark eyes. Like a Pict warrior with a Bill Gates brain.

"Between these genetics and your Falk good looks, your children are going to be awfully pretty." Branna nudged her. She noticed Aidan was watching them. "He can't take his eyes off you."

Aidan felt a pull at his shirt tail. He bent down and picked up little Cora. "Hello, darlin. Did you miss your Uncle Aidan?"

Finn was behind her, smiling. "We all did, brother. Missed you something fierce." The two men clasped each other in a one-armed man hug.

"Uncle Aidan, I dreamt of you." Sean stopped when he heard this, listening as they all were.

"You did. Was it a good dream?"

She cocked her head. "I don't really know. You were in a hospital, it was an old hospital. There was a little girl."

The hair stood up on Finn's arms, Aidan could see it. Finn asked, "What did she look like, Cora?"

She exhaled, gathering her thoughts. "She had one of those scarves around her head, like the women we see in Dublin, sometimes. She was a girl, though, dark hair and eyes. She had a doll with her. It was dirty, but she held on to it like I do to Miss Periwinkle. She said she knew Uncle Aidan." Sean's eyes were huge, looking between Cora and Aidan. The room had gone quiet.

"She wanted me to tell you something. She said to tell you thank you. She said she's okay. She's with her momma, now. She called you Mikail. I don't know why. I told her Michael was my other uncle."

Aidan's breath stuttered. He hugged his niece. "Thank you, darlin. Thank you so much. You've made your Uncle Aidan feel much better."

She patted his head. "Good, Uncle Aidan. It's time for you to be happy more."

He smiled, kissing her sweet little face. "I suppose it is."

The month went by in a flurry of activity. Aidan spent the weekdays in the North, and came during the weekends. Alanna stayed with Sorcha, and they planned the wedding with all haste. No one could throw a wedding together like Sorcha O'Brien. "If you don't mind a Thursday wedding, we can have the cottage for the party."

Branna clapped her hands. "That's where Caitilyn and Brigid and I all had our parties. Oh, Anna. I can't believe this is real."

As they sat in the kitchen of Sorcha and Sean's home, Sorcha fingered her mother's ring on Alanna's finger. "My brother John never married, so she never gave him the ring. He died almost fifteen years ago." She smiled, tears in her eyes. "Lung cancer. The mill he worked in when he was young, it had bad air. Asbestos. They weren't careful like they are now." She wiped the tears that had begun. "She was saving it for Aidan. He was always close to her. Her first grandchild."

Alanna took Sorcha's hands. "Do you mind?"

She looked surprised. "Why of course not. I have an O'Brien ring. A sapphire, like the sea. All my girls wear it on their other hand on their wedding day. I hope you will, too. But this ring. This emerald was meant for you, darling. Never doubt it."

Alanna kissed her hand. "You're the mother I always wanted. I have such a good daddy. My mom, she just never saw me as a treasure. We were all burdens. I'm so glad to be a part of your family now."

She turned to Branna. "And now we'll be sisters, as we always should have been." The three women cried together, only stopping when Brigid walked in.

"Bloody hell. I told you not to cry without me!" The women all burst out laughing.

Granny Aoife was with her. "So, how are the plans coming?"

Sorcha waved a hand, dismissively. "We've got this down to a science. Now all she needs is a dress." Alanna's jaw dropped.

"You haven't even thought about a dress? Christ, you are low maintenance. I can take you to Dublin or Shannon this week. We'll have to hurry. Do you know what you might like? Any style in particular?" Brigid asked.

Alanna lifted a shoulder. "Honestly, I always saw myself in some quaint little Southern wedding with a vintage dress. Are there any shops that rent vintage dresses? I don't even know exactly how old, I'll just know it when I see it."

Sorcha gave Aoife a look. Brigid was smiling broadly. "What? What did I say?"

Aoife stood up, putting her hand out to Alanna. "It looks like we'll be going to Granny's for tea."

Branna stood next to Alanna in Sean's childhood bedroom. "We converted it after the boys moved out, and Sean's sister moved to England. Now it is my spare room." The room was done up in beautiful antiques, an ornate vanity with silver combs and brushes, button hooks, porcelain dishes with perfumes and hair pins. There were vintage hats and ladies gloves. "I've always collected these types of things, but it all started with my grandmother's closet. I loved all of her purses and hats and the different bobbles she had."

Brigid and Sorcha walked around with Alanna, picking up different items that Aoife had collected over the decades. "Some I bought, some I inherited, but there's history in this room. Some of these things are from the fifties, when I was a young woman, some older. Some were my daughter's. Maeve loved to plunder around in here, still does. Sorcha even added a few things here and there. The best part of my collection is in here, though."

She opened a set of double doors, revealing a closet. Alanna and Branna both gasped. Wedding dresses, an entire row of wedding dresses. Sorcha touched one of them. "This was mine. It's a Gunne Sax. Sean and I got married in 1978."

Aoife pulled another out. "This was my sisters. She was very into fashion. She worked an extra job to save for this. It's Chanel. My parents thought it was terribly indulgent, but she was a beauty in it. Then Sean's sister wore it for her wedding. You'll meet her when you move to England, no doubt."

She pulled an older one out for inspection. "My tastes were a little more traditional. I wore my mother's dress."

Brigid sighed. "They knew how to dress back then, didn't they."

Aoife nodded. "Aye, they did. She wore this dress in 1928 and then I wore it in 1953."

Alanna touched the fine bead work and the intricate, crocheted lace. It had an empire waist, the silver beading cupping the bust and trimming the sweetheart neckline. Unlike the Chanel that cinched at the waist and ended at mid-calf, this was long and draped beautifully to the floor and beyond. The capped sleeves were bead strings. The white lace covered a pale, silver silk. There were threads of silver in the lace as well.

"Everyone always talked about the Venetian lace, back then, but this..." She spread it out for them to see. "This was made by the Irish lace makers. Hundreds of hours of work. You'd find nothing better in Italy. It is different than the Edwardian high neckline of the previous decade. It's not quite caught up to the look of the roaring twenties, either. It's a classic, elegant design that would look perfect in any decade. That's why she loved it. There are more, too. It's been a hobby of mine, and somehow it became a sort of museum for the family's wedding dresses. I have most of the original veils as well." Alanna touched them all, almost afraid to mar the beautiful fabrics. "Not everyone wants a vintage dress. It's a matter of taste. Brigid's dress is in here, too."

Branna cleared her throat. "I had my dress cleaned and preserved. Could I add it to your collection?"

Aoife smoothed a hand over her dark hair. "Of course, my dear. Someday, we'll show all of these to Haley and Cora. Then they'll either choose one of these to wear or add their own. This is a hundred years of history in this closet. You can try them all on, Alanna. Take your time, and I'll bet your dress is in here somewhere."

Alanna swallowed hard, "This is an unbelievable collection. I'd be afraid to wear any of it."

Aoife smiled, waving a dismissive hand. "They are meant to be worn. They've been stored properly and I always have the seams reinforced before the next bride wears it. Whichever one you choose, we will make it ready for you by the wedding. I have a special seamstress for the job, and she can adjust the size with little effort. The hard part is choosing."

The women spent the entire morning in that bedroom. Sean and David would peek in on them periodically, bringing them tea and biscuits. Alanna had known she would love Aidan's family. Any group of people capable of breaking through her best friends wall of defense had to be something special.

She'd been raised by her father and had a brother. Her mother could be fun at times, when she bothered to show up, but this was different. Brigid and Sorcha and Grandma Aoife were going to be family. She hadn't realized how much she'd missed having other women in her life until now. She'd had Meghan for a little while. She'd been the friend that spent the night too often, was too clingy to someone else's mom.

She looked at Branna from the bed she was sitting on. She was wearing a fancy hat and pretending to puff off of one of those Audrey Hepburn cigarette holders. Brigid was taking her picture. That's when the unexpected tears came.

"Are ye feeling all right, love?" Sorcha's hand was small and cool on top of hers.

She swiped her cheeks and waved a hand dismissively. "It's nothing. Hormones, probably. I just haven't had this in a long time. It's occurred to me how lucky I am, that's all. I'm getting a whole family. You've all been so kind and accepting. I just can't believe I deserve all of this."

Branna knelt in front of her. "I know exactly how you feel. It's so wonderful, the whole package is so unbelievable that it's hard to take in all at once. You do deserve it, though. We're lucky to have you."

That's when Sorcha squeezed her hand. Her voice was strained with emotion. "We prayed for you. All of us, for Aidan to find a woman who would bring him back to us. Who would see through his quiet reserve, his pain, to the heart of him." Sorcha was crying now. "Do you know how long it's been since I've seen him really laugh? He had one of those laughs that would get everyone else laughing just listening to him. We lost him for a while, but you found him. He was buried under a lot of hurt, but you found him and gave him back to us."

All the women were crying now. Alanna was looking down, unable to stand to see their tears. Then she looked up, and got a good look at Brigid. She was crying, yes. But she had a hat on with a birds nest on the top. She was wearing a pair of long fur lined gloves and fake jewels. This was all accompanying her Trinity College t-shirt and jeans. Alanna looked at the beady-eyed, fake green and yellow bird on her head and hiccuped a laugh, covering her mouth. The other women looked at Brigid, all starting to stifle giggles. Brigid scrunched her brow and put a hand to her hat. "Don't you listen to 'em birdie. You're a lovely, wee beastie."

That's when the dam broke. Soon the women were holding their sides, giggling on the bed and floor. David and Sean were at the door, peeking in. "What the bloody hell did you put in that tea, Da?" Which started a fresh wave of hysterics.

Aidan met Michael at the pub, wanting to see him alone before they joined the women. "So, what's up brother? Not cold feet, I hope."

Aidan shook his head. "No, o'course not. I just wanted to talk to you about the wedding."

Michael put his beer down. "What's there to worry about? The women have it all handled."

Aidan rubbed his neck, nervously. "I know I was the best man at your wedding."

It made sense to Michael, then. He waved a hand. "You've got a lot of good men to choose from. You won't hurt my feelings, brother. Were you thinking of John?"

Aidan said, "No. Not John. He'll need to give his attention to Maria. She won't know anyone. This is a job for family."

Michael cocked a brow. "Who then?"

Aidan gave a crooked smile. "I was thinking of Seany."

Michael's brows went up. Aidan understood his surprise. "Ye still think of him as a child, I know. It's just, he always gets left out a bit. He's so much younger. But good Christ, I wish you could have seen him in North Carolina. He's grown up and none of us have noticed. He's smart and he's brave. He drove the boat. Did he tell you that? He wouldn't stay back. When we went after her, he drove the boat. He's got nerves of steel for someone so young. He never hesitated. He wasn't my kid brother just then. He was one of my men."

Michael's face was pensive. "I guess we haven't been paying attention. He's a man in a lot of ways. It's time we acknowledged it." He slapped Aidan on the back. "He's a good choice. I think he'll be honored."

Aidan was at his mother's home, Alanna in his lap. "How are the plans going? Did you get a dress?"

Alanna smiled at the other women. "Yes, I did. I think you'll be surprised."

He cocked his head, "Scheming hens. Well, you'll be gorgeous no matter what you wear. As long as you show up, I'll be a happy man."

Seany was sitting on the sofa, more quiet then usual. Aidan went over to him and sat beside him, leaving the women to their secrets. "Staying out of the women's business, I see."

Seany snorted, "Absolutely."

He motioned to Alanna, "She's getting on well with everyone. She missed you, though. It's good you're back."

Aidan nodded, "Aye, and I her. That's not what I need to talk to you about, though."

"What, then?"

Aidan was surprised how awkward he felt. "Well, the wedding is small, as you know. Like Branna and Michael's was. I'll just have one man standing up for me."

Seany nodded, "Yes, like you did for Michael, and Michael did for Patrick."

Aidan said, "Exactly. So, I needed to ask you if you'd stand up for me."

Seany had a look of disbelief on his face. "I'm sorry, I don't understand."

Aidan shrugged, "It's simple. I want you to be my best man."

Seany swallowed, then he blinked. More blinking. "Ah, I'd be honored brother. Are ye sure you want it to be me and not one of the others?"

Aidan put a hand at the base of his skull and pulled him in. With their heads inches from each other, he looked his little brother in the eyes. "You were there for me like none of them ever have been. You had my back in singly the most terrifying hours of my life. We got her back, together. I don't want them. I love them, but I want you."

Seany put his forehead to Aidan's and exhaled, closing his eyes. "All right then, I'm your man." They hugged fiercely, the way that brothers do. Then Aidan realized that everyone was quiet. He looked up to see his mother, Brigid, all the other women tearing up.

"Good God, don't get them going again," Michael said. They laughed, but Aidan looked at his father and swore he saw tears as well.

46

Alanna stood next to her father and brother, staring out over the Cliffs of Moher. "I've seen pictures of this, many times. It just didn't prepare me for the real thing," Hans said.

"I know, Daddy. It's amazing. It's like a dream."

Erik had his arm around her. "I'm happy for you, Anna. We haven't been on a trip like this together in a long time, since we were kids. It's nice." Hans looked at his kids, all grown and out of the house, and a pang of loneliness hit him.

"Pretty soon we'll have little ones running around," Hans said with a smile.

Erik snorted. "Yeah, count me out."

Alanna nudged him. "You'll find her, Erik. You just keep the nice guy routine up and don't fall back into your bad attitude and you'll find her. I'll start looking as soon as I get to England."

He smiled at that. "You know, I can get a joint billet not too far from you. Maybe I'll look into it when it is time to rotate."

Alanna turned to him. "Really?" She flung her arms around him. "We would all be in Europe! That would be perfect!"

They started back to the car when Hans stopped. "Are you sure it's okay for us to stay with Sean and Sorcha? Maybe we should get a hotel."

Alanna shook her head. "You've met them. They won't hear of it. Mom gets in tomorrow, she's sleeping on the pull out at Branna's. She'll be thrilled to get to play with those twins. We have everyone assigned to a bed. Don't mess with the system. Just relax, daddy. When is the last time you went somewhere and just relaxed?" He grunted. "This wedding isn't complicated. With six kids, Sorcha has this down to an art."

Hans sat in the passenger seat. "Okay, baby. Just tell me when you need money and I'll be in the pub."

She laughed, "Now you're getting the hang of this."

They pulled into Gus O'Connor's Pub just before the tea time. Standing in the doorway, she saw him. She slammed the car into park and jumped out. Aidan scooped her up.

"I missed you!"

He laughed, burying his nose in her hair. "It's been three days. I told ye I'd be back." The last month had been full of periodic separations, him going back up to the North, while she stayed and planned the event. "Are you ready for this wedding, girl? I don't have to tell you that there's no backing out now."

Alanna had her arms wrapped around his neck. She gave him a sly grin. "Well, you know I hadn't seen all of your brothers. There are several good choices…Ah!"

Aidan pinched her butt. "What was that?" Pinch. Pinch. Then Tadgh came behind him to sweep her out of his arms.

"Aye, and cousins, too. You'll need to take a full account before ye settle on this crabby fecker."

Then it was Liam's turn. "Off with ye both, she might like to be a doctor's wife." At this he threw Alanna over his shoulder. "Let's get this lass a drink."

Alanna looked at Aidan as she hung like a sack of potatoes over Liam's shoulder. "You started it, girl. They'll not let you rest." His heart swelled in his chest, watching her play with his brothers.

"So, darlin. Do you have any friends that might want to be a mail order bride? America seems good hunting ground for a wife,"

Liam said, barely heard over Alanna's giggles. They went into the pub. "Jenny, I've stolen a bride. Call the priest!" He plopped her down on a bar stool.

"I don't think so, love. She's only got eyes for that one." She nodded in Aidan's direction. "Another O'Brien off the market. The lasses'll be cryin' in their cider. Tadgh, Liam, it's about time for you two to settle down. Oh, and who are these two handsome lads?"

Erik and Hans came in and took a seat at the bar as well. Aidan started introducing Jenny to his future in-laws when Dr. Mary Flynn came up to pay her lunch tab. Aidan hopped off his stool to hug her. "Mary, It's good to see you. Have you met Alanna?"

Doctor Flynn was an enigma. Pretty in a very natural way, smart, successful, and quick witted. She had chestnut hair, straight and cut to her shoulders. She had striking blue eyes, almost silver. She was trim for a woman her age and her skin was amazingly clear and smooth, more like a woman in her thirties instead of her fifties. She was unmarried and the town's family practitioner. She was also an unapologetic hard ass when she had a point to make.

Alanna gave her a wave. "Yes, I have. Branna brought her into the clinic to say hello and drop off my invitation. I'm so happy to see you've found your mate. The town loves a good O'Brien love story."

She patted Aidan's cheek. Aidan turned to Hans and Erik. "These good men are to be my father-in-law and brother-in-law. Hans, Erik, this is my friend and family doctor Mary Flynn."

She smiled, and Aidan swore he saw a flash of feminine speculation in Mary's eye when she looked at Hans. "Hans, Erik. It's a pleasure. I see where Alanna got that beautiful Scandinavian coloring. I have appointments all afternoon, so please don't think me rude. I'll certainly see you all at the wedding."

She turned to Aidan. "I took care of you when you were a lad. It is good to see you so happy, love. You can save me a dance tomorrow." Aidan hugged her again.

Then she looked at Hans and said, "It is good to meet you."

Hans stood, shaking her hand. "You as well, Mary. And if Aidan doesn't save you a dance, I certainly will."

Mary's eyes flared a bit. "I'll remember that."

As Mary left the pub, Hans watched her go. Then he realized that everyone at the bar had gone silent. "Dad, holy hell. I was starting to think you didn't have any game." Erik said. He gave his son a sharp look. Erik didn't flinch. "Don't even try it, Pops."

Alanna whistled. "Dang, daddy. Did you see that look in her eye. You've definitely still got some moves."

This of course got Tadgh and Liam in on the fun. "Doc Mary is pretty hot for her age. I'm going to have to call dibs on the coat room early."

Alanna looked at them, confused. Liam said, "In the cottage hall. The coat closet inevitably ends up occupied by some couple by the end of the wedding. At Caitlyn and Patrick's wedding, Finn and Brigid were locked in there for almost an hour. I'm still traumatized at the thought of it."

Alanna gave Aidan a steamy look. "Really?"

Erik gagged, "Please do not make sexy eyes at him in front of your brother."

Then he leaned over. "So, where is this coat closet, exactly?"

Jenny was shaking her head. "Do any of you lads want a drink before you go off on your conquests?"

"So, Alanna, when do the rest come in? You've got five others coming from the states, is that right?" asked Michael.

Alanna nodded. "Yes, Tim, John, Maria, baby Aidan, and my mother. John rented a car and they coordinated their flights. They'll all come in together from Dublin. Porter and Doc should be checking into the youth hostel this afternoon."

Tadgh groaned. "The last thing we needed was more single men. Didn't ye have some lonely girlfriends to invite? Miriam, Jenny, and Doc Mary are the only single women I can think of that are coming."

Alanna gave him poopy face. “Sorry Tadgh. My friend Izzy is deployed.”

Erik perked up. “Who’s Miriam and Jenny?” Jenny slid a drink in front of him. “I’m Jenny and I doubt I’m your type.”

Erik wiggled his eyebrows at her. “Don’t be so sure.” Jenny was pretty, and he guessed to her to be in her late twenties, early thirties.

She swatted at him. “Miriam on the other hand, she’s just about the right age. Pretty, too.”

He looked at Tadgh for confirmation. “Aye, I suppose she is. It’s just when you’ve been chasing a girl around since she was in bows and pigtails, it’s too much like family.”

Behind them, Sean’s voice came over the din. “We don’t discuss our women in pubs, boys.” They all straightened up. “Although, Mary Flynn would be quite a catch,” he mumbled to Hans.

Tim walked into the guesthouse with his bag over his shoulder. “You must be here for the wedding. So glad we could squeeze you in with that last minute cancellation.” The woman that answered the front door was in her late fifties with a soft face and red hair. “We let the two back rooms out and we’re usually booked through the fall. So nice to see another local boy getting married. So, Timothy Daniels, we have your card on file. Let’s get you to your room.”

She came around the counter and froze, her eyes going to his leg, or more specifically, where the bottom half used to be. She looked up at him sadly. “Military?”

He nodded, “Yes ma’am, Marine Corps.”

She smiled. “Well, thank you for your service. You seem to get around rather well.”

He nodded, getting that sinking feeling he got when he felt pity come his way. “My room?”

She shook herself. “Forgive me, yes. This way please.”

Tim unpacked, took a shower, and headed out to find the wedding goers. Just as he was walking around the side of the house, a younger woman came around the corner, slamming into him.

"Jesus Christ, I'm sorry!" Tim was picking papers up off the ground and noticed that they were photographs. He looked up at the woman and was struck stupid. Red hair, fair skin, but way younger and hotter than her mother. Right out of central casting for some Irish Spring commercial.

She had a camera bag clutched to her, afraid of it ending up on the ground as well. "It's okay. I should mind where I'm going. You must be here for the wedding." Beautiful, smokey Irish lilt. *Fuuuuucking hell.*

He stood up, handing her the photos. "Yes, I'm staying in the back. Do you live here?" He sure as hell hoped so. She was gorgeous.

"This is my parents' house. I was just taking some shots for the weblink. I'll see you at the wedding, no doubt. I'm the photographer."

He nodded. "Small town, everyone knows each other, I suppose. Well then, Miss?"

She said, "Fiona, Fiona Reilly." She looked at his leg briefly, then back up to his face. "Well, I bet you've got some stories. You have a grand time in Ireland, Timothy. I'll see you around." She walked away, and Tim was taken back by the fact that she hadn't flinched when she noticed his leg, and there was not one ounce of pity on her face.

"Fiona!" he called to her.

She turned.

He smiled. "It's Tim, and thanks."

She cocked her head. "For running you over?"

He laughed, "No. For not getting that pitying look in your eyes. It's a first. Especially with women."

She narrowed her eyes at him. "Well, now. You're alive, aren't you? And you're young and strong. Why would I pity you?" Then she turned and walked away.

"Tim!" Alanna and Branna both ran across the garden to greet him and he scooped them up, one in each arm.

"Well, I don't know why I came. These O'Brien men are stealing all of my high school crushes." He kissed Branna on the forehead.

"Come inside. We were just sitting down for some lunch," she said.

Alanna guided her old friend into her other old friend's cottage. "Wow, you really went old school, didn't you? This is amazing," Tim said. John, Maria, and Felicity all sat in the living room, each with a baby on their lap. "Well, not hard to tell which two are the O'Mara twins. Look at all that hair!"

Tim walked over to Felicity and scooped up little Brian. He was drooling, cutting a tooth, and chewing voraciously on his fist. He reached out as quick as a snake and grabbed two fists of Tim's hair. It was just to his shoulders and often in his eyes. The hair was something he had done when he was forced to use a hearing aid. It was chestnut brown. It shrouded pretty blue eyes and a handsome face.

"Damn, Tim. I'm loving that hair. You must be beating them off with a stick." Branna said appreciatively.

He shrugged. He'd detangled his hair from Brian and made a face at him. "Well, his grip reflex is good. Does he drive yet? I'm not digging the left side driving." He turned to the baby. "What do you think? You wanna chauffeur me around town? I need a wingman." Brian squealed and they all laughed.

"Michael is on duty. You'll get to meet him later. Aidan was making a phone call in the bedroom, but he should be done…Never mind, here he is."

Aidan came out of the bedroom and gave Tim a big man hug. "Bloody hell, it's good you made it!" he said with a grin.

"Yeah, well. Sorry, I won't be wearing my uniform. Not cutting all these pretty locks off to get within regs."

Aidan laughed, "Hans and Erik and I are the only ones in uniform. Denario, O'Malley and Porter didn't bring theirs either. Wear what ever the hell you want. I'm just glad you're here."

"Me, too. I wouldn't miss it. I like to think I helped a bit, getting you to pull your head out of your ass."

Aidan put his arm around him. "Aye, I suppose I'll have to change your nickname. Tim the Tosser seems a bit out of line this far into our relationship."

47

"Somehow I don't think this is what they had in mind when they gave us the key early." Alanna gasped, her hands going to Aidan's hair as he knelt in front of her.

He looked up and gave her a rakish grin. "Should I stop, hen?"

She arched, "Don't you dare! Ah God, yes." She rolled her hips against his mouth and grabbed the coat rack, her knees weakening. Her blouse was open, bra unclasped, and one leg was out of her pants, thrown over his shoulder. "So this is the famous coat closet," she said, looking around in a stupor. Aidan did something wicked with his lips and she moaned. "Get up here, now!"

Never one to leave a lady in distress, Aidan stood up and was freeing himself from his pants on a oner. "God, I've missed you. I've hated being away from ye, even for a few days. Come to me. Come to me, now."

She raised her bottom and slid herself down on him. She started moving, gliding against him. She shook her head back and forth, eyes closed, frantic. "Aidan!"

He held her hips. "Easy, love."

She was out of her head. "Aidan, please!"

He held her hips with one hand and curled his hand into her hair with the other. "Look at me."

She did, her eyes wild. He rolled his hips slowly, easing deeper every time. She whimpered. He pulled her to him over and over again, rubbing her deep inside. It always took a moment to accommodate him. His size and thickness was overwhelming no matter how many times they joined, but she loved the feel, the stretching and the invasion mixed with his smell, his touch, his mouth, all seducing her into physical surrender. “That’s it, my love. Feel me.” He pressed deep and her breaths became more shallow. She started to contract around him, a deep moan coming from inside her. His vision narrowed, until all he saw were her green eyes glossed over in surrender. “I feel you.Take me with you, darlin.”

No sooner did they have themselves decent, then the masses of O’Briens descended. Decorations, table linens, centerpieces. The rehearsal would be in two hours, then dinner at the pub. After that, Alanna would go to his grandparents house to sleep and get ready for the wedding. The next time he would see her, she’d be walking down the aisle to him.

Taking her in the closet had been an impulse he couldn’t deny. The last three weeks had been torture. Separated during the week, then quiet couplings in his old bedroom, trying not to gain the ear of his little brother or parents. He’d missed her screams, the feminine sighs and moans, her nails in his shoulders or his ass. He’d taken her in every room of both beach houses. On the counter, the table, against the fridge, the tub, the shower, even in the weight room below.

Watching her bite the pillow to stifle a scream, having her eyes wild and jaw clenched as she shuddered and came in silence had been fun to experience at first, but it started to chafe after a couple of weeks. She was a screamer, and he loved it. She’d been wild in that coat closet. He couldn’t wait to get her alone again. Just watching her flutter around the room, getting the tables ready, his groin was stirring to have her again.

"Easy, brother. You're almost there." Michael was grinning beside him. "Sharing a wall with Ma and Da getting to you, is it?" he jibed. Aidan let out a little growl. "That's what I thought. That's why we're giving you the cottage tomorrow night. We're taking the twins to Ma's house and giving you the entire cottage. It's all set up for your wedding night. Branna insisted. No one will hear you for miles."

Aidan looked at his brother. Then he grabbed him in a hug. "That's perfect. Jesus, thank you. It's just what we need. The fireplace, the clawfoot. It's perfect." Michael smiled, pleased to have gotten it right.

The pub was full to bursting with wedding goers and tourists alike. Alanna looked across the room to watch Aidan toasting with John, Porter, and O'Malley. Doc O'Malley and the young Sergeant hadn't bought a drink all night. The ladies in the place seem to have a thing for American military men. Aidan smiled over the rim of his glass at her.

"Jesus, you two are such saps." Tim was next to her giving her a nudge. "Do you have to look so happy?"

She wasn't fooled. He'd been scanning the room all night. "So, who is she?"

He looked at her sharply. "She who?"

Branna slid beside him. "Yeah, she who?"

He took a sip. "No one."

Alanna looked at Branna. "He's been scanning the room all night. Who's missing?"

She looked around. "No one single. Wait…where are you staying again?"

Tim took another sip of his beer. "Just a small guesthouse, off the main road."

Branna's eyes widened. "Reilly's?" Just then, they felt him tense. They both looked at the door and Branna let out a whistle. "Well, looks like the party is complete."

Alanna looked at the woman, then she leaned in. "Is that who I think it is?"

Branna answered, "Yes."

Alanna looked at Tim. "Tim, do you know that she is Michael's ex-wife?"

He shook himself. "I don't know what you two are getting at, but it doesn't matter to me who she is. You girls need a drink?"

Branna put her hand on his arm. "Listen, she's had problems in the past. She is doing really well, though. You just need to know that she wasn't always completely stable. Like I said, she doing really well and she is a hundred percent single. Just be careful. Michael would be glad to see her happy and so would I."

Tim snorted. "I've said two words to the woman and you are trying to marry me off? Just ease up girls. I'm not looking for complications."

Alanna and Branna said it at the same time. "Neither was I."

Brigid came pouncing down on the remaining chair. "I'll take you over to Gran's house whenever you're ready. You don't want to stay up too late." She looked at Tim and narrowed her eyes, then looked over her shoulder. Another whistle.

"Oh, would you three stop it."

Brigid giggled. "Small town, love. We're all up in your knickers. Best get used to it." He laughed, because that's the effect Brigid had on people. Thick Irish, heavy on the smart ass.

"That husband of yours is a lucky man."

She put her pint glass up to his. "I'll drink to that."

Fiona was up at the bar when she felt someone behind her. "Put her drink on my tab, Jenny. Thank you." She turned and fought the urge to sink to the floor, her knees having gone to jelly.

"Well, how's our small town treating you Timothy Daniels?" She turned back to Jenny briefly, as she put Fiona's drink in front of her.

"You didn't strike me as a rum and coke girl," he said.

She smiled, turning to meet his eyes again. "Diet Coke, no rum. I don't drink much anymore. It hasn't served me well and it doesn't mix with my medication."

His eyebrows popped up. She shrugged. "You'll hear it all soon enough. Michael's crazy ex, the poor dear. Hope she stays on her pills and away from the husbands." She clinked her coke to his Creans.

He cocked his head. "You sound like you're used to being disparaged. Seeing how I just met you, I couldn't care less what the town gossip circle has to say. Cheers." He took a sip. Then he said, "A little advice. Don't be so quick to warn the new guys off. I can tell you that being alone isn't all it's cracked up to be. Have a good night, Fiona."

He turned to walk away and she stopped him with an arm. "Thank you, Tim. For the drink, I mean. I'll see you tomorrow?"

His smile was easy. "Yes. If you put that camera down for a minute, I promise this isn't as bad on the dance floor as you'd think." He lifted his prosthetic leg.

She looked down at it. "I'd never think such a thing. You're obviously an athlete. I'd love to photograph you." Her eyes held speculation and a hint of heat that she was trying like hell to hide.

Tim said, "Well, you'll have to get to know me a little better before I pose like Fabio or Captain America with the peg leg."

She laughed, but there was an edge to it. "That's not the kind of photography I do. I just am light on fresh subjects. I'm more into natural shots, no posing. Your leg is a part of you of course, but I'm kind of a whole picture sort of girl. If you're going to stick around a while, I am serious about getting some shots of you."

Tim tipped his drink to her. "We'll see. I'll see you tomorrow, Fiona."

Aidan stood behind Brigid's car, holding Alanna. "It's only one night. Tomorrow is the big day."

Michael pulled Aidan back. "Off to Ma's. The Grannies will take good care of her. Don't worry."

Alanna sat in the passenger seat and sighed. "Wow, we're really here. It's almost like a dream."

Brigid reached a hand over and squeezed hers. "My brothers are the dearest things to my heart other than my children. Ye've no idea how happy this has made us all. I can never get enough sisters. They can bring all the wee yanks home they like." She winked and started the car.

Alanna walked into Gran Aoife's house and a wave of sweetness hit her. She walked into the kitchen and her heart leapt. "So this is it, my wedding cake?"

Aoife nodded, "Yes, Edith baked it and I decorated. They're in bed already. Your mother is in the living room. Come in and say hello."

Alanna looked at Brigid who shrugged. "I'll say goodbye here." She hugged her. "I'll be by in the morning, love. Sleep well."

Alanna walked into the sitting room to find her mother sitting nervously. She jumped up. "Hi honey. I just wanted to see you before tomorrow. I know you have everything set, but I wanted to give you something."

Alanna sat on the couch and her mother sat again. She pulled out a box. "Your father bought them for me, when we were first married. They're emeralds, so I thought they'd go with your ring." She seemed nervous and suddenly Alanna felt sorry for her. She swallowed hard, her eyes blurring. "They're perfect. Thank you, Momma."

Felicity's face beamed. "Well, I'll let you get your rest."

Alanna stood and caught her arm. "Wait, um, the mother of the bride is supposed to help her get ready. I have a lot of women coming over, but I only have one momma. Will you come over with Branna? You can do my make up. You were always good at bringing out my eyes without making me look like Elsa Parker."

They both said it at the same time, "Bless her heart." Then they giggled. Every southern woman knew that you could talk smack about another woman as long as you followed it up with *Bless her heart.*

"I'd like that, if you're sure. I haven't been a mom to you in a long time, but I'd like to help."

Alanna hugged her. "Then I'll see you in the morning."

Aidan was greeting friends and family as his brothers ushered people to their seats in the church. Hans had gone to find his daughter and Erik was in charge of keeping his ass calm. "So, that's Miriam? Hmmm, she's a sweetheart. Look at that perky little…"

Aidan held a hand up. "Her perky little bum is not your concern, man. She's a nice girl. This is not the time for a Marine Corps hit and run."

Erik laughed. "All right, I'll behave. You were more fun on the beach."

Hans and Sean walked to the back rooms of the church to find the women. When Hans walked in, his daughter turned around, and his heart leapt up in his throat. He was not tearing up. Nope. Shit, yes he was. "Miss Priss, you're the most beautiful thing I've ever seen."

She approached him, the dress swaying as she walked. He looked at her face, taking her in. His baby. Then he saw them. "Those look perfect on you, baby." He looked at Felicity.

"It's about time someone wore them again," she said. "She's beautiful, isn't she? Our beautiful, baby girl." Felicity came up next to him and put her arm around his shoulder. "We did this right. We didn't do everything right, but we did Anna and Erik perfectly."

He kissed her on the cheek. "That we did."

Sean approached as well. "Hello, love. Are you ready to be an O'Brien?" Alanna beamed. "Yes, I am."

He looked her up and down. "You have no idea how happy it makes me to see you in that dress."

Aidan stood at the front of the church, stoic as ever. He was resisting the urge to wring his hands like a school boy. Sean Jr. was next to him in a black, modern cut suit. He looked like a man, and it made Aidan's throat thicken to look at him. Half the town was there and a lot of family. Erik was in his dress blues, escorting his mother to the pew. Sean and Sorcha came next. The organ music was booming through the church. Next was Branna. She was as beautiful as ever. She was dressed in a simple, navy blue dress. Her hair was cascading down her back and he could hear the twins starting to babble as Michael pointed out their mother. She was smiling so brightly at Aidan when she took her place across the altar from him and Sean Jr. Then the bridal march started and Alanna came through the double doors of the church.

Whatever he was expecting, nothing had prepared him for the sight of her. She hadn't gone to some boutique and bought the big white dress. This was all together different, and familiar. It occurred to him with a wave of pride that he'd seen this dress twice before. Old black and white photos of his Great Gran and his Granny Aofie on their wedding days. He swayed a bit and he felt Sean's hand on his back, strong and true. "Easy, man. I'm here."

Alanna was radiant next to her father. She looked at him and tears glimmered in her eyes. The entire church was gasping at the sight of her. Her blonde hair cascaded, smooth and wavy, over her shoulders. The beads in her hair gathered in the back of her head to a simple lace veil. The vintage dress looked like it was made for her. She could have been thrown back in time, the entire picture was elegant and breathtaking. Her skin was pale, her make up not overdone. But the lips, they were new. Red and striking. Her pale hair and skin, her beautiful mouth, it drew Aidan's eye, and he had to stifle a groan.

Hans approached the altar with his breathtaking daughter, and it was all he could do not to cry like a girl when he looked at Aidan, then back at his daughter. Such love. A lasting love. He knew if he could see the future, these two would not be apart. Not like his marriage or Erik's. This one was going to last. Aidan O'Brien was going to love and cherish his daughter until his last dying breath, and maybe beyond.

The wedding mass went on, all the parts were there, the priest was talking. Aidan didn't hear most of it. All he could hear was his heartbeat in his ears. All he could see was his Alanna. He sharpened up when he needed to, zeroing in on the important stuff. Vows and then the rings. When she slid the platinum ring on his finger, a shudder went through him and he pulled her close, their foreheads together. "I'm yours, mo mhuirnín. I love you."

He went in for a kiss and the Father put a steadying hand on him. "Impatient lad, I'm getting to that part." The church rumbled with laughter. Aidan smirked at the priest and waited for his cue. Then she was in his arms and he took the kiss he'd been waiting for. He heard a whoop from his brothers and some ooh-rahs from his Marine and Army buddies. It was his mother who joined in the loudest. "Finally!" and she slapped Brigid a high five.

The party was in full swing. All of the local musicians took turns rotating on and off the stage along with several O'Briens. Alanna was dancing with her fifth O'Brien of the night. "He's a good man. You'll find no better. Aidan's a tough nut, but you've got him forever." Tadgh smiled down at Alanna, marveling at how lucky these O'Brien cousins were to have found their mates. Such strong, beautiful women. "Now you are one of us, so you'll have us forever as well."

Alanna smiled up at him. "Tadgh, I think I am going to like being one of you. I can't believe you all threw this together in a month. Who's next, do you think?"

He laughed. "I'd like to say it's me, but I've got no prospects. It'll have to be Liam. Hell, at the pace I'm going, it might be Seany."

She patted his cheek. "Oh, honey. Bless your heart. We're going to have to find you a nice girl. My brother, too. Maybe even Daddy."

Tadgh swirled her around and turned her to face the doorway. "Maybe not," he said in her ear.

She looked across the room and her jaw dropped. Her father was going outside for some fresh air….with Mary-freaking-Flynn in hand. "Hot damn!" she said. Tadgh laughed and twirled her around, bumping right into her new husband.

"You two are having too much fun. I'm going to have to cut in, brother."

So, Tadgh did what any reasonable man would do. He grabbed Aidan and started dancing with him. "Well, if you insist cousin, but you're not really my type."

Alanna squealed as Tadgh and Aidan strolled across the dance floor. "Christ, would you look at him. I haven't seen him this happy since he was a young lad." Brigid put her arm around Alanna. "You're good for him. So good."

Alanna watched them. "He's good for me, too. Jesus, Brigid. You have no idea what a dark place I was in. He's my salvation as much as I'm his."

Hans strolled in the beautiful garden, smelling the sea air. "I love the sea. I never want to be far from it."

Mary stopped short. "Do you smell the sea?" He nodded, thinking it an odd question. Then she asked, "Do ye hear it?"

He laughed, "Odd questions. Of course I hear it."

Mary smiled. "Interesting. Do ye have any Irish blood mixed in with that Viking?" He smiled, "Scottish grandmother, the rest are Swedes as far as I know. Am I missing something?"

She shook her head. "It doesn't matter. So, how long are you in town?"

He looked up at the stars. "Five more days. Not long enough. Not nearly long enough." Then he shrugged. "I took a job in Europe, though. That is the good news. By the time they are in England, I'll be in Spain. A good deal closer than Virginia."

Mary's eyes widened. "Spain. My, that is a good assignment."

He looked at her directly. "Yep, right on the coast. Close enough to take a train if you had a mind to visit."

Mary looked at him thoughtfully. "Are you a ladies man then, with these good looks and sly tongue?" Hans barked out a laugh. She looked a little miffed at that. "It's a perfectly logical question. You are flirting with me, Sergeant Major, most outrageously. I just want to know if it's a party trick of yours."

He narrowed his eyes. "I haven't been with a woman in seven years, and I outgrew games a long time ago. What about you? You are easily the most eligible woman in town. Beautiful, if not a little bit of a handful."

She snorted. "You try dating in a town where any man of an acceptable age comes to you to have his prostate checked."

That caused a dramatic pause and jaw drop from Hans. Then he burst out laughing. So did she. They laughed until their sides hurt. Hans took her hand. "Walk with me, Doc. Forget all the reasons this is a bad idea and just walk with me."

There were crickets and lit lanterns through the gardens, Hans was thrumming with the energy of it. "This is a special place, your County Clare. I grew up in the South. Antebellum houses and hot summers. I used to think that it had magic, but this has its own, doesn't it?"

Mary said, "Yes, I suppose it does. I never made it to South Carolina during my stint in the states. I never made it past Virginia."

Hans was surprised. "When did you live in the states?"

She shrugged. "I did part of my residency in a Navy hospital on exchange, actually. It was a very long time ago. It's how I got hooked up with Branna as my patient. Dr. Troy is retired Navy."

Hans said, "I know him. He's a civilian doc. He was our family doctor when the kids were little." He eyed her speculatively.

"So, I met your ex-wife briefly. Is she around a lot? She seems to watch you rather intensely."

Hans smirked. "She left when the kids were young, pre-teen years. She watches me now because she's never satisfied. When she had me, she wanted rid of me. Now that I don't pay her any mind, she thinks she wants…" He stopped there, blushing.

"She wants the man, not the marriage. I understand."

Hans stopped, facing her. "There's nothing left there. Hasn't been for many years. I don't do well with picking women who love me back."

She sighed, "Yes, I know the feeling. Seven years, eh?"

He laughed, "Yes, and it wasn't all that compelling. I just got lonely, I suppose. What about you? You never married?"

She put her hands in the pockets of her skirts. "I work a lot."

He cocked a head. "You ever been in love?"

She shrugged. "Once."

He finished her thought. "A Navy doctor?"

She gave him a sideways glance. "Yes, I have a weakness for uniforms."

He smiled hugely as he pulled on his uniform jacket, "Really?"

She laughed. "Aye, and it comes with a lot of long distance miles that doom it to failure."

His face changed. "Well, you were young. So was he. I'm not him. I'm a patient man, and I'm bucking up on retirement. So, Doc. Any other excuses, or would you let me take you around that dance floor?"

Mary paused, thinking. She looked right into him and he didn't flinch. "Well, hell. Did you have to be so goddamn handsome, Hans?" She said harshly, then took his hand as he led her back to the hall.

Alanna was drinking a glass of sweet tea. Liam came up to her and snatched her drink. "So, this is the famous tea Ma's been trying to perfect?" He took a sip and his brows shot up. "Christ, woman. That is certainly sweet enough. Maybe a little whiskey?"

She took it out of his hand. "No, no alcohol for me. Thanks. I'm abstaining." Liam's eyes went straight to her belly in a silent question. "No, not that I know of. I just want a clean system, in case. Keep that under your hat though. I don't want people pestering me if it doesn't happen right away…or at all."

Liam's face grew serious. "You're thinking about Caitlyn?" She exhaled and nodded. "Don't borrow trouble lass. It happens in its own time."

She cocked her head. "Is that your medical opinion?"

He laughed. "No, I'm not going OB. I'm not sure on my specialty just yet. I'm leaning toward internal medicine."

She smiled. "And what about your date? Is she pre-med?" He looked across the dance floor at Eve. She was dancing with Brigid and Cora. "No, she's a performing arts major. Dance."

Alanna looked at her. "She looks like a ballerina. How long have you known her?"

He looked away. "Only about three weeks. It's too soon to be making plans, hen. Get that sparkle out of your eye."

She put a hand on his arm. "I wanted your brother the first time I saw him. When he came back, it took one wrestling match with a baseball bat and one botched breakfast for me to know I loved him."

Liam laughed, remembering the story. "Aye, I heard about the bat. What's this about a botched breakfast?"

Before she could answer, the musician at the microphone yelled, "O'Brien Set!" and everyone cheered. Alanna was swept off to the dance floor and found herself across from Aidan. "We didn't have time to cover this. I'm sorry, love. Just don't worry. Enjoy yourself. You'll catch on by the end."

She cocked a brow at him. "Oh, I'm not worried." She winked at Aoife and Sorcha. The music started and Aidan was taken back as she fell right into step.

A big grin spread over his face. "You scheming little hens have been practicing, I see."

She took his hand, raised above their heads. Her eyes were down right steamy. "Yes, a mating song is it?"

His eyes were hooded, heavy with wanting. "Aye, it's about the chase, then the taking." His voice was a deep, husky whisper.

"Well, Porter won't give up the coat closet, so you are going to need to wait," she said.

Aidan's eyes sparkled with mischief. "Really? Who?"

She whispered. "Jenny, from the pub."

Aidan's eyes grew wide. "Going for experience, eh? Well played, young Sergeant."

She shushed him. "Pay attention, you're distracting me!"

He pulled her to him, kissing the hell out of her and causing a ripple in the dance line. "Aidan, you're making a bollocks of the family dance. Kiss your wife when it's done."

Aidan wiggled his brows at his father. "Sorry, Da." They fell back in step and Alanna was blushing.

"Behave yourself," she chastised.

"Never," he said as he picked her up and swung her around.

"I do love a good O'Brien wedding," Mary said to Hans. They watched the family dancing in unison.

He said, "She's the most precious thing in my life. I couldn't have given her up for any less."

Mary looked at him. "You're a good father. A really good father. Most men wouldn't have taken on full custody. I think I admire you."

He pulled her out of view, into a dark hallway. "Enough to give me that kiss I've been working up the nerve to ask for?" Mary was a strong spirited woman, but small in stature. Hans towered over her. But she was holding the cards, she knew that. He wouldn't make a move unless he had her permission. He had a hand above her head, her back against the wall.

She looked up at him, then at his mouth. "I'm a little rusty at this."

That's all he needed. He dipped his head and kissed her, pulling her to him with his other hand on the back of her neck. Right then, one of the O'Brien brothers came around the corner and did a one-eighty in full retreat.

Alanna and Aidan were sitting at their table taking a breather and eating some cake when Liam came skidding to a stop. He sat down, looked at Aidan's drink, then took it and drank it on a oner. He paused, collecting his thoughts. "Alanna, lass. Your da is my feckin hero."

Aidan leaned in. "And what's brought on this proclamation so suddenly?"

Liam smiled. "Because I just walked in on him in a full lip lock with Doc Mary up against the wall."

Aidan's jaw dropped. "You're takin a piss."

Liam shook his head. "I'm not. He's kind of hard to mistake."

Aidan looked at Alanna. She was grinning. "Did you know about this?"

She shook her head. "I knew he had an eye on her, but damn. Who knew he had it in him to work that fast. He hasn't had a date in years."

Liam shrugged. "He obviously hasn't had proper incentive until now. Doc Mary's a looker. She's a bit of a hard ass, but some men like that sort of woman. Good for him. Although, if they go for the coat closet, I'm putting my foot down. I've finally got that damned Marine of yours out of there." Then he hopped up and went to look for his date.

They looked around the dance floor. Finn was holding Brigid, swaying to the music, eyes full of her and only her. All of the O'Brien men had their wives in their arms as well. Felicity was dancing with Ned Kelly. Erik was dancing with Miriam. Alanna was pleasantly surprised to see Tim, who was slow dancing with Fiona Reilly.

Her heart squeezed at the sight of Tim. He was lonely. She wasn't so sure about an entanglement with this woman, but it was good to see him like this. Not alone. "He's a big boy. Don't worry about him." Aidan nudged her.

"I know. I can't help it. He's been through a lot," she said.

Aidan looked at him. "Aye, I suppose he has. War is a hard way to make a living." As he said this, he looked at John dancing with Maria. Then he looked at Porter dancing with Jenny. O'Malley was swinging around one of Caitlyn's sisters. Everyone was happy, but he worried about those men he'd trained with.

"You wish you could go with them." Not a question, but he answered it.

"Aye, I do. Not that I'd ever want to leave you, but I think about them over there. I feel responsible for them, even though they aren't mine."

Alanna rubbed his back. "And that's why I love you."

He stood up. "Dance with me, darlin. One more dance. Then let's go to the cottage. We've made nice long enough. I need you." She let him lead her out to be with the other couples, completely on board with that plan.

Tim danced with Fiona and decided that she smelled like nothing he'd ever experienced. Clean and woodsy all at once. This, he thought, is what some woodland pixie would smell like. "So, about the photos. You said you like to take pictures in a natural setting. Well, I'll agree."

Fiona's smile was full of distrust. "And the catch?"

He threw his head back and laughed. “How do you know there is one?”

She leaned in. “Ye’ve got mischief in your eye, Timothy Daniels. I see it plain as day.”

He cocked his head grinning. “Well, the problem is that I go on the road tomorrow. I didn’t fly all this way to see my old girlfriend get married. I want a tour.” Her eyes flared. “Oh, you didn’t know? Yes, school friend, then a very brief dabble into the romantic realm, failure, and back to friends. Best friends. No regrets. But…” he paused, “that is neither here nor there. The problem is that if you want to photograph me, you’ll have to pay. Don’t look at me like that. Not money.”

He pulled her back in as he swayed. “You have to pay with services. Hey, that look is very unbecoming. Get your mind out of the gutter. What I mean is, I need a tour guide. Galway, Donegal. Dublin. I’d love to hike Connemara, but I’m afraid that might be too much with this leg. I have other attachments, like some sort of action figure actually, but I don’t have them with me.”

He was babbling on and noticed that Fiona had stopped, looking at him like he was touched in the head.

As if she’d read his mind, she said, “Are ye daft? I can’t just go off with a man I don’t know. You could be some sort of lunatic.”

He looked genuinely offended. “You can ask anyone here. Aidan, Alanna, Hans, Branna. I’m no lunatic. I’d get you your own room.” He exhaled, looking at her impatiently. “Do you have so much going on in this town that you can’t just take off for a few days? I’ve seen your rates. You’re expensive. This wedding should pad your coffers for a few days at the very least.”

She was standing now, hands on her hips. “I have a life. I can’t just pick up and go.”

He shrugged. “Yes, you told me. You are the town’s Hester Prynne. That must get old. Don’t you like the idea of getting out for a few days with someone who doesn’t know every sin you’ve committed since you were in diapers?”

She bristled. He waved a hand. "Jesus, you know what, never mind the pictures. I'm sorry, I'm not going to bother you anymore. I'll head out on my own tomorrow and you can sit at the pub and drink your diet coke in peace." His voice wasn't angry. It was tired and maybe disappointed, but not angry. He stepped in, and for a moment, she thought he would kiss her. He held back, though. Her disappointment was tangible, which was stupid. She'd been doing her best to drive him off. He stroked her hair as he pulled away. "It's was nice to meet you Fiona. Goodnight." Then he walked away. She stood there, mouth agape.

"Christ, after that speech I'm ready to go with him."

Fiona jumped at the voice behind her. "Jesus, Michael. Ye scared the shit out of me!"

He was smiling. "You get jumpy when you think you're making a cock up of things but don't want to admit it."

She narrowed her eyes at him. "You don't know so much."

He laughed. "I do, and well you know it. So, what is it? You don't like him? Does the leg bother you?"

She folded her arms over her chest. "Of course not! He's strong and confident and handsome as hell." She sounded almost irritated that he be all those things at once. "Why am I discussing this with you?"

He shrugged. "I just never took you for a chicken. It's time, Fiona. Time to live again. Tim's a good man. Aidan thinks the world of him. Even if it's just five days of fun, you should go. You need a break from this town. You never go anywhere. Go learn how to have fun again."

She closed her eyes. "My problem was, if I recall, having too much fun. All at your expense."

He shook his head. "That's not you anymore. It's not me either. I have a happy life and two children. You're doing better. Time to take the training wheels off and try again. That starts with dating age appropriate, single men." She looked at him, and he softened.

He saw fear. "Don't be afraid, Fio. We've both grown up. Time to quit being so hard on yourself."

Tears pricked her eyes. She nodded. "Thanks, Michael. I'll think about it."

Aidan drew Alanna into the dim cottage and she gasped. It had been completely transformed. Michael had actually pulled their mattress out of the bedroom and put it in front of the big hearth. The place was filled with glowing candles and the smell of heather and roses. There was sparkling wine on ice and glowing peat. The windows were cracked, letting in just the tickle of a breeze. Late September was a lovely temperature in Ireland, and the cottage dripped with decadent, romantic ambience. Chocolates, flowers, honey and fruit. Silks and furs draped around the bed clothes, that made Alanna think of a medieval castle.

"She's fond of those romance novels that you like so much. She's outdone herself." Alanna twirled in the candlelight, making Aidan smile and rouse to her. "I have strict instructions on the manner in which you are to disrobe me. This dress is ninety years old." He stalked toward her, making her back away. "I'm serious Aidan. Your granny will tan your hide if you rip this." She was trying to be serious, but giggles speckled her words.

"I'm not a savage. Come, hen." He crooked his finger at her, in invitation or command, she wasn't sure.

Alanna's body glowed in the firelight. Aidan had taken his time undressing her. Then he took his time loving her. All of these hard months of fighting his feelings, of tragedy, tears, fear, and finally surrender. For once he felt no urgency. She was his, now, and he was hers. Forever. They explored each other, tasting and touching, stopping to sip wine from crystal glasses, sipping it from each other's lips, then other places. Aidan was playful and attentive at times.

Then urgent and overcome with need. They stopped and washed each other in the big clawfoot tub. Aidan oiled her down in front of the fire, rubbing her muscles until she was limp and submissive, then he took her again, feeling the orgasm roll through her like a slow, ocean surge.

She was asleep now, finally pushed to a satisfied exhaustion. He played with her hair and she sighed in her sleep. He cradled her against him and whispered in her ear. They were lover's words. She smelled like him, and he smelled of her. He covered them both and slept a deep, dreamless sleep.

48

Gus O'Connors Pub was packed to the gills with wedding goers. All in need of a stiff cup of coffee or tea and a good Irish breakfast, but too exhausted from a night of partying to make it themselves. Hans and Erik sat with Tim and John and Maria. Hans held little Aidan on his knee. "You'll have a grandchild soon enough, I'd wager," Maria said.

Hans let the baby chew his big finger. He brightened at the notion. "Whenever they want to give me one, I'll be happy. God knows I can't wait on this one." He motioned to Erik.

"What? I'm working on it. I just need stricter screening. You know, I think this whole thing has been educational. These are some fine women in this family. I'm raising my standards."

Tim leaned in. "Yes, did you notice how non-dickish their men are to them? That's the lesson you should learn. Good women don't put up with men who are dickheads." Hans was chuckling and so was John.

"Am I really that much of a dick?"

Maria patted his face. "You're adorable. Don't listen to them."

The bell to the pub dinged and they looked up. Mary Flynn came in and Hans stood, handing off the baby to Erik. "Here, start practicing. Good Morning, Doc." Mary smiled at the group and then accepted a kiss on the cheek from Hans.

Maria was grinning like a lunatic. "Mary, we've already had breakfast. Please sit down. We need to go back to Brigid's house and pack for a day trip. We're taking the Ferry to Aran."

Mary said, "Oh, you'll love it. Take the trip that shows you the ruins and the shipwreck. It won't be too long for the baby."

Erik watched in fascination as his dad attempted to woo this doctor of his. "So, Erik. Are you here for five days as well?" Mary asked.

He nodded. "Yes, I am headed with Porter and O'Malley to Dublin as soon as Porter gets his head out of the toilet. Liam is letting us sleep in his flat."

Mary said, "I'd imagine that's going to be a bit more amusing than a small fishing village with a bunch of old folk. Just be careful and watch for pickpockets."

The bell rang again and Tim looked to the door. Then he cracked a huge smile. "Good morning, Fiona." She had a bag thrown over her shoulder and her camera bag as well. "Does this mean you've had a change of heart?"

She sighed. "Don't look so pleased with yourself."

He couldn't hide his smile, however. "Well then, have you eaten?" She nodded. "Okay, let's get your stuff in the car and let me say some goodbyes. I'm all ready to go."

Mary was watching this all with amusement, as were the men. "Damn, am I the only poor sod that didn't hook up?" said Erik.

Fiona narrowed her eyes. "He has not hooked up. This is business." Then she pointed to Tim. "Business. You hear? And I own all the rights to my photos."

Tim put his hands up. "Agreed. Don't get your dander up, girl."

Tim left with Fiona, and Erik put his hands flat on the table. "Well, three is a crowd. Have fun kids." Then he left to pay his tab.

Jenny came over to the table. "The usual, Mary?" She nodded. "And how about you, Hans?"

He shrugged. "Give me whatever she's having." Jenny brought a pot of tea while they waited.

"So Hans, what are your plans for these last few days in Ireland?" Mary asked.

Hans stirred his tea thoughtfully. "Well, I'd like to see a few more towns. I saw Newgrange on the way from Dublin. I saw the Cliffs and the Burren with Alanna, already. I like the old stuff. What do you recommend? My last night in Dublin I was planning on getting a hotel and seeing Trinity."

She swallowed her tea. "It's a good start. Galway is beautiful if you are headed up. Did you want to see Belfast? Where they'll be living?"

Hans cocked his head. "I'm afraid I'd be pushing my time frame going up north. I'll have to save that for my next trip."

"Aye, well then Donegal might be a stretch as well. If you're headed toward Dublin then Galway might be best, then head inland. Do you like whiskey?"

He laughed. "Does the Pope like wine?"

She smirked. "Well then, Tullamore might be worth a look on the way back east."

"Do you like whiskey, Doc?"

She looked scandalized. "Of course." Hans looked like he was going to say something when Jenny came back with two heaping plates.

He looked down and choked on a laugh. "What on earth have you done?"

Mary shrugged. "It's a full Irish. I have a fast metabolism." Then she gave him the once over. "You don't look like you have to watch your weight with those Viking genes. You're not going to chick out on me and order a yogurt, are ye?"

Hans shook with laughter. "You cut me deep doc. I'm from the South. We know how to eat." They tucked into their breakfast with gusto. "So, do you ever get a day off from being the town doc?"

She swallowed her food, took a sip of tea, and cleared her throat. "I've been training a new doctor. He's ready, he just needs to get to know the villagers. I can't keep working forever, and honestly I don't want to. I want to retire while I'm still young enough to take some chances and hop trains without a bloody cane."

Hans perked up. "Really? I feel the same way. After this Spain tour, I am done. Retiring in my fifties was always the goal. So, can this doc in training cover your ass for a few days?"

She sat up straighter. "What, you mean now?"

He shrugged. "Why not?"

She gave him a sideways glance. "Christ, you are cocky, aren't you? Are you always so direct with women?"

He stared into her eyes. "Are you always such a hard ass? I told you, I haven't been with a woman in years."

She met his gaze. "So what's changed?"

He sat back a bit. "I met you. I like you, Mary. You're beautiful and you're smart. You've got a lion's share of smart-ass as well. I happen to appreciate a sharp tongued woman." She gave him a crooked smile with that last comment. "And I know first hand that life is short. I lost my two best friends in the span of six years. I'm tired of living my life only for my kids. They're all grown up. I can want something else."

She put her cup down. "And you want me?"

He shrugged again. "Maybe. It might be fun to find out either way. So, what do you say doc? You ready to blow this town and be a total slacker for a few days? Shirk your responsibilities and run off with some Yank? What will the town think?" He took a sip of tea and chuckled, "Worse case scenario, you leave me on the side of the road."

She took a bite, chewing and eying him thoughtfully. "Can you give me until tonight? Galway isn't that far. I need to see if he can do this. I have patients that need cared for." When he nodded, she said, "All right, then. I will go into the office and see what magic I can work with my new doctor."

She took another bite of her toast and washed it down with some tea. She eyed her watch. "Christ, I've got to go. Come by my office at four. I should be done by then." She stopped, thought for a moment, then reached over the table and gathered Hans's shirt in her fist, pulling him toward her. He went willingly as she planted a kiss on his mouth. That's when the whistles started, then some clapping.

Aidan woke in small degrees from an erotic early morning dream. He smelled jasmine, felt long silky hair across his thighs. Then he sucked in a breath at the warm, wet sensation on his cock. He opened his eyes and it wasn't a dream. He moaned and rolled his hips as he looked down at his wife, taking him slow and deep with her mouth. He didn't want to come yet, but holy shit. He watched her and could feel himself on the edge. Then she stopped, sensing how close he was. She crawled up his body and he watched her as she took him. She moaned, her body arching, breasts full and swaying. She rolled her hips and pinned his hands to the bed. She started shuddering, and that was all it took. He thrust deep, filling her up. She was flushed and tight with lust as she gripped him hard, gasping as she fell off the edge. He sat up with a violent heave grabbing her desperately, not able to get close enough. He kissed her, swallowing her cries as he pulled her to him over and over. *Mine.* He fell back on the bed, his body bowing as he spilled in her and gave a hoarse cry of his own.

"You ambushed me, ye little vixen." He was out of breath, his tone rough but amused. He felt her laugh from where her face was buried in the crook of his neck. He rolled her over, and she went willingly, limp to her toes with satisfaction. He looked down at her, touching her face gently. "Will it always be like this, do you think?"

She leaned in and kissed his hand. "Well, your parents seem to love each other very much. I'm sure it mellows to a degree, but I don't think the desire will ever leave us. Look at my dad. Here I thought he'd gone dormant for good, and he's all up on Doc Mary at my wedding."

Aidan laughed. "Aye, love was in the air last night. Or lust, in some cases. Somehow I don't think wee Jenny is looking for a ring from Sergeant Porter." They giggled as they thought about it all. "It was the best wedding I've ever been to," Aidan said.

"Oh, and you don't think you might be a little biased?" she said, cocking a brow.

He moved his head side to side. "No. Not at all. It's because it was so hard to get here. We've had a time of it, haven't we?"

She smoothed her hand over his face. "We have, and that will make this life together so much sweeter for it."

EPILOGUE

Aidan came home from work and pulled his little car into the drive of the stone townhouse. The thaw had come, and the Spring season was chilly but bursting with new life. The grass and trees had all sprouted that uniquely bright, first green of the season. Also bursting with new life, his beautiful Alanna was tending the early flowers in the garden. Daffodils, tulips, and crocus were all peeking up through the cold ground. She stood and stretched her back. He got out of the car and went to her. "Christ, woman. Would you let me do that? Ye worked all day. Put your feet up."

She smiled up at him, her belly hiding her feet at this angle. "I'm fine, Aidan. I just wanted to clear the dead leaves." She went on her toes for a kiss. Not satisfied with a small one, he pulled her to him, his tongue gliding as she moaned. The first trimester had been touch and go with sickness, but since the dust had cleared, her appetite for him was voracious. She offered a small protest, total bullshit of course. "We should eat dinner, first." For once he didn't argue with her, though. They had to talk.

He said, "I've got news from home."

Her face darkened. "Something is wrong."

He nodded. "They hesitated to tell us at all, but knew we'd hear it eventually." He rubbed his hand over her belly.

"Oh no, is it Caitlyn?" Her eyes were filled with fear.

He nodded. “Aye, she lost the baby. She was about ten weeks along.”

She put her face in her hands. “They tried so hard. It took seven months for her to get pregnant. Do they know what was wrong?”

He shook his head. “Sometimes there’s just something not right. They can try again in six weeks.” They held each other for a long while, neither of them speaking.

He wiped her tears. “Don’t worry, love. Children come to us in all sorts of ways. I think they’ll get their own in time, but if they don’t, they’ll find another way.”

She nodded. “I know, but I just feel so bad for her. It was so easy for the rest of us. You know that must play into her feeling at fault. There’s a lot of misplaced guilt when a woman miscarries.”

He kissed her forehead. “I know, darlin’. I do. Patrick told me that she wanted us to know that she’s happy for us. That we shouldn’t feel strange about bringing the baby around once it’s born. She’s a good girl. And she’s got plenty of little ones to teach at school in the meantime.”

He sharpened up. “Speaking of work, how’s the new job going?”

She smiled. “Really well. It’s a good fit. The non-profit Dr. Jennings got me hooked up with is really excited about my ideas. They are changing two of the unused rooms into yoga and alternate therapy rooms.”

He squeezed her hands. “That’s good, darlin’. And will you be able to keep working, once the baby comes?”

She nodded. “Part-time. They have a day care on the base and I’m already on the wait list.”

He brought her inside, sitting her down to pull off her wellies. They came off with a pop. “My feet are like two fat, sweaty little yams. This child of yours is making me fat, Aidan O’Brien.” Then she rubbed her belly, concern marring her features.

“The baby is fine. Don’t worry,” he said. Still, she rubbed her belly, comforting the precious cargo.

"I was thinking. Maybe we could use some good news?"

He laughed. "You are relentless. You want to look in the envelope?" She nodded, biting her lip. He sighed and went to the desk where they kept the sealed envelope. The news about Patrick and Caitlyn had darkened their thoughts. They needed this.

He handed it to her. "All right. Let's have a look. I don't think I'll make it another two months either." She giggled and looked down at the envelope as he continued. "David for my granddad or Isla for your granny?" She nodded excitedly, slipping a finger under the glued flap to tear the paper. The ultrasound picture was sealed with the gender reveal. A big smile came on her face. She pulled off a sticky note, a light blue sticky note that said, *It's a boy!*

Aidan choked down a sob, and he dropped to his knees. "A son." He put his forehead to her belly. "I never thought I'd have a son." She felt a shudder go through him.

"It's real for you now, isn't it?"

He looked up. "It's always been real, the idea of it. I feel it kick and I know it's alive inside you. I feel the movement surge inside you, when I lie with you. But when you put a name to him. When you know it's a lad, it just gets all the more real. Does that make sense?" She nodded, tears welling her eyes. His were wary. "Are you happy? I see you with little Cora and Haley. Did you..."

She put a hand up to his mouth. "I'm overjoyed. If we have ten children and they are all boys, I will still be happy. All I want is us and a family. The rest doesn't matter. The way your family spits out boys, I'm not banking on a wee Isla." Then she said, "Should we tell everyone or keep it a secret?"

Aidan thought about it. "Let's hold off with my family for a few weeks. We can tell your da and Mary."

Alanna said, "Mary will want to be there, I hope. She told Daddy that her one regret was no children, which meant no grandchildren. Now she'll get a chance. Speaking of grannies, your mother agreed."

Aidan's face lit up. "She'll catch the baby?"

"Yes, she's done with her classes, she certified again. I'll have to go home a month before the due date, but you can wait longer. We're going to try a home birth."

He stiffened, his brow furrowed. "Are you sure it's safe?"

She ran a hand through his hair. "My soon to be stepmother is a doctor and my mother in law is a midwife. I'll be fine, Aidan. We'll be fine."

He cupped her belly in his hands. "David it is then. Wee Davey, conceived in a coat check closet, the poor bugger."

Alanna burst out laughing. This was an old argument. She assured him that their first child had been conceived in the marriage bed with candles and wine and silky furs. He knew better though. His son had come to them during a tryst in the Cottage Hall coat room, the day before the wedding. He'd felt it, deep in her womb. He felt a quickening that shot straight through to his heart. He remembered every detail of it. He'd slowed her hips, looking into her eyes. *I feel you. Take me with you, darlin'.*"

She put her head on his shoulder. "I felt it, too." She said, the only hint of an admission she would ever give.

Two Months Later

Aidan walked through the corridor of the old housing complex. The musty smell of old building and poverty clouded his sense of smell. He was afraid, afraid to see her, huddled in that pile of blankets, ruined.

He opened the door to the apartment, but only light came through. Suddenly he was transported. Out of the pits of Kabul, he left in a blink. Now there was only white. A sparkling fountain with crystal water. On an alabaster bench, she sat with her doll. She, too, was free of any filth or darkness. Her face was clear, youthful, unmarred. Her hijab and abiya were pure white. He sat next to her.

"I wasn't sure I'd ever see you again. I've dreamt of you so often, but what is all of this?" He motioned around him.

Her mouth didn't move, but he heard her in his head. "I'm okay. I'm with my mother and father. I know only this life. There is no pain. You can let me go."

Aidan's eyes misted. "I failed you."

"No, my good brother. You saved me. You saved my brother and my cousin. I am at rest. You have a new child to care for." Aidan smiled at that. She put her hands on his face. "Mikail, you must wake up. It is time for you to wake up. Goodbye, my angel. I will not come again."

Aidan's eyes popped open. He was back in his childhood bedroom, his wife beside him. He heard a moan. "Alanna, what is it?" He put his hand on her tummy and felt her tensed around it. It was tight like a drum. "When did they start?"

She was breathing through it. "This is the second one." He got out of bed, popping out into the hall. "Ma! It's time!" He heard the springs pop as Sorcha jumped out of bed.

Aidan was behind his wife, her sweaty hair sticking to his cheek as she laid against him, taking a rest. Doc Mary and Sorcha were at her feet. "One more, sweet girl. I see the head." Aidan watched his mother's hand on his wife's belly.

"You can do this, Alanna. Squeeze my hands as hard as you need to," he said, kissing her temple.

Sorcha said, "Here it comes, lean forward with her Aidan. Alanna, look at me." Alanna did, "This is the one. From the depths of your body. Let the child ride the tide. Now!" Alanna clenched her teeth and growled, then it peaked to a scream the likes of which Aidan had never heard.

"The head is out! Another, lass!" Mary yelled. She screamed, and Aidan felt her let loose of his hands. She grabbed her own knees and gave it everything she had as she rose off his chest.

In the end, they face it alone. It's their battle and the child's. All we can do is bear witness. His mother's words came to him in that instant, and he finally understood. Alanna's body went loose as the cries of their first born replaced her own.

Alanna was asleep, exhausted from the hours she'd spent in labor. The sun was going down, now. Sorcha took the soup bowl from her night table and left the room, shutting the light off as she left. Her son sat in the living room, just staring down at his child as he slept soundly in his swaddling. Sorcha knelt beside him, and to her shock, he was weeping. She hadn't seen him cry since he was a small boy.

"They're both fine, lad. She did wonderfully. Mary will check her again in the morning, and the boy."

He wiped a tear off his nose. "It's not that. You were wonderful. I couldn't be happier."

She smiled, touching his face. "Tears of joy, then? It doesn't seem as simple as that."

He said, "You always saw too much when it came to me."

She laughed lightly. "You're my first born. I know you better than anyone. What is it, Aidan?"

"The girl, she came to me in my dreams."

Sorcha exhaled. "The little Afghani girl? Oh, Aidan." She pulled him close, comforting him like she did when he was small.

He shook his head. "It was different. She wasn't hurt. Everything was white. She called me Mikail. Like her brother and cousin did. She said that I had to let her go. That she was at peace." Aidan looked at his mother and tears were welling in her eyes. "She's with her parents. Then she told me to take care of him." He looked down at the baby. "She told me to wake up, and that she wouldn't come again."

Sorcha squeezed his arm. "Because you can let her go now, is that right?"

He nodded. "Aye, I think I can for him. I didn't think I'd ever be able to hold my own child. I didn't dare hope for it. But Alanna saw right through me. She dug down inside me and loved the darkest part of me."

Sorcha kissed his cheek. "She gave to you what Sean gave to me. A safe place to land. Love like I never thought was possible. You're more like me than any of my other children, even Brigid. Someday I'll tell you why. Someday we'll trade war stories. Not now, though. Not today. Today is about him." She kissed her new grandson on his soft head. Then she left them to each other.

Hans ended the call with his daughter and rubbed his eyes. He looked up just as Mary was reaching to get a cup out of the cabinet. She was wearing his Ramones t-shirt and it rose with the effort, showing him the high part of her thighs. She was talking, oblivious to how tempting she was. "How's the new mam and the little one? Are they getting some sleep?" Christ, that accent. She was appealing on every level.

"You women did good. She couldn't have been in better hands." He stalked toward the kitchen. "I like you in my shirt." He came behind her.

"You're awfully frisky for a grandpa." She squeaked when he pinched her. She wiggled away from him, her back to the counter. She liked making him work a little, but it was hard to keep her hands off him. He was in his early fifties, but he was lean and muscled and big. She looked him up and down, never quite believing that this was all hers. At the autumn of her life, she was going to get more of a husband then she ever imagined she'd want. His green eyes sparked. "You got something you need from me, Doc?" he asked, and he closed the distance between them.

It was the middle of the night, and Aidan and Alanna woke to the cries of their newborn. They finally had to order Sorcha to bed. Aidan handed little Davey to Alanna. "He doesn't want me when he knows you're in the room. I swear, it's like he smells you." The baby rooted, mouth open and searching. Alanna cradled him as he settled into his work, latching voraciously. She inhaled sharply.

"What does it feel like? Does it hurt?"

She smiled, but her face was tense. "For now. We'll get used to each other. Sorcha said I'll get sore for a while, then it will pass. I can feel when the milk comes. It's prickly. It moves down my chest to my nipple like an intense ache. When he starts to suckle, it's like the pressure gets relieved."

She put her head back, her body relaxing. "That's it. It's better now," she said dreamily. "It's like a rope that ties me to him. We pull at each other. I will start to ache if he doesn't feed."

Aidan touched her face, her mouth, traced the lines of her chest and collar bones, and over the swell of her breast, then finally over the cap of his son's soft head as he suckled. His eyes were open just a sliver, knowing only the completion and delirious fulfillment of his mother's offering. The sight of the two of them was so beautiful, it made his throat tighten. "It's like being in love, then," he said softly.

She smiled, her eyes still shut. "Yes, I suppose it is." She opened her eyes and looked at him. "Six weeks is a long time." He kissed her then, soft and undemanding. "We have our whole lives, a mhuirnín." And she laid her head back again, because she knew it to be true.

AUTHOR'S NOTES AND ACKNOWLEDGEMENTS

This story came in slow degrees while I was writing *Raven of the Sea.* The stoic older brother Aidan had a story to tell me, and he needed a good woman.

Being a military spouse, I watched my Marine rotate in and out of combat zones. It wasn't without a price. I know lots of brave men and women who do the same. My own son is a Navy medic and my eldest daughter was in the U.S.Coast Guard. One thing that no one talks about is the human rights atrocities that they witness while in the sandbox. War, fighting, combat, it all takes a toll both on the body and the mind. The other stuff, though. The soul pays the price, and some things can never be erased.

The Traumatic Brain Injury, like PTSD, is the invisible injury. Our men and women come back from these deployments having crashed, banged, and danced a tango or two with an IED. The concussion recovery clinics are real, although the names have been changed. They do great work and are breaking new ground with a whole patient approach to brain healing. They helped our family and continue to help many others.

I'd like to, as always, thank my beta readers, but most especially my friend Stacey. We had more than a few midnight chats over this book. We laughed, we cried, we made perverted jokes, but she was a huge help when it came to understanding my vision for this story.

There is some debate about the origin of Alanna's name. It's spelling has been anglicized in America and I found conflicting meanings. Some translations say that it means child. Others say it means beautiful, but regardless, I thought it suited her. Her alternative therapies are of my own design, having been boots on the ground with the families that suffer with PTSD and TBIs. Some stuff, Motrin doesn't cure. And I firmly believe that to heal the service member, the family should be involved

Some of the military details and local flavor have been altered a bit to fit the story, but I tried to keep it as authentic as possible. The Marine Corps was a huge part of our lives, and we lived in Camp Lejeune and the surrounding areas for many years. The heart and character of the military fighting man is one that is precious to me, and North Carolina will always be home.

I'd like to thank my husband for his help on the Military Transition/Embedded Team training and for bringing me into the life of the Marine Corps. All of the Marines in this book are completely fictional, but they were inspired by all of the wonderful young men I have met over the years. From every state, every socio-economic background, every race. The young, fighting men of the United States Marine Corps are the very best sort of lads. I am privileged to know just a few of you.

*The song *Ain True Love* was written by Sting. It is the perfect old war lament, which is amazing since he wrote it in modern times. The perfect duet for Aidan and Alanna.

*To learn more about my future books, my personal story, and find fun things like recipes from the book, check out my author website at www.staceylreynolds.weebly.com.

Made in the USA
San Bernardino, CA
24 January 2017